THE NUTMEG TREE

THE NUTMEG TREE

MARGERY SHARP

ISIS
LARGE PRINT
Oxford

First published in Great Britain 1937
by Collins

Published in Large Print 2002 by ISIS Publishing Ltd,
7 Centremead, Osney Mead, Oxford OX2 0ES
by arrangement with
The Estate of Margery Sharp, c/o PFD

British Library Cataloguing in Publication Data
Sharp, Margery, 1905–1991
The nutmeg tree. – Large print ed.
1. Large type books
I. Title
823.9'12 [F]

ISBN 0–7531–6801–4 (hb)
ISBN 0–7531–6802–2 (pb)

Printed and bound by Antony Rowe, Chippenham

CHAPTER
ONE

Julia, by marriage Mrs. Packett, by courtesy Mrs. Macdermot, lay in her bath singing the Marseillaise. Her fine robust contralto, however, was less resonant than usual; for on this particular summer morning the bathroom, in addition to the ordinary fittings, contained a lacquer coffee table, seven hatboxes, half a dinner service, a small grandfather clock, all Julia's clothes, a single-bed mattress, thirty-five novelettes, three suitcases, and a copy of a Landseer stag. The customary echo was therefore lacking; and if the ceiling now and then trembled, it was not because of Julia's song, but because the men from the Bayswater Hire Furniture Company had not yet finished removing the hired furniture.

On the other side of the door an occasional shuffling of feet showed that the two broker's men had not even one chair to sit on.

Thus beleaguered, Julia sang. With every breath she drew in a generous diaphragmful of verbena-scented steam, and let it out again in the form of equally generous chest-notes. She did this not out of defiance, nor to keep her spirits up, but because at that time of the morning song was natural to her. The belligerence

1

of her tone was due simply to the belligerence of the melody: her choice of the melody was due simply to the fact that she had received, the night before, a letter from France.

So Julia sang, until in the pause before the reprise a weary voice sounded huskily through the door.

"Ain't you done *yet*, mum?" demanded the voice.

"No," said Julia.

"But you bin in an hour 'n' 'arf already!" protested the voice.

Julia turned on the hot tap. She could stay in a bath almost indefinitely, and had often, during her periodic attempts at slimming, lain parboiled for two or three hours. But nothing — as was now plainly to be seen — had ever slimmed Julia. At thirty-nine — only five feet three inches in height — she had a thirty-eight-inch bust, a thirty-one waist, and forty-one hips; and though these three vital points were linked by extremely agreeable curves, Julia nevertheless hankered after a fashionable toothpick silhouette. She hankered, but not consistently. Her comfortable flesh refused to be martyred. It regarded orange juice as an appetizer, not as a staff of life; and as a result there lay Julia — recumbent in her cloud of steam, rosy-pink with heat — looking like the presiding goddess of some baroque ceiling.

The door rattled.

"If you break in," called Julia, turning off the tap, "I'll have you up for assault!"

A dead silence showed that the threat had taken effect. There was a muffled consultation; then a second

2

voice, even wearier than the first, resumed the argument.

"It's only five pound, mum," pleaded the voice. "We don't want to give no trouble —"

"Then go away," retorted Julia.

"We can't, mum. It's our duty. If you'll just let us take the stuff — or better still, pay us the five pound —"

"I haven't got five pounds," said Julia truthfully; and for the first time her brow clouded. She hadn't got one pound: she possessed exactly seven-and-eightpence, and she had to leave for France in the morning. For perhaps five minutes she lay and pondered, considering, one after the other, all those persons from whom she had borrowed money in the past. She thought also of those to whom she had lent; but one set was as hopeless as the other. With real regret, she thought of the late Mr. Macdermot. And at last she thought of Mr. Lewis.

"Hey!" called Julia. "You know that antique shop at the end of the road?"

The bailiffs consulted.

"We know a pawnbroker's, mum. Name of Lewis."

"That's it," admitted Julia, "but it's an antique shop as well. One of you nip along and fetch Mr. Lewis here. He'll pay you."

They consulted again; but after waiting (upright) for two hours, they were ready to clutch at a straw. Julia heard the tread of departing feet, and the shuffle of the feet that remained. Then she dried her hands, lit a cigarette, and reached out to the coffee table for a letter with a French stamp.

II

Though it had arrived only the previous night, she already knew it by heart.

My dear Mother,

It seems strange that you won't know my writing. I am sending this through the Bank, and unless you are abroad you ought to get it almost at once. Could you come out here and see me? It is a long way, but a beautiful place, high up on the edge of Haute Savoie, and we shall be here till October. But I would like you to come (if you can) at once. Grandmother also invites you, to stay as long as you like. As you may know, she and Sir William Waring are now my trustees. The point is (here the small, neat writing grew suddenly larger) that I want to get married, and Grandmother objects. I know there are all sorts of legal complications, but after all you are my mother, and you ought to be consulted. If you can come, the best way is by the 11-40p.m. from Paris to Ambérieu, where a car will meet you. I do hope it will be possible.

Your affectionate daughter,
SUSAN PACKETT.

From a girl of twenty, in love, to her mother, the letter was hardly expansive; but Julia understood. Because of a variety of circumstances, she had not seen her daughter for sixteen years; and the bare fact that

4

that daughter now remembered and appealed to her was so exquisitely touching that even now, on re-reading the letter for the twentieth time, Julia dropped a tear or two into the bath. But they were tears of sentiment, not of sorrow; at the thought of a trip to France, of a love affair to be handled, her spirits soared. "CATCHING TRAIN THURSDAY ALL LOVE MOTHER," she had wired back; and only then had she remembered her unusually disastrous economic situation. She had no money, no proper wardrobe, and a creditor about to foreclose. But none of these things mattered, when Susan wanted her. Susan wanted her, Susan was unhappy, and to Susan she would go . . .

"But she was christened Suzanne!" thought Julia suddenly; and was still staring at the signature when she was brought back to the present by the welcome sound of Mr. Lewis's voice.

"My dear Julia!" he shouted. "What is all this that you fetch me for? You are not really drowning yourself? This man —"

"He's a bailiff," called Julia. "They're both bailiffs. Send them away."

After a few moments the heavy footsteps retreated, the lighter ones returned.

"Now, Julia, what is it? These men —"

"Have they gone?"

"Gone and glad to," replied Mr. Lewis. "They are very modest men, my dear, and so am I. But they haven't gone farther than the stairs."

"Can they hear us?"

"They can hear me if I shout for help. They seem to think that there is stuff in there besides the usual fittings."

"There is," said Julia. "That's what I want you for. There's stuff in here I've got to sell — *good* stuff — and you've always been a sport to me, Joe, so I'm giving you first chance. There's a real lacquer table, and a new mattress, and a genuine antique grandfather clock, and a lovely dinner service, and a picture of a stag that's a real painting. I'll take thirty quid for the lot."

"Not from me you won't," said Mr Lewis.

Julia sat up with a splash.

"Of all the old Jews! Why, the stag's worth that alone, and I didn't mean to include it. I'm offering you the table and the clock and a new mattress and a dinner service, and dirt cheap at that."

"Well, let me look at 'em," said Mr. Lewis patiently.

"Of course you can't look at them. I'm in the bath."

"You mean you want me to buy blind?"

"That's it," agreed Julia. "Have a flutter."

Mr. Lewis reflected. He was a man who liked to get everything cut and dried.

"You mean you will sell me, for thirty pounds, stuff I haven't even seen, which is probably worth twenty-five bob, and which already belongs to whatever fool has been giving you credit?"

"That's right," said Julia cheerfully, "except that it's worth more like sixty, and I only owe five. What's your favourite tune?"

"The Blue Danube," said Mr. Lewis.

Julia sang it.

III

Half an hour passed. The men from the Bayswater Hire Furniture Company had taken themselves and the hired furniture away. A man from the Gas Company had come and cut off the gas. But the bailiffs remained, and so did Mr. Lewis; for even through a bolted door Julia's personality triumphed. When she was tired of singing she entertained them with anecdotes of her early life on the stage; when she ran out of anecdotes she imitated film stars, and so successfully that the grandfather clock, chiming for noon, took them all by surprise.

"That the genuine antique?" asked Mr. Lewis with interest.

"Yes," said Julia, returning promptly to business. "Now listen, Joe: I've got to go to France first thing in the morning. I've got to have ten pounds for my return fare, and a fiver for these toughs. That's fifteen quid, and I haven't a rag to my back. Make it eighteen-ten, and I'll throw in the stag."

"Fourteen," said Mr. Lewis.

"Seventeen," said Julia. "Be a sport!"

"Be a sport, guv'nor!" echoed the bailiffs — now definitely on Julia's side.

Mr. Lewis felt himself weaken. A coffee table, a dinner service, a mattress, and a grandfather clock — it all depended on the clock. The chimes had been good ones, and if it looked like an antique to Julia it would probably look like an antique to most people. It might

7

even *be* an antique, and old grandfathers fetched a lot of money . . .

Julia had known what she was about when she appealed to his gambling instincts.

"Sixteen-ten," said Mr. Lewis. "Take it or leave it."

"Done!" said Julia; and at last got out of the bath.

CHAPTER
TWO

The first time Julia had seen her future husband by daylight was on a spring morning in 1916, when she woke at about half-past ten to find him still sleeping at her side. She knew his name, Sylvester Packett, and that he was a first lieutenant in the Gunners; and in spite of the fact that for six consecutive nights he had danced with her from twelve till four in the morning, that was all she did know. He was the most silent boy she had ever met; not even the champagne loosened his tongue; and she had regretfully (but philosophically) come to the conclusion that he danced with her simply because he couldn't sleep. Boys got like that, in 1916; she wouldn't be a bit surprised if he'd come back with her the night before just to see if he could get some sleep *that* way, . . . Julia, at eighteen, considered this idea without either surprise or rancour; it was simply, like so many other things, the War.

"Poor boy!" said Julia under her breath; for she was easily sentimental, and cried over a casualty list whenever she saw one. The young man stirred in his sleep, sighed, and slept again. He had four more days' leave, and if only he stayed with her — thought Julia — he should sleep like that every single night . . .

Sylvester Packett stayed. He wanted to be down in Suffolk, but in Suffolk he couldn't sleep, and with Julia he could. It was unfortunate, but it was the War. He stayed for four more days, and at the end of that time was swallowed back into France.

Julia wept when he went. Her affection had been at least disinterested, for she refused all gifts except a Gunner brooch. But it was also ephemeral; save for one awkward and unexpected circumstance, she would never have thought of him again.

II

At the beginning of August, after a five-hour chorus rehearsal for *Pretty Louise*, Julia fainted. When her friends had brought her round, and after she had taken expert advice, she went home and wrote to Sylvester.

There was nothing of the blackmailer about her. The letter said simply that she was going to have a baby, and she was sure it was his, and if he could lend her a hand she would be very much obliged, but if not he wasn't to worry. "With love and best wishes, Julia." In answer she received the shock of her life.

He came home and married her.

He did it during a forty-eight-hour leave, and never in her life did Julia pass a more uncomfortable two days. What with relief and gratification her spirits, never low, had soared to an unexampled pitch; but he managed to damp them. He was no longer silent, but he was deadly. He talked to her for hours on end about a dreary-sounding place in Suffolk — an old, old house called Barton, in an old garden, in a village ten miles from a railway station, where his people had apparently lived, without either a car or a telephone, for hundreds and hundreds of years. He would actually have taken her there, but for lack of time; yet when Julia, happy in her escape and anxious to console, projected a visit for his next leave, he at once bit on the knuckle of his thumb and changed the subject. He behaved, in fact, as though the future had ceased to affect him. He wouldn't even buy shirts. To cheer him up Julia insisted on dining at the Ritz and going to a musical comedy; but even these measures were useless.

And if the evening was a failure, the wedding night was a flop.

Julia spent it alone. All night long her husband sat up writing a letter. It was addressed to his people, but not directly; the Bank had instructions, he said, to forward it at the proper time. When this letter was read, it was found to consist of detailed instructions for the bringing-up of his unborn child, to which he referred throughout as "the boy." The boy was to be born at Barton, and to receive the name of Henry Sylvester. He was to remain at Barton till the age of nine, then to go to a preparatory school for Winchester. After Winchester, on making his choice between the Army and Medicine, he was to proceed to either Sandhurst or Cambridge. If undecided, he was to choose the Army. "But on no account," wrote his father, with unsuspected dryness, "is he to become an Army Doctor."

Such was the main outline; there was also provision for a pony — "which must be exchanged as soon as the boy outgrows it; there is nothing worse for a child than to feel his feet trailing on the ground" — and for coaching in cricket during the summer holidays. At twelve the boy was to be given his father's old 20-bore; at eighteen, the Purdey 12: his grandfather would teach him how to handle them. All these things, and many others, had been thought of, pondered over, and put down on paper; with corrections, interlinings and much copying-out; for in this long, detailed and comprehensive document, far more than in his official will, was embodied the last testament of Sylvester Packett.

There was a brief codicil:

I never told anybody, but there is usually a tit's nest in the old pump at the bottom of the orchard. Also a bull-finch's in the red May tree at the corner of the big field. Tell him the great thing in blowing is to go *slow*. You will of course never take more than one egg.

Your loving father,

SYLVESTER PACKETT.

Two months later he was killed at Ypres; and the child born at Barton was a girl.

III

She was christened Suzanne Sylvester. The first name was chosen by Julia as both patriotic (being French) and pretty; and the Packetts let her have her way. They were unbelievably good to her. As the mother of their grandchild (even of the wrong sex) they accepted her with open arms. Affectionately, unquestioningly, she was installed as the daughter of the house. All they asked was that she and the child should stay there and be happy.

And Julia tried. For nineteen months the lay figure of young Mrs. Packett did the flowers, paid calls, went to church, and played with the baby whenever the nurse allowed. Night after night this lay figure sat at dinner with its father- and mother-in-law; every night for an hour afterwards, it played easy classics on the drawing-room piano. At such mild festivities as the neighbourhood afforded it played the same pieces on the pianos of its hosts. All its evening dresses had backs to them, and two had long sleeves.

Such was the puppet constructed by Julia's gratitude; and gratitude alone pulled its strings. Julia herself sat in young Mrs. Packett's room and wept for boredom; but even her tears, when discovered, were taken as one more sign of the puppet's faithful and tender heart. But Julia's heart was tender too: one of the worst elements in her boredom was the lack of someone to love. She had her child, indeed, and was very fond of it; but "someone," to Julia, meant a man. Loving some man or other was her natural function: only the man had to be alive, and there, and kissing her back. Love for a memory — even for the memory of a husband — was right out of Julia's line . . .

It must be admitted that to have held out as she did, under such conditions, for a year and seven months, was extremely creditable; and no less so because at the end of that time she gave up the struggle and went thoroughly back to the bad.

IV

The bad, originally, was crowd-work in a comedy film, which Julia heard of through a girl friend who had a boy friend who knew a man in the then struggling British film industry. She met the girl friend at Selfridge's, on one of her rare expeditions to Town; they encountered each other (in the stocking department) shortly after three; but what with having tea, and talking over old times, and having dinner, and going to the Bodega to meet the boy friend, and then going on to meet *his* friend at the Café Royal, Julia missed the last train back. She spent the night at the girl friend's flat, sleeping delightedly on the sofa in a bathrobe that smelt of grease paint; and that night, and that smell, settled her future. The next morning, at Barton, she told her parents-in-law that she was going back to live in Town.

"But — Susan?" said Mrs. Packett quickly.

Julia hesitated. Her husband's letter, now locked in Mrs. Packett's jewel-case, had been written on the assumption that the child was to be a son; but it was still a sort of gospel. Ponies, particularly Shetlands, were old Henry Packett's constant preoccupation, as

14

the educational requirements of Girton were the preoccupation of his wife . . .

"The child must of course stay here," said Henry Packett, speaking his thought.

"If Julia can bear to be separated —" began his wife more tactfully.

Julia felt that she could. Those nineteen months of being young Mrs. Packett had exhausted her supply of maternal affection; and she was also aware that for a young child the life at Barton was far more suitable than the life she herself looked forward to, in Town. She hadn't yet any definite plans about it, but she hoped and trusted that it would be very unsuitable indeed.

"Well — if she won't be too much trouble —"

"Trouble!" cried Mrs Packett joyfully. "Isn't this her home? As it's yours too, my dear, whenever you choose to come to it."

After that, all went smoothly. They disapproved, they were sorry, but they were unalterably good. Their patriotism had not permitted Julia to draw her pension; she had lived at Barton as a daughter, with a daughter's dress allowance; and this was now made up to three hundred a year. Julia, obscurely conscience-stricken, thought it too much, but the Packetts were adamant. They had apparently no opinion of her earning powers, and their son's widow could not possibly live on less. That was her portion, she must take it; and whenever she wished she was to come back to her home.

V

During the next year she went back five times. The year after, she went down for her daughter's birthday, but did not stay the night. On subsequent birthdays she wrote. But when Susan was nine Julia had a sudden burst of maternity and invited the child for a week's sight-seeing in Town. The opportunity was a good one, for Mr. Macdermot, whose flat Julia then shared, had been called to Menton by an invalid wife; but Susan did not come, and in answer to her invitation Julia received a counter-proposal of some importance.

The Packetts were prepared, they wrote, to take complete responsibility for the child's present, and to make her their heiress in the future, if Julia on her side would renounce all legal claim. Should she do so, she would of course see Susan whenever she wished, either at Barton or wherever else the grandparents decided; but she could not, without permission, take the child away alone. This last pill was gilded by a warm invitation from Mrs. Packett to come down at once and stay for a month.

Julia considered both these proposals carefully, accepted the first and rejected the second. She was only too glad to have her daughter's future so fully and agreeably secured, but she didn't want any renunciation scene. Also she was very busy, having interested herself, in a rather lofty, lady-patroness manner, in a new touring company then being organized by one of her theatrical friends. She would come down soon, she told the Packetts, but not just then.

Two months later she heard from them again. After that decent interval they presented her with a lump sum of seven thousand pounds in Government Stock, to take the place of her allowance. This surprising generosity Julia unresentfully interpreted as a desire to be finally rid of her; but she was only half-right. It was, also, a salve to Mrs. Packett's conscience. "With some money of her own," said Mrs. Packett (who had the frank, old-fashioned viewpoint), "she'll be able to get herself a husband."

Julia did not get a husband, but she went into management. She put on two plays within six months; and when the second came off there remained, of the seven thousand pounds, exactly nineteen-and-six.

VI

The death of Mr. Macdermot some three years later thus left Julia in a very precarious position. She was thirty-one, too old (and also too plump) to go back to the chorus; she had aquired comfortable if not luxurious tastes, and she was completely untrained for any of the respectable remunerative professions. But she managed. She was very versatile. She still got a certain amount of crowd-work, and was once (in a night-club scene) the Lady Who Fell into the Fountain. Now and again at mannequin parades she showed Models for the Fuller Figure. Her cheerful smile advertised a new baking powder and a Tonic for Women over Forty. Also, of course, she borrowed from gentleman friends, of whom she had a great many, and occasionally she accepted their hospitality. The only thing Julia never once considered was a return to Barton and the Packetts.

She was cut off from them for ever. With real humility she weighed herself up, and looked at herself all round, and acknowledged that she wasn't good enough for them. Certainly she wasn't good enough for a daughter who (as Mrs. Packett once reported) went to school at Wycombe Abbey, and who had riding lessons, and whose great friend was the daughter of a lord . . .

So Julia settled the matter in her mind, and for months on end (being extremely occupied and always hard-up) quite forgot she had a daughter at all.

It was only when Susan was in trouble that Julia's maternal instincts suddenly re-awoke; but they did so to some purpose. Their immediate effect, as has been seen, was the embarrassment of two bailiffs, and the swindling of Mr. Lewis.

CHAPTER
THREE

The address from which Susan had written was *Les Sapins, Muzin, près de Belley, Ain*; and as soon as the flat was once more at her disposal Julia went through her clothes to see which, if any, were suited to such a destination. It was in the country, of course, like Barton, and probably much the same sort of place; only naturally gayer, through being in France. Julia spread out her three evening dresses and looked at them thoughtfully: there was a midnight-blue taffeta — its bodice all boned-up to dispense with shoulder straps — which a scarf or coatee would possibly make do; but over the other two — one white, the top consisting chiefly of a black velvet poppy; one green, with sequins — Julia shook her head; even in France the Packetts wouldn't be as gay as that.

"I've got to look like a lady," she thought. "I've got to *be* a lady . . ."

The idea at once alarmed and braced her. It would be difficult, but she could do it. And on one point, indeed, Julia was more fortunate than she knew: her conception of the ladylike was as clear-cut, as lacking in ambiguous shades and small subtleties, as a dressmaker's diagram; and like a dressmaker's diagram, it was concerned with surface effects only. Nature's ladies were no ladies to Julia. They were good sorts, which was a very different thing. If you had suddenly asked Julia for a definition, she would probably have replied, Ladies never drink with their mouths full, and never pick any one up. If you had asked her why not, she would have replied, Because they are ladies. If then, with discourteous persistence, you inquired whether one must wait to see a woman eating and drinking, or being given the glad-eye, before one could tell, Julia would have enlarged her definition. You could always tell a lady by her clothes. However smart, the clothes of a true lady never hit you in the eye; and if she suddenly wanted to change her underwear — you would of course have had to get this bit out of Julia before she became a lady herself — she always could.

In the end Julia decided to take single instead of return tickets, and to buy a new dinner dress with the money saved. She also purchased a linen suit, a Matron's Model hat, and three pairs of camiknickers. She had indeed plenty of these already, but all with policemen embroidered on the legs. And on the platform at Victoria, for almost the first time in her life, she bought a book.

It was *The Forsyte Saga*, and Julia chose it partly because it seemed such a lot for the money, and partly because she had often heard Galsworthy spoken of as a Good Author. She fancied it was the sort of book Susan would like to see her mother reading; and Julia's maternal affection was so strong (though admittedly erratic) that she read three whole chapters between London and Dover.

II

Ladies, when travelling alone, never speak to anybody; so it was with but a stately inclination of the head that Julia thanked a naval officer who steadied her on the gang-way and a commercial traveller who set up her deck-chair. She had no difficulty in selecting an isolated position, for passengers were few; and with her coat over her knees, and the *Saga* open on her lap, she settled comfortably down to get on with Literature.

A schoolmistress in a mackintosh, reconnoitring for a sheltered spot, approached and paused.

"It's out of the wind here?" she speculated.

Julia inclined her head.

"Because I think," said the schoolmistress — though more formally — "that we're in for a blow."

Julia inclined her head again. The schoolmistress passed on. Julia then (with a brief interval while she watched a Daimler being swung on board) read three chapters of *A Man of Property* straight off the reel. If she found the going a trifle stiff, that rather pleased her than otherwise, for it confirmed her opinion that she was reading a really good book; and then, no one could possibly be more of a lady than its heroine. To have all that S.A. and never get any fun out of it! What could be more ladylike than that? So read, so mused Julia, a lady herself for all the world to see; and hardly lifted her eyes from one paragraph to the next.

She could not help noticing, however, a certain group composed of one woman and five men who stood leaning over the rail almost directly opposite her chair. It was the proportion of the sexes that attracted her attention. One woman to five men! Julia looked at her again, and saw nothing to merit such good fortune. She was short, plump, fifty if a day, with hair so violently golden, and lips so violently red, and such a drift of pale mauve powder on her nose, that not even an all-black ensemble could disguise her resemblance to a macaw. Julia really had to raise her eyebrows; but she also, before returning to her book, spared a glance for the five men. They varied in height from very tall to very short, but all had the same broad shoulders, straight backs, and narrow hips; there was even a vague likeness in their features, though the tallest (addressed as Fred) was also by far the best-looking. He was one of the handsomest men Julia had ever seen.

"I believe they're theatricals," she thought; and at that moment happened to catch Fred's eye. It was light-brown and boldly appreciative — just the sort of eye that Julia liked. But she did not respond. "None of that, now!" she adjured herself; and started doggedly on Chapter Eight.

Literature still kept its precarious hold on her attention when the boat, which had hitherto proceeded in a reasonable decorous manner, began to feel and transmit the increasing motion of the sea. The chops of the Channel were living up to their name, and more than one passenger stumbled hastily by, to contend with them below. Julia, in addition to many other useful qualities, had that of being an excellent sailor, and felt so little inconvenience that she decided to take a walk. Her feet were cold, and the empty decks offered space for brisk motion. A little unsteadily (in spite of her sea-legs) she walked twice up and down, then discovered that the other side would be more sheltered, and continued round. So far was she from seeking companionship that the sight of a group of five men would at once have driven her back, but that their attitudes — of bewilderment and dismay — at once drew her on. They were grouped, so far as she could discern, round a deck-chair; and as she approached a series of loud female groans told her that the victim, whether of accident or *mal de mer*, was their lady companion. She lay perfectly still, huddled in a lumpy mass, so that for one wild moment Julia imagined that the Daimler must have got loose and run over her. But it was sea-sickness only, as a sudden convulsion just then showed; and as a steward hurried up the group loosened and Fred detached himself. Julia's ladylike inhibitions melted like snow.

"If you want any brandy," she said directly, "I've a flask in my bag."

But he shook his head.

"She's had too much already. It's the pork."

"She does seem bad," murmured Julia sympathetically. The relief of opening her mouth, of returning to the common level of humanity, was so great that it brought with it a genuine flow of interest and concern. Julia, at that moment, not only would have given the sufferer her brandy, she would have held the sufferer's head. There were two men holding it already, however, and only sympathy was required.

"She *is* bad," stated Fred. "That's Ma all over — all merry and bright till the last minute, then up it all comes and she thinks she's going to die. *They*" — he nodded over his shoulder at the four mourners — "*they* want to undo her stays; but she won't let them."

"And quite right," said Julia warmly. "The stomach wants holding together, not letting loose. You ought to do them up tighter."

"You can't do Ma's stays any tighter — not without killing her. I don't know how she breathes as it is." They listened a moment in respectful silence, as the lady's groans rose a sudden octave higher. "Wonderful lung-power, hasn't she?" asked Fred with gloomy pride. "She used to be able to sing 'The Lost Chord' upside down."

"Theatricals?" asked Julia, pleased at her intuition.

With the neatness of a conjurer he produced his card. It was rather larger than usual, but then it had to be. "THE SIX FLYING GENOCCHIOS," it announced: "TRAPEZE AND HIGH WIRE. *Daring, Thrilling, Unbelievable. The Koh-i-Noor of Aerial Entertainment.*" The first line was printed in red, the second in silver, the third in blue; so that altogether it was a very imposing affair.

Julia had scarcely looked her admiration when a second card slipped over the first. On a smaller area, chastely engraved, she read the name and address of Mr. Fred Genocchio, 5, Connaught Villas, Maida Vale.

24

"That's my personal one," said Fred. "You keep it."

Julia slipped it into her bag. She was slightly mortified at not having one of her own to give in exchange, and as Fred waited expectantly had to introduce herself by mere word of mouth.

"I'm Mrs. Macdermot. I'm going to join my daughter."

"In Paris?"

"No, in Haute Savoie." Julia was pleased about that: Haute Savoie sounded so much better — more travelled, more distinguished. She should really have said Ain, of course, but did not know how to pronounce it.

"That's rather off our track," admitted Mr. Genocchio. "But then we only do Number Ones. We're opening tonight — just a hall show — at the Casino Bleu."

"It's got very beautiful scenery," continued Julia, who felt that Haute Savoie had not had its full due. "Mountains, and all that. I love scenery."

"So does Ma," said Mr Genocchio. "Take her out to Richmond and she's happy as a sandboy." He glanced over his shoulder again, evidently reawakening to his present troubles, and was at once beckoned back into the group. Not even the distressing sight that confronted him, however, could destroy his social sense.

"This is Mrs. Macdermot, Ma. She wondered —"

But Julia had now realized her error.

"Packett," she corrected firmly.

"Mrs. Packett, Ma." Fred accepted the amendment without any show of surprise. "She wondered if she could be of any help."

"No one can help me," moaned Ma in her anguish. "I wish you'd all go away. I'm dying, and I know it, and they want to undo me stays."

The five men looked first at each other, then at Julia. "Women!" that glance seemed to say. "*Women!*"

"Well, they're not going to," said Julia. "The tighter you are the better, and so I've been telling Mr. Genocchio."

Mr. Genocchio's mother — for such she was — only moaned again. She was passed all comfort, even the comfort of being let die in her corsets. "Go away!" she groaned. "Go away and leave me!"

There was evidently nothing to be done. For some minutes longer they stood sympathetic but impotent, like bystanders round a fallen horse. Then Fred slipped his arm through Julia's and drew her quietly away.

"She's right," he said. "We can't do anything. We'd better go and get a drink."

III

As they settled themselves in the bar Julia, her sympathies still engaged by so much distress, inquired whether the Sixth of the Flying Genocchios was Ma herself.

Fred shook his head.

"No. Ma doesn't fly: my old man was the sixth, and we still keep it on the card. Ma changes the number boards — you know, in tights. And between you and me, she's got past it."

"I don't think they're ever what you'd call becoming," said Julia tactfully. "At least not on a woman. A man with a good figure's different."

"You ought to see our show," said Mr. Genocchio.

With his neat conjurer's movement he produced as though from the air a fan of postcard-size photographs. All except one displayed the Six Flying Genocchios in various astonishing postures — cannoning in mid-air, pendant by the teeth; the card on top was dedicated to Fred alone. And he was superb: in black tights, against a light background, he showed as a long, slim, perfect balanced triangle, flawlessly tapered from the broad shoulders to the narrow feet. Julia gazed in admiration; she had no need to speak, her eyes were eloquent.

"You'd better come to-night," said Fred earnestly. "What time does your train go?"

"Eleven-forty," said Julia; but she hesitated. That gap of five hours at Paris was already consecrated, in her mind, to her book: she had intended to sit in the First-Class waiting-room, lost in a world of literature, while intrigued and intriguing Frenchmen vainly tried to get off with her. That, she felt, was how her journey should begin, for she had already shifted the starting-point to the Gare de Lyon. If she went to a music-hall with the Genocchios, that starting-point would have to be put off still further — till eleven-forty, in fact, which meant so much less time in which to work up her new rôle. Slapdash in everything else — and particularly in affairs of the heart — Julia nevertheless plumed herself on being a conscientious artist; and now these two sides of her character were at their usual game of Devil-pull-Baker. Then she looked at the postcard again, and the Devil won.

"All right," she said. "But I'm not going to miss my train. My daughter will be waiting for me."

His gratitude was cut short by the entrance of the four other Genocchios — three brothers and a cousin — who had followed their leader's example; and in the company of so many males Julia's spirits at once soared. Within five minutes she was the life and soul of the party. The warmth, the rowdiness, the pressure of Fred's knee against her own, all were equally agreeable to her; and only when Fred's hand went under the table as well did she suddenly remember about being a lady. It was hard, too, for those muscular fingers spoke a familiar and exciting language, to which her own cheerful flesh was only too ready to respond; but the spirit triumphed, and Julia rose.

"I'm going to have a look at Ma," she said. "It's too bad, leaving her all alone."

But she only made matters worse. As she went up the companionway a movement of the now pitching boat sent her almost off her feet. Julia staggered back, and but for the strong arm of the trapeze artist would have lost her balance. Fred had followed her up, and was holding her in an embrace so unnecessarily warm as to leave no doubts of his sentiments. He had fallen for her, flat; and Julia, always honest with herself, had no doubt that she could very easily have fallen for him. But she restrained herself nobly; perhaps *The Forsyte Saga*, which she still held under her arm, and which was pressing painfully into her ribs, lent her moral strength. In any case, instead of squeezing Fred back, she drew a little away.

"If you don't behave yourself," she gasped (for the boat was very lively indeed), "I shan't come to-night. I told you before, I'm going out to my daughter."

"All right," said Fred regretfully.

He understood. He was a perfect gentleman. Removing his arm from her waist he gave her no more support (hand under elbow) than the motion of the boat absolutely required. So, decorously, they went up on deck to the chaperonage of Ma.

Julia was sad. She felt that if only things had been different, they could have had a really lovely time.

IV

In the Paris train, which was three-parts empty, the Genocchios, with Julia, occupied two adjoining compartments. In the first lay Ma, who after being supported through the Customs had immediately collapsed again, and who was still being ministered to by Joe, Jack, Bob, and Willie; the other, Julia and Fred had all to themselves. This situation was less dangerous than it seemed, for every now and then one of the lesser Genocchios would come in to report progress, or to smoke a cigarette; but even in their solitary interludes Fred's behaviour was now impeccable. He talked quietly and seriously, chiefly about money, and displayed a most becoming family pride. The

Genocchios, he would have Julia know, were no mere buskers; Italian by origin, they had come over, if not exactly with the Conqueror, at any rate in the reign of Charles II. They had play-bills to prove it. There was a play-bill bearing their name in the Victoria and Albert Museum. He, Fred, as a nipper, had been taken to see it by his father and uncle — both notable artists; and it was his own grandfather who had actually presented it. There wasn't another family in the profession — except, of course, the great Lupinos — who could show a record to touch it. Julia listened entranced, nor did her interest wane when from the past Fred worked up to the present. He spoke of money in the Bank, of a freehold house at Maida Vale; for in addition to being artists, the Genocchios were also shrewd. Not one, in two hundred years, had been buried by the parish. They had had their ups and downs of course (and what family hadn't? Look at the Bourbons!); but for the last century neither a roof of their own, nor money in the Bank, had ever been lacking, . . .

"You must make grand husbands," said Julia sincerely.

"We do. And when we marry, we stick. No chopping and changing. Why, Ma wouldn't be with us now if Dad hadn't died six months ago. She couldn't seem to get over it, and then she took a fancy to come along, and we thought it might brighten her up. But it was a mistake," finished Fred gloomily. "Her stomach was always a bit weak."

He relapsed into silence, evidently preoccupied with professional troubles. Julia, to distract him, inquired after the rising generation; but his gloom only deepened.

"Bob and Willie are married all right, but they've only a couple of girls between them. Nice bright little kids too, but apart from the name you don't often get a woman acrobat first-class. They're learning dancing." Fred sighed. "I ought to marry myself. But there was a girl, six years ago . . ."

Julia pressed his hand. She couldn't help it, and he took it as meant.

"She fell into the net all right, but something twisted. I think she wished there hadn't been a net. Anyway, she died three months after, and for a bit I hated the whole business."

"I wonder you didn't chuck it," said Julia.

"Chuck it?" He looked at her in surprise. "Of course I didn't chuck it. But it upset me, if you know what I mean. I don't say I've never looked at a woman since, because I have; but marrying 'em was different."

"I don't suppose," said Julia gently, "she'd have wanted you not to . . ."

"She didn't. Just when she was going she said, 'Give my love to your wife, Fred' — just like that. Here, I didn't mean to upset you!"

For Julia was already weeping. No considerations of complexion had ever been able to restrain her tender heart, and the tears mingled with her rouge until Fred's handkerchief was patched with pink. When at last she blew her nose she looked five years older, but Fred did not seem to mind. He put one arm about her shoulder and tried to dry her eyes himself.

"No," sobbed Julia. "You go and see to Ma. I want to do my face."

He went at once — the perfect gentleman. Once alone, Julia's tears rapidly ceased, leaving her only pleasantly purged by emotion, and she settled down to her vanity-box with a single mind. There is no doubt that she was enjoying the journey exceedingly: her grief, perfectly genuine while it lasted, was but an extra incident in a thoroughly interesting, variegated trip. She wouldn't have missed it. Even the hasty renovation of her face was amusing to her, and she exchanged her more subdued (or Packett) lipstick for a new Kiss-proof in flamingo red. The effect was striking, but when Mr. Genocchio returned he did not appear to notice it.

"I'm worried about Ma," he said sombrely. "She's still heaving."

Julia looked up with concern.

"And what's more, when she stops heaving, she'll go to sleep. That fool Joe's been filling her up with cognac like pouring it into a flask. If you ask me" — he flung himself down on the seat — "she'll have to disappoint."

"Well, she's not really part of the show, is she?" asked Julia, in an attempt to console. "I mean, it's not like *you* dropping out."

"She gave us a breather. You can do with a breather in our act. Besides — I know you wouldn't think it to see her now — Ma's good. She's got a good smile, and a sort of way with her. Twinkle in her eye and so on. You'd be surprised the hand she gets."

"It's experience does it," said Julia rather ambiguously. "Can't you get someone at the theatre?"

32

"We might, but there's not much time, and they hate any one giving trouble. It's no use worrying. If she's all right she's all right, and if she isn't —"

"If she isn't, I'll have to help you out myself," said Julia.

The words were scarcely past her lips when she knew they were a mistake. There are occasions when one should refrain from well-doing, and this was one of them. When you are going to join your daughter — at any rate, when you are going to join such a daughter as Susan — you shouldn't step aside into borrowed tights. But already Fred was grasping her hands in almost excessive gratitude, and from his fingers into hers ran a peculiar thrill. It was the thrill of theatrical excitement, the thrill of the-other-side-of-the-curtain, to which she had so long been a stranger, and which (as she now realized) she had so sorely missed. "Just this once!" Julia told herself. "Just this one last time, before I'm too old!"

So it was that, instead of going on to the Gare de Lyon, Julia got out at the Gare du Nord.

CHAPTER
FOUR

Standing on a chair before the inadequate dressing-room mirror, Julia took a good close-up look at her legs. It was so long since she had seen them in tights that she felt both curious and apprehensive — especially as the tights worn by Ma were definitely outsize. But if Mrs. Genocchio was stout, she was also short, and the material was very elastic. By judicious pulling-up Julia had achieved an adequate degree of tautness, and the reflection in the mirror now set her doubts at rest. Stilted on the two-inch heels of her own silver shoes, Julia's legs rose strong and shapely to the silver loincloth; and if they weren't quite in the mannequin class, they had nevertheless an appeal of their own.

"Men don't care for toothpicks, anyway," said Julia complacently.

With some precaution, on account of her heels, she got down from the chair and took her upper half in turn. It was lightly covered by a sort of bathing-dress top, black like the tights, and a silver bolero. A headdress composed of black ostrich feathers, springing from a silver tiara, completed the costume; and whoever designed it (thought Julia) must have had a great deal of taste.

There was a rap at the door; she sprang away from the mirror and took up a nonchalant pose in a good light.

"It's me: Fred," called Mr. Genocchio.

"Come in!" called Julia.

Her heart was suddenly beating fast. Suppose he didn't like her? Suppose he thought her too . . . plump? With passionate repudiation she cast a backward glance over all the French pastries she had ever eaten. Why had she eaten them, when she always knew they'd be her ruin? On one occasion to amuse Mr. Macdermot, she had consumed four éclairs running . . . "He ought to have been ashamed!" she thought bitterly; and if her agitation seems excessive, it must be remembered that Julia lived ever for the moment, and that this moment was wholly Fred's.

She need not have feared, however. Fred's face, as he stood in the doorway, was positively goopish with admiration.

"You're wonderful," he said at last.

"So are you," said Julia earnestly.

For no photograph could do him justice. A photograph could give only the sheen of his black tights, not the play of muscles beneath; only the statuesque beauty of poise, not the fluid beauty of movement. Fred walked across the room like a black panther; and as he gazed in admiration Julia all unwittingly acquired something she had long coveted. She acquired a scrap of culture, and if she did not recognize it as such, that was because what one looks for among good Books one does not expect to find in the dressing-room of a music-hall. But so it happened: having filled her eyes with a best in its kind, Julia could not then turn them on a second-best without knowing it for what it was.

"I've too many bits and pieces," she stated, looking at herself in the mirror.

Fred stared in astonishment.

"You're grand. What don't you like?"

"All these." Julia slipped off bolero and headdress and held them behind her back. "They're beautiful, Fred, but I feel I ought to be neater, . . ."

Side by side they gazed at her reflection; but, without the counterbalancing feathers, Julia's hips, emphasized by the silver loincloth, now looked disproportionately large. She shook her head.

"I haven't the figure for it," she admitted sadly. "I'd best leave it alone."

"Your figure's grand," said Fred. And he meant it. He looked at her with heartfelt admiration. As Julia replaced her headdress he said suddenly, "This place where you're going — is Mr. Packett there too?"

"He's dead," said Julia. "He was killed in the war."

"You must have been an awful kid to get married."

"Sixteen," said Julia. "He was an awful kid to get killed."

"He was a hero all right," said Fred.

Julia nodded without speaking. His sympathy was sweet to her, but she had a suspicion that the spirit of her late husband might not be appreciating it. Sylvester never had liked her friends: when they tried to tell him how brave he was, he used to bite on his thumb and walk away. His shade was probably biting on its thumb now, and Julia, to placate it, hastily changed the subject.

"Isn't it nearly our call, Fred?"

"About four minutes to go. Nervous?"

"Just a bit. It's as soon as I see you bowing?"

"As soon as you see us bowing you come on and change the card — just take the top one off. You can't go wrong if you try."

He grinned at her encouragingly, and Julia suddenly laughed back. For the next hour at least they were bound to each other, they were comrades, they were fellow members of a troupe that was also a family. For the next hour she was to be, not Mrs. Sylvester Packett, but the sixth Flying Genocchio . . .

"*Allez-oop!*" cried Julia; and the call-boy knocked on the door.

II

Though Julia's legs might not conform to modern mannequin standards, they were greatly to the taste of the patrons of the Casino Bleu. Her second appearance was welcomed with acclamation, and in spite of all resolutions to the contrary she could not help casting a few glad-eyes over the crowded hall. After all, she owed it to Fred to do her best; and her best was very good indeed. There was a bonhomie about her, a willingness to give and receive pleasure, which at once brought her into contact with the audience; and as the turn advanced that contact grew more intimate. Gentlemen here and there shouted personal and appreciative remarks, and Julia's French, though scanty, was sufficient for her to keep her end up. "*Vive la France!*" she called back: "*Vive l'amour! Cherchez la femme* and many of them!" It was not wit, of course, in the classic sense, but it passed for such to her now numerous admirers, and each time she came on the exchanges grew longer and more uproarious. As for Julia, the feel of the boards under her feet, and the smell of a theatre in her nostrils, and the sound of applause in her ears, all combined to intoxicate her. Like every good actress, she was a little above herself; her personality had swelled to more than life-size; and only a sound professional conscience kept her from stealing the show. The instant she saw the troupe in position she dived for the wings; not till the last wave of applause had ebbed did she reappear. Even so, she felt qualms.

"I can't help it," she murmured to Fred in a moment when he was not performing. "I know I shouldn't have answered, but I didn't think."

He had no breath to reply — as Julia knew by the superb expansion and contraction of his chest — but his smile said everything. It was all right, he didn't mind; and when at the end of the turn she took her call with the rest his arm slipped through hers and clipped it tight to his side.

"You were grand!" he murmured, while the curtain swung down and up; and at the touch of his cheek, as he whispered, a delicious thrill ran like wine through

Julia's body. This, this, she thought, was life! The fouled air was like balmy breezes to her: the people in the audience — good and bad, clean and grimy — were her friends, her kindred, the partakers of her joy. As far as Julia ever felt a communion with nature, she felt it then. And if the nature thus communed with was exclusively human, and therefore (as is commonly believed) less pure, less elevating, than the inanimate, that was the fault of circumstance. The trees and mountains were waiting for her in Savoy.

III

Three hundred miles away old Mrs. Packett sat up and looked at the time. It was half-past ten; she had gone to bed too early. Susan always made her grandmother go to bed early when there was to be anything special next day — and then when the next day arrived, made her stay in bed late.

"Silly foolishness!" said old Mrs Packett aloud. She stretched herself out between the cool, lavender-smelling sheets: her old body felt tough and vigorous — a bit stiff in the joints, but quite capable of sitting up till a reasonable hour. She had been a trifle nervy that afternoon, no doubt; but who wouldn't, with a resurrected daughter-in-law hanging over one's head. Hadn't she a strange young man practically living in the house already? "I didn't come here to entertain a house-party," thought Mrs. Packett crossly; "I came here for rest and peace and Susan's French." But Susan was for once being unreasonable: instead of getting quietly on with her Molière she must needs go and fall in love, and adopt ridiculous martyred attitudes, and write ridiculous letters to a parent she had hardly seen! Mrs. Packett no longer feared Julia; Susan (as no one knew better than her grandmother) was past the malleable stage; but a positive invitation was more than any normal woman could resist . . .

"I let Susan domineer," thought Mrs. Packett. "It's a bad habit for both of us." Then, involuntarily, she smiled; Susan's domineering was very sweet. It made one feel — wanted. It kept one up to the mark. Susan was very particular, for example, about her grandmother's hats; she always made straight for the model department, and would look at nothing under two guineas. Once, for a plain black straw with a velvet ruche, she made the old lady pay five. "It's the *line*," Susan had explained. "It makes you look like a Romney." Mrs. Packett always submitted. She still had a tendency to woolly jackets, and to bits of embroidery on the chest, but her hats were admirable . . .

"Julia never cared," thought Mrs Packett suddenly. Julia had never cared about anything. A nice girl in her way, most docile and obliging, but always with an air of being only half-alive . . . and then she had gone off like that on her own and never come back again! So there must have been something in her, something that Barton was suppressing, was inimical to. Mrs. Packett pondered. In her own youth, before she was married off, she had often thought about living her own life and breeding spaniels: had Julia's thoughts run along the same lines? She never got that husband, it seemed; but what had she done with the seven thousand pounds? Just gone on drawing the income? "If I'd been she," thought Mrs. Packett vigorously, "I'd have started a nice little business." Perhaps Julia had; perhaps she was even now leaving behind a tea-shop, or a hat-shop, or a high-class florist's; and if so, it was to be hoped that she had a manageress she could trust.

Mrs. Packett dozed, stirred, and woke up again. The villa, like the village at its gate, was very still, and through the open window came a gust of sweet pine-scented air.

"A holiday will do her good," thought old Mrs. Packett; for somehow, during her nap, she had become firmly convinced that Julia kept a cake-shop. They would have nice long conversations about it: Julia probably had all sorts of new recipes, and if Anthelmine could be got out of the kitchen, they might even try their hands . . .

"Maids-of-honour," murmured Mrs. Packett; and on that comfortable thought went finally and peacefully to sleep.

IV

Meanwhile, in the taxi between the music-hall and the Gare de Lyon, Julia was receiving a proposal of marriage. Ardent yet respectful (Julia indeed keeping him off with an elbow against the chest) Fred Genocchio offered his hand, his heart, his money in the Bank, and his villa at Maida Vale.

"Stay here!" he implored. "Stay here where you belong, Julia, and we'll get married as soon as ever we can. As soon as the week's up the others can go back and we'll have a regular honeymoon. You're the hit of the show, Julie, you're made for it, and I want you so! And you want me, Julie, you know you do!"

She did want him. Her elbow dropped, for a long minute she surrendered to the breath-taking sensation of a trapeze artist's embrace. The motion of the taxi flung them from side to side: first Julia's back, then Fred's, thumped violently against the upholstery; and neither even noticed.

"You'll stay," said Fred.

His voice broke the spell. Julia's eyes opened, travelled vaguely past his shoulder, and focussed at last on two white patches in the darkness. They were the labels on her luggage, whose superscription she had written in London only twenty-four hours earlier: *Les Sapins, Muzin, prés de Belley, Ain*.

"I can't!" cried Julia. "I'm going to my daughter!"

She drew herself away and felt Fred stiffen beside her.

"Your daughter doesn't want you like I do!"

"She does, Fred! She's unhappy, and in trouble, and she's there waiting for me! She hasn't wanted me for years —"

"Then she can get along without you now. Julie, my darling —"

"No," said Julia.

Her distress was at least as great as his. To know him suffering, in despair, when with one word she could make all well again, was an agony so acute that she could hardly breathe. It was not her nature to deny: if she took lovers more freely than most women it was largely because she could not bear to see men sad when it was so easy to make then happy. Her sensuousness was half compassion; she could never keep men on a string, which was perhaps why only one had ever married her; and now — the bitterness! — when Fred wanted to marry her, she had to refuse him . . .

"Wait!" she pleaded. "Wait till I get back!"

"You won't come back," said Fred sombrely. "They'll get hold of you. That daughter of yours . . ."

Julia felt a sudden chill. Hitherto, unconsciously, she had been limiting that daughter's existence, and her own term of motherhood, to the next month; now she looked into the future. To marry Fred Genocchio would be to give Susan an acrobat for a stepfather. An acrobat among the Packetts! It was unthinkable, and Julia sat thinking of it, silent and in misery, while every jolt of the taxi brought them nearer to the Gare de Lyon.

"There's another thing," said Fred at last. Julia became very still; by the constraint in his voice, by the sudden casualness of his manner, she knew he was about to reveal an inner secret of the heart. "There's another thing," said Fred. "I've never been able — on the high wire — to do a forward somersault. But I've sometimes thought, if I had a son — perhaps *he* might."

V

How Julia got herself into the train, and found her sleeper, and tipped the attendant, she never quite knew. From the moment they left the taxi she had chattered aimlessly, unconscious of what she said, unconscious of Fred's replies, unconscious of everything save the pressure of his arm against her side. But she managed it nevertheless; somehow, suddenly, she was standing in the train corridor, and Fred was on the station platform, and there was a sheet of glass between them. He stood superb and statuesque, moveless as a rock — the best-built man Julia had ever seen. Then the earth seemed to slide under her feet as the train moved out; she waved once, foolishly, then stumbled into her compartment and locked the door.

She was tired as a cat, and no wonder.

She was too tired to cry, certainly too tired to lie awake. After a brief examination of the toilet arrangements — whose novelty and neat commodiousness could not fail to please — Julia hastily creamed her face and got into pyjamas. A couple of darkening bruises, one on each forearm, testified to the uncommon power of Mr. Genocchio's grip. They were the only souvenirs she had of him, and even those would fade . . .

Julia slid into her bunk and was just preparing for sleep when she noticed a narrow and hitherto unexplored door. Curiosity impelled her to get up and

44

slip back the bolt; she found herself looking not into a cupboard, but into the next (and empty) compartment.

"Handy!" thought Julia.

Then she got back into bed and slept like a log.

CHAPTER
FIVE

Ten minutes before the train stopped at Ambérieu (the time being then twenty-past six) Julia put on her Matron's Model and stood considering the effect.

It wasn't good. The hat was all right in itself, and value for money; but it didn't suit Julia. Perhaps the events of the previous day had left too many traces: there was a faint old-pro look about her, something hardy and cheerful, but a trifle worn . . .

"I need my sleep," thought Julia, tilting the hat further. It was of fine brown straw, mushroom-shaped, with a bunch of ribbons in front, but the angle at which Julia wore it was foreign to its nature. A dowager at a fête, who had been given champagne instead of claret-cup, might indeed have achieved the same effect; only it was not the one Julia sought. She took the thing off, planted it squarely on her head, and tried again. Under the straight brim her round black eyes stared in good-humoured astonishment; the full mouth, the soft chin, had no business to be there. "You're right," said Julia to her reflection, "but I'm damn' well going to wear it all the same. Don't you know it's the sort of hat she'll be looking for?"

Before the thought of her daughter all else fled. The train was slowing down already; Julia seized her smaller suitcase and hurried into the corridor. She meant to get down the steps at once and be ready on the platform, so that when Susan rushed up there would be no impediment to their embrace — and also so that the label on her suitcase would be properly displayed. For Julia was not relying on filial instinct alone: she had prepared a special piece of cardboard, seven inches by four, with MRS. PACKETT printed in block capitals. Thus not even a stranger could help knowing who she was; and as things turned out — as they so often turned out with Julia — it was a stranger who first addressed her.

"Mees' Packett?"

"Go away," said Julia sharply. He was a very little man, and she looked straight over his head, scanning the platform. No rushing daughterly figure was in sight; the few passengers and their friends were already melting away. Julia was not exactly uneasy, but she could feel uneasiness round the corner . . .

"Mees' Packett?" implored the man again. "Mees' Packett, Les Sapins, Muzin?" He was holding something out to her, an envelope, which did indeed bear her name; and as Julia looked at it her heart lightened. This time at any rate she knew the hand.

Dear Mother,
I am so very glad you have come, but I'm not meeting you because six-thirty a.m. at a railway station is such a ghastly place for reunions. The

man who gives you this is the station chauffeur, he will bring you to Muzin, and if you like you can have a bath and some more sleep before breakfast.

Affectionately,

SUSAN.

Julia folded the note away, indicated her luggage to the chauffeur, and followed him out of the station to where the car stood waiting. The freshness of the grey morning air made her shiver: as she powdered her nose again, scrutinizing her features in the little glass, she felt that Susan had perhaps been wise.

"Very sensible indeed," said Julia aloud. To her surprise, she sounded as though she were trying to convince someone. "And very *thoughtful*," added Julia angrily. Then she folded her coat over her knees and appreciated the landscape. Her dominant impression was that it went up. Just for a moment she closed her eyes; and when she reopened them the car had come to a stop.

II

They appeared to be in a farmyard. Poultry fluttered round their wheels, a dog barked, and over the half-door of a stable a horse looked at them intently.

"*Qu'est-ce que c'est?*" called Julia, rapping on the glass.

"*Muzin*," called back the chauffeur.

Julia looked at the horse, the horse looked at Julia. Directly over its head, fastened to the wall, was a very old sign advertising Singer Sewing Machines.

48

"Ah!" exclaimed the chauffeur with satisfaction; and leaning from his seat he hailed a group of three men, all bearing agricultural implements, who had suddenly materialized in his path. They wore coloured shirts, blue trousers, and straw hats vaguely moulded in the shape of sun-helmets. These gave them, to Julia's eye, an odd air of tropical explorers; but they were evidently (and on the contrary) natives.

"*Bonjour, messieurs*," called the chauffeur. "*C'est ici Les Sapins?*"

The eldest of them indicated a narrow opening between two barns. Through there, said the gesture, and up — but up! — one would find Les Sapins. The car moved slowly forward, crawled through the narrows, crossed a square with a fountain in it, and then climbed up — up — by two more lanes (or farmyards) until it was stopped by a tall iron gate. This the chauffeur opened; and as its leaves swung apart Julia saw on the farther side the first stately outposts — huge, dark, majestic — of an avenue of pines.

She was there.

III

The villa of Les Sapins, as originally constructed at the time of the first Empire, was a small white building partly of two stories, partly of one. It jutted squarely from the hillside, the upper or front door opening on a terrace at the foot of the vine, the lower door upon a terrace over the kitchen-garden. Below were the dining-room, the kitchen, and the larders; above a salon and three bedrooms. This accommodation had sufficed until about 1890, when a new owner of convivial tastes added a billiard-room and two more bed-chambers. He built straight along on the flat, thus turning the original square into a rectangle; and besides elongating the terraces to suit, he joined them by fine stucco staircases, one at either end of the house. With the construction of these staircases the glory of Les Sapins reached its height; and it lasted but two years. The jovial owner went bankrupt, the villa stood empty, or was rented and neglected by a succession of summer tenants; until finally it passed into the hands of an English spinster named Spencer-Jones, who put in a bath. Miss Spencer-Jones knew Mrs. Packett; and Mrs. Packett took it for the summer of 1936.

Even in decadence the place was charming. A great Virginia jasmine, dropping red waxen trumpets, concealed the worst deficiencies of the roof. In the deep shadow of the embowering pines the walls still looked white. Tubs of oleander flanked the broken steps, a great lime tree spread shade and perfume over the lower terrace; the rose-bushes looked like summer-houses, the summer-house like a rose-bush.

But the glory of the place was the view. From the top of the vineyard, which mounted directly behind the house, one looked straight across a vast circular plain — mountain-girdled, dotted with villages, varied by little hills, cultivated over every foot — whose centre was the tiny bishopric of Belley. It was the joke of the village that the back door at Les Sapins was two hundred feet higher than the front; and the pride of the villa that from it one could see Mont Blanc.

IV

High up amongst the topmost trees, on the morning of Julia's arrival, stood a tall, fair girl in an old mackintosh. She had been there since six, watching the Ambérieu road as a beleaguered garrison watches for the relieving force; yet as the car at last appeared her expression did not clear. She had called in, not a known ally, but a strange power. By that impulsive letter, posted as soon as it was written, she had invited a stranger to her inmost councils; had tacitly given word to throw down all defences, expose every weakness, in return for a reinforcement whose strength she did not know.

"Have I been a fool?" asked Susan Packett of the pine trees.

There was naturally no answer. But as the gates clanged open, as the car nosed up the avenue, Susan turned her back on the house and began to climb higher and higher, towards the bare rocks.

CHAPTER
SIX

Under the roses of the porch Julia was received by an elderly Frenchwoman, who at once conducted her into a wide, echoing hall. The Frenchwoman, in list-slippers, padded quietly as a cat, but Julia's heels clattered; and it was perhaps then that that she received the impression, which never afterwards left her, that she always made twice as much noise as any one else in the house.

"*La salle de bain*," said the old woman, proudly flinging open a door.

"*Je vois*," said Julia; "*très chic*."

"Madame will take the bath?"

"*Toute de suite*," agreed Julia. "At any rate, as soon as I've got a sponge out. *Eponge, savon. Dans les valises*."

"*Madame parle français!*" exclaimed the old woman politely; and a moment later Julia wished she hadn't, for while fetching the bags Claudia let out, in a volley of animated French, what Julia felt sure were messages from Susan, messages from Mrs. Packett, and general instructions for her own procedure. There was nothing for it, however, but to smile intelligently; and this Julia did.

"*Et — c'est là la chambre de Madame!*" finished the old woman with a flourish.

Julia stood still in the middle of it and looked about her. It was like no room she had ever seen — large, square, with white walls, bare boards, and two windows open on pines, sunshine and a view to a blue hill. There was a white bed in an alcove between two closets, a tiny dressing-table almost concealed behind a great bunch of roses, two chairs, and another table by the windows set with a breakfast-tray and more flowers.

"It's a bit bare," thought Julia, "but there's a lovely lot of room"; and unlocking the larger of her two suitcases she emptied it upon the bed. Her dressing-gown came out at the bottom, but she fished it up, and opened the other case to get her sponge-bag, and moved the roses from the dressing-table to make room for her toilet things. By the time her bath was ready, after only ten minutes' occupation, the whole aspect of the place was so completely altered that even Julia herself felt a slight surprise.

"I've got to be tidy," she warned herself firmly. All ladies were tidy: they had special boxes to pack their shoes in, and special boxes for their gloves, and bags marked "Linen" for their dirty vests. Julia too would have had these things, if finances had permitted; but as they didn't it seemed useless to worry over details. A broad general effect was (as always) Julia's aim; and this she now achieved by sweeping everything into a closet and shutting the door. But for the roses on the floor, and a stocking on the window-seat — and some shoes under the table and a powder-box among the breakfast things — one would never have known that she had been in the room at all.

II

And now, surely, as she lay triumphant in that French bath, was the moment for the Marseillaise. But not a note issued from Julia's throat. She was a little tired after her travelling, and a little sentimental still over Fred; but the chief reason for her silence was that she hadn't yet, so to speak, been introduced. She felt odd enough herself, lying stark naked in a house where she hadn't even met her hostess; how would Susan feel if after such careful plans for their first meeting her mother prematurely announced her presence by a song from the bath? And since splashing would be almost as bad, Julia found herself moving carefully, almost furtively, in the water: washing her back with precaution, lying down by degrees, so that not a ripple lapped. She found herself pretending, in fact, that she wasn't there; and if she closed her eyes the sensation was remarkably complete. Even the water, unscented, unmoving, didn't feel quite real. It was just a warm atmosphere in which she floated disembodied, no more real than anything else . . .

"Here!" cried Julia, vaguely alarmed, "I mustn't go to sleep!"

The sound of her own voice aroused her; she at once sat up, listening intently, to see whether any one else had been aroused as well. But all was quiet, and with a

54

sigh of relief she climbed unobtrusively out and began to dry. There were two bath-towels, beautifully large and white, besides a smaller one of linen, with embroidery on the edge; and though it was impossible to make real use of the lot, Julia had such a damn' good try that she heard the maid's slippered feet in the passage, and her own door open and shut, while she was still polishing up her thighs.

"It's my breakfast," thought Julia; and, anxious to be in the right place at the right time — another form of self-effacement — she hurried on her clothes and hastened back to her room. There was no one there, but rolls and honey had appeared on the breakfast-table; anxious to be found in the right garments, Julia exchanged her dressing-gown for a white piqué frock and hastily powdered her nose. And it was a mercy she did so, for the next moment there was a rap at the door, and behind the door was a coffee-pot, and carrying the coffee-pot was her daughter Susan.

III

At the first sight of her Julia's heart leapt up. For Susan was pretty, and pretty in a peculiarly ladylike way. She had the Packett height and slimness, the fair Packett hair, and eyes of that rare clear grey that is unflecked, unshaded, by any tint of blue. There was nothing of Julia in that face, and nothing of Julia in the sweet virginal voice.

"Good-morning," said Susan.

She was still holding the coffee-pot (could it be protectively?) so that Julia, poised for an embrace, had to sink as it were back into herself before answering.

"Good-morning," she said, trying to keep the quiver out of her voice. "Good-morning, Susan."

The girl set down the pot (could it be that she felt the danger pass?) and smiled gravely.

"Yes," she said. "I'm Susan. I hope you didn't mind my not coming to meet you. But —"

"But it's so much nicer here," finished Julia quickly.

"It shocked Grandmother, but I thought you'd understand." (That was heartening, at any rate!) "And she's also rather shocked," continued Susan, smiling again, "because I wouldn't let her get up to welcome you. She's sitting up in bed now, waiting for the moment you've finished your breakfast. But I had to have you to myself first."

Such pleasant words, spoken in so grave and charming a voice, filled Julia with maternal joy. But it was a joy still a little constrained: as she sat down to the table, and let Susan pour out for her, the odd feeling of the bathroom surged over her once again. Was this truly her daughter, standing so dutifully over the breakfast-tray? Was this strange bare house one in which she herself had truly a daughter's rights? It didn't feel real. Nothing felt real, not even the bread between her teeth, which she had to make an effort to swallow . . .

"Are you feeling shy?" asked Susan unexpectedly. "I am."

Julia beamed.

"Till you said that I was." Impulsively she got up from the table; but she was still too shy to give her daughter a kiss. Susan, in spite of so much charm, didn't look the kissing sort; and as the thought crossed her mind Julia felt an added curiosity to hear about Susan's young man. "Tell me all about him!" cried Julia impetuously; and sat down on the window-seat with ears and heart open.

Susan, however, had her own plans. She smiled affectionately, but with a shake of the head.

"His name is Bryan Relton, he's twenty-six and a barrister, and he'll be quite well off. You'll see him at lunch. Only it's no use discussing anything now, is it? I mean until you've got to know us both, it's not fair to ask for your opinion."

Nicely put, thought Julia; but she knew what it meant all the same. "Not fair" meant "no use"; and though the assumption was perfectly sound, such rationality, in a girl in love, struck her as exaggerated. Or was it rather caution? Was Bryan Relton one of those young men for whom nothing much can be said, but who have only to make a personal appearance to carry all before them? So wondered Julia, but not for long; she was too much occupied with observing her daughter. The more you looked at her — and Susan was now sitting close on the window-seat — the more perfect you saw she was. Her beautiful small ears lay flat to her head; her beautiful small hands, brown but perfectly kept, sprang delicately from the wrists as leaves from the slender stem. And then she was so clean! Julia was clean herself, she had a bath every day, so long as there was gas: but Susan's was the cleanliness of a running stream — something as much and as essential a part of her as her height or her grey eyes.

"I don't wonder he's wild about her," thought Julia, returning, though only in silence, to the forbidden topic. "I expect he's poetical." She pictured him tall and thin and very serious, the sort that adores once and for a lifetime, and she also pictured him a good deal older than his years, since it is generally to men above thirty that the virginal makes most appeal. "I bet he thinks she's a sort of angel," mused Julia, highly approving . . .

"What would you like me to call you?" asked Susan suddenly. "You look so young to be called 'Mother.'"

Julia felt a pang of disappointment. Of course she wanted to be called "Mother" — hadn't she come all the way from England for that very purpose? She wanted to be called "Mother," "Mumsie," "Mummy," "Mum"; but from Susan's tone she knew at once that none of these vocables would ever find favour. As before, it was nicely put; but behind the tribute to her appearance Julia divined a shrinking, an embarrassment which her own warm heart found difficult to comprehend.

Instead of directly answering, she said, a little wistfully, "You can't think how glad I was to get your letter. I know I've never been as much to you as I should — that was my own fault; and it made me so happy that you should still turn to me. I know I'm not really your sort —"

She broke off, for her daughter's embarrassment was now unconcealed. Susan had got up and was staring fixedly out of the window.

"I think you were perfectly right," she said rapidly. "You wanted to live your own life, and you did. I've no patience with people who sacrifice themselves to other people's ideas. If you want to know, I've always admired you."

"You — you have been happy with them?" asked Julia anxiously.

"Perfectly happy. Grandmother's an absolute darling, and so was Grandpa. And, I can't help knowing it, I've made them happy too. I've somehow consoled them for losing my father." She turned back, her face eager. "Will you tell me all about him, please?"

The moment had come — the moment for intimacy, for the long mother-and-daughter talk to which Julia had so much looked forward. But her heart, instead of leaping, sank within her. For when it came to the point — when the image of Sylvester Packett should have sprung fully-formed in her mind — she found she remembered practically nothing about him at all.

IV

"He was a first lieutenant in the Gunners —" began Julia carefully; and paused. There had been so many first lieutenants, a lot of them in the Gunners, and they had all been very much alike. Young, tired, reckless in gaiety, but never — never quite all there. Never completely with you, as though they had all left part of themselves somewhere else. You could be out dining with a man, having a perfectly lovely time, and suddenly across the room he would catch another man's eye, or a man would pause by your table, and all at once they were somewhere else and you were left behind. It had seemed as if war were a sort of fourth dimension, into which they slipped back without noticing, even out of your arms . . . So you never really knew them — at least the Julias didn't — and how could you remember any one you hadn't properly known?

"Don't, if it hurts you," said Susan gently.

In spite of her self-justification, Julia felt ashamed. She cudgelled her brains.

"He liked the Piccadilly better than Murray's," she said at last. "Most of them didn't. But then he wasn't like the rest in lots of ways."

"No?" prompted Susan.

"He was very serious. And he had very good manners. He was so good to me —" Julia broke off: impossible to tell his daughter exactly *how* good! And overcome by the effort, and by self-reproach, and by easy yet sincere regrets, she accidentally did the only right thing. She put down her head and burst into tears.

"Oh, don't!" cried Susan remorsefully. "Please, *please*!"

But Julia wept on. She might forget Sylvester for years on end, but when she did think about him it was properly. He was the best man she had ever known, he had taken thought for her, he had left her his name and

— had she wished for it — the protection of his home. He had married her! No one else . . .

"Except Fred," thought Julia.

The events of the previous evening — at the Casino Bleu, in the taxi going to the station — rose incongruously in her mind. She thrust them back, but not before they had given her, oddly enough, something she wanted.

"I've remembered another thing," she sobbed. "Something that was really *him*. Whenever he was upset he used to bite his thumb. Not the nail, you know, but down by the joint."

With a quick movement Susan stood up.

"You'd like to go in the garden," she said abruptly. "No — you'd like to see Grandmother. I'll see — I'll tell her. It's lovely in the garden. I'll tell you when Grandmother —"

Her lips trembled, she seemed to be speaking at random. Suddenly she spread out her hands and looked at them with a kind of awe.

"They got *me* out of it when I was ten," she said; and went quickly from the room.

CHAPTER
SEVEN

Julia did as she was bid. When she had made up her face — and it needed it badly — she went out by the porch, and down the broken flight of steps, and so found herself on the lower terrace. She had no impulse to explore: her instinct bade her keep close to the house; and a chair under the lime tree at once attracted her eye. It was very comfortable, and by pulling it forward she could rest her feet on the low stone wall. Emotion did not as a rule tire her — it bucked her up; but the emotion of the last hour was different. It had been constrained, not expansive . . .

"I'm a fool!" Julia told herself sharply. "Did I expect her to fall on my neck?"

The truth was that she had so expected. After that letter, after her own swift response, the actual meeting with Susan had been an anti-climax. There had been tears, indeed, but tears of the wrong sort; and none shed by Susan. "She doesn't cry easily," thought Julia. "She'd never cry before a stranger . . ." There was the rub: that Julia, who could get intimate with a trapeze artist after five minutes' conversation — who was intimate with a salesman after buying a pair of shoes — had talked for an hour to her own daughter, about the girl's own father and lover, without the least intimacy at all.

"I'm a fool," thought Julia again. "It's just because she's such a perfect lady. And what *I* need is a good sleep."

She did not sleep then, but the quiet of the morning, the sunshine, the warm odours that rose from the kitchen-garden below, gradually soothed and raised her spirits. From where she sat she could see no further than the roofs of the village: she was in a little tree-encircled world, strange but delightful in its picturesqueness. A lovely world! Julia had no eye for detail; she could appreciate only such obvious effects as the bright clear green of the tree-tops, the flaming mass of the jasmine against a white wall: but what she enjoyed she enjoyed thoroughly. She liked the oleanders — the pink ones better than the white; she admired the showy intention of the broken staircase; and it also struck her that her own white figure, against the dark-blue cushions of her chair, must be making a very pleasant effect.

Here Julia paused. Beneath the agreeable surface of her thought stirred the consciousness of something lacking. What was it? She was very comfortable, she had ceased to worry about Susan, yet that wasn't enough. She wanted something more. What was it?

"Of course!" thought Julia, surprised at her own obtuseness.

There ought to be a man there. There ought to be a man to enjoy her white frock, to admire her sensibility when she pointed out the jasmine. It wasn't because she, Julia, couldn't do without one. She didn't want a man *personally*, but because in that lovely place — with its roses and terraces and no doubt lots of little hidden nooks — the lack of one seemed such a waste.

At that moment a man appeared.

II

Julia admired him greatly. He was young, deeply sunburnt, and dressed in a blue shirt, tan-coloured trousers, and sandalettes that had once been white. Over his shoulder was slung a light jacket, on his head he wore one of the coarse straw hats, shaped like sun-helmets, which Julia had noticed in the village. This, as he approached, he respectfully doffed.

"Bonjour, Madame!"

Julia nodded affably. She hoped he was a gardener, for though obviously not a man to sit on the terrace with, she felt he would be nice to have about. He could carry cushions for her, light her cigarette; perhaps pick for her, and shyly present, bouquets of wild flowers . . .

"Bonjour, mon homme," returned Julia graciously.

The young man grinned. The change was so sudden — the flash of white teeth so altered, while illuminating, his countenance — that Julia received quite a shock. Though the hat was still in his hand, he now looked scarcely respectful at all: his regard was frankly admiring. He looked her over, evidently liked what he saw, and gave her what was practically a glad-eye. The French were like that, Julia knew, and one had to make allowances; but in a gardener it was — well, unsuitable.

"Go and get on with your work!" she said sharply. "*Allez-vous en!*"

He went at once (but apparently unabashed) towards the kitchen-garden gate; and in spite of her disapproval Julia could not help acknowledging that his figure, in its gay foreign clothes, lent a touch of picturesque interest to the landscape. Though not tall, he was very athletic: when he reached the gate he did not open it, but vaulted over. Julia heard his voice uplifted in French, apparently addressing one of the maidservants; a woman called back, a dog barked, and then all was still again.

"I bet he's a terror in the village," thought Julia.

The incident had quite wakened her up, and she had just decided to go for a walk round the house when Susan reappeared at the other end of the terrace. Julia went towards her, and when they had met — not calling out, vulgarly, from a distance — Susan gave her message.

"Would you like to come and see Grandmother? I'm afraid I've been a long time, but she'd gone to sleep again."

"I nearly slept, myself," said Julia, as they walked up the steps. "It's so lovely and peaceful."

"I do hope you won't be bored here," said Susan.

"I'm never bored where there's scenery," returned Julia grandly. "I just love a nice view."

Susan smiled, but did not look particularly reassured. "Grandmother's room has the best view of any," was all she said; and opening the door she ushered Julia in.

III

Mrs. Packett was sitting in bed wearing a very smart boudoir-cap and a woollen cardigan. She smiled as Julia came in, and held out her hand; but she also had a complaint to make, and with the frank egoism of age at once made it.

"I have been to sleep again," she announced severely. "Of course I go to sleep if Susan forces me to have breakfast in bed. It's very bad for me, and there are crumbs among the clothes."

"You'll be up in ten minutes," said Susan consolingly. "Claudia's seeing to your bath now."

"I wanted to get up *early*," insisted Mrs. Packett. "I wanted to be up to meet you, Julia, but Susan wouldn't let me. She's not going to let me lunch with you either, because —"

"Grandmother!"

"Go away, Susan." Mrs. Packett watched her granddaughter out of the room and went on where she had left off. "— Because she wants to put this young man through his paces all by herself. I'm supposed to be a disturbing influence — like in table-turning. As you'll very soon find out, my dear, Susan does anything she likes with me."

Julia smiled.

"Not altogether. You know why *I'm* here?"

"Of course I do, and I'm very glad. Draw that curtain back and let me have a look at you."

Julia did as she was told and let in a burst of sunlight not only on herself but also upon Mrs. Packett. The old woman stood it well; her plump weather-browned face was fresh and lovely, her small grey eyes looked interestedly on the world. Age suited her. As a girl she must have been pretty; in middle life, as Julia remembered her at Barton, she was scarcely distinguishable against the general background of well-bred dowdiness; now she had emerged again, complete and individual, with her prejudices elevated to principles and her dowdiness ripened into distinction. "She's *tough*," thought Julia admiringly . . .

"You've put on weight," remarked Mrs. Packett. "But you look well. What have you been doing with yourself all this time?"

Julia paused. The figure of Mr. Macdermot (and of many another) passed rapidly before her inward eye. The day at Elstree when she fell into the fountain (five times in three hours) was fresh in her memory. So were several other episodes, all as poignant and interesting at the time as they were now unsuitable for relation.

"Nothing much," she said. "I've just been living in town."

"You don't keep a cake-shop?"

"A cake-shop?" Julia was surprised. "I've never thought of it."

"I have," said Mrs. Packett energetically. "I was thinking of it only last night. It would just suit you — and you've got the capital."

Here was some of the thin ice Julia had been dreading. She cut a daring figure on it.

"Suppose I lost the lot?"

"You wouldn't, if you had any sense. Every one I know in London complains that they can never get a home-made cake. I could give you twenty addresses now. I'd write to them all personally. And if you like, while you're here, I'll show you my special maids-of-honour."

Julia listened to these plans with astonishment: she had never credited her mother-in-law with so much enterprise. But a topic involving capital was not, in her opinion, one to be too closely pursued.

"I'll think about it," she said. "At the moment I can't think of anything but Susan. I'm afraid you'll feel I've come to interfere."

"Of course you have," said Mrs. Packett. "Not that I blame you. Nor do I blame Susan, though I think she's behaving most unreasonably. I expect you thought she was locked in her room on bread and water?"

"I expected to find her . . . worse," Julia admitted.

"Instead of which I'm feeding them both twice a day on the fat of the land. You'll see at lunch-time. You'll see *him*. Susan made me promise not to speak about him until you'd met, in case I prejudiced you; but you know I disapprove, because she must have said so in her letter. Isn't that so?"

"Yes," agreed Julia, "but she didn't say why."

Mrs. Packett looked surprised: "Simply because she's too young. I've nothing against Bryan personally. But no girl should get married at twenty."

"Then you don't object to an engagement?"

"Until Susan is twenty-one I do. If they would like to announce their engagement next year, and get married when Susan is twenty-three, I have no objection at all."

This was a new light on the subject, and Julia considered it thoughtfully. Susan's birthday was in March — only eight months away — and after a formal engagement the time of waiting could probably be abridged. Then why wouldn't Susan wait? Why so desperate a measure as the fetching of her mother from London? She wasn't — Julia could have sworn it — consumed by the impatience of passion. She was escaping from no present ills. Then why . . . ?

"I can't understand it," said Mrs. Packett, meeting her thought. "She's enjoying the life at Girton, she loves it. Another two years, and one getting ready, shouldn't seem long to her. And at the beginning she agreed with me; it's only in the last few weeks that she's become so — so heady."

"And the young man?" asked Julia. "Is he willing to wait too?"

"If he is, my dear, he can hardly say so, with Susan clamouring to get married next month." Mrs. Packett sighed. "Perhaps I'm being selfish. Perhaps when I say I want her to have her girlhood, I really mean I want to keep her a little longer for myself. You know, my dear, we've always been very grateful to you?"

Julia moved uneasily. What a family they were for distributing non-existent virtues!

"I'm grateful to *you*," she said almost curtly. "When I see Susan now I know I could never have done half as well for her. She's her father's daughter much more than mine — and a very good thing too."

The old woman's glance was suddenly so shrewd that Julia was taken by surprise. "I bet it was she who wouldn't let Sue come and stay with me!" she thought. And quite right, all things considered: there were some people who shouldn't mix, however nearly they were related; the tie of the spirit was closer than the tie of the flesh, and in spirit Susan was pure Packett. Julia's spirit — "If I've got one!" she thought suddenly. "If you ask me, I'm all flesh!"

Mrs. Packett put out her hard old hand and touched Julia's plump one.

"You're my daughter-in-law, and I'm very glad to see you. Stay with us as long as you can."

"I'll stay for always!" cried Julia impetuously; but they were both wise enough to take the sentiment at its true value.

CHAPTER
EIGHT

The dining-room at the villa was a small square apartment, always rather dark because of the great jasmine, whose lower garlands drooped over its french window like a natural sun-blind. The light that filtered through was green rather than golden, and Julia, putting her head in from the bright terrace, could at first make out no more than the round table with its white cloth. She had no real business there, but she was hungry and wanted to see how lunch was getting on. The sight of cutlery and glass, laid for three, encouraged her, and so did the carafe of wine. She wouldn't have said "No" to a cocktail, but the opportunity, if Barton habits still prevailed, was not likely to arise.

"I must learn to do without them," thought Julia, as she returned to the seats under the lime tree. "They're rotten for the complexion, and it's a bad example for Susan. Besides, any one who knows about wine says they're absolute muck . . . If I could have one, I'd have a Manhattan."

With an effort she wrenched her thoughts away and directed them to the surprising metamorphosis of Mrs. Packett. The old lady's vigour had made a deep impression on her. "She wasn't like that at Barton," reflected Julia, wondering. "If she'd wanted me to start a cake-shop then, I might have done it." Or had Mrs. Packett even then hankered after commercial enterprise, and had she, Julia, been too much wrapped up in her own misery, too unresponsive to all outside impressions, to notice? Julia thought not. It seemed to her more likely that her mother-in-law was of the type, not rare among Englishwomen, in whom full individuality blossoms only with age: one of those who, at sixty-one, suddenly startle their relatives by going up in aeroplanes or by marrying their chauffeurs . . .

"Well?" said the voice of Susan. "How do you think Grandmother is looking?"

"Splendid," said Julia promptly. "Has she been up in an aeroplane?"

Susan looked surprised: "No, she hasn't. But she did talk — how odd! — of flying to Paris. I thought it might be too much for her."

"You'll have a job to stop her flying back," prophesied Julia, tucking in her feet so that Susan could pass to the second chair. But Susan did not move. She hadn't come out to talk about her grandmother.

"Lunch is just ready," she said. "And — he's here."

Julia preceded her into the dining-room and saw a young man, deeply sunburnt, who greeted her with a cheerful smile. He wore a blue shirt, tan-coloured trousers, and sandalettes which had once been white.

II

"This is Bryan Relton — my mother," said Susan from the doorway.

His smile broadened to a grin.

"*Bonjour, Madame!*"

"Well, I'm damned!" thought Julia. But there was no time to marvel. Her surprise had been patent, but she made a good come-back.

"*Bonjour, mon homme*," said Julia blandly. "We've met before, Susan, and I thought he was the gardener."

Susan joined in their laughter, but she was not quite pleased. Bryan was her property, her surprise: she was like a child who has hidden a puppy in the tool-shed, and then finds it gambolling with the grown-ups. The grown-ups couldn't help it, but it was tactless of the puppy to get out . . .

"It's those clothes," she said, with a humorous lift of the eyebrows.

"Practical, cheap, and picturesque," retorted the young man. "Don't they suit the landscape better, Mrs. Packett, than a gent's summer suiting?"

"Very much better indeed," said Julia. "And if you think you're going to make a fool of me," she added mentally, "you'll have to think again."

They sat down and ate home-grown hors d'oeuvres — eggs and radishes, chopped onion, beans in a vinaigrette sauce. The food was excellent, the meal proceeded pleasantly; Susan described the beauties of the neighbourhood. Julia (with expurgation) the incidents of her voyage. The lacunae were necessarily so

73

great that there was practically nothing left to her save the state of the Channel, the emptiness of the Paris train, and the convenience of the *wagon-lit*; but to Susan at least such uneventful voyaging seemed perfectly natural. Of Bryan, Julia was less sure.

"Poor Mrs. Packett!" he said. "Didn't you find a soul to speak to?"

"There was quite a nice woman on board — a schoolmistress, I think," said Julia.

"Very informative," said Bryan respectfully. That was the trouble — he was too respectful by half. He aroused Julia's suspicions; and as luncheon proceeded so those suspicions increased. In talking to Susan he seemed perfectly natural — affectionate, admiring, anxious to please; whenever he spoke to Julia, and however deferential the words, there was what could only be described as a look in his eye.

"I do so love the country!" announced Julia with enthusiasm.

"I'm *sure* you do," agreed Bryan warmly. But the look in his eye said — well, it practically said: "Garn!"

As for Susan, though her gaze turned constantly from her lover's to her mother's face, she appeared to see nothing of their intercourse save its pleasant surface. Perhaps that under-running current was something you couldn't see unless you could recognize it: the tacit intimacy of two complete strangers who came — how to put it? — out of the same box.

And as her suspicions thus crystallized, Julia felt a pang of sheer dismay.

74

"I believe he's the same sort as I am!" she thought. "Now what the hell am I to do?"

III

The first thing, obviously, was to find out more. It was possible that she had been mistaken; but if so, then for the first time in her life her surest instinct had let her down. It had always been her great asset — often her only asset — that she could tell at sight who was her sort and who wasn't; which of two men at a bar, for example, would stand her a dinner, which of two women in a ladies' room would put her up for the night. On such knowledge as this, indeed, Julia's dinners and beds had often depended; her highly successful partnership with Mr. Macdermot had sprung from a single glance exchanged in a railway train. No speech was possible, the compartment being full; but Julia had been absolutely certain that if she kept close to him at the station something would happen. And it did happen: "Like a lift?" said Mr. Macdermot, as they passed the taxi-rank; "I don't mind if I do," said Julia; and after that they were together for four years.

"That's no reason why I shouldn't be wrong this time," thought Julia stubbornly; but her daughter's answer, when later that afternoon she inquired where Susan and Mr. Relton had first met, struck her as a bad omen.

"In a train," said Susan.

She spoke calmly and distinctly — so very calmly, with such super-distinctness, that even Julia, who, apart from Mr Macdermot, had been meeting people in public conveyances all her life — even Julia noticed the effort. Those three words were evidently regarded by Susan as a fence to be taken; with the courage and composure of a gentlewoman she had set her teeth and taken it. But Julia's calm, as she continued, was merely natural.

"How long ago?"

"About six weeks. It was between Strasbourg and Paris, when I was meeting Grandmother before we came on here. He helped me about my baggage, and we had lunch together. You know how it is when you're travelling."

Her mother nodded. The image of Fred Genocchio waved to her from the Gare de Lyon, and in her heart Julia waved back. That was travelling — to knock up against strange men, and leave a little of your heart with them, and receive a scrap of theirs in return, and then go on with your memory by so much enriched and your forearms (if the stranger happened to be a trapeze-artist) blue with bruises.

"And then," supplied Julia encouragingly, "he asked for your address?"

"No!" said Susan. "Of course he didn't. But we were talking about France, and the various parts, and I mentioned Muzin. And then a week later — he turned up here."

Julia looked at her daughter with interest. The ice had thawed: Susan was in a positive glow. "How pretty she is!" thought Julia; and it seemed wonderful to her that so slight a cause should have produced so great an effect. But no doubt to a young girl like Susan the adventure had been both romantic and remarkable in the extreme — enough to make her fall in love with anybody. And the young man was attractive as well. That sort was, mused Julia unkindly.

Aloud she said, "He's been here nearly five weeks, then? Hasn't he anything to do?"

"He's a barrister," said Susan quickly. "They can take long holidays. And this is a special one, before he really settles down to work. It's doing him so much good!"

"Where is he staying?"

"At the lodge. At least, it isn't really our lodge, it's let out, with the vine. But Grandmother arranged it."

"Your grandmother?" said Julia, startled. "I suppose she wanted to know all about him?"

Susan glowed again.

"That's the wonderful part. She *did* know. Bryan's father — Sir James — used to know Grandfather. He actually came to Barton once. It's years and years ago, almost before the War; but Grandmother remembers him perfectly."

Julia opened her mouth and shut it again. Oddly enough, she remembered Sir James too.

IV

Her recollection of him was very clear indeed. Without even closing her eyes she could see a dressing-room at the Frivolity — the cramped, old-fashioned sort, rather dirty — six girls in various stages of pleasing disarray, and on the one sofa a large recumbent figure. The figure was that of Sir James. The six girls were discussing whether to get someone to chuck him out, or to let him sleep it off. Julia, always kind-hearted, had been for the second course: she had rashly guaranteed that if they left him there during the last part of the show he would be able at the end of it to leave under his own power. And then over the senseless form an argument arose: Julia, said one of the girls, was notoriously maternal; but where would *they* all be if his wallet was missing? Whereupon Julia, with a fortunate blow, laid the girl out upon Sir James's chest. An animated scene indeed! . . . And so different from the one immediately before her eyes that Julia felt a momentary doubt of her own identity. Could she really have taken part in that rowdy passage? And yet if she tried she could still feel, pressing against her ears, the cardboard bananas of her vegetable head-dress. The girls had been — for some long-forgotten theatrical reason — the dessert: her opponent wore grapes, piled high in a basket, and very fragile . . .

The curious thing was that Sir James never woke. He simply put up an arm and drew his unexpected bedmate into a more comfortable position. He also (still in his sleep) addressed her as "Wendy": and since this happened to be the name of the leading lady, recrimination soon gave way to happy conjecture. They were twenty seconds late for their call, and got no end of a blowing-up about it . . .

It will thus be seen that Julia had every reason for changing her mind and shutting her mouth. She had also a good deal to think about. If there was anything in heredity, it seemed to her, considerable light was thrown upon the young Bryan's conduct — and a light in which that conduct assumed other and less fair hues than those distinguished by Susan. All that family, thought Julia — perhaps unfairly — were born pursuers. If Bryan had met Susan in a country drawing-room, and been invited to call afterwards, he would probably have lost all interest; but to meet her in a train, to see her vanish into the blue just as he had begun to get going — that was very different! Circumstance, by supplying the coquetry Susan lacked, had made her desirable.

"I want you to get to know him," Susan was saying earnestly. "I want you to talk to him by himself. You'll carry so much more weight with Grandmother than I can, because she thinks you're more experienced."

Julia's tenderness, as she looked at her daughter, was not unmixed with irritation.

"It's just possible that I am," she said. "You can't learn without living."

"But some things you don't need to learn," said Susan steadily. "You *know*. Will you talk to Bryan if I fetch him now? He's in the vine."

Julia nodded. It was plain that the day had already been mapped out for her — for her, and for every one else in the Villa des Sapins. Bryan awaited his cue in the vine, Mrs. Packett lunched alone in the billiard-room, exactly as Susan bade them. Only Susan herself seemed to have freedom of movement; and she now used it to bring the most important of her puppets from the wings and plant him firmly in the centre of the stage.

"Enter Juvenile Lead," thought Julia, as she watched Bryan come down the staircase alone. Her own rôle being merely that of the confidante, she sacrificed elegance to comfort and put her feet up on the low wall.

V

Armed with her private information, Julia entered on the engagement with a good deal of confidence. Nor did the young man, as he deferentially took his seat beside her, seem at all uneasy. "He's got all his father's cheek!" thought Julia; and a moment after was shocked by her unfairness. Why shouldn't the boy be easy, when his conscience was clear? Weren't his intentions honourable? Didn't he want to marry Susan? "I can't help it, I know his sort," thought Julia vaguely, and thus, though she did not then pursue it, again touched the clue to her distrust. Bryan was waiting for her to begin.

"I'm going to ask a lot of impertinent questions," said Julia amiably.

The young man's attitude became if possible more deferential than before. It was almost too deferential to be true.

"I'll supply anything you like, Mrs. Packett, from a birth certificate to a banker's reference."

"That's not quite what I mean," said Julia. "I can leave all that to Sue's guardians. But, to begin with, when you met Susan — where were you going?"

"To Paris."

"How long had you been in Strasbourg?"

"A couple of days."

"You'd gone straight there from England? You hadn't got off at Paris, for instance?"

"Certainly not," said the young man virtuously. "I went straight as a die."

"Well it's a long way to go for two days," said Julia. "*Why* did you go there?"

"To visit friends."

"A girl?"

"As a matter of fact — yes."

"And she was otherwise occupied, so you came back," elaborated Julia.

The young man looked at her with interest.

"See here, darling" ("That's more his style!" thought Julia), "all that may be just as you say, but it has nothing to do with Susan."

"It may or it mayn't," said Julia. "I'm just establishing the facts. Were you going to stay in Paris or move on?"

"I hadn't decided. I never make plans when I'm on holiday."

"I can understand that," said Julia thoughtfully, "because I'm just the same. I like to see what turns up."

There was a long pause while old Mrs. Packett, walking slowly through the heat, passed from the shadow of the house to the shadow of the pines. Even in her unsuitable black gown, and her woolly jacket, she looked so perfectly the lady that Julia was forced to spare her a moment's attention.

"All right," said Bryan suddenly. "I *was* at a loose end. But once I got here — if you think I'm just after a holiday affair —"

"No," agreed Julia. "This house — and the people in it — aren't conducive to holiday affairs. I just wanted to know how you got here at all."

She stood up, smiled pleasantly, and left him. She had given him something to think about, and she had played confidante long enough. But even so, she did not have the last word. The last word, though unspoken, was Bryan Relton's.

"If it comes to that," said his look, "how the hell did *you*?"

CHAPTER
NINE

How indeed? wondered Julia, first with apprehension, then, as the days went by, with a secret and amused surprise. For she was getting away with it: that perfectly ordered house, that little world of perfectly bred people, accepted her as a natural inhabitant. She felt rather as a bystander might feel who, inadvertently swept off the curb into some royal procession, nevertheless manages to hold his own between the Ambassador on one side and the Admiral on the other. She had to try hard, of course; she never drank with her mouth full, and never sang in the bath, and always discussed impersonal subjects in a low, ladylike voice. And there were naturally some bad moments: there was that terrible morning, for instance, when Claudia the maid spilt a bottle of scent, and she, Julia, had said what she thought of her; the woman didn't really mind — anyway, she didn't understand half of it — but Susan's face as she paused by the open door! It had been a white mask of distaste, before which Julia and the maid equally shrank. Julia — the maid on one side, Susan on the other, the unfortunate bystander — had dropped an *h*. And then the scent itself, though expensive, had been far from a success: the night Julia wore it at dinner

Susan, on some perfectly courteous pretext, got up and opened another window . . .

If Mrs. Packett was the Ambassador and Bryan Relton the Admiral, Susan was a Bishop, walking just in front, and now and then turning back with suspicious looks. But by stepping carefully (and avoiding the Admiral's eye) Julia nevertheless hoped to hold her own.

II

The village of Muzin was tiny — so tiny that it had neither church nor schoolhouse of its own. It had not even a post office. To buy stamps, and to receive religious or secular instruction, its inhabitants had to walk a mile and a half to the bigger village of Magnieu. Belley, with its shops and market, its cathedral and promenade lay even farther — nearly four miles off, along a road for the most part unshaded; so that the occupants of the villa were almost completely cut off from the outside world. Twice a week, however, a hired car carried them into the metropolis for purposes of shopping, and on these occasions Susan, armed with a list from Anthelmine the cook, would exercise her beautiful French on the admiring tradesmen. Every one from the villa accompanied her as a matter of course, and on the second morning after her arrival Julia, warned at breakfast of the approaching excursion, was ready in her hat a quarter of an hour too soon.

"All agog?" asked Bryan, joining her on the porch.

"I hate unpunctuality," explained Julia. "I think it's so rude."

"Rude but natural," supplemented Bryan. "Like so much else. What are you going to do at Belley? Shop with Susan or come pub-crawling with me?"

"Or if you like old buildings," said Susan from the front door, "there's the cathedral — not very interesting — and a rather charming close, and one of the old gates. Grandmother doesn't walk much, but I'd love to show you them."

Julia withered Bryan with a glance. Pub-crawling, indeed, when there was a cathedral to be looked at!

"I'll come too," he said at once. "I'm good on architecture."

"You're not and you won't," retorted Susan. "We'll meet you at the Pernollet. Grandmother's taking us all there for lunch."

"Alleluia," said Bryan simply.

III

The Pernollet, as becomes a restaurant with a monument to Brillat-Savarin not a stone's throw from its door, is a very good restaurant indeed. It is better, in its kind, than the cathedral, or the close, or the old gateway, so that Julia had perhaps some excuse for preferring it to all three. The hour spent looking at architecture with Susan had not been exactly tedious, but it had been very long, and for the last quarter of it Julia was troubled by her feet. In a way this was lucky, for in order to rest them she had voluntarily sat for ten solid minutes before a stained-glass window, thus surprising and pleasing her daughter very much indeed.

"We'll come again," promised Susan willingly. But neither surprise nor pleasure could blunt the edge of her critical intelligence; as they finally walked away she was busy with a rather damaging analogy between stained-glass windows and the poetry of James Elroy Flecker. They were both *easy*; and just as there were women at college who couldn't read Milton but adored *Hassan*, so her mother's eyes were evidently shut to a Gothic arch but open to a rose window. Susan was not so foolish, indeed, as to condemn either Flecker or stained glass out and out; she knew that both made excellent stepping-stones, as it were, to better things; she only refused to countenance any confusion of the good with the best.

It was a neat analogy, and showed a great deal of intelligence; the only thing wrong with it was that it had nothing to do with the case. It was like Susan herself — strong on logic, weak on human nature. It left out Julia's feet.

So mother and daughter walked up the side of the promenade, Susan thinking in analogies, Julia thinking about her shoes, until they reached the long façade of the Pernollet Hotel. So many cars stood outside that Julia expressed her astonishment.

"They come from Aix," explained Susan. "People drive over for lunch. If Bryan hasn't got here early, we may have to wait for a table."

Bryan had been there half an hour, however, and was even then pressing Mrs. Packett to a second *apéritif*. Julia had one too; after so much architecture she felt she deserved it.

"We've ordered lunch," announced Bryan. "It ends with *fraises des bois*. You've just got here in time for them, Julia. Do you mind my calling you Julia — merely to prevent confusion?"

Julia looked across at the old lady. She herself would have preferred to be called Mrs. Packett — it helped to remind her of her new identity; but if the confusion idea originated with her mother-in-law, there was of course nothing to be said. Before the senior lady could speak, however, Susan had seized on the notion with warm approval. They would all call Julia, Julia; and Julia knew why. "It's to get out of calling me 'Mother,'" she thought with a pang. Then philosophy and food came to her aid: it was very natural — and she could never be really unhappy with a good lunch to eat and a restaurantful of people to look at. The clientele of the Pernollet, moreover, repaid attention; there were the local bourgeois, strong-stomached epicures intent on getting not only the best, but as much of it as possible, to whom a visit to Pernollet was something to be looked forward to for days and remembered for weeks; they sat for the most part in silence, eating steadily; and this silence, and the fact that they mostly wore black, and the amount they ate, somehow gave the impression that they were all celebrating substancial legacies. "Uncle Marius has done his duty; let us all — *Papa, Maman, Tante Mathilde, Monsieur le Notaire* — go and have a damned good lunch . . ." As characteristic in their way, and a striking contrast, were the visitors from Aix — youths clad lightly and picturesquely *pour le sport*, gentlemen in English tweed, beautiful ladies looking like illustrations in *Vogue*; if they lacked the bourgeois solidity, they lacked also the bourgeois waistline; in their cars outside were the tennis racquets and golf clubs with which they held fat at bay. Their eating was carefree, the bourgeois's careless; and the shade of Brillat-Savarin must have been well content.

"Grand sight, isn't it?" murmured Bryan Relton.

Julia nodded. One of the visitors in particular was holding her attention — a young woman so exquisitely appointed, and so consciously superior, both to her host and to the Pernollet, that Julia had christened her the Disgusted Lady. She wore a huge white motor-coat, cut with the utmost elegance out of the coarsest linen, which — with an air of wishing to retain as many protective layers as possible between her person and her surroundings — she refused to take off. Julia was sorry for this, since she wanted to see what the Disgusted Lady wore underneath, but the gesture filled her with admiration. A string of pearls, a white buckskin sandal, were the only accessories visible: the Lady's head was bare, either because her fair Grecian curls were too beautiful to cover, or else, and more probably, because in the whole of France there wasn't a hat she would be seen dead in. Julia could just picture her at the milliner's, flinging model after model aside and sweeping disgustedly out. That such was her practice was evident from her companion's face, which wore a permanent expression of mingled pride and apology. He was a neat little man, about fifty, but he had no other character than that of being the Disgusted Lady's appendage.

"What a dreadful woman!" observed Susan, under her breath.

Julia looked round in surprise. She hadn't thought the Lady dreadful at all. A Terror, of course — but then a Terror of such magnificence!

"The one in the white coat," said Susan.

"It's a very nice coat," said Julia foolishly.

Bryan laughed.

"It was the very *best* butter," he said; and for some reason this idiotic remark made Susan laugh as well. Julia could see no joke whatever, but was only too glad to join in. In another moment she might have started to explain, and so made a fool of herself; for what she wanted to convey was at once so vague and so complicated as to be beyond her powers of expression. She felt, roughly speaking, that while the Disgusted Lady was probably a very disagreeable and useless person, she also made the world a more interesting place. She was a fascinating specimen of humanity, just as the mosquito is a fascinating specimen of diptera. She repaid to the spectator the trouble she gave to her intimates. In short, she was worth having. "It takes all sorts to make a world," thought Julia.

But it was no use saying that to Susan.

IV

Susan was a prig. Not an objectionable prig, not a proselytizing prig, but a prig from very excess of good qualities. Like all the right-minded young, she wanted perfection; the difficulty was that her standards of perfection were unusally high. Exquisite in her own integrity, she demanded an equal delicacy and uprightness from her fellows. If they didn't come up to her standards, she would have no more to do with them. If she couldn't have the whole loaf, she would eat no bread at all. In Julia, who could extract nourishment from a crust, or even from a crumb, this attitude produced at first something like awe, then something like irritation. She found her daughter a paragon; she also, as has been said, found her a prig.

"She can't help it," thought Julia loyally, "she's been so beautifully brought up."

The latter part of this sentiment she expressed to Mrs. Packett, and the old lady was pleased.

"Every one likes Susan," she said. "She was the most popular girl at school — they all wanted her to stay with them — and now it seems to be the same at college. She's always being put on committees."

Julia could well believe it. Susan was the committee-woman born — just, tactful, and graciously dignified. She ought to be an M.P.

"I used to be so glad," continued Mrs. Packett, her words chiming with Julia's thought, "that all the Suffragette business was over, so that if Susan ever went in for politics she could do it in a graceful and ladylike manner. We once heard her speak at a debate, and her grandfather said she had a positively masculine mind." Both Julia and Mrs. Packett were the kind of women pleased by such a remark. "If Bryan ever became Lord Chancellor, she'd make a splendid hostess for him."

Julia did not answer; not because she disagreed, but because in the first place she was very sure that Bryan would never become anything of the sort, and in the second because she was by this time a little tired of talking about other people. She wanted to talk about herself for a bit; but apart from the difficulty of finding a listener, she was not, in that company, a suitable topic.

"It must have been dreadful chaining oneself to the railings," said old Mrs. Packett suddenly; "but I'm sure I could have broken a shop-window."

V

The ease with which Julia settled down at Les Sapins was due possibly to the fact that she had arrived there tired out in both mind and body; she was quite content, for the moment, to sit quietly in the sun, and go for short walks about the garden, and eat appetizing meals at regular intervals. She read the *Continental Daily Mail* and darned her stockings. She took a nap every afternoon. From Mrs. Packett she learnt several games of patience, and she also found, in a cupboardful of old books, an English manual of fortune-telling. Julia adored telling fortunes, and treated herself to three a day; the best of the three was the one she believed. This occupation brought her into friendly relations with Anthelmine the cook, who used to come up behind, as Julia sat dealing her cards at a garden table, and utter loud exclamations of sympathy and surprise. She exclaimed particularly over the three of spades, which in Julia's system stood for no more than a Slight

Disappointment; but since Anthelmine, unlike Claudia, spoke no English, Julia never discovered why. She thought of asking Susan to find out, but dreaded her daughter's disapproval. Anthelmine only looked on, of course, but she now and then sat down to do so; she had an imposing figure — not tall, indeed, but so broad in the beam that three cats at once could take their ease in her shadow — and she was naturally hard on her feet. Julia herself did not mind Anthelmine's sitting down, but she sometimes feared that to Susan, passing afar in the vine, it might seem that her mother was playing cards with the cook . . .

"And I would, too," Julia accused herself sorrowfully. "I've got no dignity." But she did not drive Anthelmine away, and Anthelmine, who was too valuable in a kitchen to fear anybody, asked Susan point-blank whether Madame her mother would like a pistachio cream. Julia was not particularly pleased by this compliment — she felt it too definitely underlined her proclivity for low company — but she finished a second helping of the cream, and but for Bryan, who ate faster, would have finished a third as well. "Done you there!" said the look in Bryan's eye; but Julia ignored it. Ignoring that young man's eye, indeed, had already become second nature to her; she feared its bright intelligence, its perpetual questioning. Contrary to her daughter's express desire, she was making no attempt whatever to get to know him; she was too much afraid that *he* might get to know *her*. Her function at Les Sapins was that of a *dea ex machina*; and the make of her car would not bear examining.

"I can lie low for another day or two," thought Julia, uneasily aware that she was neglecting her duties. But she did not really worry. Worrying was never natural to her; in that clear, fresh, pine-scented air — with all those regular, delicious, abundant meals — it was a physical impossibility. And though Susan and Bryan were evidently very fond of each other, Julia had no fear of their mutual passion flaming into any reckless and irretrievable blaze.

"There's no hurry," thought Julia comfortably. Her spirit was like a plump cat on a sunny wall. It purred. But there was a boy underneath getting ready to chase her off.

VI

"What shall you do this afternoon?" asked Susan after lunch on the fourth day.

Julia, who had her answer ready, gave it with some complacence.

"I'm going on the terrace to read *The Forsyte Saga*." She was glad Susan had asked; it wasn't boastfulness, she just wanted her daughter to know. But Susan's smile — how extraordinary! — was less respectful than indulgent.

"Grandmother adores it," she said. "You'll have a lovely peaceful afternoon."

Thus affectionately put in her place among the senile, Julia went out on the terrace in an extremely unliterary frame of mind; and this in a way was fortunate, since the afternoon, though lovely, was not destined to be peaceful. Scarcely had she settled herself when her potential son-in-law appeared with purposeful looks and an avowed desire for conversation.

"Go and talk to Sue," directed Julia. "I'm reading."

He glanced at her book — again, how odd! — with exactly the same expression as Susan's; then shut it without a word and flung himself down where he could look directly into her face. In spite of her annoyance at such cavalier manners, Julia could not help admiring that he was extremely attractive.

"Look here," he said abruptly, "what have you got against me?"

The attack was so sudden that Julia for once lacked presence of mind. Instead of protesting, she merely stared. Bryan hurried on.

"Because you have, darling, and it's no use saying you haven't. I can feel it. If you were any one else I should say you were still sore over that rise I got out of you the first morning."

"Rubbish!" cried Julia indignantly.

"As you say. And what's all the more puzzling to me is that right from the beginning — right from *then* — I thought we were going to get on. As soon as I saw you, I thought, 'Good!' If you were a bit disapproving at lunch, I'd deserved it, and didn't mind. But you've been disapproving ever since, and it isn't natural."

"Got a good conceit of yourself, haven't you?" said Julia.

He looked quite hurt.

"I never thought we should have to have all this beating about the bush, either. I should have thought that if you disliked my ties or my table manners you'd tell me straight out, and probably box my ears into the bargain. I expected any number of black eyes, Julia darling, but not the frozen mitt."

The statement was so outrageous that Julia, who had been behaving like a perfect lady for four solid days, could not let it pass.

"Do I *look* the sort of person who gives black eyes?" she demanded.

"Yes, you do, darling. You are. Just as I'm the sort of person who gets them. The fact of the matter is —"

Julia beat the bush no longer, but finished for him.

"You're the same kind as I am," she said grimly.

It was out, and she felt a certain relief; but she was also resentful. He had chased her off the sunny wall of her self-complacency; he had shown that her impersonation of a lady was not so good as she had thought. Worse still, he was going to make her say things, do things, that would have a definite effect; that might lead to scenes with Susan, to explanations with Mrs. Packett; that would put an end, in short, to the happy period of her carefree basking . . .

"Well," said Bryan, looking at her under his lids, "that's not such a bad sort to be — is it?"

Julia did not immediately reply. To marshall her thoughts, to produce an ordered sequence of ideas, was not a business which came easily to her. She had first to disentangle her own meaning, then to fit it with words; and since what she now had to communicate was of the utmost importance, so the preliminaries were correspondingly long.

"Not *bad*," she said at last. "Not out-and-out *bad*. But bad compared with people like Susan and her grandmother. Compared with other people, we're quite good. If you ask me," said Julia, "we're sort of half-and-halves. So long as we stay with our own lot, we're all right. We don't do any harm. It's only when we begin to mix with the others — with the real good — that trouble starts. If you married Susan, you'd make her miserable."

"You married Susan's father," said Bryan swiftly.

Julia shrugged.

"That was different. It was the war. If he hadn't been killed, I should have made *him* miserable."

"You'd have given him a damned good time."

"It's not a good time they want," said Julia soberly. "They want a different sort of time altogether. I'm rotten at explaining. But I remember when Susan was coming, and after, how good they were to me — you see, you can't say a thing about them without bringing in *good* — and yet we couldn't get on. They really wanted me, too; they wanted to have me for a daughter, and I was so grateful, especially as I'd half-expected to be thrown out on my neck; I thought I could do anything in the world for them. *I* tried, and *they* tried; but it didn't work."

The young man moved impatiently. "It's all dead and gone to him," thought Julia.

"I admit all that," he said; "but you must see it's a very different thing, my marrying Susan. We're both young, we're in love with each other —"

"What are you going to *do* with yourself?" interrupted Julia. "You're a sort of lawyer, aren't you?"

"A barrister, darling. At any rate, I've been called. But I'm not sure I shall ever practise."

"Why not?"

"Too much of a grind. I don't want to spend the next ten years grinding. I want to knock about the world and look at things and talk to people. I got five hundred a year from my mother, and if I married Susan I dare say the old man would stump up a bit more. He'll adore her."

Julia's thoughts flew back to the dressing-room at the Frivolity, and to the recumbent figure of Sir James Relton. Bryan was quite right: to a daughter-in-law like Susan the old rip would be generous indeed. He'd know what he was getting. And then Susan would no doubt have money too; together she and Bryan would be able to knock about — first class — to their hearts' content. Only — would Susan's heart thus be contented? Did she realize what lay in store for her? "I don't believe they know a thing about each other," thought Julia . . .

"I see your idea," continued Bryan tolerantly; "but — if you'll excuse my saying so — it's all wrong."

"If I had my way," said Julia, following her own train of thought, "I'd pack you off for a month together and let you find out for yourselves."

Bryan grinned.

"There's nothing I'd like better, darling."

"I've no doubt there isn't," said Julia sharply. "Why don't you suggest it to her?"

"Because —"

"Because you know she'd send you packing in double-quick time."

"Not at all," corrected Bryan, with a sudden return to dignity. "Because, as I should have thought you'd know, a fellow feels very differently about a girl he's going to marry and a girl he just wants to . . . have fun with. He feels — well, scrupulous."

Julia looked at him.

"You ought to have seen your face just now," she said. "There wasn't a scruple in sight."

The last word, this time, was hers.

VII

She did not, however, get much pleasure from it. She was ruffled, put out, and more than ever convinced that she would soon have to make herself extremely unpopular. And popularity, to Julia, was the breath of life; she would rather shine at a coffee-stall than eat a good dinner unnoticed. "They'll never understand," thought Julia dismally. "They'll just think I want to throw my weight about." She sighed deeply. There was another thing — her weight! She was almost certain that her stays felt tighter than they did a week ago. They weren't the sort that laced, either: they had a good stout zip-fastener, full strength . . .

It was thus in no cheerful frame of mind that Julia ascended the stone steps and met her hostess at the top.

Mrs. Packett, however, looked pleased; she held a letter in her hand, and was evidently full of news.

"Sir William comes next week!" she said. "He's Susan's guardian, you know, and so charming!"

"A man!" thought Julia.

The black clouds of depression still enveloped her; but she perceived a slight rift.

CHAPTER
TEN

Every morning, just as Julia herself had done in that long-ago time at Barton, Susan arranged the flowers. But with her it was a labour of love; she picked not only the roses, but wild flowers as well, making what she called "tangles" of them — large, and to Julia's eye rather straggling, bouquets that died almost the next day. Susan didn't seem to mind: every morning she went up into the vine and picked more. Some of them were really pretty, thin sprays of forget-me-not with tiny flowers, and clover with big purple heads, and something tall and tough that had bright-blue rosettes growing all down the stem. But Susan didn't stop even there. She actually picked grass, and dead bits of twig.

"I believe you like the tangles best," said Julia once, in her astonishment.

"Yes," agreed Susan. They were in the old garden-room, next door to the kitchen, where Susan kept her vases amongst the cobwebs and firewood. Bryan lounged in the doorway, idle as Julia: they had both expressed a wish to be of use, but so half-heartedly that even Susan's good manners had permitted her to refuse.

"Why?" asked Julia.

"Because I can do so much more with them."

Julia looked at a mass of yellow roses triumphant in their cream jar.

"They don't make half so much show as *those* . . . ?"

"No," admitted Susan. "But *that* — that's just the roses themselves. I've done hardly anything. A tangle makes a show because of *me*."

Involuntarily Julia glanced towards the door; but if this explanation reached Bryan's ears, he gave no sign. Or perhaps he didn't realize how complete an explanation it was, or how particularly ominous to a young man who didn't want to do anything special, but just knock around the world. Their conversation of the previous day was still fresh in Julia's mind: but there was something else on her mind as well, and she did not, as she no doubt should have done, seize the opportunity of showing Bryan up.

Instead, she said casually, "Aren't we expecting another visitor? Your grandmother said something — ?"

Susan looked up from her flowers.

"That's Uncle William. He isn't an uncle really, of course, but I've always called him that. He's a dear. He's coming the day after to-morrow."

"To inspect me," observed Bryan from the doorway.

Julia ignored the interruption.

"Sir William, isn't he?" she asked.

"Sir William Waring. He was a great friend of Grandfather's."

That made him seventy at least, thought Julia gloomily. Men of seventy had no interest for her: they were always, in her experience, either doddering or spry; and the spry were the worst.

"About fifty-one," said Bryan, who had been watching her face.

Julia ignored him again.

"And have you," she asked Susan cunningly, "an Auntie as well?"

"Unmarried," said Bryan.

Susan glanced at him sharply. "Are you meaning," said that look — and a very Packett look it was — "to make fun of my mother? I do not suspect you," said that look, "of deliberate impertinence; but aren't you a little forgetting yourself?"

Warm gratitude flooded Julia's breast; it was sweet to be so protected by one's daughter, and for a moment that sweetness was all she felt. Then under her pleasure, marring it, stirred a feeling of guilt, almost of shame. For she didn't deserve such protection: Susan was wrong, and Bryan right. Bryan, because his own thoughts no doubt worked the same way, knew what she, Julia, was getting at: Susan's lovely mind never even suspected it. Yet from all this complication of wrongs and rights emerged one certain good: Susan had, possibly for the first time, recognized and admitted in her lover something alien to herself.

"She's never seen him against his own background," thought Julia. "It's queer that I should be it." She looked at her daughter's stern face, and at once Susan smiled. It was the most loving smile Julia had ever received from her. "Let her find *him* out without finding me out too," prayed Julia selfishly; "I shan't be here long, O Lord!"

"Lady Waring," said Susan, addressing herself pointedly to her mother, "died about ten years ago. I hardly remember her, except that she was very nice. They never had any children: I expect that was why they made such a fuss of me."

"It must be dreadful to have no children, with a title," said Julia seriously. "It seems such waste."

Susan laughed. Like a good schoolmistress, she knew that severity should be tempered with kindness, and having properly frozen the atmosphere, she now proceeded to thaw it again.

"Uncle William isn't a baronet — he's a mere knight. He was something in the Admiralty, and they knighted him after the war. Will you have roses for your room, or a tangle?"

"A tangle," said Julia. She still liked the roses best, but she wanted to show her gratitude.

Bryan lounged in and swung himself on to the table.

"What about me?" he asked. "What about my room?"

"You've flowers enough," said Susan. "You've still the whole bunch we picked yesterday."

"But I want one now, from you. Give me a rose, Susan."

Flushed, smiling, very pretty, she broke off a yellow bud. Bryan received it with suitable gratitude. But his eyes were not on Susan; they looked over her shoulder, at Julia, with defiance.

II

That afternoon, immediately after lunch, Julia set out to look at a tree. Both Susan and Mrs. Packett were able to contemplate trees for minutes together, and her natural spirit of emulation made Julia covet the same power. There must, she thought, be something in it: some esoteric connection between garden-seats and the gentility she so much admired. For her daughter and mother-in-law were by no means isolated examples: every real lady Julia had ever met — most of whom, indeed, she had encountered actually at Barton — showed the same idiosyncrasy. On the Tuesday afternoon, therefore, Julia went out to have a whack at it herself.

She had selected her object the day before — a small *mirabelle* plum covered with hard yellowish fruit. Compared with the pines, to be sure, it had something of a twopence-coloured look; but for that very reason Julia felt it would be easier. She could work up to pines later on.

The *mirabelle* was situated on the second terrace, and as she walked up the zigzag path, dragging a garden-chair, Julia conscientiously looked about her. It was very pretty, and all the prettier because the vines were badly neglected. Between their rows the ground was green and sweet with clover and wild strawberry: where the wires had broken, full-leaved garlands, tinted turquoise-blue by sulphate, drooped and mingled with the tall flowering grass. All this Julia saw, and to a certain extent enjoyed; but the chair had a knack of hitting against her ankles, and she determined to put off all serious appreciation until she was comfortably seated. The path wound up: at the second angle it passed through a little grove of nut trees, some springing from the edge of the vine, some from the side of a great outcropping rock. There were steps cut in its base, and by peering through the nut boughs Julia could see the dilapidated shell of a tiny pavilion. But she did not allow it to distract her; she mounted steadily on, growing hotter and hotter, to the second terrace and the *mirabelle* plum.

"I'm going to bake," thought Julia, as she set up her chair: and indeed the whole circle of the plain, on whose circumference she was placed, shimmered under a heat mist. In it the roofs and steeples of Belley, the smaller groupings of the villages, showed bright yet insubstantial; here and there, exquisitely distributed over the flat, rose small cone-shaped hills, each neatly girdled by a ring of poplars, and belonging, in that light, less to Agriculture than to Art. It was the landscape of a holy picture, in which saints, not peasants, should have enlivened the foreground; and Julia needed no more than one glance to identify it as a lovely view.

She then settled back in her chair, looked at the time, and gave her eyes and mind to the plum tree. It leaned gracefully towards her, as though sensible of the compliment; its small hard fruit, already faintly speckled, made her think of birds' eggs. They would look pretty in a mossy basket — like plovers'; and Julia wondered when they would be ripe. Would the nuts have been ripe, that she passed in the little thicket? From above they looked no more than bushes, the rock was a mere boulder, the pavilion a toy. Its roof peaked up like the roof of a pagoda: a stray architect, long before the Packetts came, had identified it as late eighteenth-century chinoiserie. But Julia's interest was purely human; what a place, she thought, for assignations! Did Susan ever meet Bryan there, when the house slept and a moon shone through the nut trees? But the bushes about the steps grew thick and undisturbed; Julia very much feared that the pavilion was being wasted. Poor thing, it would probably be quite glad of someone — glad to hear a kiss again, to be filled with delicious stifled laughter and the murmuring of lovers' vows . . .

"I bet it's seen a thing or two in its time," thought Julia.

She looked at her watch. She had been sitting there twelve and a half minutes — practically a quarter of an hour. To stay longer, in that heat, would be little short of dangerous, so she folded her chair again and went down into the cool.

She was feeling extremely pleased with herself; but pride, notoriously, goes before a fall.

III

Returning by the front door, she found Susan, Bryan and the postman all in a group on the steps.

"*Il y a quelqu'erreur*," Susan was saying firmly. "Bryan give it back at once."

106

Always ready to join anything that looked like a crowd, Julia paused and craned over his shoulder. The object which Susan so eagerly repudiated was a picture postcard of extreme vulgarity.

"What things they do think of!" began Julia, much interested; and the next moment felt Bryan's elbow hard against her ribs. Susan was standing with a stony and averted face.

Furious with herself, still more furious with Bryan for the very reason that she should have been grateful to him, Julia drew back.

"Perhaps there isn't a mistake after all," said Susan.

Bryan turned the card over so that Julia could see.

It was addressed to "Mrs. Packard," and in the space for correspondence was scrawled a tender message from Fred Gennochio.

In spite of herself Julia felt the blood rise till she stood blushing like a schoolgirl. Ardently, violently, did she long to deny all knowledge of the thing; yet she had at the same time an obscure feeling that to do so would be to deny Fred himself. As though he had appeared on those steps in person, and she had cut him . . .

So torn, she could not find a word to say; and at last Susan spoke for her.

"*C'est bien*," she said calmly, addressing the postman. "*J'ai mal lu*. Coming up the vine, Bryan?"

What with anger, mortification, and sentiment — the emotions called forth, in that order, by Bryan, Susan, and Mr. Genocchio — Julia was glad to be left alone. The card now lay, in theory still unclaimed, on the stone balustrade; she took it up and bore it to her room. Fred had not written much, only four words; but a whole sonnet sequence could hardly have affected her more. "*Still thinking about you, Fred.*" He was still thinking about her! Despite her incredible hardheartedness, amid the excitement and bustle of his professional affairs, he still thought of her! In her gratitude for the sentiment conveyed Julia almost forgave the tactlessness of the vehicle. For, after all, it wasn't so bad. It wasn't *dirty*. He probably just chose it to try to cheer her up a bit, in case she was feeling blue . . .

"Then he shouldn't have," thought Julia, veering round again. "What business has he to think I'm not being happy? Conceit, that's what it is. Sheer conceit. He probably thinks I'm crying my eyes out for him!"

Then she sat down and cried hard.

IV

From her seat under the pine trees old Mrs. Packett watched Susan and Bryan going up through the vine. Susan was a little ahead, walking as usual as though all gradients were alike to her; Bryan, his hands in his pockets, loped easily behind, taking long strides over the rough places, lagging on the smooth. They made a charming pair, thought Mrs. Packett: she had just said so, in the letter she was writing to Sir William.

My daughter-in-law (continued old Mrs. Packett) seems to like him too; but she is very properly reserving her opinion, and I think she agrees with me that Susan is too young. It has all turned out *perfectly smoothly*; as you know, I was *apprehensive* (about Julia coming here), but I am glad to say that I was wrong. I feel sure that you and she between you will be able to make Susan see reason. I want you to get on with her, William, and knowing your prejudices I am going to warn you now not to be put off by her appearance, which is a little *florid*. But she is really most pleasant and amiable, quite contented in this very quiet place, and I have a feeling that everything will turn out well. When I look ahead a few years (D.V.) and see Susan married, and perhaps great-grandchildren, and Julia with her nice little cake-shop, which I shall run up to town to inspect, I feel myself to be a very lucky old woman.

★ ★ ★

Such was Mrs. Packett's view of the situation; and by a curious coincidence the amiable Julia, having wiped her eyes and blown her nose, was even then presenting the very same view to a very different recipient.

She wrote:

Dear Fred,

Thank you for your card, though I won't say it wasn't a bit common, but I know you meant well. This is a lovely place, large house and gardens and a private vineyard with most lovely views. My daughter is the loveliest girl you ever saw, so fair and distinguished, and a real daughter to me. I am having a thorough rest and holiday, and enjoying it very much. How is Ma? Poor old bird, she wasn't half done up, was she. I often think of you all, and hope you are all having every success and the hand you all deserve.

Yours sincerely,

JULIA PACKETT.

Don't send me any more of those postcards, Fred; the servants here are French, and you know what their dirty minds are.

Yours,

JULIA.

When it was finished she looked at his card and addressed an envelope to the Casino Bleu and to the house at Maida Vale. She had no French stamps, but there were some in the billiard-room; Susan and Mrs. Packett kept books of them, in the writing-table drawer.

Julia stepped out into the corridor and there paused. Could she just *take* a stamp, or ought she to pay for it? A lady, undoubtedly (thought Julia) would leave the money. She went back and fetched her bag; and on opening it in the billiard-room made the alarming discovery that when she had sent her letter to Fred Genocchio she would have only five francs left.

For almost the first time in her life Julia's courage failed. To be penniless in London was nothing; even in Paris — full of English and Americans as it was — she would not have despaired; but to be penniless among the Packetts! It was a blow so great that her knees absolutely gave under it. She sat down on the nearest chair, her bag still open on her lap, and contemplated the disaster with terrified eyes.

She ought to have thought, of course. She ought to have realized. But she had been so taken up with simply getting there, so unused to looking more than a week ahead that — well, that she just hadn't. And even if she had, from whom could she have borrowed? Who — more to the point — could she borrow from now? Involuntarily, Julia shook her head: if the sources had been dry when she left London, it would take more than long-distance work to make them flow afresh. Personality, that was what did it; and you couldn't, at least Julia couldn't, put personality into a letter. She had to be *there*. If she were only there now, she felt, she could borrow blood from a stone.

She could borrow from any one in the world except Mrs. Packett, and Susan, and Bryan Relton.

Only the world, to all intents and purposes, had at the moment no other inhabitants.

After tracing this vicious circle for perhaps the twentieth time, Julia also remembered that she had no return ticket.

V

Up in the vine Bryan was trying to make Susan quarrel with him. The occasion was purely artificial — a disagreement over the title of a book — but her cool serenity, her perfect control, was a perpetual challenge to him. He wanted to break it down, to see her hot and ruffled; it was the deep impulse to mastery which she would never satisfy. Julia, when she saw Bryan as a pursuer, was right; but she was thinking in physical terms only: if the material pursuit had been all — if by following Susan half across France he could finally have captured her — his attachment would already have worn thin. For a day or two, indeed, the apparent ease of his victory had actually disconcerted and disappointed him; he felt like a man who, setting out to climb some just-accessible peak, finds a funicular railway already installed. The railway, fortunately, did not work; though Susan had accepted him within a week of his arrival at the villa, what now bound him to her was the knowledge that he had never made any real impression on her at all.

"Why can't you admit you may be mistaken?" asked Susan patiently.

"Why can't you?"

"Perhaps I am," said Susan at once. "Anyway, it's on Grandmother's dressing-table, and I'll look when we go in."

So that quarrel came to nothing. Susan would look, as she promised, and if Bryan was right she would come and tell him at once, and if he was wrong she would wait until he asked. She was perfect, both in justice and in magnanimity.

"The lavender's nearly out," said Susan to change the subject.

They were sitting on a high gravelly slope which some bygone owner of the villa had laid out with long flower-borders; but only lavender now survived, flourishing in a bushy grey-green hedge that was sweetened but not yet coloured by the thick flower-spikes. Susan reached up and broke off a twig.

"Smell," she said, rubbing it against Bryan's nose.

He seized her hand and, still holding it, rolled over and buried his face in her palm. The smell of the lavender, the smell of Susan's warm sun-browned skin, made the blood in his temples drum.

"Susan," he said, "darling, I'm not going to wait three years."

"You won't have to," said Susan steadily.

"But if they don't budge?"

"As soon as I'm twenty-one."

"Even that's another eight months."

"Can't you wait eight months?"

For a long minute Bryan lay still. He was thinking of something Julia had said, and wondering how much of Julia was alive in her daughter. None, Julia had implied; but was she right? What did parents ever really know of their children? Bryan's thoughts flew to his finances: he had still a traveller's cheque for fifty pounds — enough to take Susan to Como, or to Rome, or perhaps down to the Riviera . . .

He turned over and sat up. That was his mistake.

"Susan —" he said.

He stopped. He oughtn't to have looked at her. With his face still buried in her palm he might have spoken; but not under that clear, level gaze.

"Well?" said she.

"Nothing. It's tea-time. Let's go down."

Hand in hand they descended the path. In the nut grove they kissed. But they were not contented.

CHAPTER
ELEVEN

For some five minutes Julia and Mrs. Packett had the tea-table to themselves. Both were preoccupied, Julia with the devastating problem of her finances, Mrs. Packett, as will be seen, less unhappily.

"I've been making a list," she announced, "of people in town who would like your cakes. I've got fifteen names already."

"I wish you wouldn't trouble," said Julia sincerely.

"It's no trouble, my dear, it's a pleasure. You must get out a nice card, and I'll enclose it with my letter. I believe Kensington would be a good place, because Susan tells me it is full of flats."

Julia looked up in surprise.

"I've never noticed it," she said. "I think they're as sharp in Kensington as anywhere else."

"They haven't proper kitchens," exclaimed Mrs. Packett, not quite taking her daughter-in-law's point. "Just a sort of cupboard and a sink, and you can't make cakes in a place like that. I'm sure you'll do well. Where *is* Susan?"

"Coming down the path," said Julia.

The young people, indeed, were close upon them, having run the last few yards in an ebullition of good spirits very pleasant to see. "Dear children!" murmured Mrs. Packett. "Damn!" said Julia softly. She wasn't damning any one in particular, least of all Susan; she was just railing at that fate which had planted her down penniless in the one place where being penniless mattered.

"The view's wonderful to-day," said Susan. "You ought to go up."

"I went up after lunch," said Julia. Susan was evidently trying to show that the incident of the postcard had now been forgiven, and Julia in turn exerted herself to appear bright and affable. She praised the view very highly, and described in some detail the appearance of the *mirabelle* plum. In other circumstances it was just the sort of conversation she would have enjoyed, but for once the spectacle of her own beautiful behaviour gave Julia no pleasure. She relapsed into silence, and let the others talk on.

It was very hot. Their table under the pines was in deep shadow, but even through those serried branches the sun here and there managed to penetrate. There was a disc of gold in Mrs. Packett's lap, another on Susan's hair; the ground from Bryan's chair to Julia's was hatched with light and shadow. Presently they were all silent together, and in the pause, from high overhead, came a staccato tap like the tapping of a knuckle on a door.

"There's a woodpecker," said Susan softly.

They all listened; the obliging bird at once tapped again. "It might be a call-boy," thought Julia. Ah, if only it were! If she were only back in a dressing-room somewhere — perhaps with bananas on her head — what would it matter that she hadn't a penny in her pocket? There would be other girls to borrow from, and boys in front, and maybe one particular boy waiting to take her out to supper! "I'd eat fried fish and be grateful," thought Julia, from the heart. Nostalgia overwhelmed her: she wanted to be back among her own kind, among people who expected you to be broke, who took it as the natural thing, who were mostly broke themselves and so could understand. "Fried fish!" thought Julia passionately. "I'd eat winkles on a pin . . ."

"One of these days," Bryan was saying, "we ought to go over to Aix."

Susan raised her eyebrows.

"What for?"

"Oh, just for the ride. To amuse Julia."

The sound of her own name brought Julia back to the present. But even the thought of an excursion could not cheer her. It would only mean spending money . . .

"I'm very well here," she said. "I like the quiet."

"Anyway, you'd hate Aix," Susan assured her. "It's full of visitors rushing about in cars. All those casino towns are the same."

Julia sat up. A casino — and a casino within reach! Hope, never long absent from her, fluttered back into her breast — no modest olive-bearing dove, but a peacock spreading its gorgeous tail. With five francs, at a casino, you could make a fortune! You could break the bank and come home a millionaire! Julia knew nothing about gambling save that beginners always won, and

116

that it was a good plan (if you weren't a beginner and so lost) to pretend to shoot yourself, and wait till the croupiers had stuffed your pockets with cash, and then get up and walk off. Either way was money for jam, and Julia was so starved for excitement that she almost hoped the second course would be necessary. But she wouldn't shoot herself: she would pretend to take poison — an aspirin would do — and drop down in a graceful appealing pose. She could see herself doing it. And perhaps the man who found her would be not a croupier but an American millionaire, and in that case she would let him bring her back to life, and he would fall in love with her and drive her about in a car the size of a house and a motor-coat like the Disgusted Lady's. If he were the right kind of American — no, an English peer would be better — she might even marry him, and so give Susan a titled stepfather.

So Julia's peacock spread its magnificent tail, and Julia, lost in contemplation of it, had been some minutes alone with her daughter before she realised that both Bryan and Mrs. Packett had taken themselves off.

"Have you talked to Grandmother yet?" asked Susan abruptly.

II

"About Bryan? Yes, of course I have." In spite of herself Julia could not quite repress a sigh. She didn't want to talk about Bryan, she wanted to go on with her beautiful dreams, to visualize more distinctly the

English peer, to rehearse scraps of her conversation with him. What was Bryan to her, beside that noble and fascinating figure? However, she knew her duty; and in any case, Susan would not have let her escape it.

"Of course I have," said Julia again.

"And can you do anything? Is she beginning to see how — how silly it is?" asked Susan eagerly.

Julia hesitated. Here was an opportunity, if she wanted one, to clear up the whole situation — to disclaim the role of ally and range herself definitely on the other side; but by doing so she would lose whatever influence she possessed. At present she was free, so to speak, of both camps; and so uncomfortably situated, with one foot in each, she feared she should remain a little longer.

"It isn't silly at all," Julia said (speaking from the Packett camp). "At any rate" (she changed over) "from her point of view. You *are* very young, Susan, and you haven't finished at college —"

"I could take my degree after I was married," said Susan quickly.

Julia thought this a very odd idea indeed. But it gave her hope.

"Only it wouldn't be the same, would it? You couldn't live in —"

"In residence," prompted Susan.

"— in residence, then, and have all the fun you do now? *Why* can't you wait, Sue?"

"I don't want to," said Susan obstinately.

It was her only argument; on it her beautiful mouth closed in a stubborn line.

118

"If you're thinking of Bryan —" began Julia again.

"Of course I'm thinking of Bryan. No one else does. No one else seems to realize that they're asking him to wait three years too."

"Oh, well," said Julia easily, "I expect he'd manage."

All at once, for one moment, Susan's composure cracked.

"I've no doubt he would," she said tartly; and with the colour high in her cheeks got up and walked away.

Julia sat on alone. "So that's it!" she was thinking. "So *that's* it!"

III

She was very sorry for Susan. She was sorry for any young girl who discovers that her lover is not perfect in fidelity; and though in this case it was undoubtedly a good thing that Susan should begin to see Bryan as he was, Julia at that moment felt more sympathetic to her than ever before. She was sympathetic, she was sorry; but she neither sympathized nor sorrowed long. Susan and her troubles could wait: the immediate problem was how she, Julia, was going to get to Aix.

Her five francs, the foundation of her prospective fortune, must be preserved intact; and for some moments Julia toyed with the idea of revising her attitude to a family excursion. If they all went together Mrs. Packett would pay for a car, and the question of transport would thus be solved; on the other hand, such a plan would considerably hamper her own freedom of movement. She might not be able to reach the casino

119

alone, and Julia had no intention of poisoning herself in the presence of her daughter. Susan would simply produce an emetic.

"I've got to get there by myself," thought Julia, "and I've got to get there free . . ."

For perhaps half an hour she sat pondering, while the garden cooled and the hillside began to glow. A great dragon-fly swooped among the rose-bushes: in the perfect stillness the creak of returning ox-wains, on the Magnieu road, was distinctly audible. But Julia's thoughts were exclusively urban; she had returned in spirit to the shifts and manouvres of her London life. The present terrain was unfamiliar to her; she could see no farther than Belley; she did not even know in which direction her Tom Tiddler's ground lay . . .

But it has been mentioned before that Julia was very resourceful, and by the time the last of the sun had faded from the vine her plans were cut and dried. She had remembered, in a beautiful heart-lifting flash, the string of cars outside the Pernollet Hotel. They came, Susan had told her, from Aix; to Aix they would doubtless return; and if she couldn't get a lift from a well-fed Frenchman — well she wasn't the good old Julia she used to be.

CHAPTER
TWELVE

At twelve o'clock the following morning Julia began to listen for the lunch-bell. Its punctual sounding was of great importance to her: if the meal was over, as it usually was, by half-past one, she would have an hour and a half for the four mile walk into Belley, since the patrons of the Pernollet would hardly get away before three. Coffee was the danger-point. On dull days they took it in the dining-room, and never sat more than ten minutes; but if the day were fine they adjourned to the garden, where Mrs. Packett at least had a tendency to linger. And the day was fine, blue and golden, with a light breeze. Julia was glad in a way, since it enabled her to wear her white linen suit (to which, before she left, she planned to add a large yellow taffeta bow); but she couldn't help fidgeting. Mrs. Packett, instead of coming straight out, went to her room; they had to wait for her; and when she did come Susan, always particular, sent the milk back to be heated afresh.

"I'll take mine black," said Julia.

She gulped it down and put the cup back on the table. Susan had a book with her, Bryan looked half-asleep; in two minutes Mrs. Packett would be asleep as well. Julia pushed back her chair and prepared for flight.

"Do you know how to make shortbread?" asked Mrs. Packett, opening her eyes.

"Yes," said Julia recklessly. "I believe I'll go for a walk."

But Mrs. Packett, like so many of the old, heard only what interested her.

"Which sort of butter do you use — salt or fresh?"

"Fresh," said Julia.

"I always use salt," said Mrs. Packett. "I must make you some. And I'll show you my special maids-of-honour."

"That will be lovely" said Julia.

"And almond buns. I always think —"

"Lovely," said Julia again. "I shall enjoy it like anything. I know how clever you are. I believe I'll go for a good walk."

It was the reappearance of Anthelmine that saved her. For Anthelmine brought out not only the milk, but also a fine plump chicken offered for sale by the man who looked after the vine and Mrs. Packett, an expert in poultry, naturally forgot everything else while she poked it in the chest. She poked, weighed, and finally approved; and when she turned back to the coffee-table, her daughter-in-law was gone.

The road to Belley covered nearly four miles, and the day was hot; but Julia — a yellow bow round her neck, her hat over one eye — did not care a damn. She felt extraordinarily lighthearted. She had a smile for every one she met, and nearly caused the death of two

122

bicycling *poilus* who kept turning round to wave to her. Julia waved back. She waved also to the car which had so narrowly missed them. Soon, very softly, she was singing as she walked.

She sang the Marseillaise.

She had reverted to type.

II

Her first act on reaching Belley was to sit down under a tree on the promenade and overhaul her face. It didn't look bad, considering the long walk, and with the help of lipstick and rouge and a touch of eyebrow-pencil she was soon as fresh as a daisy. No mere daisy, however, could display such handsome tints as those in which Julia now blossomed forth; she was not actually painted, but she was perceptibly made-up. When she had quite finished she walked once past the big café by the bus stop (just to make sure she had got the effects right) and then turned up the other side of the promenade towards the Pernollet Hotel.

There were four cars standing outside, but only one with a G.B. plate. Julia strolled by and looked at it carefully: it was an old but well-kept Daimler, in charge of an elderly but spruce chauffeur; on the back seat lay a couple of air-cushions, a couple of English magazines, and a large plaid rug. The French cars, standing behind, were all two-seaters, of the sort which gentlemen do not usually drive alone; and after some consideration Julia decided to stick to her own nationality. She looked at the Daimler once more, noted that the magazines were the *Strand* and the *Cornhill*; then walked a little way down the street and, with a philosophic sigh, wiped off most of her lipstick.

As she turned back she saw that she had been right: the owners of the car, who were just getting in, matched it perfectly. They were two middle-aged Englishwomen of the type so ably caricatured in the French press; their resemblance to horses was not strict, but it was there. As the second flat back disappeared Julia moved forward and put her head in after it.

"Excuse me," she said quietly — in her best Packett manner — "but are you by any chance going back to Aix?"

The Misses Marlowe, after recovering from their surprise, quite pleasantly admitted that they were.

"Then I wonder," continued Julia, "whether I might possibly ask you for a lift? I find there isn't a bus till four, and my children will be waiting for me."

The ladies consulted each other by a glance. If Julia had moved away they could have consulted verbally, and the younger, who had just read a novel by A. E. W. Mason, might have developed scruples; but Julia did not budge. She stayed where she was, half in the car already, and in consequence was not refused.

"Of course," said the elder lady, "certainly"; and Julia nipped in.

It was a pleasant journey. The car moved swiftly and easily along, and the two Samaritans had no cause to regret their kindness. For their new companion proved most interesting, and told them many amusing anecdotes about the three children — Ronald, Rachel and Elizabeth — whom she had left with their governess at Aix.

"I say *left*," smiled Julia, with pleasant humour, "but I've only been away from them three hours. I fancied Miss Graham — my governess — wanted them to herself for a while. I believe she thinks I'm bad for discipline."

"After all, they're on holiday," said Miss Marlowe indulgently.

Julia nodded.

"That's what I say. And they do lessons every morning. French, you know. That's why I brought them here."

"You don't find Aix too relaxing?" asked Miss Marlowe the younger. "I should have thought Geneva —"

"Ah, it's on account of my aunt," said Julia swiftly. "She's taking the cure, and wanted me to be with her. She brought me up, and we don't expect her to be with us much longer. Do you know Yorkshire at all?"

They did not, so she told them a great deal about her early childhood in a bleak stone house set among purple moors. There was no doubt that Julia's imagination, unexercised now for six days, had fairly taken the bit between its teeth. Convincing details, picturesque episodes, sprang one after another to her lips. She was run away with by unbroken ponies; she was lost in sudden mists; she struggled through the snow to the rescue of a pet lamb. The Misses Marlowe listened entranced, and so did Julia. She was not lying, she was entertaining; and the entertainment was so good that the first sight of Aix took both her and her audience by surprise.

"How quickly we've come!" exclaimed the elder lady, quite unconscious of flattery. "Where can we put you down?"

Julia hesitated. The geography of Aix was a blank to her, the only building she positively knew it to contain being the casino itself; and though there was now no real reason (the journey safely accomplished) why she should not boldly announce it as her destination, her artistic instincts rebelled. It was the pet lamb that worried them; it was all wrong to jump straight from a pet lamb to a casino, and Julia almost felt she owed her hostesses an apology. But the casino it had to be, for she dared not hesitate long; so devoted a mother could not possibly have forgotten where she was meeting her young.

"At the casino, please," said Julia. "How disreputable that sounds! But my aunt loves it!"

"It's all right in the afternoon, my dear!" said Miss Marlowe with a smile. "No one plays till night."

III

At half-past four Mrs. Packett, who had spent an agreeable afternoon writing out recipes, emerged from her room and found Susan and Bryan still under the pines. Bryan was reading *Mademoiselle Dax*, Susan had a volume of Molière; as her grandmother approached

126

she put it down and reached for the big cowbell that would summon Claudia with the tea.

"Where is Julia?" asked Mrs. Packett.

Bryan looked up.

"She said something about going for a walk. She's probably collapsed into a café."

"Dear me," said Mrs. Packett, considering the sunbaked hillside, "and there's no nice tea-shop nearer than Belley. I hope she won't be too tired."

Susan alone showed no anxiety as to her mother's whereabouts. She drank her tea, dipped into her Molière, and did not encourage conversation. It was one of her characteristics that when she did not wish to be spoken to, people rarely spoke to her: she had the faculty of wrapping herself in a cloak of silence, folded in which she courteously but firmly withdrew from society. "Packett in her cloud" was a familiar college expression; she was in her cloud now. But behind it her thoughts too were busy with the absent Julia.

"Why is it all so different?" wondered Susan. "We're here just as we used to be before she came, and yet it's all changed." A part of the change at least lay in the fact that she herself was no longer the undisputed centre of their tiny society — that the attention of Bryan and Mrs. Packett, previously concentrated on herself alone, was now liable to stray in another direction; but of this she was not consciously aware. What she was aware of, though but vaguely, was a general relaxing, so to speak, of the moral atmosphere. She couldn't put her finger on anything definite; she only knew that it was becoming more and more difficult to brace Bryan up.

This bracing of her suitor was a matter of great importance to her; she was extremely anxious that he should impress Sir William, not only with his keenness in love, but also with his keenness in his profession. She wanted to produce him as a coming young man — as he undoubtedly was, if only he would take a little trouble . . .

"It all depends on the people he's with," thought Susan. She had too nice a sense of decorum to add, even mentally, that he was in bad company when he was with her own mother; but the thought crossed her mind that Julia must by now be rather tired of Muzin.

"If Uncle William's motoring to Paris," she observed casually, "Julia might like to go with him."

Mrs. Packett looked at her in surprise.

"Has she said anything about going so soon, dear?"

"No, but she'd have a lovely run. It's the only way to see the country."

"I thought she'd stay and wait for us," said Mrs. Packett. "I want to fly the channel, and I'm sure she'd come with me if you don't care to."

Susan said nothing.

"She must be dreadfully hot if she's walking," added Mrs. Packett solicitously. "I do hope she's had some tea."

Susan said nothing to that either.

IV

Well it was for Mrs. Packett's kind heart that her vision did not reach as far as the Place du Revard; for there, at

128

that moment, stood Julia in the most deplorable state of heat and thirst. Aix was a howling wilderness to her: she had lost her five francs in five seconds, there were no millionaires (at least none unattached), and not a single coronetted car. She was too footsore even to go and look at the shops. She was so desperate that if the property aspirin had been poison indeed she would quite possibly have taken it.

To make matters worse, she had just come upon a large café of the most superior kind; its broad *terrasse* was hedged from the pavement by a row of beautifully clipped bushes just as high as her chin; and over these, as she loitered by, Julia could not help seeing the throng of happy creatures inside. There were beautiful ladies in white hats, less beautiful males who were evidently going to pay for what the ladies consumed; and at the sight of so many drinks Julia's heart fainted within her. She needed a drink. She needed a drink badly. What with heat, disappointment and weariness, she felt as though she had never needed a drink before.

By the time she reached the end of the hedge, longing had turned to resolution. She had not only needed a drink, she was damn' well going to have one.

Julia turned round and slowly retraced her steps. She was determined that if they put her in prison it should be for three Manhattans. But as she once more followed and looked over the bushes, it occurred to her that perhaps she needn't go to prison at all. Several of the tables were occupied by gentlemen alone, some obviously expectant, but one or two as obviously free, and over these last Julia ran an experienced eye. Her

129

final choice was plump and middle-aged, a prosperous-looking Anglo-Saxon whose general sobriety of demeanour was relieved by a bright and roaming glance. By great good luck there was an empty table beside him, and towards it Julia now made her way.

She had two preliminary objects — an eye to catch, an eye to avoid. The first belonged to her neighbour, the second to the waiter; and she succeeded in both, for the *terrasse* was so crowded that an inactive client could easily escape attention, and Mr. Rickaby — such was the prosperous gentleman's name — had attention to spare. Julia had not been seated two minutes before their eyes met: her own gaze was the abstracted kind, so useful for forming a sound opinion before committing oneself, and she held it at least ten seconds before starting and turning away. But she soon fell into a reverie again, and naturally the same thing happened. When it had happened three times Mr. Rickaby spoke.

"Very slow service, isn't it?"

"Terrible!" said Julia, with an encouraging smile.

It encouraged Mr. Rickaby so much that he slewed round in his chair till he was practically sitting at her table.

"Waiting for someone?" he asked.

Julia twisted her mouth and shrugged. Instinctively she had pitched on exactly the right line — a slightly mournful cynicism such as Mr. Rickaby would enjoy dispelling. She was almost certain that he was a man who liked to do good.

"What you want," said Mr. Rickaby, "is a drink." And without waiting for an answer — thus showing that

130

he was also a man who knew his way about — he energetically hailed a waiter and ordered two Martinis.

"Thanks," said Julia indifferently. She felt it was still too early for a gleam of gratitude, so she turned three-quarter face — not profile, because of the plumpness under her chin — and stared into the distance, and let him have a good look at her. Mr. Rickaby evidently appreciated what he saw, for when the drinks came he at once stated his intentions.

"Our eyes have met," quoted Mr. Rickaby softly, "our lips not yet — here's hoping. You by yourself here?"

"At the moment," said Julia.

"But not for long," suggested Mr. Rickaby.

Julia shrugged her shoulders.

"I'm alone in Aix," she said; "I haven't any luggage, and I haven't a bean. So hope is just what I need."

The mingled pathos and bravery in her voice touched them both. Mr. Rickaby made sympathetic clucking noises, and in each of her own eyes (without any conscious effort) Julia felt a tear start. It *did* sound awful, put baldly like that . . . The only thing was, was it too awful? Had it frightened him off? Just in case, Julia shifted a point farther from pathos and a point nearer to bravery.

"I'm a fool," she said gamely. "It's not really so bad as that."

"Poor little girl!" said Mr. Rickaby.

Julia's answering sigh was partly one of relief. It was O.K., she'd been quite right, he did like to do good. With a sudden flash of insight she saw him as a man

131

who liked his good times, but occasionally had trouble with his conscience, and as a man therefore to whom the combination of a good time with a Good Work would be a positive godsend . . .

"Tell me all about it," said Mr. Rickaby. "Tell me how you came here."

"With Lucien," said Julia.

"Lucien?"

"The dress designer," said Julia. How, she could not tell, but this sinister figure had at that very instant sprung fully-fledged from her brain. Lucien, the designer . . . a man about fifty; tall, heavy, with narrow, coffee-coloured eyes . . .

"Never heard of him," said Mr. Rickaby, evidently with pride. "Some dago chap?"

"Armenian," corrected Julia. "Lucien is just the trade-name."

"Armenian! My God!" said Mr. Rickaby.

Julia sighed her agreement.

"You can't trust them," she said sombrely.

"And he's left you planted here?"

Julia gulped.

"This morning — when we were leaving the hotel — there was another woman in the car . . . someone he'd just picked up. A very tall ash-blonde, with dark eyebrows."

"I believe I've seen her about," said Mr. Rickaby.

For a moment Julia was quite startled by her own powers.

"Not that one," she said hastily. "This one had only turned up last night . . . But there she was in the car,

132

and of course I wouldn't stand it. I said so. And then —
can you believe it? He simply drove off."

"No?"

"With my luggage in the back!"

There it was, a good, interesting, watertight story,
and Julia felt justifiably proud of it. It accounted for
everything, and it aroused in Mr. Rickaby the
pleasurable sentiment of righteous indignation. The
things he was saying about M. Lucien were hard
but deserved. Nothing, Julia felt, was too bad for that
devilish designer — especially when you thought how
he treated his work girls. For a moment in Julia's
imagination there hovered a vision of dreadful
Armenian excesses: for M. Lucien was by this time so
real to her that she knew exactly what happened
whenever he got a girl to stay late. But she pulled
herself up; she wasn't going to risk a libel action;
and her next cue was already overdue.

"Now tell me about *you*," said Julia earnestly.

Mr. Rickaby told her. His story was not nearly so
colourful as Julia's, but it was the one she wanted to
hear. He was alone at Aix, and finding it rather dull. He
had been overworking — overdriven, said Mr. Rickaby
— and his doctor had ordered a complete change. He
was obviously suffering for someone to talk to, and
within the next half-hour had told Julia all about the
complicated negotiations (amalgamations of two
men's-outfitting stores) which had led to his overworking and his presence at Aix. It was the sort of talk Julia
was used to, and she knew so many of the right

questions to ask that Mr. Rickaby conceived a very high opinion of her brains.

"You understand," he said at last. "You're an intelligent woman."

"It's so interesting," said Julia modestly.

Mr. Rickaby slapped the table.

"There you are. You're interested *because* you're intelligent. Now my wife isn't interested at all. The fact of the matter is, she doesn't understand me."

From sheer force of habit Julia glanced at her watch. For several years she used to have a permanent bet with one of her girl friends that every man you met said that within the first hour; the girl friend had said no, within the first half-hour; and they used to get quite a lot of fun out of jockeying their opponents (so to speak) into position — Julia holding the declaration off, Louise trying to bring it on; and then whoever lost, had to stand the other a lunch. Good old Louise! thought Julia, with quite a rush of affection; she hadn't thought of the girl for years, but it was queer how that well-remembered phrase brought her suddenly to life. Red hair, she'd had, and a way with the boys that nearly always ended in a row . . .

"You've heard that before, I expect," said Mr. Rickaby, watching Julia's face. "But what's a man to say, if it's true?"

"That's just it," murmured Julia.

"I don't say I'm easy," pursued Mr. Rickaby fairly. "I dare say I'm a bit more complicated than most men. I like all sorts of things — good music, you know, and

134

scenery. I've got — well, I suppose I've got ideals. But it takes a woman like you to understand."

Julia nodded. She had often pondered this question of why wives didn't understand when women like herself did; and the only conclusion she had reached was that to understand men — to realize the full value of their good streaks, while pardoning the bad — you had to know so many of them. Then when you came across one fellow who was a soak, for instance, you could nearly always remember another who soaked worse; and *he* in turn might have qualities of generosity or cleverness which raised him above a third man who was a teetotaller. But to know all that you had to have experience, and wives as a rule hadn't. They knew only one man, where women like Julia knew dozens; but then women like Julia rarely became wives. It was a rotten system, when you came to look at it . . .

"I expect I've left something out," meditated Julia. Her thoughts glanced at Susan, then hastily looked away, just as her eyes would have looked away if Susan had actually appeared among the café tables.

"Where are you going to-night?" asked Mr. Rickaby suddenly.

Julia hesitated. The leading-on of Mr. Rickaby, enjoyable as it was, had been the result rather of habit than of design; and she had not yet visualized any definite issue to their encounter.

"I don't know . . ."

"You must come to my hotel," said Mr. Rickaby firmly. "*I'm* going to look after you now."

She pressed his hand. She could hardly do less. And, in truth, she felt very kindly to him. A vicarious gratitude on behalf of that other Julia — the Julia who had been so shamefully used by M. Lucien — swelled her heart. But her brain remained clear.

"How can I?" she murmured. "Without any luggage?"

"I'll see to that too," said Mr. Rickaby. He was being princely, and he knew it. "We'll go shopping. We'll buy you a suitcase and some things to put inside. How's that?"

Julia was properly overcome; but her brain went on working.

V

Considering that she was a stranger to the town, Julia showed some address in getting to the lingerie-shop first. There was a leather-goods establishment directly in their path, but she got her escort past it by suddenly looking into his face and asking what she was to call him. "Bill," said Mr. Rickaby. "I couldn't call you Bill!" said Julia. "It's too ordinary." And by the time they had decided that she should call him Ronald, the suitcases were passed. The next danger-point was the actual threshold of the lingerie-shop, but here she was aided by her companion's own modest nature. "You'll wait outside?" said Julia; and did not even have to add that she wanted to give him a surprise. Mr. Rickaby simply took out his fat pocket-book and handed her a thousand francs.

"Do you know," he said, smiling at her, "you're an answer to prayer?"

"So are you," said Julia; and since those were the last words she ever spoke to him, it was just as well that they made him happy.

Once inside the shop she took the simple and straightforward line of asking the vendeuse whether there was a back way out. The vendeuse looked through the glass door at Mr. Rickaby, and smilingly said that there was. Julia then bought a pair of very nice garters, to get change, tipped the girl, and was shown out. In the street she asked the way to a garage, and there hired a car, for the sum of two hundred and fifty francs, to take her back to Muzin. It made an awful hole in the money, but she was still over seven hundred up.

VI

It was curious that, after behaving in so perfectly lady-like a manner, Julia should have been troubled by her conscience. But so it was: as she sat comfortably in the car, her bag plumped out by Mr. Rickaby's notes, she could not help feeling — well, mean.

"He asked for it," she assured herself. "He was having a gamble, and he lost. I hope it'll be a lesson to him."

For some minutes this new view of her conduct — that she had been altruistically and deliberately showing Mr. Rickaby the folly of his ways — brought a certain comfort. But the comfort did not last. In spite of herself Julia could not help picturing him waiting and wondering, and then perhaps going into the shop, and making a fool of himself in front of the vendeuse, and then stamping out again with a hot and angry face. It was all part of the lesson, of course, but men did not feel that sort of thing so . . .

To cheer herself up Julia took out the new garters and tried them on. They were black, with silver crescents. She hitched up her skirt and stretched out a shapely but solid leg, and found the effect extremely good. It was just at that moment that the chauffeur turned round to ask a direction.

"*C'est près de Belley, Madame*?"

"*Oui, oui*," said Julia, letting down her skirt again.

"Yes, yes," said the chauffeur, grinning.

"You attend to your job," said Julia.

She was furious as much with herself as with him, and the incident ruffled her. If it had been Susan in the car he would never have dared. But then Susan wouldn't have been trying on garters . . . "It's not that," thought Julia; "It's just something about me, They see they can take advantage, and they do. Mean, I call it."

Anger warmed her, and with the subconscious purpose of putting herself in the right, she directed it upon Mr. Rickaby. A man old enough to be her father — very nearly! "The old rip!" thought Julia. If she hadn't had the sense to come away, goodness knew what mightn't have happened! The idea that he was still at large in Aix, getting ready, no doubt, to entangle the next thirsty young woman who came his way, was quite distressing to her. She ought to have told the police about him. She ought to have given him in charge. He was a menace to female virtue, and it was no wonder girls went wrong . . .

"All the same," murmured the voice of Julia's conscience — and oddly enough it was also the voice of red-haired Louise — "all the same, dear, you did lead him up the path . . ."

Julia rapped on the glass and told the chauffeur to stop. They were just outside the village, and she had no wish to arouse unnecessary comment. When she gave the man his tip he did not touch his cap, but swept it off with a low bow; and though Julia was almost sure this was wrong, she dared not try to rebuke him. She had a strong presentiment that if she opened her mouth, it would be to swear.

VII

The first person she met in the villa grounds was Bryan Relton. He at once came towards her with an exaggerated air of anxiety relieved.

"My dear Julia! Where on earth have you been?"

"For a walk," said Julia.

Mr. Relton looked at her thoughtfully, but did not ask where she had gone. Though Julia had no desire to be questioned, the omission for some reason annoyed her.

"Well?" she said sharply.

Mr. Relton continued to gaze.

"You look to me," he said pensively, "like a cat who's just eaten the canary."

Julia stared at him, speechless.

"And I don't believe," continued this most objectionably perspicacious young man, "that it's going to agree with you."

Julia just managed to get to her room, and then she did swear.

CHAPTER
THIRTEEN

Whenever Julia, after a period of distress, found herself once more in funds, she gave a party; so on the next day, which was one of the villa shopping days, Mr. Rickaby played unwitting host to a second luncheon at the Pernollet. "Of course it's on me!" said Julia gaily; and for an hour and a half thoroughly enjoyed herself. At the moment of paying, however, she got a nasty jar.

"What a lovely clean note!" observed Susan idly.

Julia jumped. It *was* lovely, fresh and crisp as though it had just been drawn from the bank: a note for five hundred francs. It was hardly probable that Mr. Rickaby should have taken the number; but supposing he had — and suppose it ever got back to him — and supposing he had it traced . . .

"He'd never do anything," Julia assured herself. "He'd only think I must have had a hell of an appetite . . ." But as one fear was quieted another took its place; for the first time it struck her that Susan wouldn't be really pleased to know that Mr. Rickaby had paid for her lunch. Susan never would know, of course — but if she did! The thought turned Julia hot all over.

Aloud, and quite unconscious of the length of the pause, she said: "I got it in London. I hate dirty money."

"Filthy lucre," remarked Bryan — his tone as idle as Susan's but his eyes alert. "Personally I shouldn't mind how filthy it was, so long as it paid for this lunch. For what I have received, the Lord knows I'm truly thankful."

Susan, standing by her chair waiting for Mrs. Packett to get up, opened her mouth and on a second thought closed it again. There was evidently a lecture impending, and Julia, to pay Bryan out, at once provided an opportunity for it.

"You young ones ought to walk back," she said firmly. "It's not too hot and the exercise will do you good."

"Yes," said Susan quickly. "I was just thinking the same thing. Ready, Bryan?"

He looked at Julia, met a stony glance, and resigned himself to the inevitable. As Julia followed Mrs. Packett into the car she saw the pair of them turn along the promenade and set off at an unnaturally brisk pace.

II

"Let's stop and have a bock," said Bryan, as they reached the big café.

"Why? You can't want one now, after all you had at lunch," said Susan reasonably.

"I don't want one, I should like one," explained Bryan.

142

Susan did not answer, but merely walked on. She was in no mood for frivolity. Bryan, glancing sideways, observed, and felt it a pity, that her profile was at its best when her mouth closed in that quiet inflexible line. How different a mouth from Julia's with its full lower lip and deep corners! How different from Julia altogether, this slim young Amazon who walked looking straight in front of her, with never an answering glance for the admiring looks commanded by her silver Anglo-Saxon colouring. If only the Julia in her — and surely so vivid a mother must in a daughter live again — could be brought out and allowed to flower! And as always, in the midst of his resentment, Bryan was at once tantalized and enchanted by the vision of a Susan not silvery, but golden; not cold, but warm; of a Susan whom he felt so capable of discovering and bringing to life — if only the silver Susan would let him . . .

"Why did you say that at lunch?" demanded Susan abruptly.

"Say what, darling?"

"About not caring how dirty the money was, so long as it paid for you."

Bryan grinned. He knew well enough why he had said it: to get a rise out of good old Julia, because he was morally certain that there was something fishy about that note. Although her previous afternoon's activities were in detail unknown to him, he had given, without the least loss of appetite, a surprisingly good guess at their general outline; but he also shared Julia's opinion that Susan would not be pleased.

"That! I don't know," he said lightly. "Just for the sake of saying something, I suppose."

"I wish you hadn't," stated Susan, frowning. "If you didn't mean it, it was just foolish; and if you did it was rather rotten."

"All right, I'm just a fool," agreed Bryan amiably. "Let's try going across country." He wanted to get off the highroad, among trees, into the shelter of a hedge: he had the firmly-rooted masculine conviction that all female criticism was best met by kissing.

Rather to his surprise, Susan nodded. They turned aside, taking one of the lanes that wound to the right over a little hillock. On its summit rose the abandoned shell of a fine new villa; there was no water on that hilltop, as the impetuous architect had belatedly found out. "What an idiot he must have been!" thought Susan absently. She had no patience with people who leapt before they looked — who staked everything on a view, without considering the water supply; and since she was now (so to speak) considering a water supply herself, she did not respond to the pressure of Bryan's hand. She knew already that he could supply her with the view.

"You're not a fool," she said seriously. "And things like that — they worry me, Bryan. The things that slip out when you're not thinking."

He let go her hand and regarded the landscape with an air of exasperation.

"Darling, if you expect every word I say to be weighed in the balance first —"

"You know I don't. I should hate it."

144

"— or if you expect me to talk all the time as though I'm on oath —"

"I don't!" cried Susan again. "It's not that at all!"

"Then if you want to know," finished Bryan angrily, "I think you're making an absurd fuss over nothing."

They broke off, aghast. But to Bryan, who had often wished to provoke just such a scene, the moment was not without its compensations. He enjoyed, fiercely, the pleasure of letting his irritation get the better of him. He enjoyed Susan's wide gaze of distress, and the faint colour that stained her throat. Then the savage moment passed, and his heart dropped like lead.

"Susan — darling —"

"It's all right," said Susan quietly. She too had recovered herself; she could meet his imploring gaze with a smile. "Only — only if you feel like that, and I feel so differently, it seems pretty hopeless."

"Nothing's hopeless, if you'll stick to me," said Bryan urgently. He meant it. His penitence was so great that he felt capable of any sacrifice — more, of any long laborious toil — that would reinstate him in her graces. Susan turned away her head. To her also it was a moment for self-examination.

"I know Julia thinks I'm a prig," she said slowly.

"Damn Julia!"

For some reason Susan's expression immediately relaxed. Her next words came more easily, almost impetuously, as though a confidence withdrawn had been suddenly renewed.

"If I am, I shall be one all my life. That's what I want you to understand, Bryan: if you find me too — too difficult now, I don't believe I shall ever be easier. I can't pretend. I can't behave as though things aren't important, when I know they are. Things you think are too little to worry about. I've tried — it does sound priggish, and I know it — to set a guard about myself . . ."

There was a long silence. They were both too much moved for speech; they were both suddenly humbled, Susan before the vision of a perfect integrity, a holiness of the mind, Bryan before the reflection of it through Susan. It was the deepest emotion he had known, and so strange to him that he could not understand, but only feel. His words, when at last they came, and inadequate as they were, had at least sincerity to strengthen them.

"You're the best thing there ever was, Susan. You make me feel one of the worst."

She reached out behind her — she was now walking a little in front of him — and felt for his hand. He took it and plunged on.

"You've got such hellishly — such heavenly — high standards. You — you'll have to haul me up to them."

"Can I, my dear?"

"If you want to, you know you can. Only — pull hard."

She drew him close beside her, and they finished their walk like lovers.

III

That night, for the first time since her arrival at Muzin, Julia was unhappy. She told herself three fortunes, and each was worse than the last: she was going to have trouble in old age, and be jilted by a fair stranger, and suffer disappointment in her plans. Nor was she in the least surprised, for everything was going wrong already. Her successful raid on Aix had produced totally unexpected consequences, and so had her scheme for the discomfiture of Bryan Relton. He and Susan had returned to the villa trailing positive clouds of glory: they spent the whole evening walking up and down the terrace discussing his career. "It can't last," thought Julia; but when she looked at her daughter's face she almost doubted. Susan was so strong-minded! But even if she gained complete ascendancy, if she managed to hold Bryan's nose to the grindstone and turn him into a pillar of the law, she couldn't change his nature. He might behave like a solid pillar for year after year, but one day he would crack, and then down would come all Susan's firmly-built house. "Perhaps it's that lunch," thought Julia, quite aghast at her own gloomy prescience. "Rich food never did agree with me . . ." But she knew she was fooling herself; rich food as a rule was just what she thrived on. However, she went to her room and took a soda-mint, and either that or her long night's sleep did her good. She woke up still feeling melancholy, but only gently and sentimentally so; and since it was an instinct with her always to make the most of any emotion, she slipped out alone and bent her steps towards the ruined pavilion.

CHAPTER
FOURTEEN

It was more dilapidated than Julia had thought —
doubly so, indeed, for even the repairs were themselves
in need of repairing. A sheet of zinc under the roof
no longer kept out any but the mildest weather; in
every wall long zigzag cracks split the superimposed
plaster. There were seedlings between the boards,
cobwebs under the beams; and the only elegant thing
there was a little slender grey-green lizard that fled at
Julia's step.

Her disappointment was great. She had hoped for
true-lovers' knots, faded but still blue, perhaps
even a cupid or so; especially she had hoped for
some sign of recent occupation. A cushion, a letter,
a mere heart scratched on the wall — any of
these would have pleased and contented her. But
there was nothing. There was not even a view,
for the nut trees grew too close. "It's a shame!"
thought Julia vaguely; her pity being half for any one
else who might be similarly disappointed, half for the
pavilion itself. And the emotion (though vague)
was not a barren one: with sudden resolution
she took out her lipstick and drew a heart of her
own.

148

Scarcely had she finished when a sound of voices below brought her hastily back to the doorway. There were people on the path, Susan and Bryan and a tall unknown man. He had grey hair, and as he walked his hand rested lightly and familiarly on Susan's shoulder. Susan looked up, even her height diminished by his, and smiled affectionately. Bryan, a little behind, was wearing his best deferential air . . .

Sir William had come.

II

Julia now naturally wanted to get down unobserved and go back to the house and tidy her hair and come out again and be discovered in the garden; and as the path turned almost at once, she had every hope of being able to do so. But Bryan, already behind, let the others pass out of sight while he stopped to tie his shoe.

"*Sst!* Julia!" he hissed.

With as much dignity as she could muster, Julia advanced to the top of the steps.

"What are you doing there?" she asked severely.

"The question is, what are you? I spotted you as we came up, and thought perhaps you weren't feeling social."

"I wasn't," said Julia crossly. "I'm not now. Is that Sir William?"

"It is, darling. The ranks of the godly are increased by one. Shall I help you down?"

But Julia refused his assistance and descended alone. She had no time to waste on foolishness.

"You go on with the others," she directed, herself taking the lower path. "I've an important letter to write."

"Hi! Julia!"

Simply to stop him shouting, she turned and looked back.

"What is it now?"

"When you've written your letter — and changed your frock — where would you like us to discover you?"

Julia had a very good mind to ignore the impertinence altogether. But she didn't.

"Under the pines," she said hastily; "and *not* for half an hour."

III

Exactly twenty-five minutes later she was in position. She had on a fresh white frock, and not too much lipstick. On her knee lay *The Forsyte Saga*. She wished for a dog, but the villa could not supply one, and Anthelmine's cats were too common-looking.

The minutes passed slowly while Julia held her pose. She was afraid to lean back, in case the seat should mark her dress; there were several deck-chairs, but the rustic bench had a suggestion of Marcus Stone which strongly appealed to her. As once before, on the lower terrace, Julia was acutely aware of herself as part of a charming picture. "There ought to be a man!" she had thought; and now that a man was imminent, her consciousness was correspondingly heightened. With straining ears she listened for the voices in the vineyard;

and when at last they became audible they were so much closer than she expected that she had barely half a minute to become absorbed in her book.

To the party above she was now distinctly visible, and Susan called cheerfully down to her. Julia did not stir. She was going to look up with a start, but she was going to do it at close range. She just turned over a page and smiled slightly, as though at some cultured witticism.

"Hi, Julia!" cried Bryan, quite close at hand.

At that Julia started in earnest, for he had leapt the last bank and was speaking positively in her ear. She gave him one good glare, and turned with a welcoming smile for the more decorously approaching figures of Susan and their guest.

"This is Sir William — my mother," said Susan, also directing upon Bryan a repressive look. It was unfortunate for the young man that the return of his lady-love's favour at once produced in him those same high spirits which had been the cause of his losing it. As Susan said herself, she could not pretend; she could not pretend now to be pleased that he had leapt down that bank and made her mother jump into the air just as Sir William was about to be introduced . . .

Julia, however, noticed none of this, being too much taken up with her own deportment. It was beautiful. She graciously inclined her head, graciously extended her hand, and by moving a little along the bench, invited Sir William to sit.

"Take a deck-chair, sir," suggested Bryan maliciously. "That thing's as hard as nails."

But Sir William sat down by Julia. He was tall and thin, sunburnt, with slightly rough grey hair and the kind of profile she most admired. An aquiline nose was one of her weaknesses, and Sir William's was a real beak. "Distinguished!" thought Julia, after her first discreet glance. "He could play an Ambassador just as he stands!"

"What a beautiful place this is!" said Sir William distinguishedly.

"Remarkable," agreed Julia. "Are you fond of scenery?"

Sir William said that he was. He added that as he had his car with him, he hoped to see a good deal of it. If the next day were fine, they might all motor up the Grand Colombier and have lunch on top. They would be able to see the Rhône and Mont Blanc.

"What kind is it?" asked Julia.

Since Sir William looked a trifle puzzled, it was perhaps as well that Bryan answered for him.

"Dark-blue Daimler," he said succinctly. "I hope, sir, that barn doesn't leak?"

"I hope so, too," replied Sir William with philosophy, "but any barn a Frenchman isn't using is pretty certain to be derelict. However, the weather seems settled enough."

Susan glanced up at the blue and white sky.

"The clouds are coming from the Midi," she said, "which isn't a very good sign. Julia's had the one perfect week this summer."

These last words, in conjunction with the disastrous fortunes she had dealt herself the night before, struck

Julia as ominous. Could it be that the arrival of Sir William, to which she had so much looked forward, was to prove fatal to her peace and happiness in the character of young Mrs. Packett? Was he going to see through her, like Bryan, and — unlike Bryan — denounce her and turn her out? His aquiline features, even in repose, looked terribly stern; what would they be like when agitated by righteous indignation? "Grand!" thought Julia involuntarily; for already she admired Sir William very much indeed. She was like a passenger in a small boat who, fearful of a storm, would nevertheless enjoy seeing the ocean rage. Sir William's wrath would be terrible, but it would be a fine sight. "I'm all right so far," thought Julia, summoning her courage. "I've just got to keep my head . . ."

All through lunch, therefore, she said hardly a word. She wiped her mouth both before and after drinking, took no second helps, and was very attentive to Mrs. Packett. Bryan, after his momentary relapse, was on his best behaviour too, and almost equally silent. Susan and her grandmother talked to Sir William, asking after common acquaintances — several of them, to Julia's pleasure, with titles — and about his tour through France. But the meal as a whole was unusually dull, and no one sat long over coffee. Julia in particular was so exhausted that she went straight to her room and slept for two hours.

After tea Sir William took them all for a drive. Susan sat in front, Julia with Bryan and Mrs. Packett in the back. The car was a beauty, and they saw some very nice scenery. Then they came home and dined, and after dinner played bridge. Bryan (his behaviour was fluctuating like fever-chart) suggested poker, but Julia felt herself bound to sit on him. "I hate gambling," she said virtuously, "I think it's so bad for the character"; so they played several rubbers, Mrs. Packett sitting out, at twopence a hundred. At half-past ten Susan yawned; at a quarter to eleven Julia revoked, and no one but Sir William noticed it. Then Claudia brought in the barley-water, and they all went to bed.

"I'm so glad Sir William has come," said Mrs. Packett to Julia, as they passed through the lobby on the way to their rooms. "It will make things a little gayer for you."

"Not half," said Julia grimly.

But she said it only to herself.

IV

By next morning it was obvious that Susan's doubts had been justified; the weather was breaking, and the expedition to the Grand Colombier was by common consent put off. Julia was not altogether sorry; she had little desire to sit for another two hours — and possibly longer — cooped up with Bryan and her mother-in-law. Even in a Daimler, it wasn't worth it. The morning hours, however, now that their plan had fallen through, seemed unusually long; she would have liked to tell herself some more fortunes, but feared lest Sir William should see and despise her. He was wandering about rather aimlessly, now in the house, now in the garden; Susan had retired with her French, Bryan was nowhere to be seen, and Mrs. Packett, in the billiard-room, was busily engaged with what would probably turn out to be a small cookery-book. Julia looked in on her, and went hastily away. From the hall she caught sight of Sir William's tall figure on the porch steps. He was really beautifully set up! He had the straightest back, for his age, that Julia had ever seen, and for a moment she stood contemplating it with genuine pleasure. Then Sir William turned round, so quickly that she had no time to fall into an effective pose; and thus he too received an unexpected and attractive impression. For there was about Julia, when she forgot herself, a certain charming simplicity: she stood there admiring him with the happy candour of a child before a Christmas tree.

"Come up to the rock," invited Sir William, "and look for Susan's clouds."

"I don't mind if I do," said Julia. But her spirit, as she joined him, was weary. She was still rather afraid of his profile, and her anxiety to make a good impression almost tied her tongue. However, the opportunity was in many ways favourable; there was at least no Bryan to upset her with his too understanding looks, or with his over-emphatic agreement whenever she made a cultured remark . . .

"Do you care for Galsworthy?" asked Julia, as they began the ascent.

Sir William replied that he did. Which just showed — and Julia only wished that Susan had been there to hear.

"I've got *The Forsyte Saga*," she continued. "I think it's wonderful."

"A very fine piece of work," said Sir William. "Particularly *To Let*."

Since Julia had not yet reached that, this was rather a stumper. But she kept her end up well.

"*I* like *A Man of Property*. I think it's wonderful."

Sir William agreed with her again. Their conversation was not exactly animated, but it was of the most superior kind.

"Mrs. Packett looks remarkably well," said Sir William.

"Doesn't she?" said Julia.

It was surprising how soon a subject became exhausted. Julia, whose turn it now was, racked her brains in vain. There remained of course the whole great topic of Susan's marriage, but until she knew Sir William better — until her good impression had been made — Julia preferred to leave it untouched. He was too valuable an ally to be approached without due precaution.

"Do you like Aix?" asked Sir William.

"No, I don't," said Julia, taken unawares. "Not that I've ever been there," she added hastily. Sir William was too polite to notice the inconsistency, but the necessity for not noticing somehow killed that topic as well. They mounted for a while in silence, and soon Julia could not have spoken even if she had found anything to say. She needed all her breath to keep from panting. Sir William, with the privilege of his sex, frankly wiped his forehead; Julia made an effort to contract her pores. By the time they reached the foot of the rock her chief emotion was regret for her absent powder-box.

"Close, isn't?" she gasped, as they came to a standstill. She could feel the blood beating in her cheeks, the hair clinging to her temples: it would have astonished her to know that Sir William found the effect most attractive. "Florid," Mrs. Packett had written; "glowing," substituted Sir William; he thought that if only Julia would keep silent — or at any rate stop making genteel remarks — he could enjoy her company very much indeed.

"I love a nice view," said Julia, regaining her breath. She gazed rapidly over the plain: clouds had drifted in over the encircling hills and lay like a canopy at a level somewhat below their summits. Through great ragged gaps, however, the sun still struck down, picking out here a village, there a little hill: Magnieu lay in shadow, the roofs of Belley shone. Where, in all that, was the Midi? wondered Julia; but she did not care to show her ignorance by a direct question. Instead she asked what Sir William thought of the weather.

"It's certainly unsettled," he told her, "but I haven't Susan's local knowledge. If we do get a thunderstorm, it'll be a big one. Shall you mind?"

"Not in the least," said Julia untruthfully. Thunderstorms were a terror to her, and if one happened in the middle of the night, when she was all alone, she really didn't know how she could bear it. Louise was just the same — except that she, with the energy belonging to her red hair, at least got some excitement out of them: she used to rush out in her best nightgown and have no end of a time. "I'd better put on my pink satin," thought Julia. "I'd be too scared to change . . ." She shivered in anticipation.

"You're getting cold," said Sir William. "There's more breeze up here than one thinks."

He turned to lead the way down, and Julia willingly followed. It was lovely to have him hold aside the branches for her, and give her a hand over the rough places, but the necessity — as she conceived it — for making polite conversation was still a dreadful worry. Sir William had apparently thrown up the sponge; they descended two-thirds of the path in complete silence. At the turning under the pavilion, however, among the nut trees, an odd memory came into Julia's head, and she thoughtlessly gave it utterance.

"I had a little nut tree" —

recited Julia suddenly —

"And nothing would it bear
But a silver nutmeg —"

She broke off, feeling rather foolish; but Sir William stood smiling at her.

"— And a golden pear," he finished. "You have a wonderful gift for completing the moment."

Julia didn't quite know what he was talking about, but she nevertheless felt flattered. Her spirits rose, and on a reckless impulse she said incautiously:

"Do you know who taught me that? A Clown!"

"Circus or pantomime?" asked Sir William.

158

"Pantomime. When I was small, my mother used to play Columbine, and sometimes I waited for her in the dressing-room. And once, I don't know why, I was crying about something, and the Clown came in and took me on his knee and recited that about the nutmeg. It was ages before I found out that he hadn't made it up himself."

"And did it stop you crying?"

Julia hesitated. Since Sir William, for some reason, evidently thought highly of the rhyme, and since she herself thought highly of Sir William, she would have liked to say yes; but honesty forbade.

"I don't know," she confessed. "I *did* stop, but it was more likely because of the sausages. He let me play with them — and his poker."

"A Clown who recited nursery rhymes," said Sir William thoughtfully. "You must have had some wonderful stories to tell Susan."

Julia looked quite shocked. Tell Susan about her grandmother being a Columbine! What next! Fortunately the girl was not inquisitive, but should the question ever arise Julia had long made up her mind what to say. "Your grandmother on *my* side, dear, was the daughter of a clergyman." Which was quite possibly true, since Julia had never so much as heard her own grandfather mentioned; if she didn't know that he *was* a clergyman, she equally didn't know that he wasn't . . .

Aloud she said, brusquely, "I've never told Sue anything. As I expect you know, I haven't been much of a mother to her."

"If you had," said Sir William, "you'd neither of you be half what you are now." And irrelevantly, absurdly, he quoted the rhyme again:

". . . a silver nutmeg
And a golden pear."

"I don't know about you," said Julia, still put out, "but I'm dying for a drink."

V

It would have taken more than barley-water (which was all she got) to restore her equanimity. She had accompanied Sir William into the vine for the sole purpose of making a good impression on him; what on earth had possessed her, then, to go gadding away about Clowns and dressing-rooms? Why, with all the beautifully correct present to draw upon, must she go and dig up her peculiarly incorrect past? For he would never have guessed, thought Julia fondly; if only she'd held her tongue he'd still be taking her for a real lady.

She sat down to lunch in low spirits. It was just as dull a meal as that of the day before — with this difference, that besides being bored she was now nervous as well. She had a dreadful fear that Sir William might say something about Clowns, or Columbines, or even make some direct inquiry as to her early career; and indeed his attempts at conversing with her were alarmingly numerous. But Julia suppressed them all. Even on the subject of Galsworthy she refused to be drawn. Galsworthy had written for the theatre, and theatres had Pantomimes, and Julia was taking no risks. After a while Sir William gave up trying, and devoted himself instead to old Mrs. Packett. At that Julia drew an easier breath, and by the time Claudia was clearing the meat-plates had recovered sufficient aplomb, and also sufficient appetite, to ask Susan what was the sweet.

"Harlequins!" said Susan gaily.

Julia started. Then surprise gave way to indignation as a most appalling thought flashed through her mind. He couldn't — he couldn't have told Susan *already*?

Susan's next words showed that he had not.

"The French for 'left-over,' I'm afraid, Uncle William. There's half last night's tart to be eaten, and a cream cheese."

Julia heard, comprehended, and felt her heart sink back into its proper place. But her peace was once more shattered, for across the table, in that moment, she had just caught Sir William's eye.

CHAPTER
FIFTEEN

Julia's rôle as young Mrs. Packett now began to present greater difficulties than ever. It had been tricky enough at first — with Bryan always giving the wrong cue, Susan on the look out for slips, Mrs. Packett perpetually trying to introduce a sub-plot; but the presence of Sir William, as Julia at once perceived, was going to make everything ten times worse. He was as dangerous as Bryan, as observant as Susan, and would quite likely take an interest in the cakes. To crown all, Julia was very much attracted by him.

"I would be!" thought Julia glumly.

For the first time in her life the prospect of a new sentimental encounter — with its delicious alternations of hope and despair, its exciting approaches to intimacy, and hardly less stimulating checks — gave her no pleasure. She hadn't the time for it. She needed all her wits, all her energy, simply to keep her end up. Her only hope, and she knew it, was to lump Sir William with the rest and make no attempt at individual attention. For she had nothing to fear from him; though he might catch her out as often as Bryan did, he wouldn't give her away. Quite likely, now that they'd

162

settled down again, he'd just stop taking any notice of her at all.

Unfortunately, Julia felt that if he didn't take notice of her she wouldn't be able to bear it.

Just at this time, as if in sympathy with her distress, the weather broke. Julia looked out at the streaming skies and for a moment took pleasure in the general desolation. Then she turned away disgustedly; it simply meant that they would all be cooped up indoors at closer quarters than ever. There was no ground so favourable to love affairs (someone had once told her) as a country house on a wet day; and one horn of her dilemma was accordingly sharpened. To avoid it Julia felt she would have gone on a walking tour in the Sahara. Then Sir William shut himself up in his room with a quantity of papers, and Julia prayed for fine weather to bring him out again. She was in the most uncomfortable state of mind she ever remembered; and still it went on raining.

It rained and rained. Anthelmine, the cook, stumping up from the village under a vast umbrella, announced that it was going to last. She was in a bad temper — the umbrella, though vast, had not been vast enough for her — and dinner accordingly suffered. It rained all night, and all the next day. Even indoors, with the windows shut, one could not for a moment forget that it was raining. The sight could be shut out, but not the sound; and to the steady drumming of water on foliage the indomitable crickets added a fife obbligato. No one ventured out save Susan, who put on a mackintosh and went for a long walk. Bryan was invisible at the lodge, Sir William stayed in his room till water came through the roof, then wandered into the hall and met Julia, who at that moment happened to be taking the line of resistance. She at once bolted back into her own apartment, and Sir William retired to the billiard-room and Mrs. Packett.

The old lady was getting on better than any of them, for she had one inexhaustible resource. Whenever she had nothing else to do, she wrote letters. She was never at a loss for a correspondent, never at a loss for matter; all she needed was paper and ink; and the result was rather like planchette writing, disjointed yet unhesitating. She put down, in fact, whatever came into her head, and since her head was at that time full of Julia's cake-shop, the news of this project was being rapidly spread to the four corners of the earth.

* * *

It will be, I think, in Kensington (wrote Mrs. Packett, to a cousin by marriage who was in Australia), as Susan tells me a great many people there are forced to live in flats. Julia herself is not so certain about this, but we shall have a *good look round* when we all get back to town. You will know I am not *touting*, as you live so far away; but whenever you come home, my dear, I shall certainly take you for a nice cup of tea . . .

* * *

The only event of the morning was the arrival of a second postcard from Fred Genocchio. "Glad you're enjoying yourself," it said. "All the best, Fred." But what touched Julia chiefly was the picture of Notre Dame. It was so beautiful and refined that she left it lying in the hall in the hope that Susan would see; and when Susan made no comment Julia went and fetched it out again to show to Mrs. Packett. The old lady admired it very much, and under the impression that it was for herself turned it over and read the other side.

"Fred?" she said inquiringly. "Surely not Fred Trevelyan?"

"It's for me," said Julia hastily; "it's from a friend of mine" — and involuntarily glanced over her shoulder to see whether Sir William had heard. After that she was so annoyed with herself that she went back to her room and watched the rain from there.

About four o'clock Bryan arrived from the lodge, complaining that he had lunched off rancid cheese.

"Then why didn't you come here?" asked Susan, whose six-mile walk had left her in a kindly, reasonable frame of mind that was highly irritating to the rest of the party.

"Because I didn't want to get wet, darling," said Bryan, shaking the water from his coat. "I may be English, but I'm not mad."

"It's raining just as hard now," pointed out Susan. "Would you like a hot bath?"

"No, I wouldn't," said Bryan. "And it's hardly raining at all."

After that they played bridge for several hours, until Mrs. Packett observed frankly that it was a game very trying to the temper. After that they all went to bed. Julia looked at her best satin night-gown, which she had been wearing in case of thunderstorms, then thrust it back in the drawer and put on a pair of cotton pyjamas.

II

Precisely at three o'clock the first mutter of thunder rolled round the hills and died away. The next crash sounded directly over the roof, and a glare of lightning lit the windows. Julia woke up, not quite aware of what had happened, and lay a moment wondering at the silence. The rain had almost stopped, not a cricket was to be heard. She got up to look out, and was half-way across the room when the thunder spoke again, almost petrifying her with fear. Oblivious of her pyjamas, conscious only of the need for human companionship, she ran to the door and out into the lobby. It felt safer there, less exposed, for the one window was tightly shuttered. Julia looked at the door opposite and wondered whether Sir William had been flooded out. If he had, he was doing nothing about it; within the house all was still. "They don't care!" thought Julia bitterly. "For all they mind I might die of fright!" Never before, not even on the first morning in the bath, had she felt so utterly lost, so completely isolated, so much a stranger under that hospitable roof. She took a few steps towards Mrs. Packett's door, then paused; that

166

strong-nerved old woman was probably sound asleep, or else sitting up distracting her mind with recipes for shortbread. And Susan — Susan would be worse: sympathetic, no doubt, but faintly surprised that any one she knew could be so chicken-hearted . . . "There's no one!" thought Julia wretchedly. The thunder rolled and she found herself once more outside Sir William's door. In spite of the heavy atmosphere she was shivering from head to foot; a great wave of despair, a premonition of unhappiness swept over and shook her. She could not move, she could only stand there, her shoulders pressed against the wall, waiting for the next thunderclap.

It came at last, but from a greater distance, and followed by an appeasing, steady downpour that was the last of the rain. Julia pulled herself together, and crept back to bed.

III

At half-past six next morning, in brilliant sunshine, Bryan was on the lower terrace under Susan's window throwing up gravel. The second handful brought her head out, and some of the pebbles as well.

"Stop it!" she called. "It's going all over my bed!"

"Sorry," said Bryan, dodging the shower. "I tried with roses, but they're so rotten to throw. Are you all right, darling?"

"All right? Of course I am. Why shouldn't I be?"

"I thought you mightn't have liked the storm very much. I nearly came over to hold your hand."

167

"Thank goodness you didn't," said Susan practically. "The front door was bolted and no one would have heard you. What time is it?"

"Half-past six, and the most heavenly morning ever. Come out and smell it." He suddenly advanced and stood close under her window; it was so low that by reaching up his fingers he could touch the sill. "Jump, darling! I'll catch you!"

Susan laughed.

"You idiot! I'm only in pyjamas!"

"What the hell does that matter? There's no one about. Put on some slippers and a coat if you like, only mind you don't catch on the creeper."

Susan's golden head — so bright, so charming — abruptly withdrew.

"I'll be out of the front door in five minutes," she called. "Go and get some proper shoes and we'll climb the rock."

For a minute Bryan stood where she had left him, looking down at his sandalettes. They were soaked through, and so, as far as the knee, were his tan-coloured trousers; for he had plunged straight up to the villa without using the path. He looked down at his feet, up at Susan's window; then turned, took a running jump on to the terrace wall, changed feet like a hunter, and flung himself down into the long grass. It was soaking, and he rolled in it. The sun was hot, the raindrops were icy, the double sensation made him want to shout aloud. But he restrained himself. Susan hadn't come when he wanted her, now let her see if she could find him . . .

But Susan never thought to look in so damp a place.

168

IV

One odd result of Sir William's arrival was that the burden of Julia's ill-got gains, which she had hitherto carried without much distress, became suddenly an intolerable weight. She could not understand it herself: she knew only that the remaining four hundred francs or so weighed like lead both in her handbag and on her heart. Such a state of affairs could not continue, and in the heat of the afternoon, while every one else was resting, Julia retired to her room and there made sacrifice to an unknown god.

It would have looked better — a lot better — had she been able to return the whole amount; but no doubt Mr. Rickaby would understand. The notes, folded in a half-sheet of paper, made at any rate a respectable wad. Julia looked at them fondly, but her hand did not falter as she addressed an envelope to the Beau-Site Hotel. The idea of writing a letter was also present in her mind; it seemed so unfriendly just to return the money without a single word; but a letter might lead to an answer, or even to the appearance of Mr. Rickaby himself, and for that she had no desire. In the end she took a pen and wrote simply "From a Well-wisher" — to which the pen by itself added a couple of crosses. Then she licked down the envelope and was unfortunately compelled to steal one of Susan's stamps.

"All in a good cause," thought Julia cheerfully.

It was a hot day, but as a final penance she determined to walk into Magnieu and catch the afternoon post.

169

The village lay dozing under a sunlight that made her blink. Its inhabitants were all in the fields, and their poultry kept house for them, walking in and out over the thresholds like neighbours paying calls. In a basket at the carpenter's door slept five parti-coloured kittens: their soot-black mother, one yellow eye open, lounged on the window-sill above. All was quiet — so quiet that Julia instictively muffled her tread, stepping on the patches of straw that made sunshine even in the shade; but neither the poultry nor the cats took any notice of her.

She crossed the square with the fountain and took the Magnieu road. Like the village, it was deserted, and before she had gone far Julia began to feel as though she were the only person moving over the whole map of France. The sensation was disagreeable to her; she had a distaste for being alone with so much landscape. On her right, the breadth of a field away, towered a tree-covered bluff, brilliantly green against a sky brilliantly blue; both tones were as bright and as flat as if a child had painted them out of a new paintbox. To the left stretched the cultivated plain, more varied in colour, but robbed of all subtlety by the downright strength of the sun. Julia's sense of the theatre demanded a good-sized cloud or two, or at least a change of lighting; and she began to fix her eyes on a row of poplars that would presently break the monotony of the shadeless road.

Just before she reached it, however, the monotony was broken in a different way. From close beside her, but on the other side of the hedge, came the sound of a slight scuffle, then a half-laughing, half-angry feminine protest; and out of the next gate ran one of the village girls. She had the attractive local face — pale-skinned, blue-eyed — but also the less attractive local figure; at the sight of Julia she hesitated, then marched across the road into the field on the other side. Julia continued on her way, and thus reached the still-swinging gate at precisely the moment when Bryan Relton came through it.

"Well!" said Julia.

With great presence of mind he turned round and waved a hand towards the bluff.

"Grand view," he said, "but too damned hot."

"You've been kissing that girl," accused Julia.

"What girl?"

"The one who bounced out just now. You can't put a view across me."

Bryan grinned.

"You're right, darling. You always are. But I couldn't help it; I'd never kissed a cowherd's daughter before."

This was an attitude which Julia could well understand; but she thought of Susan and frowned.

"You oughtn't to do it," she said severely. "What was it like?"

"Overrated," said Bryan, falling into step beside her. "And how much better to have found out! Now there's one sort of girl I shan't want to kiss again."

"You oughtn't to want to kiss any sort except Susan."

"I don't — in theory."

"Susan expects theory and practice to be the same."

"But then Susan is perfect, and I'm not."

171

"I know that," said Julia. She paused. "Perhaps I ought to have told you that I knew your father."

Bryan stared.

"The deuce you did! In — er — which capacity?"

"What d'you think?" asked Julia. "I don't know what he was like at home, but in a dressing-room he was a fair caution."

"And the sins of the fathers," quoted Bryan, "shall be visited on the children. So you've been holding *him* up against me too, Julia?"

"No, I haven't. I know how little difference it can make: look at me and Susan. I'd have felt the same about you if your father'd been a bishop."

They walked on in silence for another hundred yards, keeping close under the hedge to give room to an approaching ox-wain. When it had passed, at the next gate, Bryan came suddenly to a stop.

"Does it ever occur to any one," he asked, leaning with his back to the post and his hands in his pockets, "that I may one day get a little tired of being constantly discussed and lectured?"

Julia bit back the obvious retort. She had a strong feeling that this was the mood most favourable to her own wishes.

"You'll be lectured a lot more before you're through," she said cheerfully. "Are you coming with me to the Post Office, or are you going to sulk?"

Bryan considered.

"I think I should like to get tight," he said simply. "I'll come with you to Magnieu and get tight there. There'll just be time to sleep it off before dinner."

"If there's one thing I hate," said Julia, "it's showing off. You'll go straight back to the villa now, or — or I'll tell Susan of you."

He went. With one hurt, resentful look he turned on his heel and departed, while Julia continued along the Magnieu road. It was her first attempt at blackmail, and — unlike Mr. Rickaby's money — it did not trouble her conscience at all.

CHAPTER
SIXTEEN

It was now a fortnight since Julia had had her hair washed. Being dark, she could go three weeks and still look presentable; but since the arrival of Sir William, and in spite of her determination to ignore him, presentability was not enough. She wanted a good close set, and plenty of brilliantine; and after a vain attempt to draw information from Claudia (whose own style dated from 1890) Julia went looking for Susan in the garden and interrupted her morning French.

"Where do you get your hair washed, Sue?"

"Here! I do it myself," said Susan.

Julia looked at her daughter's head — smooth, golden, with a slight natural wave — and smiled enviously.

"You *can*, of course. But me with my perm! I'd never get it set. I suppose there's a hairdresser in Belley?"

"Two or three," agreed Susan. "I'll ask about them to-morrow, if you like, when we go in shopping.'

"I'd rather get it done to-day," said Julia unreasonably. She had no ground for supposing Sir William more observant than most men, but he was always so beautifully spruce himself — as she had, at that very moment, an opportunity to note. For Sir

William had joined them, appearing on the terrace just in time to catch Julia's last words.

"Anything I can do for you?" he asked.

"It's my hair," said Julia. "I want to get it washed. I think I'll have to try Belley."

"I'll run you over in the car," said Sir William.

Julia beamed with gratification. He really must like her, then! Because as a rule men hated a hairdresser's, it made them wait about . . .

"You won't have time before lunch," observed Susan practically. "It's nearly half-past twelve now."

"We'll have lunch at Belley," said Sir William. "We'll drive in, make an appointment, have lunch, and then Julia can get it done. How's that?"

"Perfect!" gasped Julia, quite overwhelmed by the magnitude of the offer. Then she looked quickly at her daughter, to see whether Susan wanted to come too. But Susan's air, as she returned to her books, was one of amiable relief only; she seemed sincerely glad to have got her parent fixed up.

"We'll now leave Susan in peace," said Sir William. "I'll have the car out in five minutes."

II

A happy woman was Julia as she took her place in the Daimler. To be seated by a Knight, in a large car, was almost her ideal of earthly bliss; with a good lunch in front of her as well, she felt that life had nothing more to offer. And her face showed it; she beamed with pleasure.

"Comfortable?" asked Sir William.

"Heavenly!" breathed Julia.

She adored him. She had always admired him as the most distinguished man she had ever seen, but her adoration dated from that moment. Something in that one word — the way he said it, smiling, but with his eyes fixed on the road ahead — went straight to her heart. Other words had gone straight to her heart before, but never with such force.

"Tell me if you want a cushion," said Sir William. "There's one behind."

Julia smiled. Since he was not looking at her, a smile was no answer; but she dared not speak. By some miracle she had made a good impression on this superlative man; the nerve-racking part was that she had no idea how she had done it. She could not tell now, for instance, whether he would like her to move up close, so that their shoulders touched, or whether he would prefer her to keep her distance. She stole a sideways glance at his thin aquiline profile; it had such an effect on her that she had to look hastily away.

"I believe this is *it*," thought Julia uneasily. "I believe this is the real thing. If I don't look out, I shall be making a fool of myself."

Her thoughts raced on, and Sir William would have been greatly surprised at them; for by the time they reached Belley, Julia had already dedicated herself to a life of hopeless devotion. The prospect did not depress her as much as might have been expected; it rather thrilled her, and gave her a good opinion of herself. It also gave her an immediate object, for with so many sleepless and tearful nights ahead, it was absolutely essential that she should have a photograph for the tears to fall on.

"I should think you take wonderfully," she said, at last breaking the silence.

"What, photographs? I don't know," said Sir William. "I haven't been taken for years."

Julia was slightly dashed. If she made him get taken specially, he might think she was — well, interested in him. And she didn't want that; her adoration was to be unknown, unrequited, of the highest possible quality.

"I've some snaps taken on the *plage* at Cap-Martin," added Sir William, drawing up outside the Pernollet. "They make me look like a scarecrow."

"I like men to be thin," said Julia. But she said it with great detachment, so that it sounded like a general reflection only. "You should see the old geezers here — they're like a lot of pineapples."

Sir William laughed.

"The Pernollet is their only distraction. Live here a month or two yourself, and you'll see the danger."

"I wouldn't dare," said Julia seriously. "I've got to be careful. This evening I shall eat hardly anything at all."

"Then you'd better have a good lunch," he said.

III

Julia entered the restaurant with a proud and buoyant step. She did not walk, she swept. With Sir William behind her, and the Daimler outside, she felt the equal of any Disgusted Lady there. But her triumph was short; she swept only three paces; on the fourth she faltered. For the first person she saw, at a table directly in their path, was Mr. Rickaby.

Even at that peculiarly unfortunate moment Julia's first thought was an unselfish one: she was glad to see that he had consoled himself. For Mr. Rickaby was not alone, he had a companion, a handsome blonde with a good-humoured face; just the thing for him, thought Julia, as Mr. Rickaby no doubt was just the thing for *her*. Then, as the thought flashed through her mind, Mr. Rickaby glanced up.

"There's someone who knows you," said Sir William.

Julia turned round to deny it, and saw that he was looking in an opposite direction. At a table to their right sat the two Misses Marlowe.

There was nothing to do but smile and nod back, and this Julia did with admirable aplomb. Standing half the restaurant away she felt reasonably safe; she was even pleased that they should see her in the distinguished company of Sir William. So Julia smiled and nodded with her best Packett air.

It was also necessary — which Julia had not realized — to pass directly alongside their table. A beckoning *maître d'hôtel* left no option. The Misses Marlowe smiled again; the elder, who had been much taken by their new acquaintance, even put out her hand in a friendly and detaining gesture.

"We meet again!" she exclaimed cordially. "Did you find your children waiting for you?"

178

With the small of her back (as though she had suddenly developed a new nerve there) Julia instinctively felt Sir William's start of surprise.

"Yes, of course I did," she mumbled hastily. "Of course . . . Thank you very much."

"Perhaps we may all meet at Aix," elaborated Miss Marlowe. "And then you must show them to us." Her keen old eyes, as she spoke, glanced over every inch of Sir William's long figure: she evidently took him for Julia's husband, and was as evidently prepared for an introduction. But Julia, with one more incoherent mutter, passed quickly on; and a moment later found herself seated opposite Sir William's placid but inquiring gaze.

"Go on, you order the lunch," she said. "I'll tell you when I've had a drink."

"Don't if you'd rather not," said Sir William politely.

But Julia had to. She felt she couldn't sit opposite him for an hour, or maybe longer, with the shadow of an unexplained family hanging between them. As soon as the lunch was ordered, and their *apéritifs* consumed, she took the plunge.

"Those," said Julia (and the plunge was indeed a very little one), "are two ladies who live at Aix."

"I should think extremely nice acquaintances," said Sir William.

"Aren't they?" agreed Julia, gratified, even in the midst of her distress, at having given cause for his slightest approval. An odd cause it was too, when you came to think of it; and Julia thought so long that at last Sir William had to prompt her.

"I'd an idea they seemed interested in me as well?"

"They were," said Julia. "That's just it." She drew a deep breath. "I think they thought you were the father of my three children. Elizabeth, and Ronald, and — and I've forgotten the other one's name . . ."

To her extreme amazement, to her no less extreme relief, Sir William, after a moment's astonished silence, put back his head and laughed until the arrival of the *pâté*.

After that they got on famously. Julia did not tell him everything, of course — she suppressed Mr. Rickaby altogether, and substituted for her desire to visit the casino a simple desire for a jaunt — but she told him all about her assault on the Daimler, and most of the lost-sheep-and-heather stories with which she had beguiled her hostesses. Sir William seemed to find them extremely entertaining, and as her confidence grew Julia proceeded to other and equally picturesque episodes of her past life. For the first time since her arrival in Muzin she was completely herself; she had cast all care aside, she no longer bothered even about being a lady. A glorious ease flooded her soul; mentally and physically she had her elbows on the table. For Sir William wasn't being shocked, he was being thoroughly amused; he was *liking* her, enjoying her company, just as though he'd been one of the boys and not a Knight at all. If the Packetts could only see them . . .

"Gosh!" cried Julia. "You won't let out any of this to the others?"

"Of course I won't, if you don't want me to," promised Sir William. "But why not?"

180

"Why not!" Julia's round dark eyes widened with astonishment. "Because — because they think I'm a lady!"

"And so you are," said Sir William.

She loved him for it, but she knew it was only his niceness.

"Not really. Not their sort. I'm not *vulgar*, but I've got to be careful. In fact — and in a way I'm glad to tell you — Bryan's seen through me already."

At that Sir William's brows came down, and all at once he looked like a Knight indeed.

"That young man!" he said grimly. "If he's been impertinent to you —"

"He hasn't," cried Julia. "It's just that he's a bit the same sort. And that's another thing: that's why he mustn't marry Susan. I couldn't tell you before, because I didn't want to give myself away. But you don't think she ought to marry him, do you?"

"To tell you the truth, my dear," said Sir William surprisingly, "I haven't thought much about it. I'm fond of Susan, of course, and I should see she didn't get tied up to a blackguard; but I've never found her particularly interesting."

It has been remarked before that Julia's maternal instinct was highly erratic. One minute earlier such an off-hand dismissal of her marvellous daughter would have roused her to fury: she would have glared like a tigress, and like a tigress sprung; but two words from Sir William had, within the last few seconds, changed all that. He had called her "my dear"! — and those two words had so violently impinged upon her heart, and had so largely printed themselves there, as to confuse all previous inscriptions. Julia still loved her daughter, but she adored Sir William; and she had no idea of quarrelling with his judgment.

"I came to the villa," continued Sir William, thoughtfully, "purely from a sense of duty. But I'm very glad I did."

"Oh, so am I!" said Julia.

It was just at that moment that Mr. Rickaby and his friend, making for the door by a circuitous route, passed close beside the table. He saw Julia, and Julia saw him; out of the fullness of her glad heart she gave him a hearty smile. It was irresistible in its warmth and friendliness, and Mr. Rickaby smiled forgivingly back. The last wrinkle in Julia's conscience was smoothed out; she left the restaurant at peace with all the world.

The rest of the afternoon passed like a beautiful dream. They went for a long drive — but not into Aix — and Julia talked all the way. They stopped for tea at a peculiar little inn where the *patronne*, who served them, observed frankly that she had a very nice bedroom; and Sir William did not mind. "It's me," said Julia, with a frankness at least equal; she was very anxious for Sir William's dignity. She had already determined that if by any marvellous chance he asked her to go away with him — he wouldn't, of course, but just supposing he did — she would try to behave exactly like a wife.

They got back to the villa just in time, as Susan informed them, to change for dinner. The sight of her daughter roused Julia, as always, to heartfelt admiration; but it occurred to her as strange that she and Sir William, having been summoned all across France to Les Sapins solely by the question of Susan's marriage, should have found there something of so much greater interest.

IV

"Did you find a nice hairdresser?" asked old Mrs. Packett at the dinner table. She was rather short-sighted, and the question was quite without malice; what disturbed Julia more was the fact that both Susan and Bryan, who were not short-sighted at all, had preserved a discreet silence.

"No, I didn't," said Julia brazenly. "They were all horrid. I'll have to try Aix."

CHAPTER
SEVENTEEN

The trip to Aix took place, but Mrs. Packett came too. Julia did nothing to stop her, and even welcomed her company, for she was extremely anxious that the new relationship between herself and Sir William should not attract notice. She dreaded Bryan's sharp eyes and sharper tongue — not so much on her own account as on Sir William's; she could not bear the thought of causing him even a moment's embarrassment. Rather than jeopardize a morsel of his dignity, she set herself a Spartan programme of self-repression; no one was to guess that she was the least in love.

How difficult a task that was! For Julia loved with enthusiasm. She put all her heart into it. She longed to show, by her manner, by her voice, by her every action, that she regarded Sir William as the nonpareil of humanity. Flying (as usual) to extremes, she attempted at first a mask of complete indifference, and refused to take part in an expedition to the Colombier; with the result that every one at the villa immediately assumed that she was not feeling well. Mrs. Packett suggested an aspirin; Susan advised a good stiff walk and offered her company, which alarmed Julia so much — she had a vision of herself being made to tramp for three hours up a hill — that she rapidly resumed her normal habits. These now seemed to include a good many morning tête-à-têtes with Sir William in the garden. Julia erroneously fancied that they would pass either unmarked, or as common politeness to a guest at a loose end.

Her first warning, oddly enough, came from Anthelmine, the cook. Since Sir William's arrival there had been no more games of patience, and Anthelmine evidently missed them, for every now and then she would come out of her kitchen, take a look under the pines, and stump gloomily back. Julia had pointed this out to Sir William, and made him laugh at the explanation; afterwards she wished she hadn't. For Anthelmine, it appeared, began to find something under the pines even more interesting than patience; whenever Sir William and Julia were there alone she came more frequently than ever. Sometimes, benevolently, she brought them out titbits — a plate of plums, or some newly baked *petits fours*; oftener she came simply to have a look. And Anthelmine's looks were in a class by themselves — so frank in their inquiry, and, as the days went by, so frank in their congratulation, that Julia did not know how to meet them. At last she made Sir William carry a couple of chairs to the second terrace in the vine; but even thither Anthelmine followed (with some fine radishes) and made matters worse by addressing Sir William in French.

"What did she say to you?" asked Julia nervously.

"'Gather ye rosebuds while ye may,'" replied Sir William; "but this is a long way for her to climb."

After that Julia saw she must be more careful; but it was already too late. Although, by exercising the sternest self-control, she had managed to conceal about three-quarters of her sentiments, her adoration of Sir William was now so immense that the remaining fourth was enough to rouse Bryan's suspicion.

"What's the French for 'love nest'?" he asked Susan. "*Nid d'amour*?"

Susan, who happened to be doing a prose exercise at the moment, automatically put out her hand for the dictionary, and stopped half-way.

"I shouldn't think so," she said seriously. "Slang's awfully hard to translate. Why do you want to know?"

"So that I can write it up on the gate; it's time this place was rechristened. Darling, you don't mean to tell me you haven't noticed?"

"Noticed what?"

"Julia and Uncle William, of course. Our new romance."

"Nonsense," said Susan sharply.

"Not nonsense at all, darling. They're practically never out of each other's sight."

Susan laid down her pen and frowned.

"Uncle William's simply being nice to her, as I asked him to, and of course Julia enjoys being taken about. I wish you wouldn't talk like that, because it's so silly."

Bryan sat down on an open copy of Racine. The emotions he had aroused were quite incomprehensible to him; it struck him for the first time that Susan, like Queen Victoria, had a remarkable capacity for not being amused. Damn it, it was amusing — or at any rate highly interesting! — to see the distinguished and decorous Sir William fall so heavily for good old Julia . . .

"She must be such a thorough change," he mused aloud. "I wonder if she calls him Bill?"

"I loathe gossip," said Susan suddenly. "You're just like the women at college who rush round saying, 'Did you see So-and-so having coffee with Someone Else?' It — it —"

"I know," said Bryan. "It lowers the dignity of human nature."

Susan looked at him with surprise.

"Yes. Then if you see that, why do you do it?"

"Perhaps because I haven't got a particularly high opinion of its dignity to start with. On the other hand, I think a great deal of it as an entertainment."

"And that's all?"

"That's all," agreed Bryan cheerfully.

The next moment, at the sight of Susan's face, he was on his knees beside her.

"Except you, my darling! You're the only thing that matters! You're everything to me, Susan — the whole world!"

But even as he said it, as he felt her hands tighten round his head, he couldn't help wondering whether that was the sort of thing Sir William said to Julia.

II

So far, at any rate, it was not. The new romance was proceeding along such highly unorthodox lines that Sir

William, whenever he got Julia alone, spent most of his time laughing. Their luncheon at the Pernollet had put her completely at ease with him; she said whatever came into her head, introducing, without scruple, a horde of old acquaintances, and seasoning her discourse with bons mots culled admittedly from the Bodega. And Sir William was worthy of her confidence: the recurrent figure of Mr. Macdermot, for instance, seemed to arouse no unusual curiosity, and he never once inquired why it was that Julia, with her secure income, had been so patently living from hand to mouth. This last point struck Julia so forcibly, and impressed her so much, that she made a clean breast of the whole business.

"*They* don't know, of course," she said anxiously, "and that's the worst part. How can I keep a cake-shop when I haven't a bean?"

"You mean you haven't *anything*?" asked Sir William, to whom such a situation, in a person almost connected with him, was naturally startling.

"Not a cent," said Julia thankfully — for it would have been dreadful to answer that question with Mr. Rickaby's money still in her bag. "I haven't even a return ticket, and how I'm to get back I don't know."

"Don't worry about that," said Sir William. He paused, and Julia held her breath, because if he wanted an opening there was a beauty. But Sir William was still preoccupied with her extraordinary revelations.

"I'd like to know how you got here," he said, "if it won't make me an accessory after the fact."

188

"Oh, *no*!" cried Julia. "It was easy. I just sold some valuable furniture"; and since the moment for sentiment had obviously passed, she made a very good story out of Mr. Lewis and the bailiffs.

They had more weighty conversations, as well; for now that Julia knew Sir William better she was constantly on the look out for an opportunity to talk about Susan and Bryan. Such an opening, however, was surprisingly difficult to find; Sir William had apparently cast all care aside, and refused to be drawn into any serious discussion. All he wanted was to lounge about the garden and listen to Julia's reminiscences, or else drive her about in the car and laugh at her appreciations of the scenery. "But it *is* a nice view!" said Julia once, indignantly. "Of course it is," agreed Sir William. "Then why do you laugh when I say so?" demanded Julia. "It's not what you say," explained Sir William, "it's your face while you say it. You have a special landscape expression, my dear; you look so pleased with yourself . . ."

Julia finally decided to count as an opportunity the first moment she could get Sir William alone when he wasn't actually laughing out loud. This occurred one fine, very hot morning, when they were both a little lazy in the heat, and when Anthelmine's visit was safely over. She had brought them a handful of *dragées*, the white sugared almonds that announced a wedding in the village; so the opportunity was really a good one.

"These are for Jeanne-Marie," said Julia. "Claudia's niece. She's getting married next week."

Sir William grunted.

"William!"

"What is it, my dear?"

"I want to talk to you seriously. About Sue and Bryan."

Sir William stretched himself in his deck-chair and looked at the sky. Julia understood his feelings; like any man happy and contented in the moment, he did not want to be bothered. Nor did she, for that matter; for no one else but Susan would she have disturbed, by so much as a thought, their delicious silent intimacy. But for Susan she had to do it.

"It's all my fault," she said cunningly.

At once, as she had known he would — and what happiness the knowledge gave her! — Sir William roused up.

"Nonsense, my dear! You've got an absolute passion for taking blame on yourself. How could it possibly be your fault?"

"Because I ought to have been firm as soon as I got here," said Julia seriously. "As soon as I *knew* — and while Susan was readier to hear what I said. I ought to have told her straight out that he was no good. I ought to have led him on and shown him up, even if it meant showing myself up too. But I left it, partly because I did so want her to think well of me, and partly because I knew she'd be so hurt. I haven't got a really hard heart."

"That's true enough," agreed Sir William.

"You see, I'm *sure*," continued Julia earnestly. "It must seem odd to hear me say I understand a girl like Susan, but I do. She's very obstinate, and very proud.

However badly Bryan turned out she'd never leave him or divorce him or — or do any of the other things. She'd just hang on, miserable, trying to keep up appearances. She'd take up welfare work, I expect, and eat her heart out."

"I should imagine welfare work would be rather Susan's line," said Sir William.

"Of course it is. She ought to be an M.P. — her grandmother thinks so too. But how can she put her heart into anything when she's miserable at home?"

"Won't she be equally miserable if she's separated from Bryan now?"

"But only for a while," said Julia eagerly. "She'll get over it. She's only twenty. I know if she doesn't marry Bryan she won't marry any one else for a long time, but I believe that's a good thing. Susan wants someone older than herself, someone with a position, who'll appreciate her. I can't quite explain it, but she needs ideas more than people. She's got ideas about herself. If you ask me, I believe Bryan's the first young man who ever had the nerve to make love to her, and she feels if she doesn't stick to him she'll be letting herself down . . . You haven't gone to sleep again, have you?"

"No," said Sir William, "I'm considering. And I think you're right, my dear. Only what do you want me to do?"

"An awful lot," admitted Julia. "In the first place, I want you to give Bryan a bad time. Talk to him about settlements, and how you're going to tie up Susan's money, and ask when he's going to do a bit of work, and how soon you can see his father. He hates that kind of thing. If he can put it off by not being officially engaged for another year, he will. And then, for Susan — I want you to have her in town with you, and give dinner parties, and make her meet a whole lot of nice men."

Sir William considered this without enthusiasm.

"Susan's still at Cambridge," he objected. "She won't desert her French to help me entertain."

"But she gets a great long Christmas holiday," retorted Julia. "I'm not worrying about her while she's at college. A month or two back in her own atmosphere will do her good — and besides, if you begin too soon she'll smell a rat. Christmas is just the time."

"And I don't know any young men. I haven't for years."

"I didn't say young, I said nice. I know as well as you that Susan won't care for dancing. The sort you want are the serious ones — interested in the slums, and all that. If they ask her to serve on committees, she'll have the time of her life."

Sir William groaned.

"I've spent a lifetime on committees already —"

"There you are!"

"And I've had enough of them. I was going to write my last letter of resignation to-night."

"What from?" asked Julia quickly.

"A new sort of club affair in the East End. All very self-governing and educational. I had a letter from the secretary last night, asking if I'd mind submitting a provisional constitution, together with estimates for expenses and a draft appeal for public support."

"And you're not going to do it?"

"I'm going to send a cheque instead. From now on, *I'm* the public."

Julia jumped up, her face radiant.

"We won't have to wait after all," she said joyfully. "It's the very thing! Where's Susan?"

III

Susan was in the garden-room, filling her vases. For Sir William, who shared Julia's indifference to tangles, she had just completed a fine Dutch flower-piece of small early dahlias and red jasmine. She would have made a good florist, and knew it. Sometimes, in the abundance of her energy, she toyed with the idea of running a flower-shop as a sort of sideline to more important activities. She felt she could run any number of things — a career for Bryan, and one for herself, and probably her mother's cake-shop (if it ever materialized) into the bargain. At the moment, occupied by no more than French literature and a lover, she was feeling vaguely under-exercised. It was therefore with extreme pleasure, as Julia had foreseen, that she listened to her guardian's proposal.

"But of course, Uncle William!" she cried. "I've done settlement work already, for school. I'd love to help, if you think I can be useful."

"I'm sure you'll be very useful indeed," said Sir William sincerely. Not one of that extremely well-meaning committee had Susan's energy — but then not one of them had Susan's youth. A pair of charitable dowagers, an M.P., an unpaid secretary, and — yes, that fierce, rather dishevelled young man who was the prime mover. *He* had energy enough — but no tact. If he and Susan ever got together, they would make, thought Sir William, a formidable team . . .

"I ought to tell you," he said, "that there's probably another scheme being got out, by a fellow called Bellamy. He'll probably tear everything you suggest to pieces. He always does."

Susan opened her eyes.

"Bellamy! The Bellamy who wrote *Civics of the Slums*?"

"Very likely," replied Sir William, with amazing indifference. "I know he's written something. If you'll come along, I'll give you all the stuff."

Half an hour later Susan was seated in the billiard-room surrounded by a plan of the new premises, all the information so reluctantly acquired by Sir William, and a mass of pamphlets on club management. She was perfectly happy. As soon as Bryan came back from the lodge, she intended that he should share her joy.

CHAPTER
EIGHTEEN

A new and remarkable atmosphere now descended upon the villa. When Julia first arrived there she had been struck by its air of lazy peace; all that was now changed. Susan went about looking exactly like the secretary of a committee, always with a pamphlet in her hand or a bundle of foolscap under her arm. Nor did she stop at carrying the things about with her; among the papers turned over by Sir William were the plans of the proposed club; Susan traced them in triplicate (to work out alternative forms of cloakroom accommodation) and pinned them to the billiard-room wall. Whenever Julia looked up from a bridge hand she saw the words "Lavatories" in red ink. All this businesslike activity, moreover, stimulated Mrs. Packett afresh, and she telegraphed home to an estate agent for particulars of vacant shops in the Kensington district. The agent, also stimulated, telegraphed back, at such length, and detailing such enormous rents, that the old lady, as well as everybody else at the villa, was quite appalled. "What did you say in *your* wire?" they asked; but Mrs. Packett would not tell them. Undaunted, she next entered into correspondence with a number of gentlefolk who were advertising in the *Lady* for "partners with capital."

195

Some of them wired as well, saying "OFFER OPEN TWO DAYS ONLY," or "MANY APPLICANTS WILL YOU CLOSE AT ONCE?" By such innocent devices did they try to lure Julia into their tea-shops. Mrs. Packett, who was by now having the time of her life, wired back all round saying "NO SEND PARTICULARS AND BALANCE-SHEET" — and then the balance-sheets arrived, and she made Sir William check them.

"It's awful," admitted Julia gloomily; "but what can I do, William? I can't *tell* her . . ."

"I suppose not," said Sir William, looking up from the highly complicated accounts of the Singing Samovar. "But it's rather hard on me. I might just as well be back in Whitehall."

"Couldn't you make Bryan do them?"

"He can't add. Anyway, he's being roped in to draw up articles of partnership."

Julia sighed. She hated the idea of yet another link between herself and that objectionable young man, but the fact remained that she and Bryan and Sir William had instinctively grouped themselves into a passively resisting minority. In numbers, it is true, they were superior, but Susan and her grandmother had the moral ascendancy. They were Packetts. Julia resented their activities with all her heart, but she had never had a greater respect for her late husband's family.

"Here's Susan now," she said. "Give me one of those sheets to look at . . ."

Susan, however, had not come in search of assistants; she merely wanted to know Mr. Bellamy's private address.

"Because I think I'd better write to him direct, Uncle William," she said; "then if there are any of my ideas he'd like to use, he can incorporate them with his own. It's no use putting two schemes in front of a committee; they simply start to argue."

Sir William looked at her with healthy mistrust.

"Wonderful," he said. "Have you been reading Bacon?"

Susan laughed.

"I'd certainly put a committee at a long table, and not a round one. One can't approve of him, but he did know how to get things done."

Sir William looked through his diary, found Mr. Bellamy's address, and wrote it down for Susan to take away. She went without lingering, brisk and business-like; but both Julia and Sir William, instead of getting on with their work, sat gazing after her.

"She doesn't approve of Bacon," said Sir William at last. "If he were here, she'd certainly tell him so. And, of course, she's perfectly right."

"She's always right," said Julia. It was wonderful to have a daughter who was always right, but even to her own ears, and as her next words betrayed, the tribute sounded cold. "She's a darling!" said Julia firmly.

Sir William went on with his accounts.

II

The third and youngest member of the minority, Bryan Relton, was having an even harder time than his elders. Like Julia, he had found in the original atmosphere of

Les Sapins exactly the air that suited him, and the chill wind of efficiency, which now so steadily blew through it, did not brace him but simply made him shiver. Julia could at least warm herself in the comradeship of Sir William; Bryan was left out in the cold. When Susan first spoke to him of her new hobby he had been quite sympathetic and interested; if she liked that sort of thing, by all means (he felt) let her spend a wet afternoon making out plans. But the thing went on and on! Susan never forgot it! She was too strict with herself to neglect her studies, but the moment they were done she switched straight over to the Mile End Road.

"But it isn't the Mile End Road!" said Susan, in answer to one of her lover's complaints. "It's India Dock Lane." And she showed him the exact spot on a sketch map. Bryan looked at it sulkily; to him the Mile End Road — or, for the matter of that, India Dock Lane — was less an actual locality than a frame of mind.

"If you're not interested," said Susan suddenly, "I wish you wouldn't pretend to be."

"Of course I'm interested, if you are."

"That's exactly what I mean. You're working up an interest just because of me."

"But that's being in love," pointed out Bryan. "Didn't you know?"

To his astonishment — for he rather expected a quarrel — Susan abruptly folded away the plan and asked him to come for a walk. They climbed the heights above Magnieu up to the statue of the Virgin, and returned through woods. The views were magnificent, the conversation pleasantly light; but Bryan could not help feeling like a puppy being taken for a run.

III

With remarkable promptitude Mr. Bellamy replied; and Sir William, who happened to see the envelope, expressed his opinion to Julia that Susan was in for a bad quarter of an hour. For Mr. Bellamy had the habit of endorsing all suggestions which did not appeal to him with the one word "Rot!" He did it chiefly to relieve his feelings, and always meant to rub it out again if the papers were to be returned; but he was also absent-minded, and the habit had already lost him a philanthropic peer.

"He won't call Susan's scheme rot," said Julia indignantly, "because I'm sure it isn't." And as it happened she was right; Susan came out into the garden with a radiant face.

"I've had a compliment, Uncle William," she announced gaily. "Mr. Bellamy says I'm the first woman he's had to deal with who's got average common sense."

Julia looked at her daughter with wonder. If that was what Susan called a compliment . . .

"You ought to be highly flattered," said Sir William. "I suppose that's the highest praise he's ever been known to give."

"It was the cloakroom arrangements for the girls," continued Susan. "I'd got in half as many lockers again, and no overcrowding. They're going to begin converting next month, Mr. Bellamy says, and if I'm in town he's asked me to go and see him."

"Then I'm only sorry you won't be," said Sir William. "You might prevent his insulting the architect. We haven't had a libel action yet, but I expect one at any moment."

Susan gazed thoughtfully at the vineyard. Her longing was so evident that Julia marvelled again: from the expression on the child's face she might have been thinking about a hunt ball, or a new dance frock. It was really quite peculiar! But it was encouraging as well, and as soon as Susan had gone away — her visits were never long, because she had so much to do — Julia sat up with a pleased and maternal countenance.

"What's he like, William?"

"Who, my dear?"

"This Mr. Bellamy, of course. The one Susan's so struck on."

Sir William looked at her with appreciation.

"You've a wonderfully active mind, Julia. Have you been crying in the front pew already?"

"Certainly not," retorted Julia. "I've never cried at a wedding in my life." She paused, and with her usual honesty added, "Not that I've been to many. They don't seem to come my way." And at that she had to pause again, while a fine blush — the first for twenty years — overspread her face. For how dreadful if he should think . . . if she should seem to be suggesting.

"My dear —" began Sir William.

"About this Mr. Bellamy," said Julia hastily. "Tell me what he's like."

Sir William considerately did so.

"An untidy-looking beggar," he said. "Unmarried, about thirty. Too honest to be popular, but highly intelligent."

"Is he good-looking?"

"In a hungry sort of way I suppose he is. Rather like a Victorian curate gone Communist. I believe his father was an Oxford don."

Julia sighed, half-regretfully, half with relief. Though the young man sounded pretty dreadful to her, he seemed also to have most of the qualities Susan approved. It was a pity he was so far away.

"I ought to warn you," added Sir William, "that as Susan's trustee I should be forced to disapprove. If he ever makes two hundred a year, that will be his limit."

Susan's mother smiled indulgently. She knew perfectly well that if both Susan and she were set on a thing, Sir William wouldn't have a chance.

IV

Although, by comparison with her daughter and mother-in-law, Julia at this time appeared completely idle, such an impression was deceptive. She had one constant, unguessed-at occupation. She was being good.

She had often wanted to be good before. She had a great admiration for goodness; she loved it sincerely and humbly, as a peasant loves a saint. If she had never been good before it was not because her spirit was unwilling, but because her flesh was so remarkably

201

weak. She needed help — all the help she could get; and if help now came from a wholly personal and emotional source, from the fact that she loved Sir William, Julia was not proud enough to reject it.

Whether Sir William loved her in return she was not yet sure; but he at least liked her, and she could not bear that even his liking should have an unworthy object. She now knew what had made her send back Mr. Rickaby's money; it was the first instinctive step in her new direction. Looking back on her behaviour at Aix, Julia was seized by so severe a fit of remorse that for some moments she believed it to be indigestion; then she took comfort from the thought that only genuine repentance could have produced such a strong effect. If you repented, that was enough. You were forgiven and could start again. Julia wished passionately that she were a Roman Catholic so that she could make one enormous confession — from the heart, holding back nothing — and then be told she was all right. She ought, she knew, to be able to believe that by herself, out of pure faith; but she wanted telling. They might make her do things in penance — wear a hair-shirt, for instance: Julia would have welcomed one. She did give up sugar in her tea and coffee. And she carefully and conscientiously examined her wicked heart.

It wasn't, she decided tentatively, all bad. She could not remember being really unkind to any one, or mean to another woman. She hadn't been a gold-digger. Her two great faults were not having remained at Barton, and — and the Mr. Macdermots. They were black. "But I've repented!" cried Julia to herself. "I'll never do anything like that again!" And she made a great, a soul-shaking resolution: that if nothing happened about Sir William she would tell Mrs. Packett all, even how she had lost her money, and ask to be taken back to Barton for the rest of her virtuous life.

Julia did not regard this prospect exactly with gladness; but then she hadn't been good very long.

CHAPTER
NINETEEN

The next afternoon found Julia ridiculously unhappy because Sir William wouldn't be in to tea. He was driving Susan over to Belley to collect some books ordered through the local librarian, and the whole trip shouldn't have taken more than twenty minutes; but just as they were starting, and just as she, Julia, had refused to accompany them, Mrs. Packett most officiously suggested that they should stay and take tea out. This meant an absence of at least an hour, and Julia, too self-conscious to change her mind, had been suffering ever since from a sense of injury. It was idiotic, and she knew it; but to such an imbecile condition had love reduced her.

The conversation at the tea table did nothing to raise her spirits.

"Has Susan told you of her new idea?" asked Mrs. Packett. "She wants us to go back a week early."

"Why?" asked Bryan suspiciously.

"To watch them convert that club, of course," said Julia.

"Not only for that, my dear. She thinks it would be so nice," explained Mrs. Packett, "if we could all look for your shop together."

For a moment Julia was speechless. She would never have credited her daughter with so much duplicity. And yet — was it? Was it not rather just one more example of Susan's wonderful gift for tactful organization? She honestly believed, no doubt, that such a scheme would be acceptable all round; but to Julia, whose time lately had all been spent in managing Susan, it came as something of a shock to find Susan managing *her*.

"And I must say," continued Mrs. Packett, "that a week in town sounds very nice. We could go to the theatres, Julia dear; if Susan's too busy we could go by ourselves, in the evening. Susan always takes me to a matinee, in case I'm tired at night; but I'd lie down beforehand, after lunch."

"Of course we'll go!" cried Julia, suddenly touched. "And to a night club afterwards, if you like!"

The old lady looked wistful.

"I don't know about that, my dear. But we'll have dinner first, at one of the large hotels. Just a glass and a half of champagne each . . ."

Bryan whistled.

"I think I'd better come too and keep an eye on you," he said. "It sounds to me as though you'll want bailing out."

Julia looked at him severely.

"*You'll* be with Susan," she said, "down in the East End. You'd better learn how to gargle." And before he could think of an answer — before she herself could become more deeply committed to Mrs. Packett's riotous plans — Julia got up and strolled towards the house.

It was the simple and devastating truth that no plan meant anything to her unless it involved Sir William. Until she knew what Sir William wanted her to do — until she knew what he was going to do himself — she was like a ship without a course, like a weathercock waiting for a wind. If he wanted her to keep a cake-shop, she felt she could do even that. She could do anything! Anything in the world, if he would only tell her what! If he told her to go into a convent — "But they'd turn me out," thought Julia, with a sudden return to common sense. She sat down, just where she was, in the entrance hall, and tried to make that common sense work. Suppose, after all, he just wasn't interested? Suppose his own plans, already cut and dried, took no account of her whatever? Might it not be that their happy, perfect intimacy, to her the most precious thing life could ever hold, was to Sir William simply a pleasant holiday friendship, and no rarer than any other? "Then I'm done for," thought Julia. "I'll just have to grin and bear it." She tried to grin then, and found it extraordinarily difficult. She felt like a set of teeth in a dentist's window. The vigour of this image, and the fear that someone might pass through the hall, brought her to her feet; she didn't want to be found looking like a sick Cheshire cat.

"It'll all be the same in a hundred years," thought Julia gloomily; and meanwhile wandered out again, into the neglected part of the garden, where no one ever went.

II

Four miles away in Belley, at a table outside the confectioner's in the square, Susan and Sir William were finishing their tea. They were both rather silent, but whereas Susan was conscious of this, and wanted to resume, or rather redirect, the conversation, Sir William was not. His eyes were fixed on the top storey of a tall grey building immediately opposite — a top storey which was unoccupied, slightly dilapidated like the rest of the building, but which possessed a deep triple-arched loggia. There was an odd charm about the place — it was like a crow's nest over Belley, and in summer breakfast on that balcony, with the town stirring below, and a distant view of the hills, would be pleasant indeed . . .

Sir William suddenly found himself thinking that he would like to live there with Julia.

This extraordinary notion both astonished and pleased him. He had not believed himself capable — for the last twenty years he hadn't been capable — of such a juvenile emotion. He was like a man who discovers that he can still touch his toes. And other, equally juvenile, ideas came thronging after the first. He remembered a square in Cracow where all the houses were painted with bright designs, the square where they held the flower market. His eye had been caught there, in just the same way, by a little blue room, an afterthought of a room, perched like a cottage on top of a tall green-and-yellow building; now, after an interval of seven years, he mentally placed Julia at the window. And there were other places as well: Paris in springtime — "Good God!" thought Sir William. "Isn't that the title of a song?" — and the English countryside in June, and London in autumn, when dusk came down like blue smoke. He knew what Julia would say to all of them — "Isn't that pretty, William?" or "I do like a nice view!" — yet for some reason the very ineptitude of her remarks only made her company more desirable. They were so funny. They made him feel at once amused and tender . . .

"There's no doubt about it," thought Sir William, as though he had reached the end of an argument. Then his mind wandered off again, this time to the Riviera.

Susan meanwhile had eaten two chestnut-cakes, and now felt that the time had come for a little serious conversation. Serious conversation at the villa was always liable to interruption, either from her suitor or her mother, and while she had been quite genuine in her desire to visit the librarian, she was also glad of an opportunity to get Sir William to herself.

"You've never told me," said Susan abruptly, "what you think of Bryan."

Sir William detached his gaze from the balcony and came reluctantly back to earth.

"Does it matter?" he asked.

"Well," said Susan, somewhat taken aback, "I'd naturally like to know how you feel about him. I mean — isn't that what you came for?"

"So it is," said Sir William, with an air of surprise. "However, as you're determined to marry him in any case, there doesn't seem much point in a discussion. I believe I'll have another cup of tea."

Susan's eyes over the teapot, as she poured out for him, were both watchful and puzzled. She evidently suspected some trap; she simply could not believe in a genuine lack of interest.

"That sounds as though you didn't like him," she persisted. "Why?"

"I neither like nor dislike him," said Sir William. "He seems to me much the same as any other young man. He's got some money and a profession, we know who his people are, and as soon as you're twenty-one if you want to marry him you can. Now what about getting home?"

Susan obediently rose and accompanied him back to the car. Her countenance was placid, but she felt a vague dissatisfaction. Put into words — into such words as Julia used — it would have amounted simply to this: Sir William wasn't making enough fuss.

"If you've any real objection —" she began.

"I haven't," said Sir William swiftly.

"I'm perfectly willing to listen to you. Just as I've listened to Grandmother and to Julia. I'm not unreasonable."

"It is the height of unreason," pointed out Sir William, "to go on discussing a question after your mind is made up. It's a sheer waste of every one's time."

Susan was silent. She had too clear a head not to see Sir William's point, but for once a logical position was not comfortable to her. Always, before, when she thought of her marriage, she had seen it on the other side of an obstacle — an obstacle of which the chief manifestation was precisely those discussions which Sir William had just put an end to; now she saw it quite close. There was no obstacle any more. With Sir William on her side, or at any rate not opposing her, she could marry Bryan Relton the moment she was twenty-one.

Susan remained silent.

III

High up on a terrace in the vine Bryan Relton lay on his back and looked at the clouds. Like Julia, he had left the tea table in a somewhat troubled frame of mind; but the pleasantness of his situation had already made him forget the worst of his cares. They had never been heavy: they were like the clouds — small, and as yet hardly approaching the sun. Susan's new preoccupation was one of them; he was getting very tired of her continual cloakrooms, and if she were going to make a habit of them . . .

He rolled over — the clouds seemed suddenly larger than he had thought — and reached for a stem of grass. It was not the best chewing sort, but the sensuous pleasure of drawing it from its sheath for a moment completely absorbed him. He put his face down close and snuffed deeply, like a young animal. Scent of dry soil, sweeter scent of clover! By raising his head he got a whiff of cool breeze: then down to the warm earth again, and the clover sweeter than before. It was the very epicureanism of the nose. His imagination began to range — to bonfires, to tar oozing on a ship's deck, to bacon cooking for breakfast, even to the hot petrol-laden air of Piccadilly on a summer afternoon. They were all good, and the world was full of them. There simply wasn't enough time to do them all justice — nor to see all the sights, and hear all the sounds, that clamoured for attention. Probably to appreciate everything, felt Bryan, was a full-time job; and he was forced to admit, as he meditated, that the late and great Victorian, Mr. Rudyard Kipling, had exactly formulated his creed. "For to admire and for to see" — it couldn't be better put. And there was the other chap, who wanted to stand and stare . . . "Rum if I were to turn out a poet!" thought Bryan; but he knew himself too well to nourish false hopes. He wasn't creative. He'd never do any work in the world, but at least he'd be grateful.

It suddenly occurred to him that in this scheme of existence he had left out Susan. At the thought of her, and particularly at the thought of their walk back from Belley, his conscience stirred. He had promised — all sorts of things: diligence, sobriety, every human virtue. Impossible promises, which surely she had taken at their right emotional value! "She must know what I'm like!" argued Bryan. "She won't expect miracles!" He buried his face once more in the grass, drew in the fragrance, and wished she were there with him. He had an obscure conviction that if Susan could once feel the power of that warm earthy smell, he would be able to convert her.

He was back at the old place. He was still in pursuit.

"Blessed Susan!" said Bryan into the grass. The blades brushed against his lips, alive and springy; he had just time to enjoy the sensation before falling asleep.

IV

It would have been sentimentally appropriate if Susan, on her return from Belley, had gone up and found him there and waked him with a kiss; but she went straight into the house to undo her books, and it was Julia, fleeing into the vine before the approach of the car, who unromantically tripped on his shins. Bryan sat up, rubbed himself, and at once perceived that he would get no sympathy.

"That's a silly place to lie!" said Julia. "Right in the path for people to fall over you!"

"If people looked where they were going," retorted Bryan, "other people wouldn't get trampled on. Is Susan back?"

"I expect so. I've just heard the car."

"And Sir William," murmured Bryan. "Now we shall both have company again."

Under his inquisitive eye Julia walked a little along the terrace and sat down on a large rock. She couldn't go back into the garden, and her roamings had tired her.

"I expect Susan's looking for you," she said.

"I've no doubt of it," agreed Bryan complacently. "I can also take a hint. Have you an assignation, darling?"

212

Julia did not deign to answer. Instead of departing, the young man strolled over and dropped down at her feet.

"It's wonderful," he said companionably, "what a knack we both have for attracting our betters."

"I don't know what you mean," said Julia.

"Don't be modest, darling. You know perfectly well Sir William's fallen for you."

In her heart, and despite her recent sad communings, Julia did know, and the thought gave her a secret delight; but she had no intention of sharing it with Bryan.

"You shouldn't talk like that about him," she said sharply. "You ought to have more respect."

Bryan grinned.

"So you've fallen for *him*, have you? What a place this is!"

"You're right there," agreed Julia seriously. "It's all these views and rose-bushes. I remember the first morning — when you made a fool of me — I was thinking the very same thing. And that's all it is with Sir William. He doesn't mean anything."

"But even his non-meanings are sacred? You'd better look out for yourself, darling."

Julia got up and walked to the edge of the terrace. She was a good liar, but she didn't want Bryan staring into her face. For — why not admit it? — it wasn't just the rose-bushes. She could tell that. She could tell not by the way Sir William looked at her, but by the way he didn't look at her — at table, for instance, and when there were other people there. He didn't want them to see, and no wonder . . .

"When you're Lady Waring —" said Bryan behind her.

Julia turned on him.

"Don't say such things!"

"Why not? Wouldn't you like to be Lady Waring?"

"No, I wouldn't."

"Why not?" asked Bryan again.

"Because it's not my line. If you want to know, because I'm not good enough for him — just as you're not good enough for Susan."

"You mean if he asked you, you'd refuse?"

"Yes. And you've no business to talk to me like this. *We've* no business to talk about him. But there you are," said Julia harshly, "I'm the sort of woman any one talks to about anything. I can't keep them off."

She walked quickly along the terrace to where the path branched up and down. Contrary to her usual habit, she began to mount. Down — along the line of least resistance — were people, and for once Julia wanted to be alone. The truth she had just spoken was bitter in her mouth: for a moment she had seen, as though from outside herself, the kind of woman she was; and the image was hateful to her. "If only I'd known!" thought Julia desperately. If only she'd known that — that this was waiting for her, how different she would have been! It was too late now, and she knew it; the life she had been living had got under her skin, into her blood, had become a part of her that she could never now eradicate. For it was all rot about repentance, really: it was no more use repenting over spilt milk than crying over it. You could mop the milk up and squeeze it back into the jug, but it wasn't the same. It was dirty.

A tangle of blackberries barred her path; Julia pushed through, scratching her arms, and taking a queer pleasure in the pain. She was higher now than she had ever been, on a narrow ledge so closely grown with saplings that even where the cliff, on her left, dropped steeply down, she could not see out. It was like a straight green corridor, roofed against the sun. Every now and again an outcropping boulder jutted across the track, and on one of these Julia at last sat down. She had tired her body, but her mind worked pitilessly on, marshalling one after the other all the most discreditable incidents of her life. The times when she had got tight, and done things she was sorry for afterwards. The times when she had made herself cheap, hanging round bars in the hope of a dinner . . .

"O God!" prayed Julia aloud. "Don't let him ever know!"

The tears ran down her cheeks; she wiped them away, clumsily, with the flat of her hand; and as she sat there weeping a most curious image, born perhaps from that other image of the spilt milk, arose in her mind. She saw herself as a cup of clear water, which she herself was somehow bearing through a crowd, and which she should have carried carefully, steadily, losing not a drop, so that when *he* asked for it the cup was still full and unpolluted. But instead of that she had let any one drink who wished, sometimes because of what they gave her, mostly just because they were poor thirsty devils . . .

"How could I tell?" demanded Julia of her Creator. "God, how could I tell?" Ah, but how could any one tell? Suppose you carried your cup high, safe above those thirsty mouths, and at last there was no one to drink from it? Wasn't it better to have solaced a few poor devils by the way? And the strange image grew, till Julia saw all the race of women bearing their vessels of water and passing to and fro among the thirst-tormented race of men; and in the forefront she saw her daughter, carrying a cup of crystal, and holding it high above her head.

"I must be going mad," thought Julia, in real terror. She rose quickly; there was a wind among the treetops, soughing and whispering and shaking the leaves. The sound filled her with panic; she wanted to go back, yet the thought of the narrow leafy path was suddenly terrifying to her.

The air seemed darker. It wanted a full hour till sunset; but already she could apprehend the stealthy approach of night.

With quick, almost furtive steps Julia began to descend. So swiftly, so blindly had she come that the way back was now strange; twice she stood uncertain, and twice saw, or thought she saw, a movement in the trees behind. Her fear of the solitude changed to a fear of unknown company; the sensation of being watched, familiar even to those who walked habitually through woods alone, finally achieved her panic. She began to run, stumbling and hurting her feet on the upthrust

216

rocks. There were more of them than she remembered, and more blackberry arms that caught at and tore her skirts. Julia wrenched herself free and ran on, faster and faster, till at last, unaware, she had passed the nut grove and the ruined pavilion. She had not realized her safety when a tall figure seemed to rise up in her path; with a cry of sheer terror she fell forward and was caught in Sir William's arms.

"I thought you were a ghost," sobbed Julia. The feel of his coat under her cheek was such a blessed reassurance that she clung closer still, till she rasped her skin on the rough tweed. For a moment Sir William said nothing, nor was speech needed. The firm clasp of his arm, like a strong barrier against the powers of darkness, was enough. Julia made herself small within it, blessing him from her heart.

"Did anything frighten you?" he said at last.

"No," sobbed Julia. "It was nothing. Only — I'm such a fool — I stayed up there too long, and I got scared. I don't know why."

"It's untilled ground," said Sir William quite calmly, as though that explained everything. "Come down to the house, my dear, and get warm."

But he did not move, nor did Julia. She just tilted back her head to receive his kiss.

V

"I've been wanting to do that for a long time," said Sir William.

"Then why didn't you?" asked Julia, with real curiosity.

They had walked a little way down the path, not far, but just into the open away from the trees. The rose-bushes bounding the upper terrace still screened them from the house.

"Because I haven't been in love for a long time," said Sir William, "and it makes a man nervous."

Julia laughed, partly from pure happiness, partly from astonishment. That any one could be nervous because of her was something so strange, as well as so delicious, that she could hardly credit it. Her eyes widened even as she laughed; she held Sir William by the coat and made him repeat the astounding, the rapture-inducing statement.

"But why, William? How could you be?"

"In case I spoilt everything. In case you refused me."

Julia stood very still. Refuse him? Didn't he know she couldn't refuse him anything? Or was he — was it possible?

It was possible. It was a miracle, but it happened. A moment later, in the plainest of terms, Sir William had asked her to marry him.

"No!" cried Julia, almost wildly. "No, of course not! I never heard of such a thing!"

And breaking from his arm she fled down the bank and ran for the shelter of the house.

CHAPTER
TWENTY

Following the best Victorian precedent, Julia pleaded a headache, refused to come down to dinner, and drank a small bowl of soup in her room. Thither both Susan and Mrs. Packett, full of solicitude, came to visit her. "If they only knew!" thought Julia, obediently swallowing aspirins; but not a suspicion, it was plain, had crossed their minds. They talked of, and blamed, the thundery weather; they advised a quiet evening, or rather a long night in bed. Julia agreed to everything, and as soon as they were gone, dissolved — again following precedent — into a flood of nervous tears. The outburst relieved her; she washed her face, and sat down by the window, and tried to consolidate her moral position.

She had refused Sir William. For a while that one fact, so enormous, blocked out everything else. She had refused Sir William; and though her doing so had been, at the time, a simple involuntary reaction, she did not now, nor ever would question the rightness of that decision. During her talk with Bryan and her vigil on the hillside she had done all the thinking necessary; her mind was firmly made up. Sir William, in his blessed ignorance and uprightness, had asked her to marry him; only by refusing could she, Julia, reach up to his level.

"God knows how I did it," she thought, bowing her head down on the window-sill. "It must have been because I hadn't time to think . . ."

But she knew, with melancholy pride, that even if she had thought it would have been the same. For she would have thought of Susan. To marry Sir William would be to destroy the last argument against Susan's marriage with Bryan; no use talking to Bryan of incompatibility, if her own action, meanwhile, spoke louder than any words! That afternoon, for the first time, she had been conscious of making an impression on him; how much stronger it would be when he knew what she had done! For know he must, even though it meant asking permission of Sir William first — and that would be almost the hardest thing yet.

"If only I could get away!" thought Julia desperately. "If only I could cut it clean out!" The thought of the morning, bringing its renewal of their intercourse, was terrible to contemplate; she could only pray that Sir William, like herself, would be willing to wipe out and forget everything that had happened since the moment when she so literally fell into his arms. Not that *she* would forget — ever; she would warm all her life with the beautiful memory; but she would behave as though she had. Gradually, firmly, she would withdraw from intimacy; become gently reserved; so that when at last they parted it would be merely as frineds.

"If the truth were known," said Julia aloud, "I bet he's thanking his stars already."

220

Then she put her hand over her heart and pressed hard; because it really felt queer, like something heavy and bruised inside her. Renunciation scenes were all right on the stage; but in real life — and without an audience — there wasn't much fun in them. Julia got up and automatically began to tidy her hair; the face in the glass surprised her by looking very much as usual. "It's too round," thought Julia dispassionately. "I'm not built for tragedy" — and she was still scrutinizing herself when Susan tapped at the door and came quietly in.

"How are you now?" she asked. "I thought you might have gone to bed."

II

"No," said Julia, with a guilty start. "No, I haven't. I believe it's cooler."

"It is," agreed Susan. "There's almost a breeze. Uncle William thinks it might do you good if he took you for a short run in the car."

Julia started again. This was a frontal attack such as she had not contemplated, and such as she must at all costs repel.

"Thank him very much," she said quickly, "but I don't think I will. I believe I'd better stay quiet. I believe I'm going to bed."

Susan smiled encouragingly, like the best type of nurse.

"If you *can* make the effort, you know, I believe you'd feel better." Her eyes glanced over the soup bowl, which Julia, in spite of mental distress, had cleaned up with a piece of bread. "You get so much more air in a car."

"It's closed," said Julia, rashly entering into argument.

"But you can have all the windows open, and the roof. You can sit in the back by yourself and be perfectly quiet." Susan smiled again; her bedside manner was so perfect that Julia could almost smell the ether. She changed her line of defence.

"If you want to know, Sue, I don't like to give Sir William the trouble —"

"Then *that's* all right," said Susan triumphantly, "because he's getting the car out now."

Five minutes later Julia found herself being tenderly delivered to her abductor at the foot of the porch steps. The car was as open as its Daimler nature permitted, there were rugs in case the night turned chilly, and a paper fan (supplied by Anthelmine) in case it perversely turned hot.

"Back or front?" asked Susan, as Bryan leapt gallantly forward to open the door.

Sir William looked round, full into Julia's face.

"Back," said Julia.

With languid dignity she took her seat. As Bryan folded the rug over her knees, as the others stood watching from the steps, she began to feel as though she were really leaving a nursing-home for her first outing. It was a good moment in its way — and it was just like Bryan to go and spoil it.

"Bet you don't come home like that!" said Bryan cheerfully.

III

For perhaps three minutes the car and its two occupants slid silently through the dark. There was a breeze, as Susan had promised; but even physically Julia could not relax. She sat rigid in every limb, one hand clutching the rug, the other pressed hard against the seat. Totally incapable of speech herself, she equally feared and longed for Sir William's first words. When at last, from a slight movement of his head, she knew that they were coming, she could hardly draw breath.

"You must be damned hungry," said Sir William over his shoulder.

"I'm not!" gasped Julia.

"If you'd only told me," continued Sir William, unheeding, "I could have had a headache myself."

"I did have a headache!" cried Julia indignantly.

"Whether you had or you hadn't, I can quite believe you've got one now. The first thing we must do is to get you some food. Why are you sitting there in the back?"

"So that I don't have to talk," explained Julia, with as much sarcasm as she could muster. For some minutes she flattered herself that it had taken effect; but Sir William's next question was not reassuring.

"What was that young Relton said to you?"

"Nothing," snapped Julia. "At least — he said he was sorry for me being dragged out, just to please Susan, when I'd got such a headache."

223

"You'll be better when you've had some food," said Sir William.

Julia was now too exasperated to speak; but she was no longer tense. She threw herself back against the cushions with an audible thump; her brain worked naturally and furiously as she thought of more things to say to Sir William. Their skirmish had at least broken the ice, and as this thought crossed her mind Julia suddenly began to laugh.

"William!"

"My dear?"

"Did you do it on purpose?"

"Do what?"

"Make me lose my temper."

"Of course," said Sir William. "Now are you coming in front?"

He stopped the car; Julia bundled out and got in beside him. His object having been achieved, however. Sir William relapsed into silence; and indeed it was only a few minutes before the outskirts of Belley began to loom before them. They drew up not at the Pernollet, but, by Julia's choice, at a small café near the promenade. She selected it because there were plenty of people there, and because for once in her life she wanted chaperoning; she had not allowed for Sir William's English habit of lumping all foreigners with their natural and inanimate surroundings.

"Now then!" he said, as soon as Julia was supplied with an omelette and red wine. "It's customary, when refusing an offer of marriage, to give some reason. Even if you simply dislike the man, you're supposed to trump up some polite excuse as a salve to masculine pride."

"Dislike!" cried Julia, at once falling into the trap. "If you think that, you — you can't have any sense at all. I like you better than any man I've ever met."

"Thank you," said Sir William. "That's very handsome. Then why won't you marry me?"

Julia decided to tell a certain amount of the truth.

"Because it wouldn't be suitable. Because I wouldn't be the kind of wife people expect for you."

"Damn what people expect," said Sir William vigorously. "I've been doing what people expect all my life, and now I'm old enough to please myself."

Julia took a deep breath.

"You don't know anything about me —"

"I know quite enough. I know you make me enjoy things as I never thought I would again. I know that I have a most ridiculous desire, Julia — since you're so obviously capable of looking after yourself — to take care of you. You'll probably find me a thorough nuisance."

"Oh no, I shouldn't," said Julia earnestly. "I should simply love it. I've often looked at women with husbands — the nice sort, you know, who buy railway tickets for them — and thought how lovely it must be." She paused, aware that this was not the line she had intended to take, and began again. "There are things I ought to tell you —"

"Don't," said Sir William. "I haven't been a hermit myself, but I'm not going to bore you with the details."

"I shouldn't be bored a bit," said Julia, who had no tact.

"In any case I shan't tell you. We start clear from now."

"But I *must* tell," said Julia desperately. "You see, if, when we both left here, you'd asked me to go to Aix with you — or anywhere else, for that matter — I'd have come like a shot. Just for a week, or as long as you wanted me. I — I'd come now."

"I know you would, my dear."

"Well?" said Julia, staring straight in front of her.

"I don't want you just for a week," explained Sir William. "I want you for always. And I'm too old, my dear, to go about staying in hotels under assumed names. I should find it a great nuisance."

"We could take a villa somewhere," suggested Julia seriously.

"That would be even more conspicuous," said Sir William.

Involuntarily Julia sighed. She was loving him more and more all the time, and it didn't make things easier. But she thought of Susan and hardened her heart.

"There's something else, William — no, not about me; about Sue and Bryan. I've told him again and again that people as different as they are haven't a hope. But we're just as different ourselves: you're good, like Susan, and I'm the same sort as he is — and what's more, he knows it. If I go and marry you, he'll just think it's all rot."

"So it is," said Sir William.

"About us, perhaps," admitted Julia. "But then you're different again. You're not *pure* good, like Sue. You're older, and you've knocked about a bit, and you wouldn't expect so much. But Bryan won't see all that; he'll just see that I've practised one thing and preached another, and he'll never believe a word I say again. You know what the young are."

"I know one thing," said Sir William, "and that is that I strongly object to being made the sacrifice."

"He'd want a double wedding," prophesied Julia, still following her own train of thought; "it's just what he'd enjoy. He'd go and marry Susan just to see my face. I'm sorry, William dear."

Sir William was apparently following his own train of thought too.

"I can understand that you're afraid of getting tired of me —"

"No!" cried Julia, stung. "Never! You mustn't think that of me, William! I know — I could swear — that if I married you I'd never look at another man so long as I lived. I wouldn't want to. I've got an awful lot of — of faithfulness in me, if you can only believe it . . ."

"If I didn't believe it," said Sir William gently, "I shouldn't have asked you to marry me. But I think it's only for the one right man, my dear, and if I'm not he —"

"But you are!" wailed Julia, almost in tears. "I've known it all along, and that's what's so awful. You can't think how I want to — to show you. I've sometimes wished — no, not wished, just imagined — that you were a hopeless invalid, or paralysed, or something, so

227

that I could just be there looking after you for years and years. I'd love it!"

For a moment Sir William did not speak; and indeed so forcible an expression of devotion was enough to silence any man. Then he reached out and put Julia's coat round her shoulders.

"Come back to the car," he said.

"No," said Julia wretchedly. "Once you start kissing me, I'll be done."

"We've got to get back some time," pointed out Sir William.

"Not till I've made you understand." Julia sat up, and as a sign that she had fully recovered herself even managed to smile. "You've made me prouder than I've ever been in my life, William, only it's no use. There's too much against it. I can't say all I feel, I never could; but you'll always be a beautiful memory."

"Julia!" said Sir William sharply.

"What, darling?"

"You're enjoying yourself."

Julia flushed. It was only too true that in spite of her real misery, she had been conscious of speaking that last line well.

"And what's more," continued Sir William, "you're enjoying yourself at my expense. I should simply loathe to be a beautiful memory. As you can't talk sense, you'd better come home."

This time Julia rose. There was no doubt about it, Sir William possessed an extraordinary knack of tipping up the highest moral plane. Slightly ruffled by her sudden descent, Julia powdered her nose with vigour and in silence, and accompanied him back to the car.

But at least she was right about one thing. As soon as he began kissing her, she was done.

IV

"Shall I have to open bazaars?" asked Julia about an hour later.

They were driving slowly up from the Lac du Bar. Their homeward route had been by no means direct.

"Good heavens, no!" said Sir William.

Julia was reassured, but also a little disappointed. She could just fancy herself on a platform, in very good black, with a spray of orchids at the left shoulder . . .

"You won't have any of that," continued Sir William, "and we can live wherever you like. At the moment I've a flat in Town —"

"Where?" asked Julia.

"Mount Street. You may like it. And of course if we keep that on, instead of taking a house, we can go abroad whenever we want to. I'd like to take you abroad, Julia. You enjoy things so."

Julia rubbed her cheek against his coat. She couldn't kiss him, because he was driving.

"I'd like to go to Venice. Louise — a girl I used to know once — went there, and she said it was heavenly . . . William!"

"Well?"

"When I talk about people like that — people who may be a bit rum — does it worry you?"

Sir William put down his left hand and felt for hers. "Not in the least, my dear. You have the most entertaining friends of any one I've met."

"That's lucky," sighed Julia; "because I expect I shall a good bit. And Louise was an awfully good sort . . . If you're going to stop the car, darling, do it before the village."

Ten minutes later, at the villa gates, she asked him to stop it again — this time merely to let her get into the back.

"Thank you," said Sir William. "I must admit I've been curious."

"Curious?" repeated Julia in surprise. "Why, what have I told you?"

"What young Relton said as we started," replied Sir William. "And he ought to be kicked for it."

CHAPTER
TWENTY-ONE

The last action of Julia's free will, before she finally and joyfully submerged it in Sir William's, was to persuade him not to announce their engagement. Sir William wanted to do things at once, thoroughly, and get them over; he wanted to send a notice to *The Times*, tell the Packetts, and marry Julia as soon as possible. Flattering as this programme was, and much as Julia longed for its completion, she nevertheless held him back. She feared the consequences — and not only upon Bryan: she had an uneasy conviction that the Packetts wouldn't believe it. They would just think that Sir William had gone mad, and that she was abetting him. Rather to her surprise, Sir William, when she laid this view before him, was very much annoyed.

"My dear Julia," he said firmly, "if that's your only objection I shall go straight into the billiard-room and tell them now. There's no other way of showing you how foolish you are."

Julia jumped up — they were sitting in their usual place among the vines — and seized his arm.

"Don't, William! Not just yet! I'm a fool all right — I'm anything you say — but it isn't *that* only. I've got to think of Susan and Bryan. I've got to get that business settled first."

"It's settling itself," retorted Sir William. "It's settling itself perfectly. Young Relton is at last finding out what Susan's really like, and Susan — who must have found him out long ago — is beginning to realize that she'll never change him. In a couple of weeks, and especially if Susan goes to London, the whole thing will have blown over."

Julia tightened her grip.

"Then don't you see how important it is that they shouldn't be — be disturbed? It's not only that club business, William — and that was my idea too — it's partly what I've been saying to Bryan. I *have* influenced him, though he wouldn't admit it. And now if we go and get married he'll forget everything else and send their engagement to *The Times* as well, and quite likely go back to London himself and start working like hell and all" — Julia gasped for breath — "out of cussedness. We must leave things alone, William. You say yourself it's only a matter of weeks."

"And if it's longer?" inquired Sir William. "If it's two months, or two years? Are we to spend the rest of our lives waiting for two young idiots to come to their senses?"

"Now you're just being silly," said Julia comfortably. "And they're not idiots at all. They're just very young. I expect when *you* were young —"

"Thanks," said Sir William. "One of the things I like about you, my dear, is that you don't flatter me."

232

Julia slipped down on to the grass beside his chair and gave him one of her long, candid looks.

"I don't want you young, darling. I want you just as you are, experienced, and understanding, and — and able to deal with me. And besides —"

She broke off, still gazing, on a sigh of pure happiness. Sir William reached down and touched her cheek.

"Besides what, my dear?"

"You *do* look so distinguished!" said Julia simply.

An absurd glow of happiness took Sir William by surprise. There were many good reasons, he could not help knowing, why a woman in Julia's position should be glad to marry him, and in his more sober moments — when the fact that she had simply fallen in love with him seemed to pass belief — he had often enumerated them. But he had never yet included his personal appearance . . .

"I see I was wrong," he said lightly. "You're a flatterer after all."

"I'm not flattering you a bit," said Julia earnestly. "I don't say you're the handsomest — I wouldn't say you were like poor Valentino — but you're the most distinguished looking man, William, I've ever seen. It's your side-face, and your height, and the way you hold yourself. I thought it the moment I saw you."

"Then you must be in love with me," said Sir William.

As they went down to the house — the question of announcing their engagement tacitly shelved — he suddenly began to laugh. Julia asked why, but he would not tell her. She had explained so firmly that he was no longer young: and he had just caught himself wishing that instead of putting on a dinner-jacket he could appear before her in his tail-coat.

II

There was no end, Julia felt, to the good things which were now being showered upon her. As though Sir William, and all he implied, were not enough, she received that evening the first real mark of Susan's affectionate confidence. Susan came in while Julia was changing for dinner and sat down — just like a daughter — on the edge of the bed.

"Uncle William's just told me," said Susan, "that it was your idea about letting me in on this new club. What made you think of it?"

Julia smiled complacently.

"I knew it would be just the thing for you, Sue. I mean — I knew *you'd* be just the thing for them. You're so efficient, and clear-headed."

This answer, besides being for the most part true, was evidently the one Susan wanted. She looked at her mother with genuine warmth.

"You can't think how I like you to say that. The others — Bryan, and even Uncle William — seem to look on it simply as a nice hobby for *me*; they don't see the other point of view at all — that I'm possibly being of real use. You've got the right attitude."

"This is my lucky day," thought Julia; and determined to venture further.

"This Mr. Bellamy, Sue — when I'm back in Town, I think I'd like to meet him. Will it be all right if I just go down to the club?"

"Oh!" cried Susan, quite radiant at the prospect of at last making a convert. "Of course it will! I'll write and say you're coming. Only — are you quite sure it would interest you?"

Julia was certain. She had never met a man yet in whom she could not become interested at a moment's notice. It was Susan's interest she felt needed arousing — Susan's interest in Mr. Bellamy, not merely as a good worker, but as an individual young man.

"I hope he won't knock himself up," said Julia thoughtfully.

"Who? Mr. Bellamy?"

"Sir William says he isn't strong," explained Julia. "He says he's terribly thin. I expect he doesn't feed himself properly."

Susan looked serious.

"I hope he doesn't go sick, because he's really running the whole thing. He's really important. Listen, Mother —"

Julia's heart leapt. It was all she could do not to kiss Susan then and there, out of sheer gratitude. But she restrained herself. She knew that if Susan were once made self-conscious, that beautiful word would never be heard again.

"What is it, Sue?"

"I've been thinking — if I meet him in London, he'll probably want to stand me a meal, and I know he's awfully hard up. But if *you* asked us both to your flat — or I could ask him there myself, quite easily —"

"Of course!" cried Julia. "Of course you'll come! I'll give him roast beef and a suety pudding!"

At that Susan laughed, and Julia laughed too. She hadn't got a flat — she hadn't even a dining-table — and when she reacquired these things, by marriage with Sir William, Susan would quite likely disapprove and refuse to make use of them; but in spite of these obstacles Julia already saw, in her mind's eye, Susan and Mr. Bellamy sitting one on each side of her, exchanging looks of love above a well-spread board. The picture was so clear, and filled her with such confidence, that she ventured on a leading question.

"What about Bryan, Sue? Would he like to come as well?"

"Oh!" said Susan. For a moment it seemed as though she were really going to open her heart, and Julia, at the dressing-table, held her comb suspended. Then through the mirror she saw Susan slowly get up, smooth the counterpane where she had been sitting, and walk towards the door.

"No," said Susan casually, "I don't think Bryan would be interested. By the way, dinner's going to be a little early, because Anthelmine has the evening off."

Julia finished her dressing in great satisfaction. For the first time she felt herself to be completely accepted, by Susan, as Susan's ally. It was fortunate, since she enjoyed the sensation so much, that she could not see twenty-four hours ahead.

III

Twenty-four hours later an event took place in the village which had the extraordinary effect, at the villa, of ranging Julia on Bryan's side against her daughter. Jeanne-Marie, the niece of Claudia, the distributor of sugared almonds, got married; and at the ensuing celebrations Bryan got tight.

He went to the party alone, and, as afterwards transpired, was the life and soul of it. There was dancing, and he danced. There was singing, and he sang. (For several days afterwards Sir William, whenever he walked through the village, was constantly being surprised by the strains of "Forty Years On.") To support his energies he naturally needed a good deal to drink, and by the time the party broke up, shortly after midnight, it was obvious that he had had it. Even then all might have been well, for there were plenty of volunteers to escort him back to the lodge; but with the perversity of his condition he insisted on going up to the villa to bid his friends there good-night.

By chance, and because of the heat, they were still in the billiard-room. Bryan flung open the door, skidded a little over the parquet, and came to rest on the chair next to Susan's. There he began to sing.

He was not drunk, but he was undeniably intoxicated.

At once Susan, Julia, and Sir William all rose from their seats; but whereas Susan instinctively backed away, her face white with anger, Julia and Sir William as instinctively approached.

"Stop it!" said Julia severely.

Bryan looked at her, his mouth still open on a high note, with natural surprise. People had applauded his singing all evening, why should they suddenly stop now?

"Why, darling?" he asked. "Tell me why?"

"Because you're disturbing Mrs. Packett," said Julia. She glanced over her shoulder, and was briefly struck by the calmness of that lady's demeanour. Mrs. Packett didn't look disturbed at all. Bryan meanwhile had risen to his feet, not from any personal volition, but because of Sir William's firm hand under his arm.

"I wouldn't like to do *that*," he said. "Wouldn't like to 'sturb any one. Sue, darling —"

Susan walked straight past him and out of the room. He made a spasmodic effort to follow, and felt the restraining weight of Sir William.

"No, you don't," said Sir William. "Sue doesn't want disturbing either. You'd better come to bed."

"All right," agreed Bryan. "I — I'll jus' say good-night. Good-night, all!"

His innocuousness, in the face of Susan's demonstration, was almost pathetic. Sir William led him away, and all was still.

"Aspirin, I *think*," said Mrs. Packett. "There's some in my room."

"I've got some too," said Julia; and for once kissed her mother-in-law good-night.

238

IV

The following morning was an uneasy one. Bryan appeared about twelve o'clock, looking slightly pale, and apologized all round. By Mrs. Packett, Julia, and Sir William his expressions of regret were at once accepted; and they might all have been comfortable again but for the attitude of Susan. She too accepted his apology; but she could not forgive him. She did not — felt Julia — *want* to forgive; what he had done was in her eyes unpardonable, and the fact that her elders actually had pardoned it simply lowered her opinion of them as well. Julia saw this, and on Sir William's behalf was extremely annoyed; her heart was also touched by Bryan's mournful looks. Logically she should have rejoiced, but then logic was never Julia's strong point. She had made up her mind, however, not to interfere, and would probably have managed to hold aloof had not Susan deliberately brought up the subject in the garden after lunch.

"Grandmother has just been telling me," she said, with a lift of the eyebrows, "that *her* father was a three-bottle man. I suppose I'm to make a comparison."

"Your grandmother," said Julia sharply, "has more sense than any one I know."

"Then you probably agree with her," said Susan, "that last night doesn't matter in the least?"

"Of course it doesn't!" cried Julia, roused from her neutrality. "Every young man gets a bit squiffy now and again — and that's when you see what they're like. Bryan —"

"Well?"

"He was sweet," said Julia firmly. "He didn't give a bit of trouble, and he isn't being proud of himself afterwards. You're behaving as though he got rolling drunk and chased the cook."

She broke off — a little alarmed, for her own sake, by the vigour of her language. It wasn't the sort of thing she ought to have said: it implied too much experience. But Susan did not appear to notice. She was withdrawn into her cloud.

"You think, then, that I'm uncharitable?" she said at last.

"No," said Julia slowly. She also had had time to reflect. "Only . . . you don't *like* people." She thought again, and changed the intonation. "You don't like *people*. You only like — it's so hard to explain — their good qualities."

"You don't expect me to like their bad?" asked Susan grimly.

"No," repeated Julia; "but if you liked *people*, their bad qualities wouldn't worry you so much."

Susan locked her hands in her lap and stared at the tree-tops. Her young figure was stiff with pride.

"I think you're wrong," she said. "I'm sorry. But then I don't think I need people so much as you do."

Julia could only hope that she was right; but an instinctive fear as to the results of such an outlook drove her on.

"At any rate, I think you ought to make it up with Bryan. If you must quarrel with him —"

240

"I've no intention of quarrelling with him," said Susan quickly. "I can't tell him it doesn't matter, but — but I'll be nice."

And that afternoon she was nice — so charming, so lighthearted, that Bryan was quite taken by surprise when she suddenly asked for his promise not to drink wine again so long as they were in France.

"But I'll look such a fool!" he said. "It's always on the table!"

"I'll drink barley-water too," promised Susan.

"No," said Bryan firmly. Susan's niceness had rather gone to his head: he felt that for the first time her rigid will showed signs of becoming more pliant. "No, darling; it's absurd . . ."

Even then Susan only smiled. She remained charming to him all day. But on the dining-table that night he noticed, and every one else noticed, that the carafe of *vin ordinaire* was only half-full.

CHAPTER
TWENTY-TWO

In Julia's opinion it was that half-full carafe which led Bryan to view more seriously Susan philanthropic activities. His subconscious was thoroughly alarmed, but at the same time refused to admit what had really frightened it. Julia knew a lot about the subconscious from Louise, who had once been psychoanalysed with very exhilarating results. It therefore came as no surprise to her when Bryan cornered her alone in the billiard-room and observed that he was getting very tired of all this rot about clubs.

"It isn't rot," said Julia tartly. "It's a very good work."

"All right, darling. But I know Sir William ducked out of it."

"He needs a rest. He's on holiday."

"So is Susan. So — more to the point — am I. It was bad enough when she was always dashing off to read French, but this thing's the limit. She can't talk about anything else."

"Well, you'd better get used to it," said Julia calmly, "because it's the sort of thing she'll be doing all her life. I expect you will too."

"Not me," said Bryan, in genuine alarm. "I've got too much sense. I know my own limitations. All I want is a quiet life. When you open your cake-shop, darling, I shall apply for a job as errand-boy."

"I'm not going to open a cake-shop," snapped Julia, whom this subject was beginning to infuriate.

"Not even for the sake of giving me employ? What do you expect to become of me?"

Julia considered.

"I shouldn't be surprised," she said thoughtfully, "if you were to turn out a journalist."

"That's clever of you, darling, because I've had the same notion myself. I'd make a damn' good special correspondent. How did you tumble to it?"

"I used to know a lot," said Julia vaguely. "They never seemed to settle down. But what are you talking like this for? You're going to be a barrister!"

"Weather permitting, my dear. I'm not sure I should ever stick it. Besides, most barristers *are* journalists. That's how they earn the odd guineas to buy their beer."

Julia sat up in exasperation. "Can't you see," she wanted to say, "can't you *see* how hopeless it is?" But instead — for she was at last learning wisdom — she merely remarked that even if his own income proved insufficient, Susan's should at any rate be able to supply him with drinks.

"If you think I'm going to sponge on Susan —" began Bryan hotly.

"She'll have much more money than you will," Julia pointed out; "especially if you're going to be an errand-boy. I don't know exactly, but she'll have all the Packetts'."

Bryan stood up and walked quickly to the window.

"She'll probably give it all away," he said over his shoulder. "To these good works you're so keen on."

Julia nodded.

"Very likely. I expect she'll go in for them really seriously."

His fingers began to drum an impatient and angry tattoo.

"If you ask me," he said at last, "if you ask me —"

"I'm not asking, I'm telling you," said Julia. "It's what I've been telling you all along."

The next moment the door slammed behind him.

II

The party at luncheon was reduced by one: Mr. Relton had gone off on a long walk — so ran the message left with Claudia — and would not be back to tea. Julia looked quickly at her daughter, to see whether the interview which she so confidently anticipated had already taken place; judging by Susan's countenance, it had not. Susan was openly annoyed, because she had desired Bryan's company for a trip to Belley, and her afternoon's plans were thus disarranged; but she showed no sign of having been faced with the disarrangement of her whole future. Her future, as it happened, was what she chiefly talked about, and it was concerned so largely with the problems of club management that Julia could not help wondering whether the absence of Bryan would really disarrange it all. "She'll get over it sooner than I thought!" Julia told

244

herself happily. "If only she can keep her opinion of herself, she'll be right as rain!" A wound to Susan's self-esteem was the only one Julia really feared, and if the break came from Bryan — as it would — even that might be avoided: Susan wouldn't have let him down; she would have kept, scrupulously, her side of their mutual promise. For Bryan's self-esteem Julia didn't care a rap, and so she told Sir William when she met him, at three o'clock in the ruined pavilion.

They met there every afternoon, stealing up — at least Sir William walked, but Julia definitely stole — from the quiet house while its other inhabitants took their siestas. There was no actual reason, of course, why they should not have ascended boldly side by side, but Julia's romantic and sentimental heart — had she not drawn it, in lipstick, on the pavilion wall? — always missed a beat as she pushed through the nut trees and found Sir William waiting for her. She enjoyed that moment too much to forgo it, even though they never stayed longer than five minutes, because there was nowhere to sit . . .

"As for Bryan, I don't care a rap," said Julia. "He ought to be just plain grateful to me." As always on leaving the pavilion, she put out her hand and with a light caressing gesture touched the lipstick heart. Sir William turned back from the steps to watch her. "And if he isn't now," continued Julia, her rite performed, "he will be in a week or two. I've been an absolute providence to him."

"If not a mother," agreed Sir William. "Would you like to go over and dine at Aix?"

"In evening dress?" asked Julia at once.

"Certainly," said Sir William. "That's mainly why we're going. I have a craving to put on tails."

"I bet you look a dream in them," said Julia sincerely. She let him help her down to the path, and there stood a moment in thought. But she was no longer thinking about Bryan. "I can't do much myself," she said regretfully, "because my wardrobe's a bit low. I've got a lovely dark-blue taffeta, only I don't know if you'll like the top. I mean, there practically isn't any — not even shoulder straps. I don't mean it isn't *decent*, because it is; but it's a bit — well, dashing. I've got a nice lace scarf, though; it used to be white."

"And what colour is it now?" asked Sir William with interest.

"Ecru. I lent it to Louise once, and she got into a rough-house somewhere — just like she always did — and upset coffee right across the middle. So we made a lot more, in a hand-basin, and dipped the whole thing, and it came up beautifully. And then Louise went and spilt the whole basinful, right down her frock!"

"It's like the House that Jack built," observed Sir William, fascinated. "So then you made a bathful —"

"No, we didn't. Louise just smashed the basin to smithereens. It was just after she'd been psycho-analysed, and she was scared stiff of repressing herself. Not that she ever *had*, so far as I could see; but she said yes, and if she'd only known sooner there wouldn't be a whole plate left in the Café Royal." Julia paused and looked at Sir William anxiously. "She isn't *rough*, you know; it's just that she's got a rather quick temper."

246

"She sounds a most delightful and entertaining companion," said Sir William. "I won't say I'm sorry she can't come with us to-night, because I want you to myself; but when we're in London I shall have great pleasure in meeting her."

Julia looked at him adoringly.

"You don't know how lovely that is, William. I'd hate to drop her, and I'd hate to have to see her behind your back — in fact I wouldn't, because I've promised myself I'll never know any one you don't like. You'll never have to be ashamed of my friends, William — truly you won't!"

"I'm sure I shan't," said Sir William.

He spoke sincerely; he had long made up his mind to the fact that marriage with Julia would undoubtedly bring him some very queer acquaintances; but he was also convinced that her instinct for people could be perfectly trusted. Her friends might be what she called "rum"; they would also be what she called "good sorts." Their company would probably be extremely entertaining, and he had no fear of their influence, for Julia was too clever to let him be either bored or swindled. His only apprehension was that she might plunge to the other extreme and demand to open bazaars. Well, if she wanted to, she could. Sir William felt that even Julia's respectability would have something lavish and cheerful about it — like a Costers' open-air service . . .

"You'd make a first-rate Pearlie Queen," he told her; and suddenly wondered how many of his own acquaintances, given that remark, would be able to guess the context — *Sir William to the future Lady Waring*.

"Not a single one of them!" cried Julia, when he had explained why he was laughing. She thought the matter over and became slightly indignant. "And they won't even when they've seen me, either. I'm going to be the perfect lady."

Sir William bent and kissed her.

"Whether I like it or not?"

"Whether you like it or not," said Julia firmly.

Five minutes later she was being kissed again, this time by Fred Genocchio.

III

It happened in this way: Julia, anxious to see whether her taffeta needed ironing, went down to the house alone and was met on the upper terrace by Anthelmine and the woman from the lodge. They were evidently looking for her; they had a visiting-card, which Anthelmine seized out of her companion's hand and thrust with a flourish under Julia's eye.

It was Fred Genocchio's.

For a moment Julia stood still, a prey to the most violent and conflicting emotions. Astonishment came first, then dismay, then a wave of flattered excitement. She didn't want Fred any more, especially she didn't want him there and then; but how touching of him to have come! Poor old Fred!

"Where is he?" she asked. "*Où est-il?*"

"*La-bàs*," replied Anthelmine, jerking her shoulder towards the gates. She looked at Julia with a friendly, conspiratorial smile; she was evidently aware that the visitor had nothing to do with Sir William.

"*Je vais*," said Julia haughtily. "*Merci beaucoup*."

Anthelmine smiled again, and with a lavish display of tact hustled her companion in the direction of the kitchen door. Julia waited till they were gone, then hurried down the drive. *Dear* old Fred! she thought, as she rounded the bend; she would speak to him for just five minutes, very kindly and superiorly, before sending him away. She could do no less. Not to do as much would be rude, unladylike. In her anxiety to get it over Julia almost ran, so that Mr. Genocchio, watching from below, and with no clue to her real motive, may be excused for misinterpreting the situation. He saw Julia hastening towards him, catching her skirt on a rose trail, jerking it free and hastening on; and with happy (though unjustified) confidence stepped forward and caught her in his arms and kissed her soundly.

"Fred!" cried Julia.

He at once released her. There was no mistaking that repulsive note. Julia backed a little away and held out her hand.

"Why, Fred!" she said graciously. "This *is* a surprise!"

But his mental agility was not equal to hers. Instead of shaking hands like a gentleman, Mr. Genocchio merely gaped.

"What's up?" he asked bluntly. "Aren't you pleased to see me?"

249

"Of course I'm pleased to see you."

"Well, you don't seem like it."

"I'm surprised," explained Julia. "I thought you were in Paris. Is the trip over?"

"Yes, it's over," said Mr. Genocchio glumly. "Ma and the others went back yesterday."

"Is Ma all right now?"

"Yes, she's all right."

"And the others?"

"They're all right too. What about yourself?"

"Oh, I'm all right," said Julia.

"You look it," said Mr. Genocchio. "You look grand."

The old admiration was warm in his voice, bright in his eyes, and in spite of herself Julia could not repress a slight responsive glow. He *was* beautifully built, even in an ordinary suit. If he had turned up in tights she could hardly have answered for herself . . .

"Having a good time here?"

"Lovely," said Julia.

"You don't want a change? I mean, you wouldn't like to run over to Aix or somewhere — or even back to Paris — for a day or two?"

Julia took a long breath.

"I ought to tell you, Fred — I ought to have told you at once — I'm going to be married."

Mr. Genocchio stared at her a moment in silence, then turned on his heel and stared at a rose-bush instead.

"Congratulations," he said over his shoulder. "Chap staying here, I suppose?"

"Yes. Don't look like that, Fred!"

"Why not?"

"It — it upsets me."

"I'm upset myself," said Mr. Genocchio. "I know I've no right to be, but there it is." He broke off a rose switch and stood turning it in his hands. "I'd hired a car," he said.

Julia sniffed. She had so indefensibly sympathetic a nature that in another moment she would have wept.

"I'm ever so sorry, Fred. I am truly."

"Nothing to be sorry about," said Mr. Genocchio, recovering himself. "At least, I don't suppose there is. Is he a good sort?"

The phrase, so totally inadequate to Sir William, jarred on Julia's ear. But an odd shyness, a sort of modesty, prevented her from explaining the true magnificence of her prospects. As she would have put it herself, she didn't want to rub it in . . .

"One of the best, Fred. I've been damned lucky."

"I know who's got the luck all right," muttered Mr. Genocchio. "Well, it's all in the game. I suppose I'd better be going."

Julia hesitated. It seemed awful to let him come all that way and not offer him so much as a drink; but what was the good? He wouldn't be comfortable, nor would she. Indeed, when she thought of introducing him to the Packetts, and particularly to Susan, discomfort was altogether too mild a word. It would be plain bloody awful, and no offence to any one . . .

"I see I had," said Mr. Genocchio slowly. "I've put you out by coming. I'm sorry."

If only he could have swung off, glorious on his trapeze, and disappeared to the ruffle of drums! If only he could have leapt into his car and rushed away at sixty miles an hour! But twenty feet of gravel path separated him even from the gate, and that was too high to be vaulted. It was the worst exit he had ever been faced with: all he could do was to get himself off . . .

In Julia too the sense of anti-climax was strong. It was so strong as to be unbearable. All her theatrical instincts, as well as her genuine fondness for the man, rose in revolt. She caught him by the shoulder, turned him round, and held up her face to be kissed.

"Julia!"

"Fred, darling!"

He held her tight ("I hope that's not another bruise," thought Julia, already assuaged), then almost pushed her from him and hurried off. Julia too turned away, and without looking back again to reascend the drive. As far as the first landing complacency accompanied her: she felt she had handled the situation well, artistically — which meant that she had got the last ounce out of it — and, above all, in a ladylike manner. She was very much pleased with herself. But as she arrived in sight of the house, this agreeable mood changed. She felt a curious sensation of having burned her boats. That was odd and unpleasant enough, but the feeling that succeeded it was worse still. An awful doubt invaded Julia's mind. Would a lady — a real lady — have offered that last kiss without being asked? Above all, would she have *enjoyed* it? Considering these two question carefully, Julia was forced to answer yes to the first (because Fred wanted it so badly, and it would have been a shame to refuse) and no to the second. This was very bad, since she herself had enjoyed it thoroughly. She had enjoyed it just as much as if she hadn't been engaged to Sir William at all.

"I'm awful," thought Julia, with sincere melancholy.

But she repented. She repented hard, all evening, until it was time to start for Aix; and then the sight of Sir William in tails drove everything else from her head.

CHAPTER
TWENTY-THREE

After an evening of unalloyed pleasure Julia and Sir William returned to the villa at one in the morning. They had dined, they had danced a little, but chiefly they had watched the people — Julia as usual keeping up a running commentary on every one and everything she saw, Sir William as usual listening and laughing at her flights. To Julia's delight, they saw the Disgusted Lady, who, marvellous in ice-blue slipper-satin, engrossed and despised the services of the best professional partner while her companion of the Pernollet admired from the edge of the floor. "Isn't she grand?" demanded Julia. "Astounding," agreed Sir William; "a collector's piece." And Julia beamed at him, because that was just what she had tried to convey to Susan, and he understood so exactly. She was looking well herself, too; she drew many admiring glances; while as for Sir William — "You're the most distinguished man here!" declared Julia. "Look as fond of me as you can, William!" And Sir William did look fond of her, just as though he were a Frenchman — except that every one was taking him (Julia knew it) for an English lord . . .

At Muzin Sir William put the car away in its barn, so as not to wake the house, and they walked up together through the still garden. A full moon dropped silver between the trees, robbing with its brightness all brightness of colour, paling the red roses, darkening the white, but exquisitely defining, by a stroke of silverpoint and a line of charcoal, every bough and twig that daylight merged in green. Julia stood still and let the scarf slip from her shoulders. At once the moonlight flowed over them, making them whiter than milk.

"What a wonderful night!"

"Wonderful," echoed Sir William. "Whenever there's a full moon, my dear, you must wear that frock."

Julia spread out her wide skirt and let the light play over it. It was no longer blue, but black and silver.

"I'll always have one like it," she promised. "I — I'll be buried in it, William." Suddenly her voice and her hands trembled, the stiff folds dropped together with a long rustling sigh. "William!" she said. "William — I'm frightened!"

At once, as when she came running panic-stricken from the woods, the barrier of his arm held her safe.

"Frightened? Why frightened now, my darling?"

"Because it's too good. It can't last."

"Nonsense," said Sir William gently. "It's going to last all our lives."

"Then you'll die first, and I shan't be able to bear it. Or something will happen to stop us."

"Nonsense," said Sir William again. "You're tired, my dear, and excited. All this business has been a strain on you, and to-morrow I'm going to put an end to it. We'll be married straight away."

But Julia did not hear. She had started, turned away from him, and was staring into the shadows by the house.

"Something moved!" she whispered. "There's someone there!"

Sir William took three long steps from her side and laid his hand against the dark wall.

"No one," he said. "Come in, my dear; you're imagining things."

He led her into the house and turned on the hall lights. Safe within four walls, Julia was able to look up at him and laugh while he chided her for her foolishness. Then she kissed him good-night and went into her room and sat down before the mirror. Her reflection glowed back at her, flushed of cheek and bright of eye: her shoulders —

Her shoulders!

"There!" said Julia aloud. "If I haven't left my scarf outside!"

II

It was a nice scarf — it had been really good — and the dew would ruin it. Julia jumped up and went to the door, meaning to ask Sir William to fetch it in for her; but once in the lobby she paused. She had a feeling that Sir William might not like to be caught in his pants; she fancied him rather particular about that sort of thing. In the end she went out herself, and indeed had not far to go, for the scarf lay just at the foot of the porch steps. Julia picked it up, turned to reascend, and all at once felt her heart stand still.

Something *had* moved. Something was moving then.

A shadow detached itself from the shadows, took on an outline, showed a face white in the moonlight. It found a bitter and sardonic voice.

"So I wish you joy?" said Bryan Relton.

Instinctively, as though warding off a blow, Julia put out her hand. "Wait!" the gesture said. "Don't hurt me just yet! Wait!"

But he would not wait. His voice went on, hard and mocking.

"So you're going to marry him, Julia? You're going to purge and live cleanly and be Lady Waring? Do you remember what you said yesterday, Julia? Do you remember what you said to me in the vine, and what you've been saying to me for weeks — Julia darling?"

His questions pelted her like stones. She retreated before them till she stood with her back to the wall.

"Stop!" she whispered harshly. "Be quiet! You don't understand —"

Bryan looked at her and laughed.

"I understand very well indeed: when it came to the point he was too big a fish to let go. But don't think I blame you, my dear, for aren't we the same sort? Don't we both take what we can get?"

Julia moistened her lips.

"Not Susan," she said. "Not Susan!"

"Not if I can get her, darling? Isn't she still engaged to me? She wouldn't have been to-morrow, of course —

I've been running wild all day — thinking how noble you were, Julia! — rehearsing my part for the renunciation scene. I've been running wild in the moonlight — and how fortunately it's turned out! You've opened my eyes, Julia; I can see now what a fool you nearly made of me. Why shouldn't I have Susan, if I can get her?"

"Because it won't last," said Julia more steadily. "It wouldn't last two years . . ."

"Then I shall have had them. As you say, my dear, two years will probably be enough for both of us. I believe you'll miss me more than any one, Julia; you'll never find a son-in-law so much your own sort again."

At last Julia moved. She dragged herself away from the wall and set her foot on the porch step. She had to pass close to Bryan to do so, but she did not look at him.

"You're not my sort at all," she said. "You're bad."

Then she fled into the house, into her own room, and sat down once more before the table with the mirror.

III

Her reflection looked quite different. In ten minutes it seemed to have grown old. But Julia did not study it long, for she had a great deal to do.

In the first place, she had to pack.

It was strange — this struck her afterwards, when she was back in London — how little difficulty she had in making up her mind. Or rather, she did not make it up at all: she simply saw before her a series of preordained actions, like a part in a play, which had inevitably to be performed. The reasons for them she left aside: even the thought of Susan was colourless and remote.

She had to pack, get out of the house unobserved, and pick up a lift on the Paris road. At that time of year there were always cars making an early start from Aix; one of them — preferably a fast tourer driven by a solitary man — would stop for her at the Muzin fork. It would be just another of her gay adventures . . .

"I ought to get some sleep," thought Julia.

But she could not. The short night passed without her closing her eyes. First, slowly and clumsily, she filled both her suitcases; then, realizing that they would be too heavy to carry, decided to take only one. That meant unpacking both and starting again. She was very slow about it; every now and then she found herself standing motionless, with a stocking in her hand, or a nightgown over her arm; and how long she had been thus transfixed, or why, she did not know. About four o'clock her knees gave under her; she lay down on the smooth bed and turned off the light. But the room was not dark, it was grey with the twilight of early morning, and in a panic lest day should surprise her Julia pulled herself once more to her feet. Fortunately there was something she could do. She was still wearing her taffeta dress; she had forgotten to pack it, and now left it just where it fell, a heap of blackness on the white floor. She bathed her face and arms in cold water, put on her linen suit, and sat half an hour trying to make rouge and lipstick look natural instead of ghastly. Then she was ready. She decided not to take her big coat, as it was rather shabby. She thought she would look gayer without it.

There remained one other thing to be done, and it was the hardest.

My dearest William (wrote Julia), I am very sorry, but I'm not going to marry you, so this is to say good-bye.

The words looked silly to her, but she could think of no others. She stared at them till they had lost all meaning, then folded the paper in two and went out to slip it under Sir William's door.

The lobby, because of its shuttered window, was still dark; Julia suddenly remembered the night of the thunderstorm. She had stood in just the same place, outside Sir William's room, trembling as she trembled now. "What was I so unhappy about?" Julia wondered. "I couldn't have known *then*?" She put the puzzle from her mind and performed the next in the series of necessary actions. She walked to the front door, slid back the bolt, and let herself out. The action after that was to take the lower path, beside the kitchen-garden, thus avoiding the village, and pass through its wicket. Mechanically Julia did so. There was no one stirring. She walked the quarter of a mile to where the road from Muzin forked into the highway. Aix lay to her left, Paris somewhere to her right. Julia dropped her suitcase in the dust, and sat down on it to wait.

CHAPTER
TWENTY-FOUR

The Misses Marlowe prided themselves on being expert travellers in general, and particularly, when motoring, on their habit of making early starts. "From six till nine," Miss Marlowe often explained to an interested circle at Wimbledon, "one gets *cool* air and a *clear* road" — in addition to which both she and her sister definitely enjoyed the sensation of leaving their hotel while every one else was asleep. They felt they had stolen a march on time, and expecially on their fellow guests. The French, indeed, often made early starts too; but the Misses Marlowe regularly led both English and Americans.

It thus happened that at ten minutes to seven Julia, still watching by the Muzin fork, had to change her position and get behind the hedge. The old Daimler was easily recognizable: she had no wish that its occupants should recognize her. They would certainly give her a lift, but they would also want to know too much about her three children. Nevertheless Julia looked after them longingly; her spirits were low, her body was stiff, and so far she had had no luck. Of the three cars that had passed already, one had contained a mutually absorbed couple, one a large family party (with perambulator strapped on top), and the third had been going so fast that it nearly ran over her.

"I ought to start and walk to Belley," thought Julia; and with the resolution of despair — like a shipwrecked mariner stepping off a raft and beginning to swim — took a few quick steps along the dusty road. But her knees felt curiously weak; she stopped, turned, and took a last look behind. Another car had just rounded the curve and was approaching at no great speed: a disreputable, two-seater Citroën, it was not at all the sort of vehicle she had hoped for; but at least it was driven by a single male. Julia stepped out into the middle of the road and waved an arm; as the car slowed down she saw that this driver was a very young man indeed — younger even than Bryan; his hair, his complexion, and his burberry proclaimed him an Anglo-Saxon. "That's something," Julia encouraged herself. "Anyway, he'll understand what I say. He'll love me. He'll think I'm an adventuress."

The Citroën came to a stop. She advanced towards it and put a foot on the running-board.

She said, "Can you give me a lift?"

The young man looked at her. It was a queer look — not fresh, more puzzled; and there was something in it which Julia could not recognize.

"Where do you want to go?" he asked.

"I don't care," said Julia baldly. That wasn't what she had meant to say. She had meant to say, "Follow the sun!" or "Your way is mine!" — something gay and adventurous like that; but the three miserable words slipped out before she knew. With a great effort she

262

gave him one of her good-old-Julia smiles, and asked where he was bound for.

"Well, Paris, eventually," said the young man; "but I don't quite know when I shall get there. This car isn't particularly reliable."

"It's reliable enough for me," said Julia, heaving her suitcase on to the edge of the dickey. The young man hesitated a moment, then with another odd glance climbed out, placed the suitcase more securely, and opened the car door. Remarking on the heat, he also took off his burberry; and this surprised Julia, who was shivering, until he clumsily wrapped it round her knees. With a sigh of relief she sank back against the cushions: she had pulled it off, she had done it again; and automatically she felt for her powder-box. But she made no use of it. There was a mirror in the lid, and the sight of her reflected face told her suddenly, brutally, the meaning of the young man's glance.

He was giving her a lift not because he thought she was an adventuress, but because she looked such a tired, tear-stained, unhappy old woman.

II

It was just after eight o'clock when Sir William in the Daimler turned down the fork from Muzin on to the main road. Julia had thus scarcely more than seventy minutes' start of him, and the difference in speed between the two cars was considerable. The Citroën averaged twenty-two miles an hour, the Daimler forty-three. Unluckily, from Sir William's point of view, they were travelling in opposite directions.

Sir William drove towards Aix. He was not at this time unduly anxious; Julia's note had upset him, because he knew how distressed she must have been when she wrote it; but it had by no means produced despair. He drove at moderate speed, half-expecting to overtake her, either afoot or in a car, on the actual road; knowing Julia to be penniless, and to a certain extent following her thoughts, he had never had a moment's doubt of her destination. She would try to get to Paris, and thence back to London: therefore she required either money for a railway ticket, or a lift in a car; and Aix (Sir William now knew all about Mr. Rickaby) was her obvious hunting-ground. His mistake, of course, lay in under-estimating the simplicity of Julia's plan: it had not occurred to him that she would merely stand by the roadside and try to get to Paris direct. Even with his knowledge of her, he believed she would need at least half a day to establish, so to speak, her connections, and his chief speculation was as to the sort of company in which he would find her doing it.

Having failed to overtake Julia on the road, Sir William breakfasted in Aix, outside a *pâtisserie*, where he could watch the passers-by, and spent the next hour in a methodical survey of the chief cafés and streets. It was therefore not until half-past ten that the Daimler, at full speed, once more passed the Muzin fork and took the Paris road.

III

About thirty miles out of Bourg the Misses Marlowe, being driven at their usual placid rate of twenty-seven miles an hour, overtook a small and very noisy Citroën. The time was half-past ten, for they had stopped in the town to sustain themselves with a good breakfast.

"I shouldn't like to drive in that," observed Miss Marlowe. "It sounds as though it's going to break down."

With unusual agility her sister twisted round on the seat to stare out of the back window.

"But did you see who was in it?" she cried. "That nice woman we took into Aix!"

"Well!" said Miss Marlowe, also pulling herself up for a look. "That's surely not her husband driving!"

"No, he's quite young. Besides, we saw *them* go off in a Daimler — from the Pernollet. How very odd!"

The incident afforded them an interesting topic of conversation all the way to Saulieu, where they lunched rather too well at the Hôtel de Poste.

IV

Lunch at the villa was served to Susan and her grandmother alone. They were both rather silent; the curious tale brought by Claudia occupied their thoughts but tied their tongues. The young Madame Packett, said Claudia, must have left very early indeed, she was not in her room at half-past seven, and her bed had not been slept in; the Monsieur did not leave till eight o'clock. She, Claudia, had had to wake him up to give him his early tea, and the note she found on the floor . . .

"And he left no message?" asked Mrs. Packett.

None at all, said Claudia. He went like a gust of wind. He inquired was the big car still in the barn, and she ran down and looked, and ran back to say it was, and there! — he was ready to depart!

"It sounds like a paper-chase," said Susan, with a rare attempt at lightness. Something had happened which she did not understand, and instinctively she was trying to minimize it. But in truth she was deeply disturbed; there had been another incident — of which her grandmother knew nothing — the implications of which she herself was not yet ready to face. Bryan had been with them in the hall while Claudia started her tale; without a word he had gone straight to Julia's room, flung open the door, slammed it to again, and walked out of the house. Susan had waited till Mrs. Packett was gone, and then repeated his actions; she saw nothing but a blue taffeta dress lying in a heap on the floor. The sight did not strike her as odd — Julia was always untidy — and for a moment she stood puzzled: the look on Bryan's face had prepared her almost for Julia's corpse. Then, without quite knowing why, she ran out through the house, and down the drive, and seeing Bryan at the gate called to ask where he was going.

"To look for Julia," said Bryan shortly.

"But — but it's absurd!" cried Susan. She was quite close to him now, there was only the gate between them. The sound of her raised voice startled her; she lowered it, and tried to speak reasonably. "It's absurd, Bryan! Julia isn't a lost child!"

His answer was completely irrelevant. As he turned and hurried on, over his shoulder, he said brusquely:

"By the way — I've had a cable. I've got to go home to-night."

That was all. Susan went back to the house and occupied her morning, as usual, with the plays of Racine. She was not quite certain that she had heard aright. In any case, when Mrs. Packett, at luncheon, inquired why Bryan was not there, she said merely that he had gone off for one of his long walks.

But she knew, all the same, that something had happened to her.

V

Julia and the young man lunched at a small café at Arney-le-Duc, and the young man paid. Julia let him. There was nothing else she could do. She hadn't spirit enough even to tell him a tale or two in exchange. She had so far made not the slightest attempt to account for herself, nor did she do so during the long, hot, dusty afternoon. She simply sat, tongue-tied and wretched, not even hearing when her companion produced one of his brief, uncomfortable remarks. She sat like a woman in a trance, or a woman half-dead; her face was so queerly blank that the young man, in his alarm, turned off from the Paris road at Auxerre and drove into the town to procure her a cup of tea. He had great faith in tea where women were concerned — his own mother, the widowed head of a large family, was regularly revived by it five times a day. The idea was a sound one, but from his own point of view unfortunate, since Sir William's Daimler was now only twenty miles behind. Had the Citroën kept to the main road, it would have been overtaken in less than an hour, and the young man's responsibility would at once have come to a welcome end. But he turned aside; Sir William drove on; and the chance was lost.

Outside the Café de la République Julia drank her tea in silence. It did her a certain amount of good; it made her a little more able to comprehend, if not to take an interest in, her immediate surroundings. These were highly picturesque; they had been admired (the young man told her) by Walter Pater. Something in his voice made Julia look, not at the roof-line, but at him; and for the first time she realized that he was extremely worried.

"Look here," he stammered, at once abandoning the scenery to profit by what no doubt appeared to him a glimmering of intelligence, "Look here — I'm most frightfully sorry —"

"I know," said Julia wearily. "I'm a damned nuisance to you."

The young man turned crimson.

"You're not in the least. I hate driving alone. Only — the fact of the matter is — I've been running it rather fine. I mean, I've got exactly enough cash to get me to Paris — for food and petrol and so on. I mean, it's just enough for one. You see —"

"That's all right," said Julia. "I understand. You've been sweet to bring me as far as this. As a matter of fact —" she racked her tired brain for some convincing story — "I've got friends here. Staying here. I'll be quite all right now."

It didn't convince the young man. He stared in front of him, his forehead still wrinkled, and said uncomfortably:

"Look here — this may be cheek on my part — but why don't you go to a consul? There isn't one nearer than Paris, but if we went to an hotel we could make them ring him up."

Julia reached across the table, took a cigarette out of the young man's packet, and let him light it for her. To go to a consul, in her mind, was like going to the workhouse — it meant you were so down and out there was nothing left for you but public assistance. "All right," thought Julia, "I'll take it. I've got to. I've got to get back somehow . . ."

"They're doing it every day," said the young man, with a kind of clumsy tact. "I mean, sending people home. A friend of mine got stuck last year, at Genoa. Another chap I know was stuck at Paris. It's ten to one I shall be stuck there myself."

"All right," repeated Julia aloud. "You move off, and I'll go along straightaway."

"I'll come with you."

"No," said Julia, at last managing a smile. "I'll look more distressed by myself. Distressed British Subject — that's my line now."

The young man stood up, felt in his pocket, and produced a handful of crumpled ten-franc notes.

"If you try leaving any of those with me," said Julia, "I — I'll get back into the car!"

To make his farewells easier, she pretended to be very busy doing her face. It took her a long time; and when she looked up again she was quite alone.

VI

Like the young man's mother, like every other Englishwoman at half-past four in the afternoon, the Misses Marlowe wanted their tea.

"If I don't get a cup soon, I shall go to sleep," complained the elder. "It's this dreadful heat."

"It's the lunch," said her sister more realistically. "But we'll be at Joigny in ten minutes, and there's a place there."

"A *nice* place?" asked Miss Marlowe wistfully.

"A.A.," replied Miss Ann.

The two ladies sat forward in their seats, eagerly scanning the railway line for the first sign of the bridge.

On crossing it, as Sir William did half an hour later, all drivers must slow down; the Modern Hôtel stands directly and invitingly in front of them. Sir William looked at it and realized that his throat was exceedingly dry. He had been driving now, with a brief interval for lunch, for something like eight hours, and anxiety had taken possession of him. Among his fears was the dread that he might have developed a blind spot — that his eye, automatically observing every car on the road, might have ceased to transmit its messages to the brain. There was another car to be observed now, a very old Daimler standing outside the hotel; Sir William looked at it with extreme care, and this time at least his eye made no mistake.

It was the car Julia had shown him, outside the Pernollet, as belonging to two old ladies who had once given her a lift.

Sir William drew up beside it, climbed stiffly out, and entered the hotel just as the Misses Marlowe were paying for their tea. Julia was not with them. He stood a moment on the threshold, trying to frame some question which he could reasonably ask of them, resentfully aware — for he had lost all sense of humour — that owing to Julia's reprehensible habits he did not even know what name they knew her by. Then, while he hesitated, the two ladies looked up and caught sight of him.

"*Oh!*" cried the Misses Marlowe in unison. "We've seen your wife!"

Without waiting to be invited, Sir William walked over and sat down at their table. For some reason it was evidently expected that he should be anxious: the two ladies showed no surprise at his lack of ceremony.

"Young men are so reckless!" exclaimed the elder. "Hasn't she got back yet?"

"No," said Sir William, his mind all at once alert and busy. A young man — there was nothing surprising about that! But where did the recklessness come in? "Were they breaking the speed limit?" he asked. "I know on these roads —"

"No, indeed!" exclaimed Miss Marlowe. "They could hardly get along. And the car made such peculiar noises —"

"*Spluttering* noises —" put in her sister.

"— that we were really quite alarmed."

"So am I," admitted Sir William. "In fact, I'm looking for them now. This young man — a young acquaintance of ours — insisted on taking my wife for a run, and I'm afraid they may have had a breakdown. Could you tell me exactly where you saw them?"

"Not far out of Bourg," said Miss Marlowe promptly, "but that was about half-past ten. If they kept to the Paris road they ought to be somewhere behind us. Where were they going?"

"Oh, some beauty-spot or other," said Sir William vaguely. If they really were on that road, why hadn't he passed them? The blind spot, after all? Had Julia seen him go by — and made no sign?

"Auxerre?" suggested Miss Ann. "If your wife is fond of Pater —"

In spite of fatigue and anxiety, Sir William smiled; he made a mental note that he must one day give Julia *Marius*, and see what happened . . .

"That's very likely," he said aloud. "I ought to have thought of it myself: it's the only place where I could have missed them. I think" — he pulled himself up again — "I'll go back there now."

VII

Driving slowly through the picturesque streets of Auxerre, Sir William saw a small disreputable car move splutteringly off from before a small deserted café. It had only one occupant, but he was a young man such as the Misses Marlowe had described. Sir William accelerated, found himself jammed by a slow-moving cart, and changing his mind came to a sudden stop. He could catch the Citroën easily; in the meantime he got out and crossed over to the Café de la République. On the other side of the privet hedge, at an empty table, sat a woman with her elbows among the crockery and her head on her fists.

"Julia!" said Sir William.

Julia looked up, her mouth and eyes opened, she made a queer, flurried movement as though she were trying to conceal herself behind her hands. Sir William walked up to her and leant heavily on the table.

"My dear Julia!" he said. "What on earth will you do next?"

ISIS publish a wide range of books in large print, from fiction to biography. Any suggestions for books you would like to see in large print or audio are always welcome. Please send to the Editorial department at:

ISIS Publishing Ltd.
7 Centremead
Osney Mead
Oxford OX2 0ES
(01865) 250 333

A full list of titles is available free of charge from:
Ulverscroft large print books

(UK)
The Green
Bradgate Road, Anstey
Leicester LE7 7FU
Tel: (0116) 236 4325

(Australia)
P.O Box 953
Crows Nest
NSW 1585
Tel: (02) 9436 2622

(USA)
1881 Ridge Road
P.O Box 1230, West Seneca,
N.Y. 14224-1230
Tel: (716) 674 4270

(Canada)
P.O Box 80038
Burlington
Ontario L7L 6B1
Tel: (905) 637 8734

(New Zealand)
P.O Box 456
Feilding
Tel: (06) 323 6828

Details of **ISIS** complete and unabridged audio books are also available from these offices. Alternatively, contact your local library for details of their collection of **ISIS** large print and unabridged audio books.

AN INTRODUCTION TO THE BOOKS OF
THE OLD TESTAMENT

Books by
W. O. E. OESTERLEY, D.D.

Ancient Hebrew Poems.

An Introduction to the Books of the Apocrypha.

Readings from the Apocrypha.

The Wisdom of Ben-Sira (Ecclesiasticus).

The Wisdom of Egypt and the Old Testament.   In the light of the newly discovered " Teaching of Amen-em-Ope."

The Sayings of the Jewish Fathers.   (Pirke Aboth.)

Tractate Shabbath.   (Mishnah.)

The Psalms.   Translated with Text-critical and Exegetical Notes.

The Psalms, Book III (lxxiii–lxxxix).   Hebrew Text.

The Psalms, Book IV (xc–cvi).   Hebrew Text.

WITH

G. H. BOX, D.D.

A Short Survey of the Literature and Rabbinical and Mediæval Judaism.

WITH

T. H. ROBINSON, D.D.

An Introduction to the Books of the Old Testament.

Hebrew Religion: Its Origin and Development.

BY

T. H. ROBINSON, D.D.

The Book of Amos.   Hebrew Text.

———

LONDON: S · P · C · K

AN INTRODUCTION TO THE BOOKS OF THE OLD TESTAMENT

BY

W. O. E. OESTERLEY, D.D., Litt.D.

AND

THEODORE H. ROBINSON, D.D., Litt.D.
Hon. D.D. (Aberdeen), Hon. D.Th. (Halle–Wittenberg).

LONDON

S · P · C · K

1958

First published in 1934
Reprinted . 1935
Reprinted . 1937
Reprinted . 1941
Reprinted . 1946
Reprinted . 1949
Reprinted . 1953
Reprinted . 1955
Reprinted . 1958

PRINTED IN GREAT BRITAIN

DEDICATED
TO
OUR PUPILS
PAST, PRESENT
AND FUTURE

PREFATORY NOTE

In offering this book, the third work in which we have joined in happy collaboration, to Biblical students, whether in the technical or the wider sense, it has been our endeavour to strike a mean between the exhaustive work of Driver and the necessarily restricted volumes, for example, of Gray or McFadyen. Excellent as these two latter are, it is obvious that the authors were not permitted sufficient scope by their respective publishers since the size of the volumes had to conform to that of a Series. While we have, therefore, not gone into the minute details which characterize Driver's great work, it has been our aim to offer a somewhat fuller account of the Old Testament books—their contents, structure, etc.—than that given in most other English *Introductions*.

Further, we have been at pains to lay stress on some matters which have not always received as much attention as is due to them; thus, wherever needful, we have dealt as fully as space permitted with the historical background of a book; not that this has been wanting in other *Introductions*, but we venture to think that the subject demands rather fuller treatment than is usually accorded it. We have also made a point of indicating, though as a rule quite cursorily, the importance of the Septuagint for the study of the Old Testament books.

Our general approach to the problems of the prophetic literature differs from that which is to be found in most standard *Introductions*. We do not, however, claim any originality here. The line which we have followed is that taken by practically all the best writers on individual prophetic books. Here, we hope, we have been able to fill a gap in the study of the subject. The method has involved our giving more attention than has usually been done in works on Introduction to the metrical structure, *e.g.*, of the different parts of the *Book of Isaiah*. The general subject of Hebrew metre is dealt with in a special section. We are fully aware of the differences of opinion which exist on this side of Old Testament studies, but it is well, we believe, that the salient facts should be brought to the notice of the student.

Many problems arise in connexion with most of the Old Testament books; we have done our best to touch upon most of these, but it is hardly to be expected that all of them should have been dealt with.

The literature, English and foreign, which is concerned with the Old Testament is enormous; where there is a *plethora* of material it is not always easy to decide what should be said and what left aside; it is quite impossible to deal with everything in one volume, perhaps even in half a dozen. In this matter we are fully prepared to meet with criticism; we regret it, but we cannot help it.

In the first instance we are individually responsible for certain books, or parts of books; but in every case we have discussed together the various problems which arise, and in almost every case we have reached agreement; in the one instance in which we have not been able to see eye to eye the fact is indicated in a footnote.

With regard to the treatment of the individual books, it will be seen that there is not always uniformity in the headings of the sections; it is hardly necessary to apologize for this because the nature and character of the various books differ greatly, and what is appropriate in the case of some is not so in that of others.

In transcribing Hebrew words, we have deliberately avoided the use of diacritic signs to indicate quantity. For the reader who understands Hebrew these are unnecessary, for the reader who does not understand Hebrew they are meaningless. We have followed the usual method in transcribing Hebrew consonants except that we have retained the spelling—now grown familiar—of *Qinah*.

We regret that Prof. Eissfeldt's *Einleitung in das Alte Testament* did not appear until the printing of our own book was already far advanced. It has been, therefore, impossible to use it in our own work, but we note with satisfaction the extent to which we can concur in his views, especially in his treatment of the prophetic literature.

We take this opportunity of thanking Mr. H. H. Rowley, of University College, Cardiff, for having read through our MS., for having made a number of valuable criticisms, and for having also read the proofs with that meticulous care which characterizes all his work. We are also indebted to Mrs. T. H. Robinson for having read the proofs and for having checked the Biblical references.

W. O. E. OESTERLEY.
THEODORE H. ROBINSON.

April 30, 1934.

CONTENTS

PREFATORY NOTE . . . .
PAGE
vii

THE CANON OF THE OLD TESTAMENT I
    I. The term " Canon."
    II. The Purpose of a Canon of Scripture.
    III. The Hebrew Canon.
    IV. The Greek Canon.

THE TEXT OF THE OLD TESTAMENT 11
    I. Hebrew Writing.
    II. The Hebrew Text.
    III. The Versions.
    IV. The Use of the Versions.

THE PENTATEUCH 22
    I. Contents.
    II. Structure:
        i. Narrative portions.
        ii. Legal and Ritual portions.
    III. General Analysis.
    IV. Further Analysis of Sources.
    V. Deuteronomy.
    VI. The Compilation of the Pentateuch.
    VII. Characteristic Features of the Documents.
    VIII. Dates of the Pentateuch:
        i. Comparative Dating: Chronological Order of the Docu-
        ments.
        ii. Absolute Dating.
    IX. Other Views of the Structure and Dates of the Pentateuch.
        i. Structure and Analysis.
        ii. Dates.
    X. The Hebrew Text of the Pentateuch.

THE BOOK OF JOSHUA 68
    I. Place in the Canon.
    II. Contents.
    III. Structure and Date.
    IV. The Hebrew Text and the Septuagint.
    V. The Value of *Joshua* as an Historical Record.

THE BOOK OF JUDGES 75
    I. Contents, Structure, and Redactional Elements.
        (*a*) i. 1–ii. 5. (*b*) ii. 6–xvi. 31. (*c*) xvii–xxi.
    II. Sources.
    III. The Hebrew Text and the Septuagint Version.
    IV. Historical and Religious Value.

PAGE

THE BOOK OF RUTH 83
    I. Place in the Canon and Contents.
    II. Structure and Date.
    III. Historical Background.
    IV. The Hebrew Text.

I II SAMUEL 85
    I. Title.
    II. Analysis.
    III. Sources.
    IV. The Hebrew Text and the Septuagint.

I II KINGS 93
    I. Contents.
    II. Sources.
    III. Deuteronomic Elements.
    IV. Other Redactional Elements.
    V. The Septuagint.

I II CHRONICLES 109
    I. Title and Place in the Canon.
    II. Chronicles and Ezra–Nehemiah.
    III. Contents.
    IV. Date.
    V. Sources.
    VI. Compilation.
    VII. Religious Standpoint.
    VIII. Historical Value.
    IX. The Versions.

EZRA–NEHEMIAH 120
    I. The Historical Background as presented in Ezra–Nehemiah.
    II. Sources used in compiling Ezra–Nehemiah.
    III. The Compiler of Ezra–Nehemiah.
    IV. Nehemiah and Ezra.
    V. The Septuagint Versions.

THE BOOK OF ESTHER 131
    I. The Narrative.
    II. The Origin of the Book.
    III. Date and Place of Origin.
    IV. Canonicity.
    V. The Hebrew Text and the Septuagint.

THE FORMS OF HEBREW POETRY 139
    I. Parallelism.
    II. Combination of Word-Accents and Stichoi to form Lines.
    III. Mixture of Metres.
    IV. The Strophe or Stanza.

THE WISDOM LITERATURE 150
    I. Pre-Literary Wisdom.
    II. The Hebrew Wisdom Books (Uncanonical).
        i. The Wisdom of Ben-Sira (Ecclesiasticus).
        ii. The Wisdom of Solomon.
        iii. Pirke Abôth.
        iv. The Book of Baruch (iii. 9–iv. 4) ; iv. Maccabees.
    III. The Hebrew Conception of Wisdom.
    IV. The Hakamim and their Work.
    V. The Cosmopolitan Character of Wisdom Literature.

CONTENTS xiii

PAGE

THE BOOK OF JOB 166
    I. Place in the Canon.
    II. Contents.
    III. Structure and Date:
        i. Structure.
        ii. Date.
    IV. The Solution of the Problem of the Book.
    V. The Text of the Book.

THE PSALMS 179
    I. Place in the Canon: General Title.
    II. The Titles of Individual Psalms.
        i. Titles containing musical directions.
        ii. Titles containing the names of popular melodies.
        iii. Some other terms occurring in titles.
    III. Collections embodied in the Psalter.
    IV. The Dates of the Psalms.
    V. Types of Psalms.
    VI. The Psalms as Liturgical Documents.
    VII. The Psalms part of a World-Literature.
    VIII. The Hebrew Text and the Septuagint.

THE BOOK OF PROVERBS 202
    I. Title of the Book.
    II. Authorship.
    III. The Collections and their Dates.
    IV. The Hebrew Text and the Septuagint.

ECCLESIASTES 209
    I. Title.
    II. Authorship.
    III. The Character and Teaching of the Book.
    IV. The Influence of Greek Philosophy.
    V. Date.
    VI. Canonicity.
    VII. The Hebrew Text and the Septuagint.

THE SONG OF SOLOMON 217
    I. Place in the Canon.
    II. Contents.
    III. Structure and Interpretation.
    IV. Date.
    V. The Hebrew Text.

THE PROPHETICAL LITERATURE: GENERAL INTRODUCTION . . . 221
    I. Oracular Poetry (A).
    II. Biographical Prose (B).
    III. Autobiographical Prose (C)
    IV. Stages in Compilation.

THE BOOK OF ISAIAH 233
    I. Place in the Canon.
    II. Historical Background.
    III. Contents.
    IV. Structure and Date:
        1. General: the larger divisions.
        2. Chapters i–xxxix:

PAGE

    A. Ch. i. (i) Structure.
           (ii) Date.
    B. Chs. ii–v. (i) Structure.
           (ii) Date.
    C. Chs. vi–xii. (i) Structure.
           (ii) Date.
    D. Chs. xiii–xxiii. (i) Structure.
           (ii) Date.
    E. Chs. xxiv–xxvii.
    F. Chs. xxviii–xxxv. (i) Structure.
           (ii) Date.
    G. Chs. xxxvi–xxxix.
      3. Summary and Conclusions.
  V. The Man and his Message.
  VI. The Hebrew Text and the Septuagint.

ISAIAH XL–LV (DEUTERO-ISAIAH) 262
  I. Historical Background.
  II. Structure and Contents of Isa. xl–lv.
  III. The Prophet and his Teaching.
  IV. Language and Style of Isa. xl–lv.
  V. The Hebrew Text and the Septuagint.

ISAIAH LVI–LXVI (TRITO-ISAIAH) 277
  I. Historical Background.
  II. Authorship of Isa. lvi–lxvi.
  III. Structure and Contents.
  IV. Date.
  V. The Hebrew Text and the Septuagint.
  VI. The Prophet and his Teaching.

THE BOOK OF JEREMIAH 288
  I. Place in the Canon.
  II. Historical Background.
  III. Contents.
  IV. Structure and Date.
    i. Structure of A sections.
    ii. Dating of A collections.
    iii. B sections; contents, date, and authorship.
    iv. C sections: contents, origin, and date.
    v. The main compilation.
  V. Jeremiah and the Reforms of Josiah.
  VI. The Man and his Message.
  VII. The Hebrew Text and the Septuagint.

THE BOOK OF LAMENTATIONS 314
  I. Title and Place in the Canon.
  II. Contents and Structure.
  III. Authorship and Date.
  IV. The Hebrew Text and the Septuagint.

THE BOOK OF EZEKIEL 318
  I. Contents of the Book.
  II. The Ezekiel Problem.
  III. Authorship.
  IV. The Personality of Ezekiel.
  V. Conclusions.
  VI. The Hebrew Text and the Septuagint.

CONTENTS

PAGE

THE BOOK OF DANIEL 330
    I. Place in the Canon.
    II. Historical Background.
    III. Authorship and Date.
    IV. Contents of the Book.
    V. Sources.
    VI. The Languages of the Book.
    VII. The Teaching of the Book.
    VIII. The Versions.

THE BOOK OF HOSEA 345
    I. Place in the Canon.
    II. Historical Background.
    III. Structure and Contents.
    IV. Date and Authorship.
    V. Hosea's Domestic life.
    VI. The Man and his Message.
    VII. The Hebrew Text and the Septuagint.

THE BOOK OF JOEL 355
    I. Contents.
    II. Authorship.
    III. Date.
    IV. The Hebrew Text and the Septuagint.

THE BOOK OF AMOS 363
    I. Place in the Canon.
    II. Historical Background.
    III. Structure and Contents.
    IV. Date and Authorship.
    V. The Man and his Message.
    VI. The Hebrew Text and the Septuagint.

THE BOOK OF OBADIAH 369
    I. Place in the Canon.
    II. Historical Background.
    III. Structure and Contents.
    IV. Date and Authorship.
    V. The Hebrew Text and the Septuagint.

THE BOOK OF JONAH 372
    I. The Date of the Book.
    II. Historical Background.
    III. The Interpretation of the Book.
    IV. Integrity of the Book.
    V. The Hebrew Text and the Septuagint.

THE BOOK OF MICAH 381
    I. Place in the Canon.
    II. Historical Background.
    III. Structure and Contents.
    IV. Date and Authorship.
    V. The Man and his Message.
    VI. The Hebrew Text and the Septuagint.

THE BOOK OF NAHUM 387
    I. Place in the Canon.
    II. Historical Background.

PAGE

   III. Structure and Contents.
   IV. Date and Authorship.
    V. The Man and his Message.
   VI. The Hebrew Text and the Septuagint.

THE BOOK OF HABAKKUK 392
    I. Place in the Canon.
   II. Historical Background.
   III. Structure and Contents.
   IV. Date and Authorship.
    V. The Prophet and his Message.
   VI. The Hebrew Text and the Septuagint.

THE BOOK OF ZEPHANIAH 400
    I. Place in the Canon.
   II. Historical Background.
   III. Structure and Contents.
   IV. Date and Authorship.
    V. The Man and his Message.
   VI. The Hebrew Text and the Septuagint.

THE BOOK OF HAGGAI 404
    I. Historical Background.
   II. Contents of the Book.
   III. Authorship of the Book.
   IV. The Prophet and his Teaching.
    V. The Hebrew Text and the Septuagint.

THE BOOK OF ZECHARIAH 410
    I. Zechariah and Deutero-Zechariah.
   II. The Prophet Zechariah and his People.
   III. The Night-Visions.
   IV. The Hebrew Text and the Septuagint of Zech. i–viii.
    V. Zechariah ix–xiv.
   VI. The Hebrew Text and the Septuagint of Zech. ix–xiv.

THE BOOK OF MALACHI. 427
    I. Authorship of the Book.
   II. Date of the Book.
   III. Contents of the Book.
   IV. The Hebrew Text and the Septuagint.

BIBLIOGRAPHY 434
INDEX: Modern Authors cited 443
      General 445

THE CANON OF THE OLD TESTAMENT

I. The Term " Canon "

THE Greek word κανών means, in its original sense, " a straight rod "; it is derived from κάννα, " a reed," for which the Hebrew word is קָנֶה (Ḳaneh); in Ezek. xl. 3, 5, e.g., we have קְנֵה הַמִּדָּה, " a measuring rod "; the Greek word was borrowed from the Hebrew. In its earliest known Greek use (175 B.C.) it is applied to " a level " in reference to the building of a temple.[1]

Its metaphorical use in Greek is equivalent to the Latin *norma*, the " rule " or " standard " of what is right and best; cp. Gal. vi. 16: " And as many as shall walk by this rule (τῷ κανόνι), peace be upon them . . ." (cp. also ii Cor. x. 13 ff.).[2] The title κανόνες was given to the old Greek authors as those who created the best models in literature.

Its use in reference to the books of the Bible—the Old Testament in the first instance—is Christian; derivatives from the word, by the Greek Fathers, occurred before the term itself came into use; as a technical term in reference to the Scriptures it is used for the first time, so far as is known, by Amphilochius, archbishop of Iconium (*circa* A.D. 380).

By the expression " the Canon of the Old Testament," then, is meant the existence of a certain number of books which were held to conform to a standard; what constituted that norm will become clear as we proceed.

II. The Purpose of a Canon of Scripture

It is clear that the idea of a Canon necessarily presupposes the existence of a number of books, some of which, for one

[1] See Moulton, *The Vocabulary of the Greek Testament*, s.v. κανών.
[2] Cp. i Clem. vii. 2: " . . . and let us come to the glorious and venerable rule (κανόνα) of our tradition."

B

reason or another, are regarded with special veneration, and which must therefore be authoritative in a pre-eminent sense. Otherwise we should have to assume that what we now call " canonical " books were regarded as " canonical " when they first appeared, and there is nothing to suggest that this was ever the case with any Old Testament writing. Now this *idea* of a " Canon," *i.e.* of some books being more holy than others, could not have arisen all at once; it was only gradually, and by general consensus, that certain books came to have a special sanctity attached to them. The earliest actual designation of the books of the Old Testament as the " holy books," or the " holy writings," is found in Josephus, about A.D. 100; but the formulation of the Canon must have been going on for long before, because the way in which he writes shows that in his time already the Canon as we know it was accepted; and it was regarded as finally fixed, for nothing farther could be added to it. Josephus' words are so important in the present connexion that it is necessary to quote them in full:

" We have not an innumerable multitude of books among us, disagreeing from and contradicting one another; but only twenty-two books, which contain the records of all the past times, and which are rightly believed in.[1] And of these, five belong to Moses, which contain the laws and the tradition of the origin of mankind till his death for a period of nearly three thousand years. From the death of Moses until the reign of Artaxerxes, king of Persia, who reigned after Xerxes, the prophets who came after Moses wrote down the things that were done in their times in thirteen books. The remaining books contain hymns to God and precepts for the conduct of human life. But from Artaxerxes to our times all things have indeed been written down, but are not esteemed worthy of a like authority because the exact succession of the prophets was wanting. And how firmly we have given credit to these books of ours

---

[1] The word Θεῖα (believed to be) " divine," is omitted in Niese's text, as it does not occur in the Greek or Latin texts of Josephus; it is added by Eusebius (*Hist. Eccles.*, iii. 10).

is evident by what we do; for during so many ages which have already passed, no one has been so bold as either to add anything to them, to take anything from them, or to make any change in them. But it is become natural to all Jews, immediately and from their very birth, to esteem these books to contain divine doctrines, and to stand by them, and willingly to die for them." [1]

This passage shows that, according to Josephus, the essential marks attaching to the idea of " canonical Scriptures " were:

(a) that they are θεοῦ δόγματα, of unquestioned authority, and must be believed in *ex animo*; for since they all originate within the prophetical period, they are divinely inspired;

(b) that they are to be distinguished from every other form of literature in that they are holy;

(c) that their number is strictly limited;

(d) that their verbal form is inviolable.[2]

Further, it must also be noted that, according to Josephus' belief, as expressed in this passage, the canonicity of a book depended upon whether it had been written within a clearly defined period, and that period was from Moses to the death of Artaxerxes, *i.e.* within what was held to be the prophetical period. The artificiality of this test is shown by the fact that, as Ryle has pointed out, " the mention of this particular limit seems to be made expressly with reference to the book of *Esther*, in which alone the Artaxerxes of Josephus (the Ahasuerus of the Hebrew book of *Esther*) figures." [3]

This is all entirely in accordance with the teaching of official Judaism as ultimately stereotyped in the Talmud: revelation began with the Patriarchs, all the prophets up to and including Malachi were endowed with the Holy Spirit, so that the words they wrote must be regarded as having been inspired; therefore the Scriptures were " holy

---

[1] *Contra Ap.*, I. 38–42.

[2] See Hölscher, *Kanonisch und Apokryph*, p. 4 (1905).

[3] *The Canon of the Old Testament*, p. 174 (1895); see also Eberharter, *Der Kanon des alten Testaments zur Zeit des Ben Sira*, pp. 57 ff. (1911).

writings," the origin and norm of all divine teaching, and
no teaching can be recognized as true unless it can be shown
to be founded on the holy writings.[1] The Rabbis, like
Josephus, maintained that no book could be regarded as
canonical unless it had been written within the prophetical
period, which they reckoned as from Moses to Ezra.[2]

The holiness of the canonical writings was indicated by
the Rabbis by saying that it " defiled the hands ";[3] the
phrase denotes an antique conception; what is " holy " is
infected by the Deity, according to old-world ideas; but
to come into contact with the Deity, even mediately, is
dangerous, because everything holy is originally taboo;
anyone who touches a holy thing must undergo a ritual
washing.[4] Therefore a holy book imparts contagion to him
who touches it. This is what lies behind the phrase " de-
filing the hands " as equivalent to what we understand by
canonicity.

III. The Hebrew Canon

The Hebrew Bible, as we now have it, is divided into
three parts; the divisions, which are due to the Rabbis, are
artificial, and judged by their respective contents, illogical,
as will be seen; they are as follows:

(a) *The Law*, called *Torah*: Genesis, Exodus, Leviticus,
Numbers, Deuteronomy; five books.

(b) *The Prophets*, called *Nebi'im*; these are subdivided
into—

> (i) the former prophets, called *Nebi'im Rishonim*,
> viz. Joshua, Judges, i, ii Samuel, i, ii Kings
> (each of the last two being regarded as one
> book); and
> (ii) the latter prophets, called *Nebi'im 'Acharonim*,
> viz. Isaiah, Jeremiah, Ezekiel, and the Twelve
> Minor Prophets, reckoned as one book; mak-
> ing altogether eight books for this division.

[1] Weber, *Jüdische Theologie* . . . pp. 80–91 (1897).
[2] For details see Hölscher, *op. cit.*, pp. 36 ff.
[3] The term occurs frequently in reference to the Scriptures in the Mishnah, tractate *Yadaim*.
[4] Cp. Lev. vi. 27, and elsewhere.

(*c*) *The Writings*, called *Kethubim* : Psalms, Proverbs, Job, Song of Songs, Ruth, Lamentations, Ecclesiastes, Esther, Daniel, Ezra–Nehemiah (reckoned as one book), i, ii Chronicles (reckoned as one book); eleven books.[1] Thus 5 + 8 + 11 = twenty-four books. At first sight this does not seem to agree with the twenty-two of Josephus, 5 + 13 + 4; but there can be little doubt that Josephus' *Ruth* belonged to *Judges*, and *Lamentations* to *Jeremiah*.

The number twenty-four is clearly an artificial one, as can be seen, *e.g.*, by the fact that the books of the Twelve Minor Prophets, belonging to very different times, are treated as one book; on the other hand, *Ezra–Nehemiah* and *Chronicles*, which form one book, are reckoned as two. It is possible that the Rabbinical number twenty-four was chosen because it = 12 + 12; the number twelve " derived its sacred character from the fact that it is the product of three and four, and is the number of the months of the year. There are twelve tribes of Israel and the same number of tribes of Ishmael (Gen. xvii. 20, xxv. 16). The number of many representative men and things was made twelve to accord with the number of the tribes (Exod. xxiv. 4; Num. xvii. 2, 6; Josh. iv., etc.). . . ." [2]

That the way in which the books are divided is illogical is also clear, since the first division, the *Law*, consists more of narrative than of legal matter; similarly, the *Prophets*, which is very largely history.

The question now arises as to whether these three collections of holy writings represent three successive stages of canonization. It is usually held that at one time the Hebrew Canon consisted of the Law, *i.e.* the Pentateuch, only; that later the Canon was enlarged by the admission into it of the " Prophets "; and that, finally, the canonicity of the remaining books was recognized, and thus the threefold Canon came into being. This view Hölscher, in his discerning and discriminating examination of the whole sub-

[1] Of these, *Song of Songs, Ruth, Lamentations, Ecclesiastes, Esther* are known as the five *Megilloth* (" Rolls "); they were so called when they were received into the Liturgy, in post-Talmudic times; see Blau, *Studien zum althebräischen Buchwesen und zur biblischen Litteraturgeschichte*, pp. 66 ff. (1902).
[2] *Jewish Encycl.*, ix. 349, *a*.

ject, has shown to be based on insufficient and unreliable evidence, and therefore erroneous;[1] there were not three successive stages at which these three collections of books were in turn recognized as canonical in the technical sense; such stages cannot be indicated; the idea is due to post-Christian Rabbinical suppositions. What happened was that the *Torah*, as it grew from the end of the seventh century B.C., was specially venerated; but it was constantly added to until it reached its final shape about the end of the fourth century B.C.; its authoritative character increased, but no idea of canonicity attached to it. As to the *Prophets*, some of these writings existed before the *Torah* became a Law-book, and they were added to from time to time up to the middle of the second century B.C.; but nowhere is there any evidence that they became "canonical." So that, for example, what Ben-Sira says in Ecclus. xliv–1 does not indicate anything regarding the Canon as such, *i.e.* one cannot say that this is evidence that the prophetical canon was closed by that time;[2] it only shows what books had by his day (*circa* 182 B.C.) come to be regarded with special veneration—an important step in the process which ultimately led to the formation of the Canon—but the idea of a Canon had not yet arisen; and this is clearly seen by the fact that Ben-Sira can speak of himself as the latest of the Biblical writers, and therefore regards his book as the most recent addition to the Scriptures: "And I, last of all, awoke (or ' came,' as the Syriac reads), as one that gleaneth after the grape-gatherers. By the blessing of the Lord I made progress, and as a grape-gatherer, filled my winepress " (Ecclus. xxxiii. 16). Again, that Ben-Sira did not regard the books of the Old Testament as what is understood as canonical, in the sense of being separated off from other books to which no addition may be made, is seen from xxiv. 33 of his book, where he writes: " I will yet pour out doctrine as prophecy, and leave it unto eternal generations " (see also verses 30–32, 34); nor would he have taken upon

---

[1] *Op. cit.*, pp. 7–77.
[2] So *e.g.*, Buhl, *Kanon und Text des Alten Testaments*, p. 12 (1891), and Ryle, *op. cit.*, p. 113.

himself, as Hölscher points out, to assume the tone and style of the ancient prophets, as he often does (see, *e.g.*, xlvii. 20, l. 29), if the " unbridgeable cleft of canonicity " had gaped between him and the prophets.[1]

Similarly with the *Writings* ; they, too, existed in part before the *Torah* became a Law-book, and went on increasing into Christian times ; but there is no evidence to show that they, as a separate collection, obtained an individual *canonicity*.

The underlying and real cause which in course of time forced the idea of forming a Canon to arise was Greek culture and the growth of Greek literature ; the more immediate cause—which was, however, to a large extent an outcome of this—was the spread of apocalyptic books written by and circulating among the Jews. To give the reasons for this would take up far too much space here ; they are cogently presented by Hölscher. But it became necessary in view of what was regarded by the Jewish religious leaders as erroneous and pernicious literature, to gather out from the mass of current books those which they held to contain the truth ; thus the idea of a Canon came into being, and this was towards the end of the second century B.C. But the actual fixing of the Canon did not come until long after this, and it was not piece-meal ; there is good reason to believe that the Hebrew Canon as we now know it was an accomplished fact by about A.D. 100.

In what has been said the important thing to bear in mind is the distinction between books which are good and authoritative, and the same books when they have been pronounced canonical, *i.e.* as possessing the marks, mentioned above, attaching to canonicity ; the nature of books undergoes by this process, as it were, metamorphosis. But this pronouncement did not take place in three successive stages in respect of what we now call the three divisions of the Canon ; on the other hand, it did not, as it were, take place in one act ; the discussions as to whether certain of the books " defiled the hands " or not, many remains of

---

[1] *Op. cit.*, p. 20.

which are preserved in the Talmud, show that it must have taken a long time before the final fixing of the Canon was a *fait accompli* in about A.D. 100.

IV. THE GREEK CANON

By the " Greek Canon " is meant the books of the Old Testament included in the Septuagint Version of the Hebrew Scriptures; the term is used for convenience' sake; in itself it is inaccurate because the books of the Greek Old Testament not represented in the Hebrew Scriptures did not come within the purview of the Jewish religious authorities in their discussions about books which " defiled the hands " or not. So that inasmuch as these books were never even considered from the point of view of canonicity it is not, at any rate from the Jewish point of view, accurate to speak of a Greek Canon. On the other hand, from the Christian standpoint the term is justified, for the early Church regarded all the books of the Greek Bible, whether represented in the Hebrew Scriptures or not, as equally authoritative, and therefore canonical.

When exactly the repudiation by the Jewish Church of the Greek, or " Alexandrian " Canon first began to take shape is uncertain; it would seem in any case to have come gradually, for " about the middle of the first century A.D., when the Greek-speaking Christian community began to break entirely with Judaism, the narrow Pharisaic doctrine of the Canon had certainly not as yet penetrated into the domain of Hellenistic Judaism so deeply as to delete completely, or to exclude from the MSS. of the Septuagint, all the books that Pharisaism refused to recognize." [1] By the time of Josephus, however (end of first century A.D.), the Greek Bible which he used consisted substantially of the books of the Hebrew Canon as we know it; and according to ii (iv) Esdras xiv. 44, 45 (of approximately the same date) the Canon consisted of twenty-four books of the Hebrew Scriptures.

The number of the books in the Greek Old Testament

[1] Budde, in the *Encycl. Bibl.*, i. 673.

not included in the Hebrew Canon varies in the MSS. and in the lists which have come down to us;[1] but the most complete lists contain the following: i Esdras, Wisdom of Solomon, Wisdom of Sirach (Ecclesiasticus), Judith, Tobit, Baruch and the Ep. of Jeremiah, i–iv Maccabees. In addition, the *Psalms of Solomon* is sometimes included, either among the Solomonic books or at the end of the Canon; and the Greek version of the *Book of Enoch*, " although by some accident it has been excluded from the Greek Bible,"[2] was undoubtedly regarded as canonical in the early Church,[3] and must therefore have been included in copies of the Greek Old Testament.[4]

Apart from the last two, these books are comprised in what we now know as the Apocrypha; a final word in regard to this expression is called for. The Greek word *apokryphos* was originally used in a good sense in reference to books which were " hidden " from the outside world because they were too excellent for ordinary mortals. In its technical sense the term " is derived from the practice, common among sects, of embodying their special tenets or *formulæ* in books withheld from public use, and communicated to an inner circle of believers "[5] (cp. ii [iv] Esdras xiv. 44–47). " Apocryphal " was thus applied originally to books which contained hidden wisdom, and must therefore be kept hidden from the world in general.[6] But Origen used the term in reference to what we know as the pseudepigraphic books; then, in the fourth century, in the Greek Church a distinction was made between " Canonical " books and those which were read " for edification "; but these latter referred to the books of what we now call the Apocrypha; the term " apocryphal " was still used only in reference to pseudepigraphic books. Jerome (died

---

[1] For these see Swete, *Intr. to the O.T. in Greek*, pp. 201 ff. (1900).
[2] Swete, *op. cit.*, p. 265.
[3] As is well known, it is quoted in Jude 14, 15 (= Enoch i. 9).
[4] In the case of what most of the Latin MSS. call *iv Esdras* (= chs. iii–xiv of *ii Esdras* in the English Apocrypha), the Greek is not extant, excepting for a few fragments; it was originally written in Hebrew.
[5] James, in *Encycl. Bibl.*, i. 249.
[6] The equivalent term in Hebrew, *ganaz*, refers to books the contents of which were regarded as heretical, not to books of the Apocrypha, the reading of which was permitted.

A.D. 420) in the Latin Church followed the example of the Greek Church in so far that he made a distinction between the " libri canonici " and the " libri ecclesiastici "; the latter referred to those of our Apocrypha, so that these were now " apocryphal " books; Jerome was the first to use this term " apocryphal " in this new sense. It did not become general for some time; St. Augustine, for example, used " apocrypha " in the old sense, in the *De Civitate Dei*, xv. 23; but by degrees Jerome's usage of the term became generally accepted, and it has continued so to the present day.

THE TEXT OF THE OLD TESTAMENT

I. HEBREW WRITING

THE Old Testament was originally written in two languages, the greater part being in Hebrew, and portions of *Daniel* and *Ezra* in Aramaic. It has been suggested (*e.g.* by Naville) that the Law was originally written in cuneiform script and in the Akkadian language, being translated into Hebrew at a comparatively late date. This view, however, has not found general favour and lacks direct evidence.

Forms of writing may be divided into three classes. The first is called ideographic, in which the sign represents an idea and not a sound. It is often a little picture of the thing intended, or a conventionalized form of a picture in which only a few lines survive. Examples of ideographic writing may be seen in ancient Sumerian and in modern Chinese, and in the numerals commonly used by us all. The second type of writing represents syllables; to it belong the ancient Akkadian and modern Japanese writing. In the third form the syllables themselves are split up into their constituent sounds, and we have an alphabet. In comparatively early times (*c.* 1400 B.C.) we know that a Semitic dialect resembling Aramaic was written in a kind of alphabet in northern Syria,[1] and such evidence as is available supports the view that, about the same period, a Hebrew alphabet was coming into existence in the south, which

---

[1] See especially in the literary treasures unearthed at Ras-Shamra. Details will be found in *Syria*, xiii. pp. 1–27 (Schaeffer), and pp. 113–169 (Virolleaud) (1932), xiv. pp. 93–127 (Schaeffer), pp. 128–151 (Virolleaud) (1933). See also, Schaeffer, "The French Excavations at Minet el Beida and Ras Shamra in Syria," in *Antiquity*, pp. 460–466 (1930) and Virolleaud, "The Gods of Phœnicia," pp. 405–414 (1931); Montgomery, "Notes on the Mythological Epic Texts from Ras Shamra," in the *Journal of the American Oriental Society*, Vol. 53, No. 2, pp. 97–123 (1933); Gaster, "The Ritual Pattern of a Ras Shamra Epic," in *Archiv. Orientální*, Vol. 5, No. 1 (1933).

proved to be the ancestor of most of the forms of writing now current in the western world.[1]

The shapes of the letters were very different in early days from those which appear in modern printed Hebrew, being much nearer to the early Greek forms. But, in spite of changes which took place between the sixteenth and first centuries B.C., Hebrew writing preserved two characteristics which were not retained in the Indo-European languages. In the first place, the alphabet was always written from right to left, not from left to right. In the second place, it indicated consonantal signs only, like modern reporters' shorthand, and had no means of representing the vowels save by additional signs.

For details of the changes which have taken place, the reader must be referred to special works on epigraphy.[2] The peculiar nature of the Semitic languages (the group to which both Hebrew and Aramaic belong) made it possible to read with fair certainty as long as Hebrew was a spoken language. It was, however, gradually replaced by a form of Aramaic in the post-exilic period, and, by the beginning of the Christian era, apart from the regular reading of Scripture in the synagogues, it was almost confined to a body of learned men. There arose then the need for representing the vowels, in order to safeguard the traditional pronunciation and meaning. The consonantal text was gradually acquiring so high a degree of sanctity that men dared not alter it, even to make its pronunciation clearer, and two systems of vowel-representation were ingeniously devised. One of these consisted of marks placed over the consonants, and was current among Eastern Jews. The other was a system of dots and dashes, mostly placed under the consonants. This was used in the west, and is that normally found in MSS. and printed Hebrew Bibles. It may be remarked that the copies of the Law used in

---

[1] On the so-called Sinaitic alphabet cp. A. H. Gardiner, " The Egyptian Origin of the Semitic Alphabet," *Journal of Egyptian Archæology*, Vol. III. pp. 1–15 (1916); H. Bauer, *Zur Entzifferung der neuentdeckten Sinaischrift* (1918); H. Grimme, *Althebräische Inschriften vom Sinai* (1923).

[2] Cp. *e.g.*, the *Corpus Inscriptionum Semiticarum*, Lidzbarski's *Ephemeris*, G. A. Cooke's *North Semitic Inscriptions*, Driver, *Notes on the Hebrew Text of the Books of Samuel*, pp. i–xxvi (2nd ed., 1913).

synagogue worship to this day have no vowels indicated at all.

II. The Hebrew Text

Until the invention of printing, the Hebrew Bible was necessarily copied by hand. The similarity between certain letters made mistakes very easy, but this danger was largely avoided by the extraordinary care bestowed on their work by Jewish scribes. No literature has ever been copied with such absolute fidelity and accuracy as the Old Testament, and there are, probably, not many printed books which contain so few mistakes as did the average MS. of the Hebrew Bible. Among the hundreds of copies known, the variations are only slight, and the great majority of those quoted, *e.g.* by Kennicott, De Rossi and Ginsburg, affect the vowels and not the consonants. Even when scribes were sure that the text before them was wrong, they copied the consonants as they stood, though they wrote a corrected text in the margin. Sometimes the fidelity of the scribes led them to copy ungrammatical or even meaningless sentences, due in the earlier copy to the carelessness or thoughtlessness of an older copyist. But they placed the vowels of their suggested reading in the text, a procedure which often produces a curious appearance, since the vowels of one word seem to be applied to the consonants of another. The most familiar example of the process is to be found in one of the divine names. The consonants were YHWH, probably pronounced *Yahweh*. But the word was too sacred to be uttered, and readers always used the term *'Adonay* = Lord. So the vowels of the latter were actually written with the proper consonants, thus producing the composite form *Yehowah*, whence our familiar word *Jehovah*.

The task of preserving and handing down the sacred text fell to a body or class of men who are commonly known as *Massoretes*. The name is derived from the Hebrew term *Massorah*, which means " tradition." But the work of the *Massoretes* went much farther than merely copying the text accurately and seeing that it was provided with the proper vowel signs. They studied it with the utmost diligence, counting the verses in each book, identifying the middle word, and appending in the margin countless notes, calling attention to anything unusual or remarkable in the text. Even such variations as an abnormally large or small letter were faithfully copied, and a note showed that the peculiarity was traditional, not arbitrary.[1]

A great many MSS. are known, but no complete Bible can be definitely stated to be older than the ninth century A.D., though there are MSS. of portions of it which are as old as the seventh century.[2] Since the process of fixing the text seems to have been complete by the end of the sixth century, it is not surprising that the variants are few and insignificant. One MS., known as G1, in the Library of Trinity College, Cambridge, presents an abnormal number of slight differences, but clearly represents the usual text.[3] Occasional differences of reading are found in other MSS., but, in general, the text is so uniform as to make it possible to cite it comprehensively under the title Massoretic Text (MT).

There is, however, one important group of MSS. giving evidence of the pre-Massoretic text of the Pentateuch. This consists of a few MSS. belonging originally to the Samaritan community, which clearly represent the text as it was some centuries before the beginning of the Christian era. While there are many deliberate alterations, made in the interests of Samaritan as opposed to Judæan orthodoxy, yet, when allowance has been made for these, the number of variants is not extraordinarily large. It is clear that the Samaritan scribes gave to the copying of the Pentateuch almost as much care as did the orthodox Jews,

---

[1] For a general description of the Massorah, cp. Geden, *Outlines of Introduction to the Hebrew Bible*, pp. 85 ff. (1909).

[2] Perhaps an exception should be made in favour of the Nash papyrus, which contains some verses from *Deuteronomy*, though not in the usual order, and dates from the second century A.D. at the latest. Some authorities hold this to be a liturgical text; see Burkitt, " The Hebrew Papyrus of the Ten Commandments," in *The Jewish Quarterly Review* (April 1903); S. A. Cook, " A Pre-Massoretic Biblical Papyrus," in the *Proceedings of the Society of Biblical Archæology* (Jan. 1903).

[3] The MS. has been especially studied by H. W. Sheppard, who published a transcript, with notes, of Pss. i–xli. in 1920.

and the general agreement of the two lines of text carries us back with some certainty at least to the second century B.C. Like the MT, the Samaritan text can usually be cited as a general whole.

III. THE VERSIONS

All Hebrew MSS., whether Jewish or Samaritan, belong to that type of tradition which we may call Palestinian. Their practical identity greatly enhances the importance of the Versions, especially when it is clear that these latter were translated from a text far older than the archetype on which all Jewish MSS. were ultimately based. Three of these clearly belong to the Palestinian tradition, and they show how the form of text now current was gradually reached. These are:

1. The Syriac (often cited as the *Peshitta* = " The Simple ") made, probably, in the second century A.D.

2. The Targums. These were popular Aramaic renderings, which were often very free, even paraphrastic. The more important, known as the Targum of *Onkelos* on the *Pentateuch* and the Targum of *Jonathan* on the *Prophets*, reached their present form not later than the end of the second century A.D.

3. The Vulgate; a Latin translation made by St. Jerome in the fourth century A.D. There was an older Latin version, but that was based on the common Greek text, and was not rendered directly from a Hebrew original.

The differences between the text underlying all these translations and the MT are comparatively slight. But it is interesting to notice that the nearest is the Vulgate, which is the latest of the three, while the Syriac diverges more than either of the others. It is thus clear that the fixing of the text was a process which was gradually carried on down to the fourth century A.D., when it was very nearly complete. But it was already far advanced when the Syriac translation was made, a conclusion to which we are forced by the evidence of the standard Greek version. To this we may now turn.

The text which we have been considering up to this

point represents, as we have already observed, a Palestinian tradition, even in the Samaritan Pentateuch. But, after the Exile, and especially from the time of Alexander the Great, there were communities of Jews in many places outside Palestine. By far the most important of these lived in Egypt, and Jews formed a considerable element in the population of Alexandria.[1] We may assume that, when they first settled there, they took with them Hebrew copies, at least of the Law, and perhaps of later books also. Other books were from time to time introduced among them. These would be copied in Hebrew for some time, until, as the Jews forgot their ancestral language, a need for a Greek version would be felt. Probably, also, close contact with the heathen world made the Egyptian Jew anxious to exhibit the treasures of his own literature in a form intelligible to his neighbours. Jewish tradition held that the Law was translated into Greek by the orders of Ptolemy Philadelphus,[2] by seventy-two scribes, whence the version is commonly known as the Septuagint, and is normally indicated as " LXX." It may be remarked that, while the tradition refers only to the Law, the term just mentioned is applied to the whole of the Greek Old Testament, including the books now classed as *Apocrypha*. Whether the narrative be correct in placing the initiative with the Egyptian king or not, there can be no doubt that the Septuagint *Pentateuch* dates back to the middle of the third century B.C. Other books followed during the next hundred and fifty years, and it seems that by the opening of the first century B.C., practically the whole of the Old Testament was available in Greek. At the beginning of the Christian era a complete Greek Bible was in existence, largely used by New Testament writers, including, not only the books preserved in the Hebrew Bible, but also some, at least, of those which we now class as apocryphal and apocalyptic. The evidence suggests that in some books, notably in the *Pentateuch*, the text was from time to time corrected by

[1] The very much earlier settlement at Elephantiné does not come into consideration, since there is no evidence to suggest that the Jews there possessed or knew the Bible or any part of it. They were certainly unaware of some of the provisions in *Deuteronomy*.
[2] 285-246 B.C. For the story see the well-known *Letter of Aristeas.*

scribes who were familiar with the Palestinian Hebrew form, though in other cases, especially in *Samuel* and *Jeremiah*, it retained practically complete independence.

During the second century A.D. three other Greek versions appeared. These were those of:

i. Aquila, a slavishly literal translation of the Hebrew, designed to meet the Christian use of the Septuagint in argument. It was claimed that the traditional version did not fairly represent the Hebrew, and the object of this undertaking was to tell the Jews exactly what the Bible really said. It is held by some scholars that Aquila is to be identified with the Onkelos, whose name is associated with the Targum of the Law.

ii. Symmachus. This is a somewhat free translation into Greek of a more elegant literary type than that of the Septuagint.

iii. Theodotion. A very thorough revision of the Sep- tuagint, bringing it to some extent into harmony with the MT as current in the translator's time.

These last three versions (though that of Theodotion is rather a revision than an independent version), like the Syriac, Targums and Vulgate, show comparatively little divergence from the standard Palestinian text preserved in our Bibles. The Septuagint, however, often differs very widely from the MT, and is, therefore, of the highest value for textual criticism. The divergence is smallest in the *Pentateuch*, and is at its highest point in *Samuel*, *Jeremiah*, and *Ezekiel*.

We are thus able to reconstruct the history of the materials we have for textual criticism, and to represent it in graphic form: [1]

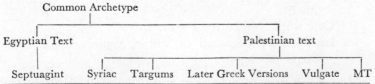

Common Archetype

Egyptian Text — Palestinian text

Septuagint — Syriac — Targums — Later Greek Versions — Vulgate — MT

---

[1] No account is taken here of the numerous secondary versions, since they are evidence, not for the Hebrew text itself, but for the version from which they were rendered. Thus the Septuagint was the parent of the Old Latin and of the Coptic and Ethiopic versions, while the Arabic was translated from the Syriac.

C

IV. The Use of the Versions

In view of the practical identity of all extant Hebrew MSS., the versions are of the highest importance for the recovery of the original text. The three later versions, together with the post-Septuagint Greek translations, can be used to help us to reconstruct the Hebrew text as it was generally accepted at the beginning of the Christian era, for where they all agree with the MT we may be sure that the readings thus attested go back to that age. But the Septuagint stands on a very different footing. The Hebrew text originally taken to Egypt clearly antedated the age of accurate copying and careful textual study. As the Samaritan form of the text suggests, we may have to make an exception in the case of the Law, though even there it is possible that Alexandrian Jews in the later Ptolemaic age had their copies revised so that they might agree with the Palestinian standard. The constant intercourse between Jerusalem and Egypt would make this almost inevitable in the case of the *Pentateuch*, while the lower grade of sanctity ascribed to other books would make Greek-speaking Jews less careful to adopt the " orthodox " forms. Where, then, we find agreement between the MT and the Septuagint, we may safely assume that we have recovered a text which, for some parts of the Bible, was as early as the fourth century B.C., and in none was later than the end of the second.

Where the Septuagint and the MT differ, we have to use our judgement in each individual case. The divergences seem to be due to three causes:

(*a*) Different pronunciation of the same Hebrew consonants.

(*b*) One word substituted for another.

(*c*) Insertion or omission of words, sentences, or even longer passages.

Variations due to (*a*) need not detain us, though we should remember that even by the time the Vulgate was translated there was no complete system of representing Hebrew vowels. A typical illustration may be seen in

Gen. xlvii. 31, where the Hebrew ran: "Israel bowed himself upon the *bed's* head." The Scptuagint, quoted in Hebr. xi. 21, reads: "top of his *staff*." Both Palestinian and Egyptian texts clearly had the Hebrew consonants MTH, but the former pronounced them *miṭṭah*, the latter *maṭṭeh*. It is usually (though not always) fairly easy to decide which of the two pronunciations gives the better sense.

Class (*b*) needs a good deal more consideration. We have to assure ourselves, in the first place, that the divergence is not due to corruption in the Greek text, rather than to a different Hebrew original.[1] Forms like ἔτι and ὅτι are often confused, while the Hebrew words which they represent (עוֹד—'odh and כִּי—ki) have no resemblance to one another. A more complicated, but very instructive, illustration may be drawn from Lam. iii. 63, where the English version, following the MT as traditionally vocalized, has "I am their song." The Septuagint has ἐπ' ὀφθαλμοὺς αὐτῶν, which seems to represent a totally different text until we realize that it is corrupted from ἐγὼ ἀπὸ ψαλμοῦ αὐτῶν, "I from their psalm." This is hardly lucid, and it is no wonder that copyists failed to produce it accurately, but it is a possible literal rendering of the Hebrew consonants, though they must have been differently vocalized. In spite of appearances, the reading of the Egyptian text was here identical with that of the Palestinian, though its meaning is by no means clear, and there may well be some corruption which crept into the text at an early period.

In countless other cases, however, the Septuagint was translated from a text which differed from the MT. A single illustration may be taken from Isa. xli. 1, "Keep silence before me." Here the Septuagint has ἐγκαινίζεσθε —"renew," and clearly read a different word—*haḥadhishu* for *haḥarishu*. As the Hebrew letters *d* (*dh*) (ד) and *r* (ר) were very similar at all stages of their development, we can easily understand how the mistake arose in Hebrew, though it would be unnatural in Greek. In choosing between two

---

[1] The textual criticism of the Septuagint is in itself a separate and elaborate branch of study, for which we have no room here. The reader is referred to Swete, *Introduction to the Old Testament in Greek* (1900), and to R. R. Ottley, *A Handbook to the Septuagint* (1920).

such readings, no general rule can be laid down, though there is a slight presumption in favour of the MT, since the Egyptian scribes would be less familiar with Hebrew than their Palestinian brethren, and would be more likely to copy a word wrongly.

When we turn to variations of the (c) class, we find that they occur most frequently in certain books. In *Jeremiah* the Septuagint is appreciably shorter than the MT; often individual words are omitted, especially expansions of the divine name; and sometimes longer passages, *e.g.* Jer. xxxiii. 14–26 is not represented in the Greek text at all. Still more striking is the fact that the collection of prophecies dealing with foreign nations, which appears in the MT (and so in the English version) as chs. xlvi–li, is placed in the Septuagint immediately after xxv. 13, instead of towards the end of the book. In *i Samuel* we find instances where the Greek text is longer or shorter than the MT; *e.g.* the former omits xvii. 55–xviii. 5, perhaps in order to avoid the difficulty raised by the suggestion that Saul did not know who David was when he went out to fight Goliath. Again, in i Kings xi, xii, the Septuagint has a much longer account of Jeroboam, differing from that of the MT in many details. Some of these additions are clearly translations from Hebrew originals, not free compositions in Greek, and this fact makes it the more difficult to decide as to the more primitive text. A scribe or reader sometimes made marginal notes which he never intended to be included in the text. Later copyists, however, did not always realize this, and often incorporated the additional matter in the text itself. Where the MT is longer than the Septuagint, there will be a slight balance of probability on the side of the Egyptian reading, since the Palestinian scribes, being the better acquainted with Hebrew, would be the more likely to expand the text.

(d) Conjectural emendation. Even when we have reached the common form which lay behind both the Palestinian and Egyptian traditions, very many passages remain which arouse suspicion. We know that, even in the comparatively short time which elapsed between the separation of the two lines of texts and the translation of

THE USE OF THE VERSIONS

both texts. Now the common archetype of the two cannot
be traced back farther than the middle of the fourth century
B.C. at the earliest, and this still leaves a gap of several
centuries for which we have no alternative evidence.[1] We
cannot but suppose that other errors will have crept in
during that long period, and again and again we meet
with passages which are unintelligible in all extant forms
of text. To correct these we can fall back only on conjectural emendation. This is often very interesting, and
countless suggestions have been made by modern scholars
for the improvement of the text. In a comparatively small
number of places we may be reasonably sure that the
emended reading is the right one. A good instance occurs
in Amos vi. 12, where the E.V. reads " shall one plough
there with oxen? " But no word for " there " is to be
found in the MT; it has been inserted by the English
translators in order to make sense of an otherwise meaningless sentence. We may add that the Hebrew itself presents
us with an anomaly which would be closely paralleled in
English by saying " shall one plough with cattles? " But,
if the last word in the verse be divided into two, and the
correct readjustment of the vowels be made, we get " shall
one plough *the sea* with cattle? ", which gives just the sense
required by the context, and is, almost certainly, the original
reading. In many instances, however, we are forced to admit
that, while a modern conjecture is often an improvement, and
may possibly restore the true text, we seldom have ground for
asserting with confidence that it has certainly done so.

Yet, in spite of all uncertainties, the great fact remains
that the text as we now have it does, in the main, represent
fairly the actual words of the authors who lived, some of
them, nearly three thousand years ago, and we need have
no serious doubt on the score of textual corruption as to
the validity of the message which the Old Testament has
to give us.

[1] We do, however, find occasionally passages which appear more than
once in the Bible, *e.g.*, Isa. ii. 2–4 = Mic. iv. 1–4, and here we may be able
to compare two ancient forms of text. But these passages are too few to
give us any general help.

THE PENTATEUCH [1]

THE Old Testament in all its forms begins with the five books of *Genesis, Exodus, Leviticus, Numbers* and *Deuteronomy*.[2] They are always grouped together, and form, in the Jewish Canon,[3] the *Torah*, or Law. They were traditionally ascribed to Moses and are sometimes cited under his name. Jewish writers often spoke of them as the " five-fifths " of the Law, and the name " Pentateuch " is a Greek way of expressing the same essential thought. In Jewish theology the collection had, and has, a degree of sanctity which is far above that of the other books of the Old Testament, and many orthodox Jews who allow themselves to accept critical conclusions regarding the *Prophets* and the *Writings* do not feel free to handle the *Torah* in the same way.

I. CONTENTS

The Pentateuch purports to present a continuous narrative which starts with the Creation of the world and ends with

[1] It has been usual among Old Testament critics to add to the Pentateuch the *Book of Joshua*, and to include the whole under the name of the Hexateuch. This is due to the fact that the final revision of these books, that of the priestly school, extended as far as the end of *Joshua*, and no farther, and it used to be held also that two of the older sources, J and E, likewise came to an end at that point. The literary work of the Deuteronomic school, on the other hand, extended beyond its limits, and certainly included the *Book of Judges*. We might even say that it was carried almost to the end of *Kings*. It is, however, now generally recognized that J and E are to be carried on through *Judges*, and, possibly, into *Samuel*, making *Joshua* much less clearly the last section of a literary unit. Further, the general habit of thinking of the first five books of the Bible together may simplify matters for the student, who should, however, remember that the term Hexateuch is still in common use in learned works on the Old Testament. He may refer for scholarly discussions to the works of Addis, *The Documents of the Hexateuch* (Vol. I, 1892, II, 1898) and Carpenter and Harford-Battersby, *The Pentateuch* (1900); Chapman, *An Introduction to the Pentateuch* (1911). By far the best book on the subject for the general reader is Simpson's *Pentateuchal Criticism* (1924).

[2] The names are derived ultimately from the Septuagint. In the Hebrew Bible the first word, or pair of words, of each book is used as its title—*Bereshith, We'elleh shemoth, Wayyiqra, Bemidhbar* (the fourth word, not the first) and *Elleh debharim. Exodus* and *Deuteronomy*, however, are usually cited by the *second* of the two words which, properly, compose the title in each case.

[3] See pp. 4 ff.

the death of Moses, as Israel is on the point of entering the
Promised Land. The story runs as follows:

Gen. i–xi. The Creation and the history of mankind
down to the time of Abraham.

Gen. xii–xxv. 18. The story of Abraham.

Gen. xxv. 19–xxvi. 35. The story of Isaac, including the
early life of Jacob.

Gen. xxvii–xxxvi. The story of Jacob.

Gen. xxxvii–l. The story of Joseph, showing how the
Israelites came to be in Egypt.

Exod. i. The oppression of Israel in Egypt.

Exod. ii–xv. 21. Moses delivers Israel.

Exod. xv. 22–xix. 25. Moses brings the people to Sinai.

Exod. xx–xxiv. A code of laws, opening with the Decalogue, is given, and a covenant is made between Israel
and Yahweh.

Exod. xxv–xxxi. Moses, in the mountain, receives
instructions as to the building of the Tabernacle, its furniture,
the priestly robes and consecration ceremonial.

Exod. xxxii. The Golden Calf; Moses breaks the two
Tables of Stone.

Exod. xxxiii. Moses' method of communication with
Yahweh.

Exod. xxxiv. Moses receives a second law, written on
another pair of tables.

Exod. xxxv–xl. Moses carries out the instructions received according to chs. xxv–xxxi.

Lev. A series of laws, mainly ritual, received by Moses
in the Tabernacle.

Num. i–iv. A census of Israel.

Num. v–vi. Further laws.

Num. vii. Dedication of the Tabernacle.

Num. viii–x. Some ritual ordinances.

Num. xi. The people murmur, and quails are sent.

Num. xii. Rebellion of Miriam and Aaron.

Num. xiii–xiv. Spies are sent into Canaan, and an
unsuccessful attempt is made to enter the land from the
south.

Num. xv–xix. Ritual regulations, including the story of the rebellion of Korah, Dathan and Abiram.

Num. xx. Incidents prior to the departure from Kadesh.

Num. xxi. 1–20. Incidents on the journey from Kadesh.

Num. xxi. 21–35. Defeat of Sihon.

Num. xxii–xxiv. The blessing of Balaam.

Num. xxv. Apostasy at Baal-peor.

Num. xxvi. A census.

Num. xxvii–xxxi. Sundry laws, mostly ritual.

Num. xxxii. Settlement of the eastern tribes.

Num. xxxiii. The itinerary of Israel.

Num. xxxiv–xxxvi. The apportionment of Canaan among the tribes, including the appointment of Levitical cities and cities of refuge.

Deut. i–iv. Moses, on the eve of his death and the entry of Israel into Canaan, recapitulates the history and exhorts Israel to fidelity.

Deut. v–xi. A second discourse of Moses, enjoining fidelity to Yahweh, and introducing the code.

Deut. xii–xxvi. A code of laws, mainly ethical.

Deut. xxvii. Arrangements for the solemn adoption of the Law in Canaan.

Deut. xxviii. Consequences of obedience and of disobedience.

Deut. xxix–xxx. Moses' third discourse.

Deut. xxxi. Moses' farewell.

Deut. xxxii. The Song of Moses.

Deut. xxxiii. The Blessing of Moses.

Deut. xxxiv. The death of Moses.

II. STRUCTURE

Even a glance over this rough outline indicates that there are two elements in the Pentateuch, a legal and a narrative, and that these have been interwoven. At once we note that *Deuteronomy* stands apart from the rest; the narrative portion is simply a recapitulation of what has been said before, and the legal section is also, in large measure, an expansion and a revision of material which is to be found in *Exodus*. The last chapter, however, with the account of Moses' death, does introduce a fresh element, and it is worth noting that it links itself naturally to the end of *Numbers*. This is clear if we read the last verse of *Numbers* and the first verse of Deut. xxxiv continuously:

" These are the commandments and the judgements which the Lord commanded by the hand of Moses unto the children of Israel in the plains of Moab by the Jordan at Jericho. And Moses went up from the plains of Moab unto mount Nebo, to the top of Pisgah, that is over against Jericho " (Num. xxxvi. 31; Deut. xxxiv. 1).

While, then, we may leave *Deuteronomy*, as a whole, for separate consideration, we should include its last chapter in any discussion of the rest of the Pentateuch.

Narrative and law are unevenly distributed throughout the Pentateuch. *Genesis* has little reference to law, introducing legal matters only to explain the origin of institutions such as the Sabbath and circumcision. *Leviticus*, on the other hand, is practically all law, with no narrative, and the two elements are combined in *Exodus* and *Numbers*. We can separate the two, and shall do best if we consider the narrative portions first.

i. *Narrative portions.* At the very start we are struck by the fact that we have two accounts of the Creation, the first ending with Gen. ii. 4, and the second continuing down to the end of ch. ii. Even to the superficial eye it is clear that these are difficult to harmonize. The first tells the story of the making of the world in six days, the general order being evolutionary and leading up to the creation of man, both sexes being made at the same time. At three points the word " create " is introduced, first in connexion with the appearance of chaotic matter, next when animal life arrives, and, lastly, when man is brought into existence. The implication is that each of these three events involves a new element, which cannot be accounted for on the basis of what has previously existed. In the second, the order is entirely different. Man is made first—there is no reference to the creation or preparation of the world of inanimate matter— and then vegetation is produced. Animals are next constructed, that the man may not be lonely, and, when these fail to satisfy him, woman is formed, but on a different method from that employed in making man and the animals.

But this superficial difference in presentation entirely fails to bring out the gulf that separates the two narratives when they are read in Hebrew. There are striking variations in the vocabulary, *e.g.* in ch. i the words used for creation are literally " create " and " make "; in ch. ii they are " model " and (used only of making the woman) " build."[1] Another obvious difference which may be mentioned here is the divine name. In Gen. i we have only " God "; in Gen. ii we have the compound phrase " Lord God," *i.e.* in Hebrew, *Yahweh Elohim,* where the second word (literally " God ") seems to be a sort of " determinative " attached to the name of the God of Israel.

These differences, however, are comparatively slight beside the contrast presented by the tone and outlook of the whole of the two passages. The second is the work of a story-teller, and is such as we should tell to children, simple, straightforward, naïve, and anthropomorphic. Yahweh is very powerful and very clever, but He can make a mistake, though, when He fails, He knows how to try another method, which succeeds. The first narrative, on the other hand, is dignified, stately, systematic, almost scientific. There is a whole area of culture lying between the two. Both express the same fundamental truth, that God made the world, but while the one presents it to an audience still in its intellectual and spiritual nursery, the other addresses an adult and " sophisticated " age. Finally, we may note that the first story of Creation leads up to the institution of the Sabbath, and this suggests an interest in, perhaps even an enthusiasm for, ritual and religious ceremonial.

We may next glance at a doublet of another type. In Gen. iv. 17–26 we have a genealogy, telling us of the descendants of Adam. In Gen. v we have another genealogy, which includes some names very like others found in ch. iv,

---

[1] For a list of terms peculiar to Gen. i and allied passages, see Driver, *An Introduction to the Literature of the Old Testament,* pp. 123–128 (1913); Skinner, *Genesis,* pp. lxiii ff. (1910).

and one or two which are identical. But, just as in the two
Creation stories, so here, we find differences in vocabulary,
still more in style and outlook. In ch. iv we have a " chatty "
account of the descendants of the first man, while in Gen. v
we have the whole fitted into a regular and formal scheme.
In other words, the second genealogy matches the first
Creation story, and the first genealogy the second Creation
story. And, as we read through the Pentateuch, we find
many another passage which presents us with the same
general characteristics as Gen. i and v. Their prevailing
interest in matters of law and ritual has led scholars to
describe them as *priestly*, and to indicate them by the letter P.

As we read further, other problems arise. In the story of
the Flood, for instance, we find at least one glaring self-
contradiction. In Gen. vi. 18–22 and in Gen. vii. 1–5 we
have accounts of the command which was given to Noah,
ending with his entry into the Ark. But in vi. 19 Noah is
bidden take one pair of *every* species, in order to preserve
them, while in vii. 2 f. he is ordered to take seven of each
" clean " species (*i.e.* of each species that may be eaten and
offered in sacrifice) and two of each " unclean " species.
Further, we have different estimates of the duration of the
Flood. The *data* supplied to us in vii. 11, 24; viii. 3–5, 13, 14,
give us a period of five months from the beginning of the
Flood before the water began to go down, nine months
before the tops of the mountains appeared, eleven months
before the ground was dry, and a total of just over twelve
months for the whole time Noah was shut in the Ark. On
the other hand, vii. 4, 12, viii. 6–12 suggest forty days' rain,
twenty-one days during which Noah made experiments with
birds as to whether the water was subsiding; and a further
seven days during which he still waited to make sure that
the ground was dry. This provides a total of sixty-eight
days. Finally, we may note that the means whereby the
Flood was produced differ. In Gen. vii. 4, 12 it is brought
about by exceptionally heavy rain, while in vii. 11 (cp. also
viii. 2) it is due to a collapse of the fabric of the universe,
which admits the waters of the great deep both from above
and from below. It is impossible to avoid the feeling that

two independent narratives have here been interwoven with one another. Actual experiment serves to confirm this impression, and the clues already given facilitate the analysis of the whole story of the Flood into two complete, distinct narratives.[1] These bear characteristics similar to those of the two stories of Creation, and the two genealogies already noticed. The narrative which speaks of *two* animals of *every* species is closely allied to Gen. i (we may note especially the use of the word " God " as the divine name, the fondness for actual figures, and the structure of the universe implied) and the genealogy in ch. v. The story which refers to *seven clean* animals, on the other hand, clearly comes from the same circles, possibly even from the same original document, as the second Creation story and the genealogy in Gen. iv. Again, we note especially the more *naïve* presentation of the record, and the use of the divine name Yahweh (" Lord "), though this time it lacks the determinative word " God." The last feature has led scholars to speak of this element in the Pentateuch as " Yahwistic," and to cite it under the letter J (Latin and German for Y).

These two elements, P and J, may be found, either singly or in combination, throughout the first four books of the Bible. It should, however, be noted that one of the distinctive marks of P in *Genesis* disappears soon after the beginning of *Exodus*. In Ex. vi. 2 ff. we have P's account of a revelation given to Moses. In verse 3 we read: " I appeared unto Abraham, unto Isaac, and unto Jacob, as God Almighty (R.V. margin ' El Shaddai '), but by my name Jehovah was I not known unto them." This explains the reason why P scrupulously avoids the use of the name Yahweh (= Jehovah, see p. 13) in the account of Creation and in the stories of the patriarchs. But now that the name has been revealed, it is no longer an anachronism to use it, and it becomes the normal, almost invariable, practice of P to use the name Yahweh in speaking of the God of Israel after this point. So, as between P and J, we have to depend on other features for the analysis of the two. Yet the style

[1] For the actual process, cp. *The People and the Book* (ed. Peake), pp. 164 f. (1925).

and outlook of P are so clearly marked that we seldom, if
ever, find serious disagreement among scholars as to the
identification and reconstruction of this document of the
Pentateuch.

This, however, does not exhaust the sources which the
compiler of the Pentateuch used in the construction of his
book.   An interesting and instructive passage is the story of
how Joseph was sold into Egypt, told in Gen. xxxvii.   In
verse 25 we hear of a caravan of Ishmaelites; in the second
part of verse 28 Joseph is sold to them, and in xxxix. 1 they
have brought him down to Egypt, and Potiphar buys him
from them.   But in the first part of verse 28 Midianites are
mentioned as having taken Joseph out of the pit in which his
brothers had left him on the instigation of Reuben (verse 22),
and in verse 36 it is they who take him down to Egypt and
sell him to Potiphar.   This is a direct contradiction and,
once more, is best explained on the theory that we have two
stories interwoven with one another.   The impression is
supported by the " doublets " which occur throughout the
whole.   There are two reasons given for the hatred felt by
the brothers—Joseph's own dreams and his father's favourit-
ism, manifested in the special coat he wore.   Two of the
brothers intervene to save his life, and by different methods
—Reuben suggests throwing him alive into a pit, and Judah
recommends that he be sold to the Ishmaelites.   Again, two
complete narratives can be disentangled.[1]   According to the
one, Joseph arouses the jealousy of his brothers and the anger
of his father by his dreams.   One day he is sent to them, and
they decide to kill him.   Reuben saves him by having him
dropped alive into a pit, where he is found, in the absence
of the brothers, by Midianites, who take him down to Egypt.
Reuben, unable to find him when he returns to release him,
is in despair, and Jacob mourns for his son.   In the other
story, Joseph is his father's favourite, and has a special coat
given to him, implying that he is to be free from the labours
which fall to the lot of his brothers.   One day, as he
approaches his brothers, they plot to kill him, but, after they
have taken his coat off, Judah persuades them to sell him to

[1] For details of the process see *The People and the Book*, pp. 155ff.

a passing caravan of Ishmaelites. The coat is dipped in goat's blood, and is taken back to the old father, who recognizes that Joseph has been devoured by a wild animal.

Though no divine name appears at all in this chapter, it is easy to see that there is no trace of P except in the two opening verses. The two stories very closely resemble one another in style, tone and outlook, and clearly belong to the same general stage of development. If differences are to be observed at all, they may be found in one or two minor points. What we may call the "Midianite" story is interested in Reuben, which suggests that its *provenance* was northern Israel, while the "Ishmaelite" story places Judah in the forefront, and, therefore, probably belongs to the south. A further characteristic feature of the "Midianite" story may be seen in its interest in dreams. The indications (especially the promises of Judah)[1] are just sufficient to enable us to associate the "Ishmaelite" story with the J element which we have already noted in the earlier chapters, while the other belongs to a different, though parallel, group of literary material.

For further investigation of the element to which the "Midianite" story of Gen. xxxvii belongs we may turn to other passages. In Gen. xii. 10–20 and xx we have two similar stories. They differ in many details, and the variations were clearly sufficient to prevent the idea that they describe the same events, and so they were not combined into a single whole, as were the two Flood narratives and the two accounts included in Gen. xxxvii. But they have the same *motif*, since both tell the reader how Abraham lied about his wife in order to avoid a possible danger to himself. We note at once a difference in the divine names; in Gen. xii we have "Yahweh," which we have noted as a sign of J, and in Gen. xx we have "God," which we have hitherto, in *Genesis*, accepted as an indication of P. But there is nothing else in Gen. xx which in the least suggests the style and outlook of P. On the contrary, but for the divine name and the presence

---

[1] Possibly also the name Israel may be added. After Gen. xxxii. 28 it seems to be used regularly by J, cp. ch. xliii. 1–12 and xlvi. 28–34; both are passages in which Judah is prominent.

of a parallel story in ch. xii, we should have been quite prepared to assign this passage to J. There is, however, one further point of distinction between the two stories. In ch. xii nothing is said as to the means whereby Pharaoh discovered who Sarah was. In ch. xx, on the other hand, the truth is revealed to Abimelech in a dream. We are at once reminded of one of the features of the " Midianite " story of Gen. xxxvii, and, in the absence of strong reasons to the contrary, we may attribute both these narratives to the same original group. From the fact that the divine name generally used is the Hebrew word *Elohim*, the term Elohistic is commonly applied to this element, and it is indicated by the letter E.

So far we have confined our attention to *Genesis*, partly because it stands first, and partly because the three elements (especially P) are fairly easy to distinguish. But the same phenomena of literary structure are to be observed also in *Exodus* and in *Numbers*. A good illustration is to be found in the story of the institution of the Passover. Exod. xii. 1–20, 24–28, 40–50, with their legal tone and their introduction of exact figures, are clearly P, while most of the remainder, with its comparatively naïve simplicity and its anthropomorphic presentation of God, suggests J. Even more striking is the combination of sources to be found in the account of the crossing of the Red Sea. Here two stories may fairly easily be disentangled. According to one of them, the passage is made possible by a natural withdrawal of the water (possibly owing to the tide—a phenomenon unfamiliar to the Israelites) and an unusually strong drying wind. The tide returns under the sand, clogs the wheels of the Egyptian chariots, and, eventually, drowns the pursuers before they can reach solid ground. This has all the marks of E, though there may be elements derived from J. In the other narrative the miraculous element is strongly brought out. The sea is actually divided, and stands up in watery cliffs on each side of the track along which the Israelites pass, falling back on the Egyptians as soon as the fugitives are safely across. This is due to P.

At the same time, it should be clearly stated that, while P

always stands out because of its peculiar style and interests, the disentanglement of J and E after the end of *Genesis* is often difficult and sometimes impossible. E still sometimes uses the divine name " God," but, after the revelation of Yahweh to Moses in Exod. iii. 1–15, that name often appears even in E. Other differences are to be noted, however, and these may serve as a guide where they appear. Amongst them we may especially mention the preference of E for the name " Amorite," as applied to the pre-Israelite inhabitants of Canaan, while J usually has " Canaanite," confining " Amorite " to peoples east of the Jordan. Still more striking is the fact that the sacred mountain, where Yahweh first appeared to Moses and where the Covenant was made, is called Horeb in E and Sinai in J and P. But, where such indications fail, though we may be conscious of a double narrative or of two parallel accounts, the differentiation is often quite uncertain.

ii. *Legal and Ritual portions.* We have already remarked [1] that P shows a deep interest in matters of law and of the cultus. We need to remember that civil and religious law, *us* and *fas*, were not distinguished in the mind of the ancient Israelite, and that a collection of laws, or " code," might include both types of regulations—indeed probably would do so. But the interest of the priestly writers was naturally focussed on matters of ritual, ceremonial cleanness, the priesthood and the like. These are not wholly absent from other elements in the Law, but they can hardly be expected to assume the same proportions as in P.

Beside P, whose characteristic style is stamped on most of the legislation in *Exodus*, and of the whole of that found in *Numbers* and *Leviticus* (with exceptions in this latter book to be noted later), we have three collections of laws in the Pentateuch, each of which was, we may assume, originally an independent code.[2] These three collections are to be found

---

[1] P. 27.
[2] At this point reference should be made to the work of Jirku, especially to his *Das weltliche Recht im Alten Testament* (1927). He redistributes the laws among a fresh series of codes from which, he believes, they have been taken to form the existing documents. His study of the subject contains valuable features, especially in his comparison of Israelite laws with those of other peoples of western Asia, but his conclusions would involve a wholly new

in: (a) Exod. xx–xxiii, (b) Exod. xxxiv. 17–28, (c) Deut. xii–xxvi. The last of these will be discussed later, when the whole of the book in which it appears is considered. The first opens with the Decalogue, followed by certain regulations for worship, and then proceeds to lay down laws for the conduct of Israelite society. Most of the laws contained in chs. xxi–xxiii are moral and social, but, especially in ch. xxiii, we find also a certain number of prescriptions dealing with worship—sacred dues, festivals and sacrifice. The little code in Exod. xxxiv is accompanied by a narrative explaining the circumstances in which Moses wrote it down at the dictation of Yahweh, together with an exhortation to root out utterly the pre-Israelite inhabitants of Palestine. It is worth noting that the prescriptions in the code itself are essentially matters of worship and ritual, and that they are all found also in Exod. xx–xxiii. Only in one instance is there a material variation: in the Decalogue *carved* images are forbidden (Exod. xx. 4–6), while in Exod. xxxiv. 17 it is *molten* figures that are prohibited. Clearly we have here a case of a doublet of the type which we have seen already in dealing with the narrative portions of the Pentateuch, and we may safely assume that the two codes belong to the two elements which we have already noted, J and E. A brief glance over the two makes it clear that, while the code in Exod. xx–xxiii has distinct affinities with the E narrative,[1] that of Exod. xxxiv is naturally connected with J, especially in the use of the name " Sinai " in the narrative framework. Here, again, we have a clear case of two parallel documents which, in this instance, seem to have been nearly identical.

---

analysis of most of the Pentateuch. His views rest on the assumption that in any one code all the laws must have been introduced by the same formula, and this appears too uncertain to justify a wholesale abandonment of conclusions which have proved themselves to be otherwise soundly based.

[1] It is enough to note here the use of the divine name " God," cp. xx. 20, 21; xxi. 6, 13; xxi. 8, 28; the interpretation "judges" suggested by the R.V. margin in some of these passages is not wholly probable. It is true that " Yahweh " occurs in this code, but, as we have seen (p. 32), this name is frequently used by E after Exod. iii, while neither of the other elements freely employs the word "God" without "Yahweh" in speaking of the God of Israel.

III. General Analysis

Detailed analysis of the whole of the Pentateuch is here, naturally, impossible. Differences in minor points are to be observed in the assignment of various parts of many passages, especially in *Exodus* and *Numbers*, but, on the whole, the following division may be accepted as a general approximation.[1]

J.	E.	P.
Genesis.		
ii. 4 b–iv. 26.		i. 1–ii. 4 a.
v. 29.		v. 1–28, 30–32.
vi. 1–8.		vi. 9–22.
vii. 1–5, 7, 10, 12, 16 b,		vii. 6, 8–9, 11, 13–16 a,
17 b, 22 a–23 a, viii.		17 a, 18–21, 23 b–24,
2 b–3 a, 6–12, 13 b,		viii. 1–2 a, 3 b–5,
20–22, ix. 18–27.		13 a, 14–19, ix. 1–17,
		28–29.

An analysis such as this looks complicated and arbitrary, but a careful reconstruction of the two narratives of the Flood, or the reading of such a translation as that found in the National Adult Schools Union's *Genesis in Colloquial English* will serve to show, by the completeness and the accuracy of the two narratives, how fully the process is justified.

J.	E.	P.
x. 8–19, 21, 25–30.		x. 1–7, 20, 22–24, 31–32
xi. 1–9, 28–30.		xi. 10–27, 31–32.
xii. 1–4 a, xii. 6–xiii. 5,		xii. 4 b–5, xiii. 6, 11 b,
7–11 a, 12 b–18.		12 a.

Ch. xiv presents problems all its own. In style and general character it is utterly unlike anything else in the Pentateuch, and is probably based on independent reminiscences, handed down through centuries, of events recorded, not in Palestine, but in Mesopotamia.

J.	E.	P.
xv. 1 bd, 2 a, 3 b–4, 6–	xv. 1 ac, 2 b–3 a, 5, 12 b–	
12 a, 17–21.	16.	

It may be remarked that verses 20, 21 are best regarded

[1] For discussions of individual points the reader is referred to any scholarly modern commentary on the separate books. *The Century Bible*, the *Camb. B.* (esp Driver's *Exodus*), and the *Westminster Commentaries* may be consulted, and still more important are the volumes on *Genesis* and *Numbers* in the *International Critical Commentary*.

as a later note appended by some scribe imbued with the style and language of *Deuteronomy*. See below, pp. 47 f.

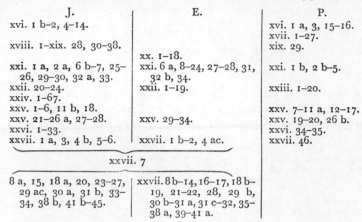

J.	E.	P.
xvi. 1 b–2, 4–14.		xvi. 1 a, 3, 15–16.
		xvii. 1–27.
xviii. 1–xix. 28, 30–38.		xix. 29.
	xx. 1–18.	
xxi. 1 a, 2 a, 6 b–7, 25–	xxi. 6 a, 8–24, 27–28, 31,	xxi. 1 b, 2 b–5.
26, 29–30, 32 a, 33.	32 b, 34.	
xxii. 20–24.	xxii. 1–19.	xxiii. 1–20.
xxiv. 1–67.		
xxv. 1–6, 11 b, 18.		xxv. 7–11 a, 12–17.
xxv. 21–26 a, 27–28.	xxv. 29–34.	xxv. 19–20, 26 b.
xxvi. 1–33.		xxvi. 34–35.
xxvii. 1 a, 3, 4 b, 5–6.	xxvii. 1 b–2, 4 ac.	xxvii. 46.

xxvii. 7

8 a, 15, 18 a, 20, 23–27,	xxvii. 8 b–14, 16–17, 18 b–
29 ac, 30 a, 31 b, 33–	19, 21–22, 28, 29 b,
34, 38 b, 41 b–45.	30 b–31 a, 31 c–32, 35–
	38 a, 39–41 a.

Here again we have a passage where the two narratives are very closely interwoven, especially in verse 7, though even here it is possible to apportion the words with some degree of certainty between them.

J.	E.	P.
xxviii. 10, 13–16, 19 (21 b).	xxviii. 11–12, 17–18, 20–21 a, 22.	xxviii. 1–9.
xxix. 2–14, 18–23, 25–28 a, 30–35.	xxix. 1, 15–17.	xxix. 24, 28 b–29.
xxx. 1 a, 3 b, 9–16, 20 b–21, 22 c–23 a, 24 b, 25, 27, 29–43.	xxx. 1 b–3 a, 4 b–8, 17–20 a, 22 b, 23 b–24 a, 26, 28.	xxx. 4 a, 22 a.
xxxi. 1, 3, 19 a, 21, 25 b, 27, 31 b, 36 a, 38–40, 44, 46, 48, 51–53 a.	xxxi. 2, 4–18 a, 19 b–20, 22–24, 25 a, 26, 28–30, 32–35, 36 b–37, 41–43, 45, 47, 49–50, 53 b–xxxii. 1.	xxxi. 18 b.
xxxii. 4–14, 23 a, 24 a, 25, 26 b, 28–29, 32–33.	xxxii. 2–3, 15–22, 23 b, 24 b, 26 a, 27, 30–31.	
xxxiii. 1–5 a, 6–10 a, 11 b–17.	xxxiii. 5 b, 10 b–11 a, 18 b–20.	xxxiii. 18 a.
xxxiv. 2 b–3 a, 5, 7, 11–13, 19, 25 b–26, 30–31.	xxxiv. 1–2 a, 3 b–4, 6, 8–10, 14–18, 20–25 a, 27–29.	
xxxv. 21–22.	xxxv. 1–5, 6 b–8 a, 14 ac, 16–20.	xxxv. 6 a, 8 b, 9–13, 14 bd, 15, 23–29.
xxxvi. 31–39.		xxxvi. 1–30, 40–xxxvii. 1.
xxxvii. 3–4 a, 12–13 a, 14 b–17, 18 b, 21, 23, 25 b–27, 28 b, 31, 32 a, 33 ac, 35.	xxxvii. 2 b, 4 b–11, 13 b–14 a, 18 a, 19–20, 22, 24, 25 a, 28 ac, 29–30, 32 b, 33 b, 34, 36.	xxxvii. 2 a.

J.	E.	P.
xxxviii. 1–30.		
xxxix. 1–25.		
xl. 1 b, 3 b, 5 b, 15 b.	xl. 1 a, 2–3 a, 4–5 a, 6–15 a.	
xli. 9 b, 14 b, 31, 34 a, 35 ac, 36 a, 41–42 a, 44–45, 48, 49 b, 53–54 a, 55, 56 b–57.	xli. 1–9 a, 10–14 a, 14 c–30, 32–33, 34 b, 35 b, 36 b–40, 42 b–43, 46b–47, 49 a, 50–52, 54 b, 56 a.	xli. 46 a.

In the earlier part of this chapter the J account is represented only by fragments. It was probably so similar to E that the compiler did not think it necessary to preserve both.

J.	E.	P.
xlii. 2, 4 b, 5, 7, 9 b–11 a, 12, 27–28 a, 38.	xlii. 1, 3–4 a, 6, 8–9 a, 11 b, 13–26, 28 b–37.	
xliii. 1–13, 15–23 a, 24–xliv. 34.	xliii. 14, 23 b.	
xlv. 1 a, 2 a, 4 b–5 a, 5 c, 7 b, 10 a, 13–14.	xlv. 1 b, 2 b–4 a, 5 bd, 6–7 a, 8–9, 10 b–12, 15–28.	
xlvi. 1 a, 28–34.	xlvi. 1 b–5.	xlvi. 6–27.
xlvii. 1–5 a, 6 b, 13–26, 29–31.	xlvii. 12.	xlvii. 5 b–6 a, 7–11, 27–28.
xlviii. 2 b, 9 b–10 a, 13, 14, 17–20 a, 20 c.	xlviii. 1–2 a, 8–9 a, 10 b–12, 15–16, 20 b, 21–22.	xlviii. 3–7.

Verse 7 may be an insertion dating from a later time, though derived from a comparatively early source. Its closest affinities, however, are with P.

J.	E.	P.
xlix. 1–27, 33 b.		xlix. 29–33 a, 33 c.

Verse 28 is a late note appended to the blessing of Jacob.

J.	E.	P.
l. 1–3 a, 4 b–10 a, 11, 14.	l. 3 b–4 a, 10 b, 15–26.	l. 12–13.
Exodus.		
i. 6, 8–12.	i. 15–22.	i. 1–5, 7, 13–14.
ii. 11–23 a.	ii. 1–10.	ii. 23 b–25.
iii. 2–4 a, 4 c–5, 7–8, 16–18.	iii. 1, 4 b, 6, 9–15, 19–22.	
iv. 1–16, 19–20 a, 21–26, 29–31.	iv. 17, 18, 20 b, 27–28.	

This passage, like many others in *Exodus* and *Numbers*, contains a certain amount of material which must have been introduced by the compilers. Such material is not especially indicated in this analysis, but is included in the passage concerned. Thus, an addition made to a section predominantly J is not separately specified, but is included in the same section as the basic sentences. For fuller discussion of the general question see below, p. 48.

J.	E.	P.
v. 3, 5–vi. 1.	v. 1–2, 4.	vi. 2–vii. 7.
vii. 14, 16–17 a, 18, 21 a, 24–25.	vii. 15, 17 b, 20 b, 23.	vii. 8–13, 19–20 a, 21 b–22.
viii. 1–4, 8–15 a, 20–32.		viii. 5–7, 15 b–19.
ix. 1–7, 13–21, 23 b, 24 b, 25 b–34.	ix. 22–23 a, 24 a, 25 a, 35.	ix. 8–12.
x. 1–11, 13 b, 14 b–15 a, 15 c–19, 24–26, 28–29.	x. 12–13 a, 14 a, 15 b, 20–23, 27.	
xi. 4–8.	xi. 1–3.	xi. 9–10.
xii. 21–27, 29–34, 37 a, 38–39, 42 a.	xii. 35–36.	xii. 1–20, 28, 37 b, 40–41, 42 b–xiii. 2.

The *provenance* of verses 21–24 is uncertain, and some editors would regard them as a redactional addition. Verses 25–27 are clearly such as addition; their tone and style strongly recall those of *Deuteronomy*.

J.	E.	P.
xiii. 3–16, 21–22.	xiii. 17–19.	xiii. 20.
xiv. 5 b–6, 7 b, 10 a, 11–14, 19 b, 20 b, 21 b, 24, 25 b, 27 b, 28 b, 30–31.	xiv. 3, 5 a, 7 a, 15 b, 16 a, 19 a, 20 a, 25 a.	xiv. 1–2, 4, 8–9, 10 b, 15 ac, 16 b–18, 21 ac, 22–23, 26–27 a, 28 a, 29.
xv. 1–2, 22–25 a, 26–27.	xv. 3–21, 25 b.	

The " Song " is possibly later than any of the main documents, and may have been inserted by a comparatively late editor.

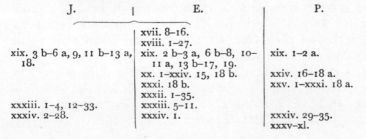

J.	E.	P.
	xvi. 4.	xvi. 1–3, 5–36.
		xvii. 1 a.
xvii. 1 b–7.		

The presence of the two elements is clear, but their assignment is very uncertain.

J.	E.	P.
	xvii. 8–16.	
	xviii. 1–27.	
xix. 3 b–6 a, 9, 11 b–13 a, 18.	xix. 2 b–3 a, 6 b–8, 10–11 a, 13 b–17, 19.	xix. 1–2 a.
	xx. 1–xxiv. 15, 18 b.	xxiv. 16–18 a.
	xxxi. 18 b.	xxv. 1–xxxi. 18 a.
	xxxii. 1–35.	
xxxiii. 1–4, 12–33.	xxxiii. 5–11.	
xxxiv. 2–28.	xxxiv. 1.	xxxiv. 29–35.
		xxxv–xl.

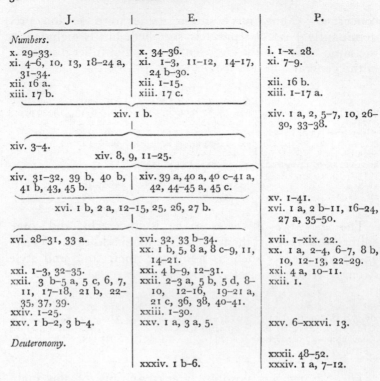

J.	E.	P.
Numbers.		
x. 29–33.	x. 34–36.	i. 1–x. 28.
xi. 4–6, 10, 13, 18–24 a, 31–34.	xi. 1–3, 11–12, 14–17, 24 b–30.	xi. 7–9.
xii. 16 a.	xii. 1–15.	xii. 16 b.
xiii. 17 b.	xiii. 17 c.	xiii. 1–17 a.
xiv. 1 b.		xiv. 1 a, 2, 5–7, 10, 26–30, 33–38.
xiv. 3–4.		
xiv. 8, 9, 11–25.		
xiv. 31–32, 39 b, 40 b, 41 b, 43, 45 b.	xiv. 39 a, 40 a, 40 c–41 a, 42, 44–45 a, 45 c.	
		xv. 1–41.
xvi. 1 b, 2 a, 12–15, 25, 26, 27 b.		xvi. 1 a, 2 b–11, 16–24, 27 a, 35–50.
xvi. 28–31, 33 a.	xvi. 32, 33 b–34.	xvii. 1–xix. 22.
	xx. 1 b, 5, 8 a, 8 c–9, 11, 14–21.	xx. 1 a, 2–4, 6–7, 8 b, 10, 12–13, 22–29.
xxi. 1–3, 32–35.	xxi. 4 b–9, 12–31.	xxi. 4 a, 10–11.
xxii. 3 b–5 a, 5 c, 6, 7, 11, 17–18, 21 b, 22– 35, 37, 39.	xxii. 2–3 a, 5 b, 5 d, 8– 10, 12–16, 19–21 a, 21 c, 36, 38, 40–41.	xxii. 1.
xxiv. 1–25.	xxiii. 1–30.	
xxv. 1 b–2, 3 b–4.	xxv. 1 a, 3 a, 5.	xxv. 6–xxxvi. 13.
Deuteronomy.		
		xxxii. 48–52.
	xxxiv. 1 b–6.	xxxiv. 1 a, 7–12.

It remains to add only that we may for the present regard the whole of *Leviticus* as coming under the general head of P.

IV. Further Analysis of Sources

Our next step must be to inquire whether we can go farther in the analysis of the three main *strata* which have been already indicated. In other words, can we assume that there ever were such documents as J, E, and P, and, if there were, is it possible that they themselves were composite before they reached the compilers who united the three into a single whole?

If we read through each of the three groups separately, the first impression made upon us, especially in *Genesis*, is that we have a number of more or less isolated stories which have been put together by a compiler. Many, if

not all, of the sections are apparently self-contained, and
can be read without reference to what precedes and what
follows. There is, admittedly, a certain unity of subject,
and there is a background with which the original reader
may be expected to be familiar. But, to take a single
example, the narratives assigned to the J and E sections of
Exodus and *Numbers* are in no sense a history of Israel during
the wilderness period, and there is no certainty that the
events between the great Covenant and the arrival in
Moabite territory (there are very few of them) are placed
even in chronological order. Such narratives as appear in
P are obviously designed to serve as a framework for the
legal (including the ritual) sections, and, as such, have a
greater appearance of unity, even on the surface. Yet
here also it might conceivably be maintained that the
narratives come from a circle of story-tellers and not from
a document in the strict sense of the term.

More detailed examination, however, shows that the connexion between the various stories is often too close to be the
result of casual synthesis.[1] The P narratives in *Genesis*, for
instance, are linked together in a way which cannot be explained simply by a theory of editorial redaction. The
final compiler would not have taken the trouble so to
modify the P story of Creation as to make it anticipate that
of the Flood, nor would he have edited the P Flood story
in such a way as to make it follow on the story of Creation.
The E narratives in *Genesis* are, perhaps, less closely connected than those of either of the other *strata*, yet a common
thread and purpose can be traced through many of them.
E in *Exodus* and *Numbers*, on the other hand, does present
us with something like a continuous history, at least up to
the Covenant and after the removal from Moabite territory. And we may make the same remark of J, though
there appear to have been several stages in the growth of
this document before it reached the form in which it was
combined with E.

The last remark introduces our second question: are the

[1] Cp. especially, Eissfeldt, " The Smallest Literary Unit in the Narrative
Books of the Old Testament," in *Old Testament Essays,* publ. Griffin (1927).

three primary documents themselves compilations from
earlier works? It may be said at once that there are
occasionally indications in the narratives which suggest
that the answer should be in the affirmative. Once or
twice, even within the limits of J and E respectively, we
find traces of doublets. We have, for instance, two presentations of Noah. In Gen. vi. 9–ix. 19 he is the hero of the
Flood, while in ix. 20–27 he is the first grower of the vine.
The two presentations are not incompatible, but they
suggest a different origin. In Gen. xii. 9–20 and xxvi.
1–10 we hear of a patriarch lying in regard to his wife for
his safety's sake. Now it is quite possible that the two
should have had the same origin, but, in view of other
facts, the natural supposition is that the studies are drawn
from different sources, and that that in which Isaac appears
is due to a later edition—we can go no further than that—
of the original collection.

It is usual, then, to recognize that in J we have a comparatively short early collection, which was gradually enlarged by the addition of fresh material, drawn from the
same general cycle of narratives, but finding its place in the
final collection at different times. The limits of the original
" book " are somewhat variously defined by different
scholars.[1]

Similar phenomena, though they are less obvious, have
been detected in E. But when we turn to P, we find, more
than anywhere else, clear and distinct evidence of compilation from earlier sources. The first, and most obvious
early element (and it should never be forgotten that all
scholars have recognized that there are very early elements
in P, whatever may be the date of its final form) is a collection of laws, mainly dealing with ceremonial purity, now
found in Lev. xvii–xxvi. The introduction: " This is the
thing which the Lord hath commanded " (xvii. 2) and the
conclusion: " These are the statutes and judgements, and

---

[1] Eissfeldt (*Hexateuchsynopse* [1922] has gone so far as to make a clear distinction between this older compilation, which he calls " L "—a Lay document,
and the later elements, to which he would confine the symbol J. Morgenstern
(see *The Oldest Document of the Hexateuch* [1927]) has isolated a primitive document
which he calls K, and which, he believes, has been subjected to repeated revision.
Most scholars, however, are content to use " J¹," " J²," etc.

laws, which the Lord made between him and the children of Israel in mount Sinai by the hand of Moses " (xxvi. 46), suggest that we have here a complete and independent code. The impression is borne out by two other considerations. In the first place, we find here a number of laws which are repeated elsewhere, though usually with slight differences. Thus we have injunctions as to the observance of the Sabbath (xix. 3, 30). Molten images are forbidden (xix. 4). A fallow year is to be observed (xxv. 2–7), though the regulations do not at all agree with those given in *Exodus*. The *Lex talionis* is repeated, almost in the same words as in Exod. xxi. 23–25. All this, and much more, suggests an independent code. Still more striking is the general tone, which resembles *Deuteronomy* (from which, however, the code is widely removed in point of style) in its humanitarianism and its exclusiveness. In substance it shows striking similarities with *Ezekiel*, especially with chs. xl ff. The greater part is devoted to laws of ceremonial cleanliness, with special reference to the priesthood, and the thought is constantly repeated that, since Yahweh is holy, His people must be holy also. It is from this latter feature that the code derives its modern name of the " Law (or Code) of Holiness," and its common designation by the letter H. We may add that, in the opinion of some scholars, even H, in its present form, has been produced by the expansion of an original nucleus.

Similar phenomena, though less clearly marked, suggest that there are other elements to be found within the limits of P, even after H has been isolated. It is possible to trace a regular continuity throughout the whole of the Pentateuch, and to observe the sections which do not fit in with it, except on the assumption that they are later insertions, due to a series of revisions. Beginning with the story of Creation, this groundwork of P proceeds, by means of genealogies, to link the beginning of the world with the birth of Moses, pausing only to describe at some length the Flood, and Abraham's purchase of the field of Machpelah. The real interest of the narrative begins with the revelation to Moses, and this is followed by the deliverance

from Egypt (P mentions five plagues only, three of which
are identical with plagues named in J, and the other two
appear to be alternative forms of two others found in the
older source), including fairly full prescriptions for the
observance of the Passover. The miraculous crossing of
the Red Sea is then described, and, after an account of the
sending of the Manna, the people are brought to Sinai.
Moses ascends into the mountain, and receives instructions
as to the making of the Ark, the building of the Tabernacle,
and the consecration of Aaron and his family. These
instructions are carried out.

The Law is then given from the Tabernacle, dealing first
with various types of offerings and sacrifices, then passing
on to forms of " uncleanness," *i.e.* that which places people
temporarily or permanently outside the religious community of Israel. This section of the Law concludes with
the ritual of the Day of Atonement. At this point the
priestly writers embodied H, adding notes from time to
time. Once or twice new laws are inserted; *e.g.* in Lev.
xxv P appends the law of Jubilee to the H law of the sab-
batical year. Laws concerning vows follow, and a fairly
long section is devoted to the priesthood. Arrangements
are made for the orderly grouping of the tribes about the
Tabernacle, and sundry ritual laws are added, possibly
belonging to a later *stratum*, though some of the ritual
involved is probably very ancient.

Then Israel moves from Sinai, and marches straight to
the Wilderness of Paran. Thence spies are sent, including
Joshua, who traverse the whole length of Palestine, finally
bringing back the report that the land is not good. The
people refuse to attempt an entry, the spies (except Caleb
and Joshua) fall by disease, and the people are condemned
to wander for forty years in the wilderness.

The remainder of P in *Numbers* contains laws of various
kinds, mostly ritual. Not infrequently incidents are described which serve to reinforce or to illustrate the priestly
law in general. Thus, the rebellion of Korah established
the Aaronic priesthood, and the case of the daughters of
Zelophehad introduces the law of female inheritance in the

absence of male heirs.[1] The account of the settlement of
the Transjordanic tribes is based on JE, but it has been
revised by a priestly hand, and P probably contained some
mention of the affair. Itineraries and a census are included, and with the appointment of Cities of Refuge on
the east of Jordan, Israel is brought to the point at which
she is about to enter the promised land.

To the later elements belongs a large number of small
notes and expansions, which, by some peculiarity in form,
or by some unsuitability to their present context, betray a
later origin. A good example occurs in Exod. xxix. 38–42,
where rules for the daily offering, repeated in Num. xxviii.
3–8, interrupt the instructions for the consecration of the
altar. Again, at the beginning of ch. xxx the construction
of the golden altar of incense is commanded. Elsewhere P
speaks as if there were only one altar, *i.e.* the great altar of
burnt-offering. Since, however, the whole represents much
the same point of view, the distinction between the various
strata of P is not of great importance for the student of
Israel's religious history, and if it be desired to enter into
details, they can readily be obtained from any good modern
commentary.

V. DEUTERONOMY

We now reach the last of the five books of the Law.
Deuteronomy covers a brief period at the end of the life of
Moses, and, in its present form, contains simply his final
charge to the people. But it stands markedly apart from
all the rest of the Pentateuch, both in style and in outlook.
Its kernel is a code (chs. xii–xxvi, xxviii), to which is prefixed a hortatory introduction in chs. i–xi. The code itself
resembles that of E (Exod. xxi–xxiii), and nearly every law
in the shorter document is reproduced in the longer, though
often in a considerably modified form.[2] There is also a

---

[1] Two other narratives of this type, the story of the man who gathered
sticks on the Sabbath and the account of the annihilation of Midian, probably
belong to a later stage in the development of the document.
[2] For a complete list of parallels between Deut. on the one hand, and JE
and P (including H) on the other, see Driver, *Deuteronomy*, pp. iv–vii (1902).

number of laws in *Deuteronomy* which find no place in the Book of the Covenant (Exod. xx–xxiii).[1]

A comparison of the two codes, E and D, makes clear one striking fact: when the same law appears in both, if there be a difference in the form, it will be found that the law of D is the milder, and carries with it a distinctly humanitarian tone. One illustration will suffice. In Exod. xxi. 2–11 and Deut. xv. 12–18 we have the law of limited slavery. In both codes the period is defined as six years. But in E it is expressly stated that the slave is to go free exactly as he entered bondage. If he has married and has begotten children, he must leave them behind, or, as an alternative, submit to the ceremony which transforms him into a permanent slave. In D nothing is said about the slave's wife or children, but his master is enjoined to give him such presents as will enable him to make a fresh start in life. Permanent slavery is still contemplated, but the motive is assumed to be love for the master himself. There is no direct contradiction here, but E, when dealing with a female slave, expressly states that she is not liable to be liberated; she is a permanent slave in any case, and the best that the legislator can do is to secure her rights if her master marries her to himself or to his son. In D, on the other hand, it is expressly stated that she stands on the same footing as the male slave. We receive the same impression of sympathy for the poor and oppressed in other instances.

The laws found in D, but not in E, are equally instructive. Some of them are ritual and ceremonial; many of these were probably intended to be condemnation of Gentile practices. Such are the prohibition of disfigurement in mourning (Deut. xiv. 1–2), of interchange of garments between the sexes (xxii. 5), and of *Asherahs* and *Maṣṣebahs*. But we have others which, again, suggest a high degree of sensitiveness to human feeling. One of the best illustrations is the law in Deut. xxiv. 16, which ordains that the family of a criminal is not to suffer with him. A like

[1] There are occasional parallels with the J code in Exod. xxxiv, but these may be neglected, since, in every instance, the law is also found in the E code.

sympathy is extended to animals; a mother-bird is not to be taken with her eggs (xxii. 6–7), the ox is not to be muzzled as he treads out the corn (xxv. 4). The most striking difference, however, concerns a matter of ritual. E evidently contemplates the possibility that there will be a number of altars on which sacrifice may be offered to Yahweh; D (Deut. xii. 1–16) insists that there can be but one.[1]

The earlier chapters of *Deuteronomy* form an exhortation, or rather a series of exhortations. They are written in a highly characteristic style with long and (for Hebrew) rather complex sentences. Again and again the text insists on right relations between Yahweh and His people, or rather on the maintenance by Israel of a right attitude towards her God. The first address of Moses occupies chs. i. 1–iv. 43. This opens with an historical introduction, in which Moses summarizes the history of the people from the giving of the Law down to the time at which he was speaking. It is a noticeable fact that this section includes nothing that is not also found in E, and may be regarded as a compendium of the history as contained in that element in the Pentateuch. Again, we note that there is little or nothing which *must* have come from J; in particular, the name of the mountain of the Law is in D invariably Horeb, as in E, and not Sinai, as in J (and P). The conclusion is almost irresistible, that the compiler of *Deuteronomy*, even in its present form, had E before him, but no other of our Pentateuchal sources.

It is generally agreed that *Deuteronomy* is not homogeneous, but has, in its present form, undergone revision from its primitive shape. What that shape was we do not know for certain, but there is little, if anything, in the code itself which suggests later addition; the principal question is as to the introductory and concluding chapters. It is generally agreed that the first exhortation, i. 1–iv. 43, was no part of the book in its original form, but opinions differ as to whether the same remark should be made of the second exhortation, iv. 44–xi. On the whole, the prob-

---

[1] As Driver has said, " Deut. xii–xxvi is an enlarged edition of the ' Book of the Covenant ' " (*op. cit.*, p. x).

ability seems to lie on the side of that view which holds that, when the Deuteronomic code was made available in its present form for general use, it was already provided with this introductory homily.[1]

Ch. xxvii bears all the marks of a later insertion. Moses is no longer the speaker, and there are internal difficulties which suggest the expansion of an original Deuteronomic nucleus, which has been transferred to this point from some other position. In chs. xxix, xxx we have another, or third, address by Moses, which, had it been original, might well have been included in the second, and is, therefore, commonly regarded as secondary. Ch. xxxi seems to contain the conclusion of the original code in verses 9–13, but the remainder is apparently derived from JE. Chs. xxxii, xxxiii consist of two poems attributed to Moses; the intervening passage, xxxii. 48–52 belongs to P. Neither of the poems has any essential connexion with the rest of *Deuteronomy*. And, finally, ch. xxxiv, describing the death of Moses, is apparently derived from the other three main elements in the Pentateuch, J, E, and P.[2]

Thus it is clear that *Deuteronomy*, like other elements in the Pentateuch, is, in its present form, the result of a process of growth. We can recognize an original document with greater clearness here than elsewhere, possibly, but it remains true that this book has undergone a process of revision. Comparatively little change seems to have been made in the main body of the work, but it has been expanded by additions both at the beginning and at the end. Some, at least, of the extra matter, is due to revisers who were imbued with the spirit and adopted the style of the main document. Finally, the incorporation of the whole into the great body of the Pentateuch led to the insertion of occasional phrases and sentences characteristic of the priestly school, and to the inclusion of a very small amount of narrative derived from the older documents J and E.

---

[1] Attempts have been made from time to time to analyse D on the basis of the pronouns used. Israel is sometimes addressed in the singular and sometimes in the plural. But the text changes so rapidly from one to the other that a satisfactory analysis on this basis is nearly impossible.

[2] See above, pp. 25, 38.

VI. The Compilation of the Pentateuch

Up to this point we have been primarily concerned with the main sources from which our present Pentateuch was ultimately derived. We have inevitably assumed an editorial process; we should now do well to sketch it briefly in detail.

We may start with the earliest form of the narrative material. This would, in the nature of the case, consist of stories told in various parts of the country—round the shepherds' fires at night, at the city gates, and, above all, at the various sanctuaries, where the priests would instruct the worshippers in the traditions of the shrine at which they offered their gifts. In course of time these would be collected, and continuous histories would be formed. Two such histories, both comparatively ancient, have come down to us; they are those indicated by the symbols J and E. In one or two other instances it seems that narratives now incorporated in the Pentateuch maintained an independent existence through the centuries till they were incorporated in the text as we now have it. A good illustration is to be found in Gen. xiv; while some scholars hold that the account of the sack of Shechem (Gen. xxxiv) contains a narrative derived, not from E, but from some source not otherwise represented in the Pentateuch, in addition to the J element, whose presence is generally admitted.

The next stage that we note is the combination of J and E, which are sometimes so closely interwoven as to defy accurate and certain disentanglement. E, however, was used as the basis for another document containing a summary of the historical element (from the giving of the Law onwards) and an expansion of the legal. This we know as *Deuteronomy* (D), and the evidence shows that it, like other parts of the Pentateuch, underwent a certain amount of revision. This document was the product of a school of thinkers and writers who did not confine their attention merely to the book of *Deuteronomy*, but also studied and revised a great deal of the older material. We find not infrequently in *Exodus* and *Numbers* (though not in *Genesis*), passages which can be explained best as due to a revision by this school.[1]

Our next " source " is a collection of laws, mainly ritual and ceremonial, to which the name " Law of Holiness " has been given. This is at present incorporated in P, apparently by the earlier compilers of that work. The Priestly document seems to have had an independent existence, but was used as a framework by the final compilers of the Pentateuch, who, imbued with its attitude, and writing in its style, took the existing works and bound them together into a single whole. It goes without saying that at each stage of development a certain modicum of editorial matter was introduced, partly to smooth over awkward joints and partly to produce a certain harmony of the whole. This latter end, however, has been very imperfectly attained, and it still remains possible to separate, in the main, the earlier documents of which the whole has been composed.

VII. CHARACTERISTIC FEATURES OF THE DOCUMENTS

Before proceeding to discuss the dating, it will be convenient briefly to glance at the characteristic features of each of these documents. J and E we can treat together. Both are written in the best style of the golden age of Hebrew prose. If there is a difference to be observed, it is to be found in the lighter and more delicate touch of J in narrative. He [2] has the gift of bringing a whole scene vividly before his readers with a few clear words, and it is in no small part due to his genius that the stories of the Pentateuch are among the best known in the world.

The principal theological distinction between the two

[1] Examples may be seen in such passages as Exod. xii. 25–27 and xiii. 8–9, where the stress is laid on the constant remembrance of the deliverance from Egypt, the expansion of the law prohibiting the graven image in Exod. xx. 4–6, where the language recalls Deut. vii. 9, and the reference to Og in Num. xxi. 33–35. The activities of this school do not end with the Pentateuch, and they are far more in evidence in *Joshua* and *Judges*. As we shall see later, we may even ascribe to it the present form of the books of *Kings*.

[2] It is, of course, admitted that J, as it now appears in the prose narratives of the Old Testament, is the work of a " school " rather than of an " author," but the present writer feels that the original nucleus around which the whole has grown was probably the work of a single hand. Cp. pp. 39 f.

documents has already been noticed. For the rest, they have much in common. Both strongly represent the outlook of that element in Israel's religious life which we may call the prophetic, though, when we use this term, we must think of Elijah and not of the canonical prophets. Both recognize only one God for Israel though neither in the least suggests a true monotheism. J carries back the worship of Yahweh by Israel's ancestors to a very early period, while E makes it originate with the revelation to Moses. The mythology of J (E has no mythological stories) at times suggests an ultimate polytheistic basis, but that has been largely eliminated. Both are interested in matters of worship, and record frequently the foundation of shrines by the patriarchs. The scanty fragment of law which appears in J is almost confined to matters of ritual, and the E code opens with regulations for the altar, besides including the provisions also found in J. In both the ethical element is clear and strong; though some acts which a more developed conscience would condemn pass without comment, yet the general stress is laid upon righteousness and fair dealing as between man and man.

The connexion between J and the south, and between E and the north, has already been mentioned.[1] J is interested in the southern sanctuaries, especially in Hebron, while E has a wider range of reference. The names which E brings into prominence are those which are connected with the north—Reuben, Joshua, etc., while in the J narratives it is Judah and the southern heroes (*e.g.* Caleb) who stand out. E is familiar with Egyptian matters, though apparently with the Egypt, not of the XVIIIth and XIXth dynasties,[2] but of a rather later period.

We have already touched on some of the characteristics of H, its hortatory passages, in which we have the beginnings of Hebrew rhetorical prose, its stress on Yahweh's holiness and on His demand for holiness in His people. We have also noted the close resemblances between H and *Ezekiel*, on which it will suffice to quote Driver: " Both breathe the same spirit; both are actuated by the same

[1] See p. 30.   [2] *I.e.* roughly between 1600 and 1200 B.C.

E

principles, and aim at realizing the same ends. Thus both
evince a special regard for the ' sanctuary ' . . . and pre-
scribe rules to guard it against profanation; both allude
similarly to Israel's idolatry in *Egypt* . . . and to the
' abominations ' of which Israel has since been guilty; both
emphasize the duty of observing the Sabbath; both attach
a high value to ceremonial cleanness, especially on the part
of the priests; both lay stress on abstaining from blood,
and from food improperly killed . . . and both further
insist on the same moral virtues, as reverence to parents,
just judgement, commercial honesty, and denounce usury
and slander. . . ." [1] In other words, in spite of differences which prohibit identity of authorship,[2] both emanate
from the same circle, *i.e.* the pre-exilic Jerusalem priesthood. H, in the form in which it came into the hands of
the priestly compiler, was clearly a manual of *toroth*, or
directions as to the religious life and practice of Jerusalem.

If H belongs to the south, D equally clearly has affinities
with the literature of the north. Its doctrine of a single
altar *may* (though this is by no means necessary) have been
originally formed in the interests of a northern sanctuary—
perhaps Bethel—for no particular place is specified. It is
certainly dependent on E rather than on J, and the hortatory
style and rhetorical prose (even more strongly marked than
in H) suggest the same period as H and the same general
stage of development. As we have seen, it is in a real
sense a revision and an expansion of the legal portion of E,
and, we may almost say, it bears roughly the same relation
to H that E does to J. It is marked throughout by an
intense fervour for Yahweh. This is not so much, as in H,
a demand for ceremonial purity and external consecration,
as an insistence on a higher moral union between God and
people. To this end must all else be subordinated. The
great deliverance, in which Yahweh first showed His choice
of, and His love for, Israel, must never be forgotten—hence
the stress on the Passover. All Canaanites ought to have
been destroyed on the entrance of Israel into the promised

---

[1] *Intr.* pp. 140 f.; cp. also the list of words and phrases on p. 140.
[2] Cp. Driver, *Intr.*, p. 141.

land, and all traces of their cults eradicated (here, especially in the condemnation of *Maṣṣebahs*, D differs from E, cp. Deut. vii. 5, xii. 3, etc.), lest Israel should be led into apostasy by them. Above all, the supreme motive from which service should be rendered to Yahweh is that of love.

We turn now to P. The literary characteristics of this element of the Pentateuch have already been noticed, especially the rather stilted, yet dignified, style, the orderly arrangement, the fondness for exact details in numbers and in dates, the careful genealogies, and the interest in all things concerned with ritual. In P, as we now have it, whatever views may have been originally suggested by earlier material incorporated in it, the theology is definitely monotheistic; nowhere is the reality of any god but Yahweh suggested. It may be possible to discover traces of anthropomorphism, but these have been for the most part eliminated. God speaks, that is all; there is little indication of the means whereby His utterance is audible, and no human form is attributed to Him. Even direct communication in this way ceases with the revelation to Moses; after his death the will of God may be ascertained through the priestly manipulation of the sacred lot, or by some similar means. The single altar is assumed, and the priesthood is strictly limited, not, as in *Ezekiel*, to the family of Zadok, but to that of Aaron, suggesting a compromise between the rigour of the pre-exilic law of Jerusalem and the wider basis on which the prescriptions of D are founded.

VIII. DATES OF THE PENTATEUCH

We must now proceed to the very difficult task of attempting to determine the dates to which we should assign the construction and combination of the documents we have discussed. Our study necessarily falls into two parts, the *comparative* dating and the *absolute* dating. The former, which consists in determining the order of the documents, is comparatively easy; the latter, which involves assigning each to a definite period, is precarious and often uncertain.

i. *Comparative Dating : chronological order of the Documents.*

For the comparative dating of the documents we may take *Deuteronomy* as a starting-point, since it is obviously related to all the rest. The general conclusion accepted by practically all modern students may be summed up in Driver's words : " It " (*i.e. Deuteronomy*) " is an *expansion* of the laws in JE (Exod. xx. 22–xxiii. 33, xxxiv. 10–26, xiii. 3–16) ; it is, in several features, *parallel* to the Law of Holiness; it contains *allusions* to laws—not, indeed, always the same as, but similar to the ceremonial institutions and observances codified in the rest of P." [1] While this represents the general judgement, it needs a certain amount of elucidation, perhaps modification.

In the first place, it is difficult to find any clear proof of D's dependence on J. The use of E is obvious, and there can be little doubt but that both the historical and the legal portions of that document were in the hands of the Deuteronomists. But, though there are references to laws which occur in J, it will be found on examination that, in every case, the law appears also in E. A similar statement may be made as to the historical references in D,[2] though we cannot speak here with the same absolute confidence. But it is clear that J and E belong to the same general age of Israelite history, and we cannot assume that D came in between them. On the other hand, the combination JE may well have been produced not earlier than the construction of D.

The relation between D and H is somewhat obscure. The matter is complicated by the close parallels between H and *Ezekiel*, which have led some writers to suppose that the prophet is the earlier. But opinion is crystallizing into the view that the dependence lies on the side of *Ezekiel*—

---

[1] *Deuteronomy*, p. xiv.

[2] There are three instances in which D has a reference to which the only parallel in our present texts is in J. The first is the mention of the " ten commandments," Exod. xxxiv. 28, and the second is the allusion to Kibroth-hattaavah, Num. xi. 34, the third is the overthrow of Sodom and Gomorrah. In the first case, however, the phrase looks like a later insertion in the text of *Exodus*—it is in any case parenthetic—and the second may well have been a tradition which was found in both documents, and taken by the compiler of J and E only from the former. This must have happened many times; practically nothing remains of E's story of the crossing of the Red Sea, but it is incredible that it should have been omitted from the original narrative. The reference to Sodom is in Deut. xxix. 22 (23), which belongs to a later *stratum*.

or rather on the side of the author of Ezek. xl–xlviii. But was H earlier than D? The only point on which clear comparison can be made is to be found in the regulations for worship. The outstanding peculiarity of D is its central-ization of worship in a single spot, and its prohibition of sacrifice at any but the one altar. Of this there is no clear evidence in H, and if H were an actual contemporary of, or only a little later than D, we should expect such evidence.[1] A really significant contrast, however, may be seen in the law which deals with the slaughter of domestic animals. In Deut. xii. 15 this is expressly permitted as a secular act —clearly an accommodation to the law of the single altar. But in Lev. xvii. 3 ff. such an act is regarded as equivalent to murder, unless performed under sacred auspices. In other words, we have here a statement—and the only explicit statement—of the ancient practice abrogated by *Deuteronomy*. We can hardly believe that the passage in H could have been formulated after the appearance of *Deuteronomy*, and, especially if, as some scholars hold, ch. xvii belongs to a somewhat late stage in the development of H, we have here very strong grounds for presuming a comparatively early date for its original nucleus. In many ways the two docu-ments resemble one another, both in form and in religious emphasis, and we are led to suspect that, while the Deu-teronomists relied for their material to a large extent on E, they represent the same stage of general religious and literary development as does the school in which H took its shape.

When we turn to P, it is at once obvious that even the groundwork of this document should be placed later than J and E. It is necessary only to compare the two stories of Creation to assure ourselves of the wide distance which separates the two. The probability is that centuries of

---

[1] Even in Lev. xxvi. 31 the destruction of the sanctuaries is threatened only as a punishment, and it does not follow that they were in themselves a reason for the punishment. The whole of ch. xxvi—at least in substance— might have come from Amos. Again, in Lev. xvii. 4 and elsewhere we have references to the " tent of meeting " or the " sanctuary." But the Hebrew phrase does not, in any case, imply that the sanctuary in question is the only one, and it may fairly be conjectured that the term " tent of meeting," at any rate, is due to the compilers who inserted H in P. On the whole subject see especially G. B. Gray in the *Encycl. Bibl.*, Art. " Law Literature," esp. cols. 2738 f., and G. F. Moore, *ib.*, Art. " Leviticus," esp. cols. 2782–2792.

intellectual and theological growth lie between them, though the old story on which the P narrative is based may be as ancient as that represented in the J narrative. When we compare P with *Deuteronomy*, however, we must base our judgement on other grounds. While the laws of P are mainly ritual and those of D mostly ethical and social, there are points of contact. One of the most obvious of these is the position of the priesthood. In D (and, incidentally, in H) all members of the family of Levi are priests; there is nothing to suggest a distinction of order within the sacred tribe. But in *Ezekiel* we do meet with a difference. Owing to their presumed apostasy, the priests of the local sanctuaries (in D placed on the same level as their Jerusalem brethren) are degraded to menial duties in the ideal scheme, while the true officiating priesthood is confined to the family of Zadok. The same distinction is made in P, though there the range of the priesthood proper seems somewhat wider, and includes all the descendants of Aaron.[1] The prescriptions for the Passover in D and P vary considerably, and even contradict one another. In J, E and P it is essentially a household festival; D attempts to centralize it and have it observed by all Israelites in the one sanctuary —clearly a part of the general policy which is characteristic of D. The P regulations strongly suggest a return, to some extent, to the older form, since the new order is clearly impracticable. The actual practice in the later Judaism was a combination of the two; the victim was killed in the Temple and then taken away, cooked, and eaten in a private house. When we add to these facts an obvious acquaintance, not only with E but also with J, we feel justified in placing P latest of the five sources we have identified.

Our general conclusions up to this point may be reinforced by reference to the social conditions presupposed in the legal codes. That of E in Exod. xxi–xxiii (and we may add the little J code Exod. xxxiv 17–18) is clearly intended

---

[1] The mention of Aaron in H, *e.g.* in Lev. xxi. 1, 16, 24, xxii. 2, 4, 18, is to be ascribed to the redaction which accompanied the inclusion of H in the body of P.

for a community which is almost entirely agricultural, and whose social and political organization is still comparatively undeveloped. D, on the other hand, while not neglecting the country and the tillers of the soil, obviously contemplates also a city life, with a higher stage of constitutional development, referring constantly, as it does, to the " gates," [1] *i.e.* to the cities, and laying down regulations for the appointment and duties of the Judges and other officers.[2] Finally, P is addressed (in its present form) to a community in which the political interests were falling into the background, and their place was taken by ritual and religious ceremonial. Its Israel is now a Church rather than a State.

So far we are on fairly safe ground, but we can be less certain when we consider the relative ages of J and E. It is clear that they come from the same stage in the history of Israelite development, and that their style corresponds closely with that which we can recognize elsewhere as being characteristic of the early or middle monarchy. There are features which suggest that E originated in a slightly more advanced community than J, particularly certain theological assumptions. These may be summed up by saying that the anthropomorphism, which is so pronounced a feature of J, is somewhat mitigated in E. Such phrases as those used of Yahweh in the J story of Creation would be unnatural in E. Revelation comes less often by theophany than by dreams—indeed the dream is a characteristic feature of E. On the other hand, in matters of actual worship J seems to be further advanced than E, especially in its avoidance of any material object of worship, except the Ark and the stones contained therein. With this may be contrasted the fact that E frequently mentions the *Maṣṣebah*, or the sacred pillar, in such a way as to make it clear that it is regarded as a legitimate symbol of the divine presence.

The general impression produced by the two documents leaves us with the feeling that J is somewhat the earlier. At the same time it must be recognized that the two come

---

[1] Cp., *e.g.*, Deut. xii. 15, 18, xiv. 27, xv. 7, etc.
[2] Cp. Deut. xvi. 18–19. Their functions in E and other early sources are performed simply by " Elders."

from different parts of Israel, the one from the south and the other from the north. The differences in outlook, then, may have a local rather than chronological explanation; Judah may have been slower to advance in theological conceptions of Yahweh than was the north. Of this, however, we cannot be certain, especially since we know that communication between the two was close and continuous,[1] and there is a slight balance of probability in favour of the priority of J.

We thus reach a probable order, J, E, H, D, P. Once again we may pause to remind ourselves that all the documents (with the possible exception of H) include much earlier material. A good illustration is to be found in E's occasional quotations of songs which seem to be more or less contemporary with the events to which they refer. The curious and almost unintelligible snatch of verse in Num. xxi. 14–15 is expressly stated to have been taken from a written collection known as "The Book of the Wars of Yahweh"; and in Josh. x. 13 [2] we hear of a "Book of Jashar," which meets us again in ii Sam. i. 18. It is universally recognized that P contains very much earlier material, including ceremonial regulations which certainly codified ancient practice, and were handed down from generation to generation, perhaps even in written form. Strength is lent to this last suggestion by the presence of a passage in D concerning "clean" and "unclean" animals,[3] which (with the omission of the names of the "clean" animals) occurs also in P.[4] Clearly both documents have taken the passage ultimately from the same source, for there are slight variations which make a theory of direct borrowing improbable. The Creation and Flood narratives in P are derived from a source which was independent of J, and must go back to an early period in Canaanite culture, though they have been profoundly modified in the course of centuries, and now bear little resemblance to what must have been their original form.

[1] It is significant that both Amos and Isaiah addressed themselves to northern Israel, the former exclusively.
[2] For the extension of the Pentateuchal elements into *Joshua* see below, pp. 69 ff.   [3] Deut. xiv. 4–20.   [4] Lev. xi. 3–20.

ii. *Absolute Dating*. With this *caveat* in mind we can proceed to the difficult task of attempting something like an absolute dating of the various elements in the Pentateuch. Our only hope of doing this with any degree of success is to find some event, recorded outside the Pentateuch, with which we can definitely connect the origin or promulgation of one of its constituent parts. A mere reference to events recorded in the Pentateuch is not enough, since the writer's knowledge might be derived from some other document, or even simply from oral tradition. Thus Hosea's mention of Admah and Zeboim, and Isaiah's references to Sodom and Gomorrah, do not entitle us to assert that they had J, still less our Pentateuch, in their hands. But in ii Kgs. xxii, xxiii, we have an account of a great reformation of religion, which was based on a book of the Law, discovered in the Temple. The measures taken by Josiah to carry out the provisions of this Law, especially the removal of all sanctuaries except that at Jerusalem, have led to the belief that the book thus discovered was our *Deuteronomy*, though possibly not in exactly its present form. The view has not passed unchallenged in recent years,[1] nevertheless it is still the most usual opinion. That the law of the single altar was regarded by the writers of *Deuteronomy* as an innovation is suggested by sundry adaptations of existing practice. One is the permission to eat the flesh of the domestic animals under secular conditions, a second is the arrangement whereby the priests of the local sanctuaries were to be permitted to come to Jerusalem and officiate there (it is expressly stated in ii Kgs. xxiii. 9 that this provision was not actually carried out, suggesting that it was enjoined in the law under which the changes were made), and we have also the provision of the Cities of Refuge, to take the place of local altars as spots to which the innocent manslayer might flee.

The principal difficulty with which this view is faced is that of explaining how a work, essentially belonging to northern Israel,[2] should have been found in Jerusalem, and the absence of a reliable and certain solution of this

[1] See below, pp. 65 f.   [2] Cp. p. 52.

problem has led some scholars to question the correctness of the identification.[1] But it is clear that the discovery of the book and of its contents was a complete surprise to the priests, especially to Hilkiah. We may assume that their manual hitherto had been H or something like it, and the law of the one altar, together with its necessary corollaries, was strange to them. It is hardly likely that a *school* of Jerusalem priests could have kept their aims and work so completely secret that all memory of it should have perished. It must have been brought from the outside as a complete document, and have represented the ideals of a group who had no official connexion with the Jerusalem Temple. This group might have been connected in some way with the eighth-century prophets, and D certainly shows more than traces of their influence. But if we have to single out one especially among them, it is Hosea, and not Isaiah or Micah, on whom our choice would fall. It would, in fact, not be unfair to describe D as E modified by the teaching of Hosea. We do not know exactly what happened to the north after the fall of Samaria, but we have no reason to doubt that, even after the formation of the Assyrian province of Samaria by Sargon in 720 B.C., there was free intercourse between the different parts of the country, and, in particular, Bethel was near enough to Jerusalem to make it easy for the one place to influence the other. We have no means of knowing how it reached Jerusalem, but the important fact remains that a law-book was found in the Temple in 621 B.C. and that all the positive evidence leads us to identify this book with the kernel of *Deuteronomy*, *i.e.* v–xxvi, xxviii.

If this identification can be accepted we have a *terminus ad quem* for the composition of the book. The only clue that we have as to the earlier limit is to be sought in the tone of the work itself. We have already observed its affinity to the work of the great prophets of the eighth century, especially of Hosea. It is clear that the prophet is the earlier, since he makes no appeal to the law in support of his demands and denunciations. In particular, we may note the insistence on love. It is true that Hosea's

[1] See below, p. 66.

favourite word is *ḥesed*, while that of D is *'ahabah*, which
suggests that we must not make the connexion too close.
But the type of appeal is the same in both cases. Further,
it is Hosea, more than any other prophet of his age, who
denounces the nominal Yahweh-cult of the local sanctuaries
as being in reality the worship of Baal.[1] It is a significant
fact that every Israelite sanctuary, except Shiloh, which
has yet been excavated, shows clear evidence of having
been used as a Canaanite shrine in pre-Israelite days.
Had the invaders been imbued with the principle which,
centuries later, was enunciated by the authors of D, and
utterly destroyed the old " high places," with all their
emblems, there would hardly have been an opportunity
for the development of that syncretism which, to Hosea,
was but a thinly-veiled Baalism.

Finally, we may note that the Jewish community at
Elephantiné knew nothing of the provisions of *Deuteronomy*.
Not only were they evidently unaware of the demand for
the centralization of sacrifice (they appealed to their
Palestinian brethren for help in restoring their Temple
after it had been destroyed by an Egyptian rising), but they
actually admitted subordinate deities, including a goddess
Anath, alongside of Yahweh, though they regarded Him
as their chief God. We do not know when the Elephantiné
Jews migrated to Egypt. They may have been descendants
of the exiled communities of northern Palestine, moving
first to Mesopotamia (where they learnt to speak Aramaic
instead of Hebrew[2]), or they may have gone as fugitives
even as early as the time of Hosea, who makes frequent
references to Israelites going down to Egypt.[3] In any case,
the evidence which their documents offer us makes it impossible to carry D back to a period earlier than the beginning of the seventh century. Many scholars believe that
the book was the work of the prophetic party which suffered
eclipse during the reign of Manasseh (696–641), and this
may have been the case, provided that we can assume the

---

[1] This view now (1941) requires some modification, since excavations at
Tell el Nasbeh (Mizpah) have disclosed the existence of an Ashtoreth temple
alongside of the temple of Yahweh.
[2] Cp. Oesterley and Robinson, *History of Israel*,[2] II. pp. 160 ff. (1932).
[3] Hos. vii. 16; ix. 6; xi. 11; xii. 1.

work to have been carried on, not in Jerusalem itself, but somewhere in northern Israel, possibly, as has already been suggested, at Bethel.

H is, as we have seen, the southern analogue to D. It breathes the same prophetic spirit, but we may suggest that the direct influence was that, not of Hosea, but of Isaiah, whose stress on holiness cannot have failed to bear fruit in the religious thinking of the best men among his people. While it includes much that is comparatively early, there are also elements which suggest a protest against the iniquities of the reign of Manasseh. As a special instance we may cite the condemnation of human sacrifice in Lev. xx. 2–5. This suggests an origin not unlike that often ascribed to D—a prophetic revision of a code already in existence, intended to help Israel to a better and purer religious life after the wicked king should have passed away. But in the case of D the earlier code was still extant, while the older basis of H, if any, must be conjecturally extracted simply from the document itself. Many of the regulations regarding sexual morality, the purity of the priesthood, the type of animal required for sacrifice, the creatures that are ceremonially clean and unclean, together with others, may have been current among the Jerusalem priesthood long before the time of Manasseh, and would not be affected by his policy. But, in its present form, or rather in the form in which it was subjected to priestly revision, it can hardly be carried farther back than the early part of the seventh century.

The *terminus ad quem* for H is obviously the date of Ezek. xl–xlviii. There is, however, a widespread conviction among scholars that these chapters are not to be ascribed to Ezekiel himself, and do not date from the exilic period at all. It is clear that they are not the latest " programme " for the ecclesiastical establishment, but they may have to be ascribed to one of the first two centuries in the post-exilic period. A more reliable point is fixed by D. As we have already seen, the central feature, alike of D and of the reform of Josiah in 621 B.C., is the centralization of sacrifice. That clearly carried with it the secularization of the flesh of the domestic animals, a regulation which is directly contradicted in H. It does not follow that H is necessarily earlier than D, but it does seem to indicate that H, in a form which included Lev. xvii, was earlier than the promulgation of D, or at least the reform of Josiah. We are thus reduced to assigning H to much the same period as D, *i.e.* to the seventh century.

The approximate dating we have reached for D and H gives a *terminus ad quem* for J and E; neither can be later than the middle of the eighth century.[1] The earlier limit for these documents is more difficult to determine. In style and general quality they resemble writings which must be assigned to the first half of the monarchical period, and they represent the general position of religion and ethics which was accepted by the best elements in the Israelite community in the ninth century. We have, however, no real clue beyond this, and it is not surprising to find that the dates assigned by different scholars vary about a century. There are those who would place E before J, though the general opinion inverts this order. Some would place J as early as 900 B.C., and others believe that E may be as late as 750. We can only say that, in all probability, the true dates lie between these extremes.

From some points of view the dating of P is simpler than that of J and E. Even the " groundwork " is admittedly later than D and H, and even later than Ezek. xl–xlviii. If these last chapters could be regarded as the work of the prophet whose name they bear, it would be necessary to assign P, at the earliest, to a comparatively late point in the Exile. But, since the probability is that these chapters themselves are post-exilic,[2] P must be later still. If further evidence is required, it may be remarked that, whereas D

---

[1] It has been held in certain quarters that Josiah's law-book is not D but the E code. The account of the reform, however, with its concentration of sacrifices, makes it impossible to maintain this view, unless we are to regard the narrative of ii Kings xxii, xxiii, as being largely *Midrash*, composed in the interests of the Deuteronomic law at a later period. Such a wholesale surrender of the historicity of ii Kings would need much stronger support than is available from the facts as known to us, though it may be admitted that there are elements in the story (some of the details which refer to the king's action at Bethel, for instance) which are probably due to later revision of the narrative.

[2] See below, pp. 320 f.

is obviously intended for a community living under a
monarchic constitution,[1] P contemplates only a theocratic
order.

The point in the post-exilic period on which our minds
fasten is inevitably the period of Ezra. In Neh. viii–x we
read of a great assembly in Jerusalem, at which Ezra
promulgated a law, solemnly accepted and sworn to by the
whole people. It is in the record of this event that we
have for the first time (outside the Pentateuch) a distinction
made between the priests, sons of Aaron, and the rest of
the tribe of Levi.[2] As we have already seen, this arrangement is the most striking difference between the community
as conceived by P and that of D, and it is not unnatural
to connect Ezra with P, just as Josiah may be connected
with D. This gives us the date 398–7 B.C.[3] for the point
at which P entered into the actual life of Israel. It goes
without saying that it was compiled at some time before
this, and, since its provisions seem to have been unknown
in Palestine (apart from features in which P overlaps D),
the place of compilation was probably Mesopotamia. At
the same time it should be observed that it shows no direct
signs of Babylonian influence, and contains much material,
even apart from H, which must have been traditional in
Israel long before the Exile.[4] The post-exilic prophets—
Haggai, Zechariah and Malachi—show no acquaintance
with P, while their utterances are quite consistent with a
knowledge of D. The same remark may be made of
Nehemiah, who is to be dated roughly two generations
before Ezra. In any case it is difficult to find any strong
reasons for denying the general identity of at least the
groundwork of P with the Law proclaimed by Ezra in

[1] Cp. Deut. xvii. 14–20.   [2] Cp., e.g., Neh. x. 28, 34, 38
[3] For the correctness of this date see below, pp. 127 ff.
[4] We may select as obvious examples the stories of the Creation and the
Flood. While both suggest ultimate Mesopotamian origin, they have been
so modified as to demand a period of many centuries for their growth, and
they must be regarded as a part of the inheritance left by the early period of
Mesopotamian influence in the West, i.e., the latter half of the third millennium
B.C. The extent to which the primitive tradition might be modified in course
of time has been recently illustrated by the discovery of the Ras-Shamra
inscriptions, which give us a form of the Creation myth very different from
that which survived in Babylonia.

398–7 B.C. As we have already remarked, P continued to receive additions, even before the general combination of all the elements into our present Pentateuch. We cannot say exactly when the whole process was completed, but early in the second century B.C. the Law was regarded as a single whole, with, apparently, no suspicion of its composite origin. We shall not greatly err, then, if we assign its final completion to a date not later than 300 B.C.

IX. OTHER VIEWS OF THE STRUCTURE AND DATES OF THE PENTATEUCH

i. *Structure and Analysis.* What has been said above forms an outline sketch of the position which has been most widely held during the last half-century. There have been, however, isolated scholars who have challenged it at one or more points, in addition to the occasional divergent views which have been noted in passing. The normal analysis has been, on the whole, almost universally accepted. Doubts have been expressed as to the possibility of separating J and E outside *Genesis*, but there are only two or three cases of scholars who have challenged the whole system.

First among these may be mentioned Eerdmans, who, in a very interesting original study of the problem,[1] has propounded the theory that the older narratives had a polytheistic basis, which was repeatedly revised and re-edited. Eerdmans' study of the question contains some important observations, but the theory as a whole has found no support. Löhr,[2] claiming Eerdmans as his predecessor, has recently developed the view that the Pentateuch was the work of a single individual, probably Ezra, who put together a great mass of earlier material.

The use of the divine names as a criterion for analysis has been attacked in a number of quarters. It will suffice to mention two scholars, Dahse and Wiener. Both call attention to variations in the text of the Septuagint, and argue from them that we cannot be certain of the use of the names Yahweh and Elohim in the original Hebrew text.

---

[1] *Die Komposition der Genesis* (1908), see also his *Die Vorgeschichte Israels* (1908), *Exodus* (1910), *Leviticus* (1912). [2] In *Der Priestercodex in der Genesis* (1924).

This has been met by Skinner [1] and Battersby-Harford,[2] both of whom show that on grounds of scientific textual criticism the MT is to be held the more reliable in this matter. Dahse himself propounded a theory which resembles that of Eerdmans in that it postulates a series of revisions, and these, he holds, were responsible for the alternations in the divine name. We may further note the type of view, represented by Möller,[3] which endeavours to save the unity of the Pentateuch (and, incidentally, its Mosaic authorship) by explaining the two names as indicating different meanings, Elohim being used when the reference is to the God of nature, Yahweh implying the God of relevation. Harford [4] has no difficulty in showing the weakness of this position.

In any case, the use of the divine names is only one of the facts on which the critical analysis is based. There are passages (*e.g.* Gen. xxxvii) where that analysis is as certain as it ever can be, in which no divine name is used at all. The whole position, however, has recently been challenged by Volz and Rudolph in a monograph entitled *Der Elohist als Erzähler* (1933). The authors believe that the grounds on which J and E have been distinguished in the narrative portions of *Genesis* are inadequate to support the theory. In many instances where there is an alternation between the two divine names it is to be explained on other grounds. Narratives which others have regarded as composite can be defended as simple. There still remain, it is true, peculiarities in the text which cannot be thus explained away, but these are due to a revision of the original J. As far as the narrative of *Genesis* goes, " E " simply represents that revision. The opinion of two scholars of the learning and ability of Volz and Rudolph entitles their view to every respect, but some will feel, even after reading Rudolph's defence of the unity of Gen. xxxvii, that here we have surely a composite narrative.

On the whole, then, we may say that the analysis hitherto accepted still holds the field; the isolation of P, in par-

[1] *The Divine Names in Genesis* (1914).   [2] *Since Wellhausen* (1926).
[3] *Wider den Bann der Quellenscheidung* (1912).   [4] *Op. cit.*, pp. 45–47.

ticular, is hardly questioned, and is admitted even by so
conservative a critic as Orr.[1] Nor is there any serious
difference of opinion as to the relative dating of the documents, beyond some uncertainty as to whether J or E is
the earlier, and as to whether H precedes or follows D.
Neither point is of serious importance. The absolute dating,
on the other hand, has been vigorously challenged from two
quarters, some scholars seeking to place the whole series
earlier than is usually done, others preferring a later date.

ii. *Dates.* As we have seen, the central point for the
absolute dating is the identification of *Deuteronomy* with the
book of the Law referred to in ii Kings xxii. As supporters
of an earlier date we may mention especially Oestreicher
and Welch. The latter has acutely observed that there is
much in D which can hardly have been applied in practice
to the conditions of the late sixth century B.C. The Passover, for instance, could not have been eaten by all Judah
in the Temple at Jerusalem. The difficulty is solved by
denying that the original *Deuteronomy* intended to enjoin
centralization of sacrifice at all. Deut. xii. 2–14, the fundamental passage in this respect, falls into two parts, which
are doublets. The former, which does unmistakeably limit
sacrifice to one spot (verse 5), is a later addition to the
original, and verse 14, which seems to have the same meaning, really means that a number of sanctuaries are recognized as legitimate, provided that they have not previously
been used for Canaanite worship. Welch notes carefully
how strong the protest still is against Baalism, and deduces
from this fact the view that the old cults were still carried
on under the old names. We have no room here to argue
the point in detail; it can only be remarked that the interpretation of Deut. xii. 14 sounds forced and unnatural, and
that Welch might have been on firmer ground if he had
assigned the whole of ch. xii to a later period than the main
body of the book. Further, there are difficulties created by
a theory which throws D back into a period earlier than
that of the first great canonical prophets.

Hölscher and Kennett, on the other hand, feel that 621

---

[1] *The Problem of the Old Testament* (1906).

F

B.C. is too early a date for D. Hölscher [1] notes the difficulties which Welch also has observed, but solves them by
assigning D to a period after the Exile, when Jewish territory
was much circumscribed and its population small. The
narrative of ii Kings xxii–xxiii is largely, if not wholly, a
pure invention. Hölscher accompanies his view of D with
a drastic and sweeping criticism of the literature of the
O. T. in general and particularly of *Jeremiah* and *Ezekiel*.
Such criticism is necessary if the theory of a post-exilic
Deuteronomy is to be maintained, but there is a strong feeling
among scholars that the extensive excisions required by the
hypothesis are not justified on other grounds. To Hölscher
D is the law-book of Ezra.

Kennett [2] seems to have felt most strongly the difficulties
created by the obvious northern affinities of D. He attempts
to meet these by supposing it to have originated at Bethel,
and to have been brought to Jerusalem during the Exile,
when sacrifices were still offered, though the Temple lay
in ruins. The theory involves a compromise between the
Jerusalem (or Zadokite) and the Bethel (or Aaronic) priest-
hoods, which was responsible for the later developments in
religious literature and practice. This theory has the
advantage of explaining how D came to Jerusalem, but it
does not account for the description of Josiah's reforms or
for the connexion between D and Jeremiah. Both these
difficulties, on Kennett's hypothesis, can be met only by a
theory of extensive interpolation in the two books mentioned. It may well be that *Deuteronomy* had its proper
home in Bethel, but most critics would prefer that its introduction to Jerusalem should involve as little interference
with the Biblical text as possible.

X. The Hebrew Text of the Pentateuch

The text is, on the whole, better preserved than that of
any other portion of the Old Testament, perhaps because
it was the first section to receive the meticulous care which

---

[1] Cp., *e.g.*, *Komposition und Ursprung des Deuteronomiums*, $ZATW$, xl, pp. 161–
255 (1922).
[2] Cp., *e.g.*, *Deuteronomy and the Decalogue* (1920.)

the scribes bestowed upon their Scriptures. We have a valuable witness to the general accuracy of the MT in the Samaritan text, which, though it must have diverged at an early date from that used in Judæa, nevertheless corresponds very closely with it. Variations in the Samaritan are often borne out by the Septuagint, which, again, shows less difference than is the case in most books. There are occasional suggestions of an Egyptian form of text which varied more widely than any extant copies, whether in Hebrew or in Greek. If, for instance, the " Nash papyrus " [1] was originally part of a Biblical MS., then *Deuteronomy* must have had two widely different recensions, of which only one has survived. It is usually held, however, that this fragment belonged, not to a Biblical MS., but to a Liturgy of some kind, which did not necessarily follow the Biblical order. The other principal versions also offer strong support to the substantial accuracy of the MT.

[1] For an account of this papyrus, which dates from the second century A.D., see S. A. Cook in *Proceedings of the Society for Biblical Archæology* for 1903.

THE BOOK OF JOSHUA

I. Place in the Canon

THE book of *Joshua* stands immediately after the Pentateuch in most versions and editions of the Old Testament, though in the Syriac version the book of *Job* usually comes in between. This is due to the theory that Moses was the author of *Job*. In the Hebrew Canon, *Joshua* stands at the head of the second group of books, *i.e.* the Prophets, and is the first of the historical books known as the "Former Prophets," a group which also includes *Judges*, *Samuel*, and *Kings*.

II. Contents

The book of *Joshua* is the record of the conquest of Palestine by Israel, under the leadership of Joshua. It takes up the story from the disappearance of Moses, and carries it down to the death of its hero. The book falls naturally into three parts: (*a*) chs. i–xii, recording the conquest itself; (*b*) chs. xiii–xxii, describing the apportionment of the land among the tribes; (*c*) chs. xxiii–xxiv, giving the last words of Joshua to the people. Its contents may be described in more detail as follows:

(*a*) i. 1–9. Yahweh commissions Joshua.

    i. 10–18. Fidelity of the Transjordanic tribes.

    ii. 1–24. Spies sent to Jericho.

    iii. 1–v. 1. Crossing of the Jordan.

    v. 2–12. The Israelites are circumcised and keep the Passover.

    v. 13–16. Joshua receives a theophany.

    vi. 1–vii. 1. Fall of Jericho and sin of Achan.

    vii. 2–26. Unsuccessful attack on Ai; execution of Achan.

    viii. 1–29. Fall of Ai.

viii. 30–35.   The Law read on Mount Ebal.

ix. 1–27.   Stratagem of the Gibeonites.

x. 1–43.   Battle of Gibeon and conquest of southern Palestine.

xi. 1–15.   Conquest of northern Palestine.

xi. 16–23.   Completion of conquest.

xii. 1–24.   A list of kings conquered by Israel.

(b) xiii. 1–xix. 51.   Partition of the land among the tribes.

xx. 1–9.   Appointment of cities of refuge.

xxi. 1–45.   Appointment of Levitical cities.

xxii. 1–34.   Transjordanic tribes return and set up a memorial altar.

(c) xxiii. 1–xxiv. 28.   Joshua's farewell address.

xxiv. 29–33.   Death of Joshua.

III. STRUCTURE AND DATE

It is generally recognized that all the documents which have gone to the construction of the Pentateuch (except H) are found also underlying the book of *Joshua* and that its history is practically identical with that of the five earlier books. For a general discussion of the sources and composition of the book reference may be made to the previous chapter. If there is a difference to be noted it lies in the fact that a good deal more material has to be attributed to Deuteronomic revision in *Joshua* than in either *Exodus* or *Numbers*. The final redaction is due to P, who accepts the Deuteronomic theory of a swift and complete conquest. The following represents in general the accepted analysis of the book:

J.	E.	D.	P.
	i. 1–2, 10–11 a.	i. 3–9, 11 b–18.	
	ii. 1–9.	ii. 10–11.	
ii. 17–21.	ii. 12–16, 22–24.		
iii. 5–6.	iii. 1–3, 8–10 a, 11–17.	iii. 7, 10 b.	iii. 4.
iv. 9–10 a, 10 c–11.	iv. 1–4, 8, 15–18.	iv. 5–7, 12, 14, 21–24.	iv. 10 b, 13, 19–20.
v. 13–15.	v. 2–3, 8–9.	v. 1.	v. 4–7, 10–12.

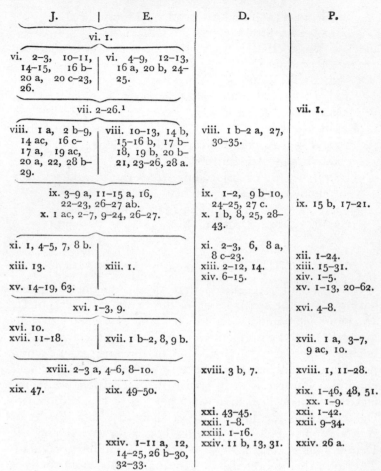

J.	E.	D.	P.
	vi. 1.		
vi. 2–3, 10–11, 14–15, 16 b–20 a, 20 c–23, 26.	vi. 4–9, 12–13, 16 a, 20 b, 24–25.		
	vii. 2–26.[1]		vii. 1.
viii. 1 a, 2 b–9, 14 ac, 16 c–17 a, 19 ac, 20 a, 22, 28 b–29.	viii. 10–13, 14 b, 15–16 b, 17 b–18, 19 b, 20 b–21, 23–26, 28 a.	viii. 1 b–2 a, 27, 30–35.	
ix. 3–9 a, 11–15 a, 16, 22–23, 26–27 ab.		ix. 1–2, 9 b–10, 24–25, 27 c.	ix. 15 b, 17–21.
x. 1 ac, 2–7, 9–24, 26–27.		x. 1 b, 8, 25, 28–43.	
xi. 1, 4–5, 7, 8 b.		xi. 2–3, 6, 8 a, 8 c–23.	xii. 1–24.
xiii. 13.	xiii. 1.	xiii. 2–12, 14.	xiii. 15–31.
		xiv. 6–15.	xiv. 1–5.
xv. 14–19, 63.			xv. 1–13, 20–62.
	xvi. 1–3, 9.		xvi. 4–8.
xvi. 10.			
xvii. 11–18.	xvii. 1 b–2, 8, 9 b.		xvii. 1 a, 3–7, 9 ac, 10.
xviii. 2–3 a, 4–6, 8–10.		xviii. 3 b, 7.	xviii. 1, 11–28.
xix. 47.	xix. 49–50.		xix. 1–46, 48, 51.
			xx. 1–9.
		xxi. 43–45.	xxi. 1–42.
		xxii. 1–8.	xxii. 9–34.
		xxiii. 1–16.	
	xxiv. 1–11 a, 12, 14–25, 26 b–30, 32–33.	xxiv. 11 b, 13, 31.	xxiv. 26 a.

It should be remarked that the analysis is rather more uncertain in *Joshua* than in the Pentateuch. It is held in some quarters that much of the material normally attributed to the Deuteronomic editing of JE really comes from an editor who revised E.[2] But the tone of so much of this matter is quite characteristic of D, and it has been felt better to retain these passages under that head. The analysis of J and E is at least as difficult as it is in the Pentateuch.

---

[1] The greater part of v. 24 is probably to be ascribed to priestly redaction.
[2] *E.g.* by Steuernagel, cp. *Josua* (1900).

It will be seen that the Deuteronomic editors often included fairly long passages, while in other places their work was limited to occasional notes. A similar remark may be made about P, which, here as elsewhere, seems to delight in formulæ and statistics.

What has been said as to the date of the various elements in the Pentateuch applies to *Joshua* also.

IV. THE HEBREW TEXT AND THE SEPTUAGINT

The text of this book has been fairly well preserved, and it is comparatively seldom that the student wishes to resort to conjectural emendation. The Septuagint, however, shows that the MT has been in places somewhat expanded by the addition of words and phrases, even after the separation of the Egyptian and Palestinian traditions.[1] In this respect it is clear that some forms of the Septuagint (particularly the recension known as that of Lucian) have been " corrected " by the Palestinian text, but there are MSS., notably the Codex Vaticanus (B), which show wider variations, and suggest a greater independence. Even so, while it is clear that the text has not received that meticulous care which was bestowed on the Pentateuch, it has obviously not suffered very seriously in the course of transmission.

V. THE VALUE OF JOSHUA AS AN HISTORICAL RECORD

A glance over the analysis of the book shows that, while the older sources, J and E (mainly the latter), are prominent in the first section, ending with ch. xii, they occupy but a small part of the second. We may almost say that the first division of the book consists of material taken from the older documents, and revised, first by D and then by P. In the second division, however, the whole seems to have been written by D or P or both, with the insertion of a few brief sentences here and there from J or E.

It is the later revisers, belonging to the Deuteronomic and Priestly schools, who have given to the whole book its characteristic presentation of the conquest. The earlier

[1] Cp. pp. 15 ff.

stories serve the purpose of giving some information as to
the details, but it is assumed that the whole land, from the
far south to the extreme north, was in the hands of Israel
before the death of Joshua.   There are, it is true, certain
exceptions suggested in xiii. 1 ff., but these are confined to
the coastal plain and the far north; the rest is already in
Israelite hands, and what is not yet occupied will soon be
conquered.   The picture is intended to be one of a complete
conquest of the land, carried out practically within a single
generation.

But interspersed in this second section (chs. xiii to xxii)
we have occasional notes, commonly assigned to J, which
tell a different story.[1]   So far from being a complete and
overwhelming success, the conquest failed to embrace some
of the most important parts of the land.   Judah could not
dispossess the Jebusites of Jerusalem (xv. 63), Ephraim failed
to conquer Gezer (xvi. 10), Manasseh left the cities of the
Plain of Esdraelon in Canaanite hands (xvii. 11–13).   There
are also, we may remark, indications of other conquests
which are not mentioned elsewhere in the book, *e.g.* the
capture of Debir by Othniel (xv. 14–19), and the sack of
Laish [2] by the Danites (xix. 47–48).

When, moreover, we come to examine the actual conquests ascribed to Joshua in chs. i–x, we are struck by the
small number of cities whose capture the older sources
report.   Jericho and Ai are taken, and Gibeon is accepted
as a subject-ally.   In ch. x the kings of Jerusalem, Hebron,
Yarmuth, Lachish and Eglon are defeated and killed, but
not one of their cities is captured, save in the Deuteronomic
conclusion to the story, x. 28–43.   The earlier documents
had nothing to say of the conquest of country to the south
and west of Gibeon.   Even after the victory over the five
kings, the camp is still at Gilgal, in the plain of Jericho, and
the great triumph shrinks to the dimensions of a successful
raid.   In other words, all that J and E had to say of Joshua's
conquests to the south of the Plain of Esdraelon was that he
secured a bridge-head in the Plain of Jericho, and a small

---

[1] It should be observed that several of these notes appear also in Judg. i,
together with additions of the same type.
[2] So probably we should read for Leshem.

triangle of territory in the heart of the mountains. No doubt both were, strategically, of the highest importance, and formed a base from which the Israelite power could gradually spread till it covered the whole land, but generations were to pass after the death of Joshua before the conquest could be called complete. Jerusalem, as we know, fell into Israelite hands only in David's time, while the first Hebrew monarch who could really lay claim to the site of Gezer was Solomon.

Ch. xi records the defeat of Jabin, king of Hazor, in northern Galilee. But a king of the same name and locality is mentioned in Judg. iv in connexion with the exploit of Deborah and Barak, and, though we may not feel able to accept the form of the story which brings him into direct political relationship with Sisera, it is clear that one line of tradition ascribed the conquest of his territory to the age of the Judges. It is difficult to see how an invading army of warriors, on the stage of development reached by Israel, could have made their way through the chain of unreduced fortresses which held the Plain of Esdraelon from Carmel to the Jordan, and on all grounds of probability it seems better to assume another crossing of the Jordan valley between the Sea of Galilee and Huleh with which Joshua had nothing whatever to do. Equally independent of him is the southern movement, whose limit (in the book of *Joshua*) is reached with the capture of Debir by Othniel, and we may suggest that here we have the memory of yet a third line of invasion, which did not cross the Jordan at all, but pressed slowly northwards from Hormah.

It is not difficult to appraise the motives which led to a belief in a complete and comparatively sudden conquest under Joshua. In addition to national pride, we have the theological outlook of that Deuteronomic school to whom we first owe the theory. From its point of view, the supreme peril of Israel from the first had been syncretism. To avoid that, the only safe measure was the complete annihilation of Israel's predecessors. Because, in view of the Deuteronomists, this ought to have taken place, and was, indeed, enjoined by Yahweh, the whole land must have been given to Israel by Yahweh at once. He would never have demanded the extermination of the Canaanites unless He had also made it possible, and He could make it possible only by giving Israel all the country.

But while the Deuteronomic theory of the conquest (accepted by the Priestly school) fails to commend itself as historical, we may safely say that we have in the older narratives an account of the first stage of the conquest on which we may generally rely. It gives us a picture, as we have seen, of three separate waves of invasion, one by Kenizzites and Calebites (clans later reckoned as Judahite) from the south, the second by the Joseph group under Joshua, which crossed the Jordan near Jericho and made good its position in the hills to the north and north-west of Jerusalem, and the third crossing the Jordan much higher up, and establishing itself in the region which extends from near the sources of Jordan down towards the Sea of Galilee and the Plain of Esdraelon. Even many of the details of these wars, especially those in which Joshua figured, may have a substantial basis in fact, handed down traditionally. The book of *Joshua*, at all events in its earlier *strata*, does give us a fair amount of material which we may accept as historical.

THE BOOK OF JUDGES

I. Contents, Structure, and Redactional Elements

THE book of *Judges* contains three clearly distinguishable divisions:

(a) i. 1–ii. 5 : the fortunes of various tribes during the conquest of Palestine.

(b) ii. 6–xvi. 31 : stories of Hebrew heroes living during the period between the conquest of the country and the establishment of the monarchy.

(c) xvii–xxi : Appendices describing events assigned to this period.

It will be convenient to start by discussing these three divisions quite independently of one another.

(a) i. 1–ii. 5. This is an introduction to the book as a whole; it contains a summary of the conquests of different districts of Canaan by individual tribes. Most of the material here included is also found in the book of *Joshua*, though that book presents, in general, a very different interpretation of the conquest. As we have seen,[1] in the main, the book of *Joshua* represents the conquest as having been completely carried out by Joshua himself; but in Judg. i the tribes wage war individually, and not wholly successfully, against their predecessors after the death of Joshua. It is, however, important to observe that there are indications of this latter view in the book of *Joshua* itself; cp. *e.g.* Judg. i. 21 with Josh. xv. 63, where the former speaks of " Benjamin," the latter of " Judah "; cp. also Josh. xvii. 12, 13 with Judg. i. 27, 28, and Josh. xvi. 10 with Judg. i. 29. Clearly the compiler of this division had at his disposal one of the sources used by the compilers of *Joshua*. He also had other sources which included more detailed narratives,

---

[1] See pp. 71 ff.

75

viz. the story of Adoni-bezek (i. 4–7), and the record of the capture of Kiriath-sepher (i. 11–15).

(b) ii. 6–xvi. 31. Here we have the kernel of the book; the contents are as follows:

Contents :		
ii. 6–iii. 6:	Introduction.	
iii. 7–11:	Othniel.	
iii. 12–30:	Ehud.	
iii. 31:	Shamgar.	
iv. 1–v. 31:	Deborah and Barak.	
vi. 1–viii. 35:	Gideon.	
ix:	Abimelech.	
x. 1, 2:	Tola.	
x. 3–5:	Jair.	
x. 6–xii. 7:	Jephthah.	
xii. 8–10:	Ibzan.	
xii. 11, 12:	Elon.	
xii. 13–15:	Abdon.	
xiii–xvi:	Samson.	

Structure. The section ii. 6–iii. 6 is an introduction which gives a summary of the whole period about to be dealt with. Particularly noticeable about this introduction is the interpretation it gives of the historical events, the accounts of which follow. Until the death of Joshua and those of his contemporaries who survived him, it is said, the people remained faithful to their God, but after the demise of these another generation arose " which knew not Yahweh, nor yet the work which he had wrought in Israel " (ii. 10). It then goes on to explain that whenever the people forsook the worship of the God of their fathers He raised up an enemy to punish them; thereupon they turned to Him again, and, as a result, He gave them a deliverer who overcame their enemy, and they lived in peace for a season. When the deliverer died, the process of unfaithfulness, punishment, and deliverance was repeated again and again (ii. 11–19).

When we pass on to the narratives we find that a number of them are prefaced by an introductory formula which offers a contrast to the body of the narrative both in the

description of the Judge and in the style of writing. In the
latter the Judge usually appears as a leader in some particular district; he calls together his followers from the
immediate surroundings, accomplishes what he has taken
in hand, and then disappears. But in the introductory
formula the Judge is represented as a ruler over the whole
people. These formulæ do, however, illustrate the theory
of history contained in the introduction proper (ii. 6–iii. 6),
the point of view being that of the Deuteronomic school of
thought.[1] They occur, though not in identical form, in
iii. 7, 11; iii. 12–14; iv. 1–3; vi. 1; x. 6–16; xiii. 1 (that
in x. 6–16 is considerably expanded). They are found,
therefore, prefixed to the narratives of the Judges Othniel,
Ehud, Deborah and Barak, Gideon, Jephthah, and Samson.
The story of Abimelech (ix) is also preceded by a short
introduction in viii. 33–35, which is thoroughly Deuteronomic in tone and style. It is clear that this " hero " could
not be treated as the other six had been, for he did not
deliver Israel from an enemy, and appears rather as an
illustration of the sinfulness of the people. We can, therefore, quite understand that the place of the usual formula
should be taken by this short introduction.[2]

The " Deuteronomic introduction " does not occur in
connexion with the other six (" lesser ") Judges. In these
cases we have another, more or less stereotyped, formula:
" And after . . . there arose to save Israel . . .," or:
" And after . . . arose . . . and he judged Israel . . ."
There is also a concluding formula: " And . . . died, and
was buried in . . ." In these cases there is no reference to
the sins of the people or to their punishment, and the
Deuteronomic view-point is entirely absent. It is possible
that originally a formula similar to this stood in the place
of the Deuteronomic prefaces to the narratives of the other
six (" greater ") Judges, and to the Abimelech section.

From this general survey two reliable conclusions may be
drawn. The first is that a writer, inspired by the ideals of

[1] See pp. 48 n.[1], 71 ff.
[2] Moore, however, following Budde, regards these verses " not as an introduction to chap. ix, but as a substitute for it " (*A Critical and Exegetical Commentary on Judges*, p. 234 [1903]).

Deuteronomy, selected a certain number of narratives about various Judges from the collections available to him in order to illustrate his theory of history.   But, in the second place, there were stories of other Judges which, clearly, he did not use, or he would have prefixed to them his characteristic formula.   These were, however, inserted by a later editor at various points in the " Deuteronomically " edited book.

We may, then, distinguish three distinct stages in the formation of this section (ii. 6–xvi. 31) of the book of *Judges* : we have, first, the writing down of various narratives ;   then the collection of the narratives of the six " greater " Judges by a Deuteronomic editor who added prefaces and concluding words expounding his philosophy of history ;   and, finally, the insertions about the six " lesser " Judges by the redactor to whom we owe the present form of this part of the book.

(c) xvii–xxi :   these chapters contain two Appendices (xvii, xviii and xix–xxi), the former (xvii, xviii) recounts the story of Micah's idols, and describes the foundation of the sanctuary of Dan ;   the latter (xix–xxi) gives the gruesome accounts of the outrage of the men of Gibeah on the Levite's concubine, and the punishment of the tribe of Benjamin.   Like the six " minor " Judges sections and the Abimelech section these Appendices cannot have been added by the Deuteronomic redactor, for they exhibit no mark of his influence ;   on the other hand, it is quite obvious that they contain ancient material ;   it would, therefore, seem probable that they, too, owe their presence in the book to the post-Deuteronomic editor who obtained them from some ancient source.   If this, as seems probable, was the case, it is an interesting fact, for it shows that at least as late as the eve of the Exile documents were extant containing *data* about the very early history of the people.

To sum up, the steps in the composition of our book may be indicated thus :   first, the " hero "-narratives in oral form ;   these were, in course of time, written down ;   then, collections of them were made ;   the first compiler of the book of *Judges* utilized more than one of these collections ;   later, a Deuteronomic redactor worked over the book thus formed with the object of explaining to his contemporaries what he believed to be the divine method of dealing with His people; later still another redactor added further material from some other early collections.

II. Sources

It is clear that the narratives included in the " Deuteronomic " book—stage (b) above—came into the hands of the compiler practically in their present form. Only so can we explain the inclusion of Abimelech among the Judges; and, as we have seen, the compiler himself felt that this figure could not be treated as the Judges proper were. But further, it is evident that even at this stage the work was already the result of a process of compilation, and we must look further for the sources used in its construction. What were these sources, and what was their origin?

The Hebrews, in common with many other ancient peoples, commemorated, at first orally, the exploits of their tribal heroes. Often, we may conjecture, a village would treasure the memory of a local warrior whose tomb was a conspicuous object in the neighbourhood; [1] and families would doubtless have preserved a record of the deeds of some great ancestor. Sooner or later these oral accounts were reduced to writing; isolated written narratives would thus have come into being. In course of time, within the different tribes, such narratives would be gathered, and thus written collections would be formed. These collections, or some of them, were clearly the documents utilized by the Deuteronomic compiler.

But there is evidence to suggest that some at least of these collections were composite. There are, for instance, two accounts of the victory of Deborah and Barak over Sisera. One of these (Judg. v) is in verse, and is probably the oldest Hebrew poem of any length preserved in the Old Testament. It is written with stirring vigour, and frequent beauty of expression, and is generally held to have been composed by a contemporary, even by an eye-witness, of the events

---

[1] Note the frequent mention of the hero's place of burial, viii. 32; x. 2, 5; xii. 7, 10, 12, 15; xvi. 31.

described. The prose version in ch. iv, though later in its present form, seems to have been independent of the poem, since the manner of Sisera's death differs in the two accounts. In the story of Gideon, again, there were probably three separate narratives from which selections were taken. It may well be that Jerubbaal and Gideon were originally different men, whose histories have been confused and combined. The account of the pursuit and capture of Zeba and Zalmunnah seems to have come from a source different from that of the story of the night attack of the three hundred, and the slaughter of Oreb and Zeeb. It would appear, moreover, that there were two recensions of even this last story, one of which attributed the surprise to the use of torches, and the other to the blowing of trumpets. And, once more, two nearly complete narratives of Abimelech's dealings with Shechem may be constructed by isolating from the rest those portions of Judg. ix. 23–45 which deal with the plot and fate of Gaal. In all these cases it is clear that the combination of the sources preceded the work of the Deuteronomic compiler, since the composite narratives in themselves show no trace of his influence.

Since a considerable portion of our book contains ancient historical material far older than the seventh century, *i.e.* long before the Deuteronomic school of thought arose, many critics have raised the question as to whether any marks of the influence of the Jehovistic and Elohistic circles are not to be discerned in it. There would be an *à priori* presumption that this should be the case since, in the book of *Joshua* which, as we have seen, has close affinities with *Judges*, there are obviously J and E elements.[1] " There is the best reason to believe," says Moore, " that neither J nor E ended with the conquest of Canaan, but that both brought the history down to a much later time, if not to their own day. The parting speech of Joshua (Josh. xxiv, substantially E) looks not only backward but forward; it is the end of a book, not of the historical work of which it formed a part; and Judg. ii. 6–10 (Josh. xxiv. 28–31), from the same hand, is unmistakeably the transition to the subse-

[1] See above, pp. 69 f.

quent history." [1] It is, indeed, quite evident that in certain parts of our book some of the characteristic marks of the writers belonging to these circles are to be traced; in the story of Gideon's call, for example, the use of the name *Yahweh* occurs throughout one form of the narrative (vi. 11 ff.), while in the other form (vi. 36–40) *Elohim* is used. But for the study of this subject, in regard to the details of which critical opinion is not unanimous, recourse must be had to the Commentaries. [2]

III. THE HEBREW TEXT AND THE SEPTUAGINT VERSION

Taking it as a whole, the Hebrew text of our book has come down to us in a comparatively pure form. Though textual corruptions of various kinds occur, especially in the Song of Deborah, the text is, generally speaking, in a satisfactory state. Where corruptions occur it is from the Septuagint that most help for emendation is to be derived. At the same time, it is to be noted that the relation between the Septuagint and the Massoretic text is very complicated. For there are two Greek translations of the Hebrew text of *Judges*. This interesting fact was first shown to be the case by Grabe; [3] it was dealt with and more fully developed by Lagarde; [4] and later it was independently treated by Moore. [5]

The earlier of these two translations is represented by the great majority of the Septuagint MSS.; especially important, however, are three groups of cursives which are related to this translation; one of these groups consists of " Lucianic " MSS., *i.e.* they contain Lucian's revision of the Septuagint, [6] which, according to Budde, is, so far as *Judges* is concerned, the oldest and best Greek text. The other translation is represented by the Vatican Codex (B) and a number of cursives, as well as the Sahidic Version; it is considerably later, Moore assigns it to well into the fourth century A.D.,

---

[1] *Op. cit.*, p. xxv; as Moore also remarks: " The symbols J and E represent, not individual authors, but a succession of writers, the historiography of a certain period and school."

[2] See especially, Budde, *Das Buch der Richter*, pp. xii ff. (1897).

[3] *Epistola ad Millium* (1705).

[4] *Septuaginta-Studien*, pp. 1–72; Lucianic text (1892).

[5] *Op. cit.*, pp. xliv–xlvi, and throughout his Commentary.

[6] Beginning of the fourth century A.D.

G

it follows the Massoretic text more closely than the other translation. Cod. B, which offers otherwise such an excellent text, must be regarded as quite secondary in importance, so far as *Judges* is concerned.

IV. Historical and Religious Value

From what has been said about the sources of our book, some of which go back in origin to an early time, it is evident that the book of *Judges* is of great historical value; indeed, without it we should lack almost all detailed knowledge of the history of Israel from the period of the gradual rise to predominance in Palestine of the Israelites to the eve of the foundation of the monarchy. It is true, the records are fragmentary and tell us only of certain outstanding episodes during the long drawn-out process of conquest; nevertheless, they give us a real insight into the way in which this process was carried out. It is but a bird's-eye view, dotted here and there with a few decisive events; but the general course of the history is unmistakeable. Moreover, the Deuteronomist has, all unconsciously and in spite of his theological ideas, indicated the true course of the history, viz. in a word, the ups and downs in the laborious task of conquest.

Of greater importance even is the insight obtainable of the nature of Hebrew religion during the pre-monarchic period. Here we are able to see plainly enough what, in spite of the acceptation of Yahweh worship, the pre-prophetic religion of Israel really was. This is not the place to go into details; [1] it must suffice to say that, together with many primitive ideas dating from time immemorial, it was a mixing-up of the worship of Yahweh with the Canaanite Baal-cult. That, in spite of several redactional processes dating from times when religious beliefs had greatly developed, the records of these early forms of worship should have been left untouched is a matter of profound interest. We are able, on the one hand, to realize the stupendous task with which the prophets were faced, and, on the other, to see an illustration of the truth expressed by the apostolic writer that God makes Himself known " by divers portions and in divers manners."

---

[1] See Oesterley and Robinson, *Hebrew Religion*, pp. 175 ff. (1930).

THE BOOK OF RUTH

I. Place in the Canon and Contents

In the Hebrew Canon the book of *Ruth* occupies the second place among the "Five Rolls," a group of short books which follows the longer poetical books, *Psalms, Proverbs, Job*, and thus belongs to the third section of the Bible. It tells a story of the days of the Judges, which has a bearing on the ancestry of David. A certain man of Bethlehem was compelled by famine to take refuge in Moab, together with his wife and two sons. The sons married Moabite women, and both they and their father died, leaving the three widows. Hearing a good account of conditions in Bethlehem, the mother-in-law, Naomi, decided to return there, and one of the daughters-in-law, Ruth, insisted on going with her (ch. i). The two women reached Bethlehem at the beginning of the harvest, and Ruth went to glean in the fields of a certain Boaz, a kinsman of the family into which Ruth had married, and was kindly treated (ch. ii). At the end of the harvest, on the advice of Naomi, Ruth sought out Boaz by night in his threshing-floor, and he agreed to see the family fortunes restored, acting in the capacity of "Go'el," or representative of the dead (ch. iii). This he did, purchased Naomi's land, and married Ruth, thus fulfilling the family duty, both in the matter of land and of posterity. Ruth bore Boaz a son, who was the grandfather of David.

II. Structure and Date

The story is very simply and beautifully told, and there is no doubt but that it was written as a complete work in practically the form in which we now have it. Possibly the genealogical note at the end is a later addition, intended to bring home the fact that a Moabitess was reckoned in David's ancestry.

The tale is obviously told as one of the distant past. The old custom of taking off the shoe to confirm a bargain

(iv. 7) was still in use when *Deuteronomy* was written,[1] and it is worth observing that the meaning of the act is no longer fully understood. In D it was a symbol of reproach; in *Ruth* it has become merely the ratification of a bargain. The refusal of the second kinsman to marry Ruth lest he should " mar his own inheritance," i.e. *fail* to continue his family line, is intelligible only in an age when monogamy was the rule, for otherwise he might have had another wife through whom he could have maintained his family. Incidentally it may be observed that the genealogies trace the descendants of Ruth, not as the posterity of her former husband, but as the children of Boaz. Finally, we may note that in the language of the book there are several indications of a comparatively late date—Aramaisms, one or two late forms, and some fairly obvious archaisms. There can be little doubt that the book was composed after the Exile.

III. Historical Background

The book itself gives us our only clues as to the conditions in which it was written. It stresses, apparently, the Moabite element in the ancestry of David. His Moabite connexions are suggested in i Sam. xxii. 3 f., where David, taking refuge himself in the cave of Adullam, commits his parents to the care of the king of Moab. Here the desire is, as it seems, to make the claims of Moab on Israel yet stronger. This suggests an age in which the Moabite was regarded with some hostility, and a broad-minded Israelite sought to mitigate this feeling by reminding his countrymen that the greatest of all Israelites since the days of Moses had Moabite blood in his veins. This would indicate a period in the latter half of the fifth century, when, under the influence of Nehemiah, an attempt was being made to eliminate Moabite connexions altogether from Israel.

IV. The Hebrew Text

The text is well preserved, and there are very few passages where there is any real doubt as to the reading. The versions do not differ greatly from the MT.

---

[1] Cp. Deut. xxv. 9, 10.

I II SAMUEL

I. TITLE

In the Hebrew Bible *i ii Samuel* figured as one book, entitled " Samuel "; but originally the books of *Samuel* and *Kings* formed one whole. The division of each of these into two books was due to the Septuagint, in which the books of *Samuel* and *Kings* were together regarded as containing a complete history of the kingdoms of Israel and Judah; so that in the Septuagint they appear as one historical work, entitled " Kingdoms " (βασιλειῶν), divided into four parts, viz. i " Kingdoms," etc. This was followed by Jerome in the Vulgate, with the difference that he called them *Regum*.

The division of these books which is familiar to us occurred first in the Hebrew Bible published by Daniel Bomberg in Venice 1517–18. Since then all printed Hebrew Bibles have followed this division.

Whatever may have been the reason for giving *i ii Samuel* the title of " Samuel " in the Hebrew Bible, there can be no question that it was an inappropriate one, and it is difficult to believe that it can originally have figured there as the title; for only in quite a few chapters does Samuel play any part, and about half-way through *i Samuel* he disappears entirely.[1] Nowhere is there any indication of Samuel having been the writer of the book; indeed in i Sam. xxv. 1 his death is recorded (cp. i Sam. xv. 35).

II. ANALYSIS

There are three main divisions: (*a*) i Sam. i–xv; (*b*) i Sam. xvi–ii Sam. viii; (*c*) ii Sam. ix–xx. 22.[2] To these ii Sam. xxi–xxiv are added as an Appendix.

[1] After i Sam. xvi. 13; the section xix. 18–24, in which Samuel is mentioned, is a Midrashic element, and of much later date.
[2] Verses 23–26 are out of place; see below, p. 87.

These divisions may be analysed as follows:

(*a*) i Sam. i–xv.   *The story of Eli.   The story of Saul to the time of his rejection by Samuel.*

i–iii.   Samuel's childhood.
iv–vii. 1.   The fall of the house of Eli.   Philistine victory at Aphek.   Loss of the Ark; its sojourn in Philistine territory; its return to the Israelites.
vii. 2–xii.   Establishment of the kingdom by Samuel; his retirement.
xiii–xv.   Saul's battles against the Philistines; defeat of the Amalekites; rejection of Saul by Samuel ("Samuel came no more to see Saul").

(*b*) i Sam. xvi–ii Sam. viii.   *Saul and David.*

xvi.   The anointing of David.   Saul is troubled by an evil spirit.   David is sent for; by his playing on the harp Saul is quieted.
xvii.   David's combat with Goliath.
xviii. 1–5.   David's covenant of friendship with Jonathan.
xviii. 6–16.   Saul's jealousy of David owing to the victory of the latter over the Philistines.
xviii. 17–xx.   Saul's ineffectual attempts to get rid of David.   The flight of David to Ramah.   The friendship of David and Jonathan.
xxi.   David flees to Nob; thence to Achish, king of Gath.
xxii.   David flees to the cave of Adullam; thence to Moab.   At Saul's command the priests of Nob are slain; Abiathar escapes and joins David.
xxiii.   David's victory over the Philistines at Keilah; he flees from Saul into the wilderness of Ziph; thence to the wilderness of Maon.   Saul pursues him, but gives up the pursuit owing to a Philistine attack.
xxiv.   David surprises Saul in the cave of Engedi, but spares his life.
xxv.   David and Nabal.
xxvi.   David steals into Saul's camp; Saul's life again spared.
xxvii.   David sojourns in the land of the Philistines.
xxviii.   Saul and the witch of Endor.
xxix.   David and Achish.
xxx.   David and the destruction of Ziklag.
xxxi–ii Sam. i.   Saul's defeat and death at the battle of Gilboa; David's sorrow; the "Song of the bow."
ii. 1–7.   David king of Judah.
ii. 8–iii. 1.   The war between David and Eshbaal ("Ish-bosheth").   The house of David and the house of Saul.
iii. 2–iv. 3.   David and Abner; the latter is slain by Joab.
iv. 4–12.   Death of Eshbaal.
v. 1–16.   David is recognized as king of all Israel.
v. 17–25.   David's victories over the Philistines.
vi.   The bringing up of the Ark to Jerusalem.
vii.   Nathan's prophecy of the permanence of the house of David.
viii.   David's valiant deeds.

(*c*) ii Sam. ix–xx.   *A record of the events which happened after Jerusalem had become the capital.   Davidic Narrative.*

ix.   David and Meribbaal, the last representative of the house of Saul.
x.   David's wars against the Ammonites and the Syrians.
xi–xii.   David and Bathsheba.   Nathan and David.
xiii.   Amnon and Tamar.   Absalom's revenge; flight to Talmai.
xiv.   Absalom is received into favour again.
xv–xx. 22.   Absalom's rebellion.   David's flight; Absalom is hindered from immediate pursuit by Hushai; David is thus enabled to reach a place of safety east of Jordan, where he gathers forces.   Absalom is defeated and slain in the ensuing battle.   Sheba's rebellion; sup-

pressed by Joab. Amasa appointed commander-in-chief of David's forces in place of Joab. Amasa is treacherously murdered by Joab. Death of Sheba.

xx. 23–26. A fragmentary list of some of David's officers.

xxi–xxiv. An Appendix consisting of a miscellaneous collection of literary pieces: xxi. 1–14 is a record of a famine in the days of David; it is interpreted as being due to Yahweh's anger because of Saul's un-avenged blood-guiltiness against the Gibeonites. David therefore delivers up the last of Saul's descendants; they are " hanged before Yahweh."

In xxi. 15–22 a brief reference is made to wars with the Philistines, and an account of the prowess of David's mighty men. The psalm contained in xxii appears in the Psalter as Ps. xviii. Another psalm, probably far more ancient, occurs in xxiii. 1–7. In xxiii. 8–23 there is a list of heroes and their valiant deeds; this is followed by another fragmentary piece (xxiii. 24–39), also containing the names of mighty men. In xxiv the narrative of David numbering the people is given.

It should be pointed out here that this Appendix, together with xx. 23–26, has been inserted in a very unfortunate place; and not less unfortunate is the division of ii Sam. from i Kgs. at this point; for i Kgs. i. 1–ii. 11 forms part of the division which begins at ii Sam. ix, *i.e.* the Davidic narrative. It is probable that i Kgs. i–ii. 11 was separated from the division to which it belonged because it seemed to be an appropriate introduction to the Solomon narrative. But this separation having once taken place there was nothing to prevent ii Sam. xx. 23–26 and the Appendix ii Sam. xxi–xxiv from being added.

This very summary analysis is merely intended to give a general idea of the subject-matter of i ii Sam.; there are many subdivisions of which no notice has been taken. But it will be found, as soon as the book is read in detail, that there are two things about it which must strike even a superficial reader. The first is that frequently the various sections follow one another without there being any con-nexion between them. The second is that in a number of instances the same narrative is told twice over. The explanation of these phenomena will be seen when we examine the sources of our book; for the present it will be well to give the most striking examples of duplicate narratives.

The account of the foundation of the monarchy occurs in two sets of passages: i Sam. ix. 1–x. 16; xi. 1–11, 15; and i Sam. viii. x. 17–25a, xii. There are two accounts of the origin of the saying, " Is Saul also among the prophets? " viz. i Sam. x. 10–12, and i Sam. xix. 18–24. Narratives of David coming to the court of Saul occur in i Sam. xvi. 14– 23 and in i Sam. xvii. 12–58. The rejection of Saul is dealt with in i Sam. xiii. 8–15 and in i Sam. xv. 10–26. There are two accounts of David's flight from Saul; the passages when gathered together are i Sam. xx. 4–10, 12– 17, 24–34, and xx. 1–3, 11, 18–23, 35–42. David's sojourn among the Philistines is recounted in i Sam. xxi. 10–15 and in i Sam. xxvii. 1–12. The treachery of the Ziphites is recorded in i Sam. xxiii. 19–28 and in i Sam. xxvi. 1–3, 25b (" So David went his way "). The narrative of how David spared the life of Saul when in his power is given in i Sam. xxiv. 1–22 and in i Sam. xxvi. 4–25a. There are two accounts of the death of Goliath, a detailed one in i Sam. xvii. 1–58, according to which he was slain by David, and another in ii Sam. xxi. 19, where it is merely said that Elhanan " slew Goliath the Gittite, the staff of whose spear was like a weaver's beam "; with this contrast i Sam. xvii. 45. The death of Saul is recounted in i Sam. xxxi. 4–6, where it is said that he committed suicide, and in ii Sam. ii. 8–10, which says that he was slain by an Amalekite. Finally, in ii Sam. xiv. 27 the children of Absalom are said to be three sons and one daughter, while in ii Sam. xviii. 18 Absalom is made to say, " I have no son to keep my name in remembrance."

These are the most striking duplicate accounts, but there are others. Their existence can be accounted for only on the supposition that *i ii Samuel* was compiled from more than one source. This subject must be considered next.

III. Sources

The main purpose for which *i ii Samuel* was compiled was to record the origin of the monarchy, the circumstances which led up to its establishment, and its consolidation under David. In other words, apart from minor details, it is the beginnings of the history of the Israelite kingdom which is the outstanding theme of *i ii Samuel*. This is borne out by the title which, as we have seen, was given by the Septuagint to the compendium which we call the books of *Samuel* and *Kings*, namely "Kingdoms," *i.e.* Judah and Israel.

Now, in the nature of things, the compilation of such a history, which for the people concerned was of profound interest and importance, would be undertaken by more than one historian; and they would not necessarily be contemporaries. Among the records available some might be accessible to one historian, others to another. So that when the compiler of our book gathered the materials for his history he found at his disposal more than one series of narratives. Thus the majority of modern scholars discern two or more sources which were drawn upon by the compiler, though considerable differences of opinion exist as to the respective sources to which the different parts of the book are to be assigned. Whether two sources were utilized by the compiler, according to some, or three, according to others, is a question extremely difficult to decide; all that can be said with certainty is that inasmuch as there are so many duplicate narratives there must have been more than one source available. Sellin, following Wellhausen, Cornill, Budde, and Kittel, believes in a two-source theory, and assigns, in general, the following portions to the earlier source: a strand in i Sam. i, ii and in iv–vi; the whole of ix. 1–x. 16; xi. 1–11, 15; xiii. 2–6, 15–23; xiv. 1–46, 52; xvi. 14–23; parts of xviii and xx; the whole of xxii, xxiv, xxv, xxvii–xxxi (excepting xxviii. 3–25); ii Sam. i. 17–vi. 23; ix–xx (in the main). To the later source are assigned: i Sam. i–iii in the main; a strand in iv–vi; the whole of vii. 2–17; viii; x. 17–25a; xii; xv; xvii. 1–xviii. 5; xviii. 6–30; xix; parts of xx, of xxi, and of xxiii. 1–13, 14–18; xxvi; xxviii. 3–25; ii Sam. i. 6–10, 14–16. The following passages in the Appendix (*i.e.* ii Sam. xxi–xxiv) are assigned to the *earlier* source: xxi. 1–14, 15–22; xxiii. 8–39.

Neither of these sources, as Sellin is careful to point out, is a unity " in the sense that it can have been written down at first in the form in which we now have it." On the contrary, as he adds, both sources include earlier material of varied origin.[1]

It should also be noted that these two sources show close

---

[1] *Introduction to the Old Testament*, p. 109 (English edition, 1923).

affinities with the J and E elements, respectively, recognizable
in the Hexateuch; the earlier with J, the later with E.
Some scholars go so far as actually to assign them to these
documents, and the symbols K^J and K^E have at times been
used to indicate them.[1]

A three-source theory has been recently championed by
Eissfeldt; [2] he discerns three strands of narrative running
throughout *i ii Samuel*; but, speaking generally, in i Sam.
they are largely interwoven, while in ii Sam. they are
written consecutively. Eissfeldt makes out a strong case for
his thesis, which is handled with conspicuous ability; his
three strands of the narrative of the foundation of the
monarchy are certainly convincing, as will be seen if the
following sets of passages be read separately:

(*a*) i Sam. x. 21b^β–27; xi. 1–5, 6b–15. (*b*) ix; x. i–16.
(*c*) viii; x. 17–21b^α ; xii.

But it is questionable whether the three-source theory can
be sustained throughout in spite of Eissfeldt's most careful
analysis.[3]

Further, apart from the sources, there can be no shadow of
doubt that the book has undergone more than one redactional process; that opinions vary to some extent as to the
precise passages which belong to the different redactions is
inevitable; a certain amount of subjectivity is bound to
come into play here. Broadly speaking, however, it may be
said that (1) the book has been considerably worked over
by the Deuteronomists, probably more than one scribe of
this school is to be discerned; the Deuteronomistic revision
is evident in i Sam. ii. 36; iv. 8b; vi. 15; vii. 3, 4, 13, 14;
xii. 10, 12; xiv. 47–51; ii Sam. v. 4, 5; vii. 13; viii; and
possibly elsewhere; (2) and that later, post-exilic additions
include ii Sam. xxi–xxiv; i Sam. ii. 1–10 (Hannah's Song);
ii Sam. xxii. 1–51 (David's thanksgiving), and ii Sam. xxiii.
1–7 (the " Last words of David ") ; though with regard to
" Hannah's song," many authorities claim an earlier date.

---

[1] This has been rightly discountenanced by Kittel, *Das erste Buch Samuel*
in Kautzsch-Bertholet, i. 408 (1922).
[2] *Die Komposition der Samuelisbücher* (1931).
[3] *Op. cit.*, pp. 56–62. See also Hylander, *Der literarische Samuel-Saul-Komplex*
i Sam. i–xv (1933).

IV. The Hebrew Text and the Septuagint

It is recognized on all hands that, with the exception of the books of *Ezekiel* and *Hosea*, no book of the Old Testament contains so many textual corruptions as *i ii Samuel*. For some reason which cannot now be known, the MS. or MSS. of our book used by those who constructed the Massoretic text [1] were in a particularly corrupt state; the Septuagint translator, on the other hand, had before him a MS. which in numberless cases contained a purer form of text. It happens, therefore, over and over again that the form of the Hebrew text as we now have it presents corruptions which can be rectified by means of the Greek text. Many of these rectifications may not be of much importance, but they certainly often make the meaning of a text clearer. An example occurs in i Sam. i. 9, where the Revised Version reads: " So Hannah rose up after they had eaten in Shiloh, and after they had drunk "; [2] the Septuagint has, it is true, " in Shiloh " which should be emended to " in the feast chamber," attached to every sanctuary where the sacrificial meal took place [3] (see i Sam. ix. 22); with this emendation added, it reads: " And Hannah rose up after they had eaten in the (feast-) chamber, and stood up before the Lord " (*i.e.* to pray, as the words which follow show). Or, again, in i Sam. iv. 13 the Hebrew has: " Eli sat upon his seat by the way side watching " (R. V.), but it is not clear as to what he was watching; the Septuagint reads: " Eli sat beside the gate, looking along the road," *i.e.* looking out for the messenger from the field of battle, which is more graphic. At times the Septuagint has passages which have fallen out of the Hebrew; thus in i Sam. iv. 1 before, " Now Israel went out against the Philistines to battle," which reads as though the Israelites were the attackers, the Septuagint has: " And it came to pass in those days that the Philistines were gathered together against Israel to war," which shows

---

[1] See above, pp. 13 f.

[2] The impossible form of the Hebrew as it now stands cannot, of course, be realized by the English paraphrase.

[3] The two words are very similar in Hebrew, and would easily have been confused by a copyist.

that the Philistines were attacking, and that is in accordance with the conditions of the times. Other important omissions in the Hebrew text are supplied by the Septuagint. On the other hand, passages are sometimes missing in the Septuagint which are preserved in the Hebrew, the most notable examples of which occur in i Sam. xvii, xviii.

It is, therefore, quite clear that *i ii Samuel* cannot be studied without constant reference to the Septuagint; at the same time, the Septuagint is by no means always reliable, and caution is always needed in making use of it.

I II KINGS

I. Contents

THESE books record the history of the kingdoms of Israel and Judah from the accession of Solomon to the fall of Jerusalem, approximately 970–586 B.C. There are three main divisions:

(*a*) i Kgs. ii. 12–xi.[1] The history of the reign of Solomon, 970–933 B.C.
(*b*) i Kgs. xii–ii Kgs. xvii. The history of the kingdoms of Israel and Judah to the fall of the northern kingdom, 933–721 B.C.
(*c*) ii Kgs. xviii–xxv. The history of the kingdom of Judah from the reign of Hezekiah to its fall, 721–586 B.C. (more strictly, to the release of Jehoiachin from his prison in Babylon, 562 B.C.).

Within these main divisions there are many subdivisions; it will not be necessary to enumerate these in detail, for many of them will come into consideration later.

II. Sources

i. The oldest source was a document which contained the history of the period immediately preceding the foundation of the monarchy; it included also the history of a large part of Solomon's reign, and was probably written towards the end of this reign. It is characteristic of this source that the historical narratives which it contains are told in a pleasant, one might almost say a chatty style. It is a source of high value, for it reveals an intimate knowledge of David in his old age, and of the court intrigues which led to Solomon's usurpation of the throne, Adonijah being the legitimate heir.

ii. The next source is mentioned by name in i Kgs. xi. 41 : " Now the rest of the acts of Solomon, and all that he did,

[1] i Kgs. i–ii. 11 belong to the preceding division, *i.e.* ii Sam. ix–xx. 22; see above, p. 87.

and his wisdom, are they not written in the book of the
' Acts of Solomon ' ? " Here we have definite reference to
a work with its title which was clearly well known. It is
important to note that the compiler of *i Kings* does not give
an exhaustive transcript of this book, otherwise he would
not refer to it for further information; we have, thus, only
extracts from it. As to the date of this source, from the
nature of the case it cannot have been written very long
after the reign of Solomon, so that one may date it approximately as belonging to the earlier part of the ninth century.
The contents and nature of this source can be gathered from
extracts in *i Kings*: it is much more a biographical than an
historical narrative. It begins by telling of Solomon's
marriage with the daughter of the king of Egypt (iii. 1),
then of the dream he had in Gibeon (iii. 4–15). In iii. 16–
28 we have the narrative of Solomon's judgement; the
parallels to this which are found in other Oriental literatures
make it probable that Solomon's biographer culled it from
some extraneous source and applied it to his hero. Then in
iv. 1–19 there are lists, (*a*) of Solomon's princes or ministers
(1–6), and (*b*) of his household officers. Whether these
lists were actually in the book, or were taken from some
official record and added, cannot be said with certainty;
but as they seem to be Solomon's personal officials it is
likely that the lists figured in his biography. We then come
to three long sections; first, Solomon's treaty with Hiram
of Tyre, and the preparations for the building of the Temple
(v. 1–18, Hebr. 15–32); then, the building of the Temple and
of the royal palace (vi. 1–vii. 51), and, lastly, the dedication of
the Temple (viii. 1–66). These have been very greatly worked
over by later hands; but the kernel, it may be confidently
asserted, was found in the " Acts of Solomon." The remaining extracts tell of further dealings between Solomon
and Hiram (ix. 11–14); the building of Millo (ix. 23–25);
Solomon's wisdom and the visit of the Queen of Sheba
(ix. 26–x. 29); and possibly, though this is rather uncertain,
the account of Solomon's two enemies, Hadad the Edomite
and Rezon of Damascus (xi. 14–25); wherever this last
came from it certainly contains some reliable historical
matter. A final fragment may well be the words telling of

how Solomon sought to kill Jeroboam, who, however, managed to escape, and found an asylum with Shishak, king of Egypt, until the death of Solomon (xi. 40).

These complete the extracts from the " Acts of Solomon," and it will be seen that they are really *biographical*, so that this source was not an historical one in the strict sense.

iii and iv. These two sources, which may be taken together, are of the greatest importance. They are both mentioned by name, the " Book of the Chronicles of the kings of Israel," and the " Book of the Chronicles of the kings of Judah." They are referred to for the first time in i Kgs. xiv. 19 and 29, respectively, where Jeroboam and Rehoboam are spoken of; from this it is evident that these two sources begin their history after the division of the kingdom; this is what might be expected, inasmuch as the " Acts of Solomon " brings the history down to the end of the reign of Solomon. The sources in question are mentioned in connexion with nearly all the kings of Israel and Judah, and since they are referred to for further details about these kings it is clear that they were utilized only in part. That these sources were drawn upon for some of the passages in i ii Chron. which have no parallel in i ii Kgs. is certain,[1] though to what extent this was the case cannot be determined.

Regarding the nature and contents of these two sources, it is to be noted that since we have only extracts from them we can only surmise what they actually consisted of; but one thing is clearly indicated by the nature of many of the extracts, viz. that the sources cannot have been official documents; they did not contain the official annals of the two kingdoms respectively, for they are too human and unconventional for that. A good illustration of this is the account, in i Kgs. xii. 2–20, of Rehoboam's dealings with Jeroboam and his following who came to ask for a remission of imposts; there we get a graphic and interesting narrative as far removed as anything could be from what an official document would contain, and written in a style quite unthinkable in such a document. Since, then, these two sources were not official documents, they must have been

[1] See below, p. 113.

compiled by private individuals; this is not to say that
public records were not made use of; they certainly were,
it would be an obvious course for any historian writing the
history of his country; so that when wars are described, or
political events, or public acts by the king, or accounts of
public buildings, such as fortifications, royal palaces, etc.,
in all such cases it is more than likely that official documents
were utilized; but the putting together of the material thus
gathered was, in the case of the two sources under consideration, the work of private individuals.   In general, it is
not difficult to indicate the various extracts from these two
sources occurring in i ii Kgs., and for the most part scholars
are agreed here; they are as follows; to which of the two
sources each passage belongs is, in almost every case, so
obvious that it will not be necessary to indicate this:

> i Kings xii. 2–20; xiv. 25–28, 30; xv. 16–28; xvi. 9,
>   10, 15–22, 34; xxii. 44 (Heb. 45), 47–50;
> ii Kings i. 1; viii. 20–22; x. 32, 33; xi. 1–20; xii.
>   1–16, 17–19; xiii. 7, 22–24; xiv. 5, 7, 8–14, 22;
>   xv. 5, 10, 14, 16, 19, 20, 25, 29, 30, 37;[1] xvi. 5–18;
>   xvii. 3–6, 24–28; xviii. 3, 4, 8, 14–16; xxi. 23, 24;
>   xxiii. 29, 30, 33–35; xxiv. 1, 2, 7.

These forty extracts show from their contents their place
of origin; and the two types of form in which they occur,
viz. sometimes very brief entries, at others elaborated
narratives, show that, on the one hand, official records have
been utilized, and, on the other, that the writers gave their
own account of events of which they were cognizant.

These two sources in their completed form are of different
dates; with regard to the " Book of the Chronicles of the
kings of Israel," since the compiler of i ii Kgs. makes no
reference to the original work in the case of Hoshea—the
only reign which is not mentioned in the source—it seems
evident that this was completed before his reign, and that
a few additions were subsequently made by some other
writer; this would give the date of the source as near the

---

[1] It is worth noting how full ch. xv is of isolated records; they are much
in the form in which entries would have been made in official records; evidently
all these notes were taken from such.

end of the eighth century. The " Book of the Chronicles
of the kings of Judah " is carried down to the eve of the
Exile, and will therefore have been completed towards the
end of the seventh century; and here again it is likely
enough that a few records were added later.

Let it be repeated that while the nature and contents of
the passages given above justify the conclusion that, in
general, they belong to one or other of the two sources
mentioned, there are doubtless some cases in regard to
which it would be unwise to dogmatize.

v. Our next source, which is not, however, reckoned
as a special one by most commentators, may provisionally
be called the " Acts of Ahab." This king is also dealt with
in two other sources to which reference will be made later.
The reason why all of these are not treated as one source
will be explained as we proceed; here it may merely be
mentioned that the provisionally named source, " Acts of
Ahab," is sufficiently distinctive to permit of its being treated
as a separate source. As the provisional title implies,[1]
this document is concerned with king Ahab; but not, as in
the " Acts of Solomon," with the king personally; it deals
with the special episodes of Ahab's battles against the
Aramæans; so that while Ahab forms the central figure in
it, the source is not a biographical, but an historical one.
The extracts from it in i Kgs. will be found in chaps. xx and
xxii. 1–40, though these have been considerably worked
over by later hands for specific purposes. There are not
many instances in the historical books of the Old Testament
of so much space being devoted to the history or doings of
one king; where this is the case—David, Solomon, Hezekiah
—there is either proof or high probability that special
memoirs concerning them existed. And since Ahab has a,
comparatively speaking, large amount of space devoted to
his reign, and since also he appears prominently in another
source (the " Elijah narratives "), and was clearly, therefore,
one of the more important among the Israelite kings, the
supposition that a special document containing his memoirs

---

[1] Of course there is no such title in reality, it is only adopted here for convenience' sake.

H

existed does not seem unreasonable. There is a further
reason which may be regarded as supporting this supposition.
The Syrian power was at this time the most formidable of
Israel's foes; Assyria had, as yet, not come within the
purview of practical politics so far as Israel was concerned.
In the reign of Omri the land had suffered seriously from
Syrian inroads (i Kgs. xx. 34); Ahab, on the other hand,
was successful in averting this Syrian menace (i Kgs. xx.
29, 30). Further, his Phœnician alliance must have been
of great service to his country politically and commercially;
and his alliance with Judah was all to the good; the de-
famation of which he has been the victim owing to the
animus of those who lived in later times and judged him
from their religious point of view, must not blind us to the
fact that Ahab was one of the greatest of Israel's kings.
To the people of his own day he was a far-seeing, beneficent
ruler, who did a great deal in strengthening the position of
his country and furthering the general well-being. These
things being so, it is highly probable that memoirs of him
existed, quite apart from other official records. An " Acts
of Ahab " source may, therefore, be postulated, giving it a
title which, it is granted, is not used in the Old Testament.
Ahab died, approximately, in the year 853 B.C., and as the, in
the main, reliable details about his Syrian wars cannot have
been written very long after his death, we may regard this
source as belonging to the later part of the ninth century.

vi. The next source, from which long portions have been
taken, was a collection of " Elijah narratives." [1] They are
comprised in i Kgs. xvii, xviii, xix, 1–18, xxi, ii Kgs. i, and,
like all the sources utilized, they have been worked over by
subsequent scribes in the interests of later points of view.
The longest of these extracts (xviii) deals with the well-
known religious contest on mount Carmel, the introduction
to it being contained in xvii (verses 17–24, the raising of the
widow's son, is a digression). While we have in this story
some elements of the wonder-tale, there can be no doubt

---

[1] Although we are treating the Elijah and Elisha (see below) narratives
as separate sources, the possibility is recognized of there having been but one
source in which narratives concerning a number of prophets were collected;
there are references to several others in i ii Kings.

that the main narrative contains a substantial kernel of historical truth. The next narrative, quite self-contained, tells of the divine manifestation to Elijah on mount Horeb (xix. 1–18). And here again there is an undoubted historical nucleus, but overlaid by some imaginative detail. The extract in xxi, which deals with the judicial murder of Naboth, bears on the face of it the marks of historical truth; but, as in the rest of these narratives, later hands have been at work upon it for their own purposes. The last extract (ii Kgs. i) seems to be not much more than a fragment with a considerable added piece (verses 9–17).

Now in the first and last of these narratives (excluding the fragment just mentioned) Ahab plays a part; it may therefore well be asked what the reason is for the contention, not held by most commentators, that the source which we have called the " Acts of Ahab " is not part of the " Elijah narratives." Apart from the reason already given regarding the personality of Ahab and the important *rôle* he played in the history of his country, there are these two further considerations : (1) the wholly different nature of the two sources, respectively; the Ahab source is purely historical, the Elijah narratives are mainly personal, while they have a large admixture of legendary matter. Two bodies of such fundamentally different material are not likely to have been comprised in one and the same source. (2) The point of view regarding the attitude towards Syria is quite different in the two sources. In the Elijah narratives Syria is represented as Yahweh's avenger on His recreant people, so that the point of view is one favourable to Syria. But in the Ahab source it is precisely the contrary; the whole attitude is vehemently anti-Syrian. Two such opposed points of view are, again, not to be looked for in one and the same source. The probability seems thus to point to an Ahab source distinct from the Elijah narratives in spite of the fact that in two of these latter Ahab plays a not unimportant part.

vii. The seventh source is of a similar nature to that just considered; it may be termed the " Elisha narratives." These occupy a considerable portion of *ii Kings*; they consist largely of a number of popular wonder tales, and are not of the historical value of much that occurs in the Elijah narratives. The *naïveté* of the stories marks them as ancient; and in many particulars they have preserved Hebrew customs and belief as these existed in the ninth century B.C.; from that point of view this source is distinctly valuable. In addition, though not much is to be gained from it which throws light on the history of the times, here and there some fragments of tradition appear which may well reflect actual fact.

It is possible that the Elijah—and the Elisha—narratives come from a single source, as many commentators hold; but two facts militate against this: (1) the Elijah narratives, both in conception and form, stand on a distinctly higher level than the Elisha narratives; as compared with the former the latter are almost puerile. The Elijah narratives sometimes rise to a grandeur which is never even remotely touched in the Elisha narratives; and this is not due only to the vastly nobler figure of Elijah, it is certainly in part, at any rate, owing to the finer literary ability of the writer of the Elijah narratives. The compiler of *Kings* may have found the two sets of narratives in one collection, but it is difficult to believe that originally they belonged to the same source. (2) The other reason is the disorder of the Elisha narratives; one has only to read them a little carefully to see that they are chronologically out of place. But this is not the case with the Elijah narratives. That is, of course, not a conclusive argument; but this fact is more easily accounted for on the assumption that they belong to different sources.

The extracts from this source are as follows: first we have a brief notice of what may be designated the call of Elisha (i Kgs. xix. 19–21); this is quite fragmentary and entirely separated from the main body of the narratives. Then in ii Kgs. ii occur several episodes which look as though they had originally been separate entries in the book of Elisha narratives, and which have more or less been welded together by the compiler of *Kings*. Thus, ii. 1–6 tells of the journey of Elijah and Elisha from Gilgal, via Bethel and Jericho to the Jordan; ii. 7–15 describes Elijah's ascent in the chariot of fire; ii. 16–18 tells of the fruitless search for Elijah's body by fifty of Elisha's followers; ii. 19–22 is an account of the miracle of healing the waters; and ii. 23–25 contains the story of the mocking children. These give the impression of having once been short independent narratives. The next narrative is longer (ii Kgs. iii), and it is an open question whether it really belongs to the Elisha narratives or not. It tells of the battle of the allied kings of Israel, Judah and Edom against the Moabites. The Israelite king, though not referred to by name, is probably Ahab (see i Kgs. xxii. 20, 39), the contemporary of Jehoshaphat, who is mentioned. It may, therefore, be that this chapter is an extract from the " Acts of Ahab "; on the other hand, Elisha plays an important part in the narrative, which inclines one to the belief that it belonged to the Elisha narrative source. In any case we have the echo here of some actual historical episode.

A very long series of Elisha narratives, with additions by a later hand, follows in chs. iv–vii; we need not go into the details of these, they are almost wholly concerned with miracles performed by Elisha; as some of them are strikingly similar to wonders ascribed to Elijah, the possibility of a mixing-up of sources here must be reckoned with.

More important are the extracts dealing with Elisha's anointing of Hazael (viii. 7–15), and the long account of Jehu's rebellion and usurpation of the throne, prompted by Elisha (ix. x); in these a considerable element of actual history is to be discerned. The last two extracts from the Elisha narratives are contained in ii Kgs. xiii. 14–21; one tells of king Joash's interview with the prophet (verses 14–19), and the other recounts the death of Elisha; it gives us another miracle of how a dead man came to life again by being brought into contact with the prophet's corpse.

Taken as a whole, these narratives, while reflecting history in only a minor degree, are very valuable for their extraordinary human interest, quite apart from anything else.

viii. The last source is the " Isaiah narratives " contained in ii Kgs. xviii. 13–(excluding verses 14–16)–xx. 19; this occurs also almost word for word in Isa. xxxvi–xxxix. That they were not written by Isaiah himself is evident from the fact that he is always spoken of in the third person. There was certainly a collection of narratives extant describing events in the life of Isaiah; that is clear from several things which are said in chs. vii and x of his book; in all likelihood this was the source utilized by the compiler of *Kings*. It may be regarded as belonging approximately to the end of the seventh century.

There are thus eight sources which were utilized in compiling *i ii Kings*. But there are large portions in these books which cannot have come from any of these sources. To these attention must next be directed.

III. Deuteronomic Elements

i. A striking characteristic of *Kings* is the way in which the events of the reigns of each of the kings of Israel and Judah are fitted into a stereotyped framework of opening and concluding formulas. Thus, *e.g.*, in i Kgs. xv. 9, 10 we read: " And in the twentieth year of Jeroboam king of Israel began Asa to reign over Judah. And forty and one years reigned he in Jerusalem "; and in i Kgs. xv. 33: " In the third year of Asa king of Judah began Baasha the son of Ahijah to reign over all Israel in Tirzah, (and he reigned) twenty and four years." That is the introductory formula; there is likewise a stereotyped concluding formula for the end of each reign; for the southern kingdom, *e.g.*, i Kgs. xv. 7, 8: " And the rest of the acts of Abijam, and all that he did, are they not written . . .? And Abijam slept with his fathers . . . And Asa his son reigned in his stead "; and for the northern kingdom, *e.g.*, i Kgs. xv. 31: " Now the rest of the acts of Nadab, and all that he did, are they not written . . ." The exact words of these formulas often vary in detail, but in general they are the same. A further point in them is that they contain an estimate of each king; and this estimate is couched in one of three forms: it is either a condemnation pure and simple, or it is an approval modified by some words of disapprobation, or it is whole-hearted approval. The first is expressed in the words: "And he did that which was evil in the sight of Yahweh " with some specifying detail. The second runs more or less in the form: "And he did that which was right in the eyes of Yahweh . . ., howbeit, the high places were not taken away, the people sacrificed, and burned incense in the high places." And the third, which is, however, very rare, is expressed by the words: "And he did that which was right in the eyes of Yahweh," followed by the details of the king's right action (ii Kgs. xviii. 3 ff., xxii. 2). These formulas also differ, sometimes there are considerable variations, but the essential meaning is always the same.

Regarding these three latter types of formulas, it is found that, with a few exceptions to be considered presently, when a king is said to have done that which is evil in the sight of Yahweh, without any modifying addition, it is a ruler of the *northern* kingdom. When a ruler of the *southern* kingdom is referred to he is dealt with in this way: if he has done evil, there is some extenuating circumstance added; if he has done right, a "nevertheless" is added. The third formula, in reference to a ruler who has done right absolutely, is reserved for two kings of the *southern* kingdom, Hezekiah and Josiah.

As to the exceptions; out of the nineteen *northern* kings there are two: in the case of Shallum nothing is said, for the simple reason that he only reigned a month (ii Kgs. xv. 13); [1] in the case of Hoshea, the last king of Israel, for some reason which is not known to us, it is said of him that though he did what was evil in the sight of Yahweh, yet it was "not as the kings of Israel that were before him" (ii Kgs. xvii. 2). Otherwise every ruler of the northern kingdom is evil, pure and simple.

Regarding the *southern* kingdom there are several exceptions; they are these: *Rehoboam*; he is spoken of as having done evil, but the blame seems to be attached to Judah as a whole rather than to the king specifically (i Kgs. xiv. 22).

[1] On the other hand, judgement is passed on Zimri though he reigned for only one week (i Kgs. xvi. 15–20).

Jehoram, *Ahaziah*, and *Athaliah* are all evil, but the fact that they were related to Ahab, the very bad king of Israel (according to later ideas), is mentioned as an extenuating circumstance (ii Kgs. viii. 18, 27). In regard to *Ahaz*, although he is spoken of as having been as bad as any of the kings of Israel, yet the stereotyped formula, " he did evil in the sight of Yahweh," is toned down, and it is said that " he did not that which was right in the eyes of Yahweh " (ii Kgs. xvi. 2). This applies also to *Abijah* (i Kgs. xv. 3). Two other exceptions are *Manasseh* and his son *Amon*, who for the obvious reasons, which are given, are unmitigatedly evil; and finally, for a reason which we shall come to presently, the last four kings of Judah, *Jehoahaz* (but he only reigned for three months), *Jehoiakim*, *Jehoiachin*, and *Zedekiah*, are all spoken of as evil, pure and simple.

There is a further point to be considered regarding the rest of the Judæan kings. They are all (apart from the exceptions just mentioned) said to have done what is right in the sight of Yahweh, but there is a significant qualifying remark which is added; and that is to this effect: " Howbeit the high places were not taken away, the people still sacrificed and burned incense in the high places "; [1] it is significant that in regard to every single king of *Judah*, mention is made, either explicitly or by implication, of the high places (*bamoth*); even in the case of Hezekiah and Josiah, who both did what was right in the sight of Yahweh, it is thought necessary to emphasize this by adding that they did away with the high places.

With regard to the kings of Israel, on the other hand, the evil of which they are all guilty centres primarily in the fact that they favoured the high places; of Jeroboam i, who appears as the evil genius of practically all his successors, it is said that he made from among all the people priests of the high places (i Kgs. xiii. 33); his son Nadab walked in the way of his father; after that it is said of each of the kings (Shallum and Hoshea alone excepted) that " he walked in the way of Jeroboam the son of Nebat," or " he walked

---

[1] i Kgs. xv. 11 f.; xxii. 43; ii Kgs. viii. 18, 27; xii. 2, 3; xiv. 3, 4; xv. 3, 4, 34 f.

in the sins of Jeroboam the son of Nebat." This is likewise
a stereotyped phrase, and implies worship on the high places.

There can be no doubt that the formulas and stereotyped
phrases referred to are to be assigned to a Deuteronomic
redactor; this is particularly evident in the cases of the
mention of the high places, for, apart from passages which
are demonstrably of Deuteronomic inspiration, there is
never a word of condemnation of the high places; neither
Elijah, nor Elisha, nor any other prophet of this age has a
word to say against them (on the contrary, see *e.g.* i Kgs.
iii. 4, xviii. 23); but in the Deuteronomic legislation it is
very different, one illustration, of many, may be cited:
" . . . Ye shall surely destroy all the places, wherein the
nations which ye shall possess served their gods, upon the
high mountains, and upon the hills, and under every green
tree . . ." (Deut. xii. 1 ff.). The destruction of the high
places and the centralization of worship in Jerusalem were
among the outstanding features of the Deuteronomic
legislation. The introductory and concluding formulas
spoken of above are also the work of the Deuteronomic
redactor, though the chronological and other details which
they contain were doubtless derived from material to which
he had access.

But these series of passages by no means exhaust the
Deuteronomic elements in *Kings*. The style of the book
of *Deuteronomy* is very characteristic and easily distinguishable; and its religious point of view is always recognizable;
so that when in the book of *Kings* both the literary style
and the religious ideas of *Deuteronomy* appear there can be
no doubt about the origin of passages in which they occur.
Many illustrations could be given, it must suffice to indicate
the most striking: i Kgs. ii. 1–4; viii. 22–66 (omitting
41–51); xi. 9–13, 29–38; xii. 26–31; xiv. 1–24; xv. 1–15;
ii Kgs. xvii. 21–23; xxii; xxiii. 1–15, 21–28.

IV. OTHER REDACTIONAL ELEMENTS

There are a certain number of passages which are not in
the Deuteronomic style, nor do they contain indications of

belonging to any of the sources mentioned; as a rule, the reasons for regarding these as later additions are fairly obvious; one illustration may be given: in ii Kgs. xiv. 5, 6 an extract from the Judæan source records how Amaziah put to death all those who had been concerned in the murder of his father Joash (see ii Kgs. xii. 20, 21), nevertheless, that the children of the murderers were spared; but to this there is added: " according to all that is written in the book of the law of Moses, as Yahweh commanded, saying, The fathers shall not be put to death for the children, nor the children be put to death for the fathers; but every man shall die for his own sin; " this latter is a *verbatim* quotation from Deut. xxiv. 16; but it is not added by the Deuteronomic redactor because he never does *quote* from *Deuteronomy*; he impresses his point of view in his well-known style, but does not give quotations; a quotation of this kind is the mark of later usage. Various other illustrations could be given (see, *e.g.*, ii Kgs. xiii. 23). Other redactional elements are: i Kgs. iv. 20–v. 6; viii. 41–51; ix. 1–9; xx. 35–43; ii Kgs. i. 9–16; xvii. 7–20, 29–40; xxi. 7–15; xxiii. 16–20, 26, 27.

V. The Septuagint

Although the Septuagint is in many places very corrupt it is quite indispensable for the study of *Kings*. Again and again corrupt passages in the Hebrew text can be corrected by referring to the Septuagint; and what is of special interest is that it is quite evident that in many cases the Hebrew text underlying the Septuagint was a purer one than that represented by the Massoretic text. This is not to say that the Massoretic text is not often demonstrably superior to that of the Septuagint; that is quite obviously the case in many instances; but, none the less, the Septuagint cannot be dispensed with.

In a very large number of cases, the cumulative effect of which is imposing, there are small variations in the Septuagint which indicate a manifestly better type of Hebrew text

than that which we now possess; one or two illustrations
may be given:

In i Kgs. xi. 3 the Hebrew has: " And he (Solomon)
had seven hundred wives . . .; and his wives turned
away his heart;" the last sentence is omitted by the
Septuagint; it is not wanted, as it occurs in the next verse.
In i Kgs. ii. 19 it is said in the Hebrew, in reference to
Solomon: " and he set a throne for the king's mother;"
for an Oriental king to do a thing like this is extremely
improbable; the Septuagint reads: " and there was set
a throne . . .," implying that this was done by the king's
servants. In ii Kgs. vi. 11 the Hebrew has a clumsy and
improbable form in the sentence: " will ye not tell me
which of us is for the king of Israel?" In place of this the
Septuagint reads: " will ye not tell me who (it is that) is
slandering (*i.e.* betraying) us to the king of Israel?" In
ii Kgs. x. 15 the Hebrew has: ". . . And Jehonadab
answered, It is. If it be, give me thy hand." In place of
" If it be," which is meaningless, the Septuagint reads:
" And Jehu said, Give . . ." These are just a few of a
large number of instances in which the Septuagint witnesses
to a Hebrew text superior to the Massoretic; individually
they may not, as a rule, be important, but their number is
significant. Apart from these, however, there are many
passages in the Septuagint which do not occur in the
Massoretic text at all. Several of these interpolations are
not of much value, but others are important; so, *e.g.*, the
longest of them, which comes after i Kgs. xii. 24; here
there are recorded the events connected with the death of
Solomon together with a summary of the reign of Rehoboam;
then there is an account of the revolt of Jeroboam, with a
repetition of what has already been told in chs. xi, xii, and
anticipating ch. xiv; but, as Swete says, " the passage is no
mere *cento* of verses to be found elsewhere either in the
Septuagint or in the Massoretic text; it is a second and
distinct recension of the story, resting equally with the first
on a Hebrew original. So different, and indeed in some
respects contradictory, are the accounts that they cannot
possibly have stood from the first in the same volume. . . .

The present Greek version of *i Kings* has preserved two ancient accounts of the dismemberment of the kingdom of David and Solomon, and though one of these survives also in the Massoretic text, there is no *à priori* ground for deciding which of the two is the more trustworthy." [1]

Valuable from another point of view is a notice preserved in Lucian's recension of the Septuagint in ii Kgs. xiii. 22: "And Hazael took the Philistine out of his land from the Western Sea unto Aphek." This, as Wellhausen has pointed out, shows where the true position of Aphek was, on the northern border of the Philistines, and throws light on the Philistine and Syrian invasion of central Palestine, for which Aphek served as a base. Samaria was thus not attacked from the north by the Syrians, but from the west, *i.e.* it would have been a flank, not a frontal, attack; from the Philistine land there was, by way of Megiddo, a good road into the heart of Israel's land. [2]

From these two illustrations, of many, it will be realized how indispensable the Septuagint is for the study of *i ii Kings*. [3]

[1] *Introduction to the Old Testament in Greek*, p. 248 (1900).

[2] *Composition des Hexateuchs*, p. 254; Lucian's recension was published by Lagarde (Göttingen, 1883).

[3] For valuable help see Rahlfs, *Septuaginta-Studien*, 1. Heft: "Studien zu den Königsbüchern" (1904); 3. Heft: "Lucians Recension der Königs-bücher" (1911).

I II CHRONICLES

I. TITLE AND PLACE IN THE CANON

THE Hebrew title, *Dibre hayyamim*, means literally "the things of the days," *i.e.* the events of the times. The Septuagint title *Paraleipomena*, "things omitted," *i.e.* from the other historical books, would seem to be due to a misunderstanding (see below). It is followed by the Vulgate: *Paralipomenon, primus et secundus*. But Jerome (*Prologus Galeatus*) suggested the Latin title, *Chronicon totius historiæ divinæ*; and it is from this that the title in the English Bible is derived.

In the Hebrew Canon *Chronicles* belongs to the *Kethubim*, or "Writings" (*Hagiographa*), and it comes last of all the Old Testament books. Originally *Chronicles* and *Ezra–Nehemiah* formed a single work (see below, § II); that the historically earlier portion (i ii Chron.) should be placed after the later is probably to be accounted for by the fact that *Ezra–Nehemiah* first found a place in the Canon without i ii Chron., the history of which was covered by i ii Kgs. (in the main); afterwards, however, it was thought well to include i ii Chron.—though only as an appendix—for it presented the history from a point of view which appealed to the later dominant school of thought. However this may be, there cannot be any doubt that the admission into the Canon of *Chronicles* was later than that of *Ezra–Nehemiah*; had that not been the case the former would certainly have been placed before the latter in the order of the Old Testament books. That the English Bible places *Chronicles* after *Kings* and before *Ezra–Nehemiah*, differing therein from the Hebrew Canon, is due to the Vulgate.

II. Chronicles and Ezra–Nehemiah

That these books originally formed a single work is generally recognized: the reasons for this conclusion are as follows:

(1) The end of ii Chron., *i.e.* xxxvi. 22, 23, which records the opening sentences of the decree of Cyrus, is repeated at the beginning of the book of *Ezra* (cp. also iii Ezra ii. 1 ff.); but in the former the sentence is incomplete, while in *Ezra* the whole of the decree is recorded; ii Chron. has therefore, properly speaking, no ending, as the words with which its present form ends are really the beginning of the book of *Ezra* (*i.e.* ii Chron. xxxvi. 22, 23 = Ezra i. 1–3a), the narrative runs on from one to the other. This does not, it is true, necessarily mean that the two books form part of one whole; but the fact that in *Ezra* the history is taken up from the point reached in ii Chron. does give the impression that the two belong together. The repetition is probably to be accounted for in this way: originally it was, of course, not there; the whole was a continuous narrative; but the part of the narrative comprised in *Ezra–Nehemiah* was, as has been pointed out, admitted into the Canon, while this was not the case with that contained in i ii Chron.; this latter was thus left without a conclusion. Later, when i ii Chron. was also admitted into the Canon, though not in its original position before *Ezra–Nehemiah*, it became necessary to add what was deemed a fitting conclusion, and what are now the last two verses of ii Chron. offered this in so far as they made the book end on a note of triumph. That Ezra i. 1 ff., and not ii Chron. xxxvi. 22, 23, has the original text is evident, because the latter has only the opening sentences of the decree of Cyrus, whereas the former gives this in its entirety.

(2) A second reason is the identity of religious standpoint, which is peculiarly characteristic, found in *Chronicles* and *Ezra–Nehemiah*. The Temple with its worship, and all that pertains to the priesthood, are matters of central interest in both.

(3) The love of genealogies and statistical records occurring throughout also points to the work of a single compiler, apart from later redactional elements.

(4) And most convincing of all is the similarity of language and style which runs through the whole series of what now appear as four books. Details of this would be out of place here; but reference may be made to Driver's *Introduction*, pp. 572 ff. (1913).

III. CONTENTS

The work is divided into the following four main divisions:

(1) i Chron. i–ix : the earliest history presented in the form of genealogies which start from Adam. Noteworthy is the special care given to the genealogies of Judah (ii. 3–iv. 23) and Levi vi. 1–81; Hebr. v. 27–vi. 66.

(2) i Chron. x–xxix : the history of David. The importance attached to the Temple, and especially to the Levites, priests, singers, and minor officials, is seen by the long sections devoted to these (xxii. 1–xxvi. 32).

(3) ii Chron. i–ix : the reign of Solomon. Here, again, the Temple occupies the central place of interest ii. 1–vii. 10 (Hebr. i. 18–vii. 10).

(4) ii Chron. x–xxxvi. 21 : the history of the kingdom of Judah. The history of the northern kingdom is almost wholly ignored. The last two verses of xxxvi belong, as we have seen, to the book of *Ezra*.

IV. DATE

It will be shown, when we deal with *Ezra-Nehemiah*, that there is convincing evidence in support of the contention that Ezra began his work in Palestine in 397 B.C. How long his work continued there are no means of knowing; but even if it was not of long duration, the compilation of the book that now bears his name, together with that of Nehemiah, cannot well have been made before the middle of the fourth century at the earliest. Since then, as we have seen, *Chronicles* and *Ezra–Nehemiah* formed originally one work, the earliest possible date for *Chronicles* is about 350 B.C.

Further, in Neh. xii. 22 the High-priest Jaddua is mentioned; according to Josephus (Antiq. xi. 322, 347) he lived at the time of Alexander the Great (died 323); his death is recorded as having taken place soon after that of Alexander. In the same passage in Neh. the designation " Darius the Persian " occurs; this also points to the Greek period. The same applies to the title " King of Persia " (Cyrus) in ii Chron. xxxvi. 23; for the titles given to Persian rulers in earlier days were: " the King " (Hag. i. 1, 15), or " the Great King," as on the Cyrus Cylinder and elsewhere; also " King of Kings," " King of the lands," on a Darius inscription.[1]

In i Chron. there are also one or two indications of date. The genealogy of David, given in iii. 19–24, is brought down to the sixth generation [2] after Zerubbabel; his date is about 520, so that even if only twenty years to a generation are assumed, the book cannot have been written until after 400. Further, in xxix. 7 mention is made of a *daric*, a Persian coin named after Darius i (died 486); its circulation in Palestine points to a time considerably after it was first issued; this, therefore, suggests a date well on in the Persian period (538–332).

Taking these various indications into consideration, we may with considerable confidence assign the date of the book to the second half of the fourth century, but possibly even later.

V. SOURCES

The chief source utilized by the Chronicler is quite obviously part of the Old Testament itself: the *Pentateuch*, *Joshua*, *i ii Samuel*, and, above all, *i ii Kings*. He refers to " the books of the kings of Israel and Judah " (ii Chron. xxvii. 7; xxxv. 27; xxxvi. 8), and doubtless the same work, though with a slightly different title, is referred to in i Chron.

---

[1] Rogers, *A History of Ancient Persia*, p. 103 (1929).
[2] The Septuagint makes it the eleventh generation.

ix. 1; ii Chron. xvi. 11; xx. 34; xxv. 26; xxviii. 26; xxxii. 32; xxxiii. 18. In comparing the many passages in *Chronicles* with the corresponding ones in these books it is evident that they were substantially, though not absolutely, in the form in which they now appear. The question as to whether the Chronicler had before him, in addition, any of the earlier sources utilized by the compilers of the historical books, and what use he made of them, is of considerable interest. One passage certainly points to this having been the case; in ii Chron. xvi. 11 it is said: " Behold, the acts of Asa, the former and the latter, behold they are written in the book of the kings of Judah and Israel "; the passage then goes on to summarize these (verses 12–14); when this is compared with the corresponding passage in i Kgs. xv. 23, 24 (which speaks only of the book of the Chronicles of the " kings of Judah "), it is seen that ii Chron. gives some details not recorded in i Kgs. This looks, therefore, as though the Chronicler had before him the source utilized by the compiler of *Kings*, and that he made a larger extract from it than that found in *Kings*. Thus, the possibility suggests itself further that in some cases the Chronicler may have made use of sources independently of what he took from *Kings*. One such source may have been " the Midrash to the book of kings," mentioned in ii Chron. xxiv. 27. A *Midrash* is a comparatively late form of exegetical commentary which seeks out and investigates—this is the root-meaning of the word—the sense of Scripture from various standpoints, and goes beneath the surface of the literal sense in order to discover what cryptic meaning a passage may contain. The Midrashic method will, by inference or deduction, often discern in a word or passage of Scripture a meaning for which the text itself gives no justification. The *Midrash* referred to by the Chronicler was, as its name implies, a source distinct from that just mentioned. Another *Midrash*, of smaller extent as its title implies, is named in ii Chron. xiii. 22, " the Midrash of the prophet Iddo "; whether this was an independent source, or whether it was merely a section of the large *Midrash* just spoken of, cannot be said with certainty; it may have at one time circulated

I

independently, and have been later incorporated in the larger work.

In the next place, there occur a number of titles of what appear to have been collections of narratives about prophets, viz. " the words (or ' acts ') of Samuel the seer," " the words of Nathan the prophet," " the words of Gad the seer "; these occur together in i Chron. xxix. 29, and were doubtless all parts of the same book; further, " the words of Nathan the prophet," " the prophecy of Ahijah the Shilonite," " the visions of Iddo the seer "; these occur together in ii Chron. ix. 29; and " the words of Shemaiah the prophet and of Iddo the seer " (ii Chron. xii. 15). These, again, may originally have been independent writings; but that by the time they were used by the Chronicler they had been incorporated in the large history of the Kings is suggested by the fact that in two other cases it is definitely stated by the Chronicler that they had been so incorporated, viz. ". . . they are written in ' the words of Jehu the son of Hanani,' which is inserted in the book of the kings of Israel " (ii Chron. xx. 34); and ". . . they are written in ' the vision of Isaiah the prophet, the son of Amoz,' in the book of the kings of Judah and Israel " (ii Chron. xxxii, 32). It would, therefore, seem likely that all these writings belonged to what was one and the same source; to this must also be reckoned " the words of Manasseh," mentioned in ii Chron. xxxiii. 18, 19.

A further source, which at first sight appears unpromising, but which has a value of its own, is to be discerned in the large body of genealogies; they occur especially in i Chron. i–ix. These genealogies must have been gathered from official documents; they are not all of equal authority (*e.g.* the omission of i Chron. i. 11–23 in the best Septuagint text suggests that these verses are a later addition), but as a whole they are of importance as illustrating certain theories of Israelite and Judahite descent,[1] held in different circles and possibly at different times.

Finally, from ii Chron. xxvi. 22 (cp. xxxii. 32 already

---

[1] For details see Rothstein-Hänel, and Richter in ZATW 1931, pp. 260–270; and in 1932, pp. 130–141.

referred to) it is clear that the Chronicler made use of the book of *Isaiah*. The conclusion is that the sources from which the Chronicler compiled his work were: the canonical books already mentioned; the *Midrash* on Kings; the *Midrash* on the prophet Iddo; and the book of *Isaiah*.

VI. Compilation

Closely connected with the subject of sources is that of their compilation. There is much in *Chronicles* which supports the contention that the compilation of the material gathered from these sources was not the work of a single compiler, and that the whole compendium cannot be assigned to one and the same period. Both suppositions are in the nature of things. The purpose for which *Chronicles* was compiled (see § VII) was one of profound interest to certain religious circles of more than one generation; so that it is to be expected that the book should have been enlarged from time to time by those whose special interests it embodied. It is not as though the literary material utilized was all gathered ready for use like a collection of manuscripts in a modern library; doubtless there were state archives in which national records were kept, *e.g.* in the Temple; but it can hardly be supposed that among the documents there preserved were to be reckoned such very unofficial writings as the book of *Kings* or the great *Midrash* on this; these are more likely to have been in the care of guilds or schools of scribes in different localities (cp. Kiriath-sepher, " the book-city," Josh. xv. 15; Judg. i. 11). So that both from the nature of things, as well as from indications in the book itself, it may be taken for granted that the compilation of *Chronicles* extended over a period of a number of years, and that more than one compiler took a hand in it. When, however, the task is attempted of seeking to discern the hands of different compilers, it is, naturally enough, seen to be both difficult and precarious. The most important contributions to this intricate study are

those of Kittel [1] and Rothstein–Hänel,[2] the latter followed
by Rad.[3]   Kittel's searching scrutiny discerns four hands of
compilers, not necessarily individuals, but more probably
groups; the work was first undertaken by a Levite or group
of Levites, who were followed by another similar group;
the former gathered together those portions of *Chronicles*
which are identical, or almost identical, with passages from
Old Testament books; the latter were responsible for those
passages which were in part identical with those in other
books.   Then came the Midrashic scribe, or scribes, and
added the Midrashic portions; and finally there was the
Chronicler himself.   In addition to these some later scribe
inserted certain portions, which occur especially in i Chron.
i–ix, not taken from the canonical books; some of this
material Kittel believes to be, in substance, pre-exilic.   The
possibility of the correctness of Kittel's careful scrutiny is
not denied, but whether it holds good all through is at least
questionable.

The other scholars also discern several hands at work;
but according to them, there were two main compilers;
the earlier of the two follows, as a rule, but not wholly, the
Priestly Code, while the later is guided rather by the Deuteronomic Code.   The correctness of this view hardly admits of
doubt in view of the convincing evidence presented.   It is
of great interest, since it shows that even in pronounced
priestly circles there existed in the fourth century a sympathetic feeling for the prophetic (*i.e.* Deuteronomic) point
of view.

VII. Religious Standpoint

Two outstanding subjects call for brief mention in this
connexion.   The Chronicler's interest is centred in the
Temple and its worship (the same applies whether there
were one or more compilers).   The conception of these is
presented from a strictly Levitical point of view, and in a

---

[1] *Die Bücher der Chronik*, in Nowack's " Handkommentar zum A.T." (1902).
[2] *Das erste Buch der Chronik* (1927).
[3] *Das Geschichtsbild des Chronistischen Werkes* (1930).

form which can have arisen only under the influence of the Priestly Code. This priestly legislation is assumed to be of Mosaic origin, and it is the norm by which all things are governed. The liturgical service of the sanctuary is the centre of religious life; in comparison with this all other interests sink into insignificance. An ecclesiastical system rather than religion in the deeper sense is the ideal inculcated. By this is not meant that the Chronicler was lacking in religious instinct; but to one for whom the religious sense is believed to be best expressed by the rigid observance of ritual worship, ceremonial and the laws governing it necessarily assume an exaggerated importance.

Illustrations of the Chronicler's ecclesiastical bent are abundant; they are most clearly to be discerned in comparing the way in which he presents occurrences of the past with the accounts given in the earlier books; of many examples that could be offered one of the most striking is the narrative of the reign of David in i Chron. x–xxix when compared with the corresponding passages in ii Sam. and i Kgs.

The other subject under this head is the Chronicler's doctrine of divine retribution. He not only represents the traditional belief here in a very pronounced manner, but he goes somewhat beyond it by insisting that divine reward for well-doing, and punishment for wrong-doing, follows immediately upon the act. In applying this theory to the doings of men in the past he often distorts history. Yet it is only fair to recognize the motive which impels this proceeding, mistaken though it be; the Chronicler's conviction of God's direct and immediate intervention in all human affairs is thoroughly sincere, and he wishes to impress this on his readers; he is not so much concerned with the illustrations whereby he drives home this truth, as he believes it to be, as with emphasizing the truth itself; he is a Midrashist, and claims the right to manipulate history in the interests of his teaching.

VIII. Historical Value

From what has been said it will be clear that not much importance can be attached to the history as presented in *Chronicles*. It does not even pretend to be a history of Israel, for it deals practically with that of Judah only, setting this forth especially as an account of the Davidic dynasty. The many almost absurd exaggerations (see, *e.g.*, i Chron. xxii. 14 and i Kgs. x. 14, 15; ii Chron. xiii. 3, 17, xiv. 8, 9, xvii. 14–19), though sometimes these may be due to textual corruption, illustrate the unreliability of the compiler; and, above all, the tendencious cause of so much that is recorded forbids one to take the history seriously. Nevertheless, here and there some scraps may be gathered which are probably reliable *data*, but which have been overlooked in the earlier historical books (*e.g.* ii Chron. xxvi. 6–15, xxviii. 17, 18, and others).

Thus, while it is possible to form but a low estimate of both the religious and historical value of our book, we whole-heartedly endorse Buchanan Gray's words, that " as a document that preserves the spirit, and the moral, religious and ecclesiastical ideals of the Jews about 300–200 B.C., *Chronicles* is invaluable, and most so because then its meaning is most clearly expressed, when we can watch the author modifying those earlier sources which we still possess." [1]

IX. The Versions

The Septuagint is the only Version, as is so often the case, which comes into consideration, though in a few instances the Vulgate seems to have retained a right reading against the Septuagint (*e.g.* i Chron. xxvi. 26). So far as *i ii Chronicles* are concerned the value of the Septuagint lies in the large number of small details in which it has preserved the right reading against the Massoretic text. In the genealogies the form of the names differs frequently, and although the Septuagint form is quite obviously often wrong, there are

---

[1] *A Critical Introduction to the Old Testament*, p. 92 (1927)

instances in which the Massoretic reading is to be corrected by that of the Septuagint. In quite a number of cases the correction of the Hebrew by the Septuagint gives the text one might expect; these are often small points in themselves, but they make just the difference to the understanding of the text (*e.g.* ii Chron. ii, 50; iii. 21; v. 13; xxv. 8; xxvi. 5; xxviii. 22; xxx. 22, and many others). Sometimes the smaller numbers given in the Septuagint suggest that the larger ones in the Hebrew are not in their original form (*e.g.* i Chron. v. 21; ii Chron. xxii. 2). The reliability of the Septuagint is in some cases attested by its agreement, against the Hebrew text of *Chronicles*, with the corresponding passage in Sam. or Kgs. (*e.g.* ii Chron. xxxiii. 20). In one instance the best Septuagint text omits a comparatively long passage in the Hebrew (i Chron. i 11–23); but this is exceptional. There are many cases of corruption in the Hebrew text for which the Septuagint offers no help (*e.g.* ii Chron. vi. 39–66), thus indicating that the corruption was already present in the text used by the Greek translators. Upon the whole, while the use of the Septuagint is necessary, it is of less importance for *Chronicles* than for most of the Old Testament books.

EZRA-NEHEMIAH

It has already been pointed out [1] that *i ii Chronicles* formed originally with the books of *Ezra* and *Nehemiah* a single work; both on this account, and also because *Ezra–Nehemiah* is regarded as one book in the Jewish Canon as well as in the Septuagint,[2] we shall treat it as such here; it will, moreover, be seen that a good deal of the book of *Nehemiah* is concerned with the person of Ezra, so that the two books, as they are represented in the Revised Version,[3] should not be separated.

I. Historical Background as Presented in Ezra–Nehemiah

Although as will be seen later, the history as given in *Ezra–Nehemiah* is at fault in some vital particulars, it is necessary to detail this as it stands in order that one may realize clearly in what respects the history has been erroneously presented.

The book opens with a brief account of the decree of Cyrus permitting the return (in 538 B.C.) of the exiled Jews to Jerusalem for the purpose of rebuilding the Temple (i.1–4). It is then implied, though not actually stated, that the Jewish leaders, with Sheshbazzar (the governor, v. 14) at their head, had returned to their own land, but far more stress is laid upon the fact that the holy vessels belonging to the Temple, which Nebuchadrezzar had carried away in 586, were given back by Cyrus (i. 5–11). The whole of ch. ii is taken up with a list of the returned exiles, 42,360 in number. The feast of Tabernacles is then celebrated, an altar having been set up under the direction of Jeshua

---

[1] See pp. 110 ff.
[2] Under the title *ii Esdras*; this must not be confused with the book often referred to as the " Greek Ezra," called in the Septuagint *i Esdras* or *Esdras A*, which consists of our book of *Ezra*, ii Chron. xxxv, xxxvi and most of Neh. viii (in the Vulgate it is called *iii Esdras*). It will be noticed that our book of *Ezra* occurs twice in the Septuagint.
[3] This is due to the Vulgate, where *i Esdras* = *Ezra*, and *ii Esdras* = *Nehemiah*.

and Zerubbabel (there is no mention of Sheshbazzar);
the full quota of sacrifices is offered. The foundation of the
Temple, however, is not yet laid, though this is said (i. 2–4)
to have been the prime purpose of the Return (iii. 1–7).
It is not until the next year that this is done, Jeshua and
Zerubbabel being again the moving spirits (iii. 8–13). The
" adversaries " (doubtless the Samaritans are meant) ask
that they should be permitted to help in the building of the
Temple, but this is refused, whereupon they hamper the
work during the whole of Cyrus' reign until the second year
of Darius, in 520 (iv. 1–5, 24). In the meantime, so it is
recorded, the adversaries wrote an accusation against the
Jews to Xerxes on his coming to the throne (485); they
also sent a letter to Artaxerxes (464 was the year in which
he came to the throne; presumably the first king of this
name is meant), warning him of the danger involved in
building the walls of Jerusalem—no previous reference to
this has been made; as a result, the builders of the wall are
forced to desist from their work (iv. 6–23).

With ch. v Haggai and Zechariah appear upon the scene;
they persuade the people to begin building the Temple;
but this is viewed with suspicion by Tattenai, " the governor
beyond the river " (*i.e.* the Persian satrap of Syria), who
addresses a letter to Darius asking for directions; the Jews,
in the meantime, also address themselves to the king, referring him to Cyrus's decree permitting the building.
Darius thereupon makes inquiries, and the decree is found;
so he gives permission for the building to be continued. It
is completed and dedicated in 516, and a great Passover
feast is celebrated (v, vi). The narrative continues:
" Now after these things," and then goes on to tell how
Ezra went up from Babylon to Jerusalem in the seventh
year of Artaxerxes; if the first king of this name is meant
the date will be 458, so that we have a gap in the history of
fifty-eight years during which nothing is recorded (vii.
1–9). Ezra's object in coming to Jerusalem is to teach the
law to Israel (vii. 10; cp. verses 25, 26). The letter which
the king wrote to Ezra and his companions permitting them
to return is then quoted (vii. 11–26); a blessing on the

Lord, purported to have been uttered by Ezra, is appended
(vii. 27, 28). There follows a list of those who accompanied
him (viii. 1–14). Before starting on his journey Ezra
proclaims a fast, with humiliation and prayer (viii. 15–23).
Much stress is laid on the weight of gold and silver, and
the vessels which were an " offering for the house of our
God " (viii. 24–30). On the arrival of the exiles in Jerusalem an immense burnt offering is sacrificed, consisting of
twelve bullocks and an inordinate number of rams, lambs,
and goats (viii. 31–36). A complaint is then brought
before Ezra by the " princes " regarding intermarriages
between the Jews and the women of the surrounding
peoples; Ezra is overwhelmed with shame and sorrow,
and offers a long prayer of confession (ix); the people are
moved to penitence, and, on the matter being investigated,
" they make an end with all the men that had married
strange women " (x. 1–17); a list is then given of those
who had contracted these marriages (x. 18–44). Nehemiah's
arrival in Jerusalem is then dealt with; the reason for his
journey being that the returned exiles were in evil plight,
and " the wall of Jerusalem is also broken down, and the
gates thereof burned with fire." The date of Nehemiah's
arrival in Jerusalem is given as the twentieth year of Artaxerxes, the same king as the one previously mentioned;
the date is, therefore, 444. The people are persuaded by
Nehemiah to rebuild the wall; but the enterprise is looked
upon with disfavour by Sanballat, the governor of Samaria
(Neh. i. 10). A description is then given of the building of
the wall (iii. 1–32; iv. 19) A further, and fuller, account of
Sanballat's annoyance at the work of rebuilding the walls
follows, and of his attempt, which does not succeed, to
frustrate this work (iv, Hebr. iii. 33–38, iv). At this point
there is an insertion giving a long account of the overbearing
behaviour of the wealthier Jews towards their poorer neighbours; this is rectified by Nehemiah (v). The course of
the narrative is then taken up again. In spite of repeated
plots against Nehemiah, which are, however, unsuccessful,
the building of the wall is continued, and the work is
completed in fifty-two days (vi). Thereupon Nehemiah

appoints two officials over the city; he also takes measures
for increasing the population of the city (vii. 1–5). A long
genealogical list is here inserted giving the names of the
sons of the exiles who had been deported by Nebuchadrezzar
(vii. 6–73a). The narrative is taken up again at vii. 73b
(cp. Ezr. iii. 1), and the great gathering of the people is
described at which Ezra, who now appears again, reads
from the book of the law. After this the feast of Tabernacles is celebrated (cp. Ezr. iii. 4), during each day of which
the law is read (viii). This is followed by a fast and more
reading of the law, also a long prayer containing an historical
retrospect (ix). Then a covenant is made to abstain from
marriage with foreign women, to observe the Sabbath, and
to support the service of the house of God (x). In ch.
xi. 1–2 mention is again made of the increase of the population of Jerusalem—at Nehemiah's instigation since this is
from his memoirs (see below); a list is given of those that
" willingly offered themselves to dwell in Jerusalem."
This is followed by another list which gives the names of
the priests and Levites who had come from exile with
Zerubbabel (xii. 1–26). Then there is an account of the
dedication of the wall (xii. 27–47), after which the law is
again read (xiii. 1–3). At some time, which is not stated,
Nehemiah had returned to the Persian court; but in the
thirty-second year of Artaxerxes (*i.e.* 432) he returned to
Jerusalem, when his first care was to rectify some irregularities in regard to the Temple which had occurred during his
absence (xiii. 4–14). He also took measures to have the
Sabbath properly observed (xiii. 15–22), and dealt with the
question of mixed marriages (xiii. 23–31).

It has been already stated that this presentation of the
history is at fault in some important respects; these must
now be pointed out.

One of the first things which must strike one is the way in
which the Persian kings are mentioned; first of all there is
Cyrus, the year in question being 538 (Ezr. i. 1); then
Darius, with the year 520 (iv. 5, 24); then Xerxes, the year
being 485 (iv. 6), followed by Artaxerxes i, who came to
the throne in 464 (iv. 7); we then get back to Darius, with

the date of the completion of the Temple, 516 (vi. 15);
then to the seventh year of Artaxerxes, 458 (vii. 7),
and finally to the twentieth year of Artaxerxes, 444
(Neh. ii. 1). This indicates some confusion in chronological
sequence.

Then, one cannot fail to notice that there is some inconsistency as to who really took the lead in urging the
rebuilding of the Temple, the prime purpose of the Return
(Ezr. i. 2); at one time this is said to have been Sheshbazzar
(Ezr. v. 16); at another, Jeshua and Zerubbabel (Ezr.
iii. 10); and at another, Haggai and Zechariah, who
stimulated Jeshua and Zerubbabel (v. 1, 2).

But more serious are the self-contradictory statements
made with regard to the date of the laying of the foundation
of the Temple; according to Ezr. iii. 8, v. 16 this took place
in the year after the Return, i.e. 537–6; but according to
Ezr. v. 1, 2 the foundation was laid in 520. In Ezr. iv. 24
it is said that the building of the Temple ceased until the
second year of Darius, but in v. 5 this is contradicted:
"they did not make them cease till the matter should come
to Darius," and soon after the building is continued (vi.
7, 14). There is also a manifest confusion between the
building of the wall and the building of the Temple; for in
iv. 6–23 reference is made to the building of the wall in the
reign of Artaxerxes, and the narrative continues in v. 2 ff.
about the building both of the Temple and the wall in the
reign of Darius (v. 3).

One other point of considerable importance is that Ezra
is represented as having arrived in Jerusalem in 458 (Ezr.
vii. 6, 9, 10), and that he was followed fourteen years later
by Nehemiah, in 444 (Neh. ii. 1); they are also represented
as contemporaries (Neh. viii. 2, 9, xii. 26); this last point is,
of course, not impossible so far as the dates are concerned.
But evidence will be given below to show that Nehemiah
came first to Jerusalem in 444, and that he was followed
nearly half a century later by Ezra, in 397; they were,
therefore, not contemporaries, reasons for which, apart
from dates, will be given.

It will thus be seen that the history of a considerable

part of *Ezra–Nehemiah* is unreliable. This is to be accounted for: (*a*) by the fact that our book is a compilation, and the sources used have been unskilfully put together; (*b*) because the compiler's knowledge of the period of history dealt with was inadequate owing to the want of *data*; and (*c*) because the compiler had some preconceived ideas with which he coloured the history.

Our next task must be to indicate the sources utilized by the compiler.

II. The Sources used in Compiling Ezra–Nehemiah

A close examination of our book shows that the compiler utilized the following sources:—

(a) *Ezra Memoirs.* Ezr. vii. 27, 28, viii. 1–34, all written in the first person, are clearly extracts from some record which Ezra kept of his work; and they appear to be *verbatim* extracts. There are other passages in which Ezra is spoken of in the third person; these may well offer the gist of extracts from the same source, viz. Ezr. vii. 1–10, ix. 1–x, 44; Neh. vii. 73b–viii. 12, 13–18, ix, and, in the main, x.

(b) *Nehemiah Memoirs.* These extracts are more numerous: Neh. i. 1–vii. 73a, xi. 1–2, xiii. 4–31; in addition, xii 27–47, xiii. 1–3 are no doubt based on the same source; but they have been somewhat worked over by the compiler.

(c) *Lists.* These are all of persons, and for the most part they must have been taken from official records. Uninteresting as they appear, when scrutinized they contain numerous points of importance.

(d) *The Aramaic Sections.* These are Ezr. iv. 7b–vi. 18, vii. 12–26; they are official documents, but include some narrative matter, *e.g.* v. 1–5; iv. 8–23 contains the correspondence with Artaxerxes concerning the building of the wall; v. 6–vi. 12 contains the correspondence with Darius, and a copy of his decree, in which Cyrus's decree is quoted, about the building of the Temple; and vii. 12–26 is a decree of Artaxerxes giving permission to Ezra and his company to go to Jerusalem. These documents do not cover the whole of the Aramaic sections; the remainder, being written by the compiler, show that his knowledge of Aramaic was more than what would suffice to copy out documents; and this is what one would expect. This leads us to the subject of the compiler and the nature of his work; for there is a considerable quantity of our book, after the subject-matter of the sources has been deducted, which must be put down to the hand of the compiler.

III. THE COMPILER OF EZRA–NEHEMIAH

We have already seen that *Ezra–Nehemiah* formed originally the concluding portion of *i ii Chronicles*; this suggests at once that the compiler of our book was the same as the compiler of *i ii Chronicles*; and all the indications go to support this supposition. This is not the place to go into details, but a brief reference may be made to some of the outstanding characteristics of *i ii Chronicles*, the presence of all of which may be observed in *Ezra–Nehemiah*—the few references given could be greatly multiplied:—the doctrine of divine retribution (Ezr. ix. 7, 13; Neh. i. 8, ix. 26, 27); the constant stress laid on the Temple and its worship (Ezr. i. 2–4, iii. 7, vii. 27, viii. 35); the importance of the Levites (Ezr. i. 5, vi. 20; Neh. viii. 11, xii. 1, 8); and of observing the law of Moses (Ezr. iii. 2, x. 3; Neh. viii. 1, ix. 13); the fondness for lists (Ezr. ii. 2 ff., x. 18 ff.; Neh. vii. 6 ff.); and finally there is the style and phraseology which show many affinities. When these points are examined there can be no shadow of doubt that our book was compiled by the Chronicler. This gives also the approximate date of the compilation,[1] *i.e.* about 300.

The compiler wrote, therefore, more than a century after the period with which he was dealing, and he had not a great deal of material at his disposal for setting forth the history. During the intervening century, although we may not be able to follow the steps, we know from the sequel that new ideas had developed in a theocratic direction; moreover, the growth and development of the Law and the elaboration of the Temple worship had revolutionized the

[1] See pp. 110 ff.

whole point of view of early orthodox Judaism. It is hardly to be wondered at that the Chronicler should have interpreted the history which he wrote in the light of the developments of his own day. With his veneration for the Temple and its worship he naturally enough imputed to the home-coming exiles the rebuilding of the Temple as their prime desire; the fact that worship had for long been offered in a somewhat dilapidated Temple did not appeal to him; probably he did not realize that those who were left in the land during the Exile had perforce to be content to worship in the ruins of a Temple which they had not the means to renovate. It must also be remembered that by the time at which the Chronicler lived the rift between the Samaritans and the Jews had developed into permanent antagonism; this he assumed had already taken place in the early days of the Return, and he constructed his history accordingly. And finally, with his exalted ideas about the priesthood it is not surprising that the Chronicler should have assumed that Ezra the priest took the initiative in all reforming movements rather than Nehemiah the layman. With his rather vague knowledge of Persian history, with the exiguous material at his disposal, and with his not very discriminating use of this, he would easily have fallen into the error of supposing that Ezra preceded Nehemiah in returning to Palestine; this involved some difficulties and inconsistencies in his presentation of the history which he made some unsuccessful attempts to straighten out; but in any case they were, to him, minor matters in comparison with what he believed to be the true course of events.

But inasmuch as we have been so used to assume that Ezra preceded Nehemiah it will be well to present the evidence to show that Nehemiah came and worked in Palestine about half a century before Ezra.

IV. NEHEMIAH AND EZRA

The reasons which justify the statement that Nehemiah preceded Ezra are as follows: first, there is a general consideration which has been shortly, but clearly, stated by

McFadyen: " The situation which Ezra finds on his arrival appears to presuppose a settled and orderly life, which was hardly possible until the city was fortified and the walls built by Nehemiah; indeed, Ezra, in his prayer, mentions the erection of the walls as a special exhibition of the divine love (Ezr. ix. 9)." The more the details of the narrative are scrutinized the more convincing does this general consideration become.

Then, to come to particulars; twice in the Nehemiah memoirs mention is made of the need of increasing the population of Jerusalem (vii. 4; xi. 1, 2); this was an important matter, for it would not have been much use for Nehemiah to have built the city walls if there had been insufficient men to defend them in case of attack. But in Ezra's time there was clearly a large settled population in the city; in Ezr. x. 1 it says that there was a " very great congregation of men and women and children," and in x. 13 similarly: " the people are many." This can be readily understood if Nehemiah came a generation before Ezra; whereas if Ezra came first it would mean that the population was dwindling; but there are various facts which could be mentioned to show that this was not the case.

A subsidiary point, not conclusive, it is true, but worth a passing word, is the question of the mixed marriages. Nehemiah hoped that by inducing those of his own people who had married non-Jewish women to promise that their children should not marry outside the Jewish race, the evil of these mixed marriages would cease. This was not the case, however; for when Ezra came things were as bad as ever, so that he took the much more drastic step of making every man who had married a foreign wife put her away: that finally settled the matter. Now, if Ezra preceded Nehemiah this sequence would be inconsequent; worse, it would be against the well-known fact that Judaism became stricter, not more slack, in its exclusiveness as time went on. It was not a question of the priest and scribe taking naturally a stricter line than the layman, but rather the ever-increasing realization of the need of Jews cutting themselves off from the outside world—engendered and fostered first through the Exile—if they were to be loyal to their principles, their beliefs, and their God.

While this is not without weight, there is the further overwhelming argument that while, from Nehemiah's memoirs, he is a contemporary of the High Priest Eliashib (Neh. iii. 1), Ezra, according to his memoirs, was a contemporary of the High Priest Jehohanan, the son of Eliashib (Ezr. x. 6); but more, in the Old Testament " son " is sometimes used in a loose way for " grandson " (see, *e.g.*, Gen. xxix. 5, xxxi. 28, 43; Ruth iv. 17); and that Jehohanan (the shortened form is Johanan = Jonathan, see Neh. xii. 22) was thus the *grandson* of Eliashib is seen from Neh. xii. 11; *i.e.* Jehohanan is the son of Jehoiada the son of Eliashib; thus, Nehemiah lived under the High-priesthood of Eliashib, Ezra under that of his grandson Jehohanan. And this is corroborated by one of the Elephantiné papyri, which tells us that Jehohanan was High Priest in 408. We know from Neh. ii. 1 that Nehemiah came to Jerusalem in the twentieth year of Artaxerxes, and from Ezr. vii. i, 7 that Ezra came to Jerusalem in the seventh year of Artaxerxes; in neither case is it indicated which Artaxerxes is meant; but from what has been said there can be no doubt that in the case of Nehemiah it was Artaxerxes i who came to the throne in 464, so that his twentieth year was 444; in that of Ezra it was Artaxerxes ii, who came to the throne in 404, so that his seventh year was 397.[1]

V. The Septuagint Versions

As indicated above, there are two Greek Versions of our book; one, called in the Septuagint ii Esdras (= *Ezra–Nehemiah*), does not offer anything of importance; but the other, *i Esdras*, known as the " Greek Ezra," demands some notice. This latter consists of the book of *Ezra* as we know it, ii Chron. xxxv, xxxvi, and Neh. vii. 73b–viii. 13a; in addition, it contains a long passage, iii. 1–v. 6, which has no parallel in the Hebrew, but which in its present form is

---

[1] See Van Hoonacker, *Néhémie et Esdras* . . . (1890); *Néhémie . . . Esdras* . . . (1892); and in the *Revue Biblique*, xxxii (1923), pp. 481–494; xxxiii (1924), pp. 33–64.

K

"certainly unhistorical."[1] On the other hand, the obvious misplacement of Ezr. iv. 7–24 does not occur in the " Greek Ezra," where the passage in question comes in ii. 15–25. There are some other important variations from the Hebrew, e.g. the omission of the name " Nehemiah " in Neh. viii. 9 (= ix. 49); and there is much to be said for Howorth's view that it is an independent translation of an earlier Hebrew text.[2] In any case, this version is an indispensable aid to the study of our book.

[1] Swete, op. cit., p. 266.
[2] In the Academy for 1893, and see Thackeray's important art. in Hastings' D.B., i. pp. 759 ff.

THE BOOK OF ESTHER

I. THE NARRATIVE

THE scene in which the plot of this little historical novel is laid is Shushan (Susa),[1] the period represented is that of Xerxes i (485–465 B.C.). During a great feast given by Xerxes, the royal command went forth that the queen Vashti should appear before the king in order that he might show " the peoples and the princes her beauty, for she was fair to look on." But Vashti refused to come; whereupon the king was filled with wrath, and took counsel among his wise men, saying: " What shall we do unto the queen Vashti according to law, because she hath not done the bidding of the king . . .? " On the advice of Memucan, one of the seven princes of Persia and Media, " which saw the king's face," it was decreed that Vashti should no more enter into the royal presence (i. 1–22). After four years the king determined to take to himself another queen; and the royal ministers sought out the fairest maid that could be found (ii. 1–4).

Now there was a certain Jew living in Shushan named Mordecai, of the house of Saul; he had brought up a young kinswoman whose name was " Hadassah, that is Esther," who was very beautiful. This maiden, in company with many another, was brought to the palace; and in due time her turn came to appear in the royal presence; but when the king saw her he loved her above all the maidens, and set the royal crown upon her head, and made her queen in place of Vashti. But Mordecai " sat in the king's gate " (ii. 5–20).

---

[1] About 200 miles east of Babylon. Xenophon, *Cyropædia* VIII. vi. 22, says: " But Cyrus himself always lived at the centre of his dominions, seven months in Babylon during the winter season, where the land is warm and sunny, three months at Susa in the spring, and during the height of summer at Ecbatana, so that for him it was spring-time all the year." The precedent set by Cyrus was apparently followed by his successors.

Now it fell on a day, as Mordecai sat in the king's gate, that he learned of an attempt to be made on the king's life; this he reported to Esther, who informed the king. Thereupon the conspirators were taken, and hanged. The matter was written in the book of the chronicles in the king's presence (ii. 21–23).

Another character is now brought upon the scene in the person of Haman, an Agagite, *i.e.* an Amalekite (i Sam. xv. 20). For some reason, which is not indicated, the king promoted Haman " above all the princes that were with him "; and by the royal command he was honoured by " all the king's servants that were in the king's gate." All, therefore, bowed down before Haman; but there was one exception; Mordecai, as a faithful Jew, refused. This greatly angered Haman, and, to avenge himself, he determined to destroy all the Jews in the kingdom; so, " in the first month, which is the month Nisan, in the twelfth year of king Ahasuerus, they cast Pur, that is, the lot, before Haman from day to day, and from month to month, to the twelfth month, which is the month Adar "; thus, when the propitious day came Haman approached the king, and made his accusation against the Jews, *i.e.* that they had laws of their own different from all others, and that they did not observe the king's laws. His request that all the Jews should be destroyed was granted, and a decree was put forth accordingly (iii. 1–15). When this came to Mordecai's ears he grieved very deeply; Esther heard of his grief, and sought to know the cause; then Mordecai sent messengers, beseeching her to intercede for her people before the king (iv. 1–17). So Esther invited the king and Haman to a banquet; and at the banquet the king bade Esther make her request; but in reply she begged the king to come to another banquet on the morrow, accompanied by Haman. And Haman boasted to his wife, Zeresh, of the honour done him by the queen, and of his wealth and high estate; " yet," said he, " all this availeth me nothing, so long as I see Mordecai the Jew sitting at the king's gate "; for it rankled in the heart of Haman that Mordecai refused to bow down before him. But his

wife counselled him to have a gallows made, fifty cubits
high, on which to hang Mordecai. Haman thought well
of this advice, and acted accordingly (v. 1-14).

Now it happened in that same night that sleep fled from
the king; so he caused the book of the records of the kingdom to be read to him, and when it was brought to his
memory how that Mordecai had denounced the two conspirators and saved the king's life, he asked what reward
Mordecai had received; and when it was told the king that
nothing had been done for him, the king called for Haman
and commanded him to honour Mordecai in royal fashion
(vi. 1-14).

On the next day, during Esther's second banquet, the
king again invited her to make her request; then she
prayed the king that she and all her people against whom
Haman was plotting might be spared. The king, understanding the cause of Haman's design, was filled with
wrath, and commanded him to be hanged on the gallows
he had prepared for Mordecai; and Haman was hanged
forthwith; then was the king's wrath pacified (vii. 1-10).

Thereupon Mordecai was greatly honoured and rewarded; and, at Esther's request, the king's decree against
the Jews was reversed, and permission was given to them
to punish their enemies; then " the Jews smote all their
enemies with the stroke of the sword, and with slaughter
and destruction, and did what they would unto them that
hated them." At Esther's further request the ten sons of
Haman were hanged, and another massacre of the enemies
of the Jews took place in Shushan; moreover, the Jews
that were in the king's provinces " slew of them that hated
them seventy and five thousand." This was done " on
the thirteenth day of the month Adar (approximately
March); and on the fourteenth day of the same they
rested and made it a day of feasting and gladness "; and
it is added: " Therefore do the Jews of the villages, that
dwell in the unwalled towns, make the fourteenth day of
the month Adar a day of gladness and feasting, and a good
day, and of sending portions one to another " (viii. 1-ix. 19).

Here it would seem—and this is the opinion of some

scholars—the book ended originally; but in what follows (ix. 20–32) it is added that the Jews were commanded to keep the fourteenth and fifteenth days of the month Adar yearly, *i.e.* the fourteenth day in the villages and the fifteenth in Shushan; these were days " whereon they had rest from their enemies." This, it is said, the Jews undertook to do, because Haman " had devised against the Jews to destroy them, and had cast Pur, that is the lot, to consume them. . . . Wherefore they called these days Purim, after the Pur." In the last chapter of the book, consisting of only three verses (x. 1–3), the attempt is made to give it the appearance of historical authority; in phraseology imitated from that of *i ii Kings* it is said: " And all the acts of his power . . . and the full account of the greatness of Mordecai, whereunto the king advanced him, are they not written in the book of the chronicles of the kings of Media and Persia? " That this is not to be taken seriously becomes apparent as soon as the unhistorical character of the book is realized.[1]

II. The Origin of the Book

That there was originally a non-Jewish element in the story of Esther is shown by the use of the word *Pur* which is translated into Hebrew by *Goral*, " lot " (iii. 7), and the word itself is Hebraized by adding the plural termination *-im* to it; this became henceforth the name of a Jewish feast which has been celebrated annually ever since— *Purim*. Much turns, therefore, on the word *Pur*; and Zimmern seemed to have pointed to the home and original meaning of the story in contending that *Pur* was equivalent to the Babylonian word *Puhru*, " assembly (of the gods)," which, according to Babylonian mythology, was held at the beginning of each year in the month *Nisan* (approximately April), and at which lots were cast for the coming year.[2] To this, however, Gunkel [3] raises formidable objec-

---

[1] For a good presentation of the subject, see Paton, *A Critical and Exegetical Commentary on the Book of Esther*, pp. 64–76 (1908).

[2] *ZATW* xi, pp. 157–160 (1891).

[3] *Schöpfung und Chaos in Urzeit und Endzeit*, p. 310 (1895); see also Hochfeld *ZATW* xxii, pp. 282 ff. (1902), who shows that etymologically *Puhru* and *Pur* are not connected.

tions; *Puhru* means, truly enough, " assembly "—it also means " feast "—but, as we have just seen, according to Esther iii. 7 *Pur* means " lot." In addition, the Babylonian New Year festival was observed at the beginning of *Nisan*, whereas the Jewish feast of *Purim* was held on the 14th and 15th days of Adar (ix. 18), *i.e.* in the preceding month. What *Pur* really means has not yet been established. More promising, therefore, is Jensen's theory as to the origin of the book: he has shown that the name *Haman* is equivalent to *Humba* or *Humban* (= *Humman*), the chief of the Elamite gods, and that *Vashti*, or *Washti*, is the name of an Elamite goddess. *Zeresh*, Haman's wife, he equates with the goddess *Kirisha*; *Mordecai* with *Marduk*; and *Esther* with *Ishtar*.[1] Esther's other name, Hadassah, *i.e.* " the myrtle " (" wreathed ") is probably derived, according to Jensen, from the Babylonian *hadashtu*, " bride." He, therefore, holds that a Babylonian myth lies behind the Esther story, and that the myth itself is the echo of an historical episode, namely, the liberation of Babylonia from the yoke of the Elamites which happened about 2300 B.C.[2] The myth will have come through a Persian medium, inasmuch as there are a number of Persian traits in the story as we now have it.[3]

Jastrow agrees with Jensen, and holds that the Babylonian myth was " transformed in such a manner by the Jewish author of the book of *Esther* as to make it the basis of an elaborate festal legend to justify the adoption of a ' foreign ' festival into the Jewish calendar," adding that " the one link missing in the chain of evidence connecting *Purim* with the period of merry-making in honour of Marduk and Ishtar is evidence of a celebration in Babylonia or Persia in the middle of Adar—just before the New Year's season proper two weeks later." [4]

---

[1] It is also interesting to note that the relationship between Mordecai and Esther (cousins, according to ii. 7) is the same as that between Marduk and Ishtar, according to one Babylonian tradition (Gunkel, *Schöpfung und Chaos*, p. 313.
[2] *Zeitschrift für die Kunde des Morgenlandes* vi. 47 ff., 209 ff.
[3] See especially Siegfried, *Ezra, Nehemia und Esther*, pp. 137 ff. (1901).
[4] In Hastings' *Enc. of Rel. and Ethics*, x. 505 *b*, 506 *a*. The Babylonian New Year festival was called the *Sacæa*, the Roman equivalent of which was the *Saturnalia*.

Thus, the book of *Esther* affords an illustration of external influence on the Jews, inasmuch as they adapted a heathen festival to their own use.[1] In some measure we have a parallel to this in the festival of Ḥanukkah (see i Macc. iv. 52–59), which, as Rankin has shown, contains traces of elements from the Dionysian and Apollo cults, which were taken over by the Jews and Judaized.[2]

III. DATE AND PLACE OF ORIGIN

That our book must be later than the time of Ben-Sira (*circa* 200 B.C.) is evident from the fact that in the Hymn in Praise of the Fathers (Ecclus. xliv.–xlix.) no reference is made to it; some mention of Esther and Mordecai would assuredly have found a place there had the book been extant in his day. It is in ii Macc. xv. 36 (37) that the book is first mentioned (i.e. *circa* 50 B.C., possibly a little earlier); it is there said: "And they all ordained with a common decree in no wise to let this day pass undistinguished, but to mark with honour the thirteenth day of the twelfth month (it is called Adar in the Syrian tongue), the day before the day of Mordecai" (Πρὸ μιᾶς ἡμέρας τῆς Μαρδοχαικῆς ἡμέρας). The reference here is to the day on which the Jews gained a striking victory over the Syrian general Nikanor (161 B.C.), so that the "day of Mordecai" was the 14th of Adar. In the parallel passage in the older book *i Maccabees* (*circa* 100 B.C.) it is said that "Nikanor's day" was to be celebrated annually on the 13th Adar (vii. 49), but there is no mention of "Mordecai's day." Thus the feast of *Purim* had obtained an assured position in the calendar before the middle of the first century B.C., and the book of *Esther* must be dated about a century earlier.

It is important to note that there is evidence of the existence of a Greek version before the end of the second century B.C., as Swete points out: "The footnote to the Greek

---

[1] See the interesting article by Krappe, "Solomon and Ashmondai," in *The American Journal of Philology*, liv. 3, pp. 269 ff. (1933).
[2] *The Origins of the Festival of Hanukkah*, passim (1930).

Esther, which states that that book was brought to Egypt in the fourth year of ' Ptolemy and Cleopatra ' . . . may have been written with the purpose of giving Palestinian sanction to the Greek version of that book; but it vouches for the fact that the version was in circulation before the end of the second century B.C." [1] The Ptolemy mentioned must be the eighth of the name, " Lathyrus " (116–108/7 B.C.) ; he reigned with his mother Cleopatra.[2] On internal evidence we may suggest that the book assumed its present form in the earlier stages of the Maccabæan revolt.   Gunkel believes that it goes back to the early Greek period, and that it originated in the eastern Dispersion like the book of *Tobit*;[3] he may be right as far as the earliest form of the story is concerned, but as we now have it the book breathes a spirit of ruthless vindictiveness which reflects the age of Antiochus Epiphanes better than any other in known Jewish history.

IV. Canonicity

Owing doubtless to its very secular character there were strong protests against *Esther* being included in the Canon; it was only after prolonged controversy that this was ultimately acquiesced in.   It took its place, probably, because it gave an explanation of and formed the literary basis for the popular feast of *Purim*.[4] Even so, its position was not finally secured until about 120 A.D.

V. The Hebrew Text and the Septuagint

Of the Hebrew text little need be said; it has come down to us in as pure a form as any book of the Old Testament; so that for the study of *Esther* the Septuagint is of

---

[1] *Op. cit.*, p. 25; see also Schürer, *Geschichte des jüdischen Volkes*, iii. p. 450 (1909).
[2] She drove him out of Egypt in 108–7 B.C., but he returned in 88 B.C. and reigned for another eight years.
[3] In *Die Religion in Geschichte und Gegenwart (RGG.)*, s.v. " Esther."
[4] Jewish tradition identified Ahasuerus with Artaxerxes i, and so the book could be regarded as belonging to the " prophetical period," see above, p. 3. See further, Buhl, *op. cit.*, pp. 28 ff., Ryle, *op. cit.*, pp. 192 ff.

but small importance. From some other points of view, however, the Septuagint offers matter of considerable interest: first, there is the fact that there are two recensions of the Greek text; most of the manuscripts contain the ordinary Septuagint text, but a certain number have the Lucianic recension of this; it is shorter than the Septuagint text itself, and conforms more to the Hebrew text. Secondly, both forms of the Greek text have considerable additions: " Of 270 verses, 107 are wanting in the present Hebrew text, and probably at no time formed a part of the Hebrew book. The Greek additions are distributed through the book in contexts as long as average chapters." [1] These additions are six in number; [2] with one exception they cannot be said to be of much importance; the third (xiii. 8–xiv. 19 in the Apocrypha, " Additions to the Book of Esther ") is, however, of interest; it consists of prayers offered by Mordecai, Israel, and Esther, for deliverance from the danger overhanging them. These prayers breathe a deep spirit of devotion and loyalty to God. The object of the additions was to supply a religious note which is otherwise entirely lacking in the book.

[1] Swete, *op. cit.*, p. 257.
[2] Apart from the note at the conclusion of the book, see above, p. 136.

THE FORMS OF HEBREW POETRY

In all the history of man's speech we do not know of any language better adapted than Hebrew to noble poetry. This is due, in part, to the very great strength of the accent, which, falling normally on the last syllable of a word (though occasionally on the last but one), seems to gather into itself the whole weight of sound and meaning carried by the word. The result is that even Hebrew prose has a very strongly marked rhythm, of the iambic or anapæstic type (though one accent may be preceded by more syllables than would be possible in a normal anapæstic rhythm), and, even in our faint efforts to reproduce it, we can see that it must have been of extraordinary beauty to the ear.

We may well ask what there can be to distinguish between prose and poetry in such a language. The answer must be that, while the rhythms of prose may be absolutely free, those of poetry must be, if not entirely uniform, at least regular within well-defined limits. But, though this has always been admitted, it is only within the last two centuries that any serious attempt has been made to define those limits or to ascertain the nature of Hebrew poetic form, while it is barely half a century since the taking of the first steps which led ultimately to the present position. We shall best realize how young is the study of Hebrew metres if we remember that one of its earliest pioneers, Professor Karl Budde, is still[1] living and at work.

I. PARALLELISM

The only step taken before Budde's day was, however, of profound importance. It was the recognition by Lowth [2] of the principle of *Parallelism*. A line of Hebrew poetry

---

[1] 1933.

[2] Cp. *De sacra poesi Hebræorum Prælectiones Academicæ* (1753).

must always have at least two parts, which in some way balance one another. It is usual to give the name *stichos* to each of these parts; in its simplest form we shall have a line in which every word in the first *stichos* will correspond to a word in the second *stichos*, and *vice versa*. Thus in Isa. i. 3 we have:

> Israel doth–not know (*Yisra'él ló yadá'*),
> My–people doth–not consider (*'ammí ló hithbondn*).

Lowth distinguished three kinds of parallelism:

(*a*) Synonymous, where both parts mean the same thing, *e.g.* the illustration just cited.

(*b*) Antithetic, where the two *stichoi* present a contrast, *e.g.* Prov. i. 29.

(*c*) Synthetic, where the sense simply flows on. This, as later students have recognized, is hardly true parallelism in thought.

Since Lowth's day three other types have been distinguished:

(*d*) Emblematic, where one *stichos* makes a statement literally, and the other suggests a metaphor, *e.g.* Ps. xlii. 1.

(*e*) Stairlike, where a part only of the first *stichos* is repeated, and the sense is continued from it, *e.g.* Ps. xxix. 1–2a.

(*f*) Introverted, where four *stichoi* are so arranged that the first corresponds to the fourth and the second to the third, *e.g.* Ps. xxx. 8–10.[1]

The first real advance on Lowth, however, was made by G. B. Gray, in his *Forms of Hebrew Poetry* (1915). Gray pointed out that in some cases the two *stichoi* of a line were exactly parallel, in others they were not. The former type may be called *Complete Parallelism*, and represented by such a formula as:

> a. b. c.
> a'. b'. c'.

An example may be seen in Isa. i. 3, already cited.

[1] For these last three, see especially Briggs, *Psalms* (*ICC*), pp. xxxvi–xxxviii (1907).

The other type may be called *Incomplete Parallelism*, and it is to be noted that this again falls into two classes. Sometimes a part of the second *stichos* is parallel to the first, while, in the remainder, a term is inserted which has no analogue in the first *stichos*. Thus:

> Yahweh from–Sinai came,
> And–shone–out from–Seir unto–them (Deut. xxxiii. 2),

i.e.: a. b. c.
  c'. b'. d.

or: Give unto–Yahweh, ye–sons–of God,
  Give unto–Yahweh glory and–strength (Ps. xxix. 1),

i.e.: a. b. c. d.
  a. b. e. f.

A very wide variety of forms is possible, making not a little of the beauty of Hebrew poetry. This Gray called *Incomplete Parallelism with Compensation*. But there is another kind, in which a part only of the first *stichos* is repeated in the second, and there is nothing to correspond to the remainder. *E.g.*:

> And–shall–become straight, the–crooked,
> And–the–rough–places plain (Isa. xl. 4b),

i.e.: a. b. c.
  c'. b'.

We may also have a whole line parallel to that which precedes, while the correspondence between the *stichoi* of each is less obvious, *e.g.*:

> Yahweh is–my–light and–my–salvation,
>   Whom shall–I–fear?
> Yahweh is–the–strength of–my–life,
>   Of–whom shall–I–be–afraid (Ps. xxvii. 1).

This we may call *External Parallelism* as opposed to the *Internal Parallelism* of the examples we have previously considered, in which the various *stichoi* of the same line balance one another. Now, although it is impossible, in many cases, to detect a strict parallelism (cp. all instances of

Lowth's " synthetic parallelism "), yet the existence of the phenomenon and its frequency lead us to one of the fundamental principles of Hebrew poetic form. A metre is usually, in most of the languages we know, a balance of *sound*—a *phonetic* rhythm. This is true of Sanskrit, Greek, Latin, Arabic,[1] Syriac, and most modern types of poetry. But in Hebrew, and in one or two other ancient literatures, *e.g.* Akkadian, Egyptian and Chinese, the essential basis of poetic form is a balance of *thought*—a *logical* rhythm. It is profoundly important to bear this in mind, for any scheme or theory of Hebrew metres which neglects this principle, or fails to give it due place, will stand self-condemned.

It is, therefore, clear that the metrical units and the metrical divisions must correspond to the pauses in thought, greater or less. Where two words are intimately connected, as in the Hebrew " construct relation," a strong metrical division, or " cæsura," is impossible between them, and they may tend to fall under the same accent-unit. Light is often thrown on the emphasis to be placed in Hebrew on certain words (*e.g.* negatives and small words like " all ") by the way in which they are combined to form metrical lines.

II. Combination of Word-Accents and Stichoi to Form Lines

The nature of the Hebrew language, which, as we have already remarked, sums up each independent idea in a strongly accented word—often complex—makes it inevitable that the " logical rhythm " should also become a " phonetic rhythm." If a line of poetry contains three significant thought elements, balanced by three more, it is obvious that there will be three significant words in each part. And each significant word, however many syllables it and its subsidiary words (*e.g.* prepositions) contain, is dominated so fully by a single stressed syllable that the rest are usually negligible from the metrical point of view.

---

[1] An exception may be found in the Arabic " Saj'," or " rhymed prose " (cp. Gray, *op. cit.*, pp. 44 ff.).

Hence we can describe a Hebrew line of poetry by the number of significant words or accents it contains in each *stichos*. Thus the illustrations above quoted from Isa. xl and Ps. xxvii would be " scanned " as 3 : 2.[1]

It should be added that there seem to be occasions when a word carries so great a weight of meaning and of sound that it may take the place of *two* logical terms. This will occur especially where a plural word has a pronominal suffix and is preceded by a preposition.[2] Even so, the doubly-stressed word is rare, and never occurs in a two-stress *stichos*.

It may be remarked that several attempts have been made, *e.g.* by Grimme [3] and Burney,[4] still further to analyse the sound-group attached to an individual stress, but none has generally commended itself. Probably no adequate rule ever will be formulated, for such analysis must depend primarily on the phonetic element; and we may doubt whether the Hebrew poet, at least in Biblical times, was ever as fully conscious of the sound of his lines as he was of their meaning.

The simplest logical proposition must consist of two terms, a subject and a predicate. Consequently we should expect to find that the primary unit in Hebrew poetry is a two-stress *stichos*. We may cite the analogy of Babylonian poetry, in which the commonest line consists of two parallel two-stress *stichoi*, though a third stress is sometimes found in one *stichos* or the other, never in both. In Hebrew, however, poems in " 2 : 2 " throughout are very rare. Usually, in some of the lines of a poem, a third stress appears, most commonly in the first stichos and occasionally in the

---

[1] The general view here outlined was first suggested by Rabbi Azariah (sixteenth century); cp. Burney, *The poetry of our Lord*, pp. 59–62 (1925). It was noticed by Lowth, but not generally accepted till it was independently worked out by Ley; cp. esp. *Grundzüge des Rhythmus, des Vers- und Strophenbaues in der Hebräischen Poesie* (1875), and *Leitfaden der Hebräischen Metrik* (1887).

[2] It may not be superfluous to remark that in Hebrew all possessive pronouns are attached as suffixes to the nouns they qualify, forming an inflexion rather than a combination of words. In the same way, some prepositions are prefixed to the word they govern and others are so slight that, though they are written as separate words, they never take a word-accent unless reinforced by a conjunction.

[3] Cp. *Psalmenprobleme*, esp. pp. 3–20 (1902).

[4] *Op. cit.*, cp. esp. pp. 43–58.

second. Thus we have a " pentameter "—3 : 2 or (rarely) 2 : 3. As a matter of fact, the 3 : 2 is far commoner than the 2 : 2, though there are comparatively few poems which are 3 : 2 throughout. It was this metre which was first recognized by Budde in Lam. i–iv, whence he gave it the name of *Qinah*, or " dirge " metre. It is, however, used for a great variety of poems, especially in some of the prophets.[1] A very well-known example is Ps. xxiii :

The–Lord is–my–shepherd, I–shall–not–want,   3⎫
    He–maketh–me–to–lie–down in–green–pastures. 2⎭
He–leadeth–me beside–the–still waters,   3⎫
    He–restoreth my–soul.   2⎭
He–leadeth–me in–the–paths–of righteousness   3⎫
    For–his–name's sake.   2⎭
Yea–though I–walk   2⎫
    Through–the–valley–of the–shadow–of–death, 2⎭
I–will–fear–no evil   2⎫
    For–thou–art with–me.   2⎭
Thy–rod and–thy–staff   2⎫
    They comfort–me.   2⎭
Thou–preparest a–table before–me   3⎫
    In–the–presence–of my–enemies.   2⎭
Thou–anointest my–head with–oil,   3⎫
    My–cup runneth–over.   2⎭
Surely–goodness and–mercy shall–follow–me   3⎫
    All–the–days–of my–life;   2⎭
And–I–will–dwell in–the–house–of the–Lord   3⎫
    For ever (lit. for–length–of days).   2⎭

The original 2 : 2 also developed by what we may call a " triplication." An extra stress was sometimes added to each *stichos*, producing 3 : 3. This is the commonest metre in Hebrew poetry, and it is used in the majority of the *Psalms*, in the poetic portions of the book of *Job*, frequently in *Proverbs*, and in many prophetic oracles. Another method of triplication was to add a third *stichos*, producing 2 : 2 : 2. This form is rare outside the *Prophets*, where, however, it is not uncommon in combination with 3 : 3. The process was carried a step further at times, and produced a third

---

[1] It has been held, *e.g.* by Duhm, that Jeremiah wrote solely in this metre.

stichos, making 3 : 3 : 3—a " trimeter tristich." It is even possible that we may have to allow for the existence of a threefold " tetrameter," produced by three 2 : 2 lines.[1]

Yet a third type is produced by adding a fourth stress to the three-stress *stichos*, thus producing 4 : 3 or (very occasionally) 3 : 4. This metre is by no means common, and, as a rule, the 4 is capable of further subdivision, giving a 2 : 2 : 3 form. In this case the second break in the line (" cæsura ") will be stronger than the first. A good instance of a little poem in this metre is the description of the chaos-vision in Jer. iv. 23–26. It also appears in the last verse of a number of 3 : 3 psalms, though here it may have a liturgical explanation. There may even be instances of 4 : 4 which cannot be resolved into 2 : 2, 2 : 2, but these always awaken suspicion. Every Hebrew poetic line is, properly, a combination of two- and three-stressed *stichoi*.

We have thus three main types of metre:

1. *Qinah*, 3 : 2, 2 : 3, or 2 : 2.
2. Hexameter, 3 : 3, 2 : 2 : 2, or 3 : 3 : 3.
3. Heptameter (comparatively rare), 4 : 3 (2 : 2 : 3).

III. MIXTURE OF METRES

The question now arises as to whether a poem may contain more than one metre. It may be said that there are a few poems which consist of exactly similar lines. In other cases the stricter student is tempted to emend the text, by the addition or subtraction of words, so as to produce complete regularity. But, as the work of Sievers[2] and Gray has shown, the alternation of 3 : 2 and 2 : 2 is so common as to make it practically certain that it was regularly admissible. Similarly, the appearance of 2 : 2 : 2 and 3 : 3 : 3 in poems

---

[1] It is obviously incorrect to speak (as Briggs, for instance, frequently does) of a trimeter " line," since this gives no room for parallelism, and thus violates the fundamental principle of Hebrew poetic form.

[2] Esp. *Metrische Studien* (1901), a very thorough and elaborate study of the phonetics of Hebrew poetry, based on an encyclopædic knowledge of prosody in general. The chief weakness of Sievers' work is his failure to give sufficient weight to the fundamental importance of parallelism, which often leads him to class as poetry literary material which is certainly prose.

L

otherwise 3 : 3 does not, in itself, constitute irregularity.[1]
On the other hand, the much rarer appearance of a 3 : 3
in poems otherwise *Qinah*, or of 3 : 2 or 2 : 2 in a hexameter poem, is certainly suspicious, and some scholars would
resort to conjectural emendation. In this connexion it is
interesting to note how often a metrically regular text may
be obtained by following the Septuagint. Thus, in the
poetical portions of the book of *Jeremiah*, there are about
230 instances (out of over 250 separate pieces) in which a
metrical irregularity is to be found. In 170 of these the
text translated by the Septuagint was metrically regular—
nearly 75 per cent. of the cases. The illustration is particularly significant, since the Egyptian, or Alexandrian,
texts of this book were clearly affected less than most others
by comparison with the Palestinian text.[2] Strong objections have been raised against conjectural emendations
made purely in the interests of metrical theory, but there is
no reason why we should not use it as a criterion in deciding
between the two ancient forms of text. We may, then,
having regard to the vicissitudes through which the Hebrew
text has passed, well feel that, originally, the Hebrew poet
confined himself to a single metre (admitting the alternatives
already noted) for each separate poem.

Before leaving this side of metrical study, a remark should
be made about *anacrusis*. It sometimes happens that a
word appears at the beginning of a line which stands outside the metre. Such words are usually exclamations, single
words drawing a strong contrast, or interrogatives. They
affect, as it were, not the single line to which they are
prefixed, but the whole of the following passage. The
opening words of *Lamentations* are best explained thus:

How![3]

Doth–the–city sit solitary   3⎫
   That–was–full–of people,   2⎭

---

[1] It is, however, worth noting that when a 3 : 3 : 3 line appears in the MT
of *Job*, one of the *stichoi* is nearly always to be suspected on other grounds than
those of metre.   [2] See above, pp. 16, 20.

[3] Though the word is sometimes interrogative, it is clearly an exclamation
here.

Is–she–become a–widow 2
    She–that–was–great among–nations: 2
Princess among–the–provinces 2
    Is–she–become tributary! 2

Another illustration may be cited from Jer. xii. 1b–2:

Wherefore!

Doth–the–way of the–wicked prosper, 3
    All–they–are–at–ease that–deal treacherously; 3
Thou–hast–planted–them, yea, they–have–taken–root, 3
    They–grow, yea–they–bring–forth fruit. 3
Thou–art near in–their–mouth 3
    And–far from–their reins. 3

A recognition of this phenomenon often reveals a singular beauty and impressiveness in the passage in which it occurs.

IV. The Strophe or Stanza

For over a century it has been recognized that the lines of a Hebrew poem may be so grouped as to form stanzas, or, as they are more often called, strophes. It is generally agreed that there are some poems which can be thus arranged, but it does not follow that all Hebrew poetry is necessarily strophic. This view has been held by many eminent scholars, but, in a large number of cases, the position is not easy to accept.

It is, of course, always possible to divide a poem of any length into paragraphs, by noting where the larger breaks in the sense occur, just as we can do with prose. But this division cannot be an element in poetic structure unless some regularity appears. Early investigators held that the strophes in a particular poem need not all contain the same number of lines (or verses), but they must be symmetrical. A strophe of two lines must be properly balanced by another strophe of two lines. They might be arranged for instance $2+3+4+4+3+2$, or $2+3+4+2+3+4$, or even $2+3+4+5+4+3+2$, or in any other form which might be symmetrical. More recent scholars, however, tend to assume that all the strophes of a poem must have the same number of lines. This has led, in some cases, to extensive alterations in the text, lines being freely omitted if they failed to fit the chosen scheme, and the amount of conjectural emendation thus demanded has thrown discredit on the whole theory. In particular, it is improbable that prophetic utterances were normally strophic. There are several apparent instances of the phenomenon, *e.g.* Am. i. 3–ii. 6 and Isa. ix. 8–x. 4, but there is always the possibility that the somewhat artificial form of these passages is due to a compiler rather than to the prophet, though the central message is the work of the latter.

In true strophic arrangement, each stanza must be a separate entity. Neither as between two lines nor as between two strophes can there be any *enjambement*. Strophic division implies logical division, and even in the *Psalter* it is by no means every poem which falls into a series of equal-lined sense-sections. Certain external signs, however, may be generally accepted :

(*a*) The presence of a refrain occurring at regular intervals, *e.g.* Ps. lxxxvii. In some cases this may have been displaced in the process of copying the text.

(*b*) Most alphabetic acrostics are strophic. These are poems in which each letter of the alphabet in turn begins a line or strophe, though even they (*e.g.* Lam. iii) are not necessarily strophic. Sometimes each letter occurs only once, at the beginning of a group of lines, as in Lam. i, ii, and iv. In other cases each line of the group begins with the same letter; Ps. cxix, the most completely artificial Hebrew poem we have, goes through the whole alphabet, beginning eight consecutive lines with each letter. Here we have a very elaborate strophe.

(*c*) The presence of the word *Selah* at the end of a line is often held to indicate the end of a strophe, but its meaning is too uncertain for us to be sure that it was used for this purpose.[1]

In other cases the individual student must be left largely

---

[1] For a possible explanation of this term see p. 185.

to his own judgement.   It may be repeated that there are two essential conditions for the recognition of strophic arrangement.   The first is regularity in length—probably even uniformity;   and the second is a clear division in thought at the end of each strophe.   Only where these are fulfilled, are we safe in describing the structure of a given poem as strophic.[1]

[1] For recent studies of the field of strophic structure cp. H. Möller, *Strophenbau der Psalmen* in *ZATW*, pp. 240–256 (1932) ; Condamin, *Poèmes de la Bible, avec une introduction sur la strophique hébraïque* (1933).

THE WISDOM LITERATURE

I. Pre-Literary Wisdom

Long before the subject of Wisdom assumed a literary form among the Hebrews it was current in oral proverbial sayings; that is common to all peoples when a certain stage of culture has been reached. Short, pithy sayings become popular when they express something which the experience of life shows to be true; and, being employed when the appropriate occasions arise, their frequent utterance makes them generally familiar and therefore common property. Among a people like the Hebrews, in whom the religious instinct was strongly developed, such popular sayings often took a religious form. In the Old Testament, therefore, a number of sayings occur of both types, secular and religious, which were current long before the Wisdom literature came into being. A few examples are the following: " Therefore it became a proverb, ' Is Saul also among the Prophets? ' " (i Sam. x. 12); " They shall surely ask (counsel) at Abel and Dan "[1] (ii Sam. xx. 18); " Out of the wicked cometh forth wickedness " (i Sam. xxiv. 13); " Let not him that girdeth on (his armour) boast himself as he that putteth it off " (i Kgs. xx. 11; in Hebrew this is expressed in four words); " They sow the wind and shall reap the whirlwind " (Hos. viii. 7); " Do they plough the sea with oxen? " (Am. vi. 12; emended text); in Ezek. xviii. 2 an ancient proverb is quoted: " The fathers have eaten sour grapes, and the children's teeth are set on edge." Sometimes the origin of a proverb is indicated, such as one just quoted, " Is Saul among the prophets? " and " Saul hath slain his thousands and David his ten thousand " (i Sam. xviii. 7), and there are many others. Many have been incorporated in the book of *Proverbs*; they are always simple in form, and, in early times, usually straightforward in regard to meaning.

[1] Emended text.

A developed form of Wisdom, though doubtless of an early type, occurs in such things as riddles (Judg. xiv. 14), or fables, for example that of Jotham (Judg. ix. 8–15, and cp. ii Kgs. xiv. 9).

The Hebrew term applied to these popular sayings is *mashal*, the root meaning of which is " to be like," *i.e.* the word contains the idea of comparison; but in the majority of cases these proverbs are not comparisons, nor do they express likeness with anything else; " the solution of this difficulty probably is that the use of the term *mashal* has gone through several stages. While its original form and connotation was a short popular saying which contained a comparison, the history of the term entered a second stage when it came to be employed of any short popular saying which contained a truth gained from general experience." [1] When, however, the term came to be used in literature it acquired an extended sense; the oracular utterances of Balaam are so called (Num. xxiii. 7, 18, etc.), also a prophecy of woe (Isa. xiv. 4–6), a lamentation (Mic. ii. 4), and an allegory (Ezek. xvii. 2, and elsewhere). But in the first instance it is applied to the simple popular sayings to which reference has been made.

These, then, constitute the earliest forms of Hebrew wisdom. By degrees the short sayings were collected, and the various collectors, it may well be believed, added to them by composing proverbs of their own; these were then written down, and thus their literary form began; when once this literary form had been reached, then the Wisdom writers, the *Hakamim*, " Wise men," developed the Wisdom literature.

II. The Hebrew Wisdom Books (Uncanonical)

In dealing with the Hebrew Wisdom literature it is demanded that the whole body of it, so far as it has come down to us, should be taken into consideration, and not merely those books which have been admitted into the Canon; for the distinction between canonical and un-

---

[1] Oesterley, *The Book of Proverbs*, p. lxxv (1929).

canonical Wisdom books is quite arbitrary; they all treat of the same general subject, though one book may emphasize, or even concentrate exclusively upon, some special aspect of it more than others. The canonical Wisdom books will be individually dealt with below; [1] here the uncanonical ones must be briefly considered.

i. *The Wisdom of Ben-Sira (Ecclesiasticus)*. This book was written approximately between 200–182 B.C. in Hebrew; it was translated into Greek in 132 B.C., according to the Prologue to the Greek translation, which was made by the author's grandson. The writer bases a good deal of his work on the earlier Wisdom books, especially *Proverbs*, but he adds very materially to this and shows much independent thought. In a number of instances he develops some well-known proverbial saying into a miniature essay, thus exhibiting his individuality. The book contains a mass of information on the thought, life, and customs of the Jews in his day which greatly enhances its value. Like the writers of *Proverbs*, Ben-Sira addresses himself primarily to the younger generation, though his admonitions very frequently apply to old as well as young, and his intention clearly was to offer a kind of text-book for guidance of life to all. This he does with the object of setting before his people the superiority of Judaism over Hellenism. In a sense, *Ecclesiasticus* " may be regarded as an apologetic work, inasmuch as it aims at combating the rising influence of Greek thought and culture among the Jews. Hellenism had already begun to affect the Jewish people, in Palestine as well as in the Dispersion, and here and there in the book one can observe that the writer himself, in spite of his conservatism, was not wholly unaffected by it. . . . Such traces of Greek influence, however, as there are in the book are to be found in general conception rather than in definite form." [2] In *Ecclesiasticus* the religious note is more prominently and more frequently expressed than in *Proverbs*.

---

[1] They are *Proverbs, Job, Ecclesiastes*, and some of the *Psalms*, or portions of psalms. Regarding these latter Fichtner, with whom probably most commentators will agree, distinguishes between the earlier and the later Wisdom psalms; the earlier are xxxiv. 11–22 (12–23 in Hebr.), xxxii. 8–11, xxxvii, xlix, lxxiii, cxii, cxxviii, cxxxiii; the later, dating from about 300 B.C., are i, xix. 7–14 (8–15), xciv. 8–23, cxi, cxii, cxix.

[2] Oesterley, *Ecclesiasticus*, p. xxiv f. (Cambridge Bible, 1912).

ii. *The Wisdom of Solomon.* There are two clearly marked parts in this book, chs. i–ix and x–xix, of which the latter is much inferior to the earlier both in thought and diction. Authorities differ both as to the unity of the book and its date. The most probable conclusion, however, is that the two parts are not from the same author, and that chs. i–ix belong approximately to the middle of the last pre-Christian century, and x–xix to the middle of the first century A.D., at the latest. Toy [1] has well summarized the difference in style between the two parts: the earlier is " relatively simple and direct, with constant regard to the Hebrew principle of parallelism, whilst in the second part it is ambitious, grandiloquent, or turgid, complicated and artificial, often without parallelism."

The book is a product of the Judaism of the Dispersion, and is full of the Hellenic spirit; this is seen in the treatment of the doctrines of the pre-existence of the soul, of immortality, of the body as evil, and of the creation of the world out of formless matter; the influence of Stoic philosophy appears in the ideas of the *Anima Mundi,* and of the metabolism of the elements, as well as in the classification of the four cardinal virtues for which the Stoics were indebted to Plato.

iii. *Pirke Aboth* (" The Sections of the Fathers "). This is better known as the " Sayings of the Fathers," and partakes largely of the character of Wisdom literature, being often reminiscent of the book of *Proverbs* and of the *Wisdom of Ben-Sira.* It is, in part, the oldest collection, in post-Biblical times, of sayings of Jewish Sages; those who are quoted lived within the period between about 200 B.C. to the third century A.D.

iv. In addition to the books mentioned, there is a Wisdom section belonging to the book of *Baruch* (iii. 9–iv. 4), probably written soon after the destruction of the Temple in A.D. 70; and the *Fourth Book of Maccabees* which was written with the object of illustrating and proving the power of " inspired reason " ($εὐσεβὴς\ λογισμός$); but its character is very different from that of the other Wisdom books.

---

[1] In the *Encycl. Bibl.,* iv. 5338.

The date is uncertain, but it may not improbably have been written about the middle of the first century A.D.

These books, then, together with the canonical books to be dealt with later, constitute the Hebrew Wisdom literature, so far as it has come down to us. Now, in order to realize the changes of thought and the doctrinal developments which are to be observed in this literature it is necessary to distinguish between its earlier and its later parts. Speaking generally, though probably there are some exceptions, the earlier literature is represented by the canonical Wisdom books and the earlier Wisdom psalms; the later, in the main, by those of the Apocrypha and the other Wisdom psalms.

When these two sets of books are carefully examined it will be seen that in a variety of ways there are notable differences between them. Thus, in the earlier literature the Sage is a Wise *man*, irrespective of nationality, while in the later books the Sage is an *Israelite*, and the writers glory in the fact that only among their own people are the true Wise men to be found. Similarly, in the older literature it is taught that Wisdom is to be obtained by all and sundry who seek her; it is never suggested that this is the exclusive privilege of the Israelite. Quite different is the attitude taken up by the writers of the later Wisdom books; here we find that no more is Wisdom a treasure, the possession of which is the reward of any man who faithfully seeks it, but that this is reserved for Israelites only; the national God vouchsafes it to His own people, not to the world in general. Furthermore, it is now taught that Wisdom is identical with the Law. One result of this was that inasmuch as the Law contained not only ethical precepts, but also directions concerning worship, stress came to be laid on the connexion between Wisdom and cult. Again, though here the difference is discernible in emphasis and tendency rather than in direct precept, in the older literature the Wise man does what is right because of the consequent reward, while in the later literature stress is laid more on the need of doing good because it is the will of God; and it comes to the same thing when obedience to

the Law is inculcated, for the Law is the expression of the
Divine will. A further notable difference is that in the
earlier literature Scripture is hardly ever appealed to,
whereas the later Wisdom writers make constant reference
to the Biblical books. Finally, what is perhaps the most
important difference is the doctrine of divine retribution.
In the older literature the conception of God centres primarily on the fact of His righteousness and justice, therefore
He rewards the righteous man for his well-doing, but a
just retribution for his evil deeds falls on the wicked; and
this retribution always takes place on this side of the grave.
This doctrine held sway in spite of its obvious contradiction
offered by the facts of daily life. In the later literature,
however, while there is the full recognition of the justice
of God, great stress is laid on divine grace and mercy
lavished upon Israel, the people of God; in illustration of
this the later Wisdom writers frequently point to the past
history of Israel to show how God's favours were accorded
to His people; it was to them, and to none others, that
God revealed Himself. Thus it is that in the later literature the doctrine of divine retribution is much modified in
its severity, as compared with the earlier literature, through
the exercise of divine mercy. A further important point in
this connexion is that while, according to the earlier literature, retribution always takes place in this life, the later
Wisdom writers, with the exception of Ben-Sira, teach that
the punishment of the wicked and the reward of the righteous
take place in the life to come.[1]

It will thus be seen that in some important particulars
the outlook and teaching of the writers of the earlier and
later Wisdom literature respectively show a marked difference.

III. The Hebrew Conception of Wisdom

The Hebrew word for Wisdom, *Ḥokmah*, is never used
in the sense of pure knowledge, nor, in its earlier usage has
it ever a religious connotation. It is used of wisdom in

---

[1] For full references to the respective literatures in justification of what has
been said, see Fichtner, *op. cit.*, passim.

the administration of affairs (Gen. xli. 33; Deut. i. 13;
ii Sam. xiv. 20; Isa. xxix. 14, etc.); of skill in various
kinds of work, making garments (Exod. xxviii. 3), fashion-
ing idols (Isa. xl. 20), constructing furniture for the Tabernacle (Exod. xxxi. 6, 7), of spinning (Exod. xxxv. 25), and
of mourning (Jer. ix. 17); it is used also of shrewdness
(ii Sam. xiii. 3), of cunning (Job v. 13), and craftiness
(ii Sam. xx. 16 ff.). Thus, it connotes in general the
faculty of being able to distinguish between what is advan-
tageous and what is detrimental; and this both in its
earlier and later usage; but in the latter, side by side with
this meaning, more stress is laid upon its religious content.
Thus, Wisdom was at first purely utilitarian, and developed
in course of time into a quality which was ethical and
religious, while it still continued to be used in its original
sense as well. Ultimately it came to be identical with the
Law. It is in these senses that Wisdom is used in this
literature.

But of the various conceptions of Wisdom found in the
Wisdom books, that which is of far-reaching importance is
its personification. As a general rule, Wisdom is spoken of
as something abstract, but in some striking passages it is
personified. According to Fairweather, it was conceived
of as a " projection out of the Divine mind, as something
more than an attribute, but as something less than a
hypostasis." [1]

The passages, however, in which Wisdom is personified
suggest that it was conceived of as an intermediate being
between God and the world; a personality existing alongside of God, but in quite a definite sense distinct from Him.
Thus, in Prov. viii. 22–31 Wisdom is represented as saying:

" Yahweh possessed me in the beginning of his way, before
  his works of old.
I was set from everlasting, from the beginning, or ever
  the earth was.
When there were no depths I was brought forth . . .
When he established the heavens I was there, when he
  set a circle upon the face of the deep;

[1] Fairweather, *The Background of the Gospels*, p. 84 (1908).

When he made firm the skies above . . .
Then was I by him, as a master workman;
And I was daily his delight, rejoicing always before him;
Rejoicing in his habitable earth; and my delight was
    with the sons of men."

In the *Wisdom of Solomon* vii. 22 ff., the nature of Wisdom
is thus portrayed:
"For there is in her a spirit [1] of understanding, holy,
sole-born, manifold, subtil, mobile, lucid, unpolluted . . .
All-powerful, all-surveying, and penetrating through all
spirits. . . ." (Cp. also ix. 9 and Ecclus. xxiv).[2]
The special importance of this personification of Wisdom
lies not only in the fact that it forms the link between the
Palestinian and Hellenistic development of Judaism, but
also that "it represents the contribution made by the
Wisdom literature to the Christology of the Old Testament,
and has greatly influenced Christian theology." [3]

IV. The Ḥakamim and their Work

There is evidence to show that the *Ḥakamim*, or "Wise
Men," traced their origin back to the learned class of the
Scribes, from whose ranks men were chosen to occupy
important positions as State officials. In ii Sam. viii. 17,
among David's high officers, is mentioned Seraiah the
Sopher or "Scribe," a kind of secretary of State; in another
list of these (ii Sam. xx. 25) a similar office is held by Sheva;
see also i Kgs. iv. 3; ii Kgs. xix. 2; ii Kgs. xxii. 3–7; Jer.
xxxvi. 20, 21. Indications of the existence of institutions
for the training of these Scribes occur in Josh. xv. 15,
where mention is made of Kiriath-sepher, "the city of
the book," or, as the Septuagint reads, Kiriath-sopher,
"the Scribe city"; in Josh. xv. 49 this city is called Kiriath-
sannah, "the city of the palm-leaf," *i.e.* it preserved the
name of the material, or one of the materials, on which the
Scribes wrote.[1]

[1] Another reading is: "For she is a spirit."
[2] In Job xxviii. 12–28 there is also a personification of Wisdom.
[3] Fairweather, *op. cit.*, p. 84.
[4] Fries, in the *Zeitschrift des Deutschen Palästina Vereins*, xxii. 125.

The first time the *Ḥakamim* are mentioned is in Isa. xxix. 14, where the name occurs as a technical term and must, therefore, have been long in existence. In Jer. xviii. 18 the *Ḥakam* is spoken of as belonging to an order, like the priest and the prophet: " . . . the law shall not perish from the priest, nor counsel from the *Ḥakam*, nor the word from the prophet"; and in Jer. viii. 8, 9, Scribes and *Ḥakamim* are seen to be identical. This identity is more fully borne out by Ben-Sira, who speaks of himself as a *Ḥakam* and a *Sopher* (Ecclus. xxxviii. 24–xxxix. 1–11).[1]

In pre-exilic times it is likely enough that the Wise men were looked upon with disfavour by both prophets and priests; the whole mental outlook and ideals of each of these latter were so utterly different from those of the former that they must have regarded the Wise men, with their lack of zeal for God (from the prophetical point of view, cp. Isa. xxii. 15–19), and their coldness towards the cult (from the priestly point of view), with something approaching contempt. The Wise men, on the other hand, with what they would regard as their superior wisdom, may well have thought the prophets arbitrary and hard, the priests as narrow-minded and self-centred. In later days, however, all this changed; prophetism in the higher sense had ceased, and a friendly co-operation seems to have existed between priests and Wise men. Ezra was both priest and scribe; and later, in such a passage, *e.g.*, as Ecclus. vii. 29–31, l. 1 ff., it is evident that the Wise men were in full sympathy with the priesthood.

For the rest, the writers of the Wisdom literature were, above all things, practical in their teaching; with their knowledge of human nature, their ability to give counsel of real help for every-day life, and of expressing this in clear and forceful language, they were an immense power for good in guiding men in the ways of religion and ethics, and in teaching them to lead sensible lives. In speaking of the way in which the Sages supplemented the work of the prophets, Ranston truly remarks: " It is customary,

---

[1] See further, Baumgartner, " Die israelitische Weisheitsliteratur," in *Theologische Rundschau*, 1933, pp. 269 f.

and with justification, to regard the prophets as the most illustrious exponents of the Hebrew religious spirit. But it may be doubted if the influence of these spiritual experts would have been so permanent and far-reaching apart from the work of the Wise men in popularizing their ideals and creating among the ordinary people a spirit sympathetic with them." [1] At a time when Prophetism in the true sense of the word had almost died out it was the *Ḥakamim* who took the place of the prophets, and it is likely enough that their methods of teaching were more effective among ordinary mortals than their greater predecessors.

It is one of the striking things about the Wisdom writers that among the various classes of people to whom they addressed themselves, the greatest attention was accorded to different types of " fools." The Hebrew language has a number of words to describe the varieties of this type of humanity. It is evident that, according to the Wisdom writers, these types constituted the majority of mankind; nevertheless, they realized the great potentialities for good in every type of " fool," with one exception (see Prov. xvi. 22, xxvii. 22), and the very fact that there is so much guidance and instruction for " fools," of the less virulent type, is sufficient evidence that the *Ḥakamim* were not pessimists in their estimation of their fellow-creatures.

Stress must, however, be laid on the fact that the *Ḥakamim* were earnestly concerned to show that foolishness *is* wickedness; every kind of Wisdom, from the lowest to the highest, is the gift of God; to permit folly, therefore, to assert its sway is to commit a wicked act, and this not only in the case of the wanton, aggressive " fools " who glory in wrongdoing, but also in that of the careless and thoughtless who flounder in the mire of their folly without realizing it: " The way of the wicked is like darkness, they know not wherein they stumble " (Prov. iv. 19).

But the *Ḥakamim* were far from contenting themselves with indicating to " fools " normal rules of conduct regarding every-day life, important as these are; they would not have been exponents of the teaching of the prophets

[1] *The Old Testament Wisdom Books and their Teaching*, p. 19 (1930).

had they not been zealous in inculcating more directly religious precepts. It is true, the earlier literature has exceedingly little to say about worship and sacrifices, and the subject of prayer is rarely mentioned, though in the later literature all these find frequent expression (*e.g.* Ecclus. xxxii. 6 f., xxxvi. 10–12, xlv. 15 ff., l. 1 ff.; Wisd. ix. 4, xviii. 9, 21, etc.); but the intimate connexion between ethics and religion is altogether characteristic of the Wisdom literature as a whole; the *Ḥakamim* of every age are insistent on Wisdom being, in its essence, the fear of Yahweh (*e.g.* Prov. xiv. 2, xv. 9, xvi. 6, iii. 7, xxviii. 5; Ecclus. xv. 1, xix. 20, Wisd. xiv. 24 ff.), on man's relationship to God, and on the need of trust in Him (*e.g.* Prov. xxii. 4, xviii. 10, xx. 22, xxx. 5, ix. 10; Ecclus. ii. 8, xiv. 12, 22 ff.; Wisd. vii. 15, ix. 17). While in the later literature the religious element is more pronounced, it would be an injustice to say that it does not receive attention in the earlier; since the Sages regarded every form of Wisdom as a divine gift, it is evident that the religious element lay at the base of all their teaching, whether expressed or not.

On the two very important subjects, the problem of suffering, and the doctrine of retribution, which figure prominently in this literature, we do not speak here, as they are dealt with elsewhere.[1]

Speaking generally, then, it may be said that the main object of these exponents of *Ḥokmah*, "Wisdom," was to teach men how to live happy lives as long as they were on this earth. This leads them to deal with the relationship between a man and his God, between parents and children, man and wife, friend and foe, rich and poor, high and low; they teach what is right behaviour in every phase and occupation of life, how to accept adverse fortune, and the fitting attitude of him who enjoys wealth—in a word, how to live to the best advantage, to do right because it brings its own reward, to avoid wrongdoing because it entails disadvantages. Yet, stress must again be laid on the fact, sometimes insufficiently recognized in reading what appears to be predominantly of a secular character,

[1] See pp. 165, 175 ff.

that underlying this utilitarian view of life there is a religious foundation; that wisdom is the gift of God is often insisted upon (*e.g.* Prov. ii. 6; Ecclus. i. 1–10, and elsewhere), that good fortune as the result of right living, and misfortune as the result of wrongdoing, are not merely a process of cause and effect, but a matter of divine intervention in the affairs of men (*e.g.* Prov. x. 22); it is pointed out that true wisdom and piety are really the same thing (*e.g.* Ecclus. i. 14–20, 25–30), and that the origin and essence and highest form of wisdom is the fear of the Lord, so that it is incumbent on all men to observe the commandments of God (*e.g.* Prov. xxviii. 4, 7). The increasing stress laid on the religious element observable among the later Sages is further seen in that a more vital difference is recognized between piety and godlessness than between wisdom and folly;[1] and it is significant that Ben-Sira estimates a godly man of limited understanding more highly than one of greater wisdom who transgresses the Law (Ecclus. xix. 24).

V. The Cosmopolitan Character of Wisdom Literature

The fact that Wisdom was not the exclusive possession of Israel is already fully recognized in the Old Testament. Thus, in order to show how great Solomon's wisdom was it is said that it " excelled the wisdom of the children of the east, and all the wisdom of Egypt " (i Kgs. iv. 30 [Hebr. v. 10]); by the " children of the east " are meant Arabians (cp. Bar. iii. 23) and Edomites, as the context shows, and doubtless also Babylonians. The "sons of Mahol" (ver. 31) were Edomites; their wisdom is referred to in Jer. xlix. 7 and in Obad. 8; and the wise men of Egypt are spoken of in Gen. xli. 8; cp. also Isa. xix. 11–15. Further, " in Job ii. 11 the names of Job's friends show that they were non-Israelite; Teman was in Edom, Shuah in Assyria, and though Naamah was in south-west Judah, it is most

---

[1] This is brought out by Baumgartner, *Israelitische und altorientalische Weisheit*, p. 5 (1933).

M

probable that Zophar was thought of as an Edomite because the clan which settled in Naamah, viz. the Calebites (see i Chron. iv. 15, where Naam is the same as Naamah), was of Edomite extraction." [1]

The existence of this extra-Israelite wisdom to which the Old Testament witnesses has been abundantly verified in recent years by the discovery of a number of Egyptian and Babylonian Wisdom books.[2] The study of these Wisdom books and a comparison between them and those of the Hebrews shows that there existed from the Nile to the Tigris an extensive Wisdom literature essentially identical in its main characteristics, and that this literature was in the nature of common property among the peoples of the ancient East. It is interesting, too, to find that the Wisdom writers of both Egypt and Babylonia belonged to the class of Scribes and occupied important posts in the State just as we have seen was the case among the Israelites.

The translation of all these Egyptian and Babylonian Wisdom books has made it possible for non-experts in these languages to compare their contents with those of the Hebrews; and the comparison raises some questions of interest and importance to the Biblical student: (1) Were the Hebrew Sages indebted to those of other countries, and if so, in how far? (2) Was there any reciprocal indebtedness? (3) Does the Hebrew Wisdom literature differ from that of the other nations, and if so, in what respects? A brief attempt must be made to reply to these questions.

The familiarity of the Hebrews with the wisdom of other countries is evident from the passages referred to above; and the older and higher culture of Egypt and Babylon would naturally impress the Hebrew; moreover, the fact that the Wisdom literature of both Egypt and Babylon was demonstrably older than that of the Hebrews offers an à priori probability that the Hebrew Sages were indebted to extraneous sources for much of their Wisdom thought. It must also be recognized that there are certain character-

[1] Oesterley, *The Book of Proverbs*, p. xxxiv (1929); see also Pfeiffer, " Edomite Wisdom," in the *ZATW* for 1926, pp. 13 ff.
[2] Some details will be found, *e.g.*, in Baumgartner, *op. cit.*, pp. 20 ff.

istics in the earlier books of Hebrew Wisdom which are strikingly non-Israelite; these have already been mentioned,
viz. the cosmopolitan outlook, the comparatively cold out-
ward religious expression, and the reticence regarding
things which receive much emphasis in other parts of the
Old Testament—worship, sacrifices, the election of Israel,
etc.; this also points to extraneous influence. But the
evidence of this becomes overwhelming when a detailed
comparison between the Hebrew Wisdom books and those
of Egypt and Babylon is undertaken; this cannot be done
here, but the large number of passages which contain
identity of thought and word makes it impossible to deny
borrowing,[1] and it must obviously be the later writers who
borrowed from the earlier. Our first question must, therefore, be answered by an emphatic affirmative.

The answer to the second question as to whether there
was reciprocal indebtedness is more difficult. Opinions on
the subject differ, though the majority of experts are inclined to doubt Hebrew influence on the Egyptian and
Babylonian Sages.

But in one respect the possibility, to put it at the lowest,
of Hebrew influence on non-Israelite Wisdom writers must
be recognized, and this even in regard to those writings
which are demonstrably older than any Hebrew books, if
one may assume later redactional additions—a not improbable hypothesis. We refer to religious and ethical
elements, but especially the former.[2] It seems arbitrary to
suppose that among men of similar bent, be their nationality
what it may, influence should have been exercised on one
side only; in the close intercourse which must at different
periods have existed between Israelites, Egyptians, and
Babylonians, it is highly probable that the Hebrew religious
genius, which was professedly unique, impressed itself upon
the more serious thinkers of other nationalities; and they
in their turn would have communicated this to others like-
minded with themselves. In this way the Hebrew religious

---

[1] See Oesterley, *Proverbs*, pp. xxxiv–lv. The most striking instance is
Prov. xxii. 17–xxiii. 14, which seems to have been taken more or less bodily
from the Egyptian Wisdom book *The Teaching of Amen-em-ope*.
[2] Cp., among others, Causse, *Sagesse égyptienne et sagesse juive*, p. 168 (1929).

spirit would have spread within certain circles both in Egypt and Babylonia, and have been reproduced in some of the Wisdom writings of these countries. So far as Wisdom itself is concerned, Israel was undoubtedly largely influenced by both these countries; but where it is a question of religion, Israelite influence is the more likely to have been predominant. What Blackman, in a different connexion, however, has said with great truth in reference to Egypt may well apply also to Babylonia: "Just as, on the one hand, specifically native Egyptian contributions to the world's cultural and religious progress penetrated into Palestine and were absorbed into the main stream of Hebrew religious development, so, on the other hand, certain results of the Semitic genius for religion in their turn penetrated into Egypt and contributed to the formulation of what was highest and best in Egyptian religion." [1]

In answer to our last question it must be affirmed that the Hebrew Wisdom literature does differ in some important respects from that of both Egypt and Babylonia. Baumgartner maintains that by simply altering the language and the name of God of sayings from *Proverbs* and transplanting them into an Egyptian, Assyrian, or Aramaic collection, and *vice versa*, one would not know that any exchange had been made.[2] So far as the Egyptian Wisdom books are concerned this is an over-statement. There is much in these that is entirely un-Hebraic, and if put into Hebrew would at once betray non-Israelite elements.

The first point of difference in the Hebrew Wisdom literature is, naturally enough, its monotheism; Israel had but one God, and His name was Yahweh; in the other Wisdom literatures many gods and goddesses are mentioned, with a variety of names. Secondly, there can be no question about it that the ethical element constitutes one of the main differences between Israelite and other Wisdom books. This is not to say that moral precepts are wanting in the Egyptian and other non-Israelite books, the difference lies in emphasis, but that is a very marked difference, and

---

[1] In *The Psalmists*, p. xiii (1926). See further, Kittel, *Die hellenistische Mysterien-Religion und das Alte Testament*, passim (1924).
[2] *Op. cit.*, p. 23.

cannot fail to strike the impartial reader of the respective literatures. A further not unimportant point here is the difference in motive in ethical behaviour; the Hebrew Sages are often insistent on good behaviour because, as the people of Yahweh, who is holy, they too must be holy in their walk in life; it is perfectly true that again and again in the Hebrew Wisdom writings the motive pointed to is not " Be good for good's sake," but for the advantage to be derived from doing what is right; yet it is none the less true that often the will of Yahweh is pointed to as that which must be the real motive for right living, and as the norm of true Wisdom; that is specifically Israelite, and there is nothing corresponding to it in other ancient Wisdom books. Once more, though this applies only to Egyptian Wisdom; retribution for evil living takes place on this earth only according to Hebrew Sages, while those of Egypt insist also on retribution in the world hereafter; it must strike one as remarkable that the Hebrew Sages with their belief in an omnipotent God were not influenced by Egyptian belief here. As to this, however, the *Book of Wisdom* offers a notable exception; though there is no reason to suppose that the writer of this book was indebted to Egypt for this. Lastly, and this, too, is matter for surprise, the Hebrew Wisdom writers of the earlier literature, as already pointed out, show little interest in matters of worship, differing herein from the Sages of Egypt and Babylonia.

Summing up, then, it must be noted that the Hebrew Sages were in many particulars strongly influenced by their *confrères* of other lands; nevertheless, they had a remarkable faculty of adapting extraneous material and moulding it in accordance with their own ideas; they show a distinct individuality, and when the different bodies of Wisdom literature are compared, it must be admitted that that of the Hebrews shows, all in all, a marked superiority over the others.

THE BOOK OF JOB

I. Place in the Canon

Few Old Testament books have had so many different places assigned to them in the Canon as has the *Book of Job*. This is, possibly, due to different theories of authorship. The Hebrew Canon, representing the opinion of Jewish scholars to whom the book was anonymous, placed it third in the *Kethubim*, or Writings,[1] after *Psalms* and *Proverbs*. The Septuagint placed all the poetical books after the historical writings and before the *Prophets*. In the view of those responsible for the arrangement of the Greek versions, the book was anonymous, and they placed before it, not only *Psalms* and *Proverbs*, but the two shorter books also which were connected with Solomon, *Ecclesiastes* and the *Song of Songs*. The *Peshitta*, on the supposition that the book was the work of Moses, put it immediately after *Deuteronomy*, while the arrangement of the books in the Vulgate suggests a combination of this view with the order of the Septuagint, and counts it as the first of the poetical books, though in other respects its arrangement of this group is the same as that of the Septuagint. Most modern versions, including the English, follow the Vulgate.

II. Contents

The book of *Job*, which is professedly a story rather than a piece of history,[2] is the record of the intellectual struggle and the spiritual agony of a man who had plumbed the depths of human suffering and had tried to harmonize his experience with his belief in an all-powerful, all-wise, and

---

[1] See p. 5.
[2] This is made obvious by the opening words in Hebrew, where a formula of introduction is employed which is never used in books which claim to be history, even in an historical romance such as *Ruth*.

all-loving God.[1] It opens with a picture of Job in his
innocence and moral perfection (i. 1–5). The scene changes
to the court of Yahweh in heaven, where His servants come
to report on their work. One of the officials is the Satan,[2]
whose business it is to discover whether good men are really
good, and to bring the guilty before Yahweh for judgement
and punishment. He is a kind of divine Attorney-General.
Yahweh calls his attention to Job's perfections, and the
Satan, who, in virtue of his profession, is necessarily somewhat cynical, refuses to believe that Job's conduct is disinterested, and insists that he is righteous for the sake of
the prosperity with which he is rewarded. Yahweh gives
the Satan permission to test Job, and a sudden series of
disasters falls upon him, which, though reducing him to
childlessness and beggary, does not make him swerve from
his loyal submission to Yahweh (i. 6–22). Again Yahweh
asks the Satan about Job, and the latter retorts that the
suffering has not gone deep enough; Job himself must be
attacked. As a result, grievous and loathsome sickness
falls upon the victim, and he becomes an outcast. In spite
of his wife's advice he still refuses to blame Yahweh. Three
friends, Eliphaz, Bildad, and Zophar, come to " comfort "
him (ch. ii).

Up to this point the book has been written in prose, but
it now becomes poetry, which extends down to xlii. 6.
The poem consists of a dialogue between Job and his
friends, ending with the appearance of Yahweh and Job's
final submission. The subject of debate is the age-long
problem of the meaning of suffering, and it is worth noting
that it could have arisen in this form nowhere in the ancient
world except in Israel. The fact of suffering is universally
admitted, and the attempt to avoid or escape it is one of
the permanent springs of human action. But it becomes a
problem only when it conflicts with the religious theory of
a single ruler of the whole universe, who is at once omnipotent, wise, and good. This is a doctrine which does not

[1] The same problem is handled in a few other places in the O.T., *e.g.* in
Hab. i. 12 ff.; Jer. xii. 1 f.; Pss. xxxvii, xlix, lxxiii, and, above all, in Isa. lii.
13–liii.
[2] Always occurring with the definite article.

appear in the ancient world outside Israel; the question is
an inevitable corollary of that ethical monotheism in which
Judaism stood alone.

The solution of the problem maintained by the friends is
that easy misinterpretation of the prophetic doctrine of
retribution which regarded all suffering as punitive. Job
must have been wicked beyond all men to have incurred
so great a penalty. From this position the friends never
move; the only change they experience is emotional, not
intellectual, for, as the debate proceeds, they grow steadily
more angry with Job, and more outspoken in their accusations. The discussion is arranged in set form. Job speaks
first, and then each of the three friends speaks in turn, a
speech of Job following each of the others. This cycle is
repeated three times, though in our present text no third
speech is assigned to Zophar, an omission generally held
to be due to textual corruption. Finally, in chs. xxix–xxxi
Job utters his concluding speech, ending with a great oath
of purgation in ch. xxxi, and an appeal to Yahweh to appear
and pronounce on the case.

This section, chs. iii–xxxi, forms the core of the book,
and requires further discussion. The three friends are
delicately distinguished from one another; Eliphaz, the
eldest, is kindly, pious, even mystical, relying for his theology
on direct revelation; Bildad is less sympathetic, but has
the weight of ancient authority behind him; Zophar, the
youngest, needs neither divine revelation nor tradition, for
he himself knows all that needs to be known, and feels that
he can state the truth with absolute and serene dogmatism.
Yet they all represent exactly the same point of view, and
contribute nothing to the elucidation of the problem. Job,
on the other hand, moves forward, and one of the features
of the poet's skill lies in the fact that each step he takes is
made possible by something that the friends say. Thus his
first speech, ch. iii, is simply a cry of pain, whose rhetorical
questions in no way imply a real intellectual problem.
Eliphaz, seeking to offer comfort, suggests that God is
responsible for Job's calamities, and that if he will but
repent and submit to God, all will be well. Never has

the futility of orthodox consolation been more ruthlessly exposed. Job's children are *dead*, and twenty others would not make up for those that have gone. He is suffering from leprosy [1] in its most terrible form, and can expect nothing but lingering pain, with She'ol as his only release. Truly Eliphaz would "heal the breach lightly"! But he has given Job an idea—it is God who is responsible, and the sufferer must ask why it is that irresponsible Omnipotence thus tortures him. Bildad replies that God is "righteous." The term has a double meaning, originally indicating the successful party in a legal action, and thence acquiring an ethical content. Job at once seizes on the word, and from this point onward the metaphor of the law-court is always with him. He admits that God is "righteous" in the forensic sense, but that makes matters only the worse, since there is no hope either of a fair trial or of an appeal. God is against him, and God is bound to win, for He is at once accuser, judge and executioner. Zophar urges him to submit, since he can never reach God (xi. 7), and the very denial kindles in Job's mind the thought that there may some day be a chance of stating his case before God (*e.g.* xiii. 3, xiv. 15).

In the second cycle of the debate the irritation of the friends has grown through the stubbornness of Job, and they feel that his impiety must be accompanied by deep-seated sinfulness. Eliphaz calls attention to the absolute purity of God, in whose sight even perfection is imperfect. Job replies that whatever wrong he has done, he has not deserved the unique punishment which has fallen upon him. A gleam of hope springs from this belief in divine faultlessness, and for a moment the thought comes over him, as the emotional tension of the poem heightens, that God must, after all, be on his side, and he appeals away from the God of orthodox theology to God as He must be (xvi. 18–21). But instantly his new-born relief is turned to despair; he is doomed, and even God cannot help him,

---

[1] While the description of Job's disease in ii. 7 is too vague to allow of accurate diagnosis, the references to the symptoms in the poem (*e.g.* vii. 5, 14–15, ix. 18, xxx. 30) leave no doubt as to the nature of the sickness.

for the grave is his only goal. Once more Bildad intervenes, and his contemptuous rebuke, which is almost an
abusive threat, drives Job to the climax of his spiritual
agony. In frantic desperation he turns this way and that
—God, his family, the friends—finding neither help nor
hope, till, out of the very depths of his despair, he makes
the great leap of faith and reaches solid ground in the
thought that, after all, death cannot be the end. There
must be still, beyond the grave, the possibility that God
will see true justice done, and Job himself will know it—
" apart from my flesh, I shall see God, whom I shall see
for myself, and mine eyes shall behold, and not as a stranger "
(xix. 26b–27). This is not yet a general doctrine of immortality, though it contains the germ of one; but it does
restore Job's confidence in the ultimate rightness of the
universe and its Governor. To the great problem there is
a solution, and here or hereafter it is possible for Job to
know it.

This does not end the debate. The general question of
the government of the universe still remains unsolved, and
Job turns to that again. His own sorrows are not forgotten, but they have already lost the keenness of their
edge, and are much rather an illustration, in an extreme
form, of the problem to be solved. Even Zophar's violence
fails to rouse Job to passion, and his next speech, in ch. xxi,
is a new statement of the general problem. This Eliphaz
does not attempt to handle, but charges Job with definite
sins, so dramatically preparing the way for the great oath
of purgation in ch. xxxi. Otherwise Job is untouched by
these accusations, and he now addresses himself to the
problem of reaching God to lay his case before Him; the
forensic metaphor once more rises to the surface.

Chs. xxv–xxvii are apparently in some disorder. Bildad's
speech in xxv is very short, and xxvi, now put into the
mouth of Job, is almost a continuation of it. Most commentators feel that the first verse of xxvi has found its way
into the text by accident, and that Bildad's third speech
includes this chapter also. Of Job's answer only xxvii. 1–6
survives, for it seems clear that the remainder of ch. xxvii

belongs to Zophar.   Probably a section containing the end
of Job's speech and the beginning of Zophar's was lost at
an early stage in the history of the text.   Ch. xxviii, even if
original, is a parenthesis, and the debate concludes with
Job's utterance in xxix–xxxi.   The first of these chapters
is devoted to a description of his former happiness; ch. xxx
draws the contrast of his present misery, and in xxxi Job
gives a detailed statement of the moral standard he has
always attained.   This is, many will feel, the highest point
reached by the practical ethics of the Old Testament, in
its justice, purity, and humanity, transcending anything
that we find in the Law.   The chapter ends (verses 38–40
are clearly out of place and should be read earlier in the
chapter) with a proud appeal to God to appear and to hear
the case Job can present.

At this point another character intervenes in the person
of Elihu.   He is younger than the rest, and has not hitherto
been mentioned.   His views occupy chs. xxxii–xxxvii, in
the course of which he states his doctrine that the function
of suffering is purgative.   No further notice is taken of
him, either by Job or by anyone else, and in xxxviii–xli
Yahweh replies to Job's challenge, giving a picture of His
majesty and power, which reduces Job to humble submission (xl. 3–5, xlii. 1–6).   He has seen God for himself,
and in that vision all his doubts and questionings sink into
the background.   In xlii. 7 the prose narrative is resumed;
Yahweh justifies Job, condemns the friends, accepts the
prayer of Job for their forgiveness, and restores to him
double of what he has lost.   The book closes with a picture
which represents the ancient Israelite ideal of prosperity.

III. Structure and Date

i. *Structure*.   The unity of the book has been widely
challenged in recent years.   Discussion has centred, in the
main, about three points: (*a*) the relation of the prose
opening and conclusion to the poem, (*b*) the originality
of the Elihu speeches, (*c*) the originality of one or two
shorter passages, *e.g.* ch. xxviii and xl. 15–xli. 34.

(*a*) It is held by many that the prose passages at the beginning and end of the book are not the work of the poet to whom we owe the intervening chapters. A difference is to be found in the divine name; in the prose we have Yahweh, in the poem other names, *e.g.* Shaddai (a term confined to P in the Pentateuch), and especially El and Eloah, the latter being a late singular formed from the naturally plural word Elohim. The fact that Job's sufferings are explained in the introduction by reference to the Satan, who does not appear at all in the poem, is easily understood on the ground that none of the earthly characters knows of the council in heaven, though it would not have been unnatural for a reference to have been introduced in Yahweh's speeches. But the whole conception of religion is different; that patient submission which the prologue ascribes to Job is what the friends want, not what the poet approves. The characters, both of Job and his friends, differ in the two parts. Even more impressive is the atmosphere which surrounds the two. With the opening verses of ch. iii we are conscious of the same kind of contrast with which we should meet if we read the story of Creation in Gen. ii. 4 ff., and then went straight back to the beginning of ch. i. It is the difference between a nursery story with a moral, and a philosophical discussion, inflamed by personal intimacy with the problem at issue. Not only is there this wide difference in the cultural ages of the two parts, but the relation of the author to his work strikes us at once. The narrator in chs. i, ii is telling a story about someone else; he makes us feel something of the tragedy of Job, but we see it sympathetically from the outside. The poet, on the other hand, was himself his hero; *he* was the leper who, through pain and torturing doubts of God, did win his way to a faith of some kind. It is, as so many commentators have remarked, with his own heart's blood that the poem is written; it is the agony of his own soul that he lays bare before us.

At the same time it is clear that the poem presupposes the introduction. It is true that the writer once or twice forgets himself (*e.g.* in xix. 17 his children are still living),

but such lapses are rare. We hear in Ezek. xiv. 14 of a
Job who, along with Noah and Daniel, is a symbol of
righteousness, and we can hardly doubt that the old story
was used by the poet as a framework for his own work.
The only question at issue is as to whether there was a
book in which the popular story was embodied, or whether
it was simply handed down by oral tradition. One or two
small points tend to turn the balance in favour of the former
view. When God appears in xxxviii. 1 the name Yahweh
is used, suggesting that this was taken from the old story
where that term was used throughout. Further, we have
mention of a whirlwind. This is a detail which would
hardly have been retained by the poet unless it had been
before him in a written source. We are thus led to the
probability that there existed, in pre-exilic days, a tale
which the poet found in written form, giving an account
of the sufferings of Job, of his patient forbearance, of a
dialogue with his three friends, and of the appearance of
Yahweh at the end. What the friends had said we do not
know—perhaps they had given Job the same kind of advice
as his wife did (ii. 10). In any case, the old dialogue was
excised, and the poem inserted in its place.[1]

(b) The Elihu speeches have all the appearance of a later
insertion. They postpone the theophany which is logically
required immediately after xxxi. 37, and they add little to
the debate, for, in spite of the suggestion that the purpose
of suffering is for purifying, they take substantially the view
adopted by the friends. Elihu is introduced in a fashion
very different from that in which the other three friends
are brought on the scene, and there is no other reference
to him whatever. There are also important philological
differences between chs. xxxii–xxxvii and the rest of the
poem.[2] Nevertheless, several leading scholars hold to the
originality of these chapters. Budde, for instance, argues

----

[1] McFadyen, *Introduction to the Old Testament*, pp. 311–315 (1932), and E.
and K. Kautzsch (cp. Sellin, *Introduction to the Old Testament*, p. 213: 1923)
stand almost alone in ascribing the framework to the poet himself; Driver
and Gray are inclined to the same view, but do not positively adopt it (*Job*,
pp. xxxiv–xxxvii).
[2] For a detailed analysis see Driver and Gray, *A Critical and Exegetical Commentary on the Book of Job*, pp. xli–xlviii (1921).

that they contain the only real solution of the problem which the poet had to offer;[1] and Sellin,[2] following a hint thrown out by Kamphausen and Merx, believes that they were written by the poet himself, but represent a view much later than that of the rest of the book. After years of further meditation the poet felt it necessary to insert his new opinions. Sellin compares the differences in outlook exhibited by the two parts of Goethe's *Faust*. But in spite of the weight of opinion represented by these scholars, it remains true that the majority still feel that Elihu represents a redactional stage which would have been repudiated by the original poet.

(*c*) Ch. xxviii is generally recognized as having little to do with the book or with its main purpose. It is a hymn in praise of Wisdom, which is in the end (if the last verse be original in the poem) identified with the fear of the Lord. It might be regarded as an attempt to solve the problem created by the doctrine of divine omnipotence in an imperfect world by calling attention to the inscrutability of God's ways. This would almost certainly imply its insertion in the poem by a later hand, since this view is already expressed to some extent by the friends, and receives fuller amplification in the speeches of God Himself.

One other section often attributed to a later writer is the description of the two monstrous creatures, the hippopotamus and the crocodile, in xl. 15–xli. 26. The passage in which they occur does deal with the marvels of God in nature, and refers to several creatures. But the descriptions of these two are much longer, and, though they attain a high literary standard, they are not on the same level as that reached by the rest of the divine speeches.

ii. *Date.* If the account of the structure of the book above suggested be the true one, we have to consider two dates, that of the popular story and that of the poem. The former is certainly pre-exilic, a conclusion which is obvious both from the reference in Ezekiel, already mentioned, and

[1] See *Das Buch Hiob* (1913), pp. xlv–xlviii, where Kamphausen, Cornill and Wildeboer are also cited as holding the originality of the Elihu speeches.
[2] *Op. cit.*, pp. 214–220.

from the fact that the sacrificial system is clearly not developed as it was in post-exilic times. It is less easy to be sure of the date of the poem. In vii. 17 we have words which read like a bitter parody on Ps. viii. 4. But what is the date of this Psalm? The subject of the book, provided we do not place it too early, is one which might have exercised the mind of any thoughtful Israelite after the Exile. It is a universal poem, and that is one of the features which give it its value and its interest for us to-day. The implicit monotheism makes a post-exilic date practically certain, and there are peculiarities of style and language which suggest that it is not to be placed too soon after the Return. Occasionally, for instance, we meet with Aramaisms, not only in vocabulary but even in syntax.[1] In general, these considerations would seem to point to somewhere between the middle of the fifth century and the middle of the fourth. But there are few poems in all literature whose date and historical background are of less importance than they are in the book of *Job*.

IV. The Solution of the Problem of the Book

We cannot leave the book without noting the difficulty that commentators have found in satisfying themselves in regard to the answer which the book gives to the problem stated therein—the inequality of suffering and its apparent injustice. We should, however, remark that there are two problems. One is the purely personal one, and concerns God's attitude to Job himself. Is He the friend or the enemy of His faithful servant? This receives a certain answer in the great passage xix. 25 ff., where Job is at least assured that God must and will vindicate him. The other problem is more general, and the book as it stands contains no less than three different attempts to solve it.

(*a*) In the first place we have the explanation offered by the popular tale. Here the suffering of the hero is due, not to any fault of his own, but to the jealous cynicism of

---

[1] Cp. Driver and Gray, *op. cit.*, pp. xlvi–xlvii, with the literature there cited.

the Satan. " Doth Job fear God for naught? " is a valid
question, not only for ancient Israel, but for every other
age in human history—we think, inevitably, of Glaucon's
description of the perfectly righteous man.[1] Like Plato,
the story-teller could find no answer except in the humiliation and hopeless agony of the faultless man, and his suffering
becomes a test, the only valid test, of *disinterested* righteousness.

(*b*) Such a solution may help the sufferer, but it does not
touch the heart of the problem. Is God justified in torturing a perfectly good and innocent person, merely to prove
that he *is* good and innocent? It is a justification of God,
a theodicy, that is needed, and the demand for a further
explanation is the motive inspiring the poet to whom we
owe the greater part of the book. In the poem, the friends
insist that suffering can be explained only as punishment
due to, and proportioned to, sin, but one of the obvious
aims of the book is to challenge this theory. The striking
fact in the poet's discussion is that the divine pronouncement at the end contains no hint at an answer. God
simply presents Himself as He is, and Job is cowed, and
abhors himself in dust and ashes. This is no solution of
the problem, and the poet cannot have intended it to be
understood as one. In other words, it looks as though he
had deliberately told his readers that there was no solution
—at least none that the human mind could appreciate.

What, then, does Job's final attitude imply? We must
remember that we are dealing with an Eastern, especially
with a Jewish, mind, and we must not expect that our own
feelings and instincts will meet with full satisfaction in what
appeals to an ancient Jew, great poet and deep thinker
though he be. With this in mind let us look once more at
the *dénouement*. Job, at the end of ch. xxxi, has appealed
to God to appear, and is prepared " as a prince to enter
His presence " bearing a convincing statement of his case
with him. In answer to this challenge God does appear,
and presents Himself in all His creative majesty. At once
Job forgets his case, and ceases to be urged by his problems.
In the presence of God these things vanish away, and only

[1] See Plato, *Repub.*, Bk. II, 361 f.

God is left. True, the experience is one which instils into him the deepest awe and self-contempt, but these are just the aspects of the matter that would be inevitable to the ancient Oriental. Translated into modern terms, however, we may surely say that the supreme lesson of the close of this book is that when once a man has really stood face to face with God, he has no more doubts. The question may have no logical answer, the problem may find no formal solution, but that does not matter; the sufferer has seen God, and that is enough. In that vision, and in the knowledge which it brings, he can rest in patience and spiritual contentment. In him is fulfilled that which was spoken by the prophet, " he shall look away out of the agony of his soul, and shall be satisfied by his knowledge." [1]

(c) The third attempt at a solution belongs to a point of view best represented by the Elihu speeches, though it may, possibly, be detected elsewhere. Here we have the position of a reader of the popular story and of the poem, who felt that there was one very serious fault in Job's character, which needed correction. Throughout the debate he has insisted on his substantial righteousness. He may have done what was wrong in the sight of God, but such sins were insignificant and unconscious. While many will feel that this determined self-justification was the natural, almost inevitable, reaction of the sufferer to the theology of the three friends, it can also be interpreted as evidence of a self-righteous Pharisaism, and in that light it was viewed by the author of the Elihu speeches. This gives him a clue: there is a double purpose in Job's calamities. In the first place they bring to light a deep-seated and subtle weakness. Prosperity would never have shown that Job was so fatally " righteous in his own eyes "; [2] in the crucible of adversity this spiritual dross has risen to the surface. But, further, Job's sufferings have offered a remedy for the disease. The poem ended with the hero lying contrite and penitent at the feet of God. He " abhors himself in dust and ashes." His self-righteousness has gone

---

[1] Isa. liii. 11.   [2] xxxii. 1.

N

and it was the purging fires of pain that had rid him of this subtle impurity of soul.

Our first perusal of the book may have left us with the feeling that the essential theme is handled in a confusing and uncertain fashion. It is only when we recognize the fact that *Job* is the result of a growth in which three main stages can be distinguished, and that each stage presents its own view of the problem, that the various lines of thought are clear, and the book takes its proper place in the story of man's developing knowledge of God.

V. The Text of the Book

The textual criticism of the book of *Job* presents some interesting and unusual features. The MT is usually straightforward, though there are passages which defy translation as they stand. In some cases the *Peshitta* shows a certain independence, but the greatest variations are to be seen in the Septuagint. It is true that this version, as presented in our printed copies, does not differ greatly from the MT, but it is known that this is not the original Septuagint. When the translation was first made, it was much shorter than it is now, between 350 and 400 *stichoi*, which appear in the MT and the modern Septuagint texts, being omitted. That these omissions were early is clear from Origen's recension, and from the Sahidic Egyptian version, which was brought to light only in 1889. In the forms of the Septuagint generally familiar to us, this shorter text has been expanded from the later Greek versions, and so brought into closer agreement with the MT. It is, however, agreed on all hands that the Septuagint text is, as a rule, a deliberate abbreviation of the MT.[1]

[1] Gray and Driver, *op. cit.*, pp. lxxi–lxxvi.

THE PSALMS

I. Place in the Canon: General Title

In the Hebrew Bible the *Psalms* heads the list in the third division of the Canon, called *Kethubim*, "Writings" (*Hagiographa*).

There are many religious poems in the historical and prophetical books; but with the exception of *Lamentations*, this is the only book which consists exclusively of such poems.[1]

The title of our book in the Hebrew Bible is *Tehillim*,[2] the plural of *Tehillah*, meaning a "hymn of praise." This title is inappropriate, for most of the psalms cannot be called hymns of praise; and though this word occurs in the body of a number of psalms, there is only one which is called a *Tehillah* (cxlv).

At the conclusion of Ps. lxxii a note is added: "The prayers of David the son of Jesse, are ended." This suggests that at one time the general title of these seventy-two psalms had been "Prayers," in Hebrew *Tephilloth*. But this title, too, would have been inappropriate, for not many of these psalms are in the nature of prayers, and only a single one is called a "prayer" (xvii).[3]

In the Septuagint the book is called βίβλος ψαλμῶν ("Book of psalms"), or ψαλμοί ("Psalms"), or ψαλτήριον ("Psalter"); this last means primarily "stringed instrument," *i.e.* psaltery; then it comes to mean the *song* sung to the accompaniment of a stringed instrument. The Greek title comes, no doubt, from the Hebrew word *mizmor*, which is the most common title for individual psalms;[4] its root meaning is to "pluck," *i.e.* taking hold of the strings with

---

[1] The *Song of Songs* does not contain religious poems.
[2] On the masculine plural form of this feminine noun see Gesenius-Kautzsch, § 87, *i, p.*   [3] Ps. lxxxvi is also called a "prayer."
[4] Fifty-seven psalms are so called in their titles.

179

the fingers, and thus connotes singing to the accompaniment
of a stringed instrument.

II. The Titles of Individual Psalms

While these titles are in all probability due to editors,
there are good grounds for believing that in many cases they
reflect some traditional use in regard to particular psalms,
and some interesting points arise in this connexion. To
deal exhaustively with the subject would be out of place
here ; [1] we are concerned only with giving a few illustrations.

i. *Titles containing musical directions*.[2] Apart from *mizmor* the
most frequently occurring musical term in the titles is
Lammenaṣeaḥ (fifty-five times) ; it is rendered in the R.V.:
" For the Chief Musician," which is as unsatisfactory as a
number of the other various explanations which have been
offered. The term is undoubtedly a puzzle, as it was, too,
to the ancient translators. What would appear to be the
most acceptable explanation, though this also has its difficulties, is that suggested by Haupt,[3] and tentatively followed
by Gunkel ; [4] by a change in the vowel-points he reads the
word *Lamminṣaḥ* (לְמִּנְצַח), which would mean: " regarding
the musical rendering." [5] If this meaning is applied to the
term a reasonable sense is obtainable in a large number of
titles in which indications are given as to how the psalm
is to be sung; thus, *e.g.*, in the titles of Pss. iv, vi, liv, lv, lxi,
lxvii, lxxvi, the musical direction is *Lamminṣaḥ bineginoth*,
" regarding the musical rendering: with stringed instruments " (probably of some special kind), *i.e.* the psalm was
to be sung to the accompaniment of stringed instruments;
similarly it is directed that Ps. v, so far as its musical rendering is concerned, is to be sung with flute accompaniment
(cp. Isa. xxx. 29) ; Pss. lvii, lviii, lix, lxxv are to be sung to

---

[1] For details see, *e.g.*, Briggs, *The Book of Psalms*, pp. lvii–lxxxviii (1906).

[2] It should be pointed out that Briggs holds that these musical directions
in the titles indicate collections from which the poems were taken, while
Mowinckel believes that they have cultic significance.   We are unable to
concur with either of these views.

[3] *American Journal of Semitic Languages* (1907).

[4] *Die Psalmen* (1926) ; see the rendering of the titles below.

[5] Cp. i Chron. xv. 21, where the verb means " to render music," or something similar.

the tune of " Destroy not " (on this see below).   In a large
number of psalms *mizmor* is added to *Lamminṣaḥ*, which would
presumably mean that these psalms were to be rendered in
the ordinary way, *mizmor* being the most common designation
of a psalm sung to the accompaniment of the simplest
stringed instruments.   A difficulty arises when *Lamminṣaḥ*
is followed by the name of David, which occurs in the titles
of several psalms (*e.g.* xxi, xxxi, xl and others) ; possibly
this means that the psalm is to be sung in the Davidic style,
i.e. in some archaic mode (but see § III (*a*)).

In the titles to Pss. vi, xii the term *'al hash-sheminith* occurs :
the R.V. renders this : " set to Sheminith," marg. " the
eighth " ; the most obvious meaning of this would seem to
be, " on the octave," and this is the most usual explanation
given.   It is, however, practically certain that the ancient
Jewish scale was not an octave ; we have here the traditional,
as distinct from the more modern, music of the Arabs to go
upon ; and all authorities are agreed that the Arabs—at any
rate, until very recent times—have retained unchanged
their customs of millenniums ago ; this would certainly apply
to music, and more especially to religious music ; it is also
agreed on all hands that we must picture the music of the
Hebrews as very similar to that of the *primitive* type of Arab
music which can be heard at the present day.   Now it is
well known that the Arabs recognize quarter-tones as well
as semitones, therefore they have no octave consisting of
eight tones and thirteen semitones ; and the same applies
to ancient Hebrew music.   Therefore the term *'al hash-
sheminith* cannot mean " on the octave," *i.e.* that the musical
instruments played, or the male voices sang, an octave
lower.[1]   Whatever the term meant—and it is quite uncertain
what is to be understood by it—it cannot have meant this.
Some authorities think it may refer to the place of the psalm
in a particular collection, *i.e.* the eighth ; but in this case it
might well be expected that some other psalms would have
had their place in a collection designated ; but this is not the
case.   In this connexion mention should also be made of
the expression *'al 'alamoth* (R.V. " set to Alamoth "), which

[1] In i Chron. xv. 21 the term is used in reference to harps.

occurs in the title of Ps. xlvi; [1] the word means " maidens,"
and is usually held to refer to high-pitched, or soprano
voices; this is not likely to be correct, since it is used, like
'al hash-sheminith, in reference to stringed instruments (i Chron.
xv. 20). It is clear that both these terms indicated something
in connexion with the musical rendering of the psalm; but
what this was it is now not possible to say with certainty.

ii. *Titles containing the names of popular melodies.* Of greater
interest are the cases in which a psalm is directed to be sung
to some well-known melody; a few of these may be noted.
Three psalms (viii, lxxxi, lxxxiv) have in their titles " According to Gittith " (R.V. " Set to Gittith "); this has often
been held to refer to some kind of instrument which took its
name from the Philistine city of Gath, and to the accompaniment of which the psalms in question were to be sung.
This is improbable, for there is no reason why the Israelites
should have borrowed an instrument from the Philistines,
nor is there anywhere the slightest hint to this effect. The
Old Testament gives the names of a number of musical
instruments—percussion, wind, and string—but there is
never any mention of an instrument of this kind. The only
reason apparently why this explanation of " Gittith " has
been offered is because it is said in the Targum to the
Psalms that " Gittith " refers to an instrument that came
from Gath; but this is only a guess suggested by the fact
that the form " Gittith " is equivalent to " Gath-like," or
" Gathic." This, however, is equally true of the Hebrew
word *gath*, which means a " wine-press "; this is how the
Septuagint understood the word, and it is so explained in
the Midrash on the *Psalms*, where reference is made to
Joel iv. (R.V. iii) 13: " Put ye in the sickle, for the vintage
is ripe; come, tread ye, for the winepress (*gath*) is full, the
fats overflow." It is, therefore, possible that " according to
Gittith " means " wine-press-like," *i.e.* the melody to which
the psalm was to be sung was the tune of a vintage song.
This is supported by another interesting title at the head of
Pss. lvii, lviii, lix, lxxv; it is directed that these are to be

---

[1] Probably also in that of xlix originally; it figures now as the last word
in xlviii.

sung to the tune of *'al-tashḥeth,* which means, " Destroy (it)
not "—these are the opening words of the first line of a
popular vintage song which is quoted in Isa. lxv. 8:
" . . . As the new wine is found in the cluster, and one
saith—then comes the quotation—' Destroy it not (*'al-
tashḥeth*), for a blessing is in it,' . . ." This song was thus
so well known that it could be referred to by its opening
words; and to the tune of this song the psalms in question
were to be sung.

Another case of this kind occurs in the title of Ps. lvi;
here it is directed that the psalm is to be sung to the tune of
" The dove of the far-off terebinths." [1] Possibly there is a
quotation from this song in Ps. lv. 6, 7: " Oh that I had wings
like a dove; then would I fly away and be at rest." Ps. xxii,
again, is, according to the title, to be sung to the tune of the
song known as *'Ayyeleth hash-shaḥar,* "The hind of the morning"; here also it is possible that this song is quoted in
Ps. xlii. 1: " As the hart [2] panteth after the water-brooks,
so panteth my soul after thee, O God; " there are other
affinities between these two psalms. A number of other
illustrations could be given (*e.g.* in the titles of Pss. ix, xviii,
xxxvi, xlv, liii, lx, lxix, lxxx); they show that the Israelites
took over the melodies of popular folk-songs for use in the
Temple worship; and it is interesting to note that this
custom was continued in the Synagogue worship until well
into the Middle Ages.[3]

iii. *Some other terms occurring in titles.* A few other terms call
for a brief notice. *Maskil* figures in the titles of thirteen
psalms;[4] the word comes from a root meaning to have
" insight " or to show " prudence " (cp. Am. v. 13), and the
form of the verb from which *Maskil* is derived has a causative
sense, so that the word would mean " insight-giving," and
in reference to a psalm it would be one that by its contents
taught insight. But there is another possibility; in ii Chron.

[1] Reading אֵילִים, " terebinths," for the meaningless אֵלֶם, " in silence."

[2] Some authorities would read the fem. אַיֶּלֶת " hind," for אַיָּל, " hart,"
as giving a better rhythm.

[3] See the " Introductory volume " to the *Oxford History of Music*, pp. 55 ff.
(1929).

[4] Pss. xxxii, xlii, xliv, xlv, lii–lv, lxxiv, lxxviii, lxxxviii, lxxxix, cxlii.

xxx. 22 the verb, in its causative form, is used in reference to the Levites, and may therefore be applied to the quality of their singing or of their instrumental playing; in this case a *Maskil* psalm would be one which was accompanied by some special kind of music. It is, however, more probable that the former explanation is right, especially as this is borne out by the contents of the psalms in question.

Regarding the term *Miktam*, occurring in the titles of six psalms,[1] there is much difference of opinion; the root meaning of the word is uncertain, and it seems impossible to come to any definite conclusion as to what the term means.

Pss. cxx–cxxxiv are called " Songs of Ascents "; these were no doubt sung by pilgrims as they ascended up to Jerusalem, the city on a hill; hence the title.

Ps. vii is called a *Shiggaion* in the title; this, again, is explained in a variety of ways, to all of which there are objections; it is impossible to feel any certitude as to its meaning.[2]

In the title to Ps. xcii this psalm is called a " song for the Sabbath day "; the Mishnah [3] tell us that there was a special psalm for each day of the week; they are given thus: xxiv, xlviii, lxxxii, xciv, lxxxi, xciii, and for the Sabbath xcii; with the exception of the third and fifth days, for which no psalm is given, this agrees with the titles in the Septuagint.

Two psalms (xxxviii and lxx) have in their titles the word *Lehazkir*, meaning " to bring to remembrance "; it can also mean " to make confession," which would be very appropriate for xxxvii, but not for lxx. Some commentators hold, with good reason, that the word should be read, *'azkarah* " memorial," which is the technical word used in Lev. ii. 2, 9 for the meal-offering; it is, therefore, probable that these two psalms were sung during the offering of the *Minḥah*, as the meal-offering was called in post-exilic times. This is how the Targum understood the term.

Some other elements in the titles will be considered in § III.

---

[1] Pss. xvi, lvi–lx.
[2] Possibly *Shigionoth* (Hab. iii. 1) comes from the same root and has the same meaning.   [3] *Tamid* vii.

Finally, though not occurring in the title of any psalm, a word must be said about the term *Selah*. That this must be a musical direction of some kind is suggested by the fact that it nearly always occurs in psalms which have *Lamminsaḥ* in their titles. The term *Selah* figures almost always at the end of a strophe or of a section,[1] and, as a rule, it is not included in the strophic rhythm, though sometimes it is, and disturbs the metre.[2] Its meaning has been much disputed; unfortunately the two most scientific explanations make it mean two directly opposite things: the root-meaning of the word is to " lift up " (סלל), but the " lifting up " can refer either to the voices or to the musical accompaniment; the Septuagint, which may well have retained an echo of traditional liturgical usage, renders it διάψαλμα; it is uncertain what this word means, but it is obviously connected with ψάλλειν, which, as already pointed out, refers to stringed instruments; it is, therefore, probable that *Selah* refers to these. In this case the word might indicate that the music was to be " lifted up," *i.e.* the voices ceased, and the instruments played alone; this is supported by the fact that *Selah* usually comes at the end of a strophe, *i.e.* a halt in the words, and therefore a cessation of the voices.[3]

III. COLLECTIONS EMBODIED IN THE PSALTER

In its present form the Psalter is divided into five books: i–xli; xlii–lxxii; lxxiii–lxxxix; xc–cvi; cvii–cl. Each of the first four closes with a doxology, in the case of the fifth, Ps. cl, being itself a doxology, makes a fitting close. That these five divisions are artificial, made probably on the pattern of the five books of Moses, is evident, for on closer examination divisions of a very different kind are to be discerned.

In the first place, it will be seen that by the different use

[1] It is found seventy-one times in the Hebrew of the *Psalms*, in the Septuagint more frequently; in the psalm of Hab. iii it occurs three times; twice in the middle of a verse, once at the end, though not at the end of the section.
[2] On the metrical system of the *Psalms*, see above, pp. 142 ff.
[3] Briggs, on the other hand, holds that *Selah* " calls for the lifting up of the voice in praise " (*op. cit.*, p. lxxxv). On the whole subject of these titles see Mowinckel, *Psalmenstudien* iv (1923).

of the divine name three large groups of psalms are separated off; thus in Pss. i–xli (Book I) Yahweh is used; in Pss. xlii–lxxxix (Books II, III) for the most part Elohim is used; and in Pss. xc–cl (Books IV, V) Yahweh is again used. Whatever may have been the reason for this varying use of the divine name, the present point is that by this means three large divisions were marked off.

But both the five-book division and the three-group division belong to later times; the Psalter was originally formed by gathering together a number of independent collections; these collections were as follows:

(*a*) The " *Davidic* " psalms: iii–ix; xi–xxxii; xxxiv–xli; li–lxv; lxviii–lxx; lxxxvi; ci; ciii; cviii–cx; cxxii; cxxiv; cxxxiii; cxxxviii–cxlv, making altogether seventy-two psalms which are ascribed to David.

(*b*) The *Korahite* psalms: xlii; xliv–xlix; lxxxiv; lxxxv; lxxxvii; lxxxviii; eleven in number.

(*c*) The *Asaphite* psalms: l; lxxiii–lxxxiii; twelve in number.

(*d*) The *Ma'aloth*, " Songs of Ascents ": cxx–cxxxiv; fifteen in number.

(*e*) The *Hallelujah* psalms: civ–cvi; cxi–cxiii; cxv–cxvii; cxxxv; cxlvi–cl; again fifteen in number.

In each case there are a certain number of psalms with the same ascription running consecutively, which points to their having at one time belonged, respectively, to separate collections.

Further, as we have seen, at the end of Ps. lxxii occur the words: " The prayers of David, the son of Jesse, are ended "; that clearly points to a completed collection. But as there are many other psalms besides these which are ascribed to David, there was, presumably, at one time another collection of " Davidic " psalms.

Another thing pointing to separate collections is that some psalms occur twice over with only small variations; thus, xiv is the same psalm as liii with one or two minor differences; the same is true of xl. 13–17 and lxx; and lvii. 7–11 together with lx. 5–12 (Hebr. 7–14), make up cviii. Obviously, a psalm would not figure twice in the same collection, whereas this is easily comprehensible if several collections were amalgamated, for a favourite psalm might well have been preserved by more than one person in his collection.

It is, therefore, clear that a number of collections have been incorporated in the Psalter; and these collections were of gradual growth, for the individual psalms were not written with the object of forming a collection; many authors wrote psalms, and long after their composition they were collected; this process was repeated in the case of many other psalms which were current. Ultimately, all these collections were gathered together, and thus the Psalter, as we now have it, came into being.

IV. The Dates of the Psalms

In dealing with this subject it must be recognized that, generally speaking, the nature of the content of most of the psalms makes the assigning of dates precarious; certain indications will, not infrequently, help to decide within what period a particular psalm is likely to have been written, and in most cases this is as near as we can get with any feeling of certitude to the date of a psalm. The matter is also complicated by the fact that so many psalms have been subjected to revision; such revision may sometimes make a psalm appear to be of later date than it is in its origin. And there are other problems which present themselves in seeking to assign dates.

But in spite of difficulties it is possible, within certain limits, to come to some definite conclusions on the subject.

Starting from the lower limit, it may be pointed out that there is no reason why the collection known as the " Psalms of Solomon "[1] (*circa* 50 B.C.) should not have been included in the Psalter (which was not the case) unless the Canon had been closed by this time. Indeed, since this collection emanated from the Pharisees, who were by now the dominant party, it would certainly have been incorporated in the Psalter had this been possible. It is, therefore, clear

---

[1] That these psalms were originally written in Hebrew is generally recognized.

that by the middle of the first century B.C. the Psalter had assumed its present form.

Next, in the words of Swete: " The division of the Psalter into books seems to have been already made when it was translated into Greek, for though the Greek codices have nothing to answer to the headings ספר ראשון (' Book the first '), etc., which appear in the printed Hebrew Bible, the doxologies at the end of the first four books appear in the Greek as well as in the Massoretic text." [1] It follows, there-fore, that at the latest the close of the Psalter had taken place by the end of the second century B.C.; in other words, the task of gathering together the various collections of psalms circulating among the Jews was finished, at the latest, about 100 B.C.; so that it is not until this date that we can even begin to consider the question of the dates of the different collections, let alone the dates of the individual psalms com-prised in these collections. The latest psalms, therefore, were written before 100 B.C. To go back one step farther, Kittel has shown [2] that the collections of the " Korah " and " Asaph " psalms belong approximately to 300 B.C., *i.e.* to the early part of the Greek period; the detailed proof of this would take us too far afield,[3] but there is every reason to believe in the correctness of this estimate.

It would be out of the question to discuss here the dates of individual psalms; it must suffice to say that, with some exceptions, Pss. lxxiii–cl (*i.e.* Books III–V) belong largely to the Greek period and later, though a certain number must be assigned to the Persian period (*circa* 500–300 B.C.); the reason for believing that some psalms belong to this period is that while they are clearly post-exilic, they contain ele-ments which demand a date before the Greek period. It is also probable that there are some psalms in Book II (xlii–lxxii), and even isolated ones in Book I, which are post-exilic.

Our next step must be to give reasons for the contention that a large number of psalms in Books I, II are pre-exilic.

---

[1] *Introduction to the Old Testament in Greek,* p. 254 (1900).
[2] *Die Psalmen,* p. xxi (1929).
[3] See Kittel, *ibid.*

(a) There is at least a *prima facie* probability that some psalms must be pre-exilic. The Temple with its services had existed for about three centuries before the Exile; that songs of praise were sung is demonstrable (see below), and it is incredible that these should have been forgotten during the Exile when the loss of sacrificial worship enhanced the importance of other forms of worship.

(b) There is a number of passages in the Old Testament which show that in pre-exilic times there was singing with musical accompaniment as an act of worship. Apart from such passages as Judg. v. 1 ff.—the song of Deborah; Exod. xv. 1–18, the psalm ascribed to Moses; Exod. xv. 20, 21, the reference to Miriam's song; Exod. xxxii. 17 ff., the singing during the worship of the golden calf—there is an obvious reference to singing with accompaniment of musical instruments in worship in Am. v. 21–23: " I hate, I despise your feasts, and I will take no delight in your solemn assemblies. Yea, though ye offer me your burnt offerings and meal offerings I will not accept them. . . . Take away from me the noise of thy songs; for I will not hear the melody of thy viols." Quite clearly this eighth-century prophet is speaking here in reference to singing and instrumental music in public worship. Isaiah, too, has in mind the Temple worship when he says: " Ye shall have a song as in the night when a holy feast is kept; and gladness of heart, as when one goeth with a pipe to come into the mountain of Yahweh " (xxx. 29). In Ps. cxxxvii. 3, 4 there is a reference to the Temple songs sung before the Exile: " For there they that led us captive required of us songs . . . sing us one of the songs of Zion. . . . How shall we sing the Lord's song in a strange land? " The implied refusal to sing these holy songs before Gentile strangers must be balanced by the words which follow: " If I forget thee, O Jerusalem, may my right hand forget," *i.e.* how to play the stringed instrument accompaniment.

These passages, and they are not exhaustive, show then that the singing of songs in worship with instrumental accompaniment was familiar to the Israelites in pre-exilic times. Such songs would not have been forgotten, and it is certain that a number of them have been preserved in the Psalter, though not, it may well be, in their original form.

(c) There are many religious conceptions expressed in some of the psalms which mark them as pre-exilic; this applies especially to the doctrine of God. Thoughts and expressions occur in reference to Yahweh which cannot possibly have originated after the Exile, e.g. Ps. xviii. 7–10; the only way of explaining the presence of such crude ideas is that they were retained just because the psalms in which they occur had been handed down for many generations, and the tenacity of traditional use refused to part with them.

(d) Finally, there is the presence of the " royal psalms " in the Psalter, i.e. those in which reference is made to the king; these are: ii, xviii, xx, xxi, xxviii, xl, lxi, lxiii, lxxii, cx, cxxxii. These may not in every case refer to an Israelite king, and while we may not wholly agree with what Sellin says on the subject, there is a good deal of truth in his words : " The desperate attempts, there is no other word for it, to interpret these (i.e. passages in which the king is mentioned) as referring to a future Messiah, a foreign king, or a Maccabæan prince, must be regarded as one and all complete failures. The prince is always a real personage of the present world, though, no doubt, in ii, xxi, xlv, lxxii–cx, a personality in whom the poet also celebrates the expected Saviour, the divine deliverer. This excludes a foreign king as completely as the title ' king ' . . . excludes a Simon, or other prince, of the Maccabæan family." [1]

While, therefore, the great majority of the psalms must be regarded as post-exilic, there is an appreciable number which should be assigned to some period before the Exile, and possibly some which were written during the Exile.

Indications as to the period to which individual psalms belong may be summarized thus:—

Pre-exilic period : the presence of " primitive " ideas about Yahweh; references to the king; references to the northern kingdom, though the mention of " Israel " does not always

[1] Introduction to the Old Testament, p. 200 (1923).

denote the northern kingdom; references to Yahweh as king point to a psalm being pre-exilic in origin, though its present form may be later.

Exilic period : references to the Dispersion may in some cases point to this period; similarly, the mention of the enmity of Edom (cp. Ezek. xxv. 12-14, xxxv), though this will usually point to a later period. It is also possible that where affinity with the thought of prophetical teaching occurs the psalm in question may be exilic. The possibility of a similar date, or even a later one, must be recognized for a psalm in which eschatological thought is expressed. And the possibility applies to a dirge psalm.

Post-exilic : to this period belong psalms in which personal devotion to Yahweh is expressed, and in which the problem of the suffering of the righteous is dealt with; also those in which the Law and the oral tradition are mentioned, and in which a universalistic note is struck. To a late post-exilic date may be assigned those psalms which exhibit literary development in one form or another, such as acrostic psalms; also the sapiential psalms; and, finally, those in which there is a reference to atheism (Greek period).

V. Types of Psalms

In reading one or other of the English versions of the Psalter the meaning of any particular passage seems, as a rule, to be perfectly straightforward and simple; and therefore it is by no means always realized how difficult it often is to grasp the full meaning of a psalm in its Hebrew form. Nothing illustrates this more convincingly than the large variety of interpretations offered by commentators. If the essential meaning of a psalm, or a passage in a psalm, were always clear, a consensus of opinion would soon be established, and there would not be so many different explanations offered.

One reason for the difficulty of understanding the real meaning of so many verses in the psalms is that the metrical structure of Hebrew poetry is characterized by verbal exiguity; the sentences are extremely short and consist often of three, sometimes of only two, words; and such sentences follow one another without any indication of their logical connexion. Gunkel,[1] in drawing attention to this, gives a simple illustration; the Hebrew poet writes: " Yahweh is my shepherd, I shall not want; " each sentence consists of only two words in Hebrew. A Greek writer would have made it clear that the second sentence was the logical result of the first; but the Hebrew poet omits a " therefore." In the case of this simple illustration it may be said that the connexion is so obvious that no connecting link is needed; but there are very many instances in which the absence of any indication of the nature of the connexion between two laconic sentences makes it difficult to decide what the poet really meant; often several interpretations seem possible, but there is no guarantee as to which is the right one.

Another difficulty arises on account of the Hebrew use of tenses; the formation of Hebrew sentences, especially in poetry, is of a somewhat " primitive " order, and the tenses are exceedingly variable in their meaning; so that, as Gunkel says, such a thing may occur as that commentators differ on the point as to whether a psalm is to be interpreted as a lament over some present calamity, or as a thanksgiving for a happy deliverance from some past trouble (cp. Pss. xli, cxvi, Isa. xxxviii, 10–20).

The only way whereby a true interpretation is to be obtained—and it is Gunkel's great merit to have discovered this—is by recognizing to what type or family (*Gattung*) a psalm belongs, and by elucidating it in the light of other psalms belonging to the same type or family; it is, as he says, " a fundamental, scientific principle that nothing can be understood apart from its *milieu* (*Zusammenhang*)." Therefore, if psalms which, by their nature, content, and special terms, can be shown to belong to the same type, are grouped together and compared, it is evident that this must facilitate their understanding, and the purpose for which, and the occasion on which, they were written. This has been done by Gunkel, and the following are the types into which he divides the psalms (one example of each is given in brackets):

---

[1] *Einleitung in die Psalmen*, pp. 1 ff. (1928).

(a) *Congregational psalms* : among these are to be reckoned *hymns* [1] which were sung in the sanctuary on holy days during sacred rites of various kinds for the purpose of giving glory to God; these were sung on behalf of the congregation either by the choir as a whole, or by a trained singer as a solo (xcv); *national dirges*, sung by the whole congregation on occasions of some public calamity; they express the mourning and grief felt by the people, together with the hope for better times, and prayer for divine mercy (xi); *pilgrim songs*, sung during pilgrimages to the sanctuary in Jerusalem, either by the whole company of pilgrims or by one of their number, and, in all probability, antiphonally (lxxxiv); songs of *national* victory, sung on appropriate occasions by the whole congregation, and accompanied by music and dancing (cxlix); *national thanksgiving*; these like the preceding were probably sung in procession (xlviii). Some of those under the third heading were also congregational.

(b) *Psalms of the individual* : these include dirges originally sung or uttered in the Temple by private individuals in times of sickness or trouble, or during the performance of sacred rites, such as sacrifices, because it was believed that at such times the Deity was closer at hand and therefore more approachable (xxii); *thanksgivings*, said or sung in the Temple during the thank-offering (*todah*); they express gratitude for deliverance from sickness or trouble (xviii); *curses*, uttered by an individual against his enemy; the curse was believed to be more effective if uttered in the sanctuary (cix).

(c) *Miscellaneous types* : most important among these were the *sacred songs* sung by the congregation in commemoration of Yahweh's ascent upon His throne [2] (xvii); here belong also the "*royal*" *psalms* sung by the court singers on festive occasions in honour of the king and the royal house (xlv); [3] further, psalms, or parts of psalms, in which the priests in chorus called upon the congregation to pronounce a *blessing*

---

[1] Gunkel, *Einleitung*, pp. 32–94.
[2] On these, in addition to Gunkel, *Die Psalmen*, the psalms in question, *Einleitung*, pp. 94–116, see Mowinckel, *Psalmenstudien*, II, pp. 1–209 (1922); III, pp. 30 ff. (1923), and Hans Schmidt, *Die Thronfahrt Jahves* (1927).
[3] Gunkel, *Einleitung*, pp. 140–171.

O

on Yahweh (cxxxiv) ; *sacred legends,* commemorated in psalms ; such legends are brought in only incidentally in hymns of praise ; but the psalms in question are sufficiently distinctive to constitute a type of their own (viii) ; " *prophetic* " *psalms,* in which different themes of the teaching of the prophets, which exercised a great influence on the religiously-minded, were taken up and embodied in psalms ; they were sung, sometimes at any rate, by an individual in the Temple (xl) ; and Wisdom psalms.[1]

Finally, it appears that in some psalms there has been a deliberate mixing up of subject-matter in which psalms of more than one type are represented (xv).

For the justification of what has been said, Gunkel's *Introduction* and his *Commentary* must be consulted.

VI. The Psalms as Liturgical Documents

The Psalter is sometimes spoken of as the hymn-book of the second Temple ; this is a misleading title, for there can be little doubt that a large number of the psalms cannot be described as liturgical documents, *i.e.* they were not used in the public worship of the Temple, nor were they ever intended to be. It is certain that the worship of the early synagogue was based on the Temple Liturgy,[2] and if we are to be guided, as we justifiably may be, by early synagogal usage, it may be concluded that not more than about half of the psalms in the Psalter were used in public worship, or can be described as liturgical documents.[3] Apart from musical directions and the like in the titles, it is very rarely that the liturgical character of a psalm is indicated in a title (Ps. xxx is " for the Dedication of the House," and Ps. xcii is a " Song for the Sabbath Day "), and even in those psalms which are demonstrably liturgical it is not always immedi-

---

[1] See above, p. 152 n.[1], 154.

[2] See, *e.g.*, Zunz, *Die gottesdienstlichen Vorträge der Juden,* p. 2 (1892) ; Elbogen, *Der jüdische Gottesdienst in seiner geschichtlichen Entwickelung,* p. 29 and *passim* (1913).

[3] About seventy of the psalms are used in the modern synagogue, but the number in use is now larger than was originally the case, see the present writer's *The Jewish Background of the Christian Liturgy,* pp. 73 ff. (1925).

ately apparent from their content that they should be so described.

In order to discern which psalms are to be designated as liturgical documents two lines of investigation must be followed: indications in the individual psalms themselves, and the evidence to be derived from early post-biblical Jewish literature, above all from the Mishnah and the tractate *Sopherim*.[1] To indicate all those psalms which bear marks of their liturgical character, and to adduce the evidence afforded by the Jewish literature mentioned, would obviously be quite out of the question here; but a few illustrations may be offered:

Thus, the liturgical character of Ps. lxxxi is shown in verse 3 (4): " Blow the shophar (ram's horn) at the new moon, at the full moon on the day of our feast." As the feast is mentioned without further designation it is the feast of Tabernacles which is meant, *the* feast *par excellence* (cp. i Kgs. viii. 2; Ezek. xlv. 25; ii Chron. vii. 8); this was celebrated at the full moon of the seventh month, which was New Year's Day; on the first day of this month, *i.e.* the new moon, the *shophar* was blown (Num. x. 10, xxix. 1), so that, according to this psalm, the two weeks preceding New Year's Day were observed as a kind of preparation for the great feast.[2] This psalm was thus one of the special ones sung at the feast of Tabernacles; and this is further borne out by the evidence of later Jewish literature; for the Targum to this psalm speaks of the " new moon " here mentioned as that of the month Tishri, *i.e.* the seventh month, in which New Year's Day occurred, and refers to Num. xxix. 1; and the Talmud also states that it was sung on this day.[3]

Another interesting illustration is Ps. xlvii; its liturgical character is seen by the reiterated call to praise God; but at first sight there does not seem to be any indication as to the occasion on which it was sung; indeed, this was not

---

[1] One of the smaller treatises of the Talmud, which contains, however, much early valuable material, see Müller's edition (1878).

[2] Cp. Ezra iii. 6: " From the first day of the seventh month began they to offer burnt offerings. . . ."

[3] *Rosh hashshana* 30b, referred to by Elbogen, *op. cit.*, p. 147.

realized until within recent years, but, as has been shown by
Mowinckel, Gunkel, and others, the occasion is indicated
clearly enough in verses 5–8 (Hebr. 6–9): "God is gone up
with a shout, Yahweh with the sound of the shophar. . . .
For God is the king of all the earth, sing ye praises with understanding; God reigneth over the nations, God sitteth upon
His holy throne;" *i.e.* it is a psalm commemorating the
enthronement of Yahweh, sung on New Year's Day, which,
as just pointed out, was the first day of the feast of Tabernacles.[1]   In accordance with this the tractate *Sopherim* (xix. 2)
records that Ps. xlvii was one of the special psalms for this
feast.

One other illustration, of a number, may be given.   The
liturgical character of Ps. cxxxv is very clearly indicated
in the first three verses, and in this case the occasion on which
the psalm was sung is not difficult to discern; verse 4 tells
of the election of Israel, verse 5 of Yahweh's power, verse 6
of the fulfilment of His will, and verse 7 of His lordship over
Nature; then in verses 8, 9 reference is made to what happened to the Egyptians at the Exodus.   All these points
immediately suggest what happened at the beginning of the
history of the nation; and thus, as a special psalm for the
Passover feast, nothing could be more appropriate.   The
psalm is certainly not one of the early ones, and in all
probability additions have been made to it; but that it was
originally composed for Passover hardly admits of doubt;
and in any case we have the evidence of *Sopherim* xviii. 2,
where it is said that this was the morning psalm sung at this
feast.

These are but a very few examples of the psalms as
liturgical documents; in many cases, as we have said, their
liturgical character is not immediately discernible, in others
it is fairly obvious; but without the evidence afforded by
post-biblical literature it would sometimes be difficult to
indicate the occasion on which a psalm was sung.   On the
other hand, it must be repeated that many of the psalms,
probably the majority, were not originally liturgical; this
does not mean to say that they were not said in the Temple;

---

[1] See, further, *Myth and Ritual*, ed. S. H. Hooke, pp. 122 ff. (1933).

they were said by individuals in the Temple for a variety of purposes; and, possibly, they were said privately during divine service; but they must not, on that account, be regarded as liturgical documents; for these partake of an official character, and it is one of the glories of the psalms that they are, in the main, human documents, that is, they express the thoughts, the aspirations, the joys, the sorrows, the hope, the faith, of the individual heart; as such, we must welcome, rather than be surprised at, the fact that most of the psalms are non-liturgical.

VII. THE PSALMS PART OF A WORLD-LITERATURE

While it is but right and fitting that the *Psalms* should be treated primarily as the product of Hebrew religious thought, it must be recognized that the Psalter was part of a World-literature. The Hebrews were in some notable respects unique, but they lived in contact with other peoples, and were not uninfluenced by the world of their surroundings. How far the Hebrews were affected in the composition of their psalms-literature by external influences it would be difficult to say; but in this and other respects they exhibited an individuality which witnesses to a striking independence, even though they may, to some extent, be indebted to others for thought and literary structure.

As is natural enough, two opposing views are held regarding this matter; it is maintained, on the one hand, that the Hebrew psalmists were largely indebted to Babylonia and Egypt, and, on the other, that no external influence is to be discerned in the *Psalms*.

Sacred poetry is a means of expressing the relationship between man and the Deity—the nature of the Deity may, for the moment, be left aside; the belief in this relationship was common to the Babylonians, Assyrians, Egyptians, and others, as well as to the Hebrews; all alike felt impelled to approach their deities with petitions for wants, with the thanksgiving for petitions granted, with prayers for help in time of need, and for averting evil, with the offering of propitiatory gifts, and also for the purpose of honouring them with praise. With such a background common to all there would seem to be no reason for postulating any borrowing of one from the other; the initial impulse was universal.[1]

On the other hand, while each individual race would, according to its own genius, in course of time build up its own literature of sacred lyric, contact between the peoples would bring to each some knowledge of their respective literatures; in such circumstances influence of some kind, conscious or unconscious, could hardly fail to exercise itself. And when, as in the case of Babylonia and Egypt, their literatures were much older than that of the Hebrews, it is within the bounds of probability that, in some respects, the early Hebrew psalmists would have been indebted to the more ancient compositions. We have, moreover, the analogy of Babylonian sacred legends and of the Egyptian and Babylonian Wisdom literature to go upon.[2]

These are factors which should be taken into consideration in this connexion. Without going into further detail here, it may be said that the conclusion to which a comparison of Babylonian and Egyptian hymns with the Hebrew psalms leads, is that both in thought and expression Hebrew psalmody is often indebted to a Babylonian or an Egyptian prototype, but that, owing to the religious genius of the Hebrews being of a vastly higher order than that of any other people of antiquity, the psalms are in their real essence independent of external influences.

Some illustrative comparisons would have been instructive, but space does not permit of this; we must content ourselves with a reference to the following works:—for Babylonian hymns and prayers: Zimmern, *Babylonische Hymnen und Gebete* (1905); Jastrow, *Die Religion Babyloniens und Assyriens*, vol. i. pp. 393–552 (1905), vol. ii. pp. 1–137 (1912); Langdon, *Sumerian and Babylonian Psalms* (1909); Stummer, *Sumerisch-akkadische Parallelen zum Aufbau alttestamentlicher Psalmen* (1922); for Egyptian psalms and the like, Erman,

---

[1] See, on the other hand, Birkeland, '*Anî und 'Anaw in den Psalmen* (1933), and *Die Feinde des Individuums in der israelitischen Psalmenliteratur* (1933).
[2] See pp. 161 ff.

Aegyptische Religion, pp. 79 ff. (1909); *Literatur der Aegypter*, pp. 183–193, 350–384 (1923). A large collection of both Egyptian and Babylonian sacred literary pieces are given in Gressmann, *Altorientalische Texte zum alten Testament*, vol. ii (1926), and see, too, the interesting chapters on Babylonian and Egyptian psalms by G. R. Driver and A. M. Blackman, respectively, in *The Psalms*, edited by D. C. Simpson (1926).

VIII. The Hebrew Text and the Septuagint

In addition to the vicissitudes through which the texts of the books of the Old Testament in general have passed, that of the *Psalms* has undergone special redactional treatment owing to their use in the Temple worship; doubtless this applies less to the later psalms than to those which have a longer history behind them. In a few instances instructive textual variations are placed before us owing to the existence of a double form of certain psalms, and we are able to see how texts differed; by comparing Ps. xviii with ii Sam. xxii; Ps. xiv with Ps. liii; Ps. lxx with Ps. xl. 13–17; Ps. cviii with Pss. lvii. 8–12 and lx. 7–14, it will be realized that the text must have been at one time in a fluid state, with the consequent inevitability for corruptions in the text to arise. When the Hebrew text is closely examined it is found that corruptions are very numerous; sometimes these are deep-seated, so much so that in a certain number of passages it is difficult to extract adequate sense from the present form of the text (*e.g.* xxii. 16 (17); lxxxvii. 7; lxxxix. 48); in other cases (which are more frequent) there are minor corruptions which are easily emended by the sense of the passage. That the text has come down in a somewhat unsatisfactory condition is only to be expected when the circumstances are borne in mind; Briggs has well expressed these when he says that the " Psalms passed through the hands of a multitude of copyists, and of many editors who made changes of various kinds, partly intentional and partly unintentional. The Psalms were changed and adapted for public worship, just as has ever been the case with hymns, prayers, and other liturgical forms. The personal, local, and historical features were gradually effaced, and additions of various kinds were made to make them more appropriate for congregational use." [1]

The Septuagint [2] is of great value for the reconstruction of corrupt passages in the Massoretic text, but special caution is called for in the case of the *Psalms*, because the many instances of fantastic renderings show that the translator could by no means always be relied upon for his knowledge of Hebrew.[3] Not only so, but there are many cases in which Hebrew letters were misread; this has resulted in some very curious renderings being offered in the Septuagint; these are sometimes meaningless, but that does not seem to have troubled the translator. It is evident that the Hebrew text from which the Septuagint was translated differed greatly from the Massoretic text, but the condition of that early text was very variable; in a great many cases it was manifestly superior to that of our present Hebrew text, but in very many others it was certainly worse. Thus, while the Septuagint is quite indispensable for the study of the *Psalms*, great care must be exercised in weighing its evidence.

The numeration of the Psalms in the Septuagint is for the most part different from that of the Hebrew; " this is due to certain consecutive Psalms in the Hebrew Psalter being counted as one in the Greek (ix and x in Hebr. = ix in the Sept.; cxiv and cxv in Hebr. = cxiii in the Sept.), and certain of the Hebrew psalms being, *vice versa*, divided in the Greek into two (cxvi in Hebr. = cxiv and cxv in the Sept.; cxlvii in Hebr. = cxlvi and cxlvii in the Sept.)." [4] The Septuagint has a psalm, cli, which is clearly based on i Kgs. xvi. 7, 11, 26, 43, 51; ii Kgs. vi. 5; ii Chron. xxix. 26; Ps. lxxviii. 70, lxxxix. 20. " Its resemblance to the Septuagint of those passages is not so close as to suggest a Greek original,

---

[1] *Op cit.*, pp. xxxiii ff.

[2] Of special value for the study of the Septuagint version of the Psalms is Rahlf's *Septuaginta-Studien*, 2. Heft, " Der Text des Septuaginta-Psalters " (1907).

[3] Cp. Swete's words: " . . . The Psalms, and more especially the Book of Isaiah, show obvious signs of incompetence " (*op. cit.*, p. 315); a well-known example is xxix. 1.

[4] Swete, *op. cit.*, pp. 239 f.

but, on the other hand, there is no evidence that it ever existed in Hebrew." [1] These last words are particularly interesting, for in recent years a Syriac version of this psalm has been discovered, together with four others; there is strong evidence for regarding these last four as having been translated from a Hebrew original; not so, however, with the Septuagint cli psalm, which contains nothing pointing to a Hebrew original, but which seems certainly to have been composed originally in Greek. [2]

[1] Swete, *op. cit.*, p. 253.
[2] These psalms are printed in Syriac with a German translation and notes by Noth, in the *ZATW* for 1930, pp. 1–23.

THE BOOK OF PROVERBS

I. TITLE OF THE BOOK

As distinct from the titles in the body of the book (see below), the title of the book as a whole is *Mishle*, which is an abbreviation of the opening sentence: " The Proverbs of (*Mishle*) Solomon, the son of David, King of Israel." [1] The Septuagint has the title *Paroimioi*, " Comparisons," similarly taken from the opening word of the book.

II. AUTHORSHIP

Solomon is designated as the author in x. 1 as well as in i. 1. The tradition about his wisdom was doubtless due to three passages; in i Kgs. iv. 29 (Hebr. v. 11–14) it is said: "And Yahweh gave Solomon wisdom"; in i Kgs. iv. 31–34 (Hebr. v. 11–14) Solomon is said to have been " wiser than all men . . . and he spake three thousand proverbs. . . . And there came all peoples to hear the wisdom of Solomon, from all kings of the earth, which had heard of his wisdom "; and in i Kgs. iii. 16–28, where the story, borrowed in all probability from an Indian source, is told of Solomon's decision as to which of the two women was the mother of the child (cp. also i Kgs. iii. 9 ff, x. 1 ff.). There was, thus, sufficient traditional material to justify the belief that Solomon wrote the book of *Proverbs*. But so far as the evidence of the book itself is concerned, while it records the tradition, its ascriptions of authorship vary; of the ten collections it contains (see next section), three have no ascription; of the other seven, two are ascribed to Solomon, one mentions his name in the title, while the remaining four are definitely ascribed to other authors; thus, following the chronological order of the collections (see next section), we have these ascriptions of authorship:

[1] On the meaning of the word *mashal* " proverbs," see above, p. 151.

x. 1–xxii. 16 is ascribed to Solomon; the title at the head of the whole book was probably taken from here. This collection contains 375 proverbs; the numerical value of the Hebrew letters which make up the name of Solomon is also 375; in all probability some scribe brought up the number of proverbs to correspond with the numerical value of "Solomon" (in Hebrew *Shelomo*); such devices, in one form or another, occur elsewhere in the Old Testament, and are the mark of late times; so that in the present instance the device would tell against Solomonic authorship.

xxv–xxix has the title: "These are also proverbs of Solomon, which the men of Hezekiah, king of Judah, copied out." On this Toy pointedly remarks that "the verb has this sense only here in the Old Testament; elsewhere (Gen. xii. 8, Job ix. 5, xxi. 7, etc.) it means ' remove ' (in space or in time), and its signification here (' transcribe ' = ' remove from one book to another ') belongs to the late literary vocabulary. This superscription . . . only bears testimony to the disposition, in later times, to ascribe all wise sayings to Solomon, and a special suggestion of Solomonic authorship may have been found in the mention of kings with which the collection opens." [1]

xxii. 17–xxiii. 14 has no title as the Hebrew text now stands; but originally there was a title; it has inadvertently been put into the text instead of being kept separate; the Septuagint has preserved the title, which no doubt at one time stood in its proper place in the Hebrew form: " Sayings of the Wise."

xxiii. 15–xxiv. 22 has no title.

xxiv. 23–34 has the title: " These also (belong) to the Wise men."

xxx. 1–14 has the title: " The words of Agur the son of Jakeh; the oracle."

xxx. 15–33 has no title.

xxxi. 1–9 has the title: " The words of king Lemuel; the oracle which his mother taught him."

i. 7–ix. 18 has the title: " The Proverbs of Solomon the son of David, king of Israel." This, with the last-mentioned

[1] *A Critical and Exegetical Commentary on the Book of Proverbs*, p. 457 (1914).

collection (xxxi. 1–9), is the latest portion of the book, the title is therefore valueless as an indication of Solomonic authorship (see next section).

xxxi. 10–31 has no title.

It will thus be seen that the evidence of the book itself is against Solomonic authorship. It may, however, be asked whether, in view of the acknowledged antiquity of proverbial utterances and of the existence of the tradition of Solomon's wisdom, some elements may not have been preserved which trace their origin to him? In reply to which it must be granted that the possibility of this cannot be wholly excluded; a Hebrew tradition usually has some basis in fact; besides, Solomon's relations with the Egyptian royal house (i Kgs. iii. 1) may well have brought him into contact with some Egyptian sages from whom he might have heard wise sayings; the Wisdom literature of Egypt goes back far into the third millennium B.C.[1] But while granting this possibility it is certain that the great mass of the collection in question is much later than the time of Solomon, and, indeed, that a large number of the sayings are post-exilic.

III. The Collections and their Dates

Reference has been made to the various collections contained in the book of *Proverbs*; some more detailed account of these is called for.

It has been pointed out above [2] that, in common with many another people of antiquity, the Hebrews had numerous sayings which were current in oral form—sayings of a popular character which expressed truths gained from the experience of life. The existence of such popular sayings invites, sooner or later, the collection of them; and in course of time collections of this kind would tend to increase. The formation of such collections would obviously be undertaken by the Ḥakamim, the Sages, or Wise Men; and in the natural order of things the Sage, in gathering together current proverbial sayings, would increase their number by adding

[1] Erman, *Die Literatur der Aegypter*, pp. 86–121, 294–302 (1923).
[2] See pp. 150 f.

words of his own.   Thus, collections of proverbs were made at different times by Sages, and in the book of *Proverbs* we have the final gathering together of a number of these collections.   That some of these collections, apart from the additions of later scribes, belonged to pre-exilic times is suggested both by the existence of popular sayings long current, and also because, as we have seen, the *Ḥakamim* formed a recognized order already in the times of Isaiah and Jeremiah.   There are, further, two other considerations which tend to confirm the belief that collections of proverbs, in written form, were in existence before the Exile.   As has been pointed out above,[1] the earliest form of the Hebrew proverb was a single-line saying, originally oral, but existing in this form even after having been reduced to writing; in course of time, no doubt, a line was added in many cases and a couplet was formed, but this still left the first line self-contained in its original form.   Now in two of the collections in our book (x. 1–xxii. 16 and xxv–xxix) there are a number of couplets in which the first line is self-contained, showing the probability of its having originally stood alone; one or two examples may be given: in x. 15a and xviii 11a there is the proverb, " The rich man's wealth is his strong city," meaning that the rich man relies on his wealth; this is a self-contained saying.   The context differs in the two passages, showing that originally the saying stood alone.   Two single-line proverbs occur in xi. 29, they are now joined by " and," but are quite independent of each other.   In xii. 11a and xxviii. 19a there is the proverb: " He that tilleth his land shall have plenty of bread," which is again a self-contained saying; in this case the added line in each passage is similar, though not identical.   In xiv. 5b it is said: " A false witness uttereth lies,"[2] and the same proverb is copied in vi. 19a; here the context in the two passages is quite different, showing again that the saying had been current independently of any context.   Many similar instances could be given (*e.g.* xiii. 12, 14, 15, 19;

---

[1] Pp. 150 f.
[2] The different marginal renderings of the R.V. represent the same word in Hebrew.

xiv. 4; xv. 3, 26, 33; xix. 23; xx. 2; xxi. 12, 29; xxii. 8, 10;
xxv. 27; xxvii. 2; xxviii. 16, 19; and xv. 21; xix. 27.
xxi. 24 are single-line proverbs without an added context);
the presence of these, while not necessarily proving a pre-
exilic date for the two collections in question, offers an argument in that direction. More decisive are the frequent
references to the king, implying the existence of the monarchy.
It is recognized that the mention of the king can quite conceivably be in reference to a Gentile monarch, *e.g.* in viii. 15;
xxx. 22, 27; xxxi. 4 belonging to later collections; but the
way in which the king is spoken of in these two collections
makes it very difficult to believe that the writer had a Gentile
ruler in mind; how could a Jew speak of a Gentile king as
one who utters a divine oracle (xvi. 10), or as one whose
heart is in the hand of Yahweh (xxi. 1), or as one who is the
friend of Yahweh (xxii. 11), or as one whose throne will be
established for ever (xxix. 14)? And there are many other
passages in which the king is spoken of in such a way as to
make it morally certain that the writer had an Israelite king
in mind. A great deal in these two collections, then (x. 1–
xxii. 16 and xxv–xxix), must be assigned to a period before
the downfall of the monarchy, though considerable portions
were undoubtedly added by later sages.

Of pre-exilic date is also the collection contained in xxii.
17–xxiii. 14. This is very largely based on the Egyptian
Wisdom-book called the " Teaching of Amen-em-ope ";[1]
the best expert opinion assigns this to the eighth or seventh
century B.C., some authorities place it earlier. The fact
of it being pre-exilic does not necessarily prove that the
Jewish collection based on it is also pre-exilic; but there are
various sayings in this collection which may well belong to
some period before the Exile (xxii. 28–xxiii. 10, 11), and it is
joined on to two other small collections (xxiii. 15–xxiv. 22
and xxiv. 23–34) which in part are certainly pre-exilic, see
especially xxiv. 21. Thus, these three collections in their
original form may be assigned to the seventh century.

---

[1] For details, see Oesterley, *The Book of Proverbs*, pp. xlvi–l (1929), and
The Wisdom of Egypt and the Old Testament (1927); for the most recent discussion see Möller, " Kritische Beiträge zur angeblichen Abhängigkeit der
Sprüche Salomos xxii. 17–xxiv. 22 von der ägyptischen Lehre des Amen-
em-ope," in *Nach dem Gesetz und Zeugniss*, pp. 304 ff. (1932).

Of the four small collections contained in xxx and xxxi, three (xxx. 1–14, xxx. 15–33 and xxxi. 1–9) do not offer any decisive indications as to date; most commentators regard them as post-exilic; the style of the fourth (xxxi. 10–31) suggests a late post-exilic date.

In the first collection in the book, as we now have it (i–ix), there is much to show that it belongs to a time long after the Exile; quite decisive, apart from other indications, is the developed conception of Wisdom (see *e.g.* i. 20–33, ii, iii. 11–20, vii. 4, and above all viii); it belongs, in all probability, to the third century B.C., though it is likely enough that some earlier elements have been incorporated.

IV. The Hebrew Text and the Septuagint

It is interesting to note that the Hebrew text of what is certainly the oldest part of our book (the collection contained in x–xxii. 16) is in a more corrupt state than any other part of the book; it looks as though the longer history of transmission here were responsible for the less satisfactory state of the text. This collection has many passages in which the textual corruption is serious; in an appreciable number of instances emendation seems almost hopeless, while corruptions of a minor character are very numerous. Chs. xiv and xvi have suffered in a special degree. In the collection xxv–xxix the text is in a somewhat better state, though here, too, in a few cases, *e.g.* xxvi. 9, xxvii. 9, emendation seems almost hopeless, so deep-seated is the corruption; the text of xxviii is in a worse state than any other chapter in this collection. In chs. xxii. 17–xxiv. 34 the text is again less corrupt, though in a number of minor cases emendation is necessary. In the first collection (i–ix) the corruptions are far less, and even where they occur they are not important. The last two chapters are remarkably free from corruption, apart from the title at the head of each chapter.

In a great number of cases the Septuagint is invaluable for emending the Hebrew text; at the same time, since the text of the Septuagint itself is often in a bad state, much caution is called for in making use of it; but not infrequently, even where the Septuagint text is faulty, it gives a cue to what the underlying Hebrew text read, and thus helps to emend the Massoretic text.[1] Again and again omissions or additions of words in the Septuagint are seen to represent a purer Hebrew text. There can be no doubt that so far as x–xxii. 16 is concerned many verses in the Greek text presuppose a better Hebrew form than that of the Massoretic text.

Apart from what has been said, the Septuagint contains a certain amount of material which is wanting in the Hebrew; some of this has evidently been translated from a Hebrew original, and may have been taken from some collection now lost (*e.g.* the couplets after ix. 12); other parts do not read like a translation from Hebrew, these may well be insertions from collections written in Greek.

Paraphrases occur not infrequently in the Septuagint (*e.g.* x. 18, xi. 31); this is probably due either to the corrupt state of the Hebrew original, or to the fact that the Greek translator did not understand the Hebrew, for this is often ambiguous. There are also cases in which the order of passages in the Septuagint differs from that of our present Hebrew text, *e.g.* xv. 28–xvi. 9, and the relative positions of the four collections in xxx, xxxi; but these differences occur mostly from xxiv. 23 onwards. This clearly indicates that the various collections, as we should expect, originally circulated separately.

[1] Much help in studying the text will be found in Kuhn, *Beiträge zur Erklärung des Salomonischen Spruchbuches* (1931).

ECCLESIASTES

I. Title

In the Hebrew Bible the title of this book is *Koheleth*, usually translated "Preacher"; the word is feminine in form because, in Hebrew, titles and designations of office are usually indicated by the feminine *form*, " notwithstanding their occasional transference to masculine persons." The word is, therefore, to be understood in the sense of one who " takes part in, or speaks in a religious assembly," hence the Septuagint: 'Εκκλησιατής, *i.e. concionator*, " preacher." [1] It is from the Septuagint, through the Vulgate, that the title *Ecclesiastes* in the English Bible is derived.

II. Authorship

In the opening verse of the book, " The words of the Preacher, the son of David, king in Jerusalem," the claim is made that Solomon was the author; but that the book cannot have been written by Solomon is quite certain for the following reasons:

(*a*) The entire subject-matter and the way in which it is dealt with is inconceivable in the tenth century B.C.; this will become sufficiently clear when the character and contents of the book are considered.

(*b*) The language in which the book is written is late and inelegant Hebrew, very different from the classical Hebrew of pre-exilic days. " The Hebrew language, which had been pure enough for some time after the return from Babylon, began to decay from the time of Nehemiah. The memoirs of Ezra and Nehemiah, and (in a less degree) the writing of Malachi, show signs of the change, which is still more palpable in the *Chronicles, Esther*, and *Ecclesiastes*." [2] The

---

[1] Gesenius-Kautzsch, § 122 *q.v.*
[2] McNeile, *An Introduction to Ecclesiastes, with Notes and Appendices*, p. 33 (1904).

Hebrew is often reminiscent of that of the Mishnah; there
are also many Aramaic words.[1]

(c) On occasion, the author writes not as a king, but as a
subject, see iii. 16; iv. 1.

These reasons are sufficiently convincing; there are others,
of less importance, which also show that Solomonic authorship is impossible; but it will not be necessary to go into these.

Apart from a few obvious interpolations (e.g. iii. 15, vii. 18;
ix. 9b, xii. 1a and xii. 9–14, which forms an appendix), unity
of authorship is postulated by the majority of scholars.[2]
There is, however, one strong objection to be urged against
this view, namely, the contradictory points of mental outlook,
and assertions incompatible with one another, which occur
fairly frequently. Some of these demand a little attention.
In ii. 24, e.g., it is said: " There is nothing better for a man
than that he should eat and drink and make his soul enjoy
good in his labour "; of an entirely contradictory nature
are the words of vii. 2: " It is better to go to a house of
mourning than to go to the house of feasting." In ix. 2
the writer declares that " all things come alike to all; there
is one event to the righteous and to the wicked . . ."; but
in viii. 12, 13 quite a different view is put forth: " Though
a sinner do evil an hundred times, and prolong his days, yet
surely I know that it shall be well with them that fear God,
which fear before him; but it shall not be well with the wicked,
neither shall he prolong his days, which are as a shadow;
because he feareth not before God." Again, in iv. 2 it is
said: " Wherefore I praise the dead which are already
dead more than the living which are yet alive "; but in
ix. 4 a very different view is presented: " For to him that is
joined with all the living there is hope; for a living dog is
better than a dead lion. For the living know that they shall
die; but the dead know not anything, neither have they
any more a reward; for the memory of them is forgotten."
And to give but one other example: in i. 13 the writer says:

---

[1] See, for example, Cornill, *Einleitung in das Alte Testament*, p. 249 (1896).
[2] *E.g.* Ginsburg, Nowack, Cornill, Wildeboer, and, more recently, Odeberg,
Qohaeleth : a Commentary on the Book of Ecclesiastes (1930).

"I applied my heart to search out by wisdom all that is
done under heaven; it is a sore travail that God hath given
to the sons of men to be exercised therewith "; but in ii. 13
it is said: "Then I saw that wisdom excelleth folly, as far
as light excelleth darkness."

These mutually exclusive utterances are difficult to account
for on the hypothesis of unity of authorship. To explain
them by saying that they reflect the varying moods of the
author might be sufficient explanation if it were a question
of spoken words; but for one and the same man to write
down in cold blood, as it were, things which are so entirely
contradictory is repugnant to common-sense. There is
much force, therefore, in McFadyen's contention that what
appear as contradictions are in reality protests inserted in the
text, not by the author, but by some others to whom much
that was asserted was thoroughly distasteful; "doubtless
these protests," he says, "could come from the preacher's
own soul; but, considering all the phenomena, it is more
natural to suppose that they were the protests of others who
were offended by the scepticism and pessimism of the book,
which may well have had a widespread circulation." [1]

Another line of argument against unity of authorship, and
perhaps even more convincing, has been put forth by
McNeile.[2] He points to the probability that the book
would naturally have created a great stir, since much that
was written in it was not in accordance with orthodox
Jewish teaching; but instead of being suppressed as
heretical, one of the wise men of the time sought to "improve" it and enrich it "by the addition of *meshalim*—more
or less isolated apophthegms bearing on life and nature—
perhaps culled from various sources. Some of these seem
to be suggested by Koheleth's words, and correct or enlarge
upon his remarks, but many are thrown in at random with
no kind of relevance. In every case their frigid, didactic
style is in strong contrast to the heat and sting of Koheleth's
complaints." McNeile then gives a list of these insertions;
in some cases his argument is stronger than in others.[3] But

[1] *Introduction to the Old Testament*, p. 347 (1932).
[2] *Op. cit.*, pp. 22 ff.   [3] *Op. cit.*, pp. 22 f.

this was only the first step; something more was needed than the addition of maxims of worldly wisdom if the book was to be safely used by the orthodox; " it must be made to give explicit statements which should fall into line with the accepted tenets of religion." This was done, according to McNeile's theory, by one of the *Hasidim*, one of the " pious ones " often spoken of in some of the later Psalms, and mentioned in i Macc. ii. 42; he gave a religious impress to the book which was so sadly lacking by adding sentences which centre round two chief thoughts: (1) the paramount duty of fearing and pleasing God, and (2) the certainty of God's judgement on those who do not fear and please Him. " The portions which appear to be due to him are seldom complete in themselves; they are tacked on to Koheleth's remarks, sometimes separating clauses that were clearly intended to be joined. In every case but one (v. 1–7, Hebr. iv. 17–v. 6) they are in direct opposition to Koheleth's spirit, if not to his actual words." [1] Some of the instances of the list of these additions are the same as the passages quoted above.

McNeile's twofold argument against unity of authorship is decidedly convincing.

III. The Character and Teaching of the Book

The main theme of the book is the vanity, emptiness, and worthlessness of human life. A pessimistic outlook frequently finds expression, but it must be recognized, as Odeberg protests, that this is in large measure due to the aim of the book; it is intended to teach men to lead a better life, for which purpose the writer sets in vivid contrast to this the worldly life of every day, which is very hollow and foolish. Nevertheless, it cannot be denied that the book does present a somewhat dismal outlook; it opens with a note of hopelessness: " Vanity of vanities, all is vanity " (i. 2), and closes in a similar strain (xii. 8); life and labour are empty, purposeless; but inasmuch as man is placed in the world and must live his life, the only thing to do is to

[1] *Op. cit.*, p. 24.

make the best of it, to eat and drink and enjoy oneself; and he is the truly wise man who acts under every circumstance in such a way as to secure a maximum of the material good to be got out of life (ii. 24). Quite in tune with this pessimistic attitude is the theory of determinism which runs through the book; man is a helpless being, everything is fixed, and there is nothing he can do to shape or alter the events of life (vii. 13). But it is this very determinism to which is due the religious tone of the book, for all things are from God, even the power to enjoy life (vii. 14), and therefore all must be done by man with a Godward view; in spite of the many difficulties presented by the incongruities of life, there is a moral rule, for God is supreme; man may be unable to understand many things (iii. 11, vii. 24, viii. 17), but " I know that, whatsoever God doeth, it shall be for ever; nothing can be put to it, nor anything taken from it; and God hath done it, that men should fear before Him " (iii. 14).

The writer's intense belief in God, which is so often expressed in the book, would assuredly have suggested a more exalted conception of the life hereafter had the thought of the time been sufficiently advanced; but when this book was written (see § V below) a doctrine of immortality had not yet been attained; hence the author says: " For of the wise man, even as of the fool, there is no remembrance for ever; seeing that in the days to come all will have been already forgotten " (ii. 16); and more pointedly in ix. 5: " . . . the dead know not anything, neither have they any more a reward; for the memory of them is forgotten "; and in ix. 10: " . . . for there is no work, nor device, nor knowledge, nor wisdom in She'ol, whither thou goest," cp. ix. 6. In one passage, it is true, a speculation is expressed which is very suggestive: " Who knoweth (with regard to) the spirit of the sons of men whether it goeth upward, and the spirit of the beast whether it goeth downward to the earth? " (iii. 21); but beyond that the writer could not penetrate; it is clear from the whole of his book that his ideas of the Hereafter coincided with the traditional She'ol belief.

IV. The Influence of Greek Philosophy

That the language of our book shows any traces of Græcisms is very improbable; McNeile has carefully examined all the instances in which, according to the opinion of Siegfried, Wildeboer, and others, Greek idioms and expressions are reflected; [1] his conclusion, with which many other scholars agree, is that " though Koheleth has a few expressions which *might* have resulted from the prevailing Greek atmosphere of his time, there are none that *demand* this explanation; and several of the instances offered can be traced to the Greek language only by violence."

The position is somewhat different regarding Greek thought; but here again there is much divergence of opinion. In such passages, *e.g.*, as i. 4 ff.; iii. 1-8, 22; vii. 16, 17; viii. 15; ix. 3, 7; x. 19; it may well be that the influence of Greek philosophy is to be discerned; on the other hand, the thoughts expressed may be nothing more than the reflection of the general mental atmosphere among cultured Jews generated by the Greek spirit, but not necessarily implying any direct knowledge of Greek philosophy. The subject is too large to be gone into here; it has been treated with much knowledge and discernment by Ranston,[2] who holds that " the evidence strongly suggests that Ecclesiastes was not widely or deeply acquainted with the early Greek *literature, i.e.* he had not *read* much of it. Had his reading knowledge been greater, signs of it would have been more clearly apparent. . . . The conclusion reached is that Koheleth, in his search for suitable proverbs (xii. 9 f.), moved for a time in circles where the minds of the people were stored with the wisdom-utterances of the early sages mentioned by Isocrates as the outstanding teachers of practical morality, Theognis being the most important." [3]

---

[1] *Op. cit.*, pp. 39 ff.
[2] *Ecclesiastes and the Early Greek Wisdom Literature* (1925).
[3] Pp. 149 f.

V. Date

From what has been said there can be little doubt as to the approximate date of our book. The Hebrew marks it as one of the latest books of the Old Testament; its paucity of ideas shows that the religious spirit, so characteristic of the writers in Israel, had practically exhausted itself; and the influence of Greek culture, however superficial, suggests, at any rate, that it was written after the beginning of the Greek period; hence *circa* 300 B.C. is the earliest possible date, but half a century later is more probable; the Maccabæan period, advocated by some scholars, is unacceptable.[1]

VI. Canonicity

Considering the religious standpoint of *Ecclesiastes* it is small wonder that it was the last of the Old Testament books to be received into the Hebrew Canon. An echo of the controversy which raged in regard to it among the followers of Hillel and Shammai is contained in the *Mishnah* tractate *Yadaim* iii. 5, where it appears that the house of Hillel declared that *Koheleth* "defiled the hands,"[2] *i.e.* was canonical, but that the house of Shammai disputed this. The date of this was about A.D. 100–120. In the end the Hillelites won the day; not so much, however, on the ground that the contents of the book made it fitting that it should be regarded as canonical, but simply because for many years it had been tacitly accepted as Scripture. That it should ever have appealed to Jews is a matter of surprise, and we entirely agree with Margoliouth when he maintains that " without the idea that *Koheleth* was Solomon one could scarcely imagine the work ever having been included in the Canon."[3]

---

[1] The fact that it was known to Ben-Sira (*Ecclesiasticus*), written about 180 B.C., makes a Maccabæan date impossible.
[2] See above, p. 4.
[3] *Jewish Encycl.*, v. 34 a.

VII. The Hebrew Text and the Septuagint

Taken as a whole, the Hebrew text, which is more or less rhythmical, has been handed down in a fairly good condition; there are not many seriously corrupt passages—among such are ii. 12b; iii. 11; iv. 1, 17; v. 17; on the other hand, there are very many instances of the addition of isolated words, presumably inserted with the object of making the meaning clearer, though that object is by no means always achieved; frequently, too, words have dropped out of the text, due doubtless to careless copying. The Septuagint is of but small value in the case of *Ecclesiastes*; here and there (*e.g.* iii. 19, ix. 1, 2, 4) it is helpful; but as a rule it does not throw much light on corrupt passages.

From the point of view of the study of the Greek text *Ecclesiastes* is of considerable interest, for it " savours of the school of Aquila." [1] The subject is somewhat intricate; it has been dealt with by McNeile very thoroughly; [2] he shows that an old Septuagint version was superseded by Aquila's version, and that, later, Aquila revised his translation himself; thus there were at one time three forms of the Greek text extant.

[1] McNeile, *op. cit.*, p. 316.   [2] *Op. cit.*, pp. 115-134.

THE SONG OF SOLOMON

I. Place in the Canon

THE *Song of Solomon* (the Hebrew title is " *Song of Songs* ") was one of the last books to find a secure position in the Jewish Canon. Its secular nature made it difficult for Jewish scholars to accept it; but the tradition which ascribed it to Solomon and its undoubted beauty made men anxious to include it, if possible, and the problem was ultimately solved by treating it metaphorically, as a picture of the love existing between Yahweh and the ideal Israel. The headings in the English Authorized Version suggest a parallel interpretation in the Christian Church.

In the Hebrew Bible the *Song* is placed first of the " Five Rolls," [1] and so immediately follows *Job* and precedes *Ruth*. In the Greek versions it appears immediately after *Ecclesiastes* and before *Job*, being the fourth of the poetical books. A similar position is assigned to it in the Vulgate, though the fact that *Job* is placed before the Psalter makes it the fifth of these books. In the *Peshitta* it stands immediately after *Ruth* and before *Esther*. These variations are partly due to the general arrangement of the Bible in the various versions, and partly to the uncertainty as to its authorship and canonicity.

II. Contents

The *Song of Solomon* consists of a series of erotic lyrics, most of which are incomplete, and some are mere fragments. Sometimes a man speaks to a maiden (i. 9–11, 15–17, iv. 1–7, vi. 4–9, vii. 1–9, viii. 13), sometimes a maiden addresses her lover (i. 2–4, 7–8, 12–14, 15–17, vii. 10–viii. 4, viii. 14 [= ii. 7]). At other times we have a maiden addressing a company, usually of other women (i. 5–6, ii. 8–14, iii. 1–5,

v. 2–8, v. 9–vi. 3, viii. 6–7); these little poems include passages which are descriptive of the lovers' experiences. We have short dialogues between them in ii. 1–7 and iv. 8– v. 1, and brief descriptions of the lover's splendour or his beloved's beauty in iii. 6–11, vi. 10, 11–12. In vi. 13 it is the company of women who speak, while in viii. 8–10 and 11–12 we have two little lyrics; in the first some brothers describe their care of their sister, and in the second we have the parable of Solomon's vineyard.

III. Structure and Interpretation

As so often in collections of different pieces, the poems in the *Song of Solomon* tend to be shorter and more fragmentary towards the end of the book. This makes it improbable that they were arranged on any definite plan; but many commentators have, nevertheless, sought to discover a systematic structure in the book. Two types of theory may be mentioned:

(a) *Dramatic*. It has been maintained that the book is a drama. Two forms have been suggested; in the one Solomon sees a rustic maiden, is captivated by her beauty, takes her into the royal harem, and wins her love. In the other form a third character is introduced, a shepherd to whom the girl has given her heart. As in the other form, Solomon takes her into his harem, but fails to win her, and in the end she returns to her rustic lover.[1] This theory has obvious disadvantages. Apart from the possibility of dramatic scenes in connexion with some forms of ritual, we have no reason to believe that there was any kind of drama in ancient Israel; there is not the slightest hint of it either in the rest of the Old Testament literature or in any outside writer. There are no stage directions of any kind, and these must be left to the imagination of the reader; even the differences between the speakers are clear only from the grammatical forms used.

(b) *The marriage ceremony*. It has been suggested that marriage customs in ancient Israel were similar to those

---

[1] The two schemes are described at length in Driver, *op. cit.*, pp. 411–416.

which now prevail among the peasantry of northern Syria. There the bride and bridegroom are enthroned for a week as queen and king, and, on the threshing-sledge which is their throne, they receive the adoration of their village, sometimes themselves taking part in the proceedings.[1] Attempts have been made [2] to reconstruct the ceremonies of the week, but they are hardly convincing.

A recent study of the book by T. H. Meek[3] has resulted in the suggestion that the songs are derived from hymns used in the cult of Ishtar, transplanted to Palestine in the worship of Astarte. Meek cites many parallel expressions, but, though the list is impressive and suggestive, it hardly amounts to proof, and the improbability of such songs being preserved in Israel militates against the theory.

We can say with confidence only that we have here a collection of erotic lyrics which, in their extraordinary beauty and freshness, are hardly surpassed by Sappho or Burns. They may have been used in the wedding ceremonies of Palestine, and they may owe their preservation to this fact, but on that point we cannot be certain. In favour of this view, we may suggest that the name given to the woman— " Shulamite "—may have no reference (as it is commonly supposed to have) to the village of Shunem, but may simply be a feminine of Solomon. As the glorious king of Israel was the king-bridegroom, so his consort must be a " Solomoness."

IV. DATE

The date of the Songs in their present form can hardly be early. The language shows signs of lateness, many Aramaic and even some Greek words appearing in the text. The relative used is one which became common only in Rabbinic times, though there are signs which suggest that it may have been current in earlier days in the far north. But, beyond saying that they are post-exilic, it is difficult to assign any period to them with confidence.

[1] Cp. Wetzstein in Dalman's *Palästinische Diwan* (1901).
[2] *E.g.* by Haupt, in *American Journal of Semitic Languages*, Vol. XVIII, pp. 193–245, XIX, pp. 1–32.
[3] Cp. " The Song of Songs and the Fertility Cult," in *The Song of Songs, a Symposium*, pp. 48–79 (1924).

V. The Hebrew Text

The MT is often obscure, and this may be owing to corruption, though it is also partly due to the very large number of unusual words, and partly to the mutilated condition to which so many of the poems were reduced before their inclusion in the collection. Help may be derived occasionally both from the Septuagint and from the Peshitta, though neither presents any unusual features. It has been suggested that the current Septuagint version is later than that of Aquila, but this view has not found general support.

THE PROPHETICAL LITERATURE:
GENERAL INTRODUCTION

THE prophetical books of the Old Testament present us with a phenomenon which is unique, not only in ancient times, but also in the whole range of world literature. They are to be dated almost entirely between the middle of the eighth and the middle of the fourth centuries B.C. This period of four hundred years was one of the most important in the history of human thought, and it saw the rise of several of the most significant religious movements made by man. It is enough to mention the names of Buddha, Confucius, Zoroaster [1] (according to some scholars), and the Greek philosophers, from the early Ionians down to Aristotle, to illustrate the extent of the spiritual upheaval throughout the world, and the influence that this age has had upon later thinking.

These four centuries also witnessed epoch-making changes in the realm of world politics. Amos, the earliest of the canonical prophets, was probably at work in the year to which tradition ascribes the foundation of Rome. Greece had hardly attained to a national self-consciousness; Amos was probably born before the first Olympiad. The Persians were but a tribe of wild mountain shepherds, and the hegemony of civilization was contested between Mesopotamia, now represented by Assyria, and Egypt. Of these two the latter had reached her political and military zenith some seven centuries earlier, and was now drawing near to disaster and eclipse, while the former was approaching the highest point she ever reached in her career of attempted world-conquest. By the time the prophetic age closed Rome was showing signs of being the strongest power in Italy, Greece

---

[1] It should be remarked that Zoroaster's date is very uncertain, and there is a strong body of opinion in favour of c. 1000 B.C. Cp. E. Bevan in *CAH* iv. 207.

had passed her peak of high achievement, and was merging, politically, into the kingdom of Macedon, soon to attain world-dominion under Alexander—there may even be references to him in some of the latest prophetic utterances. Assyria and Egypt had both fallen before the brilliant Chaldæan dynasty of Babylon, and Babylon herself had given place to Persia. And even this last great empire, shaken by the disastrous European wars of the fifth century, was rapidly sinking into the decay which led to her complete overthrow and the introduction of the new Greek culture into the nearer East.

In this age of ferment in the world of politics, thought and religion, among the saints, philosophers, statesmen and warriors who shine so brightly on the pages of its history, there is no class of men whose influence has been greater or more durable than that of the prophets of Israel. They offered the world a solution of one of man's greatest problems, the correlation of religion and ethics. It might be possible to criticize both their theology and their moral standards as being imperfect, and few would deny that advance has been made in both directions since their time. Yet the fact remains that, but for them, as far as our records of humanity can teach us, the two lines of human development would have remained apart, and the gulf between them would have steadily widened.

It is not, however, with these larger aspects of the prophets' utterances that we have now to deal, but with the literary form in which their words have come down to us. It will be at once obvious that we cannot treat problems presented by these documents on the lines followed in dealing with the Law and the historical books. There we were concerned, for the most part, with compilations which were the result of the slow growth of generations, or even of centuries, and there is not a single passage (apart from one or two poetical pieces, and possibly a few of Samuel's utterances) which we can assign to an author whose name we know. Here, in the prophetic literature, we have before us the work of definite individuals; each book bears a name, and in every case but one it purports to contain *primarily* a record of the message

uttered by the man whose name it bears. It should, therefore, be the expression of a distinct personality, and the stress
in the criticism of the prophets has always been laid on the
attempt to determine the amount of the material which can
safely be ascribed to each prophet. Too often this consideration has been allowed to obscure all others and the
attempt has been made to distinguish the original (or
" genuine ") portions of the several documents from later
accretions, without reference to the form which the work now
takes. The dominant factors in forming opinions have been
matters of style, general outlook and theology, all of which
leave room for a broad margin of error due to subjectivity.
It is only within comparatively recent years that students
have sought more objective *criteria* in the study of the forms
which the literature takes. Many of the older conclusions
have been only the more firmly established, and the way has
been prepared for still further advance in understanding the
history of these books.

In our Hebrew Bibles, the prophets—or more strictly the
" latter Prophets "—are comprised in four " rolls." Isaiah,
Jeremiah and *Ezekiel* occupy one each, while the fourth
consists of the work of the " Twelve," commonly called in
English the " Minor Prophets." These are, in the Hebrew
order,[1] *Hosea, Joel, Amos, Obadiah, Jonah, Micah, Nahum,
Habakkuk, Zephaniah, Haggai, Zechariah, Malachi.* Apparently
the intention was, in the first instance, to arrange the
books in chronological sequence, and, though the dates of
several are doubtful or disputed, the modern critic will
probably maintain that they are, for the most part, at least
correctly grouped.

When we come to read the books themselves, we can hardly
avoid being struck by the apparent want of logical sequence
within most of them. Exceptions may be claimed, perhaps,
for *Haggai* and parts of *Zechariah* and *Isaiah*, but it is practically
impossible to read any of the other books as a continuous
whole. We are repeatedly confronted with sudden changes
of subject, with marked differences in style, and it is difficult

---

[1] The English versions follow the Hebrew; the order in the Septuagint
is slightly different, and the " Twelve " are placed before *Isaiah*.

in some cases to find anything like a serious logical arrangement. We have, rather, the impression that each is a
compilation, whose separate parts have been put together
either haphazard or on principles which are not always
obvious to the modern reader. Sometimes a special kind of
grouping is clear; several of the books, for instance, contain
little collections of utterances concerning foreign nations.
But, allowing for all this, the prophetic literature in the main
presents us with a striking lack of continuity.

This is still more obvious when we turn to the Hebrew
text. Here we notice at once that in several of the books we
have both prose and poetry; nor is each type collected by
itself; the two are usually interwoven, a section of prose
standing between two poetic groups. Prose alone is found
in *Jonah* [1] and *Haggai*, and poetry alone (except for occasional
sentences) in *Joel, Obadiah, Micah, Nahum, Habakkuk, Zephaniah* and *Malachi*; both occur (in varying proportions) in
the other books, *Isaiah, Jeremiah, Ezekiel, Hosea, Amos* and
Zechariah.

I. ORACULAR POETRY (A)

The impression of patchwork which we have noticed is
deepened in most of the books when we study the poetic
sections rather more closely. From time to time (more often
in some books than in others) we have the solemn proclama-
tion, " Thus saith the Lord," a phrase which stands naturally
at the head of an independent utterance. In other places
we find the phrase " saith the Lord," which is, apparently, a
kind of signature, authenticating the divine origin of what
immediately precedes.[2] This would be in place only at the
end of a pronouncement of the divine message. There are
occasionally poems of some length, *e.g.* the great taunt-song
over the fall of a tyrant in Isa. xiv, and the psalms at the
beginning of *Nahum* and the end of *Habakkuk*. Most of the
poetry, if not all of it, in *Ezekiel* is of this kind. But usually
within a poetic group the subject changes with bewildering

---

[1] The Psalm in ch. ii. is not to be regarded as a part of the original book.
[2] There is little resemblance between these two phrases in Hebrew; the
second means literally " The oracle of the Lord."

speed, and we seldom find half a dozen consecutive verses with no break in the sense. Sometimes a superficial reading gives an impression of continuity, which is dissipated on closer study; a good instance is to be found in Isa. i, where verses 9 and 10 both have the names of Sodom and Gomorrah, but verse 10 naturally forms a new beginning, and the subject of what follows is quite different from that of the preceding verses. Finally, we note frequent changes in the metre; [1] to cite Isa. i again, we find that the opening verses 2–3 are in 3 : 3 (2 : 2 : 2), while that which follows is mainly 2 : 2, with an occasional 3 : 2. The conclusion from these facts is almost irresistible: we have in each poetic section of the prophetic books (apart from the few longer poems already mentioned) a collection of short utterances, which may originally have had little to do with one another, and whose juxtaposition is to be attributed, not necessarily to the prophet himself, but to a collector. This does not exclude the possibility that a prophet may have been his own collector, and have been to some extent responsible for the present form of collections, but, as we shall see later, there is usually some evidence which suggests that they assumed the shape in which we now find them at a time considerably later than that of the man whose words they enshrine.

The habits and methods of these collectors have not yet received the full study which they deserve, but some features of their work are already clear. As we look over any collection, we notice that it begins with little poems which are complete and well preserved. Further, it is comparatively seldom that the earlier passages in a collection awaken doubts as to authorship. If there is any existing utterance by Isaiah, it may safely be found in the first twenty or so verses of ch. i. No one has ever seriously doubted Jeremiah's authorship of ch. iii. 19 ff., or of ch. xx. 7 ff.; each passage stands at the head of a poetic collection. But as we get nearer to the end of a collection, we often find that the material grows much more " scrappy." Sometimes we may have individual sentences which have no relation to their context; sometimes an utterance is clearly unfinished, some-

---

[1] See pp. 139 ff.

Q

times it looks as though it had lost its opening words. Indications suggesting a later age begin to appear. For example,
in Isa. vi–xii we have a "collection" which opens with
passages in prose, and most of the poetical pieces in chs. ix, x
awaken little suspicion. On the other hand, ch. xi begins
with a phrase[1] which seems to imply that the house of David
has been overthrown, though not finally destroyed, and
we think, not of Ahaz or Hezekiah, but of Zerubbabel.
Occasionally we find the same passage occurring in slightly
different forms in more than one place. The most familiar
instance is the appearance of nearly identical language in
Isa. ii. 2–4 and Mic. iv. 1–4. Here it is also to be noted that
in *Micah* the section has an extra verse, at the end of which
stands one of those formulæ which attest the divine origin
of the message—" For the mouth of the Lord of Hosts hath
spoken it." The conclusion is irresistible; two different
compilers have found this wonderful utterance and each has
used it to place, not this time at the end, but at the head of his
collection. One of the two had it in a complete form, while
the other had a mutilated copy which lacked the last sentence. Again, *Jeremiah* contains several passages found elsewhere, among which we may especially notice a parallel
within the book itself, l. 41–43 is almost identical with vi.
22–24. The main difference is that the latter passage is
addressed to Zion, the former, merely by the alteration of
the name, to Babylon. Again, we note that in ch. vi the
little poem is carried on down to verse 26, and we are led
to feel that the collector who introduced it into ch. l had
only a mutilated form in front of him.

Sometimes we suspect that the recurrence of a word or
phrase has induced the collector to place two passages side
by side. A good instance may be seen in a passage already
referred to, Isa. i, where verses 9 and 10 both mention Sodom
and Gomorrah. But this (apart from the metre) is the only
link between the two, since verses 4–9 are a cry of suffering
over the distress of Judah; and though the fact of her sin
is not ignored, the main theme is the desolation of the land.

[1] The word rendered " stem " means properly the stump left in the ground
after a tree has been cut down.

Verses 10 ff., on the other hand, are a denunciation of the
cultus and a demand for social justice, with no reference
whatever to the punishment which the country is enduring.
Grouping according to subject is very common; the passages
in *Hosea* which describe religion in terms of the marriage
relation all stand near the beginning of the book, though not
all in the same collection. This tendency is most obvious
where patriotic collectors have put together utterances which
deal with foreign nations. Thus, in Jer. xlvi we have a
little collection of poems which refer to Egypt, of which the
first two are found in verses 3–6 and 7 ff. respectively. Jer.
xlviii has Moab for its subject, and two, at least, of the pieces
are found also in a similar collection in Isa. xv. f. One book,
that which bears the name of Obadiah, consists almost entirely of such pieces; all directed against Edom, and, again,
two of these are to be found in Jer. xlix. 7 ff.

Nahum consists (apart from the opening psalm) of passages
describing the fall of Nineveh. Sometimes the separate
collections, each dealing with one nation, are combined into
longer booklets; we have such " collections of collections "
in *Isaiah, Jeremiah, Ezekiel* and *Amos*. In the case of *Jeremiah*
one whole group, comprising l, li, is concerned with the
overthrow of Babylon, and must date from a time long
after the death of Jeremiah himself.

Another striking tendency of the collectors remains to be
noticed. This is their fondness for a happy ending. Few
people like to close on a note of gloom, and ancient Israel
was particularly sensitive on this matter. In later days the
feeling was so strong that there were certain books—*Isaiah*
among them—in which the closing verse was so sad that
another was always read after it. So any collection of prophetic utterances will have at the end, if possible, a passage
containing a promise of a brighter day. The instance of
Isa. xi has already been noted, and it is followed by a pair of
happy little psalms in ch. xii, with which this particular
collection concludes. *Hosea* and *Amos* both end on a note
of hopefulness, and in the latter book, at any rate, the compiler has finished with a passage which almost certainly
comes from a later time, when the " tabernacle of David "

had fallen, *i.e.* his dynasty was no longer on the throne. It might be that a collector could find a passage which was certainly due to the prophet whose words formed his main interest, but failing that, he would do his best to provide what he needed from some other source, or even, possibly, add something of his own.

We thus reach certain general conclusions, subject to slight modifications in individual instances, as to the way in which the poetical sections of the prophetic books reached the form in which we now find them. We have the original utterances of the prophet, given in short, telling, often passionate, lyrics, remembered and written down separately. Small collections of these were made, and the collectors continued to add from time to time passages which came into their hands from one source or another. They were not particular as to the completeness of what they found, nor were they greatly concerned as to authorship, especially in the later stages of the process. The growth of the collections continued over a long period, perhaps over some centuries. Several of the prophetic books never pass beyond this stage; *Joel*,[1] *Obadiah*, *Zephaniah* and *Malachi* consist each of a single collection of this kind. In *Micah* we seem to have a combination of two, or possibly three, collections, while in *Nahum* and *Habakkuk* a psalm has been added to the true prophetic material, in the one case at the beginning, in the other at the end. The remaining books all include a certain amount of prose, and to this element in their structure we now turn.

II. Biographical Prose (B)

A superficial study of the prose sections found in the prophetic books shows us that it falls readily into two main types. In the first class, we have narratives about the prophet's experiences, written in the third person, and quite frankly the work of a " biographer." It is true that we cannot speak strictly of biography in this connexion, since there seems to have been no attempt so to arrange the

---

[1] *Joel* may, perhaps, be regarded rather as a little group of small " collections." In any case the pieces in it come from more than one hand, possibly from more than one period, see below, pp. 357 f.

material as to give a picture of the life of the man concerned. In all probability we have here again collections, this time of popular stories, such as would be told about the great heroes of Israel, including, not only the canonical prophets, but also many of their predecessors. Occasionally we have reason to suspect that imagination has played a part in their construction; some of the Elisha stories would serve as illustrations. In other cases, however—and *Jeremiah* is the outstanding instance—we have good grounds for believing that the narratives are a strictly reliable account by an eye-witness of the events described. Collections of this kind were available for the use of the compilers of the books of *Samuel* and *Kings*, especially the latter, and we have one instance in which narratives used in an historical book were also included in a prophetic book—that of *Isaiah*.[1]

One complete book, that of *Jonah*,[2] is a prose description of events in the prophet's life, and this type of writing is found also in *Isaiah, Jeremiah, Amos* and *Hosea*. One of its characteristic features is that it contains very little of the actual message delivered by the prophet. We are told simply, *e.g.* that Jonah preached to Nineveh, but we have no record of the words he used. Sometimes we have passages in which the messages are given at length, but in these cases there is generally ground for suspicion that they belonged originally to another type, and have been slightly modified to appear in the third person.[3]

III. Autobiographical Prose (C)

In the second class of prose passages we have material, written in the first person, describing actual experiences of the prophet. Where a prophet gives us an account of his initial call, it is in this form, and pieces of this type usually describe the actual message which a prophet delivered. Many of them recount visions received and conversations

[1] Jer. lii represents the reverse process. It does not mention Jeremiah and is a kind of appendix taken from an historical book.
[2] The Psalm in ch. ii is not an original part of the book; cp. pp. 379 f.
[3] This seems to be the best explanation of the form now assumed by Jer. vii and the whole of *Haggai*.

carried on between the prophet and his God while he was in the ecstatic state. Several of these are described for us in *Jeremiah* and *Amos*, while the original work of *Zechariah* belongs almost entirely to this form. As has just been remarked, there are one or two instances (*e.g.* the opening verses of Jer. vii and the book of *Haggai*) which, in style and content, attach themselves to this type, though they now appear in the third person. We may conjecture that these passages have been modified from an original first person. Sometimes we have parallels, one in each of the two prose forms. Thus it seems clear that Jer. vii. 1–20 and Jer. xxvi refer to the same occasion, and it may be maintained that Hosea i (third person) and Hosea iii (first person) are parallel accounts of the same event as seen from two different points of view. There is, in Zech. xi. 4–17, one curious, isolated passage of this type, to which the name of no prophet is attached; and it is found also in *Isaiah*, *Jeremiah*, *Ezekiel* (practically the whole book), *Hosea* and *Amos*. The probability of its occurrence in *Haggai* has already been noted.

Such evidence as is available suggests that where this type occurs it may be ascribed to the prophet himself, unless there are strong reasons to the contrary. We may suspect that where it contains his message, as it so often does, the original words were heard and uttered in the poetic form usual in prophetic oracles. But when the prophet himself wrote them down, or superintended their transcription, it seems that he turned them into prose. There are those who hold that every genuine message was what a prophet heard Yahweh say while in the ecstatic condition, and that he repeated it in poetic form to the bystanders when he recovered his normal state. Such utterances would be remembered and handed from one to another in their original form. It was only when the prophet himself had them written down, when the keenness of his memory was growing dull, that he gave the substance in prose. There is at least one instance in which we have the same little oracle in the two forms,[1]

---

[1] Jer. xxii. 10–12; verse 10 is in poetic form, while verses 11 and 12 simply repeat the substance of the brief lyric with additions and circumlocutions.

and this helps us to understand the way in which this last type of prose may have been produced.

Our first glance, then, at the prophetic books has shown us three main types of material:

A. Oracular poetry.

B. Biographical prose, *i.e.* prose in the third person.

C. Autobiographical prose, *i.e.* prose in the first person.

We meet occasionally with passages which do not come under any of these heads, particularly in the form of longer and more artificial poems, and from time to time we suspect that there have been considerable modifications of the original, but these three will always be found to serve as giving us a general outline of the material. We have now to consider the way in which it was used to form the books as we have them to-day.

IV. Stages in Compilation

We have already seen that the basis of much of our prophetic books is to be found in a number of comparatively small collections of poetic material (type A). It is this which forms the first stage, and with it we may class collections belonging to one or other of the two prose types, especially to B. A number of our books (including, as far as *form* goes, *Ezekiel*) got no farther, and are still " simple." These include most of the " *Twelve* "—*Joel, Obadiah, Micah, Zephaniah, Haggai, Malachi*, while *Jonah, Nahum* and *Habakkuk* include each a psalm in addition to the strictly prophetic material. Each of these includes only one type, though further examination may show that some of them have been formed by attaching two or more collections to one another. The other books—*Isaiah, Jeremiah, Hosea, Amos* and *Zechariah*—we may call *composite*, since they include more than one type. Nor were they produced simply by taking all the material of one type and placing it together, before or after all the material of another type. In these books the types are interwoven with one another, and usually in a way which makes it clear that the work was done deliberately, and in accordance with some definite plan. Here we have another stage, distinct from that of the *collector*, which we may call that of the *compiler*.

The methods of these compilers deserve careful study, and, since they differed somewhat in the case of different books, they must be left for discussion under the head of each individual prophet. But, in general, we may remark that a compiler seldom broke up a collection of oracular poetry. That he kept mainly intact (there are exceptions, especially in *Isaiah*), and used selections from one or other of the prose types he found to his hand to introduce or to close the collection. This is especially noticeable in cases where (as happens particularly often in the book of *Jeremiah*) the prose sections were dated.

One more step must be noted. Several oracular collections were anonymous, and it is a most interesting fact that we are ignorant of the very names of some of the men who have told us most about God. Yet their words were included, since men recognized the divine origin of the message enshrined therein. Their exact position was determined by various considerations; one of the longest of these collections was placed immediately after the book of *Isaiah*. Three others, very different in style and tone, yet all bearing at their head the word *massa*, " burden " or " oracle," were appended to the book of *Zechariah* in its original form (Zech. i–viii).[1] The last of these had a name given to it from its own text, and was called " Malachi " = " my messenger " (Mal. iii. 1). This secured its independence, but the others came to be simply attached to the books which preceded them. So to this day we include one of the larger anonymous collections in the book of *Isaiah* (Isa. xl–lxvi),[2] while two of them now form part of the book of *Zechariah* (Zech. ix–xi, xii–xiv), and perhaps other phenomena of the prophetic books are to be explained in the same way.

With this brief general introduction we can proceed to the individual prophetic books.

---

[1] Viz. Zech. ix–xi; xii–xiv; *Malachi*. The word *massa* seems to have been used both for a collection of oracles (cp. Isa. xv. 1; xvii. 1; xix. 1; xxi. 1; xxi. 11, 13; xxii. 1; xxiii. 1; xxx. 6; Nah. i. 1; Hab. i. 1; etc.) as well as for a single oracle, provided it dealt with a separate subject.

[2] There are almost certainly two collections included here, but they had probably been united into a single book before they were placed after Isa. xxxix.

THE BOOK OF ISAIAH

I. Place in the Canon

THE *Book of Isaiah* belongs to the group known to Jewish scholars as the " Prophets," and, more particularly, to that section called the " Later Prophets." [1] That section consists of four books, *Isaiah, Jeremiah, Ezekiel* and the " *Twelve,*" and they are usually placed in this order. There is, however, a strong tradition among the Rabbis to the effect that *Isaiah* should stand third of the greater prophets and not first. This seems to have been due, partly to the feeling that *Jeremiah* continued, in a certain sense, the book of *Kings*,[2] and partly to the obviously later date of Isa. xl ff. In the Septuagint there are variations, but in the best MSS. the " *Twelve*" are placed before the other three, though their order is the usual one—*Isaiah, Jeremiah, Ezekiel*. In the Peshitta *Isaiah* stands at the head of the " Later Prophets," and is followed, not by *Jeremiah*, but by the " *Twelve*," while the Vulgate has the order usually found in modern versions.

II. Historical Background

The life and ministry of Isaiah fall within the period of the great advance of the Assyrians westward. When he received his call to the prophetic work, the first expedition of Tiglath-pileser had not yet taken place, and the political horizon of Palestine was limited by the little group of kindred states on both sides of the Jordan and to the immediate north and south.

Tiglath-pileser came to the throne in 745 B.C. and spent the first few years of his reign in consolidating his kingdom, and in securing its northern and eastern frontiers. But in

---

[1] See above, pp. 4 ff.
[2] Cp. Ryle, *The Canon of the Old Testament*, pp. 237–239 (1895).

738 B.C. he was in the west, and Menahem of Samaria paid tribute to him. Dynastic changes followed swiftly both in Israel and in Damascus, and the pro-Assyrian party gave place to another which was, perhaps, pro-Egyptian, and was certainly anti-Assyrian. Rezon of Damascus and Pekah of Samaria attempted to revive the alliance which, a century earlier, had kept Shalmaneser iii at bay. They tried to force Ahaz of Judah into the coalition, and, on his refusal to join them, they made an attempt to replace him with one of their own nominees. The country seems to have suffered, and possibly Jerusalem was besieged. But the city was not taken, and in three successive years, 734–732 B.C., Tiglath-pileser was in Palestine. Damascus fell almost at once, and in 733 B.C. Pekah was replaced by Hoshea. In 732 B.C. the final settlement of the north was made, great numbers of the inhabitants being deported, and both Damascus and northern Israel being organized as provinces of the Assyrian empire. The territory left to Hoshea hardly extended north of the plain of Esdraelon.

In 727 B.C. Tiglath-pileser was succeeded by Shalmaneser v. Revolts broke out almost at once, probably instigated by Egypt, and in 724 B.C. Shalmaneser moved westwards. Hoshea was captured and killed, but the city of Samaria resisted for another three years, and was captured only by Sargon, who succeeded Shalmaneser in 722 B.C. Samaria was now formed into an Assyrian province.

Up to this point Judah had been consistently pro-Assyrian. But with the outbreak of a new revolt in 711 B.C., Hezekiah seems to have taken the other side. The religious reform attributed to him, if historical, may have been, in one of its aspects, a gesture of independence. If so, it was carried out either at this date or between 705 and 701 B.C. The chief object of Sargon's wrath was Ashdod, which he captured, and no further harm seems to have befallen Hezekiah. The country remained quiet till after the death of Sargon in 705 B.C.; but then, thanks to the energy and ability of the Babylonian Merodach-baladan, almost the whole empire broke away from Sennacherib. In the west the only vassal who remained faithful was Padi, king of Ekron, who was deposed by his subjects and sent to Jerusalem, where he was imprisoned by Hezekiah. But Sennacherib was equal to the occasion. He first defeated a concerted movement by the Babylonians and Elamites, driving Merodach-baladan finally out of the country. In 701 B.C. he marched westwards, everywhere putting down the rebellion. Judah was laid desolate, and Sennacherib claims to have captured forty-six fortified cities in addition to countless unwalled towns. Hezekiah submitted and Jerusalem was not seriously besieged. The Egyptians attempted to make a diversion, but were defeated at Eltekeh in the far south. Sennacherib carried away an enormous number of captives (he claims 200,150) and exacted a burdensome tribute from Hezekiah, whose territory he also reduced.

Judah was fortunate to escape so lightly. No doubt, one of the reasons why Assyria so easily overran Israel and Damascus is to be found in the social and moral deterioration of the country during the preceding century. Israel, especially in the north, had grown wealthy, and had succeeded in outstripping her rival, Damascus. But prosperity was confined to a small class; the rest sank into depths of poverty and even into slavery, as the wealthy became richer and more luxurious. There was an internal canker in the people which meant that, sooner or later, the nation must lose her national independence. The conditions depicted for us by the eighth-century prophets, Amos, Hosea, Isaiah and Micah, made the ruin of the country not merely intelligible but inevitable.

The religious situation, like the political and social conditions of the age, gave little hope for the future. The syncretism, the mixed cult, which meant that men worshipped Yahweh with the theories and rites appropriate to the old Canaanite Baals, could exercise no ameliorating influence. Hosea saw through this type of religion and declared it to be but the worship of Baal. The old traditional faith of Israel, traced back in history to Moses and, theoretically, imported with Israel into Palestine, retained its purity only in special places and groups of people. To the south and east, we may believe, where a large proportion of the community lived on a plane which was still pastoral, rather than agricultural and civic, the old Yahwism had a better opportunity of maintaining itself, and there were groups of men and women, *e.g.* the Rechabites, who held that the old faith was the only justifiable one. The same position was taken by a strong element in the prophetic succession from Elijah onwards, and it was to this side of Israelite religious thought that the great canonical prophets belonged. It is against this background, historical, social and religious, that we must see the work of Isaiah; and, if we can but do so, we shall value all the more the truth and the courage which marked him out and gave him the unique position he still holds in the history of man's spiritual life.

III. Contents

Like most of the prophetic books, *Isaiah* consists largely of oracles of different kinds, together with a certain number of autobiographical and biographical passages. The latter are grouped together in chs. xxxvi–xxxix, thus dividing the strictly prophetic material into two parts. A detailed discussion of the contents, however, is possible only when the structure of the book as a whole has been considered.

IV. Structure and Date

1. *General : the larger divisions.*

As we have already noted, the book of *Isaiah* falls into three main sections. The first of these is the usual type of prophetic collection, and frequently the oracles and narratives bear the name of Isaiah the son of Amoz, a prophet who lived and worked in Jerusalem during the latter part of the eighth century B.C. This division includes chs. i–xxxv. In the second place, we have narratives in the third person— type B; [1] and in the third, chs. xl–lxvi, we have another oracular collection, in which, however, the name of Isaiah nowhere appears. The second division is closely paralleled by ii Kgs. xviii. 13–xx. 19, and it is clear that, even if we cannot definitely say that one passage was copied from the

[1] See pp. 228 f.

other, they have a common origin, from which neither can have diverged very widely.

It is generally recognised that the first and third divisions had originally nothing to do with one another. The third does not claim to be the work of Isaiah, and its style and vocabulary are different.[1] There are striking differences in the theological outlook, of which the most prominent is the view taken of the relation between Yahweh and the other gods. Isaiah of Jerusalem despises them, and exalts Yahweh above them all, but in xl–lxvi their very existence is categorically denied (cp., *e.g.* xli. 24, xliv. 9). While we have in several of the pre-exilic prophets adumbrations of such a doctrine, and in all of them beliefs which ultimately and inevitably lead to it, it is in this third section of the book of *Isaiah* that we have for the first time a clear and unmistakable monotheism. And, perhaps most obvious and convincing of all, we note that the whole background of the two sections is different. We shall have to allow for the presence of later material in Isa. i–xxxv, it is true, but in those parts which are certainly to be ascribed to Isaiah himself the background is that of the eighth century B.C., during the great advance of Assyria westwards, while chs. xl ff. presuppose the last years of the Babylonian empire, *i.e.* the latter half of the sixth century B.C. This does not mean that there is no prediction in chs. xl–lxvi; on the contrary, a great deal of the material consists in utterances which foretell the future. But, as Gray has so well observed, " prophecy, unless it can be shown to be a *vaticinium ex eventu*, must have been written before what it predicts, but after what it presupposes; ix. 7–x. 4 was therefore written before 722 B.C., and xl–lv before 538; but the latter section, since it *presupposes* that Cyrus has already achieved remarkable victories, must have been written after *circa* 550 B.C." [2]

Such external evidence as is available tends to support this conclusion. While it is true that, at the beginning of the

[1] For a list of expressions which are characteristic of chs. xl–lxvi, but are never found in undisputed utterances of Isaiah, cp. Driver, *op. cit.*, pp. 225–227.

[2] *Isaiah*, p. xxxi (1912). For the historical background of xl–lv, see below, pp. 262 ff.

second century B.C., the writer of *Ecclesiasticus* attributed the later portions of the book to Isaiah himself (Ecclus. xlviii. 24 f.), it seems certain that the reference of the Chronicler in ii Chron. xxxvi. 22–23 (= Ezra i. 1–2) is to this book, there attributed to Jeremiah. The book of *Jeremiah* does contain a prediction of the return after seventy years (Jer. xxv. 12, xxix. 10), and is undoubtedly the subject of the reference in ii Chron. xxxvi. 21; but the two verses in question especially connect Cyrus with the rebuilding of the Temple, and can refer only to Isa. xliv. 28–xlv. 1. It is thus clear that at the beginning of the third century B.C. these chapters were not yet attributed to Isaiah. Probably their attachment to this book was accidental. An anonymous collection, included in the books of the prophets, was almost certain, in process of time, to be read continuously with the collection which preceded it. We have parallels in the two little collections which immediately followed *Zechariah*, and the same principle may be seen in the Rabbinic dictum that an " orphan "-psalm is to be attributed to the last author mentioned in the titles. This combination of Isa. i–xxxix, and xl–lxvi requires no further explanation than the supposition that the second, anonymous, group was at some time or other placed immediately after the book which was attributed to Isaiah himself.

2. *Chapters i–xxxix.*

The original Isaianic book, like others of the longer prophetic books, is made up of a number of older and shorter collections. Here they are particularly easy to identify, and are clearly as follows:

    A. Ch. i.
    B. Chs. ii–v.
    C. Chs. vi–xii.
    D. Chs. xiii–xxiii.
    E. Chs. xxiv–xxvii.
    F. Chs. xxviii–xxxv.
    G. Chs. xxxvi–xxxix.

A. Ch. i. (i) *Structure.* A detailed analysis of the short

collection in ch. i will serve to illustrate the method on which
we may deal with the great majority of such collections.
Verse 1 forms a title for the whole book, and we have then
the following independent pieces:

(*a*) Verses 2–3. A brief oracle in which heaven and earth
are called to witness the infidelity and ingratitude of Israel
towards Yahweh. The metre is 3 : 3. Clearly inserted at
the head as striking a keynote for the book, or at least the
collection.

(*b*) Verses 4–9. A lament over the calamity and desolation which have fallen upon the land. While the sin of
Israel is recognized as the primary cause, the stress is laid
on the result of this, *i.e.* the disaster and sufferings of the land.
The metre is 2 : 2, with an occasional 3 : 2.

(*c*) Verses 10–17. A denunciation of sacrifice as practised by Israel. The metre is the same as the last, with a
much larger proportion of 3 : 2. The subject, however, is
entirely different, and the collector has been led to place the
two together by the reference to Sodom and Gomorrah with
which the one ends and the other begins. We note further
that, while the parallelism in verses 4–9 is mainly internal,
that of 10–17 is usually external.[1]

(*d*) Verses 18–20. An appeal and a warning. The metre
is again *Qinah* (3 : 2), and the parallelism in verse 18 is internal, in verses 19–20 external. We observe that a " signature "—" for the mouth of the Lord hath spoken it "—is
appended, a phrase which has no place in the metrical
structure of the oracle.

(*e*) Verses 21–28. An elegy on the sinful city of Jerusalem.
The metre is again *Qinah*, but it seems that once or twice an
editor or copyist has added a word or two. Verse 25 has,
apparently, lost a two-stress *stichos*, and, if this can be assumed,
verses 21–23 and 24–26 look as if they might form exactly
parallel strophes, the first lamenting the corruption of
Jerusalem, and the second foretelling purification and restoration. The appearance, however, is fallacious, for 24a
can have formed no part of the oracle itself, but rather
implies that a new one is about to begin. This impression

---

[1] For the metrical references cp. pp. 141 ff.

is borne out by the exclamation " Ah ! " at the beginning of
24b, which would stand most naturally at the head of a
metrical unit, whether poem or strophe. This does not
exclude the possibility that 24a is wholly redactional, except,
perhaps, for the " Therefore " at the beginning, and if we
could accept this suggestion we might regard the whole
passage as a continuous poem. If it be felt that the two
must be kept separate, we can explain their proximity to one
another by the similarity in language. Collectors, as we
have seen, were fond of putting together pieces which had
ideas or words in common.

Verses 27–28 are clearly a fragment—or a pair of fragments—which were appended to the preceding oracle before
it was included in the collection.

(f) and (g) Verses 29–30 and 31 are again fragments, of
which the first is a condemnation of tree-worship, with an
irregular metre $(3: 3 + 4: 3)$, suggesting corruption, the
second a couple of $3: 2$ lines, threatening punishment.

(ii) *Date*. While this chapter is a very good example, on
a small scale, of a typical prophetic collection, it also serves
to illustrate the difficulties which confront us when we try
to assign dates to the individual pieces. There is no reason
to deny any oracle, or even fragment, to Isaiah, but we are
forced back on guess-work as soon as we attempt a more
exact dating.   As far as we know, there was no point during
the life of Isaiah (except possibly after the reforms of
Hezekiah) when Israel could not be described as sinful and
ungrateful, and we have nowhere any suggestion that there
was a time when sacrifices were not offered. The second
utterance, it is true, will more probably have come from a
time when the land had been overrun by a foreign enemy,
and here we are left with a choice between several possible
occasions known to us. The lament might describe the
desolation wrought by the combined armies of Pekah and
Rezon in 734 B.C. (see ii Kgs. xv. 37), or to the invasion of
Sennacherib in 701 B.C. (see ii Kgs. xviii. 13 ff.), or to some
other similar disaster of which we have no surviving account,
perhaps to damage done by Sargon in 711 B.C.[1]   701 B.C. is

[1] This campaign was undertaken primarily against the Philistines, see

the favourite date, but we may ask whether Isaiah would have so spoken of the sins of his people at a point comparatively soon after the reforms of Hezekiah.

B. Chaps. ii–v. (i) *Structure.* (*a*) The collection opens with a " floating " oracle, ii. 2–4 (metre 3 : 3), found also in Mic. iv. 1–4. It is anonymous, and was adopted by both collectors to place at the head of their booklets. The text is better preserved in *Micah* than in *Isaiah*, and the collector in the latter case had only a mutilated form, for the last sentences, including the " signature," are now found only in *Micah*. Verse 5 is a pious exhortation based on the preceding oracle.

(*b*) ii. 6–19 presents an extraordinarily difficult problem, since the text is corrupt, and, possibly, has been disarranged. We may have here a single poem with a refrain (verses 10 and 19), or we may have two different poems, to one, or both, of which the refrain had been appended at a later stage. The last suggestion derives some support from the fact that a prose addition in verses 20, 21 embodies the refrain in a totally different connexion. Probably verses 6–21 had reached something like their present form when incorporated by the collector, but verse 22 is an interpolation which must have been inserted very late, since it is not represented in the Septuagint. Metres seem somewhat irregular, but the prevailing rhythm in both parts is 3 : 3.

(*c*) In iii. 1–12 we have an oracle whose original nucleus was probably verses 1–6 (*Qinah*), but which has received additions. Possibly verses 11–12 were an independent oracle (3 : 3). Another short oracle in 3 : 3, with the " signature " at the end, appears in iii. 13–15.

(*d*) iii. 16–iv. 1, in *Qinah*, describes the doom of the women of Jerusalem, and a late scribe has inserted in verses 18–23 a regular " milliner's catalogue " which, naturally, is in prose.

(*e*) iv. 2–6 forms a little eschatological utterance, depicting the final purification of Jerusalem. The metre is somewhat uncertain, being mainly 3 : 3 (2 : 2 : 2) in verses 2–3, and *Qinah* in the rest. The passage may have

---

Duhm, *Das Buch Jesaia*, p. 123 (1914), but the proximity of Judah may well have tempted the Assyrian army to marauding expeditions over the border.

R

undergone some revision before its inclusion in the collection.

(*f*) v. 1–7 (in *Qinah* metre) contains the " Song of the Vineyard," with its application, and this is followed by a series of denunciations on various types of sinners, land-grabbers (8–10, *Qinah*), drunkards (11–17, *Qinah*, and 22–24, 3 : 3), the presumptuous (18–19, in 2 : 2 : 2 rhythm), those who confuse moral issues (20, *Qinah*), the conceited (21, 3 : 3). These passages form a little collection by themselves, and, though they can have no original organic unity with one another, they were probably put together at an early stage ; the exclamation with which each begins would form a link of the kind which often induced compilers to bring together pieces originally independent.

(*g*) v. 25 is a curious mixture of an oracle-fragment with a refrain which appears repeatedly in ix. 7–x. 4. Its insertion here may be simply accidental.

(*h*) v. 26–30 describes a coming invader who will execute Yahweh's judgement on His people. It is generally held that the section is connected with ix. 8–x. 4, which has all the appearance [1] of being a strophic poem with the same refrain as that which we find in verse 25b. If this view of ix. 8–x. 4 be right, then probably the transposition is justified, though the reason for the change of place is not clear. The metre is *Qinah*, and the piece seems to be mutilated at the end.

(ii) *Date.* Once again we find ourselves at a loss to assign accurate dates. The " floating oracle " in ii. 2–4 may be as early as Isaiah, though there is a tendency to associate it with the comforting prophecies of the end of the Exile. It seems to have been known to the author of Joel iii. 10, but this certainly does not imply an early date. The additions to the original nucleus of ii. 11–19 are probably post-exilic. The oracle in iv. 2–6 may also be comparatively late. It is eschatological (though not to be denied to Isaiah simply on that ground) and refers to the " Branch " in a way which suggests that the term was a familiar expression of eschato-

---

[1] For further discussion see below, pp. 245 f., and for various arrangements cp. Gray, *Isaiah*, p. 180.

logical language. Elsewhere we know of it first at the end of the seventh century (*e.g.* Jer. xxiii. 5, xxxiii. 15), and then it seems to be a new concept. The " Song of the Vineyard " and the denunciations which follow may come from any period in the life of Isaiah, and the last oracle, if it be correctly connected with ix. 8–x. 4, will probably have been uttered at some point during the years 736–725 B.C.

C. Chaps. vi–xii. (i) *Structure.* In this section we meet with prophetic prose for the first time. It was, probably, all of the autobiographical (C) type originally, though one or two of the sections have now assumed the third person, *e.g.* vii. 3, 13. A copyist may have mistaken the last letter of the Hebrew word " to me " for the initial of the prophet's name. There is other evidence to show that proper names were often indicated simply by their initial letter. While the main narratives are always in prose, the words, both of Yahweh and of the prophet, tend to assume a rhythmical form, often showing a certain parallelism, though no regular metre can be identified. In some instances, too, the collector has found narratives to which oracular matter has been attached.

(*a*) vi. 1–13. The opening piece is Isaiah's story of his first ecstatic experience, constituting his call to the prophetic ministry. It is too well known to need further description; suffice it to point out that it ends with a verse which is hopelessly obscure, and may well have suffered textual corruption. Or, perhaps, verse 13 may be a collector's addition to what is one of the finest pieces of descriptive writing in all known literature.

(*b*) In vii. 1–9 we have the first of a series of passages which deal with the joint attack of Israel and Syria on Judah. In its present form it is in the third person, but this may be due to accidental corruption, since, in general, the passage resembles others of type C rather than type B. The first five verses give the occasion, and the message is contained in verses 7–9. The latter can be arranged metrically (3 : 3), but is prosaic in form, and is suspected of having received later accretions.

(*c*) vii. 10–17 gives another message of the same period,

in which a symbolic child, named Immanuel, is mentioned. This is followed by a series of short utterances with an eschatological tone, which may, originally, have had nothing to do with the preceding passage. The first (verses 18-19) predicts the coming of armies both from Egypt and from Assyria against Judah. Isaianic authorship has been doubted on the ground that Isaiah never feared the military power of Egypt, though he was afraid of an alliance with that country. This however, is hardly decisive, since we must always allow for the possibilty of a change in opinion due to altered circumstances.

(d) vii. 18-25. Yahweh summons Egypt and Assyria to exact his vengeance on Israel (verses 18-19—apparently originally 3 : 3). In verses 20, 21-22 and 23-25 we have three pictures of depopulation and desolation, which, again, we cannot safely assign to any particular period in the life of Isaiah, though there is no particular reason to suspect his authorship. The metre of the two former seems to have been 3 : 3; the third was probably *Qinah* in the main.

(e) viii. 1-10. viii. 1-4 is another passage derived from the autobiographical material. It describes the birth of Maher-shalal-hash-baz, whose name predicts the fall of Samaria and Damascus. To this have been appended two short oracles, or fragments of oracles. Thus, verses 5-8a (in *Qinah*, mutilated at the end) form part of a threat of destruction, verses 8b-10, part of a promise of protection, probably in 3 : 3.

(f) In viii. 11-15 we have another extract from Isaiah's own writing which may have been expanded. The prophet is warned against following popular opinions, and, while there are traces of parallelism and rhythm, no regular metre can be detected.

(g) viii. 16-18. The last piece of autobiographical matter in this section is to be found in viii. 16-18. Here Isaiah is bidden to seal up his testimony in the minds of his disciples, leaving his name and those of his children as a memorial for later generations.

(h) viii. 19-ix. 1. The extract is followed by two short fragments, of which the first, verses 19-20, is a warning

against necromancy, and the second, verses 21–22, a threat
of desolation. To this last a prose note has been appended
in ix. 1 (in Hebr. viii. 23), mitigating the doom by a promise
of restoration for northern Israel. This note may have
been the work of Isaiah, or may have been expanded from
something he said after the desolation of the north by
Tiglath-pileser in 732 B.C.

The compiler of this collection, vi–xii, has now used all the
autobiographical material he thought suitable for his purpose, together with the oracular fragments appended to its
various sections. He proceeds to add other oracles, which,
as it seemed to him, might fit the general period to which
his collection primarily refers.

(i) The first piece he thus takes is the well-known Messianic passage, ix. 2–7 (Hebr. 1–6). The metre is *Qinah*.
Isaianic authorship has been questioned by a number of
modern scholars, but the linguistic and similar grounds are
indecisive,[1] and it is impossible to resist the feeling that
scholars have been too much influenced by the idea that
Messianic prophecy is necessarily late. In its simplest form,
that of the expectation and hope of an ideal king (and that
is all that can be claimed for this passage), it may have been
very early, and we can certainly trace it in writings a century
later than Isaiah, and, probably, also elsewhere in Isaiah
himself.[2] Perhaps too much stress has been laid on the
connexion between this and the Messianic passage in ch. xi.
As we shall see later, though there are similarities, there are
also differences, and the two do not necessarily go together.

(j) ix. 8–x. 4. ix. 2–7 is followed by a passage which has
all the appearance of being a strophic poem, to each stanza
of which a refrain has been added. It extends from ix. 8–x.
4, and, probably, v. 25b–30.[3] Including this last passage,
there are five stanzas: ix. 8–12, ix. 13–17, ix. 18–21, x. 1–4,
v. 25b–30. The first of these, whose metre is partly 3: 3,
partly *Qinah*, threatens the pride of Ephraim with punishment. The second condemns the refusal of Israel to repent;

---

[1] Cp. Gray, *Isaiah*, pp. 166–168 (1912), and, for the other point of view,
Cheyne, *Introduction to the Book of Isaiah*, pp. 41–46 (1895).
[2] *E.g.* in xxxii. 1 f.   [3] See above, p. 242.

it may be arranged in 3: 3, but its language is prosaic.   The third describes civil war in the northern kingdom, and written in 3: 3; verse 20 looks like a gloss.   The fourth condemns the corruption of justice (3: 3), and the last forms a threat of foreign invasion.   It is assumed that all refer to northern Israel.   Closer examination, however, makes the unity of the whole problematical.   The stanzas are not all of equal length (ix. 14–15 are generally held to be a later insertion in the second section), and there is not that consecutiveness which would be expected in such a poem.   The fourth section is often suspected of being a later composition, and it handles a theme slightly different from the others.   Further, the construction of a poem of this kind is, even if not wholly without parallel, strange to the peculiar literary genius of the prophets.   It is too artificial for the sudden, lyric, outburst of feeling and conviction which usually marks prophetic utterance.

We are led, then, to suspect that an early compiler has taken four or five Isaianic oracles and has attached a refrain to them—possibly it was original with one of them.   One of the oracles still maintained a separate existence, and was used by the compiler of the second collection (chs. ii–v); perhaps for this reason it was omitted from the group when the whole was absorbed into the book of *Isaiah*.   We need not doubt that the passage was already in its present form when it was placed in this collection by the compiler; the unification of the five passages belongs to a still earlier stage in the history of the development of the text.   We have no reason to doubt that Isaiah was the author of all five.

(*k*) x. 5–9 forms a poem (3: 3) in which Assyria is denounced, and the prophet's philosophy of history is enunciated.   Two additions have been made to this, verses 10–11 (*Qinah*) turn the judgement from Assyria to Judah, and verse 12 summarizes the teaching of the oracle itself.

(*l*) In x. 13–18 we have another oracle, mainly in 3: 3 metre, on the same subject as the last, with an appendix added later, in verse 19.   Two other pieces, fragmentary, now follow, in x. 20–23 and 24–27a.   The former of these is mainly in 2: 2: 2 metre, while the latter seems to be now in

prose. Both hold out a hope of restoration to Judah, and
the former of them speaks of the remnant that shall return.
This is a doctrine characteristic of Isaiah, and the promise
of deliverance from Assyria, which follows, may also be
from his lips, although such a prospect is not usual with him.

(*m*) x. 27b–34 gives us a vivid picture in *Qinah* of the
advance of an army upon Jerusalem. It might conceivably
have been the combined forces of Pekah and Rezon, but the
compiler evidently thought of the Assyrians, since the rest of
the oracles here put together deal with that people. x. 33–
34 may also have referred, in the first instance, to Assyria,
and was probably added to this little group on that theory.

(*n*) A second Messianic passage appears in xi. 1–9 (3 : 3).
It is interesting to find this passage quoted in lxv. 25, though
the words are not taken exactly and consecutively. Moreover, verse 9b is not represented in lxv, though 9a is repeated
accurately, and we may conclude that 9c, which does not fit
the metre of the rest of this piece, was a later addition which
was made before the compiler inserted the whole here. The
quotations in ch. lxv will probably have been taken, not
from the finished book, but from the isolated oracle. Unlike
ix. 1–7, this passage can hardly be pre-exilic, for the word
used for " stock " in verse 1 implies the stump of a tree left
in the ground after it has been cut down, and could hardly
have been employed if the Davidic dynasty was still on the
throne.

(*o*) xi. 10–16. The remainder of ch. xi consists of a
series of pieces which are probably fragments, and all seem
to be not earlier than the Exile. Verse 10, for instance
(3 : 3), seems to stand practically alone, though we can
readily see why a collector should have attached it to the
preceding. Possibly verses 11–14 (also 3 : 3) may be read
continuously, as a promise of the return of the exiles, though
some scholars regard verse 11 as prose. Verse 15 (*Qinah*) is
again a fragment, which has little or no connexion with the
preceding, and, while the mention of Assyria in verse 16
might imply a pre-exilic date, the language suggests dependence on the admittedly exilic and post-exilic portions of
the book of *Isaiah*.

(*p*) xii. 1–6. The collection concludes with a pair of psalms, in xii. 1–2 and 4b–6 (both in 3 : 3) ; between them stands a little introduction to the second, verses 3–4a. These small psalms are songs celebrating the deliverance of Israel from captivity, and were suitably appended by the compiler to the last verses of ch. xi. They have parallels in other writings, *e.g.* verse 2 recalls Exod. xv. 2, and 4b. is made up of phrases which occur in Ps. cv. 1 and cxlviii. 13. It does not follow that we have here deliberate quotation from those psalms; the language may have been taken by both from some common source no longer extant. But the psalms are certainly post-exilic, and probably not earlier than the fourth century B.C.

(ii) *Date.* Some of the pieces in this collection are dated, and there is no reason to doubt the accuracy of the time assigned to them. Thus, ch. vi certainly must be attributed to the last year of Uzziah, and the autobiographical material in chs. vii–viii clearly comes from 735–4 B.C. We may ascribe ix. 27b–32 either to that time or to 701 B.C. For the rest, we have no means of getting nearer than to say that some of the material is either exilic or post-exilic. Some of the pieces, as we have seen, have little appendices which cannot be earlier than the Exile, while the pair of psalms which conclude the collection and round it off into a compact whole are considerably later than the Return. This justifies us in believing that the date of the collection, as a collection, is probably not earlier than the middle of the fourth century B.C., even though the greater part of the material included comes from Isaiah of Jerusalem, and must be ascribed to the eighth century B.C.

D. Chaps. xiii–xxiii. (i) *Structure.* As in other books, notably *Amos, Jeremiah* and *Ezekiel,* we have here a collection of oracles which deal with foreign nations. Properly speaking, each is a little collection within the larger one, for in most instances we shall find that there is more than one piece dealing with each nation. We may take them in the order in which they stand.

(*a*) *Babylon* (xiii–xiv. 23). Ch. xiii is sometimes treated as a single poem. But there are points where a division

seems to be indicated by the sense and the forms used, and
we may detect oracles originally independent in verses 2–3,
4–6 (both *Qinah*), 7–8, 9–12, 13 (a little apocalyptic fragment), 14–16, 17–22 (all in 3 : 3). To these we should add
the song of rejoicing over the return of the exiles in xiv. 1–2,
a passage which has clearly suffered in transmission before
being included in the collection.

xiv. 3–4a serves as an introduction to the great mocking
elegy in *Qinah* over the fall of a tyrant, xiv. 4b–21, one of the
most striking and impressive pieces of poetry in the Old
Testament—though it is hardly prophecy. It does not
follow that this song was a part of the original set of oracles,
and there is a tendency to see in it a reference to the death
of one of the Assyrian kings—Sennacherib or Sargon. It
has even been attributed in some quarters to Isaiah himself,
though, obviously, the rest of this little collection must be
much later. Verses 22–23 form an appendix to the collection
on Babylon.

(*b*) Assyria (xiv. 24–27). Only a single oracle in *Qinah* is
included here; it may well have been Isaiah's, and have
dated from 701 B.C.

(*c*) *Philistia* (xiv. 28–32). Again we have only a single
oracle in 3 : 3 whose date has given rise to some discussion.
The best date for the death of Ahaz is 725 B.C.[1] The " broken
rod " may well be Tiglath-pileser, who died in 727 B.C. His
successor, Shalmaneser v, deposed Hoshea in 724 B.C., and it
was possibly the preparations for this expedition which
called forth this oracle from Isaiah, for its terms do not
necessarily require that it should have been uttered immediately after the death of Tiglath-pileser, but only when
symptoms of disloyalty manifested themselves.

(*d*) *Moab* (xv–xvi). Here we have a number of oracles,
two of which are found in a parallel collection in the book of
Jeremiah; both are in a more or less mutilated state in each
book. Thus xv. 2b–7a = Jer. xlviii. 34–38, and xvi. 6–11
= Jer. xlviii. 29–33, though with very frequent variations
of order and transpositions. It would seem, then, that we
have at least three separate poems preserved here, all in

---

[1] Cp. Oesterley and Robinson, *Hist. of Israel*, I, 459.

Qinah, the first contained in xv. 1–9a, the second in xv. 9b–xvi. 5, and the third in xvi. 6–12, while xvi. 13 forms a concluding note to the whole collection. The problems presented by the text, especially in view of the parallels in Jeremiah, are far too intricate for detailed study at this point.[1]

(*e*) *Damascus (and Israel)* (xvii. 1–11). We have here a series of pieces of which the first only refers to Damascus, while the rest are concerned with Ephraim. The first two oracles, xvii. 1–3 (3:3) and 4–6 (probably *Qinah*), have the " signature," showing their independence of one another. The other two, verses 7–8 (metre uncertain) and 9–11 (3:3) both begin with the eschatological phrase, " In that day." While this may be a compiler's addition, we must not be blind to the possibility that Isaiah himself made use of the expression.

At the close of this little collection we have an oracle in xvii. 12–14 (3:3) which does not obviously refer to any people. It may, however, have been assumed by the compiler to date from the same period as the preceding oracles, *i.e. circa* 735 B.C.

(*f*) " *The Land of the Whirring of Wings* " (xviii). A single oracle in 3:3, without a special title, suggests that it was originally attached to that which immediately precedes. On the other hand, it is generally agreed that the reference is to Ethiopia, and the final compiler may have inserted it immediately before the Egyptian collection on this ground. The reference is, apparently, to an Egyptian embassy, perhaps connected with the rebellion against Sargon which led to the fall of Ashdod in 711 B.C., or with the general rising against Sennacherib at the beginning of his reign.[2]

(*g*) *Egypt* (xix–xx). Ch. xix opens with three oracles on Egypt, contained in verses 1–4 (3:3), 5–10 (3:3), and 11–15 (originally *Qinah*), respectively. The remainder of the chapter consists of a series of eschatological fragments and short pieces, each introduced by the phrase, " In that

---

[1] The best discussion in English is to be found in Gray, *Isaiah*, pp. 271–295.
[2] The XXVIth Dynasty, which was ruling in Egypt when these events took place, was of Ethiopian origin.

day." Two of these, verses 18 and 19–22, are sometimes referred to the Jewish temple erected at Leontopolis in the second century B.C.[1] The acceptance of this view, however, would place the compilation of this section very late indeed.

In ch. xx we have a short biographical passage in prose, describing how Isaiah went for three years lightly clad and barefoot, in order to typify the desolation coming on Egypt.

(h) Two oracles describing the coming fall of Babylon, both in *Qinah* (xxi. 1–5 and 6–10). The first is headed " Burden of the wilderness of the Sea," [2] which may be the reason why it was not included in the collection of chs. xiii, xiv.

(i) *Dumah*, a *Qinah* fragment, whose only identifiable reference is to Edom (xxi. 11–12).

(j) *Arabia* (xxi. 13–17). Here again we have a single *Qinah* oracle, with a prose appendix in verses 16 f.

(k) *The Valley of Vision* (xxii). This section is another example of a passage whose position has been determined by its title. In reality it is quite out of place in a collection which deals with foreign nations, since its subject is Jerusalem. The first part of the chapter, verses 1–14, consists of an account of the excitement over some festival, together with the contrast offered by the doom which the prophet foresees (verses 1–5, *Qinah*). This is followed by a series of little pieces, probably fragments, in 6–7 (3: 3), 8–11 (the original nucleus has received considerable additions before its inclusion in the collection), and 12–14 (metre irregular). Any of these may have come from the period of Isaiah, perhaps when the armies of Sennacherib were likely to invade the land.

The remainder of ch. xxii deals with a domestic matter, foretelling the disgrace of a high official named Shebna, and the appointment of Eliakim in his place. There seem to be two independent sections; the first (verses 15–23) is a medley of prose and poetry, the latter being, perhaps, the basis on which the whole was built. The second (verses 24–25, *Qinah*) may have been independent, and was probably added

---

[1] But see below, p. 252.   [2] The Septuagint omits " of the sea."

here by the compiler owing to the presence of the word
" peg."

(*l*) *Tyre* (xxiii).   This collection opens with what appears
to be a fairly long poem (verses 1–14, all in *Qinah*), describing the coming doom of Tyre; though it is possible that we
should distinguish three oracles in verses 1–5, 6–9, 10–14.
This section may well date from Isaiah himself, but the two
little passages with which the section ends, verses 15–16
(*Qinah*) and 17–18 (*Qinah*, with an editorial introduction)
are almost certainly by a later hand.

(ii) *Date*.   As we have seen, this collection contains pieces
from very varying dates.   Some are, without doubt, to be
attributed to Isaiah himself, others clearly come from the
period of the Exile, or even later, while there is a strong
suspicion that one of them, xix. 19–22, may be as late as the
second century B.C.   It is not impossible that this is a later
interpolation, though we should be reluctant to assume that
a prophecy would be added in the middle of a book or of a
collection after it had reached a definite shape, for such
additions are usually placed at the end.   It is possible that
the reference in the passage mentioned is not to the Temple
at Leontopolis, but to some other; if not to that of Elephantiné, then to one whose existence is otherwise unknown to us.
No one suspected the presence of a Jewish temple at Elephantiné until the discovery of the papyri in that spot.

In any case it is clear that the collection could not have
been completed till long after the return from the Exile, and
we dare not place it earlier than the end of the fifth century
B.C.   While it is true that nothing in the collection betrays
a knowledge of the reforms of Ezra, this may be accidental,
and the collection may have reached its present form during
or after his time.   Probably the end of the fourth century
should be regarded as the later limit.

E. Chs. xxiv–xxvii.   This section, as its contents will show,
belongs to a period centuries later than the time of Isaiah.
As in most of our prophetic books, various independent
fragments have been combined.   The whole section, apart
from inserted fragments, is apocalyptic, and, as in so many
other instances, contemporary historical events are placed
in an eschatological setting.

While scholars in general are agreed as to these points, there are differences of opinion regarding details. Some authorities assign the section to the reign of Darius i Hystaspes (521–486 B.C.), others to the decade 340–330 B.C.; but the developed form of the eschatological presentation, paralleled in the *Sibylline Oracles, Daniel, Enoch* and other apocalyptic books, as well as the advanced belief in immortality, points rather to 200 B.C., or even later, as the date.[1]

The fragments (viz. xxv. 1–5, xxv. 9–12, xxvi. 1–19, xxvii. 2–5, xxvii. 6–11) clearly did not originally belong to their present contexts, so that the original oracle, perhaps not all put together at one time, consisted of xxiv, xxv. 6–8, xxvi. 20–xxvii. 1, 12, 13.[2]

The contents of the original apocalypse are as follows:

xxiv. The apocalyptist foresees a great catastrophe in the near future; all classes, irrespective of calling or social position, will suffer. The earth, with all its inhabitants, save a small remnant, will be burned. But though the immediate future is so dark, there is hope beyond, for Yahweh will come and punish the powers on high and the kings of the earth; then the moon will be confounded and the sun ashamed; but Yahweh will reign on mount Zion in Jerusalem. The metre varies; verses 1–7 seem to have a *Qinah* base; verses 8–12 are 3:3; 13–14, *Qinah*; 16–20, 3:3; 21–23, *Qinah*.

xxv. 6–8 (3:3) tells of how " on this mountain," *i.e.* mount Zion, a great feast, *i.e.* a symbol of the Messianic era, will be held; death shall be done away with, and God " will wipe away tears from off all faces; and the reproach of his people shall be taken away from off all the earth."

xxvi. 20–xxvii. 1, 12, 13 should follow after xxv. 8, where it is prophesied that the reproach of God's people shall be taken away; until then the people are bidden to withdraw " until the indignation be overpast " (xxvi. 20), and in the meantime God will come forth to punish the wicked, and to

---

[1] Rudolph (*Jesaia*, 24–27 [1933]) assigns these chapters to 330–300 B.C.; he believes that, with unimportant exceptions, they are all from the same hand. For extraneous influence on Jewish eschatology see Oesterley and Robinson, *Hebrew Religion*, pp. 344 ff.

[2] See, among others, Duhm, *op. cit.*, p. 147; Lehmann, in *ZATW* 1917, pp. 1 ff.

destroy the principle of evil symbolized by the primeval sea-monster (cp. Rev. xxi. 1, " and the sea is no more "). The threefold name given to the sea-monster, " leviathan the fleeing serpent," " leviathan the winding serpent," " the dragon that is in the sea," is believed by some commentators to denote three world-powers on the part of the apocalyptist. Media, Babylonia, Egypt, or Media, Persia, Egypt, or Persia, Greece, Egypt, or Parthia, Syria, Egypt; others interpret them as the Sea, the Tigris, and the Euphrates; yet others as the constellations Serpens, Draco, and Hydra. That three world-powers are symbolized is possible, seeing how often the apocalyptists worked current historical events into their eschatological scheme; but which three must depend upon the view taken of the date of the writing.

Ultimately the trumpet shall be sounded for the ingathering of Israel; they will come from Syria [1] and Egypt to worship Yahweh on the holy mountain at Jerusalem. It will thus be seen that by eliminating the inserted portions a logical and straightforward eschatological picture is presented. The metre is uncertain, but was probably 3 : 3 originally.

As to its date, for the reason already indicated we hold that this little apocalypse belongs to the period of the apocalyptic literature proper, i.e. 200 B.C. onwards; hence we agree with Duhm and others who make out a strong case for the latter part of the second century B.C.: " The apocalyptist had witnessed the siege of Jerusalem and the devastation of Judæa by Antiochus vii Sidetes soon after the accession of John Hyrcanus (135); he had also seen the beginning of the Parthian war, and the unfortunate expedition of Antiochus in which the Jews were forced to take part (129)." The note of triumph in xxiv. 16 is occasioned by the defeat of Antiochus; but the apocalyptist cannot join in this because he foresees as a result a Parthian invasion. [2]

As to the inserted fragments, the historical background of xxv. 1-5 (3 : 3) and xxvi. 1-19 [3] seems to be the destruction

---

[1] In xxvii. 13, " Assyria," as in Zech. x. 10, stands for Syria.
[2] Duhm, Das Buch Jesaia, p. 147 (1914). For an earlier, but post-exilic, date, see Gunkel, ZATW 1924, pp. 177–208.
[3] The metre is uncertain, but the basis seems to be 3 : 3.

of Samaria by John Hyrcanus, somewhere within the period
113–105 B.C.; "the city of the terrible nation" (xxv. 3)
is Rome. The triumphant passage, xxv. 9–12 (probably
Qinah), may well belong to the time of Alexander Jannæus
(102–76 B.C.), who greatly extended the borders of the
Jewish kingdom; he subdued, among others, the Moabites
(cp. verse 10); in the later part of his reign, it is true, he
became very unpopular among his own people; but his
earlier conquest of Moab may quite well have been the
cause of the joyous outburst of this passage. In the two
fragments, xxvii. 2–5 (*Qinah*) and 6–11 (3 : 3), there seems
nothing sufficiently decisive to suggest a date.[1]

F. Chaps. xxviii–xxxv. (i) *Structure.*

(*a*) Ch. xxviii. This collection opens with the condemnation of the nobility of Samaria (1–4; verses 1–3, *Qinah*;
verse 4, 3 : 3), to which a brief eschatological note has been
attached in verses 5–6 (*Qinah*). This is followed by a pair
of denunciations of the sins, apparently, of Judah. The
first is drunkenness (verses 7–13; mainly *Qinah*), and the
second (in which verses 14–19 are in *Qinah*) necromancy.
This latter may extend down to verse 22, though the last
three verses (3 : 3) may be a later addition to the original
oracle. Verses 23–29 form an interesting passage, describing
different methods used in agriculture. The metre seems to
have been originally 3 : 3, though there are signs of redaction
which produce a prosaic effect.

(*b*) Ch. xxix opens with an announcement of the destruction
which is to fall on Jerusalem (verses 1–6, where the metre
varies). It has been suspected that verse 5 is an interpolation
due to a later writer who wished to turn the curse into a
blessing. Certainly we may believe that verses 7–8 (*Qinah*)
were appended with this object in view. The oracle on the
blindness of the people (verses 9–11a) has received a prosaic
expansion in 11b–12. In the next short utterances, verses
13–14 (3 : 3), the hypocrisy of current worship is condemned.
Verse 15 is a fragment in which certain politicians are

---

[1] For a careful study of the text of these chapters see Liebmann in the
ZATW 1902, pp. 1–56, 285–304; 1903, pp. 209–286; 1904, pp. 51–104;
1905, pp. 145–171.

denounced, and to this, it seems, the very obscure verse 16 has been added. Both are probably to be scanned as *Qinah*. The passage which begins with verse 17 is often held to be post-exilic, largely because of its contrast between the exalted and the humble. While it is true that this contrast is characteristic of a comparatively late post-exilic period, it must not be too hastily assumed that every passage in which it occurs is necessarily late. The general tone, however, of verses 17–24 makes Isaianic authorship improbable. The metre is mainly 3:3, with certain irregularities.

(*c*) Chs. xxx, xxxi deal mainly (though not exclusively) with Egypt and the proposed alliance with Egypt. It is a little curious that many of the oracles were not included in the collection now found in chs. xiii–xxiii. The pro-Egyptian policy is condemned in xxx. 1–5 (3:3), and the fragment that follows (verses 6–7, 3:3) is directed against Egypt herself. Verses 8–11 (*Qinah*) speak of the writing down of the last message, and 12–14 (*Qinah*) threaten the people with complete punishment. These last two sections might have a general reference, but the oracle in verses 15–17 (*Qinah*) is once more directed against the Egyptian alliance. Verses 18–26 are a promise of restoration and an assurance of the continued care of Yahweh, which are almost certainly post-exilic and appear to be cast into rhetorical prose, though metre may sometimes be observed, *e.g.* in verse 18 (3:3). The remaining verses of the chapter contain three short utterances—verses 27–28 (*Qinah*), 29–30 (3:3?), 31–33 (3:3)—which may have come from the time of Sennacherib's return to Assyria after the campaign of 701 B.C. Ch. xxxi contains three pieces, in verses 1–3 (3:3), a condemnation of the pro-Egyptian policy, 4–5 (*Qinah*), to which 6 and 7 (3:3) have been added later, and 8–9 (3:3), which predict the destruction of the Assyrian army. It is possible that the latter part of verse 9 is an addition, but, with the exception of this and verses 6–7, the three oracles are probably due to Isaiah himself.

(*d*) Ch. xxxii opens with a Messianic oracle in verses 1–5, followed by a later addition in verses 6–8—all in 3:3.

Verses 9–14 (*Qinah*) are a denunciation of the women of Jerusalem, in which some commentators find so strong a contrast to the treatment of the same theme in iii. 16–iv. 1 as to be convinced that the present passage is not the work of Isaiah. Verses 15–20 (3 : 3) are a fragment, mutilated at the beginning, which depict the glory of the coming new age. Here it seems impossible either to affirm or to deny Isaianic authorship.

(*e*) Ch. xxxiii consists, in the main, of a poem, we might almost say a psalm, which first pleads for deliverance from an oppressor, and then commemorates the deliverance when it comes. This is, by general consent, a post-exilic composition, but verse 1, a fragment which seems to stand as a text on which the psalm has been composed, does more resemble the style of Isaiah. The metre is irregular, and suggests that the poem is a late compilation from several sources—perhaps much expanded in course of time.

But there is considerable difference of opinion regarding the interpretation, and therefore the date, of this self-contained chapter. Many commentators insist on a pre-exilic date and maintain that it is to be read in the light of the episode recounted in ii Kgs. xviii. 14–37, in which case the date would be 701 B.C.; but in view of verse 8, "he hath broken the covenant," this opinion can hardly stand, for Hezekiah, not Sennacherib, was the one who broke the covenant. Others are on stronger ground in regarding the chapter as late; Duhm dates it in the year 162 B.C., and sees in the enemy Antiochus Eupator; and it must be said that on reading i Macc. vi. 18–63 there is a good deal of justification for his contention. There is much in the thought and language of the chapter which marks it as late; and the eschatology, taken in conjunction with this, further supports a Maccabæan date.

(*f*) Ch. xxxiv is distinctly eschatological in tone, though it does not suggest the latest forms of Jewish eschatology. It describes the destruction of the hostile nations, especially of Edom, and often recalls ch. lxiii. The metre varies, being *Qinah* in verses 1–5a, 3 : 3 in 5b–8, *Qinah* in 9, and 3 : 3 again in verses 10–17.

s

(g) Ch. xxxv offers the other side of the picture, and in some ways resembles the prophecies of the period of the Return. It can hardly be later than the time of Ezra, and the picture of the safe journey reminds us of Ezra's refusal to demand a convoy from the Persian king (Ezra viii. 22). The metre is a fairly regular 3 : 3.

(ii) *Date.* Once more we have a collection including pieces from different periods, ranging from the eighth century, possibly down to the second. The vagueness characteristic of the later passages makes it very difficult to attempt an exact dating, but, if Duhm's date for ch. xxxiii be accepted, we must assume that the end of the second century B.C. is the earliest period to which we can assign the work of the final collector of the whole group.

G. *Chaps. xxxvi–xxxix.*[1] In these chapters we have an historical appendix to the whole book of Isaianic collections. They deal with events in the reign of Hezekiah, in which the prophet took a prominent part, and they are largely duplicated in ii Kgs. xviii. 13–xx. 19. There are differences between the two passages, among which the most important are (a) the absence of the account of Hezekiah's submission (ii Kgs. xviii. 14–16) from the text of *Isaiah*, and (b) the presence in Isa. xxxviii 9–20 of Hezekiah's song of thanksgiving. There are also, as is to be expected, minor differences of text and arrangement. It is commonly held that the chapters in *Isaiah* are directly taken from the book of *Kings*, but it seems more in harmony with what we know of the growth of Hebrew literature to suppose that there existed a collection of the acts of Isaiah (the biographical matter that we have so often elsewhere in the prophets), and that this was employed both by the compiler of *Kings* and by the final compiler of *Isaiah*. The psalm in xxxviii. 9–20 is not wholly suitable to its present position, and is best regarded as a post-exilic composition. It was included comparatively late in the narrative, or it would have appeared in *Kings*; but, again, we have no reason to bring its composition down below the fourth century B.C. This will give us the *terminus ad quem* for the whole section.

---

[1] These chapters are mainly in prose (type B), but we have a song of triumph in xxxvii. 22–34 (mainly *Qinah*) and a psalm in xxxviii. 9–20 (also *Qinah*).

Summary and Conclusions. We have now seen that the book of *Isaiah*, down to the end of ch. xxxix, was produced by the combination of no less than seven different earlier collections. The last of these is mainly historical prose, but the rest are composed normally of oracular matter, with certain exceptions, especially in the third collection. The first collection contains nothing that cannot come from Isaiah himself, while the fifth is wholly composed of much later material. The others consist of matter ranging from the eighth to the fifth (possibly even the second) century, and the date of the compilation of most of them seems to have been during the first half of the fourth century. It is to much the same period—naturally towards the end of it —that we should attribute the gathering together of the various collections and their formation into the book as we now have it. It is not impossible that later insertions may have been made after the main work of compilation, but it would be more natural for these to have been placed at the end than at the beginning, and we cannot attribute to this process more than occasional notes and comments which might have been inserted in the margin and incorporated by a copyist. We shall be justified in believing that by 300 B.C. the book existed substantially as we have it to-day, though we must allow for the possibility that the compilation did not take place till the first century, B.C.

V. The Man and his Message

Like Hosea, and unlike Amos and Micah, Isaiah was essentially a man of the city. His home was in Jerusalem, and, though he was not unfamiliar with the life and work of the farmer, it was within the walls of a town that his days were spent and his work was done. He was, further, in some sense a courtier, familiar with the nobles,[1] and, to some extent, recognized and trusted by the kings. With them he is perfectly fearless, and does not hesitate to speak the plain truth, whether in condemnation or approval. His words are received with respect, even though his advice is not always followed. Tradition [2] records the martyrdom

---

[1] Cp. viii. 2, xxii. 15–25.
[2] Cp. *The Martyrdom of Isaiah*, v–x; and see the epistle to the *Hebrews*, xi. 37.

of Isaiah in the reign of Manasseh, but, as far as we know, during the period of his active ministry he suffered no kind of persecution.

Isaiah's literary abilities were of a very high order. We have few pieces of prose in any language which can be compared with the account of his call in ch. vi, and his short impulsive lyrics have an extraordinary beauty and power. We are impressed by the vigour which marks his account of the enemy's advance in x. 28–32, by the pathos which finds expression in the lament over the desolate land (i. 4–9), the passionate denunciation of injustice and oppression (cp. v. 8–10), the bitter scorn of the heartless and fashionable women (*e.g.* iii. 16–26), and the tender appeal of the great evangelical invitation in i. 18–21. All the features of great poetry are here—sincerity, honesty, depth of feeling, beauty of expression; and while Isaiah never knew the spiritual anguish which gave such poignancy to the utterances of Hosea and Jeremiah, his words are more often read and more truly loved than those of any other prophet, save only the great anonymous writer of the Exile, whose prophecies are appended to this book.

Isaiah was at one with his great predecessor, Amos, and with his equally great contemporary, Hosea, in the main outlines of his teaching. Like them he insisted on such doctrines as the supremacy of Yahweh, the demand for morality and the futility of sacrifice as a substitute for righteousness. From his call-vision in ch. vi, however, we gather that the dominant thought in his scheme of thinking was the holiness of Yahweh. He stood apart from all gods, and Israel must stand apart from all nations. Isaiah advocated complete abstention from the political entanglements of his age, and saw that the only hope for Judah's safety lay in her holding aloof from other nations. This, however, does not seem to have sprung from an appreciation of the international situation, so much as from his conviction that Israel must deal with Yahweh alone— she must be holy to Him. If she interfered in world politics, she would be contaminated by contact with other deities, and would lose the protection that purity might have secured for her.

Yet Judah went her own way, and followed the path which led, in the end, to her doom. But Isaiah could not believe in her final extinction. Yahweh needed a people for His self-expression, and for that purpose, whatever happened to Israel a " remnant " must survive. The nation could not wholly perish, and though sin would inevitably result in appalling suffering, a spiritual nucleus would still exist.

Closely allied to the doctrine of the " remnant " is another which, as far as we know, first manifested itself in the teaching of Isaiah. This was a belief in the coming of an ideal king, who should rule over his people in strict accordance with the principles of Yahweh. The Messiah, however, is not yet an eschatological figure; he has no connexion with the great day of Yahweh. He is to be simply an earthly monarch, whose righteous government is to restore happiness and prosperity to his people. Thus was born a doctrine which was to develop into one of the most significant beliefs of the Jewish people in centuries yet to come.

VI. The Hebrew Text and the Septuagint

On the whole, the text of the book of *Isaiah* has not been badly preserved. The history of the prophetic writings in general meant that they were more subject than other parts of the Bible to textual corruption, which may often have taken place even before the collections of oracles were completed. We have, for instance, a number of oracles which are clearly mutilated, and there is no reason to doubt that this mutilation took place before the passages in question came into the hands of the collectors.

The only version that needs consideration is the Septuagint. This, however, is less helpful in *Isaiah* than in some other books, since it is often free, sometimes even paraphrastic. It is thus difficult to be sure what the original Hebrew was, as it lay before the translators. There is, nevertheless, a number of passages in which it may help us to improve the text as it now lies before us in our Hebrew Bibles.[1]

[1] The Greek text has been edited by R. R. Ottley, *Isaiah according to the Septuagint*, Vol. I (1904, 1909), Vol. II (1906).

ISAIAH XL–LV (DEUTERO-ISAIAH)

I. HISTORICAL BACKGROUND

IN the year 549 B.C., Cyrus, king of Anshan, a vassal-state of Astyages, king of Media, revolted against his suzerain and conquered him; he became thus ruler of the Perso-Median empire. In fear of the rising power of Cyrus three kings formed an alliance with the object of stemming his further advance: Crœsus, king of the Lydians, Nabonidus, king of Babylonia, and Amasis, king of Egypt. The first of these was conquered by Cyrus in 546 B.C., whereby the whole of Asia Minor came under his rule; Egypt was, for the time being, left unmolested;[1] in 539–8 B.C. Babylon fell. The *Chronicle of Nabonidus* records as follows:—" On the 16th (of the month Tishri = October) Ugbaru (Gobryas) the governor of Gutium and the troops of Cyrus entered Babylon without a battle. . . . In Marcheswan (= November) on the 3rd, Cyrus entered Babylon. . . . There was peace in the city. Cyrus proclaimed peace to Babylon, to everyone."

The period covered by these chapters is probably from 549 to 538 B.C.),[2] *i.e.* from Cyrus' victory over Astyages to the eve of the capture of Babylon; the actual fall of the city is not mentioned.

---

[1] It was conquered by Cambyses, the son of Cyrus, in 525 B.C.

[2] Torrey (*The Second Isaiah* [1928]) does not believe that any part of Isa. xl–lxvi was written during the Exile; he assigns the whole to about 400 B.C., Palestine being the place of origin. The references to Cyrus, Babylon, and Chaldæa he simply cuts out, maintaining that the metre of the passages in which they occur shows them to be later interpolations. He sums up his position thus:—" Second Isaiah is indeed a prophecy of release from bondage and a triumphant return of ' exiles ' to Jerusalem by sea and land; but the prophet is looking to the ends of the earth, not to Babylonia. There is indeed prediction, definite and many times repeated, of the speedy advent of a great conqueror and deliverer, the restorer of Israel and benefactor of the world; but the prophet is speaking of the Anointed Servant of the Lord, the Son of David, not the son of Cambyses " (p. 37). That Torrey has found but few scholars to agree with him cannot cause surprise.

The references in these chapters to the historical background are as follows:[1]

xli. 2 : " Who aroused from the east him whom victory meeteth at every step, that delivereth up nations before him, and bringeth down kings? His sword maketh them like dust, his bow driveth them away like chaff. He pursueth them, he passeth on—Peace (*i.e.* his victories bring peace, see the quotation from the *Nabonidus Chronicle*, above); he doth not tread the pathway with his feet " (in xlvi. 11 Cyrus is compared with a ravenous bird, so swift and sweeping in his progress).

These graphic words must refer, in the first instance, to Cyrus' victory over Astyages, king of the Medes; he came from Anshan, which lay to the east of Babylonia. The passage also refers to the defeat of Crœsus, king of the Lydians, and Cyrus' acquisition of Asia Minor.

xli. 25 : " I aroused up one from the north, and he came from the rising of the sun (east). I called him by his name (see xlv. 3, cp. also xliii. 1)." The north refers to Media, which lay north-east of Babylonia; the east is again in reference to Anshan.

xliii. 3 : " I give Egypt as thy ransom, Ethiopia and Seba in place of thee." The reference is again to Cyrus, who is to receive the whole of Africa, as then known, as compensation for letting the exiles go free. Our records, unfortunately, give no information as to what occurred after Cyrus' defeat of Crœsus; the prophet, presumably, expected that Egypt would suffer the same fate as Lydia; but Cyrus did not conquer Egypt; that was left to his son Cambyses to accomplish.

xliv. 28 : " . . . that saith of Cyrus, ' My shepherd,' and all my requirement shall he perform." For " shepherd " in the sense of " ruler " see, *e.g.*, Jer. iii. 15; the passage means that Cyrus rules by the will of Yahweh.[2] The remainder of this verse: " even saying of Jerusalem, Let

---

[1] The renderings here given differ in some cases from the Revised Version, which does not always take the corruptions in the Hebrew text into account, and sometimes misses the point of the original.

[2] Perhaps, by a difference of pointing, we should read, " My friend."

her be built, and of the Temple, Let its foundations be laid,"
would imply that these words were written after Cyrus'
decree, permitting the return of the exiles (see Ezra i. 2–4,
vi. 1 ff.), had been put forth, *i.e.* after the fall of Babylon;
that is highly improbable, and doubtless those commentators
are right who hold that the words have been misplaced
and that they came originally after verse 26 (emended)
thus: ". . . that saith of Jerusalem, She shall be inhabited;
and of the waste places thereof, I will raise them up; yea,
that saith of Jerusalem, Let her be built, and of the Temple,
Let its foundations be laid."

xlv. 1–4. This is too long to quote; it speaks of Cyrus
as Yahweh's anointed and describes his victorious progress.

xlv. 9–13. This is also too long to quote; it is a rebuke
to those who take exception to Cyrus being the instrument
of Yahweh; the passage ends with the words: " I raised
him up in righteousness, and I will make straight all his
ways; he shall build my city, and he shall let my exiles
go free. . . ."

xlvi. 1–2. This fragment, which also reflects the historical
background, has a special interest of its own; it stands
isolated, being unconnected with what precedes as well as
with what follows, and the Hebrew text can hardly be in
order. The prophet is so certain of the now impending
fall of Babylon that he speaks of this as having already
come to pass; the verbs are all in the perfect. It may be
rendered thus: " Bel hath stooped down (cp. Gen. xlix. 9),
Nebo hath crouched down; their images are for beasts,
for beasts of burden; their things which were carried
about (a contemptuous reference to the images) are become
loads—a burden for weary (beasts). They (*i.e.* Bel and
Nebo) have crouched down, they have stooped down
(both) together, they were not able to rescue the burden
(*i.e.* these gods could not deliver their own images), they
are gone into captivity." The meaning then is that when
Babylon fell the worshippers of Bel and Nebo, the tutelary
deities of the city, attempted to escape with these images;
but they failed in this, and the gods, *i.e.* their images, were
carried captive. In this last particular, however, the

prophet was mistaken, for Cyrus was careful not to interfere with the religious beliefs of conquered peoples; on one of his inscriptions he says: "I returned the gods to their shrines." [1]

Illustrative of the historical background is also the long passage containing a prophecy of the downfall of Babylon (xlvii, cp. also xlviii. 14, 15).

The passages so far considered refer to the external historical conditions; we have next to point to those which reflect the circumstances under which the Jews were living.

xliii. 14. That the Hebrew text is corrupt is clear even from the R.V. rendering, which is meaningless; many emendations have been suggested with more or less plausibility, but certainty as to what the original text read is out of the question; the following has some points in its favour:—" This saith Yahweh, your redeemer, the Holy One of Israel: For your sake I have sent to Babylon, and I will bring down the *bars of the prison house* (*i.e.* Babylon); and (as for) the Chaldæans, I *will still their shouting with sighs*." [2] The mention of Babylon is, in any case, indisputable; and this is the first direct reference to it in these chapters. Yahweh is about to send Cyrus to Babylon to release the Jews from captivity.

xlviii. 20: " Go forth from Babylon, flee ye from the Chaldæans . . . say ye, Yahweh hath redeemed his servant Jacob." In two other passages (lii. 11, 12; lv. 12), although Babylon is not mentioned by name, it is obvious that the prophet is thinking of the city when he bids the exiles go forth.

Further, various passages speak of the return from captivity in the near future (xliii. 5, li. 11, 14, 21–23; lii. 7–9), while others refer implicitly to the Exile (xl. 2, xlii. 14, xlviii. 10 and others).

We are left, therefore, in not the slightest doubt that the historical background points to the eve of the Return as the period to which these chapters (xl–lv) belong.

It is, however, possible to indicate more precisely the

---

[1] Gadd, *History and Monuments of Ur*, p. 250 (1929).

[2] וְהוֹרַדְתִּי בְרִיחִי כֻלָּא וְכַשְׂדִּים וְהָשַׁבְּתִּי בָּאֲנִיּוֹת רִנָּתָם :

time during which the prophet uttered these poems. On closer examination it is seen that the whole collection consists of two main divisions: xl–xlviii repeatedly speaks of the downfall of Babylon; and Cyrus, as we have seen, is mentioned as the conqueror, either directly or implicitly referred to as such. But in xlix–lv no mention is made either of Babylon or of Cyrus. This can be accounted for only on the supposition that the two sets of poems do not belong to precisely the same period.

It may, therefore, be gathered that xl–xlviii belong to the time immediately preceding the fall of Babylon; Cyrus had begun his Babylonian campaign; by his victory over the Akkadians at Opis, on the Tigris, north of Babylon, and by his capture, a fortnight later, of Sippar, only fifty miles from the capital, the prophet knew that the end was in sight. The other set of poems (xlix–lv) would then have been uttered after the fall of the city, which would explain why the prophet does not mention it; instead of this he says: " Depart ye, depart ye, go out from thence; touch no unclean thing; go ye out of the midst of her; be ye clean, ye that bear the vessels of Yahweh " (lii. 11; see also li. 14, lv. 12).[1] That the exiles would not have departed immediately after the fall of the city is evident, for they could not have done so until Cyrus had issued his decree permitting this; the decree was put forth in the same year as the fall of the city; but it is not known in what month.[2]

In support of what has been said it may also be pointed out that there is a difference of characteristic between the two sets of poems: xl–xlviii deal more pronouncedly with the relationship between Yahweh and His people, whereas xlix–lv speak more of that between Yahweh and Jerusalem, or Zion, the goal of the exiles, which after the fall of Babylon would be the more prominent thought in the mind of the prophet. In the earlier group, moreover,

---

[1] The command to go forth from Babylon occurs also at the close of the earlier set of poems, xlviii. 20, 21, which would suggest that these verses really belong to the later set.

[2] When it is said in Ezra vi. 2 that this decree was found at Acmetha, *i.e.* Ecbatana, in Media, it does not follow that Cyrus issued it from there.

there is much stress laid on the folly of idolatry and of comparing any god with Yahweh;[1] this was doubtless needed so long as the exiles were settled among the Babylonians; but in the later group idolatry is not mentioned, nor was there any need for this now that the exiles were about to depart. And finally, there is in the later group a more fully expressed and eager looking forward to the return to the homeland than in the earlier, pointing therefore to its greater imminence.

II. STRUCTURE AND CONTENTS OF ISA. XL–LV

These chapters contain a number of independent poetical pieces; a sequence of thought is, however, often to be observed. In the following table these various little poems are enumerated, but it is recognized that in some cases there are differences of opinion as to their precise scope, some scholars would further subdivide a few of the poems. It must also be pointed out that no detailed discussion of the intricate metrical problems presented by these chapters is here possible. The metre indicated for each section is that which predominates within it, and must not be understood as implying that there is necessarily no variation from it in our present text.

xl. 1–11. Mainly in the *Qinah* measure (3 : 2), though there are considerable irregularities. It is a message of consolation, introductory to others which follow, proclaiming to the exiles that the time of release is at hand. Verses 9–11 should probably come after verse 5, since they continue the tone of hope and exultation, whereas verses 6–8 speak of the transitoriness of human life, a subject which comes inappropriately between verses 5 and 9.

xl. 12–17. An almost regular 3 : 3 measure. The great things in the physical world are as nothing in the sight of Yahweh; similarly, all the nations of the earth are nothing accounted of in His sight.

xl. 18–20. To this xli. 6, 7 evidently belongs; the whole

---

[1] See xl. 18–26; xli. 6, 7, 21–29; xliv. 9–20; xlvi. 1, 2; cp. also xlii. 17; xlv. 16, 20.

is again 3 : 3. It speaks of the folly of comparing graven images with God.

xl. 21–26. Partly *Qinah* and partly 3 : 3; possibly we have here two fragments, verses 21–24, and 25, 26. The subject is the omnipotence of Yahweh, the Creator of all things.

xl. 27–31. Mostly 3 : 3, but there is some slight irregularity; the change at the beginning of verse 28 to 2 : 2, " Hast thou not known, hast thou not heard," is very effective; the 3 : 3 continues immediately after. The little poem protests that Israel's fear of being ignored by Yahweh is groundless. He is from of old, and mighty in power, and gives strength to those who wait upon Him.

xli. 1–5. 3 : 3; as already pointed out, verses 6, 7 do not belong here. It speaks of Yahweh's lordship over all nations, illustrated by His raising up Cyrus to do His will.

xli. 8–16. The metre is somewhat varied, partly 3 : 3 (verses 8–10, 14–16), partly *Qinah* (verses 11–13). God's love and care for His people; Israel's enemies will be overthrown.

xli. 17–20. While 3 : 3 predominates, there is some irregularity. It contains a description of how the wilderness will be turned into a fruitful land when the exiles pass through it on their way to the homeland.

xli. 21–29. The metre again alternates between 3 : 3 and *Qinah*; but there are some textual corruptions. Its theme is the nothingness of idols; in contrast to them Yahweh foresees and foreordains all things; an illustration of this is the advent of Cyrus.

xlii. 1–4. Regular 3 : 3. The first " Servant of the Lord " song.

xlii. 5–9. The metre alternates between 3 : 3 and 2 : 2 : 2 in verses 6 and 9. The theme of the poem is the loving-kindness of Yahweh towards His people.

xlii. 10–13. A slightly irregular 3 : 3 poem, calling upon the physical world to give glory to Yahweh, the Mighty One.

xlii. 14–17. The metre is very irregular, 3 : 3 and 3 : 2 seem to have been used originally, but some textual corruptions have made havoc with any regular metre. The poet tells of how in the past Yahweh had been silent while His people suffered (*e.g.* Assyrian invasions and the Captivity); but now He is about to show forth His mercy to His people.

xlii. 18–25. A variety of textual corruptions in this piece have again disturbed the metre; probably it was originally composed of 3 : 3 and the *Qinah* metre. It is a lament over Israel's spiritual blindness and deafness.

xliii. 1–7. Again an intermixture of 3 : 3 and *Qinah* with some other irregularities. Israel is about to be released from captivity, and with them those of the Dispersion will be brought back to the home-land.

xliii. 8–13. Though there are some irregularities, the main metre is 3 : 3. Israel, the people of Yahweh, are witnesses of His Unity.

xliii. 14, 15. This isolated fragment is in regular 3 : 3 metre. It takes up again the subject of Yahweh as the Redeemer of His people.

xliii. 16–21. The usual 3 : 3 metre occurs here again, though with some irregularity. The subject is God's mercy in bringing His people home through the wilderness.

xliii. 22–28. A fairly regular 3 : 3. Israel's ingratitude to Yahweh in spite of His having chosen them as His people; therefore punishment must inevitably come upon the nation.

xliv. 1–5. The metre is, more or less, *Qinah*. In spite of Israel's sin Yahweh will pour His spirit upon His people; as a consequence the Gentiles will join themselves to the people of God, and call upon Yahweh.

xliv. 6–8. To this section, in 3 : 3, it is probable that verses 21, 22 belong. The theme is the Oneness of Yahweh; because Israel is His servant their sins shall be blotted out.

xliv. 9–20. This is a prose section, and probably a later insertion; it deals with the folly of idolatry.

xliv. 21, 22. Somewhat irregular *Qinah*; it belongs to verses 6–8.

xliv. 23. An isolated fragment with irregular metre.

xliv. 24–xlv. 7. The metre in this comparatively long section is varied, 3 : 3 and *Qinah* predominate. Cyrus, the instrument of Yahweh, has been chosen for the sake of

Israel. It is by Yahweh that he has been called, and by no other God.

xlv. 8. An isolated fragment in 3 : 3 metre. The Creatorship of Yahweh.

xlv. 9–13. The metre is again irregular, 3 : 3 predominating. Yahweh is justified in His choice of Cyrus. Evidently spoken against some who questioned the propriety of a Gentile ruler being chosen by Yahweh.

xlv. 14–17. Irregular metre. To Israel alone has Yahweh revealed Himself.

xlv. 18–25. The metre is again irregular, but *Qinah* predominates. A striking poem dealing with the Oneness and righteousness of Yahweh; the Gentiles are called upon to worship Him.

xlvi. 1–4. In the main 3 : 3. The gods of Babylon are carried in flight from the foe, but they cannot escape; in contrast to this it is told how Yahweh carried His people Israel in the past, and will deliver them now.

xlvi. 5–13. The irregular metre alternates between 3 : 3 and *Qinah*; it is evident that verses 6–8 are out of place here; their content shows this; they must be a late insertion. The theme is again the Oneness of Yahweh; His will is supreme, and in accordance with this Israel is about to be delivered from captivity by Cyrus.

xlvii. A taunt-song of triumph over Babylon in *Qinah* measure.

xlviii. 1–11. Mainly 3 : 3, but the text has suffered through glosses. The poem deals with the stiff-neckedness of Israel; nevertheless, God will have mercy upon His people for His name's sake.

xlviii. 12–16. The metre is irregular possibly owing to textual corruption; 3 : 3 predominates. The theme is again the Oneness of Yahweh; it is by His will, and by His will alone, that Cyrus is about to conquer Babylon.

xlviii. 17–19. *Qinah.* Yahweh taught Israel, but Israel would not hearken, therefore punishment was meted out.

xlviii. 20–22. Irregular metre, with *Qinah* predominating. Verse 22 is clearly an editorial addition. The exiles are bidden to go forth from Babylon.

xlix. 1–6. Mainly 3 : 3. The second " Servant of the Lord " song.

xlix. 7–12. *Qinah* in verse 7, the rest 3 : 3. Though Israel has been oppressed and despised, yet will Yahweh re-establish her, and she shall be an object of wonder to the Gentiles.

xlix. 13. An isolated fragment in irregular measure; but possibly an introduction to the poem which follows. Heaven and earth are called upon to rejoice, for Yahweh has shown compassion on His people.

xlix. 14–21. Irregular metre, varying between 3 : 3 and *Qinah*. A message of comfort to Israel, telling of Yahweh's loving-kindness.

xlix. 22–26. There is a break after verse 24, but the whole is 3 : 3. A promise that Israel's children shall be restored to her; they shall be brought by the Gentiles; kings shall do honour to her; the enemies of Israel shall be punished ; but Yahweh will redeem His people.

l. 1–3. Irregular metre, with 3 : 3 predominating. A message of comfort to Israel; she was, indeed, punished for her sins, but Yahweh is, nevertheless, ready, in His mercy, to receive her.

l. 4–11. *Qinah*. The third " Servant of the Lord " song.

li. 1–8. Mostly 3 : 3, but with some irregularities. Yahweh's blessing on those who follow after righteousness. His salvation shall be for all the world; the evil-doers shall not prevail.

li. 9–11. Alternation between *Qinah* and 3 : 3. An appeal to Yahweh to show forth His might as in primeval times.

li. 12–16. The metre is similar to the preceding. A song of comfort for Israel which is put into the mouth of Yahweh.

li. 17–lii. 12. The metre in this poem is very varied; *Qinah* seems to predominate, but li. 21, 22 are in 3 : 3, and lii. i, 2 are prose. Jerusalem's sufferings in the past are recorded; but now her redemption is proclaimed.

lii. 13–liii. 12. With a few variations the metre is 3 : 3. The fourth " Servant of the Lord " song.

liv. 1–6. *Qinah* and 3 : 3. A song of comfort for Zion.

liv. 7–10. Almost wholly 3 : 3. The theme is the same as in the preceding piece; the loving-kindness of Yahweh shall never cease.

liv. 11–14. The metre is again 3 : 3, but in this case carried right through. The future glory of Zion is depicted.

liv. 15–17. Metre very irregular. Zion's permanent safety is prophesied.

lv. 1–5. Irregular metre, but, apparently, with a 3 : 3 basis. An invitation to the people to accept Yahweh's blessings, which are freely given.

lv. 6–13. The metre varies between 3 : 3 (verses 6–11) and *Qinah* (verses 12, 13). A beautiful little poem calling upon the people to seek Yahweh; His mercy, like His glory, is everlasting.

In most cases these poems, in their originally *spoken* form, were doubtless much longer; they would, therefore, seem to be a collection of brief summaries of the prophet's addresses, delivered at different times, and, likely enough, made by himself; in some cases, as will have been seen, a fuller form of the address has been written down.[1] This would seem to be the best way to account for the number of independent pieces on the one hand, and a certain grouping together of subject-matter on the other.

III. The Prophet and his Teaching

Of the life of the prophet his writings give us no information. It is highly probable that he lived in Babylon, though that he always addresses the exiles would not necessarily prove this; more convincing is his intimate knowledge of the manner of life of the Babylonians (xlvii. 8. ff.), and of Babylonian religion (xlvi. 1), and astrology (xlvii. 13–15); these passages suggest first-hand knowledge. Further, as

---

[1] This is not to be understood as implying that our records are in any way incorrect or deficient in essentials. The essence of the message is always there, though the prophet, when speaking face to face with all and sundry, probably delivered it in a form considerably more extensive than that which appears in our Bibles. My collaborator, Dr. Robinson, is, however, unable to agree with me on this point, and still holds it to be more probable that the words ascribed to the prophet in the Bible do (except where, as often happens, an oracle has been mutilated in the course of transmission) represent *verbatim* what the prophet said, on each occasion, as he delivered the message divinely communicated to him.—W. O. E. O.

Meinhold has pointed out,[1] the anonymity of the writer supports this; there would have been no reason for his name to be concealed had he lived in Palestine, whereas in Babylon this was necessary; had the writer of much that occurs in these chapters, especially xlvii, been identified, his career would soon have been cut short. And perhaps most convincing of all is the prophet's familiarity with certain expressions and modes of address which are specifically Babylonian; details of this cannot be given here,[2] but the use of these is a strong argument in favour of the prophet having lived in Babylon.[3]

The outstanding subjects of " Deutero-Isaiah's " teaching are, firstly, his conception of God; it is true to say that we have here the most exalted teaching in the whole of the Old Testament; his monotheism is explicit as never before, and his words concerning the greatness and omnipotence of God are unrivalled. Secondly, his teaching on the regeneration of the people; here, while following in the footsteps of earlier prophets, he handles the subject independently and develops it in a way peculiar to himself. And thirdly, his universalistic conceptions; this, again, while not in itself new, surpasses in its wideness all that had previously been taught.[4]

But, apart from the first of these, the most striking and specific teaching of this prophet is contained in the " Servant of the Lord " poems (xlii. 1–4, xlix. 1–6, l. 4–9, lii. 13– liii. 12). Each of these four pieces stands independent and could be taken out of its present position without affecting the contents. In assigning the authorship of these poems to Deutero-Isaiah, we do not lose sight of the fact that opinions vary on the subject; much can be urged for and against his authorship; either view can claim a number of outstanding authorities in its favour, supported by cogent arguments; and, naturally enough, such arguments appeal

---

[1] *Einführung in das Alte Testament*, p. 273 (1932).
[2] See Gressmann, *Der Ursprung der israelitisch-jüdischen Eschatologie*, pp. 250 ff., 305 ff. (1905).
[3] The suggestions of his having lived in northern Syria, or in Egypt, do not carry conviction.
[4] These subjects are more fully dealt with in the present writers' *Hebrew Religion*, pp. 259–270 (1930).

T

with differing force to different minds. But who the writer of these poems was is a matter of less importance than the teaching they contain; briefly summarized this may be stated as follows: in the first poem (xlii. 1–4) the Servant, the chosen one of God, will, by means of the divine spirit of which he is the recipient, proclaim the message of truth and righteousness to the world; in the second poem (xlix. 1–6) this universalistic note is further emphasized; the Servant is described as one, who through apparent failure in toiling among his own people, will, by divine help, become not only the saviour of them, but will also be for salvation to the whole earth; the third poem (l. 4–11) tells of the Servant's suffering for bearing witness to God, but with the help of God all his adversaries will be put to shame; and in the last poem (lii. 13–liii. 12) he is depicted as a leper and martyr who lays down his life for others, but who will be raised from death by God to complete his work for his fellow-men.

The identity of the Servant, whether representing the nation of Israel personified or an individual, is again a matter of divided opinions; but this, as well as that of the authorship of the poems, is a special study which cannot be dealt with in detail here.[1]

IV. Language and Style of Isa. xl–lv

It has been pointed out that the form in which the writings of " Deutero-Isaiah " are composed is poetical; that the Hebrew in which they are written is so pure shows that in spite of their foreign surroundings the Jews preserved their language uncontaminated. The style of the writing is for the most part simple and straightforward, and usually easy to understand. At the same time, in reading through these chapters one cannot help experiencing a certain sense of monotony on account of the reiteration of the same subjects; this is, however, to be explained by the fact, already mentioned, that we have here summaries of discourses uttered at different times, all being independent

---

[1] See further, Oesterley and Robinson, *Hebrew Religion*, pp. 264 ff.

pieces; they were never intended to be read as a unity; the prophet had a certain number of outstanding themes which filled his mind, and these found frequent expression when he addressed his people. This must be borne in mind when reading these chapters.[1]

V. The Hebrew Text and the Septuagint

In general, the text has come down to us in a remarkably good state; there are a certain number of corruptions, and one or two displacements due to copyists; various instances occur of later additions, a feature common to all the Biblical books, but as a rule they are fairly obvious.

For a rectification of the corrupt passages the Septuagint is often of great help; one or two illustrations of this will be of interest: at the end of xl. 19 there is a meaningless phrase [2] which disturbs the rhythm and may possibly be the corrupt remnant of a marginal note which found its way into the text; the Septuagint omits it altogether. The Hebrew text of xl. 20 reads: " He that is impoverished a heave-offering wood that doth not rot he chooseth "; the Septuagint, without which it would be difficult to make anything of this, reads, " He who prepares a likeness," *i.e.* he who sets up an image, " chooseth wood . . . "; moreover, the Septuagint enables us to see what the original Hebrew text read, and how easily, owing to the similarity of the letters, the corruption arose. Another illustration may be given which occurs in xlii. 19; taking the Hebrew text as it stands it reads: " Who is blind, but my servant, and deaf, like my messenger (whom) I send? Who is blind like one that is recompensed, and blind like the servant of Yahweh? " In view of what has been said at the beginning of the chapter about the servant of Yahweh, this reads very strangely, apart from the obvious lack of sense in the passage. Following the Septuagint this verse should be read: " Who is blind like my servants (plur. *i.e.* the Israelites), and deaf like their rulers? " (*i.e.* Jehoiakim, Jehoiachin, and Zedekiah,

---

[1] Mowinckel's careful study, *Die Komposition des deuterojesajanischen Buches,* in *ZATW,* 1931, pp. 87–112, 242–260, should be consulted.
[2] The R.V. paraphrases it: " and casteth (for it) silver chains."

largely owing to whose folly the Exile came about). The Septuagint, following the original form of the Hebrew text, makes the passage full of significance. Other illustrations could be given, and there are also a number of less important cases in which, following the Septuagint, a single word, emended, gives point to the text.

It will thus be realized how extremely important the Septuagint is for the study of these chapters. On the other hand, the Septuagint, in many instances, gives fantastic renderings, having clearly misunderstood the Hebrew. The outcome is that, while we cannot afford to do without the Septuagint, it must be used with caution and discrimination.[1]

---

[1] A valuable contribution is offered to the subject by Zillessen in *ZATW*, 1902, pp. 238–263; 1903, pp. 49–86.

ISAIAH LVI—LXVI (TRITO-ISAIAH)

I. Historical Background

The external history of the times to which these chapters belong, *i.e.* 538 B.C. onwards (see further § IV), does not offer any help in understanding them, nor does it throw any light on them. Nowhere is there any allusion to what was happening in the outside world; the suzerain power, so far as our knowledge goes, does not seem to have interfered with the Jews in any way to their detriment. Darius i (522–486 B.C.) was largely occupied with the organization of his empire into satrapies, with the Scythian and other campaigns, and later with wars against the Greeks. Practically the whole of the reign of Xerxes i (485–465 B.C.) was taken up with struggles against the Greeks on land and sea; these continued during the reign of Artaxerxes i (464–424 B.C.), who also had serious trouble with Egypt.

It can thus be well understood that the Persian rulers were too much occupied in other parts of their empire to concern themselves much about Palestine, nor was there any need for this, since the Jews were in no position to attempt to throw off Persian suzerainty; it is not until the reign of Artaxerxes iii (359–338 B.C.) that the Jews joined with others in revolt, the result of which was, however, disastrous for them.

Regarding the history of the Jews, so far as the period under consideration is concerned, our knowledge is but scanty; the important events were briefly these: in 537 B.C. a number of the exiles in Babylonia returned to Palestine under the leadership of Sheshbazzar. From 537 to 520 B.C. the historical books of the Old Testament give no information as to what took place. In 520 B.C. the rebuilding of the Temple was begun under the inspiration of Haggai and

277

Zechariah. The governor of Judah at that time was Zerub-babel—of Sheshbazzar nothing further is said; the High-priest was Joshua, the son of Jehozadak. The re-building of the Temple was completed in 516 B.C. Then again there is silence, so far as the historical books are concerned, until 444 B.C. when Nehemiah came to Jerusalem as governor of Judah. How long he occupied this position is not indicated, but it must have been for at least twelve years. The arrival of Ezra with a further contingent of returned exiles from Babylonia took place in 397 B.C.; but how long he worked among his people in Palestine is, again, not recorded. From the Elephantiné papyri we learn that in 408 B.C. Sanballat was still governor of Samaria, though his two sons, Delaiah and Shelemiah, acted for him, presumably on account of his advancing age. In the same year, we learn further that the governor of Judah was Bigvai (=Bagoas), and that the High-priest was Johanan, also written Jehohanan.

In view of these exiguous *data* it is the more to be welcomed that in Isa. lvi–lxvi a few incidental references to events in Judah may be gathered. The most important, from the religious-historical point of view, of these is what is said about a body of worshippers living among the Jews who were regarded as heretical (cp. Isa. lvii. 20). It is certain that many of the inhabitants of Judah, who had been left in the land when their brethren were led away into exile, were on friendly terms with the Samaritans and apparently joined in their worship, which was conducted in the Temple at Jerusalem (cp., *e.g.*, Neh. xiii. 28 ff.); their false worship is also spoken of in Isa. lviii. 1 ff., lxvi. 3, 4, and elsewhere; and we learn from such passages that the movement was in process of development which ultimately resulted in the definite break from Judaism known as the "Samaritan schism." It will, however, be realized that the evidence points to the fact that the Samaritans were joined by a certain number of their Jewish brethren in the south. The general state of things at this time was clearly deplorable; the religious leaders are represented as utterly unfit for their position, "blind," "without knowledge," and "dumb dogs," who dream and love to slumber; they are greedy, insatiable and intent upon gain (lvi. 9–12). As had so frequently happened before, the wealthy oppressed the poor (lviii. 7); so few are the righteous in the land that they threaten to disappear altogether (lvii. 1, 2). The worship is unreal and hypocritical; with bitter irony the prophet mocks at the external form of fasting which is deemed sufficient: "Is it to bow down his head as a rush, and to spread sackcloth and ashes under him?" (lviii. 5). The people place a bar between them and their God through their sins (lix. 1–4). The evidence of these chapters shows, therefore, that internal conditions in the land during this period (for the date see § IV) were, both socially and religiously, unhappy.

II. AUTHORSHIP OF ISA. LVI–LXVI

It has been held by some scholars that these chapters were written by the same author who wrote chs. xl–lv, chiefly because there are some notable instances of identity of thought and language in each (cp. especially chs. lx–lxii). That there are affinities between the two sets of chapters is undeniable; but, on the other hand, the differences in general outlook and religious thought, quite apart from style, between the two are so marked that it is impossible to believe that both can have come from the same author. The similarities between the two parts can be accounted for on the supposition that the writer of the later collection (lvi–lxvi) was influenced by Deutero-Isaiah, and that he adopted at times thoughts and expressions from his greater predecessor, not appearing to realize that they did not always harmonize with his less exalted ideas.

An examination of the various literary pieces which make up chs. lvi–lxvi will show that there are reasons for believing that they were written at different times. While there are good grounds for believing that most of these literary pieces are from the same author, it seems probable that a few of them were not his; but the opinions of scholars differ on the subject.

III. STRUCTURE AND CONTENTS

As in the case of chs. xl–lv, the last eleven chapters of our book consist of a number of independent literary pieces, and, like the former, they are almost wholly poetical in form. The difference of subject-matter contained in the various pieces makes it, as a rule, not difficult to separate them off; their contents are briefly as follows:

lvi. 1–8. Irregular metre; its original form is no longer to be identified. An exhortation to observe the Law; with a strongly universalistic outlook the prophet contemplates the reception into the congregation of Israel of non-Jews. All who observe the Sabbath and keep the covenant have a right to take part in the worship of the Temple.

lvi. 9–lvii. 13. The metre is variable; probably it was originally 3 : 3 alternating with *Qinah*. A denunciation against the religious leaders and against idolatrous worshippers within the Jewish community; the reference is to those who were in close touch with the Samaritans; we may see here the roots of what grew to be the " Samaritan schism."

lvii. 14–21. The metre is an almost regular 3 : 3, but the text is somewhat corrupt. The theme is the mercy of God on sinners who show a contrite heart; but for the wicked who persist in their wickedness there can be no rest.

lviii. The metre is the same as the preceding with but few irregularities due to textual corruption. A denunciation against the sins of the people exemplified by insincere worship and formalism, concluding with an exhortation to observe the Sabbath. Possibly several originally independent pieces have been combined here.

lix. The metre is again 3 : 3; but verse 21 is a prose conclusion.

A further denunciation of the sins of the people; the prophet rebukes the plea that Yahweh has no care for His people, and concludes with a promise that God will deliver the nation from its ills. The section is not a unity; verses 1–15a, consisting of three oracles (verses 1–4, 5–8, and 9–15a) are of an entirely different order from verses 15b–21,

the two pieces having been joined together by a late scribe.
The latter piece contains a good deal that is borrowed from
earlier writers.

lx. Verses 1–9 are 3: 3; verses 10–16 *Qinah*, with some
irregularity; verses 17–22 are again 3: 3 and *Qinah*, but not
consistently. A hymn celebrating the future glory of
Jerusalem; for the light of Yahweh shall shine upon it, and
the Gentiles shall flow into it; it concludes with an ideal
picture of a righteous people.

lxi. Verses 1–3 mainly 3: 3; verses 4–7 *Qinah*; verses
8–11 again 3: 3. The prophet's message of comfort to his
people.

lxii. 1–9. The metre alternates between 3: 3 and *Qinah*.
This piece is closely connected with the foregoing, the subject being the future glory of Zion.

lxii. 10–12. *Qinah*, but verse 10 is mutilated at the end,
something having fallen out.   The people are here addressed,
but the theme is again the future glory of Zion.   Verse 10
is reminiscent of xl. 3, upon which it is doubtless based.

lxiii. 1–6. The metre is 3: 3, but there are a few textual
corruptions. An independent poem. Yahweh is represented as coming from Edom, where He has overcome the
enemies of His people.

lxiii. 7–lxiv. 12.[1] Although this may be regarded as a
unity, the metre changes; lxiii. 7–17 are *Qinah*, though with
irregularity, while verses 18, 19 and lxiv. 7–12 are 3: 3;
but not invariably. The section is divided into two parts,
lxiii. 7–15, and lxiii. 16–lxiv. 12, but these are closely
connected, so that it may be regarded as a whole. The first
is a poem recognizing the divine mercy; the second is a
prayer on behalf of the people suffering through the attack
of an enemy.

lxv, lxvi. These chapters form a unity, but clearly marked
sections are discernible.

lxv. 1–7. *Qinah* (verses 1–5), followed by 3: 3 in verses
6, 7. A denunciation uttered against those who are prac-
tising a false worship. lxv. 8–12 are *Qinah* (verses 8–10),
followed by 3: 3 (verses 11, 12). The orthodox and the

[1] In the Hebrew text lxiv. 1 = 2 in the English Version.

schismatics contrasted. lxv. 13–25 are, with the exception
of verses 17, 18 (3 : 3), *Qinah*. The future of the schismatics
is contrasted with that of those who are loyal to Yahweh
and who will enjoy the happiness of the Messianic times
(verses 17–25). lxvi. 1–4, consisting of *Qinah* (verses 1, 2)
and 3 : 3 (verses 3, 4), records the intention of the schismatics
to build a temple of their own; but their false worship will
bring upon them the wrath of Yahweh. lxvi. 5–16 is mostly
Qinah, but verses 12 ff. seem to be prose. The punishment of
the schismatics, but the peace and happiness of those
faithful to Yahweh. After verse 5 it is probable that verses
17–24 should come, they seem to have been displaced;
these verses are in prose up to and including verse 21; the
last three verses are 3 : 3. This passage deals further with
the false worship of the schismatics, and the reward of the
faithful is again described.

IV. Date

Connected with the question of date is that of authorship, already dealt with; unity of authorship for these
chapters is insisted on by a number of eminent scholars,
while others dispute this. If we could be certain that the
whole of Isa. lvi–lxvi came from the prophet designated for
convenience' sake Trito-Isaiah, the question of date would
be simple. But there are certain indications appearing in
some of these sections which may point to a date later than
the time of this prophet.

There are two landmarks in early post-exilic times of
paramount importance, viz. the rebuilding of the Temple
completed in 516 B.C., and the advent of Nehemiah in
444 B.C.; owing to this reformer's influence and activity a
marked difference was created in the social and religious
life of the people. As a first step in seeking to date these
poems it will be well to gather from them any indications
which may point to their having been written within this
period (516–444 B.C.), or after it.

In the section lvi. 1–8 there are various passages which
show that the Temple had been rebuilt (verses 5–7), while

the universalistic attitude necessitates a date prior to the
advent of Nehemiah with his strongly nationalistic outlook.
A similar date, though for a different reason, must be
assigned to lvi. 9–lvii. 13; the state of the religious leaders,
the idolatrous worship, and the superstitious practices of the
people, here portrayed, would never have been tolerated by
Nehemiah; the section must, therefore, belong to a time
before his advent.   There is no direct mention of the Temple;
but its existence may well be implied in lvii. 13: " he that
putteth his trust in me shall possess the land, and shall in-
herit my holy mountain "—the mountain received its sanctity
from the presence of the Temple on it.   In the next section,
lvii. 14–21, verse 19 shows that the Temple had been rebuilt:
" I create the fruit of the lips," refers to divine grace on the
worshippers; the " fruit of the lips " means praise and thanksgiving; hence the existence of the Temple worship is implied.
Other verses in the poem (14, 17, 20) point to undesirable
elements among the people of a kind that Nehemiah would
not have permitted, so that the conditions suggest a time
before his arrival.   At first sight the words in verse 14,
" Cast ye up, cast ye up, prepare the way, take up the
stumbling-block[1] out of the way of my people," being so
reminiscent of xl. 3, 4, would suggest that the section
belonged to the eve of the Return; but that cannot be the
case; the Hebrew word for " stumbling-block " is used in
reference to those who are disturbing the religious life of the
faithful by a heretical form of worship—spoken of also in the
preceding section—they are like the troubled sea casting
up mire and dirt (verse 20).

In the next section there are indubitable signs of the
services of the Temple being regularly held (e.g. verse 2),
and the prophet's rebuke to the people for their wrong
spirit when keeping the fasts (verses 3–5), and for not observing the Sabbath (verse 13), points also to this.   That
it belongs to a time before the arrival of Nehemiah is evident
from this non-observance of the Sabbath (see Neh. xiii.
15–22); he would never have suffered the desecration

---

[1] The word is used mostly in a figurative sense; it occurs in a literal sense
in Lev. xix. 14.

referred to in verse 13. Moreover, verse 12 shows that the city walls had not yet been rebuilt, which is conclusive evidence for a period before Nehemiah's governorship.

For the next section (lix) see below.

The whole of lx–lxiii. 6, forming originally a separate collection, contains indications of the period to which it belongs similar to those accruing in the sections already dealt with: in lx. 13 the beautifying of the sanctuary is spoken of, showing that the Temple had been rebuilt; and lx. 10, 11; lxi. 4 make it clear that the walls of the city had not yet been rebuilt.

For the section lxiii. 7–lxiv. 12 see below.

Chs. lxv, lxvi, with the exception of lxvi. 5, 17–24 (see below), can be taken together as they have many features in common. That the Temple has been rebuilt is indicated by lxv. 11, lxvi. 1; the latter runs: " Thus saith Yahweh, The heaven is my throne, and the earth is my footstool; what manner of house would ye build for me, and what manner of place for my dwelling? " This does not mean that the Temple had not yet been built; the words must be understood in the same sense as those of i Kgs. viii. 27 ;[1] the context shows this, for verses 3, 4 speak of the impure sacrifices which were being offered. This idolatrous form of worship (see also lxv. 2–5, lxvi. 17), denounced also in some of the earlier sections, again points to a time before Nehemiah's arrival; such things would never have been tolerated by him.

All the sections referred to, and they constitute the bulk of " Trito-Isaiah," may thus be assigned to the period 516–444 B.C.; a more precise dating does not seem possible. There are three sections, however, which for reasons to be given, do not appear to belong to this period; they are:

lix. Of the three pieces contained in this chapter, verses 1–4 do not give any indication of date, and could belong to almost any time. But 5–8 would seem to be a later insertion. The liturgical character of verses 9–15a with the note of

---

[1] " But will God in very deed dwell on the earth? Behold, heaven and the heaven of the heavens cannot contain thee; how much less this house that I have builded."

confession points to a time at any rate after Ezra. The
section 15b–21 with its eschatological note in verse 19 must
also belong to a later time.

The section lxiii. 7–lxiv. 12 forms a complete whole,
though both as to this, as well as to the period to which it
belongs, opinions differ, some scholars holding that it is a
compilation. In lxiii. 17–19 it is said: " O Lord, why dost
thou make us to err from thy ways, and hardenest our heart
from thy fear (*i.e.* from fearing thee)? Return for thy
servants' sake the tribes of thine inheritance. Wherefore
have the ungodly despised thy temple,[1] and our adversaries
trodden down thy sanctuary? "

In connexion with this must be read also lxiv. 11, 12 (Hebr.
10, 11): " Our holy and beautiful house, where our fathers
praised thee, is burned with fire; and all our pleasant things
are laid waste. Wilt thou refrain thyself from these things,
O Lord? Wilt thou hold thy peace, and afflict us very
sore? " It is clear from these passages that the Temple had
suffered grievous damage; and were it not for the quite
obvious post-exilic character of the rest of the section, one
would naturally think of the 586 B.C. catastrophe.

But, as this seems out of the question, there are only two
other occasions to which reference can be made here: the
severe chastisement inflicted on the Jews by Artaxerxes iii
Ochus about 350 B.C., or the desecration of the Temple by
Antiochus iv in 169 B.C. as recorded in i Macc. i. 20–28.
This latter can, however, be ruled out, for in lxiii. 17 there
is an obvious allusion to a captivity; nothing in the nature
of a deportation occurred in the time of Antiochus iv, but
Artaxerxes iii carried captive " many ten thousands " of the
Jews to Hyrcania, on the shore of the Caspian Sea. It is
true that there is no reference to the desecration of the
Temple by the several ancient writers who record this
episode; but as these are all non-Jewish that is easily accounted for. The section lxiii. 7–lxiv. 12 may, therefore,
with considerable justification, be assigned to about the
year 350 B.C.

Finally, we come to the concluding section, lxvi. 17–24,

---

[1] Emended text: לָמָּה צָעֲרוּ רְשָׁעִים קָדְשֶׁה (Marti, Duhm).

to which verse 5 also belongs. Opinions again differ as to its date, and it seems difficult to reach a definite conclusion; all that can be said is that the universalistic attitude of verses 18–21, 23, and the eschatological nature of verses 22, 24, offer some grounds for assigning the section to the latter part of the fourth century.

The results of our investigation may be summarized thus:—By far the larger portion of these chapters are from the writer designated "Trito-Isaiah," the sections belonging to him being lvi. 9–lvii. 13; lvii. 14–21; lviii; lx–lxiii. 6; lxv; lxvi. 1–4, 6–16; all these pieces are to be assigned to the period between the years 516–444 B.C. The remaining sections, lix; lxiii. 7–lxiv. 12; lxvi. 5, 17–24, may be regarded as belonging probably to the latter half of the fourth century B.C.

V. THE HEBREW TEXT AND THE SEPTUAGINT

Though the text of "Trito-Isaiah" has not, upon the whole, been preserved in quite as pure a condition as that of "Deutero-Isaiah," it is, generally speaking, satisfactory. There are, it is true, serious defects here and there, and numerous small errors occur; a few displacements, notably lxvi. 17–24, are also to be noted; but, in spite of these, the text cannot be said, taking it as a whole, to be in a bad state. Redactional elements are to be discerned, but they are comparatively rare.

Nevertheless, the use of the Septuagint is very necessary, for although there are no passages of any length which in the Septuagint reflect a better form of text than that of the MT (lix. 17, which is rightly omitted by the Septuagint, is the longest), there are numerous cases in which just the difference of a word represents quite obviously a reading superior to that of the present Hebrew text, and makes the sense of a passage clearer. Sometimes, too, a word in the MT is not represented in the Septuagint, and the omission makes a better reading.[1]

[1] For the study of the Septuagint see Zillessen in *ZATW*, 1906, pp. 231–276.

VI. The Prophet and his Teaching

Apart from those elements for which the writer of these chapters was indebted to "Deutero-Isaiah," such as the omnipotence and unity of God, and universalism, there are various subjects dealt with which point to post-exilic times. To "Trito-Isaiah" the Temple, its sacrificial worship, and the Law, occupy a place of importance quite unrecognized by the earlier prophet.   In his denunciations of sin as the bar which separates Yahweh from His people, his call to repentance, and his insistence that there can be no forgiveness for those who lead unworthy lives and whose worship is insincere, "Trito-Isaiah" follows in the steps of the pre-exilic prophets.   There is in these chapters a strange alternation of threats of punishment and promises of a glorious future, due to the conditions of the time; evil spiritual leaders and irreligion among the people demand threats, while the prophet's optimistic hopes constantly assert themselves, doubtless one of the marks of "Deutero-Isaiah's" influence.   Here and there, as already indicated, apocalyptic elements are to be discerned, e.g. lx. 19, 20; in this and in other respects the prophet was influenced by Ezekiel; he also draws at times from the books of Isaiah and Jeremiah.   There is but little of originality of teaching about "Trito-Isaiah," but he lived at a time when the work of a prophet was intensely needed, and without his influence and teaching it is difficult to see how the Jews could have failed to sink down to the religious level of the surrounding peoples.

THE BOOK OF JEREMIAH

I. Place in the Canon

In the Hebrew Bible the book of *Jeremiah* stands second of the " Later Prophets," following *Isaiah* and preceding *Ezekiel*. There is, however, a Rabbinic tradition to the effect that it should come first of its group.[1] In the Septuagint, also, *Jeremiah* is usually placed between *Isaiah* and *Ezekiel*, though these three are preceded by the " Twelve." In the Peshitta *Jeremiah* stands immediately after the " *Twelve*," and the Vulgate follows the Hebrew order, retained in most modern versions.

II. Historical Background

The life and activity of Jeremiah fall in one of the great critical ages of history. His call to the prophetic ministry is dated in the year which saw the death of the last of the great kings of Assyria, Ashur-bani-pal (626 B.C.).[2] At once the empire began to break up. Babylonia asserted her independence, under the Chaldæan king Nabopolassar, and the great Scythian inroads shattered the northern defences. In 616 B.C. the new Babylonian power attacked the weak Assyria, and in 614 B.C., with the help of the Medes, they captured the old capital Ashur. The allies took and destroyed Nineveh itself in 612 B.C. and captured Harran, where resistance was still made, in 610 B.C. At this point our detailed knowledge of events breaks off, but we have grounds for believing that the last stand was made still further west, at Carchemish.

The period also saw a recrudescence of vitality in Egypt. The young king, Necho, cherished the hope of restoring the

---

[1] Cp. above, p. 233.
[2] Various attempts have been made to suggest another date, but none has secured any serious recognition.

old empire of the fifteenth and fourteenth centuries B.C., and definitely threw in his lot with Assyria, probably on the ground that she would now be too weak to injure him, while the Neo-Babylonian monarchy would prove a fatal obstacle to his ambitions. For several years he led armies into Mesopotamia, fighting with varied success. But he was unable to save Nineveh, and, in 605 B.C., he suffered a final defeat at Carchemish. This was the last occasion on which Egypt seriously grasped at world-hegemony, if we except a few spasmodic efforts in the age of the Ptolemies.

The Palestinian states had, previously, been forced to accept Egyptian dominion, but the result of Carchemish was an inevitable transfer of power to Babylon. Nebuchadrezzar, who succeeded his father, Nabopolassar, a few months after Carchemish, was satisfied with receiving tribute from the little kingdoms of the west; but, stirred up by Egyptian intrigues, they were restless and inclined to revolt. Nebuchadrezzar was forced to suppress such a rising in 597-6 B.C. Judah was implicated by Jehoiakim, but it seems that he died before an actual attack was made on the city, and it was his son, Jehoiachin, who surrendered and was carried captive to Babylon. Zedekiah, a younger brother of Jehoiakim, was placed on the throne. He was a weak ruler, and was unable to resist the nobles who were intriguing with Egypt against Babylon. The inevitable result was the invasion of Judah by the Chaldæans in 588 B.C., resulting in the capture of Jerusalem in 586 B.C.

The kingdom of Judah thus ceased to exist, crushed by the advancing power of Babylon. Palestine had suffered, as it seems, from the Scythian invasion in or about 626 B.C. Some of the oracles of Jeremiah fit this invasion better than any other, and it seems that Zephaniah was also faced with the same conditions. In 621 B.C. Josiah carried through his great reform, based on a law-book found in the Temple,[1] and we may regard his action as having a political, as well as a religious, aspect. Since it involved the eradication of all foreign cults, it was, in fact, a gesture of independence of Assyria. Thirteen years later (608 B.C.) he met his death at

[1] See above, pp. 57 f., 65.

U

the hands of Necho, who was ostensibly on the Assyrian side. The people passed over his eldest son and placed the second, Jehoahaz, on the throne. On his return from that year's Mesopotamian expedition, Necho deposed Jehoahaz, and took him in chains to Egypt, setting his elder brother Jehoiakim on the throne. The new king was a vigorous and unscrupulous tyrant, who oppressed his people much as Solomon had done. It would seem that some of the results achieved by the Deuteronomic reform were now reversed, and Judah went back to many of her old ways.

On the destruction of the city of Jerusalem, and the absorption of Judah into the Babylonian empire, Nebuchadrezzar appointed Gedaliah, of the family of Shaphan, governor of the country. He made his headquarters at Mizpah, and remained there for a period whose duration we cannot determine with certainty. It was, however, probably four or five years. He was eventually assassinated by a representative of the old royal house, Ishmael by name, on the instigation of the Ammonites, and the last remnants of the governing body fled to Egypt, in fear of vengeance from Babylon.

III. Contents

The book of *Jeremiah* is a combination of several collections of oracular material, with others, giving an account of events which took place in the prophet's lifetime and with some descriptions of the prophet's own experiences. A detailed account of its contents, however, can be appreciated only in connexion with the study of its structure.

IV. Structure and Date

The book of *Jeremiah*, like *Isaiah*, is a compilation in which all three types of source[1] have been freely used. The method adopted by its compiler, however, is quite different from that employed in *Isaiah*. In this latter book the material of each kind is more or less grouped together, while in *Jeremiah* passages from the one alternate with the others.

[1] See below.

Not infrequently the prose passages have a heading, giving the date or some other circumstance, and this is almost invariable where a prose passage precedes a group of oracular material. Once or twice a heading is followed first by type A and then by type B or C, but the other is the usual order. Occasionally little scraps of prose are found in the middle of oracular sections, and *vice versa*. The general distribution of the three types is as follows:

A	B	C
(Oracular Poetry).	(Prose in the 3rd person).	(Prose in the 1st person).
i. 15–iii. 5.		i. 1–14.
iii. 19–vi. 30.		iii. 6–18.
viii. 4–x. 25.		vii. 1–viii. 3.[1]
xi. 15–xii. 17.		xi. 1–14.
xiii. 15–27.		xiii. 1–14.
xiv. 1–10.		xiv. 11–16.
xiv. 17–xvii. 18.		xvii. 19–27.
xviii. 13–23.		xviii. 1–12.
xx. 7–18.	xix. 1–xx. 6.	
	xxi. 1–10.	
xxi. 11–14.		xxii. 1–5.
xxii. 6–xxiii. 40.	xxvi.	xxiv.
xxv. 30–36.	xxix.	xxv. 1–29.
xxx. 4–xxxi. 22.	xxx. 1–3.	xxvii.
xlvi–li. 58.	xxxiii.	xxviii.
	xxxiv.	xxxi. 23–40.
	xxxvi–xlv.	xxxii.
	li. 59–64.	xxxv.
	lii.	

We now turn to the headings which appear from time to time in the book. These are found in the following places: i. 1, ii. 1,[2] iii. 6, vii. 1,[2] xi. 1, xiii. 1, xiv. 1, xvii. 19, xviii. 1, xxi. 1, xxv. 1, xxvi. 1, xxvii. 1, xxviii. 1, xxix. 1, xxx. 1, xxxii. 1, xxxiii. 1, xxxiv. 1, xxxiv. 8, xxxv. 1, xxxvi. 1, xxxvii. 1, xxxix. 1, xl. 1, xliii. 8, xliv. 1, xlv. 1, xlvi. 1. It will be seen at once that in the earlier parts of the book these headings occur most often at the beginning of prose passages

---

[1] Except for the heading in vii. 1 (where the prophet is mentioned in the third person, and this may be due either to redaction or to accidental corruption of the text; a similar heading is found in xviii. 1 and xxvii. 1, though both passages are clearly C, not B), there is no *formal* indication of the type to which this passage belongs. But in character it identifies itself with C rather than with B, and a part of it clearly refers to the same occasion as xxvi, which is obviously B. We thus have a reference to the same event from the two types of source.

[2] Not found in the text of the Septuagint.

which are followed by poetical pieces. Later, when the poetical portions have practically come to an end, they occur in the course both of B and of C groups. This seems to imply that the compiler had before him collections of B and C material, divided into sections, all of which had headings of some kind, many of them being dated. These headings were no part of the original pieces, since in more than one instance the heading of a C passage is in the third person, *e.g.* in xviii. 1, xxv. 1, xxvii. 1 and xxxv. 1. It is possible that some of the oracular sections had such headings, and one may survive from this source in xiv. 1. This, however, is the only case in which a poetical section precedes the prose which is linked up with it.

These facts give us a clue to the methods of the compiler. He had before him a number of little collections of oracular material in poetry, some of which had prose appendices or expansions of no great length. He had also a collection of descriptive material from the hand of a biographer, and a similar collection of passages in the first person, mainly consisting of oracular material worked over into rhetorical prose form.[1]

His method was to take each small collection, or group of oracular utterances, and to prefix to it a suitable selection from one of the two prose collections. We may safely assume that if he had had but a single poetic collection, he would have made it more continuous, and the result would have been a book much more like that of *Isaiah* in general appearance. For his purpose he preferred passages of the C type, and used but little of the B class until the others were nearly all exhausted. It is not until we reach ch. xix that we have a B passage. It seems probable that the collection of C passages was much fuller for the earlier period of Jeremiah's ministry, though it included passages dating from the final siege of Jerusalem, while the B passages cover the later period only. The first of the latter (ch. xix) has no heading, while the second (xxi. 1–10) is dated

---

[1] In one illuminating passage, xxii. 10–12, we have the two side by side, first the poetic oracle, and then a prose version of it. In this instance the compiler has displaced the prose verses from their original setting in order to combine them with the poetic form.

in the reign of Zedekiah. Ch. xxvi is dated at the beginning of the reign of Jehoiakim (608–597 B.C.), but there is little else of this type that can be placed earlier than the fourth year of that king's reign, *i.e.* the time of the battle of Carchemish, when the Egyptian power was finally broken, and Babylon became the one great world-power.

i. *Structure of A sections.* We may now note in rather more detail the contents of the various little oracular collections which have been utilized by the main compiler. We can distinguish no less than fourteen in all, none of them as long as the majority of those preserved in *Isaiah* and, perhaps, in some other books. They are as follows:

(*a*) i. 15–iii. 5.[1] The first two of the pieces included here may not have belonged to the original collection. The first (i. 15–16) evidently owes its position to its suitability as a sequel to the vision of the boiling pot, and the second forms a natural conclusion to the story of Jeremiah's call to the prophetic ministry. The remainder, however, consists of utterances which may all belong to the earlier part of the prophet's work, either before or during the Deuteronomic reform. We may distinguish the following: ii. 2–3, 5–8 (verse 4 is clearly a collector's note), 9–12, 13 (probably mutilated at the end), 14–17, 18–19, 20–22, 23–24, 25 (a fragment), 26–29, 30–31a (only the beginning of this piece has been preserved), 31b–33, 34–35, 36–37, iii. 1 (this is prosaic in form, and may include a commentator's explanation as well as a fragment of an original oracle), 2–5.

Throughout all these oracles the influence of Hosea seems to be particularly strong, inasmuch as most of them present the relation between Yahweh and Israel as that of husband and wife. They are best assigned to a time not later than the reform of Josiah, and there is nothing to indicate that the compilation itself was made late.

(*b*) iii. 19–vi. 30. The separate pieces included here seem to have been: iii. 19–20, 21–22, 23–25, iv. 1–2, 3–4 (modified by addition at the end, unless it be mutilated),

[1] The " title " in ii. 1–2 is absent from the Septuagint, and may well be a scribal addition. See below on the Hebrew text, pp. 312 f.

5–8, 9–12 (worked over and recast as prose, though clear
signs of the original poetic form are to be seen, especially
in vv. 11 f.), 13–17, 18 (possibly a fragment); 19–21 (to
which 22 has been appended), 23–26, 27–28, 29–31, v. 1–6,
7, 8–9, 10–13 (this has probably been expanded towards
the end), 15–17 (with a prose introduction in 14 and conclusion in 18–19, the style of which suggests the age of
Malachi), 20–25 (much worked over near the beginning),
26, 27, 28–29, 30–31, vi. 1–5, 6–8, 9–12, 13–15 (mutilated
at the beginning; the complete form appears in viii. 10–12),
16–19, 20, 21, 22–26, 27–30. Many of the pieces in this
collection date from a time of foreign invasion, possibly that
of the Chaldæans in 596 B.C. or 587 B.C., but more probably
that of the Scythians in 626 B.C. While there is nothing
which we cannot ultimately ascribe to Jeremiah, several
of the pieces have been worked over and recast, and there
appear to be traces of the style of the age of Malachi. It
is possible that we must date the final form of this collection
as late as the end of the fifth century B.C. It may here be
noted that the last piece but one (vi. 22–26) appears in
l. 41–43, in a form which has been mutilated and adapted
to Babylon instead of to Jerusalem.

(c) viii. 4–x. 25. We may note the following pieces:
viii. 4–7, 8–9, 10–12, 13–14 (with a verse taken from xiv.
19 appended), 16–18, 19–23, ix. 1–2, 3–5, 6–8, 9–10, 11–13,
14–15, 16–18, 19–21, 22–23, 24–25, x. 1–10 (a late passage
which has received considerable accretions since the translation of the Septuagint, and is followed by an Aramaic
verse which must be a late addition), 12–16 (an extended
doxology, probably post-exilic, which appears again in
li. 15–19), 17 (a fragment), 18 (probably also a fragment),
19–21, 22, 23–25.

While there are portions of this collection which are
certainly due to Jeremiah, there are others which are
equally certainly derived from a much later source,
especially in ch. x. The first sixteen verses cannot be
earlier than the Exile, and may well be much later. The
curious Aramaic verse (x. 11) is apparently a sort of charm
to be used by pious Jews when confronted with heathen

gods. We cannot place this collection earlier than the end of the fifth century, and it is probably somewhat later still.

(*d*) xi. 15–xii. 17. This section includes pieces which, though resembling the usual oracles in their poetic form, yet differ from them in that they tell us of the prophet's inner experiences rather than of his message to his people. These are among the most valuable and important passages in the book. The collection, however, includes other oracles as well: xi. 15–17 (text corrupt and often obscure), 18–20, 22–23 (verse 21 is introductory to this), xii. 1–3, 4–6 (possibly not originally a single piece), 7–13 (this has been considerably modified at the end, but it is no longer possible to restore the actual conclusion of the original oracle), 14–17 (a promise of a restoration which, in its present form, can hardly be pre-exilic, though its basis seems to have been originally the work of Jeremiah).

Here again, amid much that is obscure and uncertain, we have some undoubted utterances of Jeremiah, and unmistakable signs of a much later worker. While the collection cannot be very early, it need not be placed much later than the return from the Exile.

(*e*) xiii. 15–27. This contains only two poems, the first (15–16) being a rather vague warning, and the second (17–27) a denunciation and threat against the king and the queen-mother, especially the latter. It would seem that an attempt has been made to transfer the threat from the queen-mother to the city of Jerusalem, but the real character of the poem is quite clear.

The prominence given to the queen-mother makes it practically certain that the second poem comes from the short reign of Jehoiachin (597–6 B.C.). The other might be from almost any period, though its style suggests Jeremiah himself.

(*f*) xiv. 1–10. Verses 2–6 describe a drought, and the remainder seems to be a prayer of national confession, possibly used in some ritual which was intended to secure the favour of Yahweh in such a time.

There is no clue to the dates, except that the interest

shown in wild life in the former poem would be quite characteristic of Jeremiah, and inclines us to accept his authorship of it.

(g) xiv. 17–xvii. 18. This is another of the sections in which we have material describing Jeremiah's immediate experience in his dealings with Yahweh. xiv. 17–22 forms a prayer for deliverance, followed by xv. 1–4 (an oracle much worked over), 5–9, 10–14 (the original form much expanded, partly by the inclusion in 13, 14 of material also found in xvii. 3–4), 15–18, 19–21, xvi. 1–4, 5–8, 9, 10–13 (much modified), 14–18 (a prose passage apparently from near the close of the exile), 19–21, xvii. 1–4 (modified and worked over), 5–8 (a psalm which forms the basis of Ps. i), 9–10, 11, 12–13 (the last two mere fragments), 14–18.

(h) xviii. 13–23. This seems to contain only two pieces, 13–17 and 18–23, the latter being an imprecation on Jeremiah's personal enemies.

(i) xx. 7–18. The little collection opens with Jeremiah's complaint in 7–10, to which fragments from various sources have been appended in 11, 12, and 13. Verses 14–18 were the model for Job iii.

(j) xxi. 11–14. A single oracle which may have been originally included in the next collection; it has received additions to its original form.

(k) xxii. 6–xxiii. 40. The nucleus of this collection is a group of oracles dealing with the various kings contemporary with Jeremiah. The opening section, 6–7, is a mutilated oracle, which has been continued in prose. This is followed by other oracles in 10–12 (Jehoahaz), 13–17, 18–19 (Jehoiakim), 20–23 (Judah in general), 24–27, 28–29, 30 (all three refer to Jehoiachin, though they have been worked over and are now prose in form). Ch. xxiii. 1–8 consists of a group of Messianic prophecies, which seem to have been gathered round 5–6. These last may be a relic of a dirge over Zedekiah, promising a better king whose name shall be the reverse of his. Verses 7–8 have appeared already in xvi. 14–15. The remainder of the chapter is a conglomeration of utterances, mostly small fragments, which have the prophets as their subject. As usual in such cases, a few oracles are clearly defined near the beginning of the little collection, *e.g.* 9–11, 13–15, 21–22, 23–24, 25–29 (much modified), 33–40 (also much worked over).

(*l*) xxv. 30–36. Evidently taken from a collection of oracles dealing with foreign nations, perhaps that which is now found in chs. xlvi–li. It contains several more or less fragmentary pieces: 30–31, 32–33, 34–36.

(*m*) xxx. 4–xxxi. 22. This collection owes its position in the book to the fact that it is primarily composed of promises of a happy future. This, however, is not the only type of oracle found in it, though the gloomy utterances tend to have a happy ending affixed to them. Thus we have: xxx. 4–7 (with 8–9 appended), 10–11, 12–15 (text very doubtful in parts), 16–17, 18–21, 22, 23–24 (also found in xxiii. 23–24), xxxi. 2–6, 7–9, 10–14, 15–17, 18–20, 21–22.

While there is a good deal in this collection which suggests the tone of the later years of the Exile, there is also a certain amount of material which we can certainly attribute to Jeremiah.

(*n*) xlvi–li. A collection of oracles dealing with foreign nations. Each group contains several oracles, and the phenomena of their composition resemble those of the other collections. The nations dealt with are as follows: Egypt (xlvi. 1–26, with an appendix in vv. 27 f., which is also found in xxx. 10 f.), Philistia (xlvii. 1–7), Moab (xlviii. 1–47, including passages also found in Isa. xv, xvi), Ammon (xlix. 1–6), Edom (xlix. 7–22, including two oracles also found in *Obadiah*), Damascus (xlix. 23–27), Kedar (xlix. 28–33), Elam (xlix. 34–39), and Babylon (l. 1–li. 58).

This brief outline survey of the general structure of the book has made certain facts evident. Of these we may select three as being the most significant for the history of the book, and, indeed, of much of the prophetic literature. The first is the brevity of most of the independent pieces we have isolated from one another. To some extent this is due to the "scrappiness" of the material which the various collectors found ready to their hands. There are many mutilated pieces; sometimes we have definite proof

of the fact in the appearance of a fuller form, either in this
or in some other book. In many cases we have nothing
but brief fragments, whose original context it is impossible
to guess, and these have been flung together, almost haphazard, by some of the collectors. There is more of this
type of material in *Jeremiah* than in any other prophetic
book, and it tends to make exegesis difficult and uncertain.

The second point which strikes us is the frequency with
which we meet with little prose pieces in the midst of what
are, otherwise, poetical collections. Naturally, there is
seldom, if ever, enough evidence to show whether the
prophet was mentioned in the first or in the third person
in these small sections, but, since they consist of messages
and not descriptions of events, they attach themselves more
readily to the C type than to the B type. They are, in
fact, oracles which were probably once poetic in form but
written down in prose form before the formation of the
collections. Often we have snatches of the poetic rhythm
and parallelism in these pieces, and in one instance (xxii.
10–12) we have the two forms side by side, and can see
something of the process which resulted in these " prose
oracles."

There is one feature of these pieces which deserves special
notice. The style and language in which they are cast
is usually reminiscent of *Deuteronomy*, especially of the
hortatory portions of that work. It has been usual to suspect
that they, or many of them, were produced by the " Deuteronomic School," but a little consideration will show that
this hypothesis is not necessary to account for the facts.
The so-called " Deuteronomic style " is simply the form
which Hebrew rhetorical prose took in the latter part of
the seventh century and the first part of the sixth. The
aims and ideas expressed in these passages would often
be acceptable to the compilers of *Deuteronomy*, but that is
not inconsistent with their being ultimately of Jeremianic
origin.[1] We are justified in believing that these passages
were originally poetic oracles, many of them uttered by

---

[1] For the relation between Jeremiah and the Deuteronomic position see
below, pp. 307 ff.

Jeremiah himself, which have been reduced to prose (and expanded in the process), either when they were first written down, or at some point in their transmission. The former is the more likely explanation.

The third point which strikes us at once is the number of oracles and fragments in *Jeremiah* which occur elsewhere, either in this or in other books. We have passages which are common to *Jeremiah* and *Isaiah* (especially in the Moabite sections, Isa. xv–xvi and Jer. xlviii), and others which are found in *Jeremiah* and *Obadiah* (among the oracles on Edom, Jer. xlix. 7–22). We have a fair number of parallel passages in the book of *Jeremiah* itself. The most striking of these is the parallel vi. 22–26 = l. 41–43, where, by a very slight change, the same oracle is made to refer to both Judah and to Babylon. Further, the form in ch. l has been mutilated at the end, though in other respects its text seems to have been rather better preserved. These facts lead us to the conclusion that, in the age when the collections were made, a great deal of the oracular matter attributed to Jeremiah was fairly widely known, and that independent collectors found a number of " floating " oracles, in whose Jeremianic authorship they had reason to believe.

ii. *Dating of A collections.* In our brief survey of the material contained in the oracular sections of *Jeremiah* we have had occasion to note, from time to time, that certain sections cannot be attributed to the prophet himself, and that, therefore, some of the collections must be exilic or post-exilic. The most obvious case of a late date is to be found in x. 1–16, which is almost universally regarded as being fairly late post-exilic. Few commentators to-day would be prepared to argue for a date earlier than the end of the fifth century, and to many this would seem far too early. The fact that it is followed by fragments whose Jeremianic authorship is hardly disputed, shows that it cannot be merely a late appendage to its collection, but must have been included in the original form. Another passage on which there would be general agreement is xvii. 21–27 (insistence on the observance of the Sabbath). This inevitably reminds us of Nehemiah's regulations on the same subject, and may well come from his time, or, perhaps, a little later. While it is impossible to fix with any certainty on a period for the compilation of the collections, we may safely say that some of them cannot have existed (in the form in which they came into the hands of the main compiler of the book) until the end of the fifth century or the beginning of the fourth.

iii. *B sections : contents, date, and authorship.* We may now turn to the passages we have classed as type B, which consist of narratives describing the events in the life of the prophet, making no claim to have been written by himself, and containing little of his message, except so much as is necessary to explain or illustrate the events recorded. Most of the incidents are carefully dated. The first of these pieces (xix. 1–xx. 6), however, lacks both introduction and date, and describes Jeremiah's breaking of the clay vessel over the valley of Hinnom, together with the resultant imprisonment by Pashhur. It contains rather more of the preaching of Jeremiah than the majority of the passages in this class, and the " Deuteronomic " style is evident in the prophet's utterances.   xxi. 1–10 records a message given by Jeremiah in answer to an inquiry by Zedekiah. Ch. xxvi contains an account of an address given by Jeremiah in the Temple, early in the reign of Jehoiakim. The occasion is clearly the same as that indicated in the opening verses of ch. vii, and some commentators have gone so far as to attempt a reconstruction in which both passages are used. But, while ch. vii gives a much fuller account of what Jeremiah said, ch. xxvi narrates the effect of his utterance and the peril into which it brought him. It is noticeable that we have here the only instance in which one of our canonical prophets is expressly quoted by name in the work of another— there is a direct reference to Mic. iii. 12 in verse 18. Ch. xxix describes a letter written by Jeremiah to certain exiles in Babylon after the deportation of Jehoiachin. In xxx. 1–3 we have little more than an expanded heading for what follows, but the order to write down the prophecies which follow may justify us in classing the verses with this type of material. Ch. xxxiii gives, in another form, the message of ultimate hope already communicated in the preceding chapter. It is to be noted that from verse 14 onwards this passage has no representation in the Septuagint, which suggests that the latter part of the chapter is a very late addition. Ch. xxxiv dates from the final siege of Jerusalem, and the latter part (from verse 8 onwards) deals with those who liberated their slaves during the siege, only to claim them again when the Chaldæans had temporarily departed. In ch. xxxvi we have the account of the way in which Jeremiah's prophecies were first written down, of the burning of the document by Jehoiakim, and the preparation of a new roll. This is dated in the fourth year of Jehoiakim, *i.e.* the year of the battle of Carchemish. Chs. xxxvii–xlv give a nearly continuous record of events, especially those in which Jeremiah was most concerned, from the early part of the final siege of Jerusalem until the flight of the last remnant and their settlement in Egypt. It closes with a pronouncement of a final breach between Yahweh and Judah. Ch. xlv records a private oracle given to Baruch; li. 59–64 records a journey taken by Zedekiah to Babylon in the fourth year of his reign. Jeremiah sends a copy of oracles he has uttered against Babylon; these are to be read and then sunk in the Euphrates. The Jeremianic authorship of the surviving oracles against Babylon is a matter of very serious doubt, and we have no other record of, or reference to, this visit of Zedekiah's to Babylon, either from Israelite or from other sources. The originality, therefore, of this passage has been widely contested, and it is generally held to be a piece of " Midrash " attached by a later hand to the " Babylonian " oracle collection. Finally, ch. lii is an extract, either from ii Kgs. xxiv. 18 ff., or from a source employed by the writer of that section. It adds a certain number of details to the record as we now have it in *Kings*, and may represent an earlier form of the source. It has little or nothing to do with Jeremiah himself.

Except for certain obvious additions and expansions, this collection of the " Acts of Jeremiah " has all the marks of being the work of a contemporary, and there are good grounds for the general opinion that Baruch was the writer. It will suffice to mention two of them. It was in the fourth year of Jehoiakim (*i.e.* the year of the battle of Carchemish), as far as we know, that Baruch came into official contact with Jeremiah. Only one incident recorded in this collection can be placed earlier than this date, and that is the attempt made by the religious leaders of the people to put Jeremiah to death after his address in the Temple. Here we have a date given to us in the early part of the reign of Jehoiakim. The incident was a very public one, and Baruch must have been aware of the details—as every other inhabitant of Jerusalem would have been. The probability thus created by the general body of the collection becomes a practical certainty when we note that it includes a private oracle delivered to Baruch himself. It is hardly likely that another would have known of this, and still less likely that he would have troubled to record it.

While the greater part of this collection consists of narrative, there is still a certain amount of space devoted to the actual message delivered by Jeremiah. If we may judge by the one instance in which we can form a comparison, *i.e.* that of the parallels between chs. vii and xxvi, the utterances of the prophet were condensed and abbreviated. Nevertheless, the whole carries the stamp of the " Deuteronomic " style. This is less obvious in the narrative portions, since the plain telling of a story, in the simple style imposed by the very nature of Hebrew syntax, does not leave very much room for wide differences. But where the words of the prophet are recorded the style is unmistakable. As we have seen, this " Deuteronomic " style is nothing more than the form which Hebrew rhetorical prose took from the middle of the seventh century and for some time onwards. Every consideration points to the same general conclusion as to date and authorship of this " biography " of Jeremiah.

iv. *C Sections : contents, origin, and date.* This group of material opens, appropriately enough, with the call of the prophet, followed by two introductory visions (i. 1–14). The next passage (iii. 6–18) is dated in the time of Josiah, and is either connected with, or earlier than, the Deutero-

nomic reform. It shows strongly the influence of Hosea.
In vii. 1–viii. 3 we have a series of utterances which begins
with the " Temple-sermon," and is dated by the parallel
in ch. xxvi in the early part of the reign of Jehoiakim. The
latter part of this section, from vii. 21 onwards, is devoted
to condemnation of the *cultus,* especially of sacrifices in
various forms. Ch. xi. 1–14, apparently, is a statement
of Jeremiah's early attitude towards the Reform. Ch.
xiii. 1–14 falls into two parts, of which the first recounts
Jeremiah's acted parable of the girdle, and the second is a
prophetic application of a popular saying. Since the
oracular matter which immediately follows belongs to the
short reign of Jehoiachin, it is possible that the compiler
attributed these two passages to the same time. In xiv.
11–16 we have a short denunciation of insincere worship,
xvii. 19–27 insists on Sabbath observance. The passage
looks late, and may come from the time of Nehemiah.
Ch. xviii. 1–12 (supplied with a heading which speaks of
Jeremiah in the third person) gives Jeremiah's parable of
the potter and the clay. Ch. xxii. 1–5 is a general introduction to the group of oracles on the kings. The vagueness of its language suggests a comparatively late date.
Ch. xxiv, which comes from the reign of Zedekiah, records
the vision of the two baskets of figs, and draws the contrast
between the exiles and those who remain in Jerusalem.
In xxv. 1–29 (like ch. xviii supplied with a heading) we
have a group of utterances belonging to the critical year
of Carchemish, in which first the consequences to Judah
of the epoch-making battle are indicated, and then the
results for the rest of Jeremiah's world are described. From
the beginning of the reign of Zedekiah (so read for " Jehoiakim " in xxvii. 1) we have chs. xxvii, xxviii, a series of
utterances in which Jeremiah sought to impress on his people
the supremacy of the Chaldæans, and the necessity of remaining loyal to them. The immediate occasion was the
prediction of certain prophets, especially of Hananiah,
that Babylon would shortly fall and Jehoiachin and his
fellow-exiles be restored. Ch. xxxi. 23–40 consists of a
group of utterances concerning the happy future of Judah,

which probably Jeremiah expected under the rule of Gedaliah, after the fall of Jerusalem. It includes the great prophecy of the New Covenant. Ch. xxxii tells the story of the purchase of a piece of land by Jeremiah during the final siege of Jerusalem. Finally, ch. xxxv draws a lesson for all the people from the fidelity of the Rechabites. This is dated in the reign of Jehoiakim.

It is at once obvious that these passages are no longer in their original order—if that order was chronological. In contrast to the B passages there is comparatively little that can be placed after the year of Carchemish. The tone and style are strongly " Deuteronomic," though there are passages, such as vii. 21 ff., which suggest that the prophet did feel, at some time in his life, that the Reform had not gone far enough. He would have abolished sacrifices altogether, and would have secularized the " burnt-offering " as well as the " peace-offering."

The Deuteronomic flavour which these passages carry with them has led some modern commentators [1] to believe that they had, for the most part, nothing to do with Jeremiah whatever, but that they were the free inventions of the Deuteronomic school, who sought to use the name of the prophet to secure acceptance for their own views and theories. Even so, there are several passages whose Jeremianic authorship is universally admitted; no one has denied the " authenticity " of i. 1–14. And when the remainder are more closely examined, it will be seen that the question of authorship is not to be dismissed in summary fashion. Granted that there are passages which are probably due to a much later age than that of Jeremiah, there remain a number, probably the larger number, against which no real objection can be urged. It may at once be admitted that the style is Deuteronomic, but, as we have observed more than once, this is no more than the rhetorical prose of the period, which begins about the time of Jeremiah and extends probably till after the Return. As we have seen, the style of the B passages, almost universally accepted as the work of a contemporary, is also strongly Deutero-

---

[1] Particularly Duhm, Mowinckel and Hölscher.

nomic. We meet from time to time with words, phrases, metaphors, ideas which are not to be paralleled in the Deuteronomic literature, strictly so called, *i.e.* in *Deuteronomy* itself, or in the Deuteronomic framework of the historical books.[1] And certainly the Deuteronomists would not have approved of Jeremiah's attitude towards sacrifice.[2]

We have, however, more direct evidence of the comparatively early date of some of these passages in the relation which they bear to *Ezekiel*. The latter book has been subjected to some very drastic criticisms of late, but the passages universally recognized as original include chs. xviii and xxiii. When these are compared with Jer. xxxi. 29–30 and iii. 6–11 respectively there can hardly be any doubt that the *Ezekiel* passages are based on those found in *Jeremiah*—in fact they look like sermons on the *Jeremiah* texts.[3]

We must not, however, assume that every section and sentence we find in this type is to be accepted *ipso facto* as being from *Jeremiah*. Each must be judged on its merits, and there is a good deal which a commentator would wish to refer to a time long after that of Jeremiah. In iii. 14–17, for instance, we have a passage which, at the earliest, belongs to the close of the Exile, and may be post-exilic. It has been inserted in the collection in the place where it now stands on account of the use of the words " return " and " backsliding "—both being derived from the same Hebrew root. We may even suspect that these verses were written by a scribe of a later age for the position they now occupy. And in most of the sections that we have we may suspect, occasionally, a later addition; the most obvious, xvii. 21–27, has already been mentioned.

When, then, we speak of the " origin " of these passages, we must think of the original form, the nucleus around which the final structure was built up. The material is clearly the " prose oracle." We have no reason to doubt that, when an oracle was first uttered, it was poetic in form,

---

[1] As a single instance we may take the use of the word " conspiracy " in xi. 9.   [2] Cp. vii. 21–26.

[3] For a discussion of one of the main grounds for rejecting these passages (the attitude of Jeremiah to the Deuteronomic reform), see below, pp. 307 ff.

x

and that a prose edition of it would come only later, possibly when it was written down. We have already referred to xxii. 10–12, where we have both forms, a short, yet full, poetic utterance, followed by an expansion in prose of the latter part of it.

If we may hazard a conjecture as to the origin of this collection of C passages, we may surmise that it is to be found in the " roll " which Baruch wrote at Jeremiah's dictation in 605 B.C. (see Jer. xxxvi).[1] It has been usual to try to reconstruct this document by putting together all the oracles which seem to have been delivered before 605 B.C. This, naturally, leaves room for subjectivity in determining the dates of the various passages. Our present suggestion does not wholly eliminate this possibility, since there certainly are some passages in the C collections which are later than Jeremiah. But we are on more solid ground when we recognize that such a document as that prepared by Baruch will probably have been couched in the rhetorical prose of the age, and that the scribe is very likely to have prefixed from time to time such headings as we have in vii. 1, xviii. 1 and xxi. 1–2. The greater number of the oracles included in this collection belong to the period which closed with the battle of Carchemish—the time at which they were first written down—but, as we are expressly told in xxxvi. 32, in the second edition of the roll " there were added besides unto them many like words." This surely means that the process was continued after 605 B.C., and that, so long as Jeremiah and Baruch were associated, additions were made from time to time to the roll. As we hear in xliii. 3, the connexion between the prophet and the scribe lasted till after the fall of Jerusalem. At the same time, many of Jeremiah's utterances were heard and remembered in the usual way, and were handed down by oral tradition till they were included in various oracle-collections.

v. *The main compilation.* As we have seen, there appear to be three main collections lying behind our present book of *Jeremiah*. All three of them contain material which must

---

[1] Cp. T. H. Robinson, *Baruch's Roll*, in *ZATW*, 1924, pp. 209–221.

be a good deal later than the prophet himself; some of it may be as late as the early part of the fourth century B.C., and it is to that century to which we can most safely assign the main compilation. Even then the book was subject to additions and alterations, though most of these can be ascribed to the zeal of the scribes who copied them. There are, however, instances of longer insertions, *e.g.* xxxiii. 14-26, which must be deliberate enlargements of the book. Moreover, we have reason to suspect that the collection of oracles against foreign nations was not included in the book till a much later period still—after the divergence of the Palestinian and Egyptian texts.

V. Jeremiah and the Reforms of Josiah

In attempting to understand Jeremiah's position there is one point which requires fuller mention. This is the relation of the prophet to the Deuteronomic reform. A number of modern scholars—it is enough to mention Duhm and Kennett—believe that Jeremiah could not possibly have approved of a movement which permitted sacrifice still to continue. His utterance in vii. 21, " Add your burnt offerings unto your sacrifices and eat ye flesh," is interpreted as a universal condemnation of sacrifice. The limitation of sacrifice to a single altar would not satisfy Jeremiah; he would have had neither victims nor altar, but a purely spiritual form of worship. It is true that in ch. xi Jeremiah appears to be an enthusiastic supporter of the Reform, but ch. xi is among the C sections whose authenticity is so widely suspected. (Incidentally, it may be pointed out that ch. vii usually falls under the same condemnation as ch. xi.) But in ch. viii. 8 we have a less equivocal expression of opinion, " How do ye say, We are wise, and the law of the Lord is with us ? But, behold, the false pen of the scribes hath wrought falsely." In other words, Jeremiah believed that *Deuteronomy*, the first law-book of which we know that it claimed absolute authority, was nothing but a forgery. " But for this passage," says

Duhm,[1] " we might believe that he was not a contemporary of the Reform, or that he intentionally ignored it. And this solitary passage is hostile ! "

These considerations create a difficulty which cannot lightly be set on one side. Yet there are others which may be set against them. In the first place there hardly seems to be enough reason to reject all the C passages; on the contrary, as has been already suggested, at least a large nucleus of them may reasonably be ascribed to Jeremiah's own dictation. We have, further, especially in the earlier chapters of the book, a number of undisputed oracles which might well have been delivered either before or during the progress of the Reform. Certainly they would have been out of place for some time afterwards.

Further, it may be that we should assume too much if we insisted categorically that Jeremiah was opposed to sacrifice *throughout the whole of his career*. Room must be granted to him to make further discoveries, to change his mind, to take into consideration new factors as they appeared. If vii. 21 belongs to the same date as the passage which precedes it, it comes from the early years of the reign of Jehoiakim, thirteen years after the Reform. If Jeremiah, as a young man, had seen in the Reform a means of achieving some part of the ideals for which he stood, he might well have been prepared to compromise, and it does not follow at this stage that he was opposed to sacrifice in principle. With the local cults he was familiar, as a member of a family which probably officiated at one of them, and he realized their dangers. So did the compilers of *Deuteronomy*, and Jeremiah may well, at this stage in his life, have shared their belief, that a cult centralized in Jerusalem could be controlled and kept pure.

Doubtless the years brought disillusionment. It would be difficult to find a more emphatic pronouncement than that already cited from viii. 8, where the most natural rendering of the Hebrew consonants in the latter part of the verse is that actually adopted by Duhm—" The lying pen of the scribes has made it into a lie." But Duhm's interpretation

[1] *Jeremia*, p. 89 (1901).

that the "scribes" are the authors, not the copyists, of *Deuteronomy*, is *not* the most natural explanation. On the contrary, the idiom used implies that the document in question had not always been " a lie," but had been turned into one since it first came into being. Thirteen years is ample time in which a man may discover that a document was being misused, misquoted, and misinterpreted—perhaps even deliberately altered to suit the convenience of the priesthood. At first the Reform looked likely to succeed, and Josiah retained the respect and admiration of Jeremiah till his death, though not necessarily on theological grounds. But, as time passed, it became clear that the movement had certain fatal weaknesses, and Jeremiah was forced to admit that it had failed. It was, as he suggests in viii. 8, too much exposed to manipulation and corruption. At the same time, the prophet may well have grown into the belief that *all* sacrifice was contrary to the will of Yahweh, at least as expressed in the Mosaic age. Finally, he saw the truth; its fundamental weakness was that, however perfect in itself, it was externally imposed, and a law of this kind would never be worth more than a "scrap of paper." So he was led to the enunciation of the profound truth that a covenant, to be effective, must be written on men's hearts, and his new conviction ultimately found expression in the great prophecy of the New Covenant— xxxi. 31-34.

VI. The Man and his Message

"Ah, Lord, I cannot speak, for I am a child," was the response Jeremiah made to the divine call. It was typical of the man's character. All his life he felt himself to be a person of extreme insignificance, carrying no authority of his own, and temperamentally unfit for public work of any kind. Tender, shy, and sympathetic as he was, his modest spirit would have been satisfied to the full with the peace and joy of quiet domestic life in his village home. He loved wild nature, and had observed the ways of beast and bird as carefully as Amos had done, while he had watched them with an understanding and a sympathy which we do not find in the older prophet. His affections were strong, and no small part of the cross he had to bear lay in the barrier which kept him from forming the closest and dearest of human relationships.

Jeremiah—perhaps owing to the unfortunate tradition which fathered on him the book of *Lamentations*—stands to most men as the type of the mournful pessimist. Unhappy he certainly was, and could not have been otherwise. He was a man with a double passion and a twofold loyalty, devoted equally to his people and to his God. His patriotism was of that supreme quality which makes a man identify himself with his country, feel her troubles as his own sorrows, and repent for her sins with a personal remorse. His consuming desire was to see a permanent union established between Israel and Yahweh. Not only was he intensely conscious of the spiritual peril to Israel involved in her separation from her God, but he realized that the course she followed throughout the greater part of his ministry could end only in her material ruin. For forty years he pleaded that his people should return to Yahweh, and, save for the last half of Josiah's reign, he pleaded in vain. So for forty years, with his prophetic experience, he lived through the horrors of her coming fall, helpless to turn her into safe paths or to ward off the fatal blow. He could have been happy only at the cost of truth, only by saying (as men about him said) " Peace, Peace " where there was no peace. Yet his prophetic vision could carry him beyond the worst disaster and see recovery and restoration in the future, however distant it might be. The destruction of Jerusalem, city and Temple falling together, would not be the final issue, and, though for himself life ended with the last apostasy of his fellows in Egypt, and the bond between Yahweh and the Israelite fugitives was there irreparably snapped, he left the world the grandest triumph that true optimism ever achieved in his prophecy of the New Covenant.

As a poet Jeremiah is surpassed in the Old Testament only by Hosea, some of the Psalmists, and the poet of *Job*. Stirred to the depths of his passionate soul by the sin and by the inevitable doom of his country, he gave to his lyrics an intensity and a power which thrill us to this day. It is impossible to read without a sense of wild horror such a passage as the great chaos-vision,[1] which we may, albeit feebly, paraphrase somewhat thus:

> " I looked on the earth—
> And saw chaos' rude birth,
> At the heavens—and from them no light brake;
> I looked on the hills
> In their agony-thrills—
> All the mountains did totter and quake.
> I looked o'er the ground—
> No man there I found,
> All the birds had winged far their flight;
> Unto Carmel I faced—
> And its gardens were waste,
> All was blasted beneath the fell blight."

In a sense this overwhelming picture of tossing mountains and lifeless plain was a reflection of Jeremiah's own spiritual experience. In doctrine (apart from the New Covenant) he added little to the teaching of his eighth-century predecessors. He reminded his contemporaries of Micah, and his positive demands recall to us little more than that threefold insistence on justice, love, and holiness which summarizes for us Amos, Hosea, and Isaiah. But Jeremiah was himself greater and more significant than his message. He had received at his call the promise that he should be as a pillar of iron and walls of bronze, and as far as we know, he never once flinched in the face of king, priest, or hostile crowd. It was otherwise in his dealings with his God. His ministry became an intolerable burden to him, an unquenchable and devouring flame within him; like others of his day, he believed that the prophet whose word remained unfulfilled was " seduced " by Yahweh Himself to his utter ruin, and for forty years Jeremiah's word was unfulfilled. Not once only, but again and yet again, he struggled to free himself from the toils of divine inspiration, and always in vain. Yet his meaning for the world lies in his very failure to rescue his own soul. Religion implies a relation between God and man, and, in the older view, the human unit was not the individual but the community. Jeremiah, first

---

[1] iv. 23–26.

of all men, as far as our records go, was cut out from among his people in his spiritual life. He was left alone, and God wrestled with him.

So, out of this agony of spirit, human religion won a new aspect. Historically, it is to the lifelong torture of Jeremiah's soul that man owes one of his most glorious possessions. While the conception of the group or of the community as a religious unit has never been, and must never be, wholly lost, it is the birthright of every individual that he can claim personal fellowship with God. When we realize the incalculable wealth of spiritual life which this discovery has meant to later ages, we shall be inclined to feel that Jeremiah, not through his words, but through his experience, gave the world more than any other single person in the whole history of Israel.

VII. The Hebrew Text and the Septuagint

There is no book in the Old Testament in which the differences between the MT and the Septuagint are more striking than they are in *Jeremiah*. Hints of this have already been given, and, even here, it is impossible to enter into great detail. It must, however, be said, that the Greek text is very much shorter than the Hebrew; it has been computed that there are about 2700 words in the MT which are not represented [1] in the translation, while the text followed by the translators had about 100 words not found in our present Hebrew texts. In many cases the " omissions " of the Greek are small matters, expansions of the divine name, and occasional words which take little or nothing from the sense. But there are very many instances in which the differences go further than this; in particular, we have already noticed how often the shorter text of the Septuagint gives us a metrical regularity which is lacking in the MT.[2] In these cases we may assume that the preference lies with the Egyptian tradition. Once or twice we have longer passages omitted in the Septuagint,

[1] Giesebrecht, *Jeremia*, p. xix (1894).
[2] See above, p. 146.

e.g. xxxiii. 14–26, and in these cases the presumption is that the sections in question have been imported into the MT at a point later than the divergence of the two lines of tradition.   But the most striking difference of all is to be found in the arrangement of the oracles against foreign nations.   In the MT this collection stands at the end of the book, and the chapters containing it are numbered xlvi–li.   But in the Septuagint they are placed immediately after xxv. 13, verse 14 is omitted altogether, and the text proceeds with xxv. 15 after the foreign oracles have been inserted.   Not only so, but the order of the oracles in the two recensions is different.   It runs as follows:

MT.	*Septuagint.*
Egypt	Elam
Philistia	Egypt
Moab	Babylon
Ammon	Philistia
Edom	Edom
Damascus	Ammon
Kedar	Kedar
Elam	Damascus
Babylon	Moab

Differences such as this carry us beyond the borders of textual criticism proper into that of higher criticism.   It is useless to discuss which was the original order of the prophecies, or what was the original place of the collection in the completed book.   It is fairly clear that this group must have maintained a separate existence until after the divergence of the two texts.   Only later than this point in the history of the book was it included in either form, and even then there were two recensions in existence.   The Palestinian scribes put it at the end of the book, while those of Egypt, not unnaturally, included it in the short section already devoted to the same subject, displacing a verse (xxv. 14) which was no longer necessary.

THE BOOK OF LAMENTATIONS

I. Title and Place in the Canon

LIKE the books of the Pentateuch, the book of *Lamentations* derives its name in the Hebrew Bible from its first word, *'Ekah*—" How!" It is, however, often referred to under the descriptive title *Qinoth*—" Dirges," which is a fairly accurate description of its contents.

In the Hebrew Canon it is included among the " Five Rolls," where it is placed third, following *Ruth* and preceding *Ecclesiastes*. In the Septuagint and practically all other versions it is placed immediately after the book of *Jeremiah*. This is due to the theory that Jeremiah was its author.

II. Contents and Structure

The book consists of five poems, of which the first four deal with the desolate state of Jerusalem during and after the siege of 587–6 B.C., while the last is a prayer which might be interpreted as referring to the same period.

The first four poems are all alphabetic acrostics, but each has its own peculiar character.

Ch. i is arranged in three-line stanzas, in *Qinah* [1] metre, each stanza beginning with its own letter of the alphabet. The letters are in the usual order. The poem is a lament over the sad plight in which Jerusalem, representing the people, finds itself. The writer contemplates now this, now that, part of the nation—the pitiable state of those left in the home-land, and the sorrow of those in exile; in each case the visitation has come upon the people because of sin (i. 5). But the thought of sin and of Yahweh is only fleeting; the poet's heart is over-full with grief as he contemplates the forlorn and disconsolate city, once so proud

[1] See above, pp. 142 f.

in her glory, the envy of all, now bowed down in humiliation and sorrow; her foes triumphant within her, and her children starving; and the writer pathetically appeals for the pity of all who pass by (i. 12). His main thought is not of sin, but of the present distress; and this leads him to cry out for vengeance against the enemies who have caused it (i. 22).

Ch. ii resembles ch. i in form, save that in the alphabetical order the letter פ comes before ע instead of after it. In this lament the main theme is similar to that of the preceding. Very prominent in the earlier portion is the emphasis laid on the part that Yahweh has taken in the punishment of the city. Noticeable also is the contention that one cause of the great calamity is to be sought in the remissness of the prophets for not having warned the people (ii. 14). As a final result of this the outlook is dark and hopeless; one thing, and one only, there is now left to do: let heartfelt supplication be made to God (ii. 18–20). Striking is the fact that in this dirge there is scarcely any reference, to sin; and the cry for vengeance on the enemy is absent.

Ch. iii. This piece differs markedly from the rest of the poems. It is composed in single lines, with no true strophic arrangement. The lines, however, are grouped in threes, and each of the three in every group begins with the appropriate letter. Taken as a whole, therefore, the poem is arranged in sixty-six single-line verses, instead of being in twenty-two three-line verses as are chs. i and ii. But it seems probable that this was not its original form; it may well be that we have here a collection of four psalms; three are "individual" psalms, like the "I"-psalms in the *Psalter* (verses 1–24, 25–39, 52–66), and one is spoken in the name of the people (verses 40–51). Löhr suggests a slightly different arrangement; he thinks that there were originally two psalms (verses 1–24 and 52–66) in which the compiler makes Jeremiah address the people; and he shows by a comparison with various passages in the book of *Jeremiah* that the author did intend to make Jeremiah the speaker. The psalm in verses 25–51 he believes to be the composition of the compiler, who finally made the whole an acrostic.[1] There are many points of similarity between these compositions and some of the *Psalms* (see especially Pss. lxxxviii and cxliii). It is quite possible that in its present form the poem was used in the Temple Liturgy.

Ch. iv resembles ch. ii closely, except that each stanza contains two lines instead of three. The lament over Jerusalem and its inhabitants is taken up again; sin is once more declared to be the cause of all that has come upon the land and the people. All, prophets, priests, and people, have sinned. According to verse 22, however, the chastisement has come to an end, and Israel is no more in captivity, while Edom, Israel's inveterate foe, will suffer for her iniquity (verses 21, 22).

Ch. v is not a dirge, but a prayer for deliverance from tribulation. Though it contains twenty-two verses, the right number for an alphabetic acrostic, there is no sign of the acrostic itself. Each verse contains a single 3 : 3 line.

III. AUTHORSHIP AND DATE

Tradition assigned the whole of the book to Jeremiah. This seems to be based on a misinterpretation of ii Chron. xxxv. 25—" And Jeremiah lamented for Josiah; and all the singing men and singing women spake of Josiah in their lamentations, unto this day; and they made them an ordinance in Israel: and, behold, they are written in the lamentations." Whatever these " lamentations " were, they cannot have been those preserved in our book, for we have here no reference to Josiah. Nor is it easy to believe that Jeremiah was the author of any of them. Though the passionate feeling expressed, especially in chs. ii and iv, reminds us of the prophet, the style is entirely unlike anything that we can confidently assign to him. The artificial device of the acrostic, while it does not necessarily conflict with a high degree of genuine feeling, would be unnatural to such a poet as we know Jeremiah to have been. Further, the thought is sometimes at variance with

---

[1] *ZATW* for 1904, pp. 1 ff.

that which we associate with the prophet.[1] Finally, we may observe that it is very improbable that all five poems are the work of a single author.

Of the five chapters, ii and iv seem to be the nearest in date to the calamity which they describe, and are, possibly, the work of the same author. The writer has lived through the horrors of the siege and sack of Jerusalem, and, though some time has now elapsed, and the first poignant anguish is over, the poems are an expression of deep sorrow. Ch. i seems to be somewhat later, it fails to reach quite the same high literary standard; moreover, the different order in the alphabet suggests a different author from the writer of chs. ii and iv. Ch. iii is later still, and may even come from the period after the return from the Exile. And, finally, ch. v might have come from any one of a number of periods in the history of Israel when the people were distressed by cruel oppression.

IV. The Hebrew Text and the Septuagint

The Hebrew text of *Lamentations* has been well preserved, and there are few places where we suspect serious corruption. The Septuagint often suggests a variation, but a fair proportion of these instances are demonstrably due to corruption during the transmission of the Greek text itself, and do not indicate that the translators had a Hebrew text different from ours.

[1] For a summary of the discussion, see Driver, *op. cit.*, pp. 433–435.

THE BOOK OF EZEKIEL

I. CONTENTS OF THE BOOK

IN its broad outlines the book consists of two main divisions:

i–xxiv deals with the approaching fall of Jerusalem and the dissolution of the State, while xxv–xlviii (apart from xxv–xxxii) has for its central theme the restoration of Jerusalem and the reconstitution of the State as a religious community.

These two main divisions may be sub-divided as follows:

i–xi: The prophet's call; the announcement of the fall of Jerusalem and of the fate of its inhabitants as a punishment for their idolatrous worship, in consequence of which Yahweh departs from " the midst of the city " (xi. 23).

xii–xix: A continuation of the same theme; prophets, priests, people and rulers have all gone astray; retribution will come upon them; a special denunciation is uttered against Jerusalem, the " harlot " (xvi).

xx–xxiv: A further denunciation of the people for their many sins, and reiterated prophecies of the fall of the city.

xxv–xxxii: Oracles against the surrounding nations.

xxxiii–xxxix: In the main, these chapters contain promises of restoration; but xxxiv. 1–22 is a denunciation against the " shepherds of Israel," and xxxv is a prophecy of the destruction of Edom.

xl–xlviii: The ideal Temple, and (xlvii, xlviii) the renewed fertility of the land when Yahweh comes to dwell once more among His people.

II. THE EZEKIEL PROBLEM

Strictly speaking there are two problems which present themselves in our book: (a) the historical situation; (b) the person of the prophet; but, as will be seen, the solution of the former necessarily brings with it the solution of the latter. Nevertheless, for the sake of clearness, we will indicate each separately.

(*a*) Ezekiel is represented as living among the exiles in Babylon who were deported in 597 B.C. The theme of his preaching is the coming destruction of Jerusalem. But though he is living in Babylon he addresses himself exclusively to the people in Jerusalem in chs. i–xxiv. He has no word of comfort or encouragement to those exiles among whom he is living; however deserving the people of Jerusalem were of the prophet's denunciation, it must strike one as strange that he has nothing to say to those of his immediate surroundings. A prophet always exercised his ministry by word of mouth to those among whom he lived; here they are ignored, while he addresses himself to a far-off audience who cannot hear him, and performs symbolic actions for the instruction of those who cannot see him. Under such circumstances how can Ezekiel be regarded as a prophet in the true sense? And yet in these first twenty-four chapters everything points to Ezekiel as a prophet exercising his activity face to face with his people; he speaks as if in their very midst, his words pulsate with passion; the earnestness and sincerity of his utterances, generated by a sense of responsibility, do not read like a written message penned far away from the scene of action. So that, explain the matter as we may, the problem is there.

(*b*) And closely connected with this is the question as to what we are to make of the prophet as depicted in the book. On the one hand, as we have just seen, the book represents Ezekiel as a prophet in the truest sense of the word; on the other hand, much that we read in the book is of a purely literary character, the outcome of calm reflection, and it is difficult to see how the writer of chs. i–xxiv, which record prophetic activity, can be the same as the meditative philosopher who expresses his thoughts in the later chapters. This twofold problem, therefore, turns upon the question of authorship.

III. Authorship

Up to within recent years it was held almost unanimously that the book of *Ezekiel* was a literary unity. A notable exception was Ewald, who pointed to the contrast between the two main divisions of the book, the former representing clearly the utterances of a prophet, the latter, however, not suggesting the picture of a prophet active among his people, but rather one given to literary labours; the implication was that unity of authorship could with difficulty be postulated. But from the time that Ewald wrote, three-quarters of a century ago, until comparatively recently, he had few, if any, to follow him. Thus, McFadyen, in the latest edition of his *Introduction,* writes: "We have in Ezekiel the rare satisfaction of studying a carefully elaborated prophecy whose authenticity has, till recently, been practically undisputed. It is not impossible that there are, as Kraetzschmar maintains, occasional doublets, *e.g.* ii. 3–7 and iii. 4–9; but these, in any case, are very few and hardly affect the question of authenticity. The order and precision of the priestly mind are reflected in the unusually systematic arrangement of the book." [1] McFadyen remarks, however, in reference to the problems raised by Hölscher,[2] James Smith,[3] and Torrey,[4] that "the new problems raised by these scholars have not yet had time to receive adequate discussion." [5] It will be worth while to set in review quite briefly the opinions regarding its authorship held by some recent writers on the subject. We may begin with Kraetzschmar, though his work was published some time ago.[6] He argues strongly against literary unity, pointing to the many instances in which the narrative breaks off incontinently, to the large number of chapters in which want of order is discernible, and to numerous parallel texts and doublets; he also draws attention to several sections in

---

[1] *Introduction to the Old Testament,* p. 187 (1932).
[2] *Hesekiel, der Dichter und das Buch* (1924).
[3] *The Book of the Prophet Ezekiel* (1931).
[4] *Pseudo-Ezekiel and the Original Prophecy* (1930).
[5] *Op. cit.,* p. 203.
[6] *Das Buch Ezechiel* (1900).

the book which have opening and closing *formulæ*, giving the impression that they are independent pieces. He concludes that there were two recensions of the book, in one of which the prophet spoke in the first person, in the other he is spoken of in the third person;[1] that, therefore, Ezekiel cannot have put the book together himself, but that this was done by a redactor who made various alterations and additions. Herrmann[2] agrees with Kraetzschmar in not regarding the book as a connected literary production, but disagrees entirely with the conclusion drawn from this. He points to the fact that the books of *Isaiah* and *Jeremiah* contain collections of independent sections which are the work of these prophets, respectively, and maintains that the same is the case with *Ezekiel*. He holds that the book was put together by degrees by Ezekiel himself, who made alterations, modifications and corrections from time to time; he sees, therefore, no need for the two recensions theory of Kraetzschmar. This remodelling theory of Herrmann's will account, as he maintains, for all the literary difficulties presented in the book; the many marks of the redactor's hand he fully recognizes. Herrmann agrees, therefore, with the hitherto dominant view as to unity of authorship, though he would assign more to the work of the redactor than has, until recently, generally been the case.

Much more drastic is Hölscher's treatment of the book; he insists that a more rigorous distinction must be made between the prophet's writing and the redactional elements, of which there are various kinds. Hölscher maintains that in the first instance a redactor worked over the book in its original form, making numerous additions; then, from time to time, other editors added their quota, the last of these being one who belonged to the Deuteronomic school of thought, but who attempted to imitate the style and thought of Ezekiel much in the same way as Trito-Isaiah wrote under the influence of Deutero-Isaiah. This redactor

---

[1] As a matter of fact there are but two instances in which Ezekiel is spoken of in the third person (i. 3; xxiv. 24), and in the second of these it is in a speech of Yahweh's.

[2] *Ezechiel* (1924).

Y

is held to have lived in the fifth century. Hölscher's discernment and ingenuity demand every recognition, but his work is vitiated by arbitrary assumptions which lack adequate proof; thus, for example, he insists that Ezekiel was not a prophet in the ordinary sense, but a poet, and therefore only the poetical passages in the book belong to him; and sometimes he manipulates the text (e.g. in xv, xvi) in an unwarrantable way in order to make poetry out of prose. A poet, he argues, does not mix up symbolism and concrete fact, therefore any passage in which this appears cannot belong to Ezekiel; it must be the work of a redactor. Very arbitrary is Hölscher's contention that the doctrine of individual responsibility must be post-exilic, and that therefore any passage in which this is dealt with cannot have been written by Ezekiel. There are various other instances of à priori assumptions which necessitate the relegation of many passages to the hands of redactors; in the final result only about a sixth of the book is assigned to Ezekiel himself.

Far more sober is Kittel's [1] treatment of the book; he believes that its literary problems can be solved by recognizing that Ezekiel's experiences in the two very different environments of Palestine and Babylonia generated in him a kind of dual personalty; he was a priest, but he had to turn his back on the functions of the priesthood; he was a prophet, yet his thoughts constantly reverted to the Temple; Babylonia was so different from Palestine. He was thus a prophet full of burning passion; yet he was a priest full of pedantic casuistry, a theologian who reflected in calm consideration. Moreover, he was a poet, not wanting in poetic ardour, yet often descending to wearisome prose. These different elements in the personality of Ezekiel, due to the great change of environment, explain, according to Kittel, some otherwise puzzling features in the book. He holds, therefore, apart from redactional elements, to unity of authorship.

A very different picture is presented by Torrey.[2] In one

---

[1] Geschichte des Volkes Israel, iii. pp. 144–180 (1927).
[2] Pseudo-Ezekiel and the Original Prophecy (1930).

important respect he puts forth a theory which is likely
to be widely accepted. He argues with much force that
we have in chs. i–xxiv (apart from redactional elements)
a prophecy uttered in Jerusalem; the theme of these chapters,
as we have seen, is the coming calamity upon the city;
the hearers are addressed as a " rebellious house," and the
" prophet "—though not, according to Torrey, Ezekiel—
is spoken of as dwelling " in the midst of a rebellious house "
(xii. 2); that Jerusalem is meant is universally recognized.
The most obvious and natural conclusion is that the prophecy was uttered in Jerusalem, and that the people addressed were the inhabitants of the city. Were it not for
what is said in i. 1–3, a confessedly worked-over passage,
and certain other references in the book to Babylonia,
nobody would think of denying that Ezekiel had lived and
worked in Jerusalem during some period of his life before
being taken with the exiles to Babylonia. This part of
Torrey's argument (excepting his refusal to regard Ezekiel
as the prophet in question) must be regarded as convincing.
But apart from this his thesis is quite unacceptable. He
maintains that our book is a pseudepigraphic work written
about 230 B.C. by one who gave it the appearance of having
been penned by a prophet during the reign of Manasseh
(696–641 B.C.). This supposed late author is represented as
wishing to show that the people were warned by the fictitious
prophet about the coming calamity on Jerusalem. The
author, according to Torrey, took ii Kgs. xxi. 1–17 as his
starting-point; on this he constructed his work of fiction.
Subsequently a redactor worked over this book, though as
little as possible, and skilfully interpolated various passages
in order to give it a Babylonian dress. Apart from these
interpolations, which Torrey finds no difficulty in designat-
ing, the book forms a literary unity.[1]

James Smith [2] offers a very different, but likewise original
view; he holds that Ezekiel's prophetic activity extended
approximately from 722–669 B.C., partly in Palestine and
partly among the *northern* exiles; in each of these two

[1] A searching criticism of Torrey's work is offered by Shalom Spiegel in
The Harvard Theological Review, Oct. 1931, pp. 245–321.
[2] *The Book of the Prophet Ezekiel* (1931).

centres he composed oracles, one set in Palestine and the other among the exiles in Assyria from the northern kingdom; both were artificially united together by a redactor. In confirmation of this James Smith recalls the tradition preserved by Josephus (Antiq. x. 79), that Ezekiel wrote two books, and the Jewish belief that Ezekiel's prophetic activity commenced in Palestine. According to this view Ezekiel was not connected with Judah and Jerusalem, but with northern Israel and Gerizim. That Ezekiel worked as a prophet in Jerusalem is believed, on the other hand, by Herntrich[1] to have been the case, and he also disagrees with James Smith regarding the period of the prophet's activity, as well as with Torrey's views. He holds that Ezekiel exercised his prophetical office in Jerusalem during the years 593–586 B.C., and that chs. ii–xxiv, in the main (see below), and xxv–xxxix belong to him. These Jerusalem prophecies were later worked over by an exilic redactor who clothed them in a Babylonian dress; he was responsible for ch. i, for the framework of the vision of Ezekiel's call in chs. ii, iii, similarly for the Babylonian elements in chs. viii and xi, for xxxiii. 21–23, and with " considerable probability " for chs. xl–xlviii. Besides this, the exilic redactor's hand is to be discerned in various other minor additions;[2] it is also probable that still later redactors have in numerous instances further amplified, and sometimes corrupted, the text; this, however, applies mainly to chs. xl–xlviii. The contents of the book, in Herntrich's view, present us with the pictures of two different worlds: the world of the genuine Judæan prophet, and the world of the exilic redactor; the latter has constructed a framework around the genuine prophecy, and by means of theosophical speculations and a widely embracing scheme of revelation, has sought to prove the unity of his God in opposition to the Babylonian pantheon. Signs of his work are to be discerned throughout the book; the genuine prophecy forms the central picture around which the redactor has constructed his framework; at the close of the book he has added his religious programme of the future,

---

[1] *Ezechielprobleme* (1932).　　　[2] *E.g.* xiv. 21–23, xxxiii. 30–33.

which is not a prophecy, but a " sacerdotal " polity. Thus, our book received its present form in Babylonia. It is probable, though this cannot be proved, that Ezekiel was among the exiles of one of the later deportations, and brought with him his written prophecies;[1] this would explain how they came into the hands of the Babylonian redactor.

Whether Herntrich's conclusions be accepted or not, it must be allowed that they go a long way in solving the problem of the book.

IV. THE PERSONALITY OF EZEKIEL

As already pointed out, this presents us with a second problem closely connected with the preceding. Taking the book as it stands there is much to show that Ezekiel was a prophet pure and simple; there is also much to show that he was a writer and nothing else; and there is, furthermore, much to show that he was a mystic. While it must be recognized that it is possible for the characteristics of the prophet, the author, and the mystic to be centred in one man, it will not be denied that this is a very difficult and improbable combination. To the question of the mystic we shall turn presently; apart from this there are, broadly speaking, two views held with regard to Ezekiel: to many earlier critics, who saw in the book purely a literary production, Ezekiel was no prophet, but only a writer, who constructed an artificial picture; and since, according to some who held this view, the city had already fallen when he wrote, his " prophecy " was nothing more than a literary device. With this view many scholars, foremost among whom is Herrmann, disagree; he protests that one must have but a meagre apprehension of the power of religious witness not to discern the impassioned fervour which quivers in many of Ezekiel's utterances, prompted as they were by

[1] In further support of Herntrich's view, we may point out that, except for some rather long and artificially constructed poems, the book belongs in form to what we have called type C (see above, p. 229), the prophetic message delivered in prose and placed in the first person. As we have observed elsewhere, it seems probable that this was the form which a prophet's oracles assumed when he himself was responsible for their being written down, whether he did the work himself, or whether he dictated it to a scribe. This would account for the form the book assumed in such portions as were really Ezekiel's.

the needs and conditions of the times. " His historical-
philosophic solution of the cause of the present tragic state
of affairs is anything but the theorizing product of the
study," says Herrmann; on the contrary, it is clearly the
outcome of practical experience, intended to be of present
help and service. Similarly, when he deals with the subject
of individual responsibility and retribution; this is not
the product of quiet meditation and calm reflection; it
is forced upon the prophet through the dire reality of what
he sees around him.

It will, therefore, be seen, that the view taken of the
prophet's personality has a direct bearing upon the literary
problem which the book presents.

But there is one other matter in connexion with Ezekiel
which demands attention. In Ezek. viii. 1 ff. we read:
" And it came to pass . . . as I sat in mine house, and the
elders of Judah sat before me, that the hand of the Lord
God fell upon me . . . and he put forth an hand, and took
me by a lock of mine head; and the spirit lifted me up
between the earth and the heaven, and brought me in the
visions of God to Jerusalem. . . ." In the chapters which
follow a vivid description is given of what the prophet
sees in Jerusalem. It is nowhere told how Ezekiel was
brought back to Babylonia, though in ch. xiv it is clear that
he is again in the land of exile (cp. verse 1 with viii. 1).
How is the strange narrative here contained to be explained?
Many solutions have been attempted; they fall, roughly,
into two categories. It is held by some that Ezekiel was
psychically abnormal and had the gift of second sight, so
that we have here a case of clairvoyance. Others insist
that the apparently supernatural episodes are to be explained on simpler and more rational lines. As perhaps
the best representative of the former point of view Kittel [1]
may be designated. He acknowledges that modern scientific
psychologists do not recognize the existence of occurrences
such as are told of Ezekiel; if such are recorded, it is contended that they are mere coincidences or pure chicanery.
Kittel does not dogmatize, but in view of the advance of

[1] *Op. cit.*, iii. 147.

knowledge in the domain of psychology and of modern conceptions of time and space, he doubts whether we are justified in denying the possibility of clairvoyance; or in refusing to recognize any element of mystery in connexion with such a confessedly remarkable personality as that of Ezekiel. He recalls the interesting narrative of xxiv. 15–27; here the prophet foresees in a vision the death of his wife, and is told that he is to regard this as a symbol of what is to overtake the people, and that his dumbness will pass (cp. iii. 24–26). While this may certainly be regarded as a genuine case of clairvoyance, it can hardly be contended that it stands in the same category as the former narrative. A somewhat different explanation is offered by other scholars;[1] it is rightly pointed out that there were abnormal elements in the personality of Ezekiel; he had periods of unconsciousness, and that he suffered from catalepsy is evident. It is known that people thus afflicted will remain sometimes for weeks bereft of the faculty of speech and of movement, though they do not necessarily lose consciousness altogether, but apprehend to some extent what is going on around them; sometimes, too, this state is attended by hallucinations; moreover, at such times both sight and hearing may be affected; though, on the other hand, cases are on record in which, when in a state of catalepsy, the patient's perceptive faculties become in some inexplicable way abnormally acute. From our book it may be gathered, according to this view, that all these things would apply in the case of Ezekiel; while in some such condition he could well have believed himself to have been transported to Jerusalem.

As to the other school of thought a number of opinions are expressed; they may be summarized thus: it is held by some that the visions must be regarded as realities, but that the prophet adopts the device of making it appear that he was in the presence of the people of Jerusalem; in other words, he places himself in imagination in the home-land. Another explanation is that the visions were not really experienced, but that they are a purely literary

[1] *E.g.* Meinhold, *Einführung in das Alte Testament*, p. 260 (1932).

description of an imaginary picture constructed by the prophet.

A different view is put forward by recent commentators who maintain that the hand of the redactor is to be seen in the accounts of the visions; it is said that Ezekiel experienced these visions while still in Jerusalem, and that he wrote them down before he was taken to Babylonia; then at some later time a redactor—one of the exiles—added the passages about Ezekiel being transported to Jerusalem, since from this redactor's point of view Ezekiel was in Babylonia when he received the visions.

The subject is a difficult one, for much is to be said for and against the various theories held; whichever is adopted must to some extent depend upon the view taken of the literary problem; if the book is a literary unity, as most earlier scholars held, then one must accept in a literal sense all that the prophet says about his abnormal experiences, however one may explain them. The more modern view as to the composition of the book, though this is not yet quite free from difficulties, makes the whole subject much easier to understand.

V. CONCLUSIONS

The conclusion to which we are led by the study of recent investigations of our book may, in general outline and omitting details, be put thus: Ezekiel began his ministry in Jerusalem soon after Jehoiakim's revolt against Nebuchadrezzar in 602 B.C.[1] His denunciations against the people of Jerusalem and his prophecies of the fall of the city were soon after put into writing by the prophet himself. In 597 B.C. he was carried captive to Babylonia, and took with him his written prophecies. While in exile he added to his writings prophecies of restoration; these were addressed to his fellow-exiles; but whether they were written before or after the fall of the city in 586 B.C. cannot be stated with certainty.[2] At some later period during the Exile the prophet's writings came into the hands of one

[1] According to others 598 B.C.
[2] Herntrich maintains that " in no case may we assume that Ezekiel exercised his prophetical activity after 586 " (op. cit., p. 126).

of his co-religionists who edited them in such a way as to make it appear that the whole material was written in Babylonia. Further minor additions were made still later by one or more redactors.

This represents, for the most part, Herntrich's standpoint; to him students of the book of *Ezekiel* will be permanently indebted.

VI. THE HEBREW TEXT AND THE SEPTUAGINT

The trustworthiness and importance of the Septuagint, and therefore its value for the study of the Hebrew text, have been amply shown by Cornill,[1] after a minute examination and comparison of the two. As illustrating the honesty of the translator it is found that in many cases, rather than make a guess at the meaning of an unfamiliar word, he transliterates the Hebrew; in numberless cases he follows the Hebrew by giving minute equivalents, such as particles, etc.; often he gives literal translations of the Hebrew which make almost incomprehensible Greek; in such cases it is usually easy to discern the form of the underlying Hebrew text. On the other hand, free translations are frequent, and many small additions are made in order to make the language of the translation run more smoothly. Further, at times whole sections, some short, others long, occur in which the translation is freer than that of the immediate context, almost giving the impression that a different translator had been at work (*e.g.* iii. 3–7, xxxiii. 5, 6, 22, 32).

In the numerous cases in which the Massoretic text has words or sentences which do not occur in the Septuagint it may be confidently asserted that these did not figure in the form of the Hebrew text used by the Greek translator.

There is thus no doubt that both in general as well as in detail the Septuagint is an absolutely faithful translation, and therefore a trustworthy witness of the Hebrew text extant in Alexandria during the third pre-Christian century; its value for text-critical purposes can scarcely be over-estimated.

---

[1] *Das Buch des Propheten Ezekiel*, pp. 96–103 (1886).

THE BOOK OF DANIEL

I. Place in the Canon

In the Hebrew Canon *Daniel* does not figure among the *Nebi'im* (" Prophets "), but towards the end of the third division, *Kethubim* ("Writings "),[1] viz. *Daniel, Ezra–Nehemiah, i ii Chronicles*. Although in the later Jewish lists of the order of the Biblical books there are some variations in this third division, the position of *Daniel* never varies; it always comes immediately before *Ezra–Nehemiah*, almost at the end of the list.[2] In the Septuagint, Cod. B has *Daniel* at the end of the whole list; but in Cod. A, with a great following, it comes after *Ezekiel* among the prophets; and this order, so far as *Daniel* is concerned, is followed in the Patristic and Synodical lists of the Western Church.[3] This is the order in the Vulgate, and is followed by the English versions.

II. Historical Background

The struggle between the Seleucid and Ptolemaic dynasties for the conquest of Syria ended with the victory of Antiochus iii at the battle of Panion (199 B.C.) over the Egyptian forces led by Scopas. We have but little knowledge of the internal state of Jewish affairs during the reign of Antiochus iii and of his son Seleucus iv; but the little that we do know is significant and highly suggestive, and it is of importance for the understanding of the subsequent history. During the later part of the reign of Antiochus iii we have the earliest indications of the rivalry between the houses of Onias and Tobias. The original root of this rivalry is to be traced to the fact that while the High-priesthood was

[1] See above, p. 5.
[2] Ryle, *The Canon of the Old Testament*, p. 280 (1892).
[3] See Swete, *Introduction to the Old Testament in Greek*, pp. 210–214 (1900).

vested in the family of Onias, the important office of tax-
farmer was possessed by Joseph of the house of Tobias,
first under Ptolemy iv, and, after the conquest, under
Antiochus iii. The two highest offices in the State, the
spiritual and the financial—the latter by far the more
influential under the circumstances of the times—were
thus held by representatives of these two houses respectively.
For those Jews who were loyal to their faith the spiritual
head was naturally the real head of the community; but
for the hellenized Jews the holder of the purse, who received
his appointment from the king, and who represented the
nation before its suzerain, was the more important
functionary. It will be readily understood that with the
existence of two supreme officers of State, independent of
each other, and with diverse interests, occasions of friction
might easily arise; and this would more especially be the
case when the two parties had opposed religious views.
Greek influence had already been exercised on certain
sections of the Jews for some time previously.[1] The house
of Onias, supported by the Ḥasidim, the "pious ones,"
was loyal to the Law, and strict in its adherence to the
ancestral religion; opposed to the orthodox party were
the partisans of the house of Tobias, who favoured Greek
ideas and practices. It was at the instigation of a hellenistic
Jew, Simon, of the tribe of Benjamin, that the attempt was
made by Seleucus iv to appropriate the Temple treasures;
he sent his "chancellor," Heliodorus, to lay hands on these;
the attempt failed, owing to what was believed to be some
supernatural appearance.[2] The episode is important as
showing that the Syrian ruler could count on the support
of pro-Greek Jews in his dealings with his Jewish subjects.
It also shows that there existed at this time a very unsatisfactory state of affairs among the Jews themselves;
indeed, the bitterness between the two parties must have
reached serious proportions, for very shortly after this the
High Priest, who was now Onias iii, found it necessary

[1] Hecatæus of Abdera (circa 300 B.C.) records: "Under the later rule of
the Persians and of the Macedonians, who overthrew the empire of the former,
many of the traditional customs of the Jews were altered owing to their intercourse with aliens."
[2] See ii Macc. iii. 1-13, 22-30; Simon was the "guardian of the Temple."

to journey to Antioch for the purpose of inducing Seleucus iv to intervene and to put an end to the unrest that was going on in Jerusalem. It was at this time, in 176–5 B.C., that Heliodorus headed a conspiracy against Seleucus, and murdered him. With the accession of his brother, Antiochus iv Epiphanes, a very critical period for the Jews dawned; for the hellenistic Jews found in him an ally who supported them whole-heartedly in their conflict with their orthodox brethren.

The absence of Onias iii from Jerusalem (whither he had gone while Seleucus iv was still living) at the accession of Antiochus iv was taken advantage of by Jason, the brother of Onias, to secure for himself the High-priesthood; he succeeded ultimately in this by offering a bribe to the king; the bribe was accompanied by a request which Jason knew would appeal, viz. for permission to establish a gymnasium on Greek lines in Jerusalem and to have the inhabitants of the city registered as citizens of Antioch; the account continues: " And when the king had given assent, and he (Jason) had gotten possession of the office, he forthwith brought over them of his own race to the Greek fashion." [1] It will be noted that the initiative in the movement to hellenize the Jews is taken, not by Antiochus, but by the leader of the Jewish hellenistic party. The appointment to the High-priesthood by the king, quite apart from the fact that the true High Priest was still living, was, naturally enough, bitterly resented by the orthodox party, and served to intensify the mutual hatred between them and their hellenistic brethren. For three years Jason retained the High-priesthood; then Menelaus, by offering a higher bribe to the king, received the office. Jason had to flee from Jerusalem. [2] In order to raise the money for his bribe to the king, Menelaus plundered the Temple treasury; Onias, the legitimate High Priest, rebuked him for this; but Menelaus revenged himself by having him murdered. In the meantime, Jason, who had taken refuge in Ammonite territory, had not given up hopes of regaining the High-

[1] ii Macc. iv. 7–10, and cp. i Macc. i. 11–15.
[2] ii Macc. iv. 23–29.

priesthood; his opportunity occurred in 169 B.C., when he heard that Antiochus, who was warring in Egypt, had fallen in battle. He hastened to Jerusalem, and drove out Menelaus. But the rumour about the death of Antiochus was false; he returned at the end of the year, and vented his wrath on the orthodox Jews for receiving Jason back by appropriating many of the Temple vessels; afterwards he instituted a " great slaughter." [1] Jason managed to escape, and Menelaus was confirmed in the High-priesthood. Further trouble, however, broke out, for the Jews refused to recognize Menelaus. Although Jason had been illegally appointed, according to the Jewish law, he was at least a member of the High-priestly family, and on the death of Onias iii the Jews recognized him; but Menelaus could make no such claim; the orthodox Jews would therefore have nothing to do with him. Tumults broke out in Jerusalem, and the position of Menelaus became precarious. The king had to protect him by sending a Syrian official, Apollonius by name,[2] to take vigorous measures against the orthodox Jews.

It is necessary here to take note that the immediate cause of Antiochus' step was a political, not a religious one; in refusing to acknowledge the king's nominee to the High-priesthood the Jews were, from the king's point of view, committing an act of rebellion; that had to be punished, and from i Macc. i. 30–32 it is clear that the cruelties perpetrated were merely a vindictive object-lesson to show the consequences of disobedience. What followed must be put down, in the first instance, to the hellenistic Jews; from what is said in i Macc. i. 30–40 one can see that the *religious* question which now came to the fore was due to these hellenistic Jews; they seized the opportunity to combat orthodox Judaism; Antiochus, an ardent Hellenist, was only too ready to take a lead in this, and he did so with fanatical ardour. He forbade the observance of the Sabbath and the practice of circumcision; the worship of the Temple was abrogated, copies of the Scriptures were destroyed, to possess them was for-

---

[1] i Macc. i. 20–28.   [2] ii Macc. v. 24; cp. i Macc. i. 29.

bidden, the Temple was laid waste, the city walls were thrown down, and a fortress was erected which overlooked the Temple enclosure; heathen altars were commanded to be set up all over the land upon which swine's flesh was to be offered. Disobedience involved the death sentence. To crown all, an altar to the Olympian Zeus was placed upon the altar in the Temple.

These cruel measures had the effect of inducing many Jews to deny their faith; among the greater number who resisted many were put to death.[1] This resistance was at first passive; but that could not last, and very soon resolute action was taken against the oppressors. The revolt was started by Mattathias and his five sons at a village named Modein, near Lydda; they were at once joined by the loyal Jews from all parts of the country, the *Ḥasidim* are especially mentioned.[2] The religious fervour and the valour of Mattathias' followers enabled them to achieve some remarkable initial successes; but these untrained bands, poorly armed and numerically inferior, could not expect to cope successfully for any length of time with the Syrian forces; if ultimate success were to be attained it must be by divine intervention. It was at this critical time, in the year 166–5 B.C., that the book of *Daniel* was written to encourage the loyal Jews in their resistance to their enemies, and to give the promise of the overthrow of Antiochus and the Seleucid empire, and the establishment in the near future of God's kingdom on earth.

III. AUTHORSHIP AND DATE

In what has been said the date of the book has been assumed; it will now be necessary to give the reasons for assigning the book to the year 166–5 B.C.

The author of our book purports to be one of the exiles at the court of Nebuchadrezzar and his successors. It will, therefore, be necessary, first, to show that this is not to be taken literally.

---

[1] i Macc. i. 41–64.   [2] i Macc. ii. 42.

The author makes erroneous statements about the history of the sixth century B.C., which would be incredible on the part of one who had really lived during that period; thus, in the opening verse of the book Nebuchadrezzar is said to have besieged Jerusalem and to have captured the city in the third year of Jehoiakim, *i.e.* 605 B.C. But this did not happen until 597 B.C. when Jehoiachin was king. Again, in v. 2 Nebuchadrezzar is spoken of as the father of Belshazzar; but Nabonidus, not Nebuchadrezzar, was the father of Belshazzar. In v. 1, 30 Belshazzar is called " king," but he was never king; the inscriptions speak of him as " Crown Prince." In v. 30, 31 Darius, represented as the ruler of the Median Empire (!), is made to succeed Belshazzar; the writer presumably did not know that Cyrus and Cambyses reigned before Darius. In addition, three points of less importance likewise show that the writer's knowledge of this historical period was very faulty: in a number of verses (i. 4; ii. 2, 4, 5, 10; iv. 7; v. 7, 11) the term Chaldæans is used in reference to a caste of wise men; as Charles says: " This use of the word is unparalleled throughout the rest of the Old Testament, and there is no trace of it in the inscriptions." [1] The writer assumes that the court language at Babylon was Aramaic; to quote Charles again: " The wise men would have addressed the king in Babylonian or Assyrian, which is declared in Jer. v. 15, Isa. xxviii. 11, xxxiii. 19, to be unintelligible to a Jew." [2] And finally, he uses the Persian title " satrap " as though it were a Babylonian one.[3]

It is, therefore, extremely difficult to believe that any writer could be so ignorant of the history of his times as this writer would have been had he lived in the sixth century; so that when he represents himself as having lived at that time he does so for a particular purpose, to be spoken of later.

On the other hand, our author has an accurate knowledge of the history of the Greek period down to and including

---

[1] *A Critical and exegetical commentary on the Book of Daniel,* p. 14 (1929); Charles holds that ארמית in ii. 4 is a corruption of ויאמרו.

[2] *Op. cit.,* p. 30.   [3] See, further, Charles, *op. cit.,* p. 61.

the reign of Antiochus Epiphanes;[1] the details which he gives agree with other historical sources. The conclusion is, therefore, irresistible that he lived during the period of which he has an accurate knowledge; and, as the details of ch. xi show, the actual time at which he wrote must have been shortly before the end of the reign of Antiochus Epiphanes, for he does not record his death (163 B.C.); this he would certainly have mentioned had he written after the death of this king. But a more exact date can be given: from viii. 11 ff. it is clear that the author wrote after the erection of the heathen altar in the Temple on the 15 Chisleu (= December), 167–6 B.C., and before the dedication of the new altar on the 25 Chisleu 164–3 B.C.; as the Jewish year began in the spring, the exact year, according to our reckoning, will be 165–4 B.C.[2] The late date of the book is supported by the form of both languages; the Aramaic is held by expert opinion to be of a later type than that of the book of *Ezra* ;[3] similarly, the Hebrew is of a late date and poor style, quite different from the exilic writings of Deutero- and Trito-Isaiah.

Whether the whole book comes from one hand or whether the narratives are of different authorship from that of the visions is difficult to decide; but Charles in his exhaustive study of the subject offers a strong plea for unity of authorship, and in this respect Rowley agrees with him. There is, however, an increasing consensus of opinion that the book is composite; the arguments of those who hold this view are not always convincing, and they clash with one another on important points.[4]

In common with all the apocalyptic writers our author issued his book under an assumed name. Various reasons have been put forward to account for these pseudonymous titles; the most convincing is that given by Charles. He points out, firstly, that when once the Law had assumed absolute supremacy, " the prophets were practically reduced to a position of being merely its ex-

[1] For details see Charles, *op. cit.*, pp. 272–322.
[2] Kolbe, *Beiträge zur syrischen und jüdischen Geschichte*, pp. 28 f. (1926).
[3] See Rowley, *The Aramaic of the Old Testament*, passim (1929).
[4] See Rowley, *ZATW*, 1932 (pp. 259 f.).

ponents, and prophecy, assuming a literary character, might bear its author's name or be anonymous." Then, when the Law claimed to be " all-sufficient for time and eternity . . . there was no room left for new light and inspiration, or any fresh or further disclosure of God's will; in short, no room for the true prophet. . . ." [1] So that if a servant of God felt that he had a message to offer his people, there was no chance of his obtaining a hearing unless he wrote under the name of one or other of the great ones of the past. He might, moreover, well feel convinced that what he had to say expressed what the patriarchs of old and other worthies of the past would have thought and said. That would seem to account satisfactorily for the pseudonymous titles of this and other apocalyptic books.

IV. CONTENTS OF THE BOOK

The two main divisions of the book are: i–vi and vii–xii; the former contains narratives, the latter visions.

i. 1–19. Introductory narrative. Jehoiakim and many other Jews are carried captive to Babylon. Nebuchadrezzar shows favour to certain of the noble Jewish youths; among these are Daniel, Hananiah, Mishael, and Azariah. These, out of loyalty to the Jewish Law, refuse the food provided for them by the king. In spite of the simple fare which they choose in place of the king's bounty, they appear stronger in every way than those who partake of the royal food. They are received into the king's favour. Verses 20, 21 belong before the words of ii. 49, " but Daniel was in the gate of the king."

ii. 1–49; i. 20, 21. Nebuchadrezzar seeks from his wise men the interpretation of his dream; on their being unable to give an interpretation they are condemned to death. Daniel intercedes for them and they are saved; for he not only describes the dream without having been told about it, but also gives the interpretation of it. The dream with its interpretation occurs in verses 31–45. Daniel is placed over all the wise men of Babylonia.

---

[1] *Op. cit.*, pp. xxii f.; for a different view see Rowley, *loc. cit.*, pp. 266 f.

Z

iii. 1–30. The narrative of Shadrach, Meshach, and Abed-nego in the fiery furnace.

iv. 1–37 (Aram. iii. 31–iv. 34). Nebuchadrezzar has another dream; Daniel again interprets it, and prophesies that the king, because of his pride, will be punished by the loss of his reason for a certain period; this comes to pass (verses 34–37 (Aram. 31–34); see the Septuagint). The king repents and his reason comes back to him; his kingdom is restored.

v. 1–30. Belshazzar's feast; the handwriting on the wall which Daniel alone can interpret. The death of Belshazzar.

vi. v. 31–vi. 28 (Aram. vi. 1–27). Daniel in the lion's den. He is rescued and set over the whole kingdom.

vii. 1–28. The vision of the four beasts, interpreted by an angel.

viii. 1–27. The vision of the ram and the he-goat, interpreted by Gabriel.

ix. 1–3, 21–27 (verses 4–20 are an interpolation). Daniel seeks an interpretation of Jeremiah's prophecy concerning the seventy years' desolation of Jerusalem; the interpretation is given by Gabriel.

x. 1–xi. 1. A vision concerning the latter times.

xi. 2–xii. 4. An historical retrospect, followed by a prophecy of the latter times.

xii. 5–10. A vision of two angels. Verses 11–13 are a later addition.

V. Sources

As we have seen, the first half of our book contains narratives in which the leading part is played by Daniel, though others, namely the companions of Daniel and various kings, also have important *rôles*. The question arises as to whether the writer of our book composed these stories himself, or whether he made use of some earlier sources. The question is not superfluous, for one or two considerations suggest the possibility, perhaps the probability, of earlier material having been utilized.

Thus, the figure of Daniel was borrowed; that legends

of this mythical hero of old were current is certain, for his righteousness and wisdom are spoken of in Ezek. xiv. 14, 20; xxviii. 3, as well known.[1] In the two former of these passages Daniel is mentioned together with Noah and Job; of these two later stories have been preserved; this justifies the presumption, or at any rate the possibility, that our Daniel stories were based upon earlier legends. It is also worth noting that in *Ezekiel* the mention of Daniel in conjunction with Noah and Job shows that, like them, he was a hero of primeval times, and therefore a non-Jew; but in our book he is represented as a true son of the Law. Moreover, Ezek. xiv. 18, 20 suggest that Daniel had children; but in our book that element of the legend is left aside. These things point clearly to the manipulation of earlier material.

In the second place, it must be conceded that some elements in the narratives are not appropriate, considering the conditions of the times; that they should have *originated* during a time of persecution is difficult to believe. With the exception of Belshazzar the stories end in the conversion of a Gentile ruler; this is not likely to have been the attitude of the Maccabæans towards Antiochus Epiphanes; see, *e.g.*, ii Macc. vii. 34–36; iv. Macc. ix. 9, 31; x. 11, 21; xii. 19.

And, lastly, it is generally recognized that all the apocalyptic books make use of traditional material; so that if this is the case with the apocalyptic portions of *Daniel*, the same might well apply to the narrative portions.

Thus, while it is not possible to indicate what the sources were to which the writer of our book had access, of the fact that such were utilized there can be no reasonable doubt.[2]

VI. The Languages of the Book

Chs. i–ii. 4a, viii–xii are in Hebrew, ii. 4b–vii in Aramaic;[3] this fact will be found to raise some difficult problems,

---

[1] There is also a reference to him in the recently found Ras-Shamra texts.

[2] See, in general, Kuhl, *Die drei Männer im Feuer* (1930).

[3] On the Aramaic of our book Baumgartner's art. in *ZATW*, 1927, pp. 81–133, will be found useful. See also the important article by H. H. Rowley, "Early Aramaic Dialects and the Book of Daniel," in *The Journal of the Royal Asiatic Society*, pp. 777–805 (1933).

the attempts to solve which differ among scholars; but this whole question has been so admirably and convincingly dealt with by Charles that his conclusions are likely to be generally accepted. We shall return to the subject. A point of less importance, but one which has been used as an argument for the theory of composite authorship, is that Daniel is spoken of in the third person in chs. i–vi, while in chs. vii–xii the first person is used. This may, however, be accounted for by the difference of subject-matter in the two parts of the book; for chs. i–vi contain narratives, while chs. vii–xii describe visions. But the real difficulty arises from the fact that the change of language does not correspond with the change of subject-matter; for, as we have seen, i–ii. 4a is written in Hebrew, but ii. 4b–vii. 28 is in Aramaic; if the change of subject-matter corresponded with the change of language, the whole of chs. i–vi ought to be written in Hebrew, and chs. vii–xii in Aramaic, or *vice versa*.

The difficulty is dealt with in great detail by Charles; we can offer here but a summary of his conclusions; the book was originally written entirely in Aramaic; this was necessary because the author wrote for the purpose of encouraging his people to be loyal to their ancestral religion at a time when they were suffering grievous persecution; Aramaic was the vernacular; Hebrew would not have been understood by the bulk of the people. An important point in support of this contention is that the Aramaic sections do not give the impression of being translations; this cannot be claimed for the Hebrew sections. Chs. ii. 4b–vii are therefore in the original language of the book; the reason why ii. 4b–vii was not translated into Hebrew was because at this point the Chaldeans begin to speak: " Then spake the Chaldæans to the king in Aramaic," then begins the Aramaic: " O king, live for ever . . .," *i.e.* the writer lets them speak in what he thinks was their language. The evidence given by Charles shows that ii. 4b–vi and vii come from one and the same writer. Since ch. vii records the first vision, and is written in Aramaic, " there is no rational or conceivable ground for the author's forsaking the vernacular language of his day, and having recourse to Hebrew for his remaining three visions in viii–xii, seeing that his visions, no less than his narratives, were addressed, not to a small educated minority who understood Hebrew, but to the uneducated many who understood only Aramaic." The question then arises: since ii. 4b–vii have been left in their original language, how comes it that i–ii. 4a and viii–xii are in Hebrew? In reply to this Charles writes: " The original of the entire book of *Daniel* was of course in the Aramaic vernacular, but, if the book was to be embodied in the Canon and made of lasting significance, this end could not be achieved otherwise than by commending itself in a Hebrew form, at all events in its opening and closing chapters, to the scholars of the day, who could admit its canonical authority, as they did that of the bilingual *Ezra*, though they refused to include it in the Canon of the prophets." [1]

There may have been a further reason for the apocalyptic portions viii to xii being in Hebrew; for since these are of a prophetic nature it would have been thought more appropriate to have them in the language of the earlier prophetic literature.

A matter of less importance is whether the author himself translated the portions in question into Hebrew, or whether this was done by someone else. Here again opinions

---

[1] *Op. cit.*, p. xlix; so, too, Marti, in Kautzsch-Bertholet, *Die Heilige Schrift des A.T.*, ii. 460. Rowley (*ZATW*, 1932, pp. 256–268) disagrees with Charles; but his own theory, though very ingenious, strikes us as unnecessarily complicated; he holds that " Daniel was a legendary hero, concerning whom popular stories were current in the post-exilic period, and that a Maccabæan author worked up some of these stories and issued them separately in Aramaic for the encouragement of his fellows. Chs. ii–vi were thus issued. Later, ch. vii was similarly issued in Aramaic. The author had now passed over, however, to a different type of literature, which was less suitable for popular circulation. This he recognized by writing subsequent eschatological visions of this type in Hebrew. When he collected his stories and visions into a book, he wanted a fuller and more formal introduction than he had used for the first story when it was issued separately. He therefore rewrote the first part of the story of Nebuchadrezzar's dream, and since this was now intended as an introduction to the whole book, it was written in Hebrew, the language of the more recent sections. The point of transition was thus determined by the amount of the earlier material he desired to rewrite." Other scholars maintain that the whole book was written in Hebrew originally; yet others that the first part was written in Aramaic and the second in Hebrew, and that there was a translation of the beginning of each half into the other language.

differ. Charles, in a searching examination of the linguistic character of the Hebrew portions, comes to the conclusion that the work of three translators is to be discerned (i–ii. 4a; viii–x, xii; and xi).[1] Rowley, in an acute criticism of Charles' contention, says: " The differences Charles finds are quite insufficient to distinguish between the style of the sections, and, moreover, if they were valid, they would each divide the Hebrew sections differently. They do not support one another, and certainly they give us no evidence whatever of three separate documents, each marked by a distinctive group of literary usages." [2] This is somewhat over-stated; but it must be confessed that it is a question very difficult to decide; fortunately it is not one of great moment.

VII. THE TEACHING OF THE BOOK

As is generally recognized, the apocalyptic literature presents us with two greatly differing eschatological points of view. Our book is in some notable particulars an illustration of this. For example, while, on the one hand, the kingdom is for Israel alone, and Israel is to be supreme over all the nations of the world, there are, on the other, passages which certainly suggest that the kingdom is something more than a worldly one: " And in the days of those kings shall the God of heaven set up a kingdom which shall never be destroyed, nor shall the sovereignty thereof be left to another people; but it shall break in pieces and consume all these kingdoms, and it shall stand for ever "; similarly in vii. 18–27; the kingdom is clearly an earthly one in so far as it will overcome all other kingdoms; but since it is an everlasting kingdom it must be something more than a purely earthly one. The incongruity is quite comprehensible when it is remembered that throughout this literature two forms of eschatological teaching find a place.

The teaching concerning the future life shows developments of great interest; xii. 2, 3 is one of the very few

[1] *Op. cit.*, pp. xlvi ff.　　　　[2] *ZATW*, 1932, p. 264.

passages in the Old Testament which express belief in the resurrection: " And many of them that sleep in the dust of the earth [1] shall awake, some to everlasting life, and some to shame and everlasting contempt. . . ." Of the " many " that sleep in the dust of the earth, *i.e.* She'ol, some who are raised are righteous and some are wicked; but presumably the great mass of the departed continue their sleep in She'ol; nothing is said of these; nor is anything said of the places wherein the risen righteous and the risen wicked, respectively, remain for ever. So far as one can gather, it would seem that, according to our author, She'ol is an intermediate state for both the righteous and some of the wicked, but an eternal abode for the great mass of departed spirits, whether good or bad. It must, therefore, be acknowledged that our author does not present his ideas on this momentous subject very clearly; his belief in the fact of resurrection is definite; but otherwise what he says raises questions to which he gives no answer.

The main fact in his conception of God is the emphasis he lays upon the divine transcendence. The Almighty is spoken of as " the God of Heaven " (ii. 18, 19, 44), " the heavens " (iv. 26), " the great and dreadful God " (ix. 4), and see also vii. 9, 10. This is also brought out by the place assigned to angels as the intermediaries between God and men; angels interpret visions to Daniel (vii. 16, viii. 16, ix. 22), and they act as guardians of nations (x. 13, 20, 21, xii. 1).

Like all the apocalyptists our author observes the precepts of the Law; thus in the matter of clean and unclean foods (i. 8–16), doing the works of the Law (iv. 27, Hebr. 24), keeping the hours of prayer (vi. 10, Hebr. 11).

VIII. The Versions

By far the most important are the Greek versions; of these there are two: the Septuagint and Theodotion's revision of the Septuagint. The former exists, however, in only one late and very corrupt MS.; for, whatever the

---

[1] The Hebrew has: " in the land of dust."

reason may have been, it was Theodotion's version and not the Septuagint which was mainly used by the early Church Fathers. But, further, a matter of special interest about Theodotion's version is that it represents a version which was in existence long before his time; this is proved by the fact that in large numbers of quotations from *Daniel* occurring in the writings of Church Fathers before his time, the characteristics of his version already appear. Thus, there was a " pre-Theodotion " version. It seems, therefore, reasonable to conclude that Theodotion had at his disposal a MS. which presented a type of text—so far as *Daniel* was concerned—superior to that of the ordinary Septuagint text; this would, at any rate, account for the preference for his version, rather than for that of the Septuagint, on the part of early Church writers. However this may be, Theodotion's version as well as that of the Septuagint are of great value for the study of our book, for in the frequently corrupt form of the original these versions supply what in all probability represents the true text; this help is greatly needed, for, as Charles points out, the Massoretic text is in hundreds of passages " wholly untrustworthy as to the form of the original and occasionally as to its subject-matter." [1]

In both the Greek versions there are large additions not found in the Massoretic text; thus, the *Story of Susanna* precedes Dan. i. 1; after Dan. iii. 23 follows the *Prayer of Azarias* and details about the heating of the furnace and the preservation of the three men in the furnace; and after Dan. xii. 13 we have the story of *Bel and the Dragon*.[2] In the early Church these additions were regarded as belonging to the canonical Scriptures. In the Septuagint text various further additions of minor importance appear.

Of less value, but not to be ignored, are the Peshitta and the Vulgate.

[1] *Op. cit.*, p. lix.
[2] On these additions see Kuhl, *op. cit.*, pp. 84–104.

THE BOOK OF HOSEA

I. Place in the Canon

THE book of *Hosea* always occupies the first place among the *Twelve Prophets*, and its general position varies with that of the latter. Thus, in the Hebrew Bible it comes immediately after *Ezekiel*; in the Septuagint it is the first of the Prophets; in the Peshitta it stands next to *Isaiah*, and in the Vulgate, followed by modern versions, it is placed next to *Daniel*. It owes this position mainly to the fact that it is the longest of the *Twelve*, but partly, possibly, to the theory that Hosea was the first of them in chronological order.

II. Historical Background

The activity of Hosea falls within the lifetime of Isaiah, and the background of external politics is the same for both prophets. In northern Israel the time was one of utter confusion. The great age of the successful Jeroboam ii was over, and Israelite prosperity was rapidly fading. Jeroboam's son, Zechariah, was assassinated by Shallum, Shallum by Menahem. This king won a temporary security by submission to Tiglath-pileser in 738 B.C., but his son, Pekahiah, was murdered by Pekah in the interests of the anti-Assyrian party. Pekah perished in a vain attempt to stem the tide of Assyrian advance, and the greater part of his kingdom was organized into Assyrian provinces. His successor, Hoshea, revolted after a nine-years reign, and was put to death by Shalmaneser v, who succeeded Tiglath-pileser in 727 B.C. Samaria was then besieged, and fell after a three-years' resistance (721 B.C.), and the kingdom of Israel came to an end.

III. Structure and Contents

The book seems to contain two collections of oracular matter, one of which is a good deal longer than the other. The first is introduced by a biographical passage (type B),[1] and the second by a chapter in which the prophet describes his own experiences (type C).[2]

The first section comprises chs. i–ii. In i. 2–9 we have an account of Hosea's domestic history from the pen of a third party, who describes his marriage and the birth of his three children. To this has been appended a short oracle, in i. 10–ii. 1 (Hebr. ii. 1–3), describing the happy future that awaits Israel. It may be a good deal later than Hosea, for the names in ii. 1 suggest that it was written for its present position, and the substance points rather to a period after the fall of Jerusalem in 586 B.C.

The little collection which follows includes verses 2–5 (Hebr. 4–7) (a mutilated oracle), 6–7 (Hebr. 8–9), 8–13 (Hebr. 10–15). All these are messages of condemnation and of doom, but in the rest of the collection we have promises of forgiveness and restoration. These are contained in the following verses (the numeration in the Hebrew Bible is two higher than the R.V. throughout this chapter): verses 14–15, 16–17 (fragmentary and, probably, worked over before its inclusion in the collection), 18–20, 21–23 (apparently the end only of a rather longer passage). Some scholars reject these and other passages on the ground that Hosea could not have held out any hope for his people. This, however, seems to be an assumption which it is difficult to justify, and there is nothing else in these pieces (except perhaps in verse 23) which suggests the work of a later prophet. We may note the fact that the collector has placed these happier utterances at the end of his collection in accordance with a principle which is abundantly illustrated in the Old Testament.

The second, and much longer, collection, is introduced by the prophet's own account of his marriage. The relation between chs. i and iii will be referred to later. Again we

---

[1] See above, p. 228 f.   [2] See above, pp. 229 ff.

note a happy expansion at the end.   This (verse 5) is probably the work of a Judæan scribe some time between the
fall of Samaria (721 B.C.) and that of Jerusalem (586 B.C.).

Ch. iv contains six or seven pieces, or fragments.   Verses
1–3 (probably the latter part of verse 3 is a later expansion)
are followed by 4–6 (of which the opening is corrupt and
unintelligible), 7–11 (mutilated at the beginning), 12–13a,
13b–14 (mutilated at the end), 15 (a later addition by a
Judæan scribe, apparently a good deal later than Amos),
16–19 (where the text is extraordinarily corrupt, though
not necessarily hopeless).   Ch. v. 1–7 gives us one of the
longest continuous sections in the book, and is followed by
two oracles in v. 8–9 and 10–14.   Chs. v. 15–vi. 3 suggests
an extract from some current Liturgy, and there is no need
to reject it as some scholars do.   Ch. vi. 4–6 seems to be
closely attached to the foregoing.[1]   Ch. vi. 7–11 forms an
independent whole.   Ch. vii appears to contain the following pieces : verses 1–2, 3–6, 7–10 (placed after the preceding owing to the mention of the " oven "), 11–12, 13–14
(probably mutilated at the end), 15–16.   In ch. viii we
have verses 1–3 (mutilated at the beginning), 4a (an isolated
fragment), 4b–7, 8–10, 11–13.   Ch. ix contains seven oracles
or oracle fragments: verses 1–4, 5–6, 7–9, 10, 11a (the last
two are mere fragments), 11b–15 (of this the opening words
have not been preserved), 16–17.   In ch. x we have verses
1–2, 3–4 (regarded as a late insertion by some scholars,
though it must belong to the age of the monarchy), 5 (an
isolated fragment), 6–8, 9–10 (the beginning only of this
oracle has been preserved), 11–13a, 13b–14 (here we seem
to have the beginning and end of two separate oracles,
which have been telescoped in our text), to which a prose
note has been appended, at some time before the end of
the Judæan monarchy, in verse 15.

It is not impossible that a fresh collection opens with
ch. xi.   The main theme of the first two collections was the
apostasy of Israel, the " wife " of Yahweh ; here the people
become His sons.   This is especially brought out in the

---

[1] On v. 1–vi. 6 see Budde in the *Journal of the Palestine Oriental Soc.*, vol. xiv
(1934).

first piece, xi. 1–3. This is followed by verses 4–6, with an addition in verse 7 taken from some other utterance of Hosea's, 8–11, 12–xii. 1 (in the MT xi. 12 is counted as the first verse of xii), 2–6, 7–10 (of which the beginning and end have not been preserved), 11–13 (again incomplete at both ends), 14 (an isolated fragment). Ch. xiii is commonly divided into two parts at the end of verse 11, but metrical and other considerations make the following analysis more probable: verses 1–3, 4–6, 7–8, 9–11, 12–14c, 14d–16 (something has been lost at the beginning). Ch. xiv has aroused more discussion than any previous oracular section. Many editors would deny Hosea's authorship, mainly on three grounds: (a) it offers hope for the future, which Hosea would not have done; (b) a compiler always tried to find a hopeful passage to place at the end of his work; (c) there are words and phrases which do not occur elsewhere till long after the time of Hosea. The first two are of little importance, since we must allow a prophet to change his tone with altered circumstances, and the fact that a compiler found a hopeful section for the conclusion of the book does not prove that this section was not the work of Hosea. The later words and phrases are not numerous, though verse 7 seems to be dependent on Pss. xxxvi. 9 and lxv. 11, 12. We should, however, note that the passage has a distinctly liturgical form, and may have been cited by Hosea and modified by a later age. In verses 1–3 the officiating priests appeal to Israel to repent, and in verses 4–7 the people respond. Verses 8 and 9 are isolated sentences which a compiler—or even a scribe—has appended to the whole.

IV. DATE AND AUTHORSHIP

It is clear that the work of Hosea is to be placed during the last generation of the existence of the northern kingdom. The earliest suggestion of a definite date is to be found in viii. 9, which may well refer to the tribute paid by Menahem to Tiglath-pileser in 738 B.C. There is no direct reference to the fall of Samaria, though it is clear that the prophet often felt the calamity close at hand. If, however, we accept some of the more hopeful passages as original, we may conjecture that they were uttered after 721 B.C., when the kingdom, so obnoxious to Hosea, had vanished, and there might be hope of a spiritual new beginning.

There are two classes of passages which have awakened the suspicions of commentators. One is that already mentioned, in which the prophet looks forward to the possibility of a brighter future. These occur usually at the end of sections or of collections, and may be the additions of a later age. This, however, does not necessarily follow, and the evidence does not justify us in dogmatically asserting that they are not the work of Hosea himself. The other class is that in which Judah is mentioned. Here we must face the possibility, even the probability, that southern scribes have deliberately modified the text to make it fit their own community, or have inserted such sentences as xi. 12b, which contrast the fidelity of Judah with the apostasy of the north. Apart from these two classes of passage, there is little, if anything, which modern scholars would deny to Hosea.

The date of the compilations seems quite uncertain. We have occasional hints of an exilic, or of a post-exilic, date, especially in the Judah passages, and that suggests that the oracles were not formally collected till long after the time of Hosea. The corrupt state of the text, and the mutilated condition of a great many of the separate pieces, are also indications of a fairly long period between the utterance of the words and their inclusion in collections. Jeremiah seems to have been acquainted with the work of Hosea, but it does not follow that the book, or even the individual collections therein, had reached the form in which we have them now. Probably we shall not be far wrong if we assign the actual compilations to the exilic or post-exilic age.

V. Hosea's Domestic Life

The problem of Hosea's marriage has aroused a great deal of discussion in recent years, and numerous attempts have been made to reconstruct the actual course of events.

The primary sources are chs. i and iii; and some of the oracles, especially those contained in ch. ii, have been used to supplement the prose narratives.   We may briefly indicate several of the views that have been held:

(*a*) It has been maintained that the whole story is symbolical, and that it does not represent historical fact.   This is rendered improbable by certain details, particularly the name Gomer.

(*b*) The narrative in ch. i has been held to be historical, and ch. iii allegorical—a position for which there seems to be no good ground, unless we are to assume that all C passages in the prophets are due to later Midrash.

(*c*) The two have been combined, and it has been held that, after the birth of the third child, Gomer left her husband and fell ultimately into slavery, whence she was purchased by Hosea and taken again to his home.   This has been popularized by the brilliant exegesis of Sir George Adam Smith, and is the form of the story best known to English readers.   On the other hand, it has been maintained, especially by those who have taken into account the difference in type between the two chapters, that ch. iii is a more intimate account of the actual marriage, emanating from the prophet himself.

A further question is as to whether Gomer was innocent at the time of her marriage, and whether, if she were not, Hosea was aware of her character.   The language of i. 2 and iii. 1 seems definitely against the former view, though it might be explained as prophetic.   A literal acceptance is extremely difficult, especially in view of Hosea's obvious repugnance to the sexual immoralities prevalent in Israel. This might be met psychologically by the suggestion (probably sound) that Hosea suffered from sex-obsession, which drove him into the thing of which he had the greatest horror.   It might be defended also on religious grounds by the supposition that Gomer was originally a temple prostitute.   This would explain Hosea's feeling that his marriage was a religious act, and would offer a reason for several of the details preserved in ch. iii.

Even the conjugal infidelity of Gomer is not to be deduced

with certainty from the narratives of chs. i and iii. The names of the two younger children have been interpreted as implying this, and a further argument is to be seen in the use of the word " adulterers " in iii. 1. But the word used here may have a wider significance than that implied in the English rendering, and the names Lo-ruhamah and Lo-ammi, like those of Isaiah's children, may be signs merely for Israel, with no reference to their father's home-life.

But even if this be true, we have no right to assume that these two fragments of narrative give us the whole of Hosea's story. On the contrary, there was much in his domestic experience which profoundly influenced his thought and feeling, though there is no direct account of it. Ch. xi surely implies that Hosea suffered, not only from a faithless wife, but from ungrateful and rebellious children. So also, even though Gomer's adultery may not be actually mentioned in the prose narratives, it is difficult to understand Hosea's message and teaching except on the theory that she was false to him, and fell back into her old ways. We should beware of reading too much into the connexion between chs. i and ii, but we are probably justified in assuming that the oracles contained in ch. ii—and elsewhere —are based on bitter experiences which befell Hosea after the events described in chs. i and iii.

VI. THE MAN AND HIS MESSAGE

Modern psychological science has helped us to see that we have in prophecy the emergence of elements from the subconscious, facilitated—indeed made possible—by the peculiar psychic state which made the prophet what he was.[1] In other words, what the prophet said and did was the expression of that real basic personality of which he himself was often unaware. Like many another great soul in the history of man's religion (we may, not unfairly, cite Tertullian and Augustine as examples), Hosea was, at any rate in his youth, subject to what recent psychology would call a " sex-complex." Such natures as his have a

[1] Cp. especially Haeussermann, *Wortempfängnis und Symbol* (1933).

peculiar intensity and passion which run through all their life, and often, when duly " sublimated," give them an extraordinary power and impressiveness.   In Hosea we have the struggle between the subconscious obsession and the purity of conscious thought resulting in his involving himself in the thing he most hated.   Seen from another point of view (that which the prophet himself may have more nearly realized) he seems to have felt that the supreme act of surrender to the will of God was to take the step most horrible to him, and to bind his life to that of a woman belonging to the class he most loathed.   More simply still, he found himself swept away by an overwhelming love for a woman who belonged to a class against which his better nature revolted, and, in his love, he found a reflection of that which Yahweh bore to Israel, faithless and disgusting as she was.   It was an awful thing to Hosea that he should so love Gomer, but Yahweh was immeasurably nobler and purer than he, and Israel stood on a lower moral level than the erring woman to whom he gave himself.   So, in the agony of his own spirit, and in the deathless love he knew, he found an image of the heart of God, broken by the constant rejection of His love, and by the endlessly repeated apostasies of His beloved people.

That is, in fact, all that we know of Hosea, and all that we need to know.   Of his life outside his own home we have no record whatever.   We are told the circumstances in which his various oracles were delivered, but we hear nothing of the reception accorded to them.   We know that he was unheeded by his people, but that we learn, not from the book of Hosea, but from the fact that Israel went her way to ruin.

In later life, as it seems, the loving passion which consumed the prophet was directed as much to his children as to his wife.   Yet they too proved a crushing disappointment, and once more he realized the meaning of divine sorrow over human sin.

Hosea's poetic style is characteristic of the man.   In spite of the mutilation which so many oracles have suffered and the grave corruptions of the text, we can recognize in his verse the staccato quality of utterances forced from the man by intense emotion. This often makes the meaning obscure, but, in *Hosea*, the literal sense is always subordinate to the feeling which the poetry expresses. His metaphors are taken less from life and Nature than those of Amos and Jeremiah, and his language is much more that of a towns-man than is theirs.

Hosea was not oblivious to the evils which called forth the denunciations of his predecessor, Amos, and of his con-temporaries, Isaiah and Micah. He was aware of social injustice and has much to say of political folly. To him, as to Isaiah, close association with foreign peoples involved apostasy, and it was the religious shortcomings of the nation on which his attention was fixed. The cultus was evil—sheer Baalism—and he was the first, as far as we know, expressly to condemn the bull-worship at Bethel.

But, above all things, Hosea insisted on Yahweh's demand for *Love*. For its lower manifestations he uses the common term *'ahabhah*, but his favourite word expresses a higher " sublimated " type—*Hesedh*.[1] Here we have a term which defies translation. It is love always in the light of some definite relationship—husband–wife, parent–child, God-worshipper. It has, therefore, an element of *duty* in it, and from this side is better represented by the Latin *pietas* than by any other rendering. But it is more than *pietas*, for it has a far deeper emotional content; it may be the love of the higher to the lower, or of equals to one another, as well as that of the inferior to the superior. It implies, too, always a full recognition of the nature, rights, and demands of personality, and, in one of its aspects, may be described as consecration to personality. It goes deeper than the justice which Amos required; it is a fundamental quality of soul which serves as a spring and motive for all right action in personal relationships.

For Israel Hosea saw little hope. There are passages (of disputed authorship, as we have seen) which suggest the possibility of repentance and restoration. But the former was an indispensable condition of the latter, and, if it were

---

[1] Rendered " goodness " in vi. 4; " mercy " in vi. 6 and elsewhere.

A A

lacking, the people's ruin was inevitable. It was better that the nation should cease to be than that it should continue as it was. Yahweh loved Israel with a passion so great that, while He would restore her if she would allow Him, He would yet, if need be, destroy her utterly.

VII. The Hebrew Text and the Septuagint

There is no book in the Old Testament which has suffered more from textual corruption than *Hosea*. There is hardly a single verse of which the reader can be sure that it has not been more or less altered, generally by accident. A large part of the text, as it stands, is meaningless, though good sense can often be obtained by very slight changes. Illustrations may be seen in iv. 4, 5, vii. 5, ix. 6, 7, 8, x. 10, xi. 4, 7. Sometimes additions have been made by later scribes, *e.g.* in ii. 4, ix. 9, xiii. 6, xiv. 4, 5. The text before the Septuagint translators was hardly better, though a superior reading is sometimes suggested, as in ii. 20, v. 15, viii. 10, x. 10, and the worst corruptions must have taken place before the divergence of the two lines of tradition.

THE BOOK OF JOEL

I. Contents

A BRIEF survey of the contents will show wherein the problem of this book lies. It contains two elements—narrative and apocalyptic.

1. *The narrative portion* is as follows:—The book opens with a description of a plague of locusts from the ravages of which the land has suffered (i. 2–5). So terrible has been the scourge that the swarms are compared with an invading army (i. 6, 7). The prophet calls to lamentation; let the priests mourn because the offerings cannot be brought to the sanctuary; corn, wine, and oil, which formed an important part of the offerings, are unprocurable; let the vine-dressers and agriculturists mourn because everything has been devastated; all the inhabitants are called upon to fast and to cry unto Yahweh (i. 8–14). The prophet points to the ravages before the very eyes of the people, and leads them in a plaint to the Almighty (i. 16–20). Let them now at once turn to Him in fasting and weeping and mourning, for He is very merciful; it may be that He will hear their cry (ii. 12–14). So the prophet commands a fast and a solemn assembly (ii. 15–17). As a result the answer comes from Yahweh that He is about to give them once more all that they need; the enemy, *i.e.* the locust swarms, are being driven away, the land may rejoice, the beasts of the field need fear no more; there shall again be plenty in the land, let the people praise God, for He is in their midst (ii. 18–27).

That is the narrative; it is not quite clear whether there was only the promise of returning fertility in which the people implicitly trusted, or whether this had actually taken place—in which case the lapse of some time must be assumed between ii. 17 and 18–27—but otherwise the narrative in

itself is perfectly straightforward.   It covers i. 2–20 (excepting verse 15), ii. 12–27 (excepting verse 20).

2. *The apocalyptic portion* begins abruptly at i. 15, which
breaks the course of the narrative portion: " Alas for the
day ! for the day of Yahweh is at hand, and as destruction
from Shaddai shall it come." It continues in ii. 1 ff.;
here the locust swarm is allegorized; the day of darkness
and gloom is at hand; a description of the advent of a
mighty people follows; they will overrun the land and
leave it waste; all men will be in fear of them, they will
come in serried ranks and overwhelm the city; the earth
will quake before them; the heavens will tremble, sun and
moon and stars will be darkened; who can abide the day
of Yahweh? (ii. 1–11).   After these terrors have passed the
Almighty will pour His spirit on all flesh.   Then there will
be further wonders in the heavens and on earth, the sun
and moon turned to darkness.   But the remnant of the
people, *i.e.* those who call on the name of Yahweh, will be
delivered from all the terrors (ii. 28–31 [Hebr. iii. 1–5]).
The dispersed of Israel will be brought back, but all the
nations shall be gathered together in the valley of Jehoshaphat to be punished for the evil which the people of God
have suffered at their hands; Tyre, Zidon, Philistia, and
the Greeks are specially mentioned (iii. 1–8 [Hebr. iv. 1–8]).
The nations are again bidden to gather themselves in the
valley of Jehoshaphat, when the sun, moon and stars will
be darkened, and Yahweh will utter His voice from Jerusalem, and the children of Israel will no more be troubled;
but fruitfulness will be poured out upon the land, the
people will dwell in prosperity, for Yahweh will dwell in
Zion (iii. 9–21 [Hebr. iv. 9–21]).

The apocalyptic portion is thus contained in i. 15, ii. 1–11,
20, ii. 28–32 (Hebr. iii. 1–5), iii. 1–21 (Hebr. iv. 1–21).   Like
the narrative portion it is written in poetry.[1]

---

[1] Duhm (*ZATW* 1911, pp. 184–188), however, maintains that it is in prose;
it must be allowed that the metre is not always clear, and even where the
poetical form is evident it is not always uniform, *e.g.* iv (E.V. iii) 9–14 is irregular
while iv (E.V. iii) 15–17 is 3 : 3.

II. Authorship

The question now arises as to whether these two portions are to be assigned to the same author or not. If the narrative portion be understood in a literal sense, which is the most obvious and natural, then it is a little difficult to understand how an author can intermix in one and the same writing such very different themes as a locust visitation and an apocalyptic prophecy regarding the end of the present world. Placing oneself in the position of the writer of the narrative portion one cannot fail to notice how terrible to him was this visitation, with its awful ravages, and with the consequent danger of famine. Not less intense was the feeling with which he exhorted priests and people to fast and mourn and pray, in order that by the mercy of God better times might come. Clearly his thoughts were concentrated on these things, his whole attention absorbed by the present distress and the means to be adopted for ensuring a happier future. Under such conditions it seems extremely unlikely that he could at the same time be thinking about the end of the world and the various apocalyptic elements with which the later part of the book is full. Later thought might well suggest an allegorical interpretation of the visitation in the sense of its being a symbolical heralding of the Day of Yahweh; so that it could with justice be contended that the apocalyptic portion was a subsequent addition by the author to his earlier writing, setting forth his reflections as he looked back upon the dire episode. In itself this would be a perfectly acceptable solution of the problem. On the other hand, an equally satisfactory explanation would be to suppose that the narrative portion was written by a prophet, and that subsequently it was utilized by an apocalyptist for the purpose of driving home his teaching concerning the coming Day of Yahweh. That the latter inserted some minor verbal additions in the narrative, such as i. 15, would be a natural process.

But why, it may be asked, is the idea of dual authorship suggested at all, especially when the great mass of Old

Testament scholars believe in single authorship?[1] The reason is that there are indications in the two portions of the book, respectively, which point to difference of date. To this subject we turn next.

III. Date

It was, no doubt, due to the position of our book in the Canon, viz. between those of *Hosea* and *Amos*,[2] which induced the belief, held for long, that it belonged to pre-exilic times. But the place of a book in the Canon is no indication of its date, as is clear, *e.g.*, from the positions of *Ruth, Daniel* and *Jonah.*

1. The *narrative* portion must be regarded as post-exilic for the following reasons; not that these are all decisive, but taken in the aggregate they offer a convincing case:

In the titles of almost all the pre-exilic prophetical books the name or names of the kings during whose reigns the prophet worked is given. That this is not the case with our book does not necessarily point to a post-exilic date, for the same is the case with Nahum and Habakkuk; but it must be noted as not being in accordance with the general usage of pre-exilic prophetical books.

More convincing is the fact that not only is there no reference to the northern kingdom, but " Israel " is used as synonymous with Judah; this usage occurs only after the time of Ezra. In ii. 27 it is said: "And ye shall know that I am in the midst of Israel "; but the people addressed are those of Judah: " Be glad then, ye children of Zion " (ii. 23). In iv. 2, again, we read of " my heritage Israel," but the reference, as verse 1 shows, is to "Judah and Jerusalem." And, once more, in iv. 16 Israel is mentioned, but it is from Zion, from Jerusalem, that Yahweh will make His voice heard; clearly, therefore, by " Israel " is

---

[1] Dual authorship is held by Duhm (*ZATW* for 1911, pp. 184–188) and Marti, in Kautzsch-Bertholet's *Die Heilige Schrift des A.T.*, ii. p. 23 (1923); but they reckon ii. 1–11 as belonging to the narrative portion, though with apocalyptic insertions. We had reached our conclusion as to dual authorship independently.

[2] In the Septuagint it occupies the fourth place, after *Micah*.

meant the people of Judah. This points unmistakably to post-exilic times.

Again, Jerusalem is the only sanctuary; not that this necessarily points to post-exilic times, for it could be argued that inasmuch as the prophet belongs to the south there would be no need to mention the northern sanctuary. But what is of real significance is that no reference whatsoever is made to the high-places (*bamoth*); this must mean that either this narrative portion was written some considerable time before Amos, or else after the Exile. But as there is not a single argument which will bear examination for such an early date, the only alternative is to place the narrative portion in the post-exilic period. It should also be noted that i. 14, ii. 15, 16 give the impression that the people are all living in close proximity to Jerusalem, which points to post-exilic conditions.

But there are yet stronger arguments in favour of this date. The priests are the leaders of the people; a king is never spoken of. Interest is centred on the worship of the Temple; the threefold reference to the meal offering (*minḥah*) and the drink offering (*nesek*) in i. 9, 13, ii. 14 is quite conclusive as to date, for these refer to the daily morning and evening offering to which the abbreviated name *Tamid* (" continual " offering) is given; in pre-exilic times the burnt offering was offered in the morning, the meal offering in the evening (see ii Kgs. xvi. 15); but in the Priestly Code of post-exilic times these were combined and were offered together both morning and evening;[1] to these was then added the drink offering (Exod. xxix. 38–42, Num. xxviii. 3–8); so that the mention in *Joel* of the drink offering in connexion with the other offering points indubitably to post-exilic times.

The importance of offerings shown in this narrative portion is very different from the attitude of the pre-exilic prophets, to whom the sacrifices were of small account, if

---

[1] In Ezek. xlvi. 13–15 the morning burnt offering and meal offering are already combined, but the drink offering has not yet come into vogue; no evening offering is mentioned. In the *Joel* passages burnt offering (*'olah*) is not used, but it was probably included in the *minḥah*, which was a general term for sacrifices (see Gen. iv. 3–5; Num. xvi. 15; i Sam. ii. 17, xxvi. 19).

not unnecessary, at any rate when offered in the wrong spirit. And striking, too, in contrast to the earlier prophets, is the entire absence of ethical teaching. The pre-exilic prophets would assuredly have pointed to the locust visitation as a mark of divine wrath for the sins of the people (see, *e.g.*, Am. iv. 9); there would have been a call to forsake sin and refrain from evil; but here the prophet exhorts to fasting, weeping and mourning; only once does the phrase " turn unto Yahweh your God " occur (ii. 13).

And, finally, as Marti has pointed out, the easy and smooth style of the writer of this book, so far from being a sign of early date, is in fact a proof of the contrary; smoothness of style and simplicity of expression are qualities which the earlier prophets do not possess, and it is certain that from about 400 B.C. onwards the art of writing good and smooth Hebrew was cultivated.[1] It has also been shown by Holzinger that our book contains various words and expressions which belong to late Hebrew style.[2]

These considerations make it certain that the narrative portion of our book belongs to the post-exilic period. The marked influence of the Priestly Code points to a period after the time of Ezra; so that we may with some confidence assign this part of the book to about the middle of the fourth century B.C.

2. Turning now to the *apocalyptic* portion, there are some interesting indirect indications of date. In iii. 1 (Hebr. iv. 1) it is said: " For, behold, in those days, and in that time, when I shall bring again the captivity of Judah and Jerusalem . . ."; here the words " when I will bring again the captivity " do not represent the meaning of the original; in an exhaustive study of the Hebrew phrase (*shūb shĕbûth*) Dietrich[3] has shown that this is a technical term which, in its original sense, occurs only in eschatological passages, and means " to bring back as of old " or " re-establish as in primeval times," *i.e.* it expresses the hope of the return of the Golden Age at the end of the present world-order.

---

[1] *Das Dodekapropheton*, p. 113 (1904).
[2] In *ZATW* ix. pp. 89 ff.
[3] שׁוּב שְׁבוּת *Die endzeitliche Wiederherstellung bei den Propheten* (1925).

This is borne out by the context in which the term stands in *Joel*; and this context contains all the outstanding traits of the developed form of the eschatological drama presented in the apocalyptic literature of the last two centuries B.C., viz. the salvation of Jerusalem; the judgement on the nations; followed by the time of general well-being, fruitfulness of the land, etc.; the permanent abode of Yahweh on Zion—in a word, the Messianic Age. In another part of the eschatological portion of our book (ii. 11, 12), which is repeated in iii. 15, 16, the usual signs in the heavens and the shaking of the earth are also mentioned. While not an absolute proof, the fact that this portion of the book is so closely similar in content to the central eschatological traits contained in the apocalyptic literature makes it highly probable that it belongs approximately to 200 B.C., or slightly later.

Further, as will be seen in the chapter dealing with Zech. ix–xiv, this portion of *Zechariah* was written after 200 B.C. The close affinities between Joel iii and Zech. xiv, therefore, make it highly probable that a similar date is to be assigned to each. The identity of thought between these two books is so striking that it is worth while placing them in parallel columns:

Joel iii.	*Zech. xiv.*
2. I will gather all nations and will bring them down into the valley of Jehoshaphat.	2. And I will gather all nations against Jerusalem to battle.
11. . . . thither cause thy mighty ones to come down, O Yahweh.	5. . . . and Yahweh my God shall come, and all the holy ones with thee.
17. So shall ye know that I am Yahweh your God, dwelling in Zion my holy mountain.	9. And Yahweh shall be king over all the earth (*i.e.* in Jerusalem, see verses 3, 4).
18. . . . and there shall no strangers pass through her any more.	21. . . . and in that day there shall be no more a trafficker in the house of Yahweh of hosts.
18. . . . and a fountain shall come forth of the house of Yahweh.	8. and it shall come to pass in that day that living waters shall go out of Jerusalem.

A few other points may be noted. In Joel iii. 4 ff. (Hebr. iv. 4 ff.), it is said of the Phœnicians and Philistines that they had sold the Jews as slaves to "the sons of the Grecians." In Zech. ix. 13 "the sons of Greece" are also

mentioned, and there are good reasons for believing that by
these the Seleucid empire is meant, for this had been part
of Alexander's dominions, and the Seleucids were ardent
Hellenists. It is possible that a similar meaning is to be
attached to " the sons of the Grecians " in Joel iv. 6.
Jewish slaves would be at least as likely to be sold to the
Syrians as to the Greeks. Besides, Phœnicia and Philistia
come to the front again and again during the Seleucid era
(*e.g.* Zech. ix. 2, 6). And, once more, in Joel ii. 20 " the
northern (army) " is spoken of; there is no mention of
" army " in the original, it is " the northern one," which
may well be " the king of the north " in Dan. xi. 11,
i.e. Antiochus iii; [1] if so, the reference would be to the
abortive attempt made by this king in 218-217 B.C. to
wrest Cœle-Syria from Ptolemy iv Philopator.

The many affinities between this part of *Joel* and the
apocalyptic portion of Isa. xxiv–xxvii [2] would also point to
a date not earlier than about 200 B.C.

IV. The Hebrew Text and the Septuagint

With but few exceptions the text of *Joel* has come down
to us in a very satisfactory condition. The few corruptions
which occur are not serious (*e.g.* i. 7, 17, 18; ii. 11; iii. 11,
Hebr. iv. 11); in these the Septuagint gives, once or
twice, some help. Additions to the Hebrew text are to be
discerned here and there (*e.g.* in ii. 11, 20, 26; ii. 31 [Hebr.
iii. 4]), but they are of no importance. In about half-a-
dozen places the Septuagint contains additions to be noted,
though they are not of much importance (*e.g.* i. 5, 8; ii. 12;
iii. 11); in only two or three of these does it represent a
better Hebrew text (*e.g.* i. 18).

---

[1] Torrey thinks the reference is to Alexander the Great (*Martifestschrift*,
pp. 281 ff. (1925). For extraneous influence on Jewish eschatology see
Oesterley and Robinson, *Hebrew Religion*, pp. 344 ff.
[2] See above, p. 252 ff.

THE BOOK OF AMOS

I. PLACE IN THE CANON

THE book of *Amos* stands third in the order of the " *Twelve* " in the Hebrew Bible. In the Septuagint, however, it is placed second, the book of *Joel* coming later. The Peshitta, Vulgate, and modern versions follow the order of the Hebrew Bible.

II. HISTORICAL BACKGROUND

The reign of Jeroboam ii was the most brilliant period in the history of the northern kingdom. The old rivalry between Israel and Damascus was ending with Israelite supremacy, and even districts to the east of Jordan were recovered for Israel. Egypt was too weak to interfere, and Assyria had not yet begun the movement which ended in the conquest of Palestine.

For the internal condition, Amos himself is our chief witness. He shows us a people, rich and luxurious, but selfish and careless of human rights; the upper classes have all that they want, while the poor, especially the peasants, are sinking into misery and even slavery. Beneath the fair surface the whole country is rotten, and its doom cannot be long delayed.

III. STRUCTURE AND CONTENTS

All three types of material [1] are found in the book of *Amos*, though B is confined to a short passage in ch. vii, and C to a series of visions in the last three chapters. The general construction of the book presents some peculiar features. There appear to be headings of a kind at the beginning of chs. iii and v, which may mean that there

---

[1] See above, pp. 224 ff.

were minor oracular collections. Other oracles are found attached to the visions in chs. vii–ix; a large proportion of these must be classed as eschatological. They have, apparently, been selected by the main compiler, or by the compiler of this last section, as being suitable to the general trend of the visions.

The first section opens with a collection of oracles against foreign nations, preceded by a general statement of the prophet's message in i. 2. The peoples denounced are: Damascus (i. 3–5), Philistia (6–8), Phœnicia (9–10), Edom (11–12), Ammon (13–15), Moab (ii. 1–3), Judah (4–5), and at the end we have Israel (6–7a). The originality of the section dealing with Philistia, Phœnicia and Edom has been challenged, but the reasons have not generally been deemed decisive. For instance, the absence of Gath in the list of Philistine cities has been held to prove that its fall in 711 B.C. had already taken place. Clearly, there may have been other reasons for the omission. On the other hand, it is generally agreed that the oracle against Judah (ii. 4–5) is a later insertion.

A more serious problem is created by the structure of the oracles. They are all couched in the same form, and in almost identical language. The chief difference lies in the crime for which each nation is condemned. It is as though a framework has been used and filled in with different names and different charges, and it may be observed that the inserted portion is in most cases metrically discordant with the framework. Is it likely that this was the work of the prophet himself? Against the inherent improbability of his adopting such a method, we have the fact that Amos does seem to use formulæ which he adapted to various needs, e.g. in the series of little utterances which we have in iv. 6–11. In view of all the facts, we may take it for granted that Amos did utter threats against the peoples mentioned, on the grounds given, even though we suspect that a collector or editor was responsible for the identity of the mould in which all are cast.

The list of nations concludes with Israel, introducing a further and more detailed account of her iniquities. Two oracles are added in this section, ii. 7b–12 and 13–16, the first (in *Qinah* 3:2) dealing with ritual sins, and the second (metre 3:3) announcing punishment.

The second group of oracles opens with a rhetorical statement of the law of causation (iii. 2–8), followed by a summons to foreign powers to witness the iniquity of Samaria. Then we have a fragment in verse 11, short threats of punishment in verses 12–13 and 14–15, a denunciation of the women in iv. 1–3, and of the cultus in iv. 4–5. Then comes a group of utterances each of which describes some calamity and ends with the formula: " Yet ye have not returned unto me." The signature " saith the Lord " suggests that they were originally independent utterances, which have been connected either by the prophet himself or by an early collector. They mention famine (verse 6), drought (7–8), blight (9), pestilence (10), earthquake (11), and conclude with a final threat of the coming of Yahweh Himself to execute His final vengeance (12–13).

The next group opens with the lovely dirge over Israel, the fallen virgin (v. 2), to which, perhaps, verse 3 should be attached, eliminating its introductory clause as redactional. Verses 4–6 denounce the sanctuaries; verse 7 is an isolated fragment; 8–10 are clearly taken from a hymn to Yahweh as Lord of Nature; 11–13 contain two fragmentary denunciations of social iniquity; 14–15 are an exhortation to see Yahweh; 16–17 a threat of punishment; 18–20 a description of the Day of Yahweh; and 21–27 a condemnation of the cultus. In vi. 1–7 we have a denunciation of the ruthless luxury of the rich, and verse 8 expresses Yahweh's loathing of the pride of Israel. This will result (verses 9–11) in pestilence and earthquake—apparently two oracular fragments have been worked over in prose form, and verses 12 and 13–14 are isolated fragments.

With ch. vii begins the series of visions. These are described in prose (type C), and the first (vii. 1–3) is that of locusts, followed by a devouring fire (4–6), and Yahweh Himself standing with a plumbline against a wall (7–8a). To this last a short oracle has been appended in 8b–9. Ch. vii. 10–17 is the only instance of biographical prose in the book, and it describes the conflict between Amos and Amaziah, the priest of Bethel. The fourth vision is that of a basket of summer fruit (viii. 1–3), which is followed by a series of short oracles; most of these are eschatological in tone--viii. 4–8, 9–10, 11–12, 13–14. Ch. ix opens with the fifth vision, that of Yahweh smiting the sanctuary (at Bethel?), with which is closely linked a prediction of the complete annihilation of Israel (ix. 1–4). Next, we have another fragment from a hymn of praise (ix. 5–6), and two oracular fragments in verses 7 and 8a. Verse 8b to the end of the chapter consists of a series of hopeful oracles, all of which seem to presuppose the Exile, and one of them (ix. 11–12) certainly does so, since it speaks of the tabernacle of David as having fallen.

IV. Date and Authorship

Apart from one or two passages and small fragments, which seem to come from the compiler, and especially the small collection of exilic prophecy at the end of the book, there is little that we cannot ascribe to Amos himself. In v. 8 we have language which suggests that the prophet may have actually witnessed an eclipse. This can only have been that which took place in June 763 B.C., and we can thus date the prophecies of Amos with some degree of probability, shortly after that date. They were, as it appears, delivered in Bethel and Samaria, and his boldness aroused official hostility against him. He is not likely, then, to have remained long in the north, and the whole of his activity may be placed within the reign of Jeroboam ii.

V. The Man and his Message

Amos, as he himself tells us, was a shepherd and a dresser of coarse figs, whose home lay in the semi-wilderness of the Tekoa region in southern Judah. He was essentially a countryman, intimate with all the creatures of the wild— the vulture, the lion, the bear, the serpent. But he had visited famous sanctuaries and great cities, and knew both

Bethel and Samaria. His home life, far away, enabled him
to come to them with a certain detachment, and to see
them from the outside. Thus he is free alike from the
drugging influence of familiarity and from the numbing
sense of inevitable complicity in the evils which he so
clearly sees. His detachment gives him a certain austerity,
and we miss the passionate horror of sin and the equally
passionate sympathy for the doomed sinner which we find
in Hosea and in Jeremiah.

Yet Amos, from his external standpoint, can fasten on
the real spiritual dangers of Israel. His poetry, with its
vigour and its wealth of imagery, casts a fierce light on the
condition of Israel as he saw it. Beneath the fair surface of
prosperity he could detect the rotting mass of spiritual
corruption, and could expose it to men's eyes. He saw the
falsehood of worship, the foulness of professional religion,
and the commercial dishonesty of his day. More terrible
and perilous to him was the total neglect of the rights and
demands of human personality. Men were crushed below
the human level by the reckless luxury of the rich and by
the sordid corruption of justice. Ruin stared Israel in the
face, but he alone could recognize its form, and he knew
that, without righteousness, fair dealing, truthfulness, and a
recognition of the status of humanity, the nation was
doomed.

Amos had a remedy to offer the people for their social
and national disease. He had inherited the traditions of
the true Yahwism which traced its history back to Moses,
and stood for the faith of old times, uncontaminated by
Canaanite syncretism. Let men seek Yahweh—which involved establishing true justice—and they might live; otherwise they must perish. He did not, like the Nazirite and
the Rechabite, condemn, and seek to escape from, the
higher civilization of the agricultural and civic community,
but he did insist that Israel's only safety was to be found in
transfusing that more complicated social order with the
true spirit of Yahweh. It was not enough merely to
observe the old commandments in literal simplicity; their
essence must be applied to the life the people now led.

No consideration, political or religious, must be suffered to dam the stream of righteousness. Spiritual worship, purity of life, and above all, justice, must be established and maintained as the indispensable conditions of a safe and happy future.

Religiosity was no substitute for the fulfilment of Yahweh's moral demands; unaccompanied by righteousness sacrifice was merely loathsome. Men believed in the approach of a Day of Yahweh, in which Israel should triumph over all her enemies. Amos accepted the belief, but insisted that Yahweh would come, not to vindicate indiscriminately His own nation, but to assert the claims of His moral character on all who had denied them in practice. His message was primarily a " cry for justice."

VI. The Hebrew Text and the Septuagint

In spite of the fragmentary character of much of this book, the text seems, on the whole, to have been well preserved, though there are some places where emendation seems necessary (e.g. ii. 7; iii. 12, 14; iv. 3, 5, 9; v. 6, 26; vi. 2, 10; vii. 2; viii. 3; ix. 1). The Septuagint and other versions offer no striking variations from the traditional Hebrew text, but the Septuagint is sometimes of real help (e.g. ii. 16; iii. 5; iv. 7; v. 9; vi. 12; viii. 4).

THE BOOK OF OBADIAH

I. Place in the Canon

In the Hebrew Bible this book occupies the fourth place among the " *Twelve*," being placed after *Amos* and before *Jonah*, and this position is retained in the Peshitta, the Vulgate and the modern versions. In the Septuagint, however, it stands fifth in this collection, following *Joel* and preceding *Jonah*.

II. Historical Background

Among the tribes which remained outside Israel, yet were akin to them, Edom, to the south of the Dead Sea, was that which was held to be nearest. This people had attained to an ordered government before the foundation of the Hebrew monarchy, and, when David established his kingdom on a firm basis, the conquest of Edom was one of the steps which he took to protect his southern frontier. Its subjugation was also necessary if the southern trade, especially through the Red Sea port of Ezion-geber, was to be maintained, and the assertion of its independence in the reign of Solomon was an important factor in the decline of Israelite prosperity. Throughout the period of the monarchy the mark of a strong king of Judah was that he conquered Edom; but Judahite hold on the country was never secure. Edomites took a prominent part in the attacks on Jerusalem which preceded the fall of the city, and took advantage of the partial desolation of the land during the Exile to press northwards. The rivalry and hostility continued until about 127 B.C.; John Hyrcanus subdued Edom, and compelled its people to become Jews. The Herod family was of Edomite origin.

III. Structure and Contents

The book of *Obadiah* is a collection of oracles directed against Edom, and resembles such collections as those found in Jer. xlvi–li. Two of the oracles which appear in the Edom section of the Jeremiah collection appear also here, though one of the two is represented only by a fragment. It would seem that the following oracles or fragments were originally distinct: Verses 1–4 (= Jer. xlix. 14–16) condemning the pride of Edom; verse 5, a fragment from an oracle which appears in fuller form in Jer. xlix. 7–11, where the completeness of the destruction of Edom is emphasized; verses 6–7 describe the foes arrayed against Edom; verses 8–9 predict the doom of the wise men for whom Edom was famous; verses 10–11 ascribe the punishment to the part Edom had played in the humiliation of Jerusalem; verses 12–17 (which may include some later additions at the end) deal with the same theme, though the metre and style are rather different from the preceding; finally, verses 18–21 foretell the part that Israel will play in carrying out vengeance on Edom. This also seems to have suffered from accretions at the end.

IV. Date and Authorship

It is impossible to be certain that all the oracles included in this collection are to be ascribed to the same prophet, or even to the same time. But the age in which the hostility between Judah and Edom was most strongly developed was that which followed the fall of Jerusalem, and even the forcible conversion of the Edomites to Judaism by John Hyrcanus did not end the sense of antagonism. These oracles might have come from almost any time between the end of the sixth and the middle of the second centuries B.C., though an earlier date rather than a later is the more probable.

Of the author we know nothing; we do not know that a prophet Obadiah ever existed. The name is one which might easily have been applied to a collection of anonymous

prophecies, since it means simply " Servant of Yahweh,"
and the inclusion of two of the oracles in the book of
Jeremiah proves that these were known in one form, at any
rate, as anonymous. This, however, does not preclude the
possibility that there were other prophecies which were
known to have been uttered by a man of this name.

V. The Hebrew Text and the Septuagint

The text of this book has been, on the whole, badly preserved; much of it is obviously corrupt. Some help may
be derived from the Septuagint, and some from parallels in
Jeremiah, though, it must be admitted, the text as it stands
in that book is in no better condition.

THE BOOK OF JONAH

I. THE DATE OF THE BOOK

THE opening words of the book, " Now the word of Yahweh came unto Jonah the son of Amittai," would point to its having been written in the reign of Jeroboam ii (788– 747 B.C.), since, according to ii Kings xiv. 25, the prosperous years of this king of Israel were foretold by " Jonah, the son of Amittai, which was of Gath-Hepher." For it is evident that we are intended to understand by the Jonah of this book the prophet mentioned in ii Kgs. xiv. 25. This would indicate a date for the book soon after 800 B.C.

The arguments against such an early date are, however, overwhelming. Much stress need not be laid on the fact that the author of our book seems to have known the book of *Joel* (cp. iii. 9 with Joel ii. 14, and iv. 2 with Joel ii. 13), the narrative portions of which belong to the middle of the fourth century B.C.,[1] though this indication of date must not be ignored; but more convincing is the language of the book. Thus, when we find words used by the writer which are common in post-Biblical Hebrew, but which do not occur elsewhere in the Old Testament, or only in writings which are recognized on all hands to be of late date, the presumption is irresistible that their presence in the book denotes a late period. It might be urged that the words or phrases in question are merely marks of " working over " by a late editor; but the objection is not valid, for they do not at all give the impression of being the work of an editor; moreover, they belong too much to the general style of the writing to suggest that they are not part of the original form. A few illustrations may be offered: in i. 5 the word translated " mariners " is Aramaic and is never found in classical Hebrew, but it is common in the Talmud and in Midrashic works. In the same verse the Aramaic

[1] See above, pp. 358 ff.

word for " ship " occurs, and it is interesting to note that
the Hebrew word for this is used in the preceding verse,
which shows that it was not yet superseded; in the Mishnah
and the Gemara it is the Aramaic word which is used.   In
iii. 2 the word translated " preaching " (better " proclama-
tion ") never occurs elsewhere in the Bible, but it is common
in post-Biblical Hebrew;   and, once more, in iii. 7 an
Aramaic word is used for " decree," and this, too, is never
found elsewhere in the Old Testament, but is common in
the Talmud.

Of verbs we have, *e.g.* in i. 6 an Aramaic root used,
meaning to " think upon " or " take thought for "; it occurs
in Dan. vi. 3 (Aram. 4), though the verbal form is different,
otherwise it is not found in the Old Testament, but it is
frequent in this form in the Targums.   In i. 11, 12 the
verb meaning " to be calm " is Neo-Hebrew, occurring in
the Old Testament in late passages only, Prov. xxvi. 20,
Ps. cvii. 30; it is the usual word in late Hebrew, and is common
in the Talmud and Midrash.   So, too, the verb for to " prepare," in i. 17 (Aram. ii. 1), iv. 6, 8, is found in the form used
only in Neo-Hebrew and Aramaic.   Likewise in iv. 10 the
word for to " labour " is late Hebrew, found elsewhere in
the Bible only in *Ecclesiastes* and in the later portions of
Proverbs, but it is common in post-Biblical Hebrew.

But still more important are modes of expression which
are alien to classical Hebrew; these are perhaps the most
telling signs of late composition.

In the R.V. the phrase in i. 4 is rendered: " so that the ship
was like to be broken " (*i.e.* on account of the mighty
tempest); literally it is, " so that the ship was minded to
be broken "; this verb is never used in reference to
inanimate objects like a ship in classical Hebrew.   The
R.V. avoids the difficulty, as it would sound to us, by
rendering " was like to be broken."   Again in iv. 10, in
reference to the gourd, it is said: " which came up in a
night, and perished in a night."   This is necessarily a paraphrase; literally the Hebrew might be translated: " which
was the son of a night, and perished the son of a night ";
the form of the relative is late (so, too, elsewhere in the

book), and the mode of expression is Neo-Hebrew, and it is not found elsewhere in the Old Testament. To late Hebrew belong also the forms for " on account of whom " (i. 7), and " for my sake " (i. 12); similar forms occur in other late books, *e.g.* Ecclus. viii. 17, Song of Solomon i. 6, iii. 7, and they are the usual forms in post-Biblical Hebrew and in the Targums. Finally, in iv. 11 the word for 10,000 in the original is an Aramaism; it is a form of the absolute found only in late Biblical books and in post-Biblical literature.

These examples constitute a strong argument for the late date of the book of *Jonah,* especially on account of the approximation to Aramaic which they exhibit. It is true that as early as the reign of Hezekiah (725–696 B.C.) we find a knowledge of this language existent in Palestine; but this was exceptional. In writing about the prevalence of the Aramaic language in general during the Persian period, Nöldeke remarks that " this preference for Aramaic, how- ever, probably originated under the Assyrian empire, in which a very large proportion of the population spoke Aramaic; in it this language would naturally occupy a more important position than it did under the Persians. Thus we understand why it was taken for granted that a great Assyrian officer could speak Aramaic (ii Kgs. xviii. 26 = Isa. xxxvi. 11); and why the dignitaries of Judah appear to have learned the language; namely, in order to communicate with the Assyrians." [1] While the nobles knew Aramaic, the common people did not understand it, and that was why the princes asked Rabshakeh to use it. We must not, therefore, conclude that because at this com- paratively early period Judæan officials knew Aramaic, it was in any way generally known in Palestine at that period. Although the influence of Aramaic steadily grew, this did not really begin until well after the Exile. The book of *Jonah,* to judge from its language, must belong to an early stage of this period of gradual transition from Hebrew to Aramaic, approximately 350 B.C. or thereabouts; some scholars would put it a little later.

---

[1] *Encycl. Bibl.,* i. 281 f.

II. Historical Background

In the case of the book of *Jonah* the historical background
must be considered from a point of view different from that
of the prophetical books in the stricter sense; here it is not
the external historical surroundings which concern us, but
the internal state of the country and its people. During
and after the Exile circumstances arose which accentuated
the antagonism between Jews and Gentiles. The work of
Ezra in inculcating the observance of the Law had, in
course of time, the effect of exaggerating in their own eyes
the importance and superiority of the " people of the Law,"
and of causing them to look upon all other peoples as
inferior to themselves. Moreover, as the elect people of
God, the Jews, upon whom alone—as was believed—the
marks of divine favour had been showered, and above all,
who had alone been the recipients of divine revelation,
regarded all other nations as outside the pale of God's
mercy and care. This was, more or less, the official attitude
towards the non-Jewish world. But not all the Jews
assumed this narrow, uncompromising position; a deeper
conception of the Personality of God and a higher ideal of
human relationship impelled them to oppose the self-centred
particularism of many of their brethren, and to think and
speak of the Gentiles, too, as objects of the divine solicitude
and compassion. Instead of the belief in a coming vengeance of God upon the Gentiles, culminating in their utter
destruction, the Jews, according to this view, were to be
God's instruments for the salvation of the nations of the
world. These opposing standpoints find expression in some
of the post-exilic writings of the Old Testament; but
nowhere are they presented in more convincing contrast
than in the book of *Jonah*. The writer sets forth Jonah as
the type of the narrow-minded, exclusive Jew, who not only
despises all non-Jews, but conceives of the Almighty as the
God of the Jews only, and as a God who has no care for
the rest of His creation. The author himself, on the other
hand, not only makes Jonah the unconscious or unwilling
cause of the conversion, first of the mariners, and then of

the Ninevites, but also teaches the divine truth of the universal Fatherhood of God.

Our book thus reflects the two opposing schools of thought, the particularists and the universalists, within Jewry. The author was, thus, a propagandist, and accordingly it may well be that he chose the name of Jonah as his leading *persona dramatis* for the purpose of propaganda; we suggest that there was here a twofold reason:

(i) The historical Jonah lived at a period during which the Assyrian empire was growing to great power. It was, at the most, very shortly before his activity that an Assyrian monarch, Shalmaneser iii, came for the first time into direct contact with the land of Israel, and the result was humiliating to the Israelites, who had, therefore, no reason to love the Assyrians; indeed, the fear and hatred of them grew with the centuries, and their very land became detestable. The feelings entertained towards this land to the north-east are well depicted in one of the visions of the prophet Zechariah; he sees in his vision a woman named *Rish'a*, who is the personification of " Wickedness," lifted up and carried away to the land of Shinar, the land to the north-east (Zech. v. 5–11), *i.e.* Babylonia,[1] which had been part of the Assyrian empire. Not only is this land the most fitting dwelling-place for " Wickedness," but, what is more important, the land where " Wickedness " has her abode must inevitably go to ruin. Nothing could more pointedly illustrate the hatred of the Jews for the Gentiles who lived in this land of " Wickedness " than this prophetical vision. Now it was in the reign of Shalmaneser iii that direct contact between Israel and this land began. It may or may not be a point of significance that, unlike his immediate predecessors, Shalmaneser iii made Nineveh the royal residence.[2] At any rate, the historical Jonah lived at a time when Assyria had become the leading world-power, and when it had come for the first time, and with dire consequences, into direct contact with Israel; and this may well have been one reason why the writer of our book chose

[1] See Isa. xi. 11, Dan. i. 2.
[2] Hommel, *Geschichte Babyloniens und Assyriens*, p. 589 (1885).

the name of Jonah the son of Amittai as that of his hero, for there was a point of contact between Jonah and the land to the north-east which applied to no other prophet.[1]

(ii) It is conceivable that the name of Jonah appealed to the writer of our book for an additional reason. The name means " dove "; and Nineveh, the city to which he goes, was the chief sanctuary of the goddess Ishtar whose sacred bird was the dove. It is possible that the writer of our book wished to place in contrast Jonah, the " dove " sent by Yahweh, the God of Israel, and the dove sacred to the tutelar goddess of the city. The idea may seem fanciful at first, but our author, as we shall see, was not unfamiliar with some of the mythological *data* regarding ancient Nineveh, in which case he may have desired, quite in the Jewish fashion, to point a moral by showing the difference of purpose between his God in sending His messenger, the " dove," and the heathen goddess with her debased cult, who was symbolized by her sacred dove.

III. The Interpretation of the Book

Apart from the traditional interpretation which takes the story of Jonah in a literal sense, and which is now discarded by all modern scholars, there are two methods of explaining it, one or other of which is adopted by commentators: the mythological and the symbolic. The main objection to the mythological interpretation, as it seems to the present writers, is that from the point of view of the narrative itself it has no *raison d'être*. The mythological interpretation necessarily postulates that the great fish which swallowed Jonah is *Tehom*, the dragon of the subterranean deep. But this sea-monster was the embodiment of the principle of evil, inimical to God and man; whereas in our book the fish is represented as beneficent, since it saves Jonah. *Tehom* would be altogether out of place in our story. The fact

---

[1] There is no reason why the writer of *Jonah* should not have known something about Assyrian history, especially when it touched that of his own people.

that neither *Tehom* is used in reference to the big fish,[1] nor
yet *Tannin*, nor yet *Leviathan*, both likewise mythological
monsters, and harmful, is in itself an argument against a
mythological interpretation. Moreover, on the supposition
of such interpretation, it may well be asked: What is the
application? Cheyne, one of the most thorough-going of
this school, says that " it is the all-absorbing empire of
Babylon which swallowed up Israel—not, however, to destroy
it, but to preserve it and to give it room for repentance." [2]
But what has this to do with the subject-matter of the
book? The repentance and conversion of the *Gentiles*
through the mercy and long-suffering of God, not the
captivity and spiritual condition of Israel, is the burden of
the story. Having regard to the author's evident love of
symbolism, as exemplified by the name Jonah, and by the
story of the gourd, it seems much more natural to interpret
the sojourn of Jonah in the great fish for three days and
three nights symbolically, and to regard this as the symbol
of Nineveh, the " great city of three days' journey "; while
his being vomited out is symbolic of his going out of the
repentant city; he was out of place there. In this connexion attention must be drawn to an illuminating article
by the late J. C. Ball: he gives the written symbol denoting
Nineveh and its tutelar goddess in cuneiform characters;
this in the linear character, or ideogram, appears as the
outline of a two-storied building, with a fish on the lower
floor. With the determinative prefix for " city " the character was read *Ni-nu-a*, i.e. Nineveh; and with its determinative of deity, " god " or " goddess," it denoted the
tutelar divinity of the place. " It is," he says, " surely a
fact of capital importance for a right estimate of the character of the Biblical book of *Jonah* that the name of the
city to which the prophet was sent was expressed in writing,
from the earliest period, by a combination of the symbols
for *house* and *fish*. For this fact at once suggests that the
three days' sojourn of Jonah in the *House of the Fish*, i.e.
Nineveh, might be symbolized or haggadically represented

---

[1] It is always the ordinary Hebrew word for " fish " that is used (i. 17,
ii. 1, 10), viz. *dag*.   [2] *Encycl. Bibl.*, ii. 2568.

as a three days' abode in the bowels of a ' Great Fish ';
much as Israel's enforced sojourn in Babylon could be
compared with being swallowed up by a dragon " (Jer.
li. 34).[1]

The objection that " there is no trace of the writer of
Jonah having been a man of learning " [2] is hardly valid;
the constant intercourse between the Jews of Babylonia and
Palestine would make many ideas and traditions current in
the former generally familiar, and there is no reason why
the writer of *Jonah*, with his wide outlook, should not have
been acquainted with these.

IV. INTEGRITY OF THE BOOK

With one notable exception the book forms an obvious
unity; the exception is the psalm contained in ii. 2–9
(Hebr. ii. 3–10). In ii. 1 it is said: " Then Jonah prayed
unto Yahweh out of the fish's belly. And he said . . ."
Then follows the psalm; this, however, is not a prayer, but
a thanksgiving for deliverance from a watery grave. But
this thanksgiving is uttered before the deliverance has taken
place, for it is not until the end of the psalm that the words
occur: " And Yahweh spake unto the fish, and it vomited
out Jonah upon the dry land " (verse 10). Moreover, it
will be acknowledged that if this psalm occurred elsewhere,
e.g. in the Psalter, there would not necessarily be anything
in it to suggest its connexion with Jonah in the fish's belly.
It is only its present position which suggests such a connexion. Nowhere in the psalm is there any mention or hint
of Jonah being inside the fish; indeed, such an idea is excluded by the words of verse 5: " The weeds were wrapped
about my head "; as Wellhausen pointedly remarks:
" Weeds do not grow in a whale's belly." [3] It is evident
that the psalm expresses the grateful outpouring of one who
had been nearly drowned, whereas in the case of Jonah

---

[1] The ideogram is: *Proceedings of the Soc. of Biblical Archæology*,
xx. pp. 9 ff. (1898).

[2] Cheyne, *ibid.*   [3] *Die kleinen Propheten*, p. 221 (1898).

there is no question of drowning. The psalm was clearly not an original part of the book, but was added later by one who felt that it would be appropriate to insert what he thought would represent the words which Jonah would have uttered. That the text runs perfectly smoothly without it is seen by reading ii. 10 immediately after ii. 1: " Then Jonah prayed unto Yahweh out of the fish's belly. And Yahweh spake unto the fish, and it vomited out Jonah upon the dry land."

Whether the psalm is earlier or later than the book itself cannot be decided; that it was inserted after the book had been written does not necessarily imply that it was later in date; all that can be said is that it is post-exilic; [1] various passages in it are reminiscent of the *Psalms*.

V. THE HEBREW TEXT AND THE SEPTUAGINT

Apart from a very few glosses the Hebrew text has been preserved in remarkably good order. One displacement seems to have occurred, iv. 5 does not read logically in its present context; its proper place is after iii. 4. It should also be noted that there is a change in the use of the divine names, Yahweh and Elohim; on the basis of this Böhme [2] has propounded a theory that the book is combined from two sources; this is highly improbable. It is far more naturally explained by Marti, who holds that a later reader of the book took exception to the use of the Tetragrammaton and substituted Elohim for it; in iv. 6, where both occur together, he presumably forgot to make the alteration.

The Septuagint is of little value so far as this book is concerned. It is, however, of interest to note that " in certain MSS. and a large proportion of cursives the *Psalms* are followed by a collection of liturgical *cantica* "; [3] among these is the psalm in ch. ii.

[1] See further, Sellin, *Das Zwölfprophetenbuch*, p. 241 (1922).
[2] *ZATW* vii. pp. 224 ff. (1887).
[3] Swete, *op. cit.*, p. 253.

THE BOOK OF MICAH

I. Place in the Canon

In the Hebrew Bible, the Peshitta, the Vulgate and modern versions, the book of *Micah* stands sixth among the " *Twelve*," following *Jonah* and preceding *Nahum*. In the Septuagint, however, it stands third, being placed after *Amos*, probably on account of its length.

II. Historical Background

Micah was a contemporary of Isaiah, and witnessed the same series of historical events as he. But he was far more impressed than Isaiah by the condition of the rural population, since he lived in the agricultural district of the Shephelah.[1] Life as he saw it was very similar to that which Amos observed in the north, with the rich oppressing the poor, and the working peasant often reduced to the most distressing and humiliating position. Like Amos, Micah realised that this state of affairs could not continue, and that destruction was the only possible outcome. The book is quoted in Jer. xxvi. 18, and we gather from that passage that his message did effect some improvement in conditions. Certainly, apart from one or two passages in *Isaiah*, we hear comparatively little elsewhere about social injustice in the Judæan countryside.

III. Structure and Contents

The book of *Micah* falls into three clearly marked sections. The first, consisting of chs. i–iii, is a collection of oracles in which the sins of Samaria and Judah are denounced. Chs. iv–v are eschatological, and even Messianic, in tone, while chs. vi–vii contain both threat and promise. We may look at these in rather more detail.

[1] The tract of land lying between the hill country of Judah and the Mediterranean.

1. Chs. i–iii. This collection opens with an oracle in which the whole world is summoned to witness the catastrophes which will take place as a result of the sins of Judah and Israel (i. 2–5a).   5b–6 fastens the sin more particularly on Jerusalem and Samaria, and in 7–9 we have another account of the doom which befalls these places. Verse 7 is sometimes regarded as a later addition; if so, it must have been appended to 6 at an early stage.   If, on the other hand, it belongs to what follows, we must assume that something has been lost before it.   Verse 9 seems to be incomplete, and this oracle was almost certainly mutilated. Verses 10–16 constitute a dirge over the disasters which have come upon various cities in Judah.   It is especially marked by *paranomasia*.

The first three verses of ch. ii are in dirge form, but are a complaint of the oppressiveness of the country magnates. Another dirge—or fragment of a dirge—follows in verse 4, to which an explanatory note has been attached in verse 5. Verses 6–7 are a remonstrance by the prophet's hearers, which is answered in verses 8–10.   Verse 11 seems to be isolated unless we can suppose that it is the retort of the people to what the prophet has just said.   Verses 12–13 are a consolatory utterance which, apparently, assumes that the Exile has already taken place.   Unless we can suppose that the scattered remnant to be restored are the exiles of the north, taken away by Tiglath-pileser and Sargon, this must date from the sixth century at the earliest.

Ch. iii opens with a bitter denunciation of the local magnates of the countryside (iii. 1–4).   This is followed by a condemnation of the false prophets, with whom Micah contrasts himself (verses 5–8).   The section concludes in iii. 9–13 with a further denunciation of the local powers.

2. Chs. iv–v. This collection opens with a passage, verses 1–4, which occurs also in Isa. ii. 2–4; though here it is in a more complete form, and an isolated fragment has been appended to verse 5.   iv. 6–8 depict the restoration of the exiles and Zion's recovery of her ancient sovereignty. Verses 9–10 tell of the Exile (now in the near future) but with a promise of restoration.   In 11–13 this promise is

realized, and v. 1 [1] is a summons to mourning, which suggests that Israel is actually suffering foreign invasion. Ch. v. 2–4 foretell the coming of a Davidic king; to this has been appended a prophecy of the seven princes which is assigned by many to the Maccabæan age (verses 5–6). Verses 7–9 predict miraculous prosperity to the Diaspora, while verses 10–15 threaten Israel with disaster in terms which are more suited to the pre-exilic than to a later period.

3. Chs. vi–vii. In this section also we have a collection of different pieces, but they vary in character, not only from what has gone before but also from one another. The collection opens with what appears to be a fragment of an appeal to the people, based on their history (vi. 1–5). It recalls passages like Am. ii. 9–11, but lacks a conclusion. This is followed by the best known passage in the book, vi. 6–8, dealing with the essentials of true religion. Verses 9–12 are a denunciation of commercial iniquity, and 13–16 foretell punishment because the people have followed in the sins of the house of Omri. vii. 1–3 offers a lament over the moral state of the people, and perhaps verse 4 belongs to this passage, though its meaning and text are not clear. Verses 5–7 afford a parallel to the last oracle. In verses 8–10 we have a fragment of a Psalm of justification, in which the speaker tells his accusers that, though he has suffered from the just anger of Yahweh, he will yet rise triumphant from his sorrows. Verses 11–13 predict the restoration of the walls of Jerusalem, and the concluding passage, vii. 14–20, is a prayer for the forgiveness and restoration of the whole people.

IV. DATE AND AUTHORSHIP [2]

We learn from Jer. xxvi. 18 that, at the end of the seventh century B.C., Mi. iii. 12 was held to be the work of Micah the Morashtite, a prophet who had lived in the days of

---

[1] Heb. iv. 14; the numeration of verses in ch. v differs in the Hebrew Bible accordingly.

[2] An adequate summary of the history of the criticism of this book will be found in J. M. P. Smith, *Micah (ICC)*, pp. 9–16 (1912). The most recent contribution to the subject is that of Lindblom, *Micha literarisch untersucht* (1929).

Hezekiah. Since this passage is to be dated only a hundred years after the time to which it refers, it may be accepted as reliable. Further, we may assume that everything in the first collection which corresponds with this verse may be assigned to the same prophet. But the language used in *Jeremiah* makes it evident that Micah was not known to have said anything that was inconsistent with, or contradictory to, this condemnation. It does not follow that the words of Micah were current in book form; they may still have been at the stage of oral tradition, or known in isolated oracular pieces, and we have to allow for the possibility that the collection in Mic. i–iii was made later than the time of Jeremiah. This possibility becomes a probability when we notice that the collection includes a passage (ii. 12–13) which presupposes the Exile. It is true that it mentions a "king," but the parallel in the second part of the line shows that this is Yahweh, and it is so much the clearer that the utterance reflects the theocratic ideals of the late exilic and the post-exilic period. Where we have indications of date elsewhere in this collection, they invariably point to a pre-exilic date, and usually, to the period to which Jer. xxvi. 18 assigns Micah, *e.g.* in i. 5 f. we have references which show that Samaria was still standing, though its fall was expected. This collection, then, composed mainly of the oracles of Micah of Moresheth-Gath, was probably made not long after the return from the Exile.

The second collection, on the other hand, must be a good deal later than the first. There may be pre-exilic passages in it, *e.g.* iv. 9–10 may come from the age of Jeremiah, v. 6–7 suggest the last quarter of the seventh century B.C.,[1] and v. 10–15 would suit a pre-exilic period at least as well as a later age. On the other hand, the Messianic passage in v. 2–4 can hardly be earlier than the Exile, and may be very much later, while the references to the Diaspora in iv. 6–8, and the eschatological tone of iv. 11–v. 1, suggest a comparatively late date. On the whole, we cannot assign

[1] The alternative is the Maccabæan age, when Syria was spoken of as Assyria. But it is less likely that the name of Nimrod would have appeared in a prophecy of this age.

the compilation of the collection to a period earlier than the fifth century B.C., and, if the references in v. 5–6 are really to be ascribed to the Maccabæan age, then the collection must be very late indeed.

It is interesting to note that the third collection contains some passages which might quite well be by Micah himself. Thus vi. 14–16 have been held [1] to refer to Samaria before 722 B.C., and it has been suggested that in the great passage vi. 6–8 we have an answer given by the prophet to the doubts of the new settlers, after the destruction of the northern kingdom.[2] On the other hand, in vii. 11–13 we have a passage which may be nearly as late as the age of Nehemiah, and cannot be earlier than the Return from the Exile. Here, again, we have a collection which can hardly have reached its present form before the latter part of the fifth century B.C., and may be later still.

V. THE MAN AND HIS MESSAGE

Since the reference in Jer. xxvi. 18 confirms, but does not add to, what we know of Micah from the book that bears his name, it is to that that we must turn for our information. As with most of the prophets, there is little for us to learn. Micah came from Moresheth-Gath, whose site has not been identified, though it clearly lay in the Judæan Shephelah. Unlike Isaiah, he was thus a countryman, and his outlook resembles that of Amos more than that of any other prophet. He differs from Amos, however, in being more deeply in sympathy with the sufferings of the oppressed peasantry; we are left with the impression that he was himself under the harrow. Micah had a fervid and vigorous personality, and employed powerful modes of expression. No prophet is more bitter—we might almost say more savage—in his condemnation of the social evils of his day. The denunciation of the rural magnates and of the prophets in iii. 1–4, 5–7 breathes an extraordinary vindictiveness and passion. Like Amos, he stood for righteousness, and for a

---

[1] By Lindblom; cp. *Micha literarisch untersucht.* pp. 116–120.
[2] Cp. ii Kgs. xvii. 24–31. The suggestion is due to Burkitt; see *The Journal of Biblical Literature*, xlv. pp. 159–161 (1926).

C C

type of righteousness which gave full value to the rights and needs of human personality. Any other ruling principle must lead to ruin. Micah thus adds nothing to the doctrines of Amos, Hosea, and Isaiah, but he does reinforce them and apply them to the conditions of his own time with peculiar effectiveness.

It is impossible even to speculate on the authors of the later passages in the second and third sections of the book. But, again, their message has little significance beyond the fact that it represents the general trend of prophetic, Messianic, and early eschatological teaching. The only point specifically used by later times was the identification of Bethlehem as the birthplace of the Messiah.

VI. The Hebrew Text and the Septuagint

The Hebrew text of this book is often corrupt, though it is not in such a bad state of preservation as that of *Hosea*. Illustrations may be seen in i. 10, ii. 4, 8, 12, vii. 11, while scribal additions are probably included in ii. 3, iii. 8, vi. 5 and elsewhere. Occasionally the versions, especially the Septuagint, offer some help, as in iv. 13, vii. 12, 19, though it is clear that many of the erroneous readings had already found their way into the book before the separation of the Egyptian from the Palestinian text.

THE BOOK OF NAHUM

I. Place in the Canon

In all forms of the Bible this book stands seventh in the list of the " *Twelve*," following *Micah* in the Hebrew Bible, the Peshitta, the Vulgate, and the modern versions, and *Jonah* in the Septuagint. It invariably precedes *Habakkuk*.

II. Historical Background

After the death of Ashur-bani-pal, the last of the great kings of Assyria, in 626 B.C., the empire fell rapidly to pieces. Babylon at once secured its independence under the vigorous Chaldæan dynasty, now headed by Nabopolassar, and henceforward a dangerous enemy to Assyria. The Scythian inroads,[1] though no permanent dominion resulted from these, weakened the northern defences of the kingdom, and made it impossible to maintain the Assyrian supremacy over the western parts of the empire. Egypt had finally revolted before the death of Ashur-bani-pal, and the reform of Josiah of Judah, in 621 B.C., may be regarded, in one of its aspects, as a gesture of independence.[2] We shall probably be justified in assuming that all the outlying dependencies threw off the Assyrian yoke about the same time.

Such details as we have of the next few years come to us from a Babylonian Chronicle, which belongs to the reign of Nabopolassar.[3] The story of Assyria's last war begins with the advance of Nabopolassar northwards in 616 B.C. He won a great victory, but Necho, king of Egypt, joined forces with the Assyrians and compelled the Chaldæans to retreat. Nabopolassar met with no better fortune in the

---

[1] See also below, p. 400.
[2] Cp. Oesterley and Robinson, *Hist. Israel*, i. pp. 423 f.
[3] See Gadd, *The Fall of Nineveh* (1923).

following year, but, in 614 B.C., the Medes took the field and destroyed Ashur, the ancient capital of Assyria. The Chaldæans joined the victors, and in 612 B.C. the joint armies succeeded in capturing and sacking Nineveh itself. Resistance was still maintained further west, and in 610 B.C. Harran was captured. Here our records break off, but there are grounds for believing that an attempt was made to preserve the old kingdom at some centre still further east, possibly at Carchemish. We know, at least, that Necho continued his pro-Assyrian expeditions; one is mentioned as having taken place in 608 B.C., and he suffered a decisive and crushing defeat at Carchemish in 605 B.C.

III. Structure and Contents

The book of *Nahum* opens with a portion of a psalm, which extends from i. 2 to ii. 2,[1] and originally formed an alphabetic acrostic. It has, however, suffered badly in course of transmission, and the acrostic is not obvious after verse 8 (the Hebrew letter *Kaph*, כ), though it may be recovered conjecturally down to verse 10 (*Samekh* ס). Various attempts have been made to restore the remainder, but without much success. Verse 11 is sometimes regarded as belonging to the prophetic portion of the book, and it is possible that i. 12–ii. 2 did not belong to the original psalm at all, but were attached to it, or rather to the fragment which survives. The oracles proper are contained in ii. 3–iii. 19. It seems that not more than five or six can be distinguished, and all refer to the sack of the city. It should be remarked that most modern commentators put together the fragments now found in i. 11, 14, ii. 1, to form a part of the oracular section, but this arrangement is difficult to justify, since there seems to be no reason why such pieces should have been inserted in the midst of a psalm. But we can certainly find a continuous passage in ii. 3–9, where the street fighting and the plundering are described. ii. 10–13 depict the desolation of the

---

[1] Heb. ii. 3; the numeration of verses in ch. ii differs accordingly in Hebrew and in English.

city after its sack. In iii. 1–4 we have another picture of
the horrors of the assault which, possibly, continues down
to iii. 7. In iii. 8–13 there is a comparison between the
fate of Nineveh and that of the Egyptian Thebes, sacked
by Ashur-bani-pal in 663 B.C. Ch. iii. 14–17 describes the
feverish but futile efforts of the defenders, and the whole
collection closes with a brief dirge over the fallen city,
iii. 18–19.

IV. DATE AND AUTHORSHIP

The book of *Nahum* resembles that of *Obadiah* in being
(apart from the introductory psalm) a collection of oracles
directed against a single foreign people. In every other
respect, however, it is unique. There is little doubt as to
the common authorship of all the oracles; they present us
with a style which, for vividness and force, has no parallel
elsewhere in the Old Testament and very rarely in other
literature. The prophet is a master of word-painting; he,
as it were, flings words at the reader, yet his clipped, disjointed sentences are pregnant with meaning; here is an
example, being more or less a literal translation of the
Hebrew:

" Crack of whip; and rumbling wheels; Galloping riders;
Rattling chariots; Plunging steeds; Flashing sword; Glit-
tering spear; Mass of slain, and weight of corpses " (iii.
2, 3). That describes the entry into Nineveh!

In a miscellaneous collection, such as we so often find in
other books, differences of style are usually noticeable. The
homogeneity of these oracles makes their common authorship practically certain, especially when we remember the
extraordinary character of the whole.

The earliest possible date is determined by the reference
to the sack of Thebes (No-Amon) in iii. 8, which, as we
have seen, took place in 663 B.C. The latest possible limit
is supplied by the fall of Nineveh itself in 612 B.C., and the
actual date must lie somewhere between these two. The
fact that the fall of the city was expected would tend to
place Nahum's oracles during the final war, *i.e.* in or soon

after 616 B.C. The only objection to this is the long time which had elapsed since the fall of Thebes. There does not seem, however, to be any decisive difficulty here, since so striking an event might well be remembered for fifty years.

The date of the psalm is more difficult to determine. While a superficial reading of it might suggest that it, too, referred to the fall of Nineveh, closer examination shows that this is very unlikely, since the language of i. 15 implies that the enemy had interfered with the cultus. This is generally held to point to a Maccabæan date, and, if this be correct, we must assume that the book had existed for some centuries before the psalm was prefixed to it.

V. THE MAN AND HIS MESSAGE

We know nothing of Nahum except what we can gather from the book itself. Elkosh is named as his birthplace, but the site has not been identified; tradition held that he lived and died in Mesopotamia, but the evidence of the book itself makes it clear that he was a Judæan. No details of his life have been preserved, but his style shows him to have been gifted with a vivid imagination and an extraordinary power of expression. No writer in the Old Testament suffers so much in translation; his vigour defies reproduction in any other language.

We do not expect much of the characteristic teaching of the prophets in a book which is wholly occupied with songs of gloating exultation over the fall of a hated enemy. Yet we have hints of the inexorable law of retribution; as Assyria had done to others, so shall it be done to her. We have also, underlying the whole, the sense of the supreme prophetic demand for the recognition of the rights and needs of humanity. In the last resort, it is because Nineveh has neglected these, and has used her power tyrannously, that she must perish. The book might serve as a commentary on Isa. x. 5-15.

VI. The Hebrew Text and the Septuagint

Except in the psalm, where the aberrations from the acrostic suggest corruption, the text is fairly well preserved. The versions exhibit no peculiarities, though they, especially the Septuagint, are sometimes helpful in restoring difficult passages, *e.g.* in ii, 4, 9, 12; iii. 9, 17.

THE BOOK OF HABAKKUK

I. Place in the Canon

THIS book always occupies the eighth place among the " *Twelve*," its position being after *Nahum* and before *Zephaniah*.

II. Historical Background

The events against which we must see this prophet's work will necessarily be determined by the date to which we assign it. While we shall probably be right in placing Habakkuk in the age of Jeremiah, several scholars [1] would put him as late as the time of Alexander the Great. The foundation of the Macedonian power was the most sudden and spectacular of all the great events of the ancient world; even the rise of Cyrus was slower and achieved less. In 334 B.C. Alexander fought his first battle on Asiatic soil at the river Granicus. In the following year he defeated the full force of the Persian empire at the battle of Issus. The next year he devoted to the subjugation of Syria and Egypt, meeting with serious opposition only at Tyre, and in 331 B.C. he won, at Arbela, the battle which gave him undisputed possession of the whole Persian empire. He seems, on the whole, to have favoured the Jews, and did no harm to Jerusalem or to the Temple. They submitted to him, and Jews were to be found in his armies. He also used them freely for purposes of colonization, and gave them special privileges in their new homes. It will be necessary to bear these facts in mind when considering the date of the prophecies of Habakkuk.

III. Structure and Contents

The book of *Habakkuk* at first sight falls into two clearly distinguished parts. The first comprises oracular matter in chs. i–ii, while ch. iii takes the form of a psalm.

[1] *E.g.* Duhm, Sellin.

The first oracular piece is contained in i. 2–4, and forms
a statement of the prophet's problem: Why does God
allow iniquity to flourish? This is followed by a prediction
of the coming of the Chaldæans, "that bitter and hasty
nation," in i. 5–11. It may be observed that in verse 9 the
subject changes from the plural to the singular. Since it is
a nation that is contemplated, either construction is possible,
but it seems a little strange, and it may be that we should
take verses 9–11 as a separate piece. In i. 12–13 we have
the problem of the opening verses repeated, even more
strongly and forcibly. This develops naturally, in verses
14–17, into a further complaint of the violence done by
some enemy, presumably the same that is mentioned in
verses 5–11. In ii. 1–4 the prophet puts himself in the
proper attitude of receptivity, and is assured that there is
an answer to his problem: while the wicked will suffer,
the righteous shall live through his fidelity. The exact
meaning of verse 5 is not clear, but in the rest of the chapter
we have a series of denunciations, each introduced with
"Woe!" and each condemning a different sin, though the
sinner may be the same in all. Thus, in verses 6b–8 the
man who violently steals land is threatened, in verses 9–11
it is he who builds his house by injustice, in verses 12–13
(to which is attached a sentence closely resembling Isa.
xi. 9) it is the city builder, in 15–16 the drunkard, and in
19–20 the idolater. Verse 17 is a curious appendix to the
preceding piece—curious, because it has no reference to
drinking—and verse 18 is an introduction to the two verses
that follow.

Ch. iii in its present form consists of a psalm, which has
been taken from a collection such as those which were used
for the construction of our present Psalter. It is, however,
clearly an adaptation of an earlier poem for this purpose.
The original piece consisted of iii. 2–16, where we have a
vivid description of a great theophany when Yahweh comes
to destroy His foes. To this has been appended an expression of unshakeable confidence in Yahweh, by a pious
reader of a later age (iii. 17–19).

IV. Date and Authorship

Of the prophet and of his circumstances nothing whatever is known except what can be deduced from the book itself, and the evidence afforded by the text has raised very serious difficulties. The main problem may be simply stated. We have two threads running through the whole; on the one hand, we have the problem raised by the ruthless persecution of the righteous by a wicked tyrant, and, on the other, we have the judgement pronounced on the tyrant. As the text stands, the Chaldæans, introduced in i. 5–11, are Yahweh's instrument of vengeance on the tyrant, while, apparently, in the rest of the book they are identified with the tyrant himself.

Various attempts have been made to solve the problem thus created. Some [1] have assumed that the original prophecy has received numerous additions and interpolations, to which its present confusing character is due. Budde seeks to elucidate the question by placing the description of the advancing Chaldæans (i. 5–11) after ii. 4, thus producing a continuous development of thought. The Chaldæans are not now the oppressive tyrant, but only the instruments of Yahweh's vengeance. To this it has been objected that the description does not fit the Chaldæans at all, for they were not a comparatively unknown people, as is suggested by the way in which they are introduced, nor did they move from west to east as is implied in i. 9.

A most interesting theory has, therefore, been worked out by Duhm, and is accepted by Sellin and others. On this view the appearance of the Chaldæans is due to textual corruption, and it is really the victorious Greeks under Alexander the Great whom the prophet has in view. The whole is to be dated shortly after the battle of Issus (333 B.C.). Instead of " Chaldæans " in i. 6 we should read " Kittians " (properly Cypriotes, but possibly used of Greeks in general), and in ii. 5 instead of " wine " we should read " Greek." [2] It may be said at once that both these textual changes are easy, and no objection could be

---

[1] *E.g.* Marti.   [2] The two words in Hebrew are very similar.

raised to them if the theory were justified on other grounds. It is further pointed out that Alexander, alone among the conquerors of the ancient world, can be spoken of as having subdued so many nations, and that his habit of building cities as centres of Greek influence is referred to in ii. 12–14. We may regard these as the main points in an attractive and brilliant theory.

When we look further into the matter, however, we are less certain that Duhm has found the right solution to the problem. It is by no means clear that the advancing conqueror is moving from west to east. The word for " east (wind) " is in the accusative, it is true, but in a Semitic language the accusative does not necessarily imply " motion towards." The Septuagint actually had " from the east," which may be an interpretation or (more probably) a difference of reading. There is no evidence whatever to suggest that Alexander ever ill-treated the Jews, and their later experiences with the Persian empire, especially under Artaxerxes Ochus, would tend to make them welcome a new conqueror as a deliverer. There is, moreover, evidence to show that the term " nations " might be applied to different clans or groups of people resident in Palestine, perhaps even in Judah.[1] Even if this be not deemed a sufficient explanation of the use of the plural, there remains the possibility that the text has been modified in an eschatological sense. We should do well to examine the matter afresh before committing ourselves to a fourth-century date.

A great deal of the difficulty has been due to the feeling (perhaps an unconscious feeling) that the book was originally written by a prophet as a single, continuous whole. As soon as we remember that it, like other prophetic books, is a collection of oracles made, possibly, long after the time of the prophet to whom they are ascribed, a large part of the problem disappears. We do not need Budde's reorganization of the text, for there is no reason to believe that the priority in the book of i. 5–11 points to priority in the actual delivery of the oracles concerned.

Further, we may remark that much of the language of

[1] Cp. Jer. iv. 7, 16.

the book suggests the age of Jeremiah, if not actual dependence on the utterances of that prophet. The main problem
of the book is raised in Jer. xii. 1 ff. The description of
the " Chaldæans " can hardly fail to remind us of the foe
whom Jeremiah envisaged,[1] while the condemnation of the
tyrant in Hab. ii. 9, 12, inevitably recalls the judgement
pronounced on Jehoiakim in Jer. xxii. 13 ff. These last
passages also suit a domestic tyrant rather than a foreign
oppressor, and we are faced with the possibility that the
prophet was troubled by a wicked ruler as well as by a
heartless conqueror—not necessarily the same person.

One of our difficulties is certainly that the oracles have
been modified before their inclusion in the present book.
We cannot regard ii. 14, for instance, as the original conclusion of the oracle which begins with verse 12, since it
appears also as the final sentence of the great Messianic
passage in Isa. xi. 1 ff. We may go so far as to suspect
that most of the " Woes " in ch. ii consisted originally of a
single short sentence, which has been modified, either by a
collector or, more probably, before it came into his hands.

We have, then, to find a time at which a righteous man
was overwhelmed by a cruel opponent, probably a foreign
conqueror, and about the same time the country suffered
from the exactions of a ruler who erected magnificent
buildings at the expense of his people. Is there any period
which fits these facts better than the years 608 B.C. and
those which followed? The good Josiah,[2] overwhelmed by
the cruel Egyptian king, and followed by Jehoiakim—these
would fit the circumstances as no others known to us would
do. It must be admitted that there are still several problems
left for solution. We do not know that the Egyptians
offered sacrifice to their nets (i. 16), but we do not know
that Alexander did so either. We may make the same
remark of the " violence done to Lebanon " (ii. 17).
Archæology may some day be able to throw real light on
these problems, but at present we are completely in the

[1] Cp. e.g., Jer. iv. 13, v. 6; Hab. i. 8.
[2] We need to remember that it was the democratic and ethical features
of Josiah's government which appealed to the prophetic mind rather than
his religious policy. It was here that Jehoiakim was so strongly contrasted
with his father. Cp. Jer. xxii. 15–17.

dark.   In the meantime, the end of the seventh century B.C.
is probably the period which best suits the conditions of
most of the oracles included in this book, though there are
certainly later additions.   The final Woe (ii. 19–20), for
instance, can hardly be pre-exilic, since it breathes the
spirit of Deutero-Isaiah.

The dating of the psalm in ch. iii is more difficult.   Duhm
and Sellin regard it as the crown and climax of the book,
and therefore attribute it (except the final verses, 17–19) to
the prophet himself.   But this conclusion is necessarily
based on the very improbable hypothesis that the prophet
himself was responsible for the book in practically its present
form.   If the book as we now have it does lead up to the
poem, it is the collector or compiler who is responsible for
this arrangement, and the fact gives us no clue to the
authorship.   There is, however, little or nothing in it which
makes a pre-exilic date impossible, though the combination
of a theophany with an historical retrospect would be more
natural from the pen of a post-exilic writer.   In any case,
the final compilation of the book cannot be placed earlier
than the beginning of the fifth century.

V. The Prophet and his Message

We know nothing, as we have said, of Habakkuk except
what we can gather from the book itself; even his name is
somewhat of a puzzle.   Apart from all questions of date
there are two points in which the book is important.   In
the first place, we have in ii. 1 a very valuable light on the
methods of the canonical prophet.   All prophecy, at least
until a comparatively late post-exilic period, was based on
a peculiar psychological condition to which the name
ecstasy is often given.   It was characteristic of the false
prophet as well as of the true, but the former often, if not
always, resorted to artificial means for its production—
music, drugs, mass excitation, or other methods.   As far as
we know, the true prophet, represented by those whose
words have been handed down in our Bible, eschewed such
means of producing the necessary condition.   At the same

time, he could do something at least to prepare himself for its reception; he could place himself in a mental attitude in which it might occur. Sometimes, even then, the phenomenon was delayed (cp. ii. 3); Jeremiah, on one occasion, had to wait ten days before receiving the communication which he and his people sought (Jer. xlii. 7). But, while we should, perhaps, have guessed this, we have nowhere else so clear an indication of it as in this prophet's statement that he will "stand upon watch" and post himself on his "tower."

Of far greater importance is the question which Habakkuk asked. Given a righteous and omnipotent God, how are we to explain the injustice of the world? Why are the guilty not punished at once, and the righteous rewarded? This problem could have arisen nowhere except in the Israel that had learnt of Yahweh's moral character from the eighth-century prophets. But, given their teaching, it was bound to arise sooner or later.

Unfortunately, we do not know what the prophet's real answer was. It seems to be offered to us in ii. 4—" the righteous shall live through his fidelity." But what does this mean? Are we to understand that the righteous would survive all his disasters, if he were only faithful, and would, in the end, attain the vengeance and the prosperity which he sought? Or is it implied that a righteous man's real *life* consists, not in the things that befall him, good or bad, but in his character and spiritual qualities—in fact, in his fidelity? To some the latter may seem to be too advanced a doctrine even for a Hebrew prophet, but it is a possibility which cannot be ignored. We should not expect to find a complete answer in Habakkuk, whether his date be the seventh or the fourth century B.C., for the problem is one with which the human mind still grapples unsuccessfully. But he was one of the first to ask the question, and the search for an answer, even if not wholly successful, has led man into some of his greatest discoveries in the realm of things divine.

VI. The Hebrew Text and the Septuagint

The text has not been particularly well preserved, and there are places in which conjectural emendation seems inevitable. Illustrations may be cited from i. 3, 9, 11, ii. 4, etc., while the psalm (ch. iii) is in many places obviously corrupt. The versions, especially the Septuagint, sometimes provide us with a clue, though not as often as in some of the other prophetic books. The Septuagint, for instance, seems to have a better reading in i. 6, 15; iii. 10.

THE BOOK OF ZEPHANIAH

I. Place in the Canon

The book of *Zephaniah* occupies the ninth place among the " *Twelve* " in all forms of the Old Testament, following *Habakkuk* and preceding *Haggai*.

II. Historical Background

The weakening of the northern defences of the Assyrian empire in the last days of Ashur-bani-pal (669–626 B.C.) left open the path for invasions by hordes of the wilder peoples whose home lay in eastern Europe and west central Asia. These are variously grouped under such titles as Scythians and Cimmerians, and there are frequent references to their inroads in Mesopotamian records. Herodotus states that they dominated western Asia for twenty-eight years, that they marched through Palestine, where they sacked the temple of Aphrodite at Ashkelon, and were prevented from entering Egypt only by heavy bribes.[1] They appear in Assyrian inscriptions as early as the reign of Esarhaddon (681–669 B.C.), under the name of Ashkuza.

The story of their invasion of Palestine has been doubted, but on inadequate grounds.[2] The peril to Judah passed, and there seems little doubt that their incursions brought to an end the Assyrian power in the west. It is probable that their appearance was the occasion of the first utterances of Jeremiah, and we may conjecture that Zephaniah's call came through the same series of events.

III. Structure and Contents

The book of *Zephaniah* consists of a single collection of oracles, mostly short. In i. 1–6 we have a general threat of destruction uttered against the worshippers of Baal. i. 7–8

---

[1] i. 105, 106.   [2] Cp. Oesterley and Robinson, *op. cit.*, i. pp. 412–415.

announce a great sacrificial feast prepared by Yahweh. i. 9–11 and 12–13 are little pieces which foretell punishment to different groups of sinners. i. 14–18 supply a further description of the Day of Yahweh. In ii.1–3 the prophet appeals to his people to repent, and ii. 4–7 describe the ruin that is to fall on the Philistine cities. In ii. 8–11 Moab and Ammon are threatened, and verse 12 seems to be an isolated fragment from some threat against Egypt. The doom of Assyria is pronounced in ii. 13–14, to which an addition has been made in verse 15, based on Isaiah xlvii. 8. Ch. iii opens with a threat against Jerusalem in 1–7, followed by a prediction of a general overthrow in verses 8–10.[1] In iii. 11–13 the prophet is once more dealing with Jerusalem and her fate. The book closes with two exultant songs of deliverance in iii. 14–15 and 16–20. The latter has probably received additions in verses 19 and 20.

IV. Date and Authorship

The general authorship of the book has not been seriously doubted, though different editors have found reason to suspect considerable interpolations. These, however, are to be explained, for the most part, by reference to the structure of the whole; there can be little doubt that some of the independent pieces were expanded before their inclusion in the collection. In one case, as we have observed (on ii. 15), the addition can hardly have been made before the close of the Exile, and the final compilation of the book must be set down to the usual age of such compilations, *i.e.* the fifth century B.C.

The ministry of this prophet is dated in the reign of Josiah by the heading of the book, and this is generally accepted as historically accurate. The first oracle, and some other phrases, suggest a time before the reform of Josiah, and it is possible that Zephaniah, like Jeremiah, was concerned in the promulgation of the principles on which the reform was based. The threats against the

---

[1] The universal application of this oracle has been disputed; Sellin, for instance, regards the mention of the foreign nations as due to interpolation.

D D

foreign nations may have extended over a series of years. There are traditions of a siege of Nineveh (recorded by Herodotus) [1] in 625 B.C., and this may be referred to in ii. 13–14. On the other hand, it seems more likely that this should date from a time some ten years later, when the Chaldæans and the Medes were slowly drawing their net closer around the doomed city.

It should be added that some scholars regard iii. 16 ff. as an exilic or post-exilic utterance. But the signs of the Exile are not obvious until we reach verse 20, which, in any case, is a later addition, and the unsuitability of the passage as a continuation of verse 15 cannot be held to be decisive.

V. THE MAN AND HIS MESSAGE

Zephaniah has a longer recorded pedigree than any other prophet, and it goes back to Hezekiah, who is usually, and with some reason, identified with the king of that name. If that identification be correct, we have in Zephaniah a person unique among the canonical prophets, since no other is connected with the royal house of Judah. For the rest, we are dependent on the book for our knowledge of the man.

Zephaniah, as shown in the oracles which have come down to us, is not a great original thinker, nor is he the kind of person who would be a real leader to his people. But he does stand in the line of the great prophets; he has the same passion for righteousness, and the same ethical conception of the character and demands of Yahweh. Like many another weaker spirit, he takes refuge, in a time of danger and calamity, in eschatology. His hope lies in an unprecedented interference of Yahweh in human affairs, in the vengeance that shall be taken on evil-doers in his own and other lands, and in the forcible righting of all wrongs. His eschatology is of a comparatively early form; its most striking feature is the great sacrifice which Yahweh will hold in " the day." The thought appears also in Isa. xxxiv. 6 and Jer. xlvi. 10, but in neither case is it strictly

[1] i. 103.

eschatological, and the former passage is later than the time of Zephaniah. In the " darkness " (i. 15) which is to mark " the day " we may have a reminiscence of Amos (cp. Am. v. 18, 20), and we may take it for granted that most of the features which he envisaged are a part of the traditional eschatology. Zephaniah is, however, the first of our Old Testament writers whose mind is dominated entirely by eschatological ideas, and it is this which gives him his importance in the history of Israel's religion.

VI. The Hebrew Text and the Septuagint

The text is, on the whole, fairly well preserved, and where we suspect error the Septuagint often helps us,[1] e.g. in ii. 2, 11, etc.

[1] It should be noted that many of the points mentioned in the footnotes to Zephaniah in Kittel's Biblica Hebraica (1906) belong to the sphere of higher criticism rather than to that of the text.

THE BOOK OF HAGGAI

I. HISTORICAL BACKGROUND

As Haggai and Zechariah were contemporaries the historical background of their respective books is the same.[1]

During the last few years of the reign of Cambyses (he died in 522 B.C.), the son of Cyrus and the second king of the Persian empire, this monarch was absent from his kingdom, and during his absence a Magian [2] pretender, Gaumata by name, personated the king's brother Bardes (Smerdis), and usurped the throne. Persia, Media, and other provinces fell away from Cambyses.[3] The great hold which this usurper managed to obtain over the people is shown by the words of Darius i (Hystaspis): " There was no man, Persian or Median, or one of our family, who could deprive Gaumata of the kingdom; the people feared him for his tyranny . . . no one dared to say anything against Gaumata until I came." [4] The rebellion was quelled in 521 B.C. with the death of Gaumata. But there were other troubles awaiting Darius; in the Behistun Inscription he tells us of widespread revolts, the empire was seething with restless discontent; Babylonia, Media, Armenia, Hyrcania, Parthia, Bactria, Sagartia, Persia,

---

[1] By the book of *Zechariah* we mean Zech. i–viii, the remainder of the book which now bears his name belongs to a later century (see pp. 419 ff.).

[2] The Magi were a high-priestly caste among the Medes, and belonged to the sect of the Zoroastrians; they were mainly occupied in carrying out the ritual in the worship of the gods (of later Zoroastrian belief); they were also healers of sickness; in addition, the giving of oracles was part of their activities; and, of course, they were also concerned with occult practices.

[3] For the details of this formidable revolt we are indebted to Herodotus iii. 61–87, and the Behistun Inscription of Darius i. This inscription, recording the victories and great deeds of Darius, occurs on the face of the rock of this name, and is 500 ft. above the main caravan road between Baghdad and Teheran, 65 miles from Hamadan. The inscription, which covers a space of 58 ft. 6 in., is in cuneiform characters, and is written in three languages, Persian (the official language), Susian (the language of the great province of Elam), and Babylonian. For further details, see Rogers, *A History of Ancient Persia*, pp. 95–98 (1929).

[4] Behistun Inscription.

Arachosia on the borders of India—in a word, the whole of the eastern parts of the empire had risen, the various vassal rulers intending to gain independence.

The knowledge of these convulsions would soon have spread to all parts of the empire; and the intercourse which we know to have existed between the Jews of the east and those of Palestine (see, *e.g.*, Zech. vi. 10) would have been the means of keeping the latter informed of what was happening. To Haggai and Zechariah this tumult of nations meant the prelude to the advent of the Messianic kingdom, hence the former says: " Yet once, it is a little while, and I will shake the heavens, and the sea, and the dry land; and I will shake all nations, and the desirable things of all nations shall come, and I will fill this house with glory, saith Yahweh Ṣebaoth " (ii. 6, 7). And again: " I will shake the heavens and the earth, and I will over-throw the throne of kingdoms, and I will destroy the strength of the kingdoms of the nations. . . . In that day, saith Yahweh Ṣebaoth, will I take thee, O Zerubbabel, my servant . . . and will make thee as a signet; for I have chosen thee " (ii. 20–23). This was all spoken during the seventh and ninth months of the second year of Darius. But Zechariah, on the other hand, speaking in the eleventh month of the same year, says: " All the earth sitteth still, and is at rest " (Zech. i. 11); this is, however, entirely in accord with what we know of the history; for by the end of the second year of his reign Darius had subdued all his enemies, and there was peace—for the time being. But we have the record of a second revolt of Babylonia, which was not suppressed until the spring of 519 B.C.; this will per-haps explain why Zechariah, in viii. 1–7, written presumably soon after what he had said in i. 11, looks forward with certainty to the coming of the Messianic times.

The historical background explains why both Haggai and Zechariah regarded the approach of the Messianic kingdom as imminent, and why Haggai was so insistent on the need of the Temple being renovated; it was necessary that this should be ready for the dawn of the Messianic kingdom. There was no need for Zechariah to urge the rebuilding of the Temple, for by the time that he arrived upon the scene this had been seriously taken in hand (Zech. iv. 9).

II. Contents of the Book

Small as the book is, it is of importance for the insight it gives of early post-exilic conditions in Palestine of which we have at the best but scanty knowledge.

The book consists of a series of very short addresses, and two pieces of narrative, also very fragmentary.

i. 1 gives the date of the *first two addresses*, viz. the first day of the sixth month of the second year of Darius; as he came to the throne in 522 B.C., his second year was 520 B.C.; the sixth month was approximately the last week of August and the first three weeks of September. The first two addresses then follow: i. 2–6 and i. 7–11. Both are spoken to the people, and both contain rebukes to them for not undertaking the rebuilding of the Temple. There follows (i. 12–15) a short piece of narrative describing how the people began the work of rebuilding; this is said to have been begun on the twenty-fourth day of the same month; but the sequel shows that something must have interfered with the actual starting of the work.

The *third address* occurs in ii. 2–9; this, too, is preceded by the date, the twenty-first day of the seventh month (the year, though not mentioned, is the same as before). This is again an exhortation to rebuild the Temple, so that it looks as though the people, for some reason, had soon lost heart in their resolve, and needed further urging from the prophet. Then follows another short piece of narrative (ii. 10–14) recording a discussion between Haggai and the priests about clean and unclean; this, too, is dated; but the date, which is *the* one of real importance in the book, is given because, as the sequel shows (ii. 18), it was that on which the rebuilding of the Temple was actually begun, viz. the twenty-fourth day of the ninth month of the second year of Darius, *i.e.* about the middle of December 520 B.C. Following upon and joined to this narrative-piece comes the *fourth address* (ii. 15–19), which tells of the prosperity now to be looked for since the work had been seriously taken in hand; this was uttered on the same day. Lastly, there is the *fifth address* (ii. 20–23), also delivered on the same day; it is spoken to Zerubbabel, who is designated the Messiah by the prophet; the overthrowing of kingdoms, which indicates the near approach of the Messianic kingdom, is announced.

III. AUTHORSHIP OF THE BOOK

The opening verse of the book mentions Haggai as having uttered these short addresses, and there can be no doubt that they were originally spoken by him. But that the book as it stands came from his hand cannot be the case; the addresses as we now have them are very greatly curtailed *résumés*; if the prophet himself had written them he would assuredly not have contented himself with such fragments.[1] But more decisive is the fact that the prophet is always spoken of in the third person; that is very unlikely to have been the case had Haggai himself penned the writing. In all probability it is the work of a contemporary who has recorded the salient points of the prophet's addresses. To him will also be due the exact dates so characteristic of the book; it is probable that we have in this particular a mark of Babylonian influence. On the other hand, some scholars hold that we have here the writing of the prophet himself, which, in the first instance, was written in the first person and later modified to the third person by an editor, probably a contemporary, who was familiar with the facts; to this editor was due the introductory sentence prefixed to each oracle. It is pointed out in justification of this view that elsewhere narratives in the third person are devoted mainly to the experiences of the prophets, and have little to say of their teaching.[2]

[1] Some authorities believe the book to be an extract from some historical work; this is a possibility which cannot be dismissed off-hand; but there is not sufficient evidence to make it certain.

[2] If this explanation be correct the book will have belonged originally to type C (see above, pp. 229 ff.), though in its present form it must be classed as type B.

IV. The Prophet and his Teaching

The short period of Haggai's activity, so far as the evidence of the book goes, extended from the beginning of September to the middle of December 520 B.C. That he came from Babylonia, where he had hitherto lived among the exiles, is suggested by the prominent mention of Darius at the opening of the book, and by the fact that the Babylonian chronological system is followed; according to this the year began in the spring. But what makes this practically certain is his attitude as recorded in ii. 12–14; this passage shows clearly that Haggai belonged to the circle of priests and scribes who during the Exile were busily occupied with the study and elaboration of the Law; not that Haggai was himself a priest, for he says: "Ask now the priests concerning the law" (ii. 11); but his knowledge of the *minutiæ* of the Law shows that he must have been in close touch with the priestly circles. There is nothing at all to show that any priestly activity in this sense existed in Palestine at this period; it was in Babylon that legalistic Judaism took its rise; the priests to whom Haggai refers came with him from Babylon.

Haggai is called a prophet; but as compared with the pre-exilic prophets he is hardly deserving of the title. The chief activity of the prophets had been the teaching of the ethical righteousness of Yahweh and His demand that his chosen people should show their faithfulness to Him by moral living and spiritual worship; stern denunciation of sin, whether in the social, political, or religious life of the people; the certainty of divine judgement on the wicked, and the promise of a restored people when purified. Of all this there is scarcely a trace to be found in the teaching of Haggai. Drought and unfruitfulness are not spoken of as being a punishment for moral wrong (contrast Am. iv. 6–11), but simply because the people had not taken in hand the rebuilding of the dilapidated Temple. Haggai is almost wholly concerned with urging the people to undertake this renovation and with the promise of the advent of the Messianic time when this is accomplished. His designation of Zerubbabel as the Messiah shows that his mind was concentrated only on earthly things; of higher religious thought or of the reign of righteousness in the Messiah's kingdom there is not a word. His whole mental outlook and utilitarian religious point of view (see i. 9–11) is sufficient to show that he can have no place among the prophets in the real sense of the word.

V. The Hebrew Text and the Septuagint

Upon the whole, the Hebrew text is in good order; but a certain number of corruptions occur (*e.g.* in i. 7, 9, 10, 12; ii. 6, 15, 17); glosses are inserted in i. 13; ii. 5, 15. The Septuagint represents an obviously better text in most of these passages, so also in i. 8; ii. 7; it contains an addition in ii. 9 which does not occur in the Hebrew text, but which certainly stood there originally. Thus, in spite of the generally good state of the Hebrew text, the use of the Septuagint is demanded.

THE BOOK OF ZECHARIAH

I. Zechariah and Deutero-Zechariah

That the two parts of this book, i–viii and ix–xiv, are of different date and authorship is now generally recognised. The reasons for this view are briefly as follows:

1. The historical background of the two portions of the book, respectively, is quite different; that of the former half has already been dealt with,[1] that of the latter will be considered in detail below;[2] here it will suffice to notice that the division i–viii belongs quite obviously to the early Persian period; in ix–xiv there is nothing at all that points to this period; it deals with peoples which during the time of Zechariah had no relationship with the Jews; viz. Damascus (ix. 1), Tyre and Zidon (ix. 2), "Assyria,"[3] and Egypt (x. 10, 11), and, above all, Greece (ix. 13). In i–viii there are no indications of unrest in the land, while in ix–xiv there are constant references to war and tumult (ix. 4–6, 8, 13–15; x. 3–7; xi. 1–3, xii. 1–9; xiii. 7–9; xiv. 12–19).

2. In i–viii the main subject matter is concerned with *the rebuilding of the Temple* and the imminent approach of the *Messianic Age*; in ix–xiv the former is never even hinted at; the one reference to the Messiah is of an utterly different nature (ix. 9–12), and the apocalyptic ideas in ch. xiv place us within a mental environment of a character far removed from the Messianic conceptions of Zechariah.

3. In i–viii *prominent leaders* are mentioned by name, Zerubbabel and Joshua; but in ix–xiv the leaders are called "shepherds," and they are never named; they are, moreover, of a type as different as possible from Zerubbabel and Joshua.

4. In i–viii *exact dates* are given (i. 1, 7; vii. 1), as well as ascriptions of authorship (i. 1, 7; vii. 8), and it is definitely

---

[1] See pp. 400 ff.   [2] See pp. 419 ff.   [3] See p. 422.

stated that Zechariah received the visions (i. 7, 8); but in ix–xiv there are no dates, and no name of an author, the only title that occurs is quite indefinite, " the burden of the word of Yahweh " (ix. 1; xii. 1).[1]

5. The style and diction of the two parts of the book are strikingly dissimilar; even in English this is noticeable; in reading the Hebrew this argument for difference of authorship is overwhelming.

6. Apart from the last point, the most compelling reason against unity of authorship is the *difference in religious conceptions* between the two parts; this cannot be dealt with in detail here; it must suffice to give one illustration: in i–viii the Messiah is Zerubbabel (iv. 6–10, 14); but in ix–xiv the person of the Messiah is thus described: " Behold, thy king cometh unto thee; he is just and victorious, lowly, riding upon an ass, even upon the foal of an ass " (ix. 9). Elsewhere in this second part of the book the Messiah is represented as a wholly insignificant figure in the Kingdom of God which is to come; in xiv. 9 it is said: " And Yahweh shall be King over all the earth; in that day shall Yahweh be one, and his name one." That is, on the one hand, a theocratic conception quite incompatible with that of an earthly Messianic ruler; and, on the other, it is a universalistic ideal unimaginable in the mouth of Zechariah.

The question of diversity of authorship will come before us again in dealing with ix–xiv.

II. The Prophet Zechariah and his People

Of the personality and life of the prophet we know, apart from his book, nothing; that, unlike Haggai, he was in the true line of the prophets is clear from his teaching, as shown, above all, in his visions; but that, like Haggai, he was a son of the Exile may be gathered from the fact that he was a grandson of Iddo (i. 1), who, according to Neh. xii. 4 (see also verse 16),[2] was one of the priests who returned from Babylon; the family had, presumably, settled down in the land of Exile. The record of his activity extends from

---

[1] See the section on the Prophetical Literature, p. 232.
[2] In Ezra v. 1; vi. 14 he is called " the son of Iddo."

520–518 B.C., so that, if we are to be guided by what his book tells us, he never saw the completion of the Temple, in 516 B.C., which was the main object of his return to Palestine.

His advent among the returned exiles was intensely needed ; towards the end of the Exile great hopes had animated the hearts of the people owing to the stirring words of a brilliant future uttered by Deutero-Isaiah ; the return to their native land was looked forward to by the exiles as the beginning of an era of prosperity and well-being.   But these expectations came to nothing ; Yahweh had not, after all, had mercy on them ; they were disillusioned as to the restoration of the kingdom ; the Gentiles did not pay them homage ; they were still but the remnant of a once prosperous and God-favoured people.   Small wonder that they became a prey to gloom and misgiving.   It was, therefore, the duty and aim of Zechariah to rouse and hearten his people, to draw them out of this dejected state, and to reanimate the hopes which had been so cruelly shattered.

The condition of the people, social and political, can be pictured by noting the following points :— It was not a kingdom to which they belonged ; they formed but a sparse colony.   The thought of what their nation had been but a generation or two ago, contrasted with their present state, filled them with bitterness.   They were not an independent people ; their freedom was to some extent, at least, restricted ; they had to obey the dictates of a far-off monarch.   They were not a unity ; their brethren were scattered in different lands ; there was no national cohesion ; concerted action, had such been contemplated, was out of the question.   The consciousness of their ineffectiveness was demoralizing.   The attempt to start a new national life had been begun under very unfavourable circumstances ; they were poverty stricken ; they depended, in the main, on agriculture for gaining a living, but the seasons were unpropitious, the crops disappointing, the harvest inadequate.

It was, thus, to a people dejected because of disappointed hopes, embittered because of their political state, dissatisfied because of material wants, and lacking in religious fervour, that Zechariah came.   The message whereby he sought to inspire new hope in his sorely tried people was embodied in a series of visions; to these we must now turn.

III. The Night-Visions

These eight " visions " form a unity; the centre of unity is the thought of the Messianic era, now about to begin. Each vision has something specific to say in regard to this; but the prophet, in constructing them, has made them pairs; the first and the last (eighth) are not pairs in quite the same way as the middle six; but, as will be seen, they belong together. The first pair (the second and third visions) declare that the world-powers will not be able to hinder the advent of the Messianic era, for it is Yahweh Himself who will overcome Israel's enemies and protect them in the Holy City. The second pair (the fourth and fifth visions) show that the Messianic era has, in essentials, really begun; and the third pair (the sixth and seventh visions) describe the moral preparation of the people for the opening of the Messianic era. The first and eighth form a fitting opening and closing, respectively, of the whole cycle, inasmuch as the first heralds the dawn of the Messianic era, the eighth its imminent beginning.

The date given in i. 7 (the 24th day of the 11th month of the 2nd year of Darius = February–March 519 B.C.) at the head of the visions clearly applies to all of them, otherwise further dates would have prefaced the other visions; so that the prophet experienced these visions one after another, and probably, as will be seen, within a very short period of time.

The first night-vision (i. 8–17). The prophet sees in a deep valley a rider on a red horse; behind him are dark-red, pink,[1] and white horses; riders are not mentioned, nor is this required, since these horses are symbolic. The riders are taken for granted. They are represented as having been riding to and fro on the earth, and report that there is peace and quiet everywhere. Since the *shaking* of the earth, and not quietude,

---

[1] The precise meaning of the Hebrew word is uncertain, but if the interpretation of the vision given below is correct, pink probably comes nearest to the colour that is meant.

is to be the sign of the coming of the Messianic age (Hag. ii. 6, 7), the angel asks Yahweh—for the prophet's information—how long He will refrain from having mercy on Jerusalem, *i.e.* how long it will be before the Messianic age dawns. Yahweh replies the He is about to return[1] to Jerusalem, and that the cities of the land shall he prosperous.

The purpose of the vision is to assure the prophet, and through him the people, that the advent of the Messianic age is close at hand. It is a night-vision ("I saw in the night"), but the rider on the red horse symbolizes the sun, *i.e.* the bright time that is about to come; the dark-red horse is a symbol of the first stage of the glory which the prophet sees in his mind's eye; it is the indistinct glimmering in the dark recesses of the valley; the pink horse denotes the brightening of the sun beginning to rise in the east; and the white horse symbolizes the sun in the fullness of its glory. Similarly, the myrtle trees beginning to shoot forth their buds in newness of life (it is spring-time) are a symbol of the coming renovation of the nation.[2]

The vision is thus an introduction to the whole series; it presents, in symbolic form, a picture of the coming Messianic age, the preparation for which is dealt with in the visions which follow.

The second night-vision (i. 18–21; Hebr. ii. 1–4). The prophet sees four horns, symbols of strength, they represent the Gentiles in general, comprehended in the four corners of the earth. He then sees four smiths, symbols of destruction (cp. Isa. liv. 16, 17, and Ezek. xxi. 31, Hebr. 36), and is told that these have come to destroy the four horns. This destruction of the Gentiles, preparatory to the advent of the Messiah, becomes a prominent element in eschatological drama; in its origin it is a mythological trait, and came to Judaism, in all probability, through the medium of Persian eschatology.[3]

The third night-vision (ii. 1–5; Hebr. ii. 5–9). The prophet sees a man with a measuring-line who is about to measure the extent of Jerusalem in order to see how long and how wide

---

[1] It is the "prophetic perfect" which is used here.
[2] See Rothstein, *Die Nachtgesichte des Sacharja*, pp. 26 ff. (1910).
[3] See Böcklen, *Die Verwandschaft der Jüdisch-christlichen mit der Parsischen Eschatologie*, pp. 125 ff. (1902).

the city is to be. But he is told that Jerusalem will not need
to be enclosed with walls because the multitude of men and
cattle who will come there will be so great; it must not be
circumscribed with walls. This, however, is a subsidiary
reason; the real point is, as the prophet goes on to say, that
Yahweh will be a wall of fire around the city; for His advent
is imminent, and His glory will appear in the midst of Jerusalem, *i.e.* in the Temple (cp. Mal. iii. 1).

There is a close connexion between this and the preceding
vision, for, according to the Jewish eschatological drama, the
onslaught of the Gentiles would be directed against Jerusalem,
hence the prophet's words about Yahweh forming a wall of
fire around it (see ii [iv] Ezra xiii. 9–11); this is to be its protection against the Gentiles.

The actual vision occupies only five verses; what follows
in verses 6–13 (Hebr. 10–17) contains a group of prophetic
utterances which are not part of the vision. It is to be noted
that both in the vision and in the passage which follows it the
conceptions regarding the age to come, *i.e.* the Messianic
times, differ fundamentally from those in the two visions
which follow. It is evident that Zechariah had been greatly
impressed with eschatological traits, during his life in Babylon, which later became stereotyped in Persian eschatology;
it is, otherwise, difficult to understand how he could at one
time make Yahweh (God) the central figure of the Messianic
age, and at another, the Messiah, in the person of Zerubbabel; he appears to have been at pains to adapt the eschatological ideas he had imbibed in Babylon to the Messianic
expectations of his people.

The fourth night-vision (iii. 1–10). In the first three visions
the prophet's thoughts were largely centred on Jerusalem;
he is now concerned with his people. In this vision he deals
with the moral condition of the people in the sight of God.
The prophet sees the high-priest standing before the angel
of Yahweh and being accused by Satan. The latter is, however, dismissed, and the angel of Yahweh commands his servants to take away the filthy garments wherewith the high-
priest is clothed, and to put on him clean garments, and to
place the high-priestly head-dress upon his head. The high-

priest, Joshua, then receives a promise from Yahweh that if
he will walk in His ways he shall rule in the Temple and have
access to God.   It is further declared that Joshua and his
fellows, *i.e.* the priesthood, are a sign, or pledge, of the near
approach of the Messiah.   It is noteworthy that the Messiah
is spoken of as the "servant" of Yahweh, and is called the
Ṣemaḥ, "Branch," or "Sprout."   The gem which is to adorn
his crown is ready, and Yahweh Himself is about to engrave
thereon a fitting inscription.   When the Messiah comes God
will obliterate the sins of the people, and there will be peace
upon the land.

The meaning of the vision is, briefly, as follows:—The
high-priest Joshua is the representative of the people; his
filthy garments symbolize their pitiable present condition;
the clean garments are symbolic of national restoration.
Satan is dismissed because his accusation is futile, the people
have atoned for their sins through the Exile (cp. Isa. xl. 2).
The facts that the full functions of the priesthood are
about to be re-inaugurated and the Temple worship restored
are an earnest of the near advent of the Messiah (cp. Hag. ii.
1 ff.).   The stone for his diadem points to the Messiah's
coronation; his name is to be engraved upon it.   With the
advent of the Messiah will come peace and prosperity, for
the people will have become a purified nation.

The fifth night-vision (iv. 1–6a, 10b–14).   This vision is a
development of the preceding one.   The prophet sees a
lamp-stand with seven branches; each branch bears seven
lamps; over each of them is a bowl from which oil is supplied to the lamps.   On either side of the lamp-stand is an
olive tree.   The angel explains to the prophet that the seven
lamps represent the eyes of Yahweh—the seven times seven
express intensity—and that the two olive trees are the two
"sons of oil," *i.e.* the two anointed ones, the high-priest and
the Messiah, Joshua and Zerubbabel.[1]

On the dislocation of the text here see below.

The sixth night-vision (v. 1–4).   The prophet sees a great roll
of writing being blown by the wind over the land of Judah;

---

[1] Some scholars regard the mention of the two "sons of oil" as a later
addition.

upon it a curse is written, a curse upon the guilty among the people. The roll flies into the dwellings of the wicked, bringing punishment upon them and destroying their houses.

The vision is a symbolical picture of the purging of the land of sinners preparatory to the advent of the Messiah.

The seventh night-vision (v. 5–11). This vision is closely connected with the preceding one; in that the destruction of individual sinners was symbolized; this one describes the taking away of the principle of evil from the land; again, it is preparatory to the advent of the Messiah. The prophet sees a woman in an *ephah*—a large dry measure; she is " Sin " personified, having the name of *Rish'a* (" wickedness "); she is carried away in the *ephah* by two women who have wings " like the wings of a stork "—their journey is a long one, hence the wings of a stork, which flies for great distances; she is taken to the land of Shinar, synonymous with Babylon,[1] the land of Israel's captivity, and therefore the arch-enemy; the land is thus an appropriate one for the permanent abode of Wickedness.

The eighth night-vision (vi. 1–8). Between this and the first vision there is a certain external similarity, but this must not be unduly pressed, for the function of the differently coloured horses is not the same in the two visions. In the first they are symbolic of the coming glory of the Messianic era; here, attached to chariots, they are Yahweh's instruments of punishment; in the first vision their colours represented phases of the rising sun of glory; here the colours indicate the four quarters of the compass.

The prophet sees four chariots with differently coloured horses, coming forth from between two mountains. They go towards the four quarters of the earth after having stood before the face of the Lord of the whole earth, *i.e.* to receive His commands as instruments of the divine wrath against the Gentiles. The chariot with the black horses goes towards the north, *i.e.* to Babylon; in regard to this it is said: " Behold, they that go toward the north country have quieted my

[1] This identification is not accepted by all scholars.

E B

spirit[1] in the north country " (vi. 8), *i.e.* punishment upon this country has been inflicted by Yahweh's messengers, therefore His wrath [1] is appeased.

This vision thus records the final act preparatory to the advent of the Messiah.

. . . . . .

What follows the series of night-visions (vi. 9–15) is an appendix connected with the fourth one; in iii. 8 ff. it is pointed out that Joshua and the priests are " men of sign," or a pledge that Yahweh will bring forth the Messiah, and that the stone for the diadem is ready to receive upon it an inscription which Yahweh Himself will inscribe; in this appendix the command is laid upon the prophet to cause a crown to be made out of the gifts from the exiles still in Babylon; no doubt we are intended to understand that the inscribed stone is to be set in the crown, or diadem; in verse 11 it is said that the crown is for Joshua the high-priest, but everything has pointed to Zerubbabel, the Messiah, as the one for whom the crown is destined (see also verse 12 and Hag. ii. 20–23); the name of Joshua was put in place of Zerubbabel at a later time when the high-priest was the head of the theocratic government.

Chs. vii, viii belong together; in the former the question is asked whether certain fast-days, hitherto kept, are still to be observed; the prophet replies in the form of prophecies and admonitions in which he gives as a reason why the fast-days should be discontinued the fact that God had not commanded the fathers to keep them; what God did command was justice and righteousness; but His commands were disregarded, and therefore punishment came. In ch. viii the prophet gives a further reason for the abrogation of the fast-days: the Messianic age is about to dawn, therefore fast-days must be turned to festivals.

[1] " Spirit " is here used in the sense of " wrath," as frequently, see, *e.g.*, Judg. viii. 3; Isa. xxv. 4, xxx. 28.

IV. The Hebrew Text and the Septuagint
of Zech. I–VIII

The somewhat unsatisfactory state of the Hebrew text of these chapters is due not only to the corruptions to which all MSS. in the course of transmission are subject (*e.g.* vii. 2), but also, as for example vi. 11, to deliberate alteration in the interests of a later religious point of view. One considerable dislocation of the text, not easily to be accounted for, occurs in ch. iv, where verses 6b–10a should come after verse 14. There are a number of minor interpolations which mar the text, *e.g.* in i. 19 (Hebr. ii. 2), v. 6, vii. 1, 8, 9, viii. 13; a few doublets occur, *e.g.* iv. 12, v. 11; and in some cases what appears to have been a marginal note is inserted in the text, such as ii. 8 (Hebr. ii. 12), iv. 12, vi. 6, and some others. These blemishes are not always apparent in the Revised Version.

In many cases the Septuagint gives valuable help where the Hebrew text is obviously corrupt (*e.g.* ii. 3 (Hebr. ii. 7); ii. 6 (Hebr. ii. 10); iii. 4, 5; vi. 12; viii. 9), but not infrequently the Septuagint presents corruptions found in the Hebrew text itself, *e.g.* iv. 12, v. 3, vii. 2, and the dislocation of iv. 6b–10a. Upon the whole, the Septuagint is indispensable, but it has not, for these chapters, the same importance as for many others of the Old Testament books.

V. Zechariah IX–XIV

These chapters contain two small collections (ix–xi and xii–xiv), each of which, like the book of *Malachi*, bears the title *Massah* (*i.e.* a prophetic " utterance ").

In two respects these chapters resemble, in external form, most of our prophetic writings: they consist of a number of independent literary pieces, and they are, for the most part, written in poetic form. That they were not written by Zechariah is generally recognized, but there are considerable differences of opinion as to their date and historical background. It will be necessary to consider each piece separately; but to enter into a detailed argument for the position here taken up in regard to them would occupy too much space; references will be given where the arguments in support of the statements to be made can be found.

ix. 1–8 and xi. 1–3. These two pieces may very likely refer to the same event, which is clearly an invasion of Syria, including Phœnicia and Palestine; in ix. 1 it is said: " Oracle. The word of Yahweh concerning the land of Hadrach, and Damascus is its resting-place " (*i.e.* it is specially concerned with Damascus); the context goes on to mention a number of places in western Syria to the south of Palestine which fall into the hands of the conqueror. The invasion of Syria is still more clearly referred to in xi. 1: " Open thy doors, O Lebanon . . . "; the context describes the invasion of the land east of Jordan. The " doors " of Lebanon are the fortresses constructed by the Egyptian power in defence of Cœle-Syria. The reference in these two passages is to the invasion of Syria by Antiochus iii; but this monarch invaded Syria twice, in 218 B.C. and 199 B.C., and one cannot be quite sure as to which of these the passages refer.[1]

ix. 9–12 and 13–17. These two passages probably belong to the same period, though somewhat later than those just considered. The first of them is a Messianic passage in which the Messiah is pictured in a way entirely different from that usually presented. In itself it might have been written by Isaiah, or by a Deutero-Isaiah, but that its content does not suggest an historical background of such early periods; it runs: " Behold, thy king cometh unto thee; just is he and victorious, lowly, and riding upon an ass, even a she-ass's colt." War has ceased, there is peace among the nations, and the Messiah's dominion is to be world-wide; the Jews, scattered abroad, are to return to the homeland (" the stronghold "). We have here an ideal picture, prompted during a period of peace; and there are reasons justifying our assigning it to the year 164 B.C., when the victory of Judas Maccabæus over the Syrian forces marked a turning-point in the Jewish struggle for independence, since by it religious freedom was gained. Owing to the preoccupations of the Syrian forces

---

[1] See further, Oesterley and Robinson, *A History of Israel*, ii. pp. 203 ff., 212 ff. (1932).

elsewhere the Jews enjoyed a comparatively long period of peace; the re-dedication of the Temple, after its pollution by Antiochus iv, made possible once more the full celebration of the Temple worship; the episode is reminiscent of the hopes and rejoicings at the dedication of the Temple after its re-building in 516 B.C. (Ezra vi. 15 ff.). Just as Haggai and Zechariah had believed that the renovated Temple would herald the approach of the Messiah, so the writer of this passage saw in the re-dedication of the Temple a sign of the coming of the Messiah. Like Zechariah ("Not by an army, nor by power, but by my spirit, saith Yahweh Ṣebaoth," Zech. iv. 6), this Ḥasid also looked for the conquest of the world by the Messiah by spiritual means ("he shall speak peace unto the nations").[1]

The other passage (ix. 13–17), while also belonging to the time of Judas Maccabæus, is to be dated about a year earlier; that it is of different authorship must be supposed owing to its warlike spirit. In verse 13 it is said: " I will stir up thy sons, O Zion, against the sons of Greece ";[2] this cannot refer to any period in Jewish history other than the Maccabæan, for the Jews never fought at any other period against the Greeks; it is entirely appropriate that the Syrians should be called " Greeks," both because the Seleucid empire had formed part of Alexander's eastern dominions, and because the Syrians were whole-heartedly hellenistic. The passage refers to the beginning of the leadership of Judas Maccabæus, when the warlike zeal of his followers was roused to fever-heat by his victory over Apollonius, the Syrian general; we read in i Macc. iii. 12: " . . . and Judas took the sword of Apollonius, and therewith he fought all his days "; it is likely enough that this martial spirit leading to victory is reflected in Zech. ix. 13: " I have bent for me Judah as a bow, I have filled it with Ephraim (i.e. Judah is the bow, Ephraim the arrow), I will stir up thy sons, O Zion, against the sons of Greece, and I will make thee as the sword of a mighty man " —the last words are possibly an allusion to the sword captured by Judas. In this connexion the words of verses 14,

[1] See further, Oesterley and Robinson, op. cit., ii, pp. 243 ff.
[2] Following the, doubtless correct, reading of the Septuagint.

15 are also full of significance: " And Yahweh shall be seen over them, and his arrow shall go forth as the lightning, and the Lord God shall blow the trumpet with the whirlwinds of the south. Yahweh Ṣebaoth shall defend them, and they shall prevail, and shall tread down the slingers; and they shall drink their blood (Sept.) like wine, and they shall be filled like the bowls—like the horns of the altar "; the picture in the mind of the writer expressed by these last words was that of the blood of the sacrifices splashed upon the altar; the somewhat bloodthirsty spirit displayed can be understood when one reads such passages in i Macc. i. 20–28, 54–64, ii. 38, and remembers the unrestrained fury which religious persecution will prompt.[1]

x. 1–2. Of this fragment there is little to be said; it has nothing to do with what precedes or follows; it is difficult to account for its presence.

x. 3–12. There are a number of indications in this passage which suggest that it was written towards the end of the high-priesthood of Jonathan, the brother of Judas Maccabæus; with the victories of Jonathan it looked as though the Maccabæan struggle had reached a triumphant conclusion. In verse 4 the "corner stone," the "nail," and the "battle bow" may well refer respectively to the three Maccabæan leaders, Simon, Judas, and Jonathan. In the words of verse 6, "And I will strengthen the house of Judah, and I will save the house of Joseph . . . " and of verse 10, the writer expresses the conviction that final victory and the return of all Israel from the Dispersion is about to take place. Tyre and Gebal, the great sea-ports, and Syria and Egypt shall all be done away with; in conformity with his love of figurative expression he uses "Assyria" for Syria, as in Isa. xxvii. 13, Mic. v. 5 f. (Hebr. 4 f.), and Egypt is the Ptolemaic empire.[2]

xi. 4–17 and xiii. 7–9. As many commentators recognize, these two passages belong together; the latter has been misplaced and should come immediately after xi. 17.[3] Their full significance can be grasped only in the light of the

---

[1] See further, Oesterley and Robinson, *op. cit.*, ii. pp. 242 f.

[2] See further, Oesterley and Robinson, *op. cit.*, ii. p. 259.

[3] We note, however, that in form xi. 4–16 belongs to type C (see above, p. 229), while the remainder is of the usual oracular type.

internal conditions of Judæa during the period of the Maccabæan struggle; with these we cannot deal here.   It must
suffice to say that two deplorable factors brought shame and
suffering on the people during a considerable part of this
period—we are referring to *internal* conditions; one was the
buying and selling of the high-priesthood, the other was the
internecine strife between the hellenistic and orthodox Jews.
The " shepherds " spoken of in these passages are the high-
priests Jason, Menelaus, and especially Alkimus; in xi. 8 it is
said that these three shepherds are to be cut off " in one
month "; this is meant to be taken figuratively, " within a
short period," which we know from i Macc. and Josephus to
have been the case.   All three, and especially Alkimus, were
guilty of leaving the flock (verse 17) both in the literal sense
as well as in the sense of neglecting their charge.   It is in
reference to Alkimus that the words of this verse are spoken:
" The sword (used figuratively for ' destruction ') shall be
against his arm and against his right eye; his arm shall be
clean dried up, and his right eye shall be utterly darkened ";
this description of a paralytic stroke agrees with what is said
in i Macc. ix. 55, 56: " At that time was Alkimus stricken,
and his works were hindered, and his mouth stopped, and he
was taken with a palsy ($\pi\alpha\rho\epsilon\lambda\acute{v}\theta\eta$) . . ."
    Then with regard to the conflict between hellenistic and
orthodox Jews, this centred, in the first instance, in an antagonism between Jerusalem and Judah, and is referred to
specially in xi. 7–11; the two " staves " called " Beauty "
and " Bands," but more correctly " Pleasantness " and
" Union," are used figuratively of Judah and Jerusalem; [1]
both the staves are broken to indicate that the brotherhood
which should naturally exist between the Jerusalem Jews and
those of the rest of Judah was severed; this was bitterness to a
true Jew such as the writer of this passage, and verse 9 reflects
his feeling of irritation at the existence of such an unnatural
animosity between brethren.   These sections are thus the
reflections of one who stood aloof from the turmoil of the
times, but who was impelled to record what he felt; they are

---

[1] The Hebrew text reads " Judah and Israel," but, apart from the fact
that two MSS. and the Lucianic text read " Jerusalem " for " Israel," the
circumstances of the time demand that we should read " Jerusalem."

important as witnessing to the internal affairs of the Jews during the middle of the second century B.C., of which we have evidence in extra-Biblical sources.[1]

xii, xiii. 1–6. These difficult passages in which eschatological thought is attached to current historical events—a common trait in Jewish eschatology—has clearly been influenced by some parts of the book of *Ezekiel*. The eschatological portion is contained in xii. 1–9; an historical event lies behind xii. 10–14, and in xiii. 1–6 the conditions which will obtain in the Messianic age are contrasted with those of the present time, the two subjects referred to being idolatry and the prophetical order, which had fallen into decay. It is the second of these passages (xii. 10–14) which is the most difficult to understand on account of its cryptic references; and the difficulty is increased by a number of corruptions in the Hebrew text. The following brief explanation is taken from the volume already referred to more than once; to it recourse must be had for further details: [2] the reference in the passage is to the death of Simon the Maccabee and to the mourning for him; verses 10, 11 contain two corruptions in the Hebrew text; emended, we may read them thus: " And I will pour [3] upon the house of David the spirit of deep emotion and of supplication, and they shall contemplate him (*i.e.* Simon) whom they (*i.e.* his murderers) have pierced; [4] and they (*i.e.* the Jews) shall mourn for him, as one mourneth for an only son. . . . In that day there shall be a great mourning in Jerusalem, like the mourning of women lamenting Tammuz-Adon." [5]   In the description of the mourning that takes place (verses 12–14), the first point to note is the strict separation of the sexes, a definite mark of a very late period; there is, further, much significance in the order of the mourning families enumerated; " the family of the house of David " comes first, in reference to the ruling family, *i.e.* the high-priestly house, of which

---

[1] See further, Oesterley and Robinson, *op. cit.*, ii. pp. 258 ff.

[2] Oesterley and Robinson, *op. cit.*, ii. pp. 267–271.

[3] The future form is somewhat misleading, it is a statement of actual facts which is recorded.

[4] See i Macc. xvi. 14–17.

[5] See Ezek. viii. 14; the " weeping for Tammuz " was always enacted by women.

John, the son of the murdered Simon, was now head; then
" the family of the house of Jonathan," [1] this would naturally
be mentioned next as being nearest of kin to the new high-
priest; " the family of the house of Levi " is in reference
to the priesthood; and lastly, " the family of the Simonites," [2]
the more distant relatives of Simon.

Thus interpreted the passage is full of meaning.

xiv. This is an apocalyptic section dealing with the final
safety and glory of Jerusalem in the last times. In verses 1–5
it is told of how Yahweh will come and save Jerusalem from
all the nations who gather against the city; verses 7, 8 speak
of the light of the presence of Yahweh, so that there will be no
difference between day and night; then in verses 8–11 there
is the promise of living waters proceeding from Jerusalem
east and west, and Yahweh alone will reign over all the earth;
in verses 12–19 the apocalyptist tells of the punishment of all
who fought against Jerusalem, and of those who will not
come to Jerusalem to worship Yahweh; finally, verses 20, 21
speak of the sanctification of Jerusalem and Judah in that
day. The writer is strongly nationalistic; and he offers
some of the bizarre pictures characteristic of the later
apocalyptic writings.

VI. The Hebrew Text and the Septuagint of Zech. ix–xiv

The Hebrew text of this part of the book has, like the
earlier part, suffered considerably; the corruptions in a number of instances are small, but nevertheless they often spoil the
meaning of a text, and must be emended; in other cases they
are more serious. The text is at fault in the following passages (they do not profess to be exhaustive): ix. 8, 15, 16, 17;
x. 2, 5, 9, 12; xi. 2, 7, 8, 13, 14, 16; xii. 1, 5, 10; xiv. 5, 6, 10,
12. Dislocations of the text occur in xiii. 7–9, which belongs
after xi. 17; and xiv. 13, 14 is a passage which is clearly out
of place. Glosses are inserted in xi. 6 and xiv. 2.

In numerous instances the Septuagint witnesses to a better

---

[1] The text has " Nathan " by mistake.
[2] " Shimeites " is again a textual error.

form of the Hebrew text, *e.g.* ix. 2, 5, 10, 13, 15; x. 9, 11, 12; xi. 5, 16; xii. 2, 5, 8, 13; xiii. 7, 9; xiv. 5, 6, 18. Sometimes it is only a word which is in question, but it makes all the difference to the sense of a passage; so that the study of the Septuagint text cannot be ignored.

THE BOOK OF MALACHI

I. Authorship of the Book

WE are accustomed to regard the name of the writer of this book as Malachi; but " Malachi " is not a proper name, as can be seen by the Septuagint rendering of i. 1: " Oracle; the word of Yahweh unto Israel, by the hand of his messenger " (ἄγγελος αὐτοῦ). The idea of Yahweh's messenger who is sent to prepare the people for His coming is taken from Isa. xl. 3–8. " Malachi " is simply the Hebrew for " my messenger." The writer of the various literary pieces of this book is anonymous like so many others whose writings have been preserved in the prophetical books.[1]

But if we do not know his name, we learn from his book something about the personality of the writer. He has the spirit of the true prophet in him in his denunciation of insincere worship; he believes in the necessity of the sacrificial system, but he insists upon the right spirit in offering, otherwise it is a dishonouring of God (i. 6–8). Better no sacrifices at all than the kind of offerings which were being presented on the altar by priests who by doing so were despising the name of God (i. 6); he says: "O that there were one among you that would shut the doors, and that ye might not illuminate mine altar to no purpose " (i. 10); he wishes that there were even one priest who had sufficient strength of character to keep the Temple gates shut so that the mockery of the altar fire might cease.

But this prophet is equally zealous for the honour of the sanctuary in another direction; he finds that the people have been neglectful in paying tithe which was so necessary for the upkeep of the Temple and its services. He speaks in very strong language to the people on this subject: " Will a man rob God? Yet ye rob me [he speaks in the name of

---

[1] See above, p. 232.

God]. But ye say, Wherein have we robbed thee? In tithes and heave offerings (cp. Deut. xii. 11). Ye are cursed with a curse, for ye rob me, ye, the whole nation! " (iii. 8, 9).

This is all in the spirit of the true prophet.

Another striking trait is his universalistic outlook. When speaking in the name of God, he says to the priests, " neither will I accept an offering at your hand "; and he goes on to say: " For from the rising of the sun unto the going down of the same my name is great among the Gentiles; and in every place a pure offering is burned to my name; for great is my name among the Gentiles, saith Yahweh Ṣebaoth " (i. 11). A word of explanation for this rendering is demanded. The point is that the prophet wishes to set in contrast against the polluted sacrifices of the Jewish priesthood and the insincere worship of the people (or a section of them), the religion of the Gentiles; the prophet holds that the God Who is inadequately worshipped in Jerusalem is the same Who is acknowledged by the Gentiles, who did revere " the highest God "; for a monotheistic tendency was beginning to show itself in many quarters, as Wellhausen has shown. The "highest God " worshipped in the Gentile world *is*, the prophet maintains, Yahweh. It is extremely doubtful whether there is any reference to incense; the word used for " incense " in the R.V. is not a noun formation, and never occurs as such; but the form is a past-participle (מָקְטָר Hophal),[1] and means, as in Lev. vi. 15, making the smoke of sacrifice. In any case, the passage exhibits an extraordinary universalistic attitude on the part of the prophet.

One other point must be mentioned as showing the type of man this prophet was; his ethical sense makes him regard divorce with abhorrence; and this not because the men who divorced their wives married daughters of " strange gods " (ii. 11), but because divorce in itself is an evil thing. His words are: " Yahweh hath been witness between thee and the wife of thy youth, against whom thou hast dealt treacherously, though she is thy companion, and the wife of thy covenant " (ii. 14); the next verse is difficult because the

---

[1] The *Oxford Heb. Lex.* in one place calls it Hoph. partic., in another, a substantive!

Hebrew text is obviously corrupt; emended, we must read:
"Did not One (*i.e.* God) make us and preserve our spirit
alive? And what does the One desire? A godly seed!
Therefore take heed to your spirit, and let none deal faith-
lessly with the wife of his youth. For I hate divorce, saith
Yahweh, the God of Israel. . . ." That is very fine, and
shows an infinitely higher ethical ideal than Ezra. Altogether this prophet, whose name we do not know, was an
exceedingly admirable man; some of his ideas, it is granted,
were *naïve*—he was a child of his time—but that makes his
fine ideas all the more remarkable. Note especially that his
teaching on the indissolubility of the marriage-tie is quite out
of harmony with the Judaism current at the time; it has its
only parallel in the teaching of the Gospels.

II. DATE OF THE BOOK

There are not many books in the Old Testament which
can be dated with more certainty than this one. That it is
post-exilic cannot admit of doubt; thought, teaching, and
diction make this self-evident; and the land is ruled over by
a *pekah* or "governor." It was written after 516 B.C., because the Temple has been rebuilt and the full sacrificial
system is in vogue; thus, in iii. 1 it is said: " . . . and the
Lord, whom ye seek, shall suddenly come to his temple ";
and in iii. 10 " mine house " is spoken of; besides, the offerings of sacrifices in the Temple is assumed all through (i. 7-14,
and elsewhere); and the gates of the Temple are mentioned
in i. 10, as we have already seen.

On the other hand, the condition of the priesthood and of a
large section of the people is such that the reforms of Nehemiah and Ezra cannot possibly have taken place yet; this
necessitates a date before 444 B.C. In passing it is worth
noting: in *Malachi* no distinction is made between priests
and Levites (ii. 4-9, iii. 3), all the sons of Levi are priests; but
in the Priestly Code there is a great difference between them,
the Levites being quite a subordinate order. On the other
hand what Malachi says about the temple-tithe (iii. 7-10)
agrees with Nehemiah and the Priestly Code (*Deuteronomy*

knows nothing of a tithe for the Temple, but only for the
Levites every third year); but this is no argument for the book
having been written in the time of Nehemiah or of the Priestly
Code, because the Priestly Code has preserved a number of
ancient laws, much older than *Deuteronomy*, many of which
do not appear in that book.

"Malachi" therefore belongs to the period between 516
B.C. and 444 B.C., towards the end of it rather than at the
beginning, so as to allow time for the development of the
sacrificial system.

III. Contents of the Book

i. 2–5. The prophet opens his book with asseverating that
Yahweh loves His people: they had doubted this, probably
on account of some calamity that had fallen on the land, see
iii. 10, 11. So the prophet cites a concrete example to show
the people that God loves them: Yahweh's love for Jacob, he
says, is shown by his hatred of Esau; He has made their land
a desolation, and even if the Edomites (the descendants of
Esau) build the waste places, Yahweh will destroy them again.
Then the people of Israel will recognize that Yahweh is great
beyond the borders of Israel. The argument cannot, of
course, appeal to us; but we must remember the time and
that "Malachi" was the child of his age; it makes it all
the more remarkable that he exhibits such exalted traits, as
already pointed out.

i. 6–ii. 9. The prophet rebukes the priests because the
offerings they bring are dishonouring to God; they think
that anything is good enough for the purpose of sacrifice.
Herein they show themselves, however, inferior to the Gentiles, who offer pure offerings to the name of God. Since
the priests are guilty in this respect it is small wonder that the
people in general follow their example; they bring animals
with blemishes instead of a male from the flock. A prophecy
of punishment is then uttered. The prophet, further, contrasts the conscientious way in which, in the past, the offerings
were made with what is now done by the priests.

ii. 10–16. The prophet then condemns the marriages

with " daughters of a strange god " ; and this for two reasons :
the practice involves disloyalty to Yahweh ; and it has also
meant that the lawful wife has been divorced. Such faith-
lessness is an abomination to Yahweh.

ii. 17–iii. 5. The prophet now addresses himself to those
impatient ones who, illogically enough, conclude that because the day of Yahweh does not come, therefore God is not
really zealous for what is right—" Where is the God of judgement? "—" Everyone that doeth evil is good in the sight of
Yahweh! " But Yahweh will send His angel before Him,
who will prepare the way ; and then He will Himself come to
His Temple with the angel of the covenant. Then there
will be a purging of the sons of Levi, *i.e.* of the priesthood ;
and offerings will be brought as of old. But punishment
shall overtake all evil-doers.

iii. 6–12. The paragraph division in the R.V. is wrong ;
this section begins at verse 6 (not 7). Because of the troubles
of the times (verses 10, 11) the people say that Yahweh has
changed, and is not as He used to be in His treatment of His
people. This idea the prophet combats : " For I, Yahweh,
change not " ; it is the people who have changed ; this they
have shown by not bringing the tithes and offerings. If they
will bring the whole tithe again with the proper offerings, the
curse which is upon them will be taken away, and the people
will be happy again.

iii. 13–iv. 4 (Hebr. iii. 13–22). This section is in part
parallel to ii. 17–iii. 5. The prophet denounces those who
say it is useless to serve Yahweh, and who assert that the
wicked are to be envied because they are prosperous. But,
says the prophet, Yahweh has a book of remembrance wherein are inscribed the names of those who fear Him. These
shall be His when His day comes ; and He will be a Father to
them. In that day the eyes of the wicked will be opened, and
they will discern between the righteous and the wicked.
Then there will be a burning, and those who have done evil
will be burned up like stubble. The God-fearers, on the
other hand, shall bask in the sun of righteousness, which shall
bring healing to them. Then shall they tread upon the
wicked, " for they shall be ashes under the soles of your feet "

(iv. 3, iii. 21 in Hebr.). The prophet concludes with an admonition to remember the law of Moses. Some commentators regard this verse (iv. 4) as a later addition, joining it on to the last two verses, because, it is said, it is incongruous to call upon the righteous, who have just been mentioned, to keep the law, which is just what they have been doing. It seems, however, to be an appropriate final reminder; yet, it must be noted what is to be said presently. In any case, the mention of Horeb points to its having been written before the Priestly Code, because in this it is always Sinai, while in *Deuteronomy* it is always Horeb, which is the scene of the giving of the law.

iv. 5, 6 (Hebr. iii. 23, 24). With iv. 4 the book would have had a fitting close, and doubtless this did originally conclude it; but some scribe added these two verses which are evidently intended as an allusion to iii. 1, " Behold, I send my messenger, and he shall prepare the way before me "; Elijah was the most obvious man to choose because he was taken up in the fiery chariot, *i.e.* he never died, and therefore his return might be expected at some time; and what more appropriate time than the eve of the day of Yahweh? These last two verses (and also iv. 4) are regarded by some modern commentators as a later addition on account, mainly, of the difference of function of the messenger in iii. 1 and here. But otherwise the integrity of the book is not seriously questioned.

The reference to the " law of Moses "—it occurs in no other prophetical book [1]—and the conjunction of Moses and Elijah certainly point to a late date; both belong to developed Judaism; the expression " law of Moses " always refers to the whole of the Pentateuch, and therefore belongs to a time after the final redaction of the Priestly Code; and Elijah legends arose also in later days. Elijah would never have been given this precedence over all the great prophets had it not been for the traditional legend of his having gone up to heaven in a fiery chariot.

[1] ii Kgs. xxiii. 25, where the words " according to all the law of Moses " occur, belongs properly to a very late edition of the book.

IV. The Hebrew Text and the Septuagint

The Hebrew text has been well preserved; in only two passages are there corruptions which make emendation difficult (ii. 3, 15); minor corruptions are more frequent (*e.g.* i. 13, ii. 12, 15, iii. 6, 8), but they are not serious. The Septuagint is often helpful, sometimes it supplies an additional word which seems to have fallen out of the Hebrew text (*e.g.* i. 6, ii. 2, 3, iii. 5), and makes a better reading; the only omission of any note is iv. 3 (Hebr. iii. 21), though not all MSS. omit it.

BIBLIOGRAPHY

THE following list of works does not profess to be exhaustive; with every book mentioned one or other of us is more or less familiar; articles in learned journals are not included, but in many cases references in footnotes indicate them.

There are a number of series of Commentaries, both English and German; many volumes from these find mention below, but we cannot profess to be familiar with all of them. These series are:

The International Critical Commentary (*ICC*)
The Cambridge Bible (*Camb. B*)
The Westminster Commentaries (*W. Com.*)
The Century Bible (*CB*)
Nowack's Series: "Handkommentar zum Alten Testament" (*HKAT*)
Kautzsch-Bertholet's Series: "Die heilige Schriften des Alten Testaments" (*HSAT*)
Marti's Series: "Kurzer Hand-Commentar zum Alten Testament" (*KHAT*)
Sellin's Series: "Kommentar zum Alten Testament" (*KAT*)
Eissfeldt's Series: "Handbuch zum Alten Testament" (*HAT*)
Gressmann and others: "Die Schriften des Alten Testaments" (*SAT*)

BOOKS ON INTRODUCTION

Bertholet, *Kulturgeschichte Israels* (1920); Engl. ed.: *Ancient Hebrew Civilization* (1926)
Bewer, *The Literature of the Old Testament in its Historical Development* (1922)
Bleek, *Einleitung in das Alte Testament* (1886)
Budde, *Geschichte der Althebräischen Litteratur* (1906)
Cornill, *Einleitung in das Alte Testament* (1896); English edition by G. H. Box (1907)
Creelman, *Introduction to the Old Testament* (1917)
Driver, *An Introduction to the Literature of the Old Testament* (1913)
Eissfeldt, *Einleitung in das alte Testament* (1934)
Gray, *A Critical Introduction to the Old Testament* (1927)
Hempel, *Die Althebräische Literatur,* in "Handbuch der Literatur-Wissenschaft" (undated) (not yet completed)
Kent, *Growth and Contents of the Old Testament* (1926)
McFadyen, *Introduction to the Old Testament* (1932)
Meinhold, *Einführung in das Alte Testament* (1932)
Moore, *The Literature of the Old Testament* (1913)
Sellin, *Introduction to the Old Testament* (1923); latest German ed. 1933
Steuernagel, *Lehrbuch der Einleitung in das Alte Testament* (1912)
Strack, *Einleitung in das Alte Testament* (1906)

THE CANON OF THE OLD TESTAMENT

Budde, *Der Kanon des Alten Testamentes* (1900)
Buhl, *Kanon und Text des Alten Testamentes* (1891)
Eberharter, *Der Kanon des Alten Testamentes bis zur Zeit des Ben-Sira* (1911)
Hölscher, *Kanonisch und Apokryph* (1905)
Robertson Smith, *The Old Testament in the Jewish Church* (1892)
Ryle, *The Canon of the Old Testament* (1895)
Wildeboer, *The Origin of the Canon of the Old Testament* (1895)

434

THE TEXT OF THE OLD TESTAMENT

Bauer-Leander, *Historische Grammatik der Hebräischen Sprache*, I. Band, pp. i-55 (1922)
Bertholet, *Kulturgeschichte Israels* (1920); English edition: *Ancient Hebrew Civilization* (1926)
Geden, *Outlines of Introduction to the Hebrew Bible* (1909)
Ginsburg, *Introduction to the Hebrew Bible* (1897)
Kahle, *Masoreten des Ostens* (1913)
—— *Masoreten des Westens* (1927)
Ottley, *A Handbook to the Septuagint* (1920)
Swete, *Introduction to the Old Testament in Greek* (1900)
Weir, *A Short History of the Hebrew Text of the Old Testament* (1907)

THE PENTATEUCH

Addis, *The Documents of the Hexateuch*, Vol. I (1892), Vol. II (1898)
Battersby-Harford, *Since Wellhausen* (1926)
Carpenter and Harford-Battersby, *The Composition of the Hexateuch* (1892)
—— *The Pentateuch* (1900)
Chapman, *An Introduction to the Pentateuch* (1911)
Eerdmans, *Alttestamentliche Studien* (1908)
Eissfeldt, *Hexateuchsynopse* (1922)
Holzinger, *Einleitung in den Hexateuch* (1893)
Jirku, *Das weltliche Recht im Alten Testament* (1927)
Klostermann, *Der Pentateuch* (1907)
Simpson, *Pentateuchal Criticism* (1924)
Smith, J. M. P., *The Origin and History of Hebrew Law* (1931)
Wellhausen, *Die Composition des Hexateuchs . . .* (1889)

GENESIS:

Driver, S. R., *The Book of Genesis* (1904) *W. Com.*; rev. by G. R. Driver (1926)
Gunkel, *Genesis* (1910) *HKAT*
Procksch, *Genesis* (1913) *KAT*
Skinner, *A Critical and Exegetical Commentary on Genesis* (1912)

EXODUS:

Bacon, *The Triple Tradition of the Exodus* (1894)
Baentsch, *Das Zweite Buch Mose* (1903) *HKAT*
Beer, *Exodus* (1939) *HAT*
Driver, *Exodus* (1911) *Camb. B.*
Holzinger, *Exodus* (1900) *KHAT*
McNeile, *The Book of Exodus* (1908) *W. Com.*

LEVITICUS:

Baentsch, *Leviticus* (1903) *HKAT*
Bertholet, *Leviticus* (1901) *KHAT*

NUMBERS:

Baentsch, *Numeri* (1903) *HKAT*
Binns, *The Book of Numbers* (1927) *W. Com.*
Gray, *A Critical and Exegetical Commentary on Numbers* (1903) *ICC*
Holzinger, *Numeri* (1903) *KHAT*

DEUTERONOMY:

Bertholet, *Deuteronomium* (1899) *KHAT*
Driver, *A Critical and Exegetical Commentary on Deuteronomy* (1902) *ICC*
Kennett, *Deuteronomy and the Decalogue* (1920)
König, *Das Deuteronomium* (1917)

DEUTERONOMY:

Puukko, *Das Deuteronomium* (1910)
Robinson, H. Wheeler, *Deuteronomy and Joshua* (1907) *CB*
Smith, G. A., *Deuteronomy* (1918) *Camb.* B
Steuernagel, *Das Deuteronomium* (1923) *HKAT*
Welch, *The Code of Deuteronomy* (1924)
—— *Deuteronomy, the Framework of the Code* (1932)

THE BOOK OF JOSHUA

Cooke, G. A., *Joshua* (1918) *Camb. B.*
Friedeberg, *Joshua, an annotated Hebrew Text* (1913)
Garstang, *Joshua, Judges* (1931)
Holmes, *Joshua, the Hebrew and Greek Texts* (1914)
Holzinger, *Das Buch Josua* (1901) *KHAT*
Noth, *Das Buch Josua* (1938) *HAT*
Steuernagel, *Josua* (1900) *KHAT*

THE BOOK OF JUDGES

Budde, *Das Buch der Richter* (1897) *KHAT*
Burney, *The Book of Judges* (1918)
Cooke, G. A., *Judges* (1918) *Camb. B.*
Eissfeldt, *Die Quellen des Richterbuches* (1925)
Garstang, *Joshua, Judges* (1931)
Kittel, *Das Buch der Richter* (1909) *HSAT*
Moore, *A Critical and Exegetical Commentary on Judges* (1903) *ICC*
Nowack, *Das Buch der Richter* (1902) *HKAT*

THE BOOK OF RUTH

See under *i, ii Samuel*
Kennedy, *The Book of Ruth* (1928): for the Hebrew Text

I II SAMUEL

Budde, *Die Bücher Samuelis* (1902) *KHAT*
Driver, *Notes on the Hebrew Text of the Books of Samuel* (1913)
Eissfeldt, *Die Komposition der Samuelisbücher* (1931)
Hylander, *Der literarische Samuel-Saul-Komplex i Sam. i–xv* (1933)
Nowack, *Richter, Ruth und Bücher Samuelis* (1902) *HKAT*
Smith, H. P., *A Critical and Exegetical Commentary on the Books of Samuel* (1899) *ICC*
Wellhausen, *Der Text der Bücher Samuelis* (1871)

I II KINGS

Benzinger, *Die Bücher der Könige* (1899) *KHAT*
Burney, *Notes on the Hebrew Text of the Books of Kings* (1903)
Kittel, *Das Buch der Könige* (1900) *HKAT*
Mowinckel, *Die Chronologie der israelitischen und jüdischen Könige* (1932)

I II CHRONICLES

Benzinger, *Die Bücher der Chronik* (1901) *KHAT*
Curtis, *A Critical and Exegetical Commentary on the Books of Chronicles* (1910) *ICC*
Elmslie, *Chronicles Camb. B.* (1916)
Kittel, *Die Bücher der Chronik* (1902) *HKAT*
Rad, *Das Geschichtsbild des Chronistischen Werkes* (1930)
Rothstein-Hänel, *Das erste Buch der Chronik* (1927)

EZRA–NEHEMIAH

Batten, *A Critical and Exegetical Commentary on the Books of Ezra and Nehemiah* (1913) *ICC*
Bertholet, *Die Bücher Esra und Nehemia* (1902) *KHAT*
Browne, *Early Judaism* (1920)
Oesterley and Robinson, *A History of Israel*, ii. pp. 111–156 (1934)
Rothstein, *Juden und Samaritaner* (1908)
Siegfried, *Esra, Nehemia, und Esther* (1901) *HKAT*
Torrey, *Ezra Studies* (1910)
Van Hoonacker, *Néhémie et Esdras* (1892)

THE BOOK OF ESTHER

Gunkel, *Esther* (1916)
Paton, *A Critical and Exegetical Commentary on the Book of Esther* (1908) *ICC*
Siegfried, *Esra, Nehemia und Esther* (1901) *HKAT*

FORMS OF HEBREW POETRY

Burney, *The Poetry of Our Lord* (1925)
Cobb, *A Criticism of Systems of Hebrew Poetry* (1905)
Condamin, *Poèmes de la Bible . . .* (1933)
Gordon, *The Poets of the Old Testament* (1912)
Gray, *Forms of Hebrew Poetry* (1915)
Grimme, *Psalmenprobleme* (1902)
Kautzsch, *Die Poesie und die poetischen Bücher des alten Testamentes* (1902)
Ley, *Grundzüge des Rhythmus, des Vers- und Strophenbaues in der Hebräischen Poesie* (1875)
—— *Leitfaden der Hebräischen Metrik* (1887)
Lowth, *De sacra poesi Hebraeorum Praelectiones Academicae* (1753); Eng. ed. (1843)
Müller, D. H., *Strophenbau und Responsion* (1898)
Rothstein, *Grundzüge des hebräischen Rhythmus und seine Formenbildung* (1909)
Schlögl, *Die echte biblisch-hebräische Metrik* (1914)
Sievers, *Metrische Studien* (1901)

THE WISDOM LITERATURE

Baumgartner, *Israelitische und altorientalische Weisheit* (1933)
Box and Oesterley, The Book of Sirach, in Charles' *The Apocrypha and Pseudepigrapha of the Old Testament*, Vol. I (1913)
Causse, *Sagesse égyptienne et sagesse juive* (1929)
Cheyne, *Job and Solomon* (1887)
Cowley, *Jewish Documents of the time of Ezra* (1919)
—— *Aramaic Papyri of the fifth century B.C.* (1923)
Davison, *The Wisdom Literature of the Old Testament* (1894)
Eissfeldt, *Der Maschal im Alten Testament* (1913)
Elmslie, *Studies in Life from Jewish Proverbs* (2nd impression, undated)
Erman, *Die Literatur der Aegypter* (1923); English translation by Blackman, *The Literature of the Ancient Egyptians* (1927)
Fichtner, *Die altorientalische Weisheit in ihrer Israelitisch-Jüdischen Ausprägung* (1933)
Goodrick, *The Book of Wisdom* (1913)
Gressmann, *Israels Spruchweisheit im Zusammenhang der Weltliteratur* (1925)
Humbert, *Recherches sur les sources égyptiennes de la Littérature Sapientiale d'Israël* (1929)
Langdon, *Babylonian Wisdom* (1923)
Lange, *Das Weisheitsbuch des Amenemope* (1925)
Meinhold, *Die Weisheit Israels* (1908)

BIBLIOGRAPHY

BIBLIOGRAPHY
438

Oesterley, *The Wisdom of Jesus the son of Sirach, or Ecclesiasticus* (1912) Camb. B.
—— *The Wisdom of Egypt and the Old Testament* (1927)
—— *The Wisdom of Solomon* (1917)
—— *The Book of Proverbs* (1929) W. Com.
Ranston, *The Old Testament Wisdom Books* (1930)
Schencke, *Die Chokma (Sophia) in der jüdischen Hypostasenspekulation* (1913)
Smend, *Die Weisheit des Jesus Sirach* (1906): Commentary
—— *Die Weisheit des Jesus Sirach, Hebräisch und Deutsch* (1906); Text and
translation

THE BOOK OF JOB

Ball, *The Book of Job* (1922)
Budde, *Das Buch Hiob* (1896) *KHAT*
Cheyne, *Job and Solomon* (1887)
Dhorme, *Le Livre de Job* (1926)
Dillmann, *Das Buch Hiob* (1891)
Driver and Gray, *A Critical and Exegetical Commentary on the Book of Job* (1921)
    ICC
Duhm, *Das Buch Hiob* (1897) *KHAT*
Hölscher, *Das Buch Hiob* (1937) *HAT*
Kissane, *The Book of Job* (1938)
König, *Das Buch Hiob* (1929)
Kraeling, *The Book of the Ways of God* (1938)
Peake, *Job* (1905) *CB*
Sellin, *Das Problem des Hiobbuches* (1919)
Strahan, *The Book of Job interpreted* (1913)

THE PSALMS

Baethgen, *Die Psalmen* (1904) *HKAT*
Barnes, *The Psalms, with Introduction and Notes* (1931) W. Com.
Briggs, *A Critical and Exegetical Commentary on the Book of Psalms* (1906, 1907)
    ICC
Buttenwieser, *The Psalms* (1938)
Calès, *Le Livre des Psaumes* (1936)
Cheyne, *The Book of Psalms* (1888)
—— *The Origin and Religious Contents of the Psalter* (1891)
—— *The Book of Psalms* (1904)
Duhm, *Die Psalmen* (1899) *KHAT*
Gunkel, *Die Psalmen* (1926) *HKAT*
Gunkel-Begrich, *Einleitung in die Psalmen* (1928, 1933)
James, *Thirty Psalmists* (1938)
Kittel, *Die Psalmen* (1929) *KAT*
Mowinckel, *Psalmenstudien* (1922, 1923)
Oesterley, *The Psalms*, Book III, 73–89 (1933); Book IV, 90-106 (1936): for the
    Hebrew Text
Peters, *The Psalms as Liturgies* (1922)
Schmidt, *Die Psalmen* (1934) *HAT*
Simpson, ed. by, *The Psalmists* (1926)
Wutz, *Die Psalmen textkritisch untersucht* (1925)

PROVERBS

Frankenberg, *Die Sprüche* (1898) *HKAT*
Gemser, *Sprüche Salomos* (1937), *HAT*
Kuhn, *Beiträge zur Erklärung des Salomonischen Spruchbuches* (1931)
Oesterley, *The Book of Proverbs* (1929) W. Com.
Toy, *A Critical and Exegetical Commentary on the Book of Proverbs* (1914) *ICC*
Wildeboer, *Die Sprüche* (1897) *KHAT*

ECCLESIASTES

Barton, *A Critical and Exegetical Commentary on Ecclesiastes* (1908) *ICC*
Ginsburg, *Coheleth, commonly called the Book of Ecclesiastes . . .* (1861)
Haupt, *The Book of Ecclesiastes* (1905)
Hertzberg, *Der Prediger* (1932) *KAT*
Kuhn, *Erklärung des Buches Koheleth* (1926)
McNeile, *An Introduction to Ecclesiastes, with Notes and Appendices* (1904)
Odeberg, *Qohœleth* (1930)
Ranston, *Ecclesiastes and the early Greek Wisdom Literature* (1925)

THE SONG OF SONGS

Budde, *Das Hohelied* (1898)
Jastrow, *The Song of Songs* (1921)
Rothstein, *Das Hohelied* (1893)
Schoff, *The Song of Songs : a Symposium* (1924)

GENERAL INTRODUCTION TO THE PROPHETICAL LITERATURE

Bennett, *The Post-Exilic Prophets* (1907)
Buttenwieser, *The Prophets of Israel* (1914)
Cornill, *Der Israelitische Prophetismus* (1896); Engl. transl., *The Prophets of Israel* (1917)
Davidson, *Old Testament Prophecy* (1912)
Duhm, *Israels Propheten* (1916)
Gordon, *The Prophets of the Old Testament* (1916)
Hölscher, *Die Profeten* (1914)
Micklem, *Prophecy and Eschatology* (1926)
Peake, *The Roots of Hebrew Prophecy and Jewish Apocalyptic* (1923)
Robertson Smith, *The Prophets of Israel* (1897)
Robinson, T. H., *Prophecy and the Prophets in Ancient Israel* (1928)
Welch, *The Religion of Israel under the Kingdom* (1912)

THE BOOK OF ISAIAH

Box, *The Book of Isaiah* (1908)
Cheyne, *Introduction to the Book of Isaiah* (1895)
Condamin, *Le Livre d'Isaie ; Traduction critique avec notes et commentaires* (1905)
Duhm, *Das Buch Jesaia* (1914) *HKAT*
Elliger, *Die Einheit des Tritojesaia* (1928)
Gray, *Isaiah i–xxvii* (1912) *ICC*
Marti, *Das Buch Jesaia* (1910) *KHAT*
Skinner, *Isaiah xl–lxvi* (1917) *Cam. B.*
Torrey, *The Second Isaiah* (1928)
Volz, *Jesaia II* (1932) *KAT*
Wade, *The Book of the Prophet Isaiah* (1911) *W. Com.*
Whitehouse, *Isaiah* (1908) *CB*

THE BOOK OF JEREMIAH

Binns, *The Book of the Prophet Jeremiah* (1919) *W. Com.*
Condamin, *Le Livre de Jérémie : Traduction et Commentaire* (1920)
Cornill, *Das Buch Jeremia* (1905)
Driver, *The Book of the Prophet Jeremiah* (1906)
Duhm, *Das Buch Jeremia* (1901) *KHAT*
Erbt, *Jeremia und seine Zeit* (1902)
Lofthouse, *Jeremiah and the New Covenant* (1925)
Nestle, *Das Buch Jeremia, Griechisch und Hebräisch* (1924)
Peake, *Jeremiah* (1912) *CB*

440 BIBLIOGRAPHY

Robinson, H. Wheeler, *The Cross of Jeremiah* (1925)
Skinner, *Prophecy and Religion : Studies in the life of Jeremiah* (1922)
Smith, G. A., *Jeremiah* (1924)
Volz, *Studien zum Text des Jeremia* (1920)
—— *Der Prophet Jeremia* (1922) *KAT*

THE BOOK OF LAMENTATIONS

Budde, *Die Fünf Megilloth* (1898) *KHAT*
Löhr, *Klagelieder* (1894) *HKAT*

THE BOOK OF EZEKIEL

Bertholet, *Hesskiel* (1936) *HAT*
Cooke, *A Critical and Exegetical Commentary on the Book of Ezekiel* (1938) *ICC*
Cornill, *Das Buch des Propheten Ezechiel* (1897)
Davidson, *The Book of the Prophet Ezekiel* (1906)
Herntrich, *Ezechielprobleme* (1932)
Herrmann, *Ezechielstudien* (1908)
—— *Ezechiel* (1924) *KAT*
Hölscher, *Hesekiel, der Dichter und das Buch* (1924)
Jahn, *Das Buch Ezechiel auf Grund der LXX hergestellt* (1905)
Kessler, *Die innere Einheitlichkeit des Buches Ezekiel* (1926)
Kraetzschmar, *Das Buch Ezechiel* (1900)
Rothstein, *Das Buch Ezechiel* (1922)
Smend, *Der Prophet Ezechiel* (1880)
Smith, James, *The Book of the Prophet Ezekiel* (1931)
Torrey, *Pseudo-Ezekiel and the Original Prophecy* (1930)

THE BOOK OF DANIEL

Bentzen, *Daniel* (1937) *HAT*
Bevan, *A Short Commentary on the Book of Daniel* (1892)
Charles, *A Critical and Exegetical Commentary on the Book of Daniel* (1929)
Driver, *Daniel* (1922) *Camb. B.*
v. Gall, *Die Einheitlichkeit des Buches Daniel* (1895)
Jahn, *Das Buch Daniel nach der LXX hergestellt* (1904)
Kuhl, *Die Drei Männer im Feuer* (1930)
Marti, *Das Buch Daniel* (1901) *KHAT*
Montgomery, *A Critical and Exegetical Commentary on the Book of Daniel* (1927) *ICC*
Welch, *Visions of the End* (1922)

THE TWELVE MINOR PROPHETS

Marti, *Das Dodekapropheton* (1904) *KHAT*
Nowack, *Die kleinen Propheten* (1897) *HKAT*
Oesterley, *Codex Taurinensis* (Y) (1908) : for the text of the Septuagint
—— *The Old Latin Texts of the Minor Prophets* (1905)
Robinson and Horst, *Die Zwölf Kleinen Propheten* (1936–38) *HAT*
Sellin, *Das Zwölfprophetenbuch* (1922) *KAT*
Smith, G. A., *The Book of the Twelve Prophets* (1895, 1905); rev. ed. 1928
Wellhausen, *Die kleinen Propheten . . .* (1898)

HOSEA:

Allwohn, *Die Ehe des Propheten Hosea in psychoanalytischer Beleuchtung* (1926)
Brown, *The Book of Hosea* (1932) *W. Com.*
Cheyne, *Hosea, with Notes and Introduction* (1899) *Camb. B.*
Harper, See under *Amos*
Lindblom, *Hosea literarisch undersucht* (1927)
Valeton, See under *Amos*

BIBLIOGRAPHY 441

JOEL:

Driver, *The Books of Joel and Amos* (1898) *Camb. B.*
Knieschke, *Die Eschatologie des Buches Joel in ihrer historischgeographischen Bestimmtheit* (1912)
Merx, *Die Prophetie des Joel und ihre Ausleger von den ältesten Zeiten bis zu den Reformatoren* (1879)

AMOS:

Cripps, *The Book of Amos* (1929)
Driver, See under *Joel*
Harper, *A Critical and Exegetical Commentary on Amos and Hosea* (1905) *ICC*
Oesterley, *Studies in the Greek and Latin Versions of the Book of Amos* (1902)
Robinson, T. H., *The Book of Amos* (1928): for the Hebrew text
Schmidt, Hans, *Der Prophet Amos* (1917)
Valeton, *Amos und Hosea* (1898)
Weiser, *Die Prophetie des Amos* (1929)

OBADIAH:

Wade, See under *Micah*

JONAH:

Döller, *Das Buch Jona* (1912)
Mitchell, Smith and Bewer, See under *Haggai*
Schmidt, Hans, *Jona, eine Untersuchung zur vergleichenden Religionsgeschichte* (1907)
Wade, See under *Micah*

MICAH:

Cheyne, *Micah, with Notes and Introduction* (1895) *Camb. B.*
Lindblom, *Micha literarisch untersucht* (1929)
Wade, *Micah, Obadiah, Joel, Jonah* (1925) *W. Com.*

NAHUM:

Davidson, *The Books of Nahum, Habakkuk, and Zephaniah* (1899) *Camb. B.*
Driver, *Nahum, Habakkuk, Zephaniah, Haggai, Zechariah, Malachi* (undated) *CB*
Stonehouse and Wade, See under *Zephaniah*

HABAKKUK:

Davidson, See under *Nahum*
Driver, See under *Nahum*
Duhm, *Das Buch Habakkuk* (1906)
Peiser, *Der Prophet Habakkuk* (1903)
Stonehouse and Wade, See under *Zephaniah*

ZEPHANIAH:

Davidson, See under *Nahum*
Driver, See under *Nahum*
Stonehouse and Wade, *Zephaniah, Nahum, and Habakkuk* (1929) *W. Com.*

HAGGAI:

Mitchell, Smith and Bewer, *A Critical and Exegetical Commentary on Haggai, Zechariah, Malachi and Jonah* (1912) *ICC*
Rothstein, *Juden und Samaritaner* (1908)

ZECHARIAH:

Mitchell, Smith and Bewer, See under *Haggai*
  G G

ZECHARIAH:

Rothstein, *Die Nachtgesichte des Sacharja* (1910)
Sellin, *Das Buch Zacharjas* (1901)

MALACHI:

Mitchell, Smith and Bewer, See under *Haggai*

INDEX OF MODERN AUTHORS

A

Addis, 22

B

Ball, 378
Battersby-Harford, 64
Bauer, 12
Baumgartner, 158, 161, 164, 339
Bevan, 221
Birkeland, 198
Blackman, 164, 199
Böhme, 380
Böklen, 414
Briggs, 140, 180, 185, 199 f.
Budde, 8, 77, 81, 89, 139, 144, 173, 394, 395
Buhl, 6, 137
Burkitt, 14, 385
Burney, 143

C

Carpenter, 22
Causse, 163
Chapman, 22
Charles, 335 f., 340 ff., 344
Cheyne, 245, 378, 379
Condamin, 149
Cook, S. A., 14
Cornill, 89, 174, 210, 329

D

Dahse, 63, 64
Dalman, 219
De Rossi, 13
Dietrich, 360
Driver, G. R., 199
Driver, S. R., 12, 26, 43, 45, 49, 50, 173, 174, 178, 218, 317
Duhm, 144, 241, 253 f., 304, 307 f., 356, 358, 392, 394, 395, 397

E

Eberharter, 3
Eerdmans, 63, 64
Eissfeldt, 39, 40, 90
Elbogen, 194, 195
Erman, 198 f., 204
Ewald, 320

F

Fairweather, 156, 157
Fichtner, 152, 155
Fries, 157

G

Gadd, 265, 387
Gardiner, 12
Gaster, 11
Geden, 14
Gesenius-Kautzsch, 179, 209
Giesebrecht, 312
Ginsburg, 13, 210
Grabe, 81
Gray, Buchanan, 53, 118, 140, 142, 145, 173, 174, 178, 245
Gressmann, 199, 273
Grimme, 12, 143
Gunkel, 134, 135, 137, 180, 192 ff., 196, 254

H

Haeussermann, 351
Harford-Battersby, 22
Haupt, 180, 219
Herntrich, 324 f., 328 f.
Herrmann, 321, 326
Hochfeld, 134
Hölscher, 3, 4, 5, 7, 65, 66, 304, 320 ff.
Holzinger, 360
Hommel, 376
Hooke, 196
Hoonacker, Van, 129
Howorth, 130
Hylander, 90

J

James, 9
Jastrow, 135, 198
Jensen, 135
Jirku, 32

K

Kamphausen, 174
Kautzsch, 173, 358
Kautzsch-Bertholet, 341
Kennett, 65, 66, 307

Kennicott, 13
Kittel, 89, 90, 116, 164, 188, 322,
    326 f., 403
Kraetzschmar, 320 f.
Krappe, 136
Kuhl, 339, 344
Kuhn, 208

L

Lagarde, 81, 108
Langdon, 198
Lehmann, 253
Ley, 143
Lidzbarski, 12
Liebmann, 255
Lindblom, 383, 385
Löhr, 63, 315 f.
Lowth, 139, 143

M

McFadyen, 128, 173, 211, 320
McNeile, 209 ff., 214, 216
Margoliouth, 215
Marti, 341, 358, 360, 362, 380, 394
Meek, 219
Meinhold, 273, 327
Merx, 174
Möller, 64, 149, 206
Montgomery, 11
Moore, 53, 77, 80 f.
Morgenstern, 40
Moulton, 1
Mowinckel, 180, 185, 193, 196, 275,
    304,
Müller, 195

N

Naville, 11
Niese, 2
Nöldeke, 374
Noth, 201
Nowack, 116, 210

O

Odeberg, 210, 212
Oesterley, 151, 152, 162, 163, 206,
    274
Oesterley and Robinson, 59, 82, 249,
    253, 362, 400, 420 ff.
Oestreicher, 65
Orr, 65
Ottley, R. R., 19, 261

P

Paton, 134
Peake, 28, 29
Pfeiffer, 162

R

Rad, 116
Rahlfs, 108, 200
Rankin, 136
Ranston, 158 f., 214
Robinson, T. H., 306 (see under
    Oesterley).
Rogers, 112, 404
Rothstein, 414
Rothstein-Hänel, 114, 116
Rowley, 336 f., 341 f.
Rudolph, 64, 253
Ryle, 3, 6, 137, 232, 330

S

Schaeffer, 11
Schmidt, Hans, 193
Schürer, 137
Sellin, 89, 173, 174, 190, 380, 392,
    394, 397, 401
Sheppard, 14
Siegfried, 214
Sievers, 145
Simpson, D. C., 22, 199
Skinner, 26, 64
Smith, James, 320, 323 f.
Smith, J. M. P., 383
Spiegel, 323
Steuernagel, 70
Swete, 9, 19, 107 f., 129, 136 f., 138,
    188, 200 f., 330, 380

T

Thackeray, 130
Torrey, 262, 320, 322 f., 362
Toy, 153, 203

V

Virolleaud, 11
Volz, 64

W

Weber, 4
Welch, 65, 66
Wellhausen, 89, 108, 379
Wetstein, 219
Wiener, 63
Wildeboer, 174, 210, 214

Z

Zillessen, 276, 286
Zimmern, 134, 198
Zunz, 194

INDEX: GENERAL

AARON, 42, 54, 62
Aaronic Priesthood, 66
Abdon, 76
Abed-nego, 338
Abijah, 104
Abijam, 102
Abimelech, 76, 77, 78, 79
Abraham, 30, 41
Absalom, 88
Acrostic poems, 148, 191
Acts of Ahab, 97 ff., 101
Acts of Jeremiah, 301
Adam, 111
Adar, 132, 133 ff.
Admah, 57
'Adonay, 13
Adoni-bezek, 76
Adonijah, 93
Adullam, 84
Africa, 263
Agriculture, Methods of, 255
Agur, 203
Ahab, 97, 98, 99
'Ahabhah, 59, 353
Ahasuerus, 3, 131 ff., 137 n.¹
Ahaz, 104, 226, 234, 249
Ahaziah, 104
Ahijah, 114
Ai, 72
Akkadian, 11, 142, 266
'Al-'alāmôth, 181
Alexander Jannaeus, 255
Alexander the Great, 16, 112, 222, 362 n.¹, 392, 394 f., 421
Alexandria, Alexandrian Judaism (see also Dispersion, Egypt), 16, 18
'Al-hash-sh'mînîth, 181 f.
Alkimus, 423
Alphabet, 11
Altar(s), 43, 45, 49, 50, 53, 57, 336
'Al-tashhēth, 183
Amalek, 88
Amasis, 262
Amaziah (King), 106
Amaziah (Priest), 366
Amen-em-ope, Teaching of, 163 n.¹, 206
Ammon, 290, 297, 313, 364, 401
Amon, 104

Amos, 53 n.¹, 221, 224, 227, 230, 231, 235, 248, 259, 260, 309, 311, 347, 353, 358, 359, 363 ff., 369, 381, 385 f., 403
Amphilochius, 1
Anacrusis, 146
Analysis of Joshua, 69 f.
Analysis of Pentateuch, 34 ff.
Analysis of Samuel, 86 f.
Anath, 59
Anima Mundi, 153
Anshan, 262 f.
Anthropomorphism, 26, 31, 51, 55
Antioch, 332
Antiochus III, 330 f.
Antiochus IV (Epiphanes), 137, 285, 332 ff., 421
Antiochus Eupator, 257
Antiochus VII (Sidetes), 254
Antiphonal singing, 193
Aphek, 108
Aphrodite, 400
Apocalyptic elements (see also Eschatology), 7, 252 ff., 337 ff., 355 ff., 424 f.
Apocrypha, 9 f., 16, 154
Apollo, 136
Apollonius, 333, 421
Aquila, 17, 216
Arab, Arabia(ns), 161, 181, 251
Aramaeans (see also Syrians), 97
Aramaic, Aramaisms, 11, 12, 59, 84, 126, 164, 175, 210, 219, 294, 335, 336, 339 ff., 372 ff.
Aramaic documents, 125 f.
Arbela, 392
Aristeas, Letter of, 16 n.²
Aristotle, 221
Ark (Noah's), 27
Ark (of Covenant), 42, 55
Artaxerxes I, 2, 3, 121, 123 f., 125, 129, 137 n.⁴, 277
Artaxerxes II, 129
Artaxerxes III (Ochus), 285, 395
Asa, 102, 113
Asaph, Asaphite Psalms, 186, 188
Ascents, Songs of, 186
Ashdod, 234, 250
Asherah, 44

Ashkelon, 400
Ashkuza, 400
Ashur, 288
Ashur-bani-pal, 288, 387, 389, 400
Assyria(ns), 98, 161, 164, 197 f., 222,
    233 ff., 237, 244, 246 f., 254 n.[1],
    256, 288 ff., 324, 335, 345, 363,
    374, 387, 400 f., 410
Astarte, 219
Astrology, 272
Astyages, 262 f.
Athaliah, 104
Atonement, Day of, 42
Augustine, 351
Autobiographical Prose in the
    Prophets (C), 229 ff., 243, 245,
    291 f., 302 ff., 321, 346, 350, 363,
    365 f., 407 n.[2], 422 n.[3]
'Ayyeleth hash-shaḥar, 183
Azariah, 337
Azarias, Prayer of, 344
'Azkārāh, 184

Baal, Baalism, 59, 65, 82, 235, 353,
    400
Baasha, 102
Babylon, Babylonia(ns), 62, 93,
    131 n.[1], 134, 135, 161 ff., 197 ff.,
    209, 222, 226 f., 234 f., 237, 248,
    251, 254, 262 ff., 288 ff., 297,
    299 ff., 313, 319, 387
Bagoas (Bigvai), 278
Balaam, 151
Bamoth, 104, 359
Barak, 73, 76, 77
Bardes, 404
Baruch, 300 f., 306
Baruch, Book of, 9, 153
Beauty and Bands, 423 f.
Behistun, 404 n.[2]
Bel, 264
Bel and the Dragon, 344
Belshazzar, 335, 338
Benjamin, 75, 78
Ben-Sira (see also Ecclesiasticus), 9,
    136, 152, 155, 158, 161, 215 n.[1]
Bethel, 60, 66, 100, 353, 366 f.
Bethlehem, 83, 386
Bildad, 167 ff.
Biographical prose in Prophets (B),
    228 f., 231, 243, 258, 291 ff., 300 ff.,
    346, 363, 365 f.
Blessings on Yahweh, 193 f.
Boaz, 83, 84
Branch, 242, 416
Buddha, 221
Burden of the Wilderness of the Sea,
    251
Burns, 219

Caleb(ites), 42, 49, 74, 162
Calendar, Jewish, 135
Cambyses, 263, 335, 404
Canaanites, 50 f., 56, 59, 75
Canon, 1 ff., 151
Carchemish, 288 f., 293, 301 ff., 388
Carmel, 73, 98
Carved images, 33
Catalepsy, 327
Centralization of Sacrifice, 43, 57, 103
Chaldæans, 265, 288 ff., 294, 301,
    335, 340, 387 f., 392 ff., 402
Chief Musician, 180
Chinese poetry, 142
Chinese writing, 11
Chisleu, 336
Christology, 157
Chronicles, Books of, 109 ff., 120, 209,
    330
Chronicles and Ezra–Nehemiah,
    Books of, 110 f.
Chronicles of the Kings of Israel,
    Book of, 95 ff., 113
Chronicles of the Kings of Judah,
    Book of, 95 ff., 113
Cimmerians, 400
Circumcision, 25, 333
Clairvoyance, 326 f.
Cleopatra, 137
Codes, 32, 43 ff.
Cœle-Syria, 362, 420
Collections (Collectors) of Prophetic
    Material, 225 ff., 232, 238 ff., 291 ff.,
    321, 346 ff., 364 ff., 370, 382 ff.,
    395 ff.
Collections of Proverbs, 204 ff.
Collections of Psalms, 185 ff.
Compilation of Pentateuch, 47 ff.
Compilers of Prophetic books, 232,
    291
Composite nature of Prophetic books,
    231 ff.
Confucius, 221
Congregational Psalms, 193
Conjectural emendation, 20 f.
Conquest of Palestine, 68, 72, 75, 80
Cosmopolitan character of Wisdom,
    161 ff.
Covenant, 39
Covenant, Angel of, 432
Covenant, Book of, 44, 45 n.[1]
Covenant, New, 304, 309, 311
Creation, 22, 27, 39, 56, 62 n.[4], 172
Criticism of Prophetic Literature,
    221 ff.
Crocodile, 174
Crœsus, 262 ff.
Curses, 193
Cypriotes, 394

Cyrus, 110, 112, 120, 123 f., 131 n.[1], 237 f., 262 ff., 335, 392, 404

Damascus, 234 f., 244, 250, 313, 363, 364, 420
Dan(ites), 72, 78
Daniel, 5, 173, 253, 330 ff., 345, 358
Darius i, 112, 121, 123 f., 253, 277, 335, 404, 406, 413
Dates of the Pentateuch, 51 ff., 65 f.
David, 20, 73, 83, 84, 87 f., 93, 97, 108, 112, 117, 157, 179, 181, 186, 209, 226, 247, 366, 369, 424
Davidic Psalms, 186
Day of Yahweh, 357, 365, 368, 401, 402 f.
Debir, 72, 73
Deborah, 73, 76, 77
Deborah, Song of, 79 f., 81, 189
Decalogue, 33
"Dedication of the House," 194
Defilement of hands, 4, 7, 215
Delaiah, 278
"Destroy not," 181, 183
Determinism, 213
Deutero-Isaiah, 262 ff., 279, 286, 321, 336, 397, 420
Deuteronomic redaction, 48 n.[1], 69 f., 71, 77, 90, 102 ff., 304 f., 321 f.
Deuteronomic Reform. See Reform, Josiah's.
Deuteronomic style, 45, 298, 302, 304 f.
Deuteronomic theory of history, 76 f., 82
Deuteronomy (D), 43 ff., 47 f., 52 ff., 65 ff., 69 f., 71, 84, 166, 298, 302, 304 f., 307 ff., 429 f., 432
Deutero-Zechariah, 410, 419 ff.
Dionysus, Cult of, 136
Dirges. See Lamentations, Qinah.
Dirges, National, 193
Dispersion, Diaspora, 152, 191, 383, 384
Divorce, 429
Domestic animals, Slaughter of, 53, 57, 60 f.
Doublets, 25 ff., 40, 87
Dove, 377
Draco, 254
Dramatic interpretation of Song of Solomon, 218
Dreams, 55
Drink-offering, 359
Dumah, 251

Ecbatana, 131 n.[1]
Ecclesiastes, 5, 166, 209 ff., 217, 314, 373

Ecclesiasticus (see also Ben-Sira), 9, 152, 238
Eclipse, 366
Ecstasy, Prophetic, 230, 243, 397 f.
Edom(ites), 161 f., 227, 251, 257, 281, 297, 313, 364, 369 f., 430
Eglon, 72
Egypt(ians), 49, 50, 59, 94, 161 ff., 196, 197 ff., 204, 222, 235, 244, 250, 254, 256, 262, 288 ff., 313, 330, 363, 387, 392, 401, 410, 420
Egyptian poetry, 142
Egyptian text (see also Septuagint), 16 ff., 67, 71, 307
Ehud, 76, 77
'Ekah, 314
Ekron, 234
Elam(ites), 235, 297, 313
Elamite deities, 135
Elders, 55 n.[2]
Elephantiné, 16 n.[1], 59, 129, 252, 278
Elhanan, 88
Eli, 91
Eliakim, 251
Eliashib, 129
Elihu, 171, 173, 177
Elijah, 105, 236, 432
Elijah narratives, 97, 98 f., 100
Eliphaz, 167 ff.
Elisha, 101, 105
Elisha narratives, 99 f.
Elkosh, 390
Eloah, 172
'Elohim, 26, 31, 63, 64, 172, 186
Elohist (E), 31 ff., 47, 48 f., 52 ff., 65, 69 f., 71, 72, 80
Elon, 76
El Shaddai, 28
Eltekeh, 235
Enjambement, 148
Enoch, Book of, 9, 253
Ephraim, 72, 245, 250
Erotic poetry, 217 ff.
Esarhaddon, 400
Esau, 430
Eschatology, 241, 250, 252 ff., 257, 342 f., 402 f., 414 f., 424 f.
Esdraelon, Plain of, 72, 74, 234
Esdras, 120 n.[2]
Esther, 5, 131 ff., 209, 217
Ethiopia, 250, 263
Euphrates, 254
Exodus, 196
Exodus, Book of (see also Pentateuch), 22 ff., 69
Extermination of Canaanites, 73 f.
Ezekiel, 41, 52, 54, 60, 66, 223, 224, 227, 230, 233, 248, 288, 305, 318 ff., 330, 339, 345, 424

Ezion-geber, 369
Ezra, 62, 66, 121, 158, 252, 258, 278, 336, 358, 360, 375, 429
Ezra Memoirs, 125
Ezra–Nehemiah, 109, 120 ff., 330

Fallow year, 41
Fas, 32
Fasting, 418
Fathers, Sayings (Sections) of, 153
Faust, 174
Fish, symbol of Nineveh, 378 f.
Five Rolls, 5, 83
Floating oracles, 299
Flood, 27 f., 39, 56
Fools, 159
Formulæ of *Judges*, 76 f.
Formulæ of *Kings*, 102, 103

Gaal, 80
Gabriel, 338
Gad (seer), 114
Galilee, Sea of, 73
Gath, 182, 364
Gaumata, 404
Gedaliah, 290, 304
Gemara, 373
Genealogies, 26 f.
Gentiles, Divine care for, 375 f.
Gerizim, 324
Gezer, 72, 73
Gibeah, 78
Gibeon, 72, 94
Gideon, 76, 77, 80, 81
Gilgal, 72, 100
Gittith, 182
Gobryas, 262
Go'el, 83
Goethe, 174
Golden Age, 360
Goliath, 20, 88
Gomer, 350, 352
Gomorrah, 52 n.[2], 57, 225, 226, 239
Granicus, 392
Greece, 254, 277, 356, 361, 394 f., 410, 421
Greek Canon, 8 ff.
Greek Ezra, 120 n.[2], 129 f.
Greek poetry, 142
Greek thought, 214, 222
Greek vocabulary, 219
Gutium, 262

Habakkuk, 223, 228, 231, 358, 387, 392 ff., 400
Hadad (Edomite), 94
Hadassah, 131
Hadrach, 420

Haggai, 62, 121, 124, 223, 224, 229 n.[3], 230, 231, 400, 404 ff., 411, 421
Hagiographa (*see also* Kethubim), 109, 179
Hakamim, 151, 157 ff., 204
Hallelujah Psalms, 186
Hallucinations, 327
Haman, 132 ff.
Hananiah, 337
Hananiah (Prophet), 303
Hannah, 91
Hanukkah, 136
Happy endings, 227, 346, 349
Harran, 288, 388
Hasid(îm), 212, 331, 421
Hazael, 101
Hazor, 73
Hebrew, Decadence of, 209 f.
Hebrew influence on foreign writers, 163 f.
Hebrew writing, 11 ff.
Hebron, 49, 72
Heliodorus, 331, 332
Hellenism, 152, 153, 331 ff.
Hellenistic Judaism, 8, 157
Herod, 369
Herodotus, 402
Heroes, Local, 77, 79
Hesedh, 353
Hezekiah, 93, 97, 103, 104, 203, 226, 235 f., 240 f., 257 f., 374, 384, 402
High places, 103, 104, 105
High Priesthood, 330 ff.
Hilkiah, 58
Hillel, 215
Hinnom, Valley of, 300
Hippopotamus, 174
Hiram, 94
Historical value of *Chronicles*, 118
Historical value of *Joshua*, 71 ff.
Historical value of *Judges*, 82
Hokmah, 155 ff., 160
Holiness, 41, 260
Holiness, Code of (H), 41 ff., 49 ff., 52 ff.
Horeb, 32, 45, 99, 432
Hormah, 73
Hosea, 57, 58, 59, 223, 224, 227, 229, 230, 231, 235, 259, 260, 293, 303, 311, 345 ff., 358, 367, 386
Hoshea, 96, 103, 234, 249, 345
Huleh, 73
Human sacrifice, 60
Humban, 135
Hydra, 254
Hymns, 193
Hypostasis, 156
Hyrcania, 285

Hyrcanus, John, 254 f., 369

Ibzan, 76
Iddo the Seer, 114, 115
Immortality, 170, 213
Indian stories, 202
Individual, Psalms of the, 193
Individual thanksgivings, 193
Individualism in religion, 311 f.
Inspiration of Scripture, 3
Ionian philosophers, 221
Isaiah, 57, 58, 60, 114, 189, 205, 223, 224, 225, 229, 230, 233 ff., 288, 290, 299, 311, 321, 345, 353, 385 f., 420
Isaiah, Main divisions of Book of, 236 ff.
Isaiah narratives, 101 f.
Ishmaelites, 29 f., 290
Ishtar, 135, 219, 377
Israel, Kingdom of, 89, 93, 234, 345, 353 f., 363, 364 f., 367
Issus, 392

Jacob, 29, 430
Jaddua, 112
Jahvist (Yahwist) (J), 28 ff., 47 ff., 52 ff., 69 f., 71, 72, 80
Jair, 76
Japanese, 11
Jashar, Book of, 56
Jason, 332 f., 423
Jehoahaz, 104, 290, 296
Jehohanan (= Johanan), 129, 278
Jehoiachin, 93, 104, 275, 289, 296, 303, 335
Jehoiada, 129
Jehoiakim, 104, 275, 289 f., 293, 296, 300 ff., 308, 328, 335, 396
Jehonadab, 107
Jehoram, 104
Jehoshaphat, Valley of, 356
Jehovah (see also Yahweh), 13, 28
Jehu b. Hanani, 114
Jehu b. Nimshi, 101, 107
Jephthah, 76, 77
Jeremiah, 66, 205, 223, 224, 225, 226, 227, 229, 230, 231, 233, 238, 248, 249, 260, 288 ff., 314, 315, 316, 321, 349, 353, 367, 371, 384, 392, 396, 401
Jericho, 72, 74, 100
Jeroboam I, 20, 95, 104 f., 107
Jeroboam II, 345, 366, 372
Jerubbaal, 80
Jerusalem, 50, 57, 58, 65, 66, 72, 73, 121, 123, 124, 209, 234 f., 236, 239, 247, 255, 257, 264, 266, 271, 278, 281, 303. 319, 323 f., 327 f.,

332 ff., 382, 401, 423, 424, 425, 428
Jerusalem, Destruction of, 289, 290, 304, 314 ff., 328
Jerusalem, Population of, 128
Jeshua, 120 f., 124
Joash, 101
Job, 161, 339
Job, Book of, 68, 166 ff., 217, 296, 310
Joel, 223, 224, 228, 230, 231, 355 ff., 372
John Hyrcanus, 254 ff.
Jonah, 223, 224, 229, 231, 358, 372 ff., 381
Jonathan (Hasmonean), 422, 425 f.
Jonathan, Targum of, 15
Jordan, 43, 73, 74, 100, 233
Joseph (patriarch), 29 f.
Joseph (Tobias), 331
Joshua, 42, 49, 68, 73, 74, 75
Joshua, Book of, 22 n.¹, 68 ff., 75, 80
Joshua (High-priest) (see also Jeshua), 410 f., 415 f.
Josiah, 57, 60, 61, 66, 103, 104, 289 f., 293, 302, 307 ff., 310, 316, 387, 396, 401
Jotham, 151
Jubilee, 42
Judah (Nation), 89, 93, 104, 118, 161, 226, 234 ff., 278, 289 ff., 324, 349, 381 ff., 395, 423 f.
Judah (patriarch), 29
Judah (tribe), 49, 65, 72, 75
Judas Maccabæus, 421 f.
Judges, Book of, 22 n.¹, 68, 75 ff.
Judith, Book of, 9
Jus, 32

Kedar, 297, **313**
Kenizzites, 74
Kethubim, 5, 109, 166, 179, 330
Kibroth-hattaavah, 52 n.¹
King, Bridegroom as, 219
Kings, Book of, 22 n.¹, 68, 85, 93 ff., 229, 233, 258
Kiriath-sannah, 157
Kiriath-sepher, 115, 157
Kirisha, 135
Kittians, 394
Koheleth, 209, 215
Korah, Korahite Psalms, 186, 188
Korah, Rebellion of, 42

Lachish, 72
Laish, 72
Lamentations, Book of, 5, 144, 310, 314 ff
Lammenaṣeaḥ, Lamminṣah, 180 f., 185
Land of the Whirring of Wings, 250

Latin poetry, 142
Latin versions, 15
Law, 4, 5, 11, 16, 17, 22 ff., 154 f., 156, 337, 343, 408, 432
Lay Document of Hexateuch (L), 40 n.[1]
Lebanon, 396
Legal elements in Pentateuch, 32 ff.
Legends, Sacred, 194
Lehazkir, 184
Lemuel, 203
Leontopolis, Temple at, 251, 252
Leprosy, 169
Leviathan, 254, 378
Levi(tes), 54, 62, 116, 123, 425, 429
Lex talionis, 41
Liturgical services, 67, 117, 194 ff., 316, 347
Lo-ammi, 351
Locusts, 355 f.
Lo-ruhamah, 351
Love, 59, 353
Lucianic text of Septuagint, 81, 108
LXX. *See* Septuagint.
Lydda, 334
Lydia(ns), 262 f.

Ma'aloth, 186
Maccabæan Age, 257, 330 ff.
Maccabæan revolt, 137, 334, 339
iv Maccabees, 153
Macedon(ians), 222, 331 n.[1], 392
Machpelah, 41
Magians, 404
Maher-shalal-hash-baz, 244
Mahol, 161
Malachi, 62, 223, 224, 228, 230, 231, 232, 294, 419, 427 ff.
Manasseh (King), 104, 114, 260, 323
Manasseh (Tribe), 59, 60, 72
Manna, 42
Marduk, 135
Marginal notes, 20
Marriage ceremonies, 218 f.
Marriage of Hosea, 346, 349 ff.
Martyrdom of Isaiah, 259 f.
Mashal, Meshalim, 151, 211
Maskhil, 183 f.
Massah, 419
Massebah, 44, 51, 55
Massorah, Massoretes, Massoretic text, 13, 106 f., 118 f., 178, 200, 208, 220, 312 ff., 344, 348
Mattathias, 334
Meal-offering, 184, 359
Medes, Media, 131, 254, 262 f., 288, 335, 388, 402, 404
Megiddo, 108
Megilloth, 5 n.[1], 83, 217, 314

Memoirs of Ezra and Nehemiah, 125
Menahem, 234, 345, 348
Menelaus, 332 f., 423
Merodach-baladan, 234 f.
Meshach, 338
Mesopotamia, 59, 62 n.[4], 221, 289
Messiah, 190, 261, 410 f., 420 f.
Messianic prophecy, 245, 247, 253, 256, 282, 296, 361, 386, 396, 405 f., 409, 413 ff.
Metres, Hebrew, 142 ff., 225, 239 ff., 267 ff., 314 ff.
Micah (Ephraimite), 78
Micah (Prophet), 58, 223, 224, 228, 231, 235, 241, 259, 353, 381
Midian(ites), 29 f., 43 n.[1]
Midrash, 61 n.[1], 85 n.[1], 113 f., 115 f., 182, 301, 350, 372
Miktam, 184
Millo, 94
Minhah, 359
Minor Prophets, 223
Miriam, Song of, 189
Mishael, 337
Mishle, 202
Mishnah, 184, 195, 210, 215, 373
Mixed marriages, 122 f., 128, 430 f.
Mixtures of metres, 145 ff.
Mizmor, 179, 181
Mizpah, 290
Moab(ite), 83, 84, 249, 255, 297, 313, 401
Modein, 334
Molten images, 33, 41
Monarch, 206
Monarchy, Foundation of, 87
Monotheism, 49, 51, 164, 168, 428
Mordecai, 131 ff.
Moses, 2, 23, 32, 33, 41, 45, 46, 49, 51, 68, 84, 117, 185, 235, 367, 432
Moses, Song of, 189
Music, 180 ff.
Mystics, 325
Mythology, 49

Naamah, 161, 162
Nabonidus, 335
Nabonidus, Chronicle of, 262 f.
Nabopolassar, 288 f., 387
Naboth, 99
Nadab, 102, 103
Nahum, 223, 227, 228, 230, 231, 358, 381, 387 ff., 392
Naomi, 83
Narratives of Pentateuch, 25 ff.
Nash Papyrus, 14 n.[2], 67
National Psalms, 193
National records, 115
Nazirite, 367

Nebi'im, 4, 330
Nebo, 264
Nebuchaddrezzar, 120, 123, 289, 290, 328, 334 ff.
Necho, 288 ff., 387 f.
Necromancy, 255
Nehemiah, 62, 84, 122 ff., 278, 282 f., 303, 385, 429 f.
Nehemiah and Ezra, Dates of, 127 ff.
Nehemiah, Memoirs of, 125
Neo-Hebrew, 373
Nesek, 359
New Covenant, 304, 309, 310, 311
New Year, 135, 195 f.
Nikanor, 136
Nile, 162
Nineveh, 227, 288, 376 ff., 388 ff.
Nisan, 132, 134
Noah, 27, 173, 339
No-Amon, 389
Northern origin of D, 67
Numbers, Book of, 22 ff., 69

Obadiah, 223, 224, 228, 231, 297, 299, 369 ff.
Octave, 181
Official records, 94, 96
Og, 48 n.[1]
Omnipotence, 167, 169
Omri, 98, 383
Oneness of Yahweh, 269, 270
Onias iii, 331 ff.
Onias, House of, 330 ff.
Onkelos, Targum of, 15, 17
Opis, 266
Oracular poetry, 224
Oreb, 80
Orthodoxy, 169 f.
Othniel, 72, 73, 76, 77

Padi, 234
Palestinian text (*see also* Massoretic text), 15 ff.
Panion, 330
Parallelism, 139 ff.
Paran, Wilderness of, 42
Paroimioi, 202
Parthia, 254
Parties in Jewish State, 331 ff.
Pashhur, 300
Passover, 31, 42, 65, 121, 196
Patristic lists, 330
Pekah (King), 234, 240, 247, 345
Pekah, 429
Pekahiah, 345
Pentameter, 144
Pentateuch, 5, 14, 17, 22 ff., 69, 185, 432

Persia(ns), 121, 131, 221, 222, 254, 392
Peshitta, 15, 166, 178, 217, 220, 344, 345, 363, 387
Pessimism, 212 f.
Pharaoh, 31
Pharisaism, 8, 177, 187
Philistia, Philistines, 88, 91, 92, 108, 249, 297, 313, 356, 361 f., 364
Phœnicia(ns), 98, 361 f., 365
Phylogeny of versions, 17
Pietas, 353
Pilgrim songs, 193
Pirke Aboth, 153
Plagues, 42
Plato, 153, 176
Poetry, Hebrew, 139 ff., 224 ff.
Polytheism, 164
Potiphar, 29
Prayers, 179
Pre-exilic Psalms, 189
Priesthood, Position of, 54
Priestly writings (P), 27, 28 ff., 69 f., 116, 359, 360, 429, 432
Prophet(s), 4, 5, 6, 15, 22, 68, 158 f., 166, 221 ff.
Prophetic literature, 221 ff.
Prophetic poetry, 224 ff., 291 ff.
Prophetic prose, 228, 243, 291, 300 ff.
Prophetic Psalms, 194
Prophetic teaching, 260, 272 ff., 287, 309 ff.
Prose oracles, 305
Proverbial sayings (*see also Mashal*), 150
Proverbs, 150
Proverbs, Book of, 150, 151, 164, 166, 202 ff., 373
Psalms, Book of, 5, 166, 179 ff., 310
Ptolemies, 289, 330
Ptolemy Lathyrus, 137
Ptolemy Philadelphus, 16
Ptolemy IV (Philopator), 331, 362

Qinah, 144 f., 239 ff., 314
Queen, Bride as, 219
Queen-mother, 295
Queen of Sheba, 94

Rabshakeh, 374
Ras-Shamra, 11 n.[2], 62 n.[4]
Rechabites, 236, 304, 367
Red Sea, Crossing of, 31, 42
Reform, Josiah's, 57, 303, 307 ff.
Refrain, 148, 246
Refuge, Cities of, 43, 57
Rehoboam, 95, 103
Remnant, Doctrine of, 261
Resurrection, 343

Retribution, 117, 165
Returned exiles, 122, 411 ff.
Return of exiles, 120 ff., 247, 248 f.,
    258, 277, 304, 385
Reuben, 29, 49
Rezon, 94, 234, 240, 247
Rhetorical Prose, 49, 298, 302, 304
Rhythm, Hebrew, 139, 142 ff.
Riddles, 151
Rish'a, 376, 417
Roll, Baruch's, 306
Rome, 221
Royal Psalms, 190, 193
Ruth, 83 ff.
Ruth, Book of, 83 ff., 217, 314

Sabbath, 25, 41, 43 n.[1], 123, 194,
    280, 283 f., 299, 303, 333
Sacæa, 135 n.[4]
Sacred Legends, 194
Sacrifice, 45, 53, 160, 163, 193, 239,
    240, 303, 307 ff., 359, 427, 436
Sacrifice, Human, 60
Sahidic Version, 17 n.[1], 81
Saj', 142 n.[1]
Samaria, 108, 122, 255, 278, 366,
    367, 381 f.
Samaria, Fall of, 58, 234, 244, 345,
    348, 382
Samaritan(s), 121, 127, 278
Samaritan Pentateuch, 14 f., 16, 67
Samaritan schism, 127, 280
Samson, 76, 77
Samuel, 222
Samuel, Books of, 22 n.[1], 68, 85 ff.
Sanballat, 122, 278
Sanctuaries, Local, 45, 53 n.[1], 57,
    59, 65, 308
Sanskrit, 142
Sargon, 58, 234, 240, 249, 382
Satan, 167, 176, 415 f.
Satrap, 335
Saturnalia, 135 n.[4]
Saul, 88
Scansion of Hebrew poetry, 142 ff.
Scopas, 330
Scribe(s), 157 f.
Scriptures destroyed, 333
Scythians, 288 f., 294, 387
Sea, 254
Seba, 263
Selah, 148, 185
Seleucids, 330 ff., 362
Seleucus IV, 331 f.
Semah, 416
Sennacherib, 234 f., 240, 249, 251,
    256, 257
Septuagint, 8, 16 ff., 63, 67, 71, 81 f.,
    85, 88, 91 f., 108 ff., 112 n.[2], 114,

118 f., 129 f., 137 f., 166, 178, 179,
    182, 185 n.[1], 200, 202, 203, 207 f.,
    216, 226, 261, 275 f., 286, 293 n.[1],
    294, 312 ff., 317, 329, 330, 338,
    343 f., 345, 354, 362, 363, 368, 369,
    371, 380, 386, 387, 391, 395, 399,
    403, 409, 419, 425 f., 433
Seraiah, 157
Serpens, 254
Servant songs, 268, 271, 273 f.
Sex-complex, 351 f.
Shadrach, 338
Shallum, 103, 104, 345
Shalmaneser III, 234, 376
Shalmaneser V, 234, 249, 345
Shamgar, 76
Shammai, 215
Shaphan, 290
Sheba, Queen of, 94
Shebna, 251
Shechem, 47
Shelemaiah, 278
Shemaiah, 114
She'ol, 169, 213, 343
Shephelah, 381, 385
Sheshbazzar, 120, 277 f.
Shiggaion, 184
Shigionoth, 184 n.[1]
Shiloh, 59, 91
Shinar, 376, 417
Shishak, 95
Shoe, Loosing of, 83 f.
Shophar, 195, 196
Shua, 161
Shulamite, 219
Shunem, 219
Shushan (Susa), 131, 133
Sibylline Oracles, 253
Simon (Benjamite), 331
Simon Maccabæus, 190, 422, 424 f.
Sinai, 32, 33, 42, 45, 432
Sinaitic writing, 12 n.[1]
Sippar, 266
Sisera, 80
Slavery, 44, 301
Social deterioration, 235, 363, 367,
    381
Social orders, 54 f., 62, 367
Sodom, 52, 57, 223, 224, 239
Solomon, 87, 93, 97, 107, 108, 166,
    202 ff., 217, 369
Solomon, Acts of, 93 ff.
Solomon, Psalms of, 9, 189
Solomon, Wisdom of, 153
Song of Songs (of Solomon), 5, 166,
    179, 217 ff.
Sopher, 158, 195 f.
Sources, 38 ff., 79 ff., 88 ff., 93 ff.,
    112 ff., 125 ff., 338 ff.

Stanza, 147
Stichoi, 140 ff.
Stoicism, 153
Stress-accent, 143 ff.
Strophe, 147 ff.
Structure of Pentateuch, 24 ff.
Suffering, Problem of, 166 ff., 175 ff., 393, 398
Sumerian Writing, 11
Susanna, 344
Susian, 404 n.³
Symmachus, 17
Synagogue, 183
Syncretism, 59, 73, 82, 367
Synodial Lists, 330
Syria(ns), 98, 99, 108, 243, 254, 330 ff., 362, 420 ff., 429 f.
Syriac poetry, 142
Syriac version, 15, 17, 68, 201

Tabernacle, 42
Tabernacles, Feast of, 120, 123, 195 f.
Talmud, 3, 8, 195, 372 ff.
Tamid, 359
Tammuz-Adon, 424
Tannin, 378
Targums, 15, 17, 182, 184, 195, 374
Tattenai, 121
Tehillah (-im), 179
Tehom, 377
Tekoa, 366
Teman, 161
Temple, 110, 115, 116, 123, 126, 127, 183, 194 ff., 333 f., 359, 427 f.
Temple, Building of, 94
Temple, Rebuilding of, 120 ff., 124, 125, 238, 264, 282 ff., 406 f.
Tephilloth, 179
Terebinths, 183
Tertullian, 351
Textual variants, Origin of, 18 ff.
Thanksgiving, Individual, 193
Thanksgiving, National, 193
Thebes, 389 f.
Theodotion, 17, 343
Threshing-sledge, 219
Tiglath-pileser (III), 233 f., 245, 249, 345, 348, 382
Tigris, 162, 254, 266
Tishri, 195, 262
Tithes, 427 f., 431
Titles of Psalms, 180 ff.
Tobias, 331
Tobit, Book of, 9
Todah, 193
Torah, 4, 6, 22 ff.
Trito-Isaiah, 277 ff., 321
Twelve Prophets, 223, 233, 288, 345 ff., 381, 387, 392

Types of Psalms, 191 ff.
Tyre, 94, 252, 356, 410

Ugbaru, 262
Uncanonical Wisdom Books, 151 ff.
Universalism, 375 f., 428
Utilitarianism, 156, 161
Uzziah, 248

Vashti, 131
Vengeance of Yahweh, 365, 394
Versions, 15 ff.
Victory, Psalms of, 193
Vineyard, Song of the, 242 f.
Vintage-song, 183
Vision, Valley of, 251
Visions, Apocalyptic, 338
Visions, Prophetic, 303, 413 ff.
Vowel-representation, 12 f.
Vulgate, 15, 17, 85, 109, 120 n.², ³, 166, 344, 345, 363, 387

Walls of Jerusalem, Building of, 122 ff.
Wars of Yahweh, Book of, 56
Whirring of Wings, Land of the, 250
Wine-press, 182
Wisdom, 154, 155 ff., 174, 207
Wisdom Literature, 150 ff.
Wisdom Psalms, 154, 194
Wise, Sayings of the, 203
Wise Men. See Hakamim.
World-literature, Psalms in, 197 ff.
World-literature, Wisdom in, 161 ff., 204 ff.
Worship, 117, 126, 154, 183, 333, 359, 427
Writing, Hebrew, 11 ff.
Writings (see also Kethubim), 5, 109

Xerxes, 2, 121, 131, 277

Yahweh (Yehowah, Jehovah), 13, 26, 32, 33, 41, 50, 56, 59, 63, 64, 73 f., 77, 81, 82, 103, 164 f., 167, 171, 173 f., 186, 190, 194, 196, 217, 235 f., 253, 256, 269 ff. passim.
Yarmuth, 72

Zadok, 54
Zalmunnah, 80
Zeba, 80
Zeboim, 57
Zechariah (King), 345
Zechariah (Prophet), 121, 124, 223, 230, 231, 232, 278, 361, 376, 405 f., 410 ff.
Zedekiah, 104, 272, 289, 293, 296, 300 ff.

Zeeb, 80
Zelophehad, Daughters of, 42
Zephaniah, 223, 230, 231, 289, 392, 400 ff.
Zeresh, 132
Zerubbabel, 112, 121, 123 f., 226, 278, 405, 409, 410 f.

Zeus, 334
Zidon, 356, 410
Zimri, 103 n.[1]
Zion, 253, 266, 271, 272, 356, 361
Ziphites, 88
Zophar, 162, 167 ff.
Zoroaster, 221

PRINTED IN GREAT BRITAIN BY RICHARD CLAY AND COMPANY, LTD., BUNGAY, SUFFOLK.